I0524639

The
Angel
Brings Fire

Book One : *Angel of Mailànkh*

(Second Edition)

by

Marcus B. Shields

Copyright © Marcus Shields / Telostic Corporation, 2010-2015.
All rights reserved.
ISBN : (978-0-9939221-1-4)

Song "Believe In You" lyrics © Human Boy Music; MetaTune Inc.; Sony Music Publishing (Canada)

For additional information about *The Angel Brings Fire*, surf to :
http://abfbook.telostic.com

For K.M.S... and for somehow putting up with the author

Table of Contents

Prologue

The President of the United States – looking every bit the gray-haired, tall and fit Anglo-Saxon father-figure that had, after a fashion, "won" him the last election – had insisted on wearing his standard, well-pressed business-suit, complete with expensive Italian silk tie and shiny, black leather dress-shoes.

His outfit had appeared out-of-place, while he was striding down the dirt road that led from the heli-pad to this isolated survival-bunker, high in the inaccessible, densely-forested Elk Mountain Range of western Colorado. Everyone else – save Bezomorton (the National Security Adviser), several big, glowering Secret Service agents and the most senior military-guys – was wearing mufti.

"You know I *hate* doing this," complained the U.S. leader, as he stared unhappily at the mud and dust that now encased the soles and bottom-parts of his shoes. "Leaving it with those, uhh, 'stand-ins', in charge of the place, I mean... just doesn't feel *right.*"

Without having to be told, an Air Force orderly immediately dashed forward from the throng of Secret Service and Marine guards.

The junior warrior took out a wet towel and began the clean-up job.

Bezomorton – whose portly frame had been having a hard time keeping up, especially in the rarefied air of a place more elevated still than Denver – was now close enough to comment.

"I know, sir," he acknowledged in his usual, unctuously-solicitous tone, "But it's part of the plan – we obviously can't have you there when... well, *you* know. And it's not the *first* time we've had to do it... as you're aware."

"Brave men don't hide in holes," grumbled the President. "But somehow... that's what I'm about to do... right?"

Wisely, none of the courtiers took the bait.

After an involved set of access-authorization locks had been duly dealt with, the group entered the bunker-complex, going down one, two, three sets of stairs, thence to an elevator large enough to accommodate a bulldozer, done all around in shining, stainless-steel.

The trip continued downward a very long way, until, finally, it terminated in an quarter-size underground facsimile of the old NORAD command-post at Cheyenne Mountain. The place had been hewn from the very rock, and – so he'd been told – could survive anything except a direct hit by a megaton-range nuke.

"Home away from home," muttered the President, as he walked forward. "Where's the briefing-room?"

"Straight ahead – end of the hall," noted Bezomorton. "Everybody's already there, sir."

He purposefully strode into the meeting-room, which was a huge one, with a twenty-five-foot-long-table of oak and granite in the precise middle, illuminated by some kind of elongated overhead light; this had been set up to clearly reveal only those with a seat at the table, while allowing the functionaries arrayed on the peripheral walls to fade into the shadows.

The place had a gloomy, "five minutes to midnight", feel to it.

Well... at least that part of it, makes sense, mused the American leader.

I wish it was just a nuke that we had to deal with.

"Mr. President," greeted the white-haired, LeMay-esque Air Force General, Harry Anderson, while all but the most high-up mucky-mucks retreated to the edges of the room.

The President surveyed the crowd.

Half of the seats were occupied with members of the uniformed military, and though there were some cabinet-members here, there were also a number of people with whom he was only familiar in the most casual way. But at least, there was Bezomorton, and the dapper, lanky, mid-thirties, immaculately-manicured figure of Jerry Kaysten, the White House Chief of Staff.

Two guys who I can always count on, reflected the U.S. leader,

Now, if only they didn't hate each other's guts.

Well... taking everything else that's going on these days, it's the least of my problems...

"Good afternoon, Harry... everyone," politely returned the President, as he took the seat at the front end of the table. "Let's get started. I want to keep this to a few minutes... tops. After that, I'm out of here and back to the airborne command-post, for as long as that's possible... I'll leave the implementation-details to the rest of you. As you're aware, I only made the trip out here because of the legal requirement that decisions of this type, have to be witnessed, in-person."

No doubt, his underlings would have preferred a longer meeting; but they knew such wasn't this man's style, so none disputed the pronouncement.

"We have a status-report," offered the many-creased, "old-before-his-time" Science Adviser, Fred McPherson.

"And...?" asked the American leader, dreading what he was about to hear.

"No change, I'm afraid," commented McPherson, with a grave head-shake. "We've had NASA, DoD and every space-telescope that we can get our hands on, tracking the damn thing. It's still on the same path."

"Okay," neutrally replied the President. "Options?"

"Only what we had discussed earlier this week, Mr. President," remarked Anderson. "I'd like to state for the record, that it's very risky to devote *all* the nukes, to this project... what if we do, the Russians and Chinese hide some... and then on the day after, they've got 'em, and we don't?"

Several of the military-types murmured agreement.

"That's a bridge that we'll cross when we come to it," parried the American leader. "Jeremy... how are the civil preparations going?"

Another gray-haired, Caucasian face spoke up.

"Slowly, sir," mentioned Jeremy Franklin, the Emergency Measures Coordinator. "I'm afraid the message isn't really sinking in, among the civilian

the Chief of Staff pleaded, "Let them go *on*, sir. Let them finish what they set out to do."

"But –" started the President; uncharacteristically, Kaysten cut him off.

"Sir," he pressed, "I got a *feeling* about this one... remember the feeling I got, just before the South Carolina primary, five years back?"

For another long moment, the American leader stood and hesitated, staring the adviser, long in the eye.

Then the President said,

"Ah... let's let this Jacobson guy, do what he's going to do."

"But Mr. *President* –" protested DeWitt.

"You know, Arthur," observed the U.S. leader, with a mordant shrug, "Even if he's next up... you've got to have *somebody*, to write your epitaph."

Then, to the stony faces of his military advisers, the President said,

"Let's go, gentlemen."

He turned and headed out of the meeting-room, heading for the elevator.

Mars

Touchdown

Thud.

There was a cloud of rusty-red, slightly-brownish dust.

After four months, they had... *landed.*

Major Brent Boyd, second-in-command of Landing Vehicle *"Eagle II"* – the smaller component of Earth's first manned mission to Mars – exhaled with relief, though he had slightly violated standard NASA procedure by holding his breath in the suspense of the final descent to the Red Planet's surface.

This had been planned, rehearsed and re-rehearsed, dozens of times previously; but no test could have obviated the excitement of the final act.

They were on Mars.

They were the first humans there.

One for the history-books – as all were acutely aware.

"We... *made* it!" Boyd heard Captain Sam Jacobson, the heavy-set, Caucasian commander of the *Eagle*, the surface expedition and, of the *Infinity* orbital module circling overhead, exclaim out loud, in no particular direction.

It seemed rather pedantic, given the gravity of the occasion, but neither Boyd nor the rest of the 4-person crew – three elite U.S. Air Force pilots, if you didn't count the Russian in the orbital module, and one female civilian scientist, Ms. Cherie Tanaka, PH.D – could think of anything more memorable to say.

Jacobson *would* have tried his hand at a little *ad hoc* oratory, but, per pre-determined orders, this phase of the trip wasn't being broadcast back to Earth in real-time, anyway (that is, if such a description could properly be applied, when even radio-waves took many long minutes to travel back and forth between the two planets).

After the last attempt at a manned Mars-landing, the politicians had decided that there wouldn't be any more news of space-disasters; or, at least, news that couldn't be appropriately massaged, before it had to be released to the *hoi polloi.*

"Yep," Boyd replied, grinning broadly. "Piece of cake... unlike the simulations, the computers were working *for* us rather than against us this time, and they weren't rigging 'em to make Mars dodge."

"Unbuckle. Start-up protocol," ordered Jacobson.

All three of the others, and the commander himself, un-clicked the various straps and harnesses that kept them locked in the G-chairs on the way down, standing up slowly and deliberately in the thin Martian gravity, then attending to the baroque collection of computer displays, buttons and switches that controlled this tiny, isolated oasis of Planet Earth, on the face of its mysterious, oft-fictionalized cousin.

Boyd caught a glimpse of the handsome, African-American face of the Communications Officer, Major Devon White, activating the high-bandwidth comm-link.

"NASA, this is *Eagle II* Oberg Base Mars, reporting. I say again, *Eagle II* Oberg Base, Elysium Plantia Mars. The *Eagle* has *again... landed.*"

Being at a high angle from the Earth-link video-screen, Boyd could only imagine a fraction of the celebration that would shortly occur back at home, but, nonetheless, he could almost *hear* the roar of cheers and congratulations.

It felt good.

No matter *what* might happen hereafter, his place in history was assured. His mission in life, from first time he saw a science-fiction show as a small boy, was now fulfilled.

He felt a tap on his shoulder and turned to see Professor Tanaka's attractive, thirty-something Eurasian countenance.

"Time to get up, Major – I need your station," she requested.

"Very much my pleasure," he replied, with the obligatory, side-to-side grin, "And please tell me that we have a nice thick atmosphere to breathe out there, so I don't have to wear that damn suit".

Smiling, the science officer sat down, punched in a few computer commands, observed a video-display and said, amicably, "No such luck, I'm afraid, Major... looks like those seventy years of scientific observations and space probes were right, after all. You'll have to suit up."

Men weren't supposed to giggle; but Boyd did anyway, upon hearing this.

Not that he hadn't known, ahead of time.

He shot a glance out of one of the *Eagle II*'s two portholes.

"Hard to believe that you could freeze-dry your skin and burst your lungs out there in only a few minutes," he observed. "Those mesas to the south look just like Nevada, minus the cactus, plus the red sky."

He had expected Mars to be a strange, alien place; but in truth, it looked familiar, almost boring, to an instructor pilot who had spent years in the U.S. desert, training Tom Cruise wannabes how to fly old F-18s, -22s and -32s, while not being shot down in the process.

"Well, I'd advise you not to test *that* theory any time soon," counseled Tanaka. "However much you don't like those suits."

"Cherie," interjected Jacobson, "Have you got a fix on our exact location yet?"

"Got it," she replied, "Minus 0.1 north, 172.1 east. Almost perfect set-down. Could have maybe been one or two kilometers further south, towards the mesa, but we're pretty much inside the bulls-eye, anyway."

"Excellent," responded the commander. "Well, keep on the touchdown science protocol. I guess we're all a bit anxious to get out there, but we got to get the preliminaries out of the way. How long till sundown and no comm to Houston?"

"About 6 hours, Captain. More than enough to get the necessities done, first."

She sent him a knowing glance.

He nodded, saying, only, "Message... *received.*"

Boyd noticed the a guarded look on Tanaka's face; but he said nothing; there was – as he well knew, from close contact with the woman, for many long months – no point in asking.

Toss Of The Dice

The next few hours passed fleetingly, until the pale Martian sun waned near the horizon.

There was a great deal to do – landing on an alien world and establishing one's home for the next week there *is*, after all, an involved process – but Boyd could only think of the same thing that all else, save Tanaka who had gracefully declined the opportunity, could think of, after the celebratory video calls back to Earth had been dealt with.

Nobody wants to be the second *man to set foot on Mars*, he mused.

"Comm-link off," directed the Captain.

The video-screen and little red "camera on" lights went dark. Knowing what this meant, the other three gathered around the central light-table, a minor technological marvel that doubled as a holographic map display projector, a touchscreen computer display or just as a plain old eating-place, as appropriate.

"Well, folks, it's time for the dice, I guess," continued Jacobson. "We had better settle it tonight, or none of us, including me, are going to get any sleep."

"Don't know how y'all got those past NASA," joked White, "But y'all'd fit right in with my homies back in Compton, honky or not, for being that good a smuggler."

"Heh, yeah," replied Jacobson, "Well, I'm not putting my trick into the reports... probably be safer trying to pirate this crate to Jupiter, Major. Now we had better get this over with *fast*, before those guys back in Houston get interested in what's going on here."

"Alright," said Tanaka, "You space cowboys all know the rules. Two dice, for each of you, but I roll 'em on your behalf, unless there's a tie, in which case you get to re-roll for yourselves. High score wins, second and third place determined by score. Agreed?"

"Agreed," said Jacobson and Boyd, together.

White just nodded, nervously, fingering his crucifix.

"What order?" asked Boyd.

"I suggest by rank, descending," concluded the Professor. "Since you and Major White are equivalent, I'll go by age, which makes him last."

"Good as anything I can think of," said White. "Let's go."

Jacobson handed a pair of Vegas dice – themselves, no doubt, to become the most famous of their ilk, thought Boyd – to the science officer.

He noticed that even the normally sedate Captain, his muscular, crew-cut countenance ridged with poorly disguised tension, was now crossing his fingers.

"Wow, talk about *responsibility*," she joked. "Here we go. First, for Captain Jacobson."

She threw the dice uncertainly, not being sure of how hard to do so considering the thin gravity, and they almost skidded off the table before coming to rest.

"7. Lucky number," observed Jacobson.

"Now for Major Boyd," announced Tanaka. "Good luck."

She threw the dice again, this time more precisely. When they came to rest, one showed six pips, the other four.

Trying not to look his superior in the eye, Boyd said, "Sorry, Captain."

"Don't be," replied Jacobson. "Anyway, we've still got one to go."

"Very true," said Tanaka. "Here goes."

She threw, again, but White's eyes were now cast downward, perhaps in anxiety, perhaps for the same reason that Boyd had avoided seeing the Captain. But he heard a gasp, and summoned up the will to look.

He saw Boyd looking in disbelief.

"Boxcars," exclaimed the science officer. "A big score for a big decision, I'd say. Congratulations, Major."

"Listen, guys, y'all don't have to... I... uhh... don't know what to..." stammered White.

"It's okay," reassured Jacobson. "I'm just glad that we had a fair way to decide it. Major White, you will be the first human being to set foot on Mars. A great honor. Let me second the Professor – congratulations."

Forcing a grin, Boyd added, "Just don't stumble on the way down, Devon. Remember, you'll be on TV – eventually."

They all laughed, semi-hysterically.

It *had* to be settled, somehow, and this way was as good as any. Now it was, thankfully, over with, and they know who would be first, second and third down the ladder to Mars.

Opening The Kimono

"Earth setting, comm-link interrupted," stated White, matter-of-factly. "We're out of sight and out of touch for the next few hours, folks."

The Martian night had fallen, enveloping the surrounding landscape in inky blackness.

Boyd again glanced out the porthole and now, being only able to make out a few rocks here and there, he began to appreciate the alien unfamiliar loneliness of the place. It somehow *felt* colder and more desolate, though they had not moved and though the *Eagle*'s cabin temperature had not changed past a comfortable 20 degrees Celsius.

"Set comm-link off manual," requested Jacobson, "And team, I need you all here for something *very* important."

"But sir," replied White, "Why do we need to do that? Earth can't see us anyway."

"Set comm-link off manual," replied the Captain, neutrally but forcefully.

White got the message. The camera and video lights went from yellow – "functional but unconnected" – to red.

Whispering, Boyd asked the science officer, "What's going *on*, Professor? You know anything about this?"

"You'll see," she evaded.

They all gathered around the central light-table, again.

"Sorry for the skulduggery, gentlemen," – Jacobson shot a glance at the Professor – "And ladies. But I have something about our mission that I have to tell you now in the strictest confidence, something that even *I* didn't know about, prior to setting off from Canaveral."

"Whaddya *mean*, sir?" asked White. "Our mission is to be the first to explore Mars, isn't it?"

Jacobson smiled. "That hasn't changed, Devon," he said, "But we now also have something potentially more important to deal with, something that may be even *more* interesting."

Boyd felt the sense of excitement of a thousand science-fiction stories come rushing at him. He shot a glance at White, who was no doubt thinking exactly the same thing.

"What's *that*, sir?" inquired White, as evenly as he could.

"Now, wait a minute, I *know* what you're probably thinking, but it's not quite *that* historic, at least, not so far," said Jacobson. "Let me explain, so we don't all go off on a tangent, here. Halfway through our trip, I got a specially-coded message from Houston that only the Professor here had the keys to decipher, and here's the upshot of it."

He continued, "Basically, the fact that we have landed where we have, in Elysium Plantia just north of the mesa-formations, is no accident – there's something down there, that is, to the south of us, in which the folks back at NASA are quite interested. But they're not sure what it is, and they want us to have a look at it, while we of course go about all the other things that you already know about."

"Exactly what *is* this, sir?" said Boyd.

"I will defer to the science officer for that," Jacobson replied. "Cherie, I think this is where you take over."

Not missing a beat, Tanaka chimed in.

"During one of the more recent Mars Micro-Mapping Orbiter missions," said the science officer, "That spacecraft detected an unusual electromagnetic anomaly centered around one the mesa-formations in the out-wash basin, about three kilometers to the south of us. It's very strange; it seems to radiate energy at various wavelengths, always at a very low level, but much more intensely during the day than at night, when the output drops down to almost zero."

She continued. "At first, we thought it was just an unusually rich mineral deposit, maybe naturally-occurring uranium or something like that, but if so it's unlike anything we have any experience with, back on Earth. There's *nothing* that we can see in visible light or infrared from the orbiter, that is, there are no structures or otherwise remarkable rock-formations... so maybe whatever is causing this effect is buried. From the sky, it just looks like any other Martian mesa, basically."

"You think we've found the Martians, Professor?" exclaimed White, only half in jest.

"I don't *believe* so," disingenuously replied a smiling Tanaka, "But since we just happen to be in the area, we might as well check it out... don't you think?"

"Those are my orders," added Jacobson. "So that's what we'll do. But," he warned, looking each of the others in the eye, one by one, "I need you to understand that for now, since all we have is something of *geological* interest, there is to be no mention of this to either Houston, NASA or anyone else, under *any* circumstances, until I say otherwise. *Any* circumstances, as a condition of your duty and membership on this mission. Do I make myself clear, gentlemen?"

Boyd and White both responded with one voice. "Yes, sir," they said, with military precision.

"Dismissed," said Jacobson. "Now let's try to get some sleep. We have a lot of work to do tomorrow and there's also that little walk down the ladder, isn't there?"

"Yes, *sir*," replied the two men.

Short Step To History

After a fitful night of semi-sleep – the excitement of the upcoming day, mingling with the new-found unknowns of the upcoming quest, having affected all (except Tanaka, serene and professional as ever) – Boyd shook off the doldrums, courtesy of the alarm function on his wristband, and found himself awake.

He partook of his carefully prescribed portion of NASA's ingenious "S-Rations" (supposedly enough to keep a grown man alive for two days, yet all compressed into a single tube the size of a cigar; well, he hadn't expected a *restaurant*, after all), cleaned his teeth with a mist of recycled water (he swore that he could taste where it had come from, but no use dwelling on *that*) and managed, with some difficulty, to answer nature's needs in the W/C closet on the top floor. He then moved, deliberately in the thin Martian gravity, down the ladder from the *Eagle*'s top sleeping deck to its main area.

The other three were already there.

"Good morning, team," said Jacobson. "I trust you all slept well?"

Boyd noticed that the camera-lights were green again, which meant, "On".

"Uhh... yes, absolutely, Captain," Boyd semi-prevaricated. "But I guess we're all just a bit excited. How about you?"

"I'm good," Jacobson replied, "I had a late-night bulletin from Houston that kept me up awhile, but I got enough sleep afterwards."

He continued, "Well, right to business, then. Daybreak is in three minutes with egress to follow twenty after that, as you know, all to allow us to offer our deathless words to the folks back home before we go out there. So start thinking of things to say, in between making sure you have executed nourishment, bodily function and bio-check protocols prior to suiting up."

Jacobson was being very matter-of-fact about it; but then again, he *had* lost the dice roll.

"Dismissed. Let's suit up," he ordered.

"*Yeah!*" exclaimed White.

They all broke up momentarily, then regained their composure for the cameras, as each of the three former Air Force (technically, Boyd had been Navy, but he had transferred midway through his career) pilots slowly checked and re-checked each space-suit component as it was put on.

Following protocol, Boyd checked White's suit, piece-by-piece, White checked Jacobson's and Jacobson checked Boyd's; nothing was left to chance. On Mars, only slightly less so than in the deadly void of space, taking chances was a luxury none could afford.

They all remembered the first expedition to Mars and how it had aborted under still-not-fully-explained circumstances, with the loss of two fine astronauts, midway through.

Sure, Boyd wanted to be a hero; but a *live* one, not a dead one.

All three repeated the protocol confirmations. "Communications Officer suited up and checked, sir," said White.

"Pilot suited up and checked, sir," echoed Boyd.

"CO and Co-Pilot suited up and checked," said Jacobson.

After a few fairly nervous moments of back-and-forth joking, the Earth link video-screen lit up, revealing the familiar face of Hector Ramirez, Houston Mission Commander for the expedition.

Boyd had expected to see a kid-in-the-candy-shop grin from the normally ebullient Ramirez, but he looked strangely stony-faced, considering the space-exploration accomplishment that was about to happen.

"Greetings from Earth, Oberg Base," said Ramirez. "We wish you well, when you make history as the first members of the human race, to set foot on Mars."

Boyd made a mental note to remember that the message must have been sent at least ten minutes ago. Mars, though just a baby-step in the long march to the stars, was still a long way from Earth.

Jacobson stood in front of the camera and said, in a genuine, but no doubt carefully rehearsed manner, "Houston, I think I speak for the entire crew of the *Eagle* when I say, we feel tremendously lucky to have been given the honor of being the first on Mars, on behalf not only of the United Nations Space Program but also of the whole human race."

"And, in this context, I'm very pleased to announce that we have selected Major Devon White, our communications officer, to be the first man to set foot on the Red Planet, followed by Major Brent Boyd, my second-in-command and co-pilot, followed finally by myself. Chief Science Officer Cherie Tanaka will remain on-board the *Eagle* to supervise our first egress and report back to Earth as developments warrant, while Cosmonaut Major Sergei Chkalov, as you know, is currently on-board *Infinity* – *Eagle's* mother ship in orbit around Mars – keeping everything ready to provide our way back home. I want to say to Sergei that each and every one of us down here understands the great sacrifice that he is making in coming so close to Mars, yet not joining us down here, so that we can all get safely back to Earth. His contribution to this mission is perhaps the most important of all, so Sergei, we all salute you."

Jacobson paused a second or two, then said, "Houston, that is all. We will now commence egress."

He turned to the other two astronauts. "Well, Brent, Devon, I guess the time has come. Congratulations, in advance. Let's put our hats on."

"Man," commented White, "I never thought I'd get rubber legs... but this is a *big* thing, isn't it, Captain? Y'all gonna catch me if I fall off that ladder?"

"Devon," Jacobson replied, helpfully, "You're on your own... you're ahead of *me*... remember?"

They all shared a laugh, then, again following protocol, put each other's space helmets on, then had each installation checked by another crew-member.

Boyd caught a glimpse of Tanaka, gazing introspectively out the porthole, towards the mesa formation in the southern distances.

She seemed rather detached, considering what was about to happen... but then, *she* wasn't going to be even the *fourth* person on Mars, if the plans stayed as they were, even though there *were* four space-suits.

Like so many other things about personal ambition in the space program, this wasn't something that Boyd could do anything about, even if he had wanted to.

He turned away, towards the airlock, following White, ahead of Jacobson, who closed the door and then sealed it shut with a rather obsolete-looking, manual wheel, reminiscent of the same ones found in submarines and warships. This was not something that astronauts wanted to entrust to computers, even if those inscrutable techo-things *were*, in fact, overseeing the whole process, in the background.

Now Jacobson came in, over the intercom.

"Comm check, gentlemen," he instructed.

"Co-pilot, confirmed," replied Boyd.

"Communications officer, confirmed," said White.

"Can you hear us, Professor?" Jacobson continued.

"Hear you and see what you're seeing, loud, clear and in color, Captain," chimed in the voice of the science officer, now seated in front of the multi-screen display, connected in real-time to the cameras attached to each space-helmet. "You have a good day to make history, Captain. Very little dust and we're warming up, about minus 20 Celsius, nice and warm for you. Good luck."

Jacobson nodded, then said, "Outside airlock release."

Whoosh.

Though most of the air inside the airlock had already been silently recaptured into the *Eagle II*'s main compartment – oxygen being a priceless commodity on this forbidding world – there was still enough to make the first sound heard, if indirectly, by human ears on Mars.

The door opened slowly, revealing a russet-colored, desert-like landscape, halfway between serene and desolate, with small boulders and rocks strewn haphazardly across a wide plain with the occasional deep gully, extending to the horizon in the north. It appeared to end abruptly a few kilometers to the south in a series of towering, mesa-like formations.

"Devon, your turn. Hope you've got something to say," said Jacobson, facing White and pointing to the now-open outside door.

"Yessir," replied White. He reached the door, turned uncertainly and, step by careful step, proceeded about halfway down the ladder.

"Brent, you now."

"Thanks, sir," said Boyd. "It all seems unreal. Wow," was all he could think to say.

Following the first man, Boyd turned and started down the ladder, taking care not to put a foot on White's head; something like *that* wouldn't look very good in the history-books, after all. He was followed by Jacobson, who closed the door and secured the airlock with a sequence of button-presses on the command pad just to the right of the entrance-way.

"Brothers and sisters of Earth," he heard White declare, "This is the voice of a man born poor, a man who has come all the way from Compton, Los Angeles, to the surface of another planet."

He paused for a long second, and then continued, "One night, a long time ago, this man promised his dying father that he would live out a dream; and the next step that I will take, will be on behalf of the millions who *also* had that dream... and who *also* made that promise. I will show that there's *nothing* that human beings can't do, if we boldly set sail in search of far shores... even though we may only see them, through the eyes of our children. Today,"

Boyd heard a soft, "thud".

"The least of Earth... are the first of Mars," said White.

Best And Worst Of News

The other two stepped off the ladder, one by one, each making their own comments for history.

When all had reached the surface, Boyd remarked, "Devon, that was *inspired*. Don't know where it came from, man, but I don't think anybody could have said it better. Well done."

"Came from the *heart*, man... *that's* where. Only place I could find it," White replied.

"Amen to that," said Jacobson. "Now back to the plan, gentlemen. Let's get the flag."

A flag bearing the emblem of the United Nations on one side, with Old Glory on the other – kept rigid in the now-soft Martian breeze by internal stiffening ribs – was duly planted on the face of the planet.

They saluted, with all the ceremonies relayed back to Earth after the obligatory delay.

"Let's get the Rover, team," directed Jacobson, "We're heading south to the mesa complex. As you know, it's a routine scientific mission. We'll record our activities for relay to Earth as we go," he said, giving the pre-arranged hand-signal that meant "relay off", when seen by Tanaka, back in the *Eagle II*.

"Is the communications setup properly configured?" he asked the science officer, via interlink.

"Yes, sir," she replied, "All is working as planned."

Then a voice they had not heard recently – that of Sergei Chkalov in the orbital module – echoed the message.

"Captain," he said, "All is working as planned".

That is, Earth could no longer see them, even if it *thought* that it could. Lapses in communication could be explained later, by experts.

As they had trained for so many times before, the three set immediately to work, freeing the dune buggy-type Mars Mobility Vehicle, a four-seater with a top speed of perhaps forty kilometers per hour (and a safe speed of half that), from its holding-bay on the side of the *Eagle*'s lower module.

As he boarded the MMV from the port driver's side, Boyd said, "If those street punks I used to road race back in Jersey could just see me driving *this*, here, now. I lost lots of races... but I guess I won the prize, eh, Captain?"

"You're probably right, Major," agreed Jacobson. "But let's not do any racing here – we don't know the track, after all. Fifteen kilometers per hour, max, please. To the south, please, avoiding anything and everything in our way."

"Aye aye, sir," replied Boyd. "Engaging Long-Range GPS for general route track. I'll steer past the bumps. Here we go."

Slowly, the MMV began to move, powered partly by its spread-out solar wings, partly by an on-board nuclear reactor, itself a marvel of, so it had been claimed, 'safe atomic miniaturization'.

The vehicle's on-board computer and communications equipment steered it inexorably in the direction of each pre-programmed way-point, these being confirmed in turn by GPS signals relayed from the *Infinity* orbiter. Nothing, other than the minor adjustments made by the driver to avoid potentially damaging terrain-hazards, could set them on the wrong course.

Which was fortunate, considering that they were traversing the most hostile, isolated deserts that human beings had ever ventured forth upon.

Boyd noticed that despite the relative clarity of the atmosphere – a *real* one, however thin the science-books said it to be – his visor had to be wiped clean of Mars' fine, red dust every ten minutes or so. No doubt, it wouldn't be fun to inhale that stuff, even if the air itself had been fit to breathe in the first place.

The trip to the mesa formation did not take long; after all, the *Eagle II* had landed not too far north of this area, and Boyd had, perhaps, "pushed the speed" of the MMV just a bit, with the benign indulgence of the Captain.

As they neared the formation, all three started to come to the stark realization that they *were*, indeed, on another planet, far different from the familiar confines of Earth.

"Holy Smokes," exclaimed White, looking up at the scenery in awe. "I did three tours at Red Flag, but I've *never* seen a mesa *that* high – the damn things must be 1500 meters or more."

"Yeah," added Boyd, "And look how far the top parts of those things overhang the lower parts, gives me the creeps to think that we're going to be underneath them... they'd *never* be able to support the weight on Earth, but I guess in this weak gravity, they stay up there. At least, I *hope* they're gonna stay up, when we get there."

The voice of Cherie Tanaka interrupted.

"Actually, according to our best estimates, the mesa-formations that you're nearing have been more or less intact for at least 200,000 years, maybe as many as ten million," she mentioned. "We don't think that there have been any significant erosive or tectonic events since those times, but we're not precisely sure, of course..."

"Gives me all the confidence I need," said White, semi-sarcastically. "Y'all remind me to bring my umbrella next time, like Wile E. Coyote, man."

"Okay, *enough*, folks," demanded Jacobson. "NASA wouldn't send us anywhere hazardous, you know that, gentlemen. Professor, how far are we from the objective? Can you give us a relative fix?"

"Yes, sir, just a minute," she replied. "You're looking good, about another kilometer and a half, past the first three outer mesa units, follow the out-wash channel that you're now on, the objective is the fourth unit which will be to your right. Can you see it now?"

"Hold on..." replied Jacobson, now standing in place, having swung his integral thermal imaging and telescopic vision enhancement goggles into the 'down' position. "Yes... I can just make it out... doesn't look any different from the surrounding units, but then, we're still a fair distance from it, and there's all this dust in the air. Will give you another report and a close-up visual when we get there."

"Understood, Captain," said the science officer. "Standing by."

They were now in the midst of the mesas, the gigantesque majesty of which was all the more breathtaking, up close. Boyd tried to think of something – maybe, a California redwood, only fifty times the size and with a top made of stone, not wood – that he could use as a simile for the folks back home, when trying to describe what he was now seeing.

This was, however, an *alien* landscape, unlike anything on Earth. There really was nothing you could use as an analogy. Especially with those overhanging cliffs, at the top, which seemed to go impossibly far from the center parts of each mesa-structure.

Boyd hoped that there weren't any Mars-quakes, any more.

"Captain," interjected Tanaka's voice, "We have another bulletin from Houston."

"Can it wait?" replied Jacobson.

"I think you should hear it now," she said. "I'll pipe it through on a private link."

"Very well," he said. "Major, if you could stop the MMV for a minute, please? Excuse me for a moment, gentlemen, I'm going to take a short walk."

He got off the vehicle and walked a few meters away, with his right boot perched on a Martian rock, listening to the incoming message; it would have made a great picture, had anyone remembered to bring a still camera.

The other two waited, worriedly. Eventually Jacobson came back and got in his seat, without saying a word.

"Captain?" asked White.

"Yes?" said Jacobson.

"Anything you care to share with us, sir?" Boyd added.

"I'm afraid not, right now at least," Jacobson replied. "Except, since I know that it's what you are thinking, no, it *doesn't* have anything to do with our current objective."

"Sir," Boyd said, trying to be as militarily correct as he could, "I think we both understand that as Commander of this mission, there are things that you may not be comfortable in disclosing to us, but, frankly, I don't think that the Professor would have interrupted this expedition for something unimportant, isn't that right? I'm just concerned that not understanding what the situation is, might affect our performance out here... that's all."

Jacobson sat and looked into space for two or three seconds, then said, "Without getting into the details, Brent, I can tell you that what it's all about isn't important... no, let me rephrase that, at least, it's not important... to *us*, given where we are, and given what we're out to do. The moment that this information becomes relevant, you have my assurance that I will bring you up to date, immediately. Now, we have *work* to do. Let's get going."

"Aye aye, sir," Boyd replied.

Even through a dusty visor, he could see a look of concern on White's face.

After perhaps another ten minutes of minimal verbal communication, other than for obligatory procedure checks and confirmations, the MMV was finally nearing the objective. Which was now clearly visible as just another one of the towering, glowering mesa-things surrounding them, like so many elephantine toadstools.

"*Eagle II* and *Infinity*, this is MMV reporting at the objective," stated Jacobson over the cross-link. "We're here. Cherie, please advise and direct investigation from this point on."

"Excellent, MMV," replied a ghostly voice. "There's a bit of interference, but I can see what you're seeing quite clearly. Hard to make out distances and relative size scales, from this end. Can you deploy your EM sensor array, now? You're a lot closer than we'll ever get; let's see if you pick up something."

"Understood, *Eagle*," said White. "Communications officer now deploying EM subsystem. I'm pointing it at the mesa. Engaging. Tell us what you get here, Professor."

He got out of the vehicle and retrieved a multi-antennaed object from the back, pointing an arrowhead array at the mesa. It powered on and began to work, noiselessly.

"Interesting," said the science officer, over the two-way. "Getting a few ambient readings... above the expected baseline, especially in UV and gamma, but the actual energy's very low. Could be an instrumentation malfunction."

"Above safety-limits?" inquired Jacobson. "Remember, Cherie, these suits don't do a good job of keeping out hard radiation."

"Don't worry," replied Tanaka. "Levels are notably more than what's around you, but what's around you is almost nil. You're in no danger, as long as you don't spend the next six months there, outside your space-suits."

"I'm relieved, man," said a voice that had to be Devon White. "I don't even like microwave ovens."

"Professor," asked Boyd, "You say that you're getting readings; we believe you, but we don't see *anything*. Have you got a false-color visual? Is there a hot-spot you can direct us to?"

"Two steps ahead of you, Brent," she replied. "I have it... I think... about fifty meters up the central column. Is there any visible marking there?"

Engaging his vision-enhancers, Boyd paused for a second, focused where he had been told to, then responded, "Negative, *Eagle*. Looks just like sheer rock to me, and there's no *way* that we could get up there anyway, it's much too high. Also there's a collection of spalled rock at the base of the mesa which would make for some pretty rough going, just to get up next to it."

"Please hold on a second, Major," said Tanaka. "The signal's fluctuating unusually... hmm. I think that maybe we're not looking directly at it..."

"What do you mean, Professor?" said Jacobson.

"I think that whatever is making this radiation may be closer to the outside surface of the mesa, on one of the mesa's other sides. Is there any way you can take a trip around it and see?" she requested.

"Yes, I think so," confirmed Boyd. "Captain, look there – a lot of big boulders, but there's a path I can get the MMV through. We could go south, around the circumference, it would be a bit out of our way, but we have plenty of air and battery left."

"Sure, let's," replied Jacobson. "Cherie, we might as well, there's nothing here, just a huge rock formation like all the others. Maybe we'll have better luck around the side. Devon," – he gestured towards White – "Can you just hold the EM array in your lap, as we go for the ride? I think it will be okay as long as Brent doesn't drive too fast."

"You can be sure I won't," Boyd pledged. "Alright... everybody aboard."

They all clambered back into the vehicle, White in the back, holding the array so that it was continuously pointing at the mesa.

They now diverted from the outflow path between the main mesa-forest, turning instead into a more narrow path between the objective formation and the mesa just to the south of it. Boyd had to maneuver sharply in a couple of places where rock-spalls had evidently crashed down from above, but there was otherwise ample room in which to drive.

Soon they were southwest of their original target.

"Wait –" they heard Tanaka's voice caution. "Readings are climbing, but still way under danger levels, lest that worry you. What do you see?"

"Nothing unusual," answered Jacobson, "Just rockfalls everywhere... nothing that – "

"What's *that*, sir?" interrupted White, pointing at something between two large boulders at the foot of the mesa.

"What's *what*?" replied the Captain. "It looks just like some sand, to me. *Lots* of sand around here, you know."

"I *know*, sir," persisted White, "But it looks too... *neat*, somehow. See how it goes behind them big rocks there?"

Boyd engaged his vision-enhancers. "I see what he means, Captain," he said. "Definitely different from most of the surrounding terrain. Looks much more regular and undifferentiated than the rest of this stuff. Professor, what do you think?"

"Can you focus on it please, Major?" requested Tanaka. "Thanks – wait – yes, indeed, that's interesting. Looks like a fine silica-deposit, perhaps. Please investigate if you can."

"Easily done. Sir, may I take us up there?" said Boyd.

"Proceed," replied Jacobson. "Cherie, keep an eye on that rad-hazard setting, please. I want to know the *moment* that things begin to get into the danger-zone."

"Certainly, Captain," she said, "But as of now, it would have to be a thousand times stronger to really be dangerous. I'll let you know if we get anywhere near that."

The MMV approached the formation and stopped about fifteen meters in front of its base. Boyd and White debarked to investigate. As they neared point-blank range, Boyd heard a whistle of amazement over the intercom.

"Brent... what do you make of *that*?" White said, excitement rising in his voice.

"Damn interesting, *that's* for sure," he replied. "Looks like an out-wash of fine-grained sand, mineral composition obviously different from the other stuff around here, that got kind of frozen in place, all of a sudden. Professor, can you see the greenish tinge to this deposit? Looks almost *glassy*, in places, but I thought that this isn't a geologically-active area?"

"Fascinating," came Tanaka's voice over the two-way. "It looks like a pyroclastic outflow of some kind, but you're right, I wouldn't expect to see anything like this at all, in this part of the planet. Is it stable? Can you stand on it or sample it?"

Bending over, Jacobson, who had now joined them, attempted to break a piece of the unusual rock flow free with a hand-pick. "Negative," he said. "It's *very* tough stuff, at least as resilient as granite. We'll have to bring the power-drills from the *Eagle* if we want a piece of this."

"Captain?" called White.

"Yes?" answered Jacobson.

"Don't you *see*, sir?" demanded White.

"What do you mean?" asked the commander. "I see it just fine. It's interesting."

Jacobson seemed a bit annoyed, at this.

"No sir, that's not what I mean," retorted White.

"I think you'd better get to the point, Devon," suggested Boyd.

"Sir, it's a *ramp*," explained White. "An artificial *path* that goes up, up the side of the mesa."

For a second, all of them just stood there, stunned, absorbing the impact of White's hypothesis. Then, hardly daring to believe, Boyd stepped off to the right side, hoping to see, hoping not to see, all at the same time.

The shining, greenish-white stone path, smooth enough to have rolled a shopping-cart up or down, curved up, up and around the far side of the mesa, out of sight. Boyd was soon joined by the others.

"Professor," Jacobson quietly spoke, "Are you getting this?"

"Yes... I am... yes, that's an affirmative, MMV," confirmed the science officer. "But let's not jump to conclusions, here. I know the Major's idea is one that we'd all like to *believe* is true... but there are probably many natural explanations for what we're looking at here, so let's continue our investigation, which we would have to do either way. How are you all for air and battery?"

Even Tanaka sounded excited.

"Air still good at average 80 per cent remaining, battery at 73, we're still nominal," indicated Jacobson. "Major White, since you're the one who proposed this thing, I think it's only right that you lead Major Boyd up there to explore it. I'll remain down here for the time being so that if you get into trouble we have a local resource for rescue. I'll watch your progress on the screen down here in the MMV. You may proceed."

"You *bet*, sir," said White. "It doesn't look too steep, anyway. Professor, y'all got a lock on my camera?"

"A bit more interference now, Devon," she replied, "But I'm compensating for it, you're still very clear. Get yourself going! Now you've got *me* very interested, too."

They were all scientists and – in one way or another – believers in intelligent extraterrestrial life. But on *Mars*? How could that be *possible*? The planet was geologically and biologically dead and had certainly been so for millions of years. There was simply no logical explanation. None at all.

Step by step, tied together with an improvised mountaineering cable, over the next twenty minutes, White and Boyd advanced up the side of the mesa, along the path, a trip that would have been only moderate exertion on Earth, but which, with the ever-present danger of falling and being exposed to the hostile environment of this alien world, seemed both physically and mentally tiring.

The ramp wound around the mesa structure in a gentle curve, ending on an even plane with the floor of a perhaps ten meter-wide rock-shelf, fifty or so meters up the south-facing side.

And it was obvious why this feature had never been noticed from the many overhead scans that had been done by various telescopes and space probes; the overhang of the surrounding terrain, would have blocked it from being seen by a top-down onlooker.

The two astronauts took the opportunity to catch their breath for a second, upon reaching the rock-shelf; after all, the Mars exploration plans, to the extent that they had been known prior to departure, did not anticipate mountain-climbing, and both men were becoming acutely aware of how effectively their space-suits trapped heat and perspiration.

"Man," said White, sitting on a boulder, "It don't look like much, but that's a *long* way up..."

But there was no reply from Boyd, who was staring, stunned beyond comprehension, straight forward at the rock wall of the mesa.

"*Holy Jaysus, it's a door!*" was all White could think to say. "Professor, y'all receivin'? Can y'all confirm what I'm seein' here?"

There was a long pause.

"*My God*," they heard her astonished voice say, "You *have* to be right. There's no other explanation... Captain, do you see it too? Cut right into the rock! There's something *inscribed* in it, too! I can't *believe* what I'm seeing... Major, can you get a bit closer? We need to get a good look. Wait – I'm checking for radiation. Higher, but still safe. Go ahead."

"*Mozhde buyt*," they heard faintly over the intercom. None of them really understood Russian, but Sergei's amazement was palpable as well.

They both approached the 'door', or whatever-it-was.

Here was the 'smoking gun', the incontestable evidence, the definitive piece-of-the-puzzle that would forever end the "are we alone" debate back on Earth.

They were the first humans on Mars and this structure had definitely *not* been made by natural means.

Someone, or something, *else*, had to have made it.

The idea was thrilling, frightening, intimidating and amazing, all at once.

The history of Earth, once they would be allowed to communicate the news, would be even more irrevocably changed than they had ever dreamed imagine.

"Can you get a zoom on the thing?" requested the voice of Jacobson, from down at the secondary MMV video station. "We should get dimensions, surface appearance, as much as we can get before nightfall. Let's put on our scientist-hats, gentlemen."

"Aye aye, sir – my pleasure," vowed White. "Appears about two meters or so high by about a meter and a half wide, slightly inset into the rock-face. I'm scannin' the inscriptions... four groups of them, each contained in a sunken-relief box of some kind... these square shapes are deployed horizontally across the door. There's a rectangle above the boxes and below them there are three undulating lines – looks a bit like the symbols we use for waves or water, maybe. Above the rectangle I see circular glyphs that might be celestial objects, stars, planets, Deimos and Phobos, maybe. Don't really see anythin' else, no signs of a door-handle or a lock – too bad, there. Brent, have I missed anything?"

"Nope... not that *I* can see," replied Boyd. "Except, those inscriptions in the four boxes kind of remind me of Maya-writing... but of course the letters are completely different."

"Y'all want to try to open it?" White mischievously proposed. "But where's the handle?"

"Needless to say, Major," interrupted Jacobson, "That wouldn't be allowed, even were it possible. For now, don't even *touch* it. We're looking at an archaeological project that will probably take *decades* and several large-scale expeditions, to complete. We've already achieved more than any exploration party in human history – let's leave it on that high note, at least until we know what Houston wants us to do. Professor, do you have what you need in terms of remote sensing?"

"Affirmative, Captain," responded Tanaka. "I'm already running the symbology against my internal databases, but I'd really need to send them to Earth for proper analysis. I also have the spectroscopy and EMF profiles of the door – some unusual results there, but again, interpreting them will take time."

"Very well, then," replied Jacobson. "Major White, Major Boyd, all I can say is, 'job well done'. Now get yourselves down from there, safely. We need to get back to *Eagle*, ASAP. We have a great deal of science to do, gentlemen."

The two stumbled down the pathway back to the MMV, faster than they should have gone, considering the incline. But no reprimand was forthcoming, only a look of utter amazement and professional admiration from the Captain.

"Men," he stated, shaking his head, "The rules say I can't go there today, but as a personal favor, would one of you take me up tomorrow? I *have* to see it with my own eyes."

"Of course, sir," agreed Boyd. "It's really not that hard a climb, we were just panting away because we weren't used to doing it in the space-suits, even in this gravity. Should be a piece of cake, tomorrow."

"Great!" replied Jacobson. "Now, I guess we had better get back to the ship. We're nowhere near nightfall, but we obviously have some reporting to do, which I would prefer you leave to myself, unless directly asked a question by one of the NASA boys. Oh, and one other thing..."

"Yes, sir?" said White.

"You two got down the ladder first," mentioned Jacobson. "Now you're the first men to ever see an extra-terrestrial artifact. The next one's *mine*, you understand?"

Grinning broadly, White offered, "Sure, Captain, but I can't imagine what could top *this*. I guess this trip is full of surprises, though... maybe there's a few more in store."

Sharing a chuckle, all three boarded the MMV and did an about-face towards the *Eagle*, with Boyd pushing the speed envelope even a bit more. Stowing the vehicle in an anti-dust enclosure underneath the spacecraft – the local forecast was largely benign, at least by Martian standards, no windstorms – Jacobson ascended the ladder and opened the airlock using the control-pad, followed by Boyd and White.

"Bio-scan nominal," announced Tanaka over the internal intercom, as the airlock gradually filled with breathable air. There was no surprise here, since repeated robot probes had found the place utterly dead, devoid even of microbes. They took off their helmets, instantly appreciative of the freedom to move.

A bit of dust rubbed off on Boyd's finger, as he disrobed.

"I've touched Mars, with my bare hands," he said.

They all gathered around the center-table.

"Transmission from Earth in 5 minutes," said White, back at his normal duties for a nonce. He heard Jacobson say, "Set comm-link off manual," but Tanaka had, perceptively, already turned off the local video-cameras, although Earth would still see normal activity around the *Eagle II* otherwise.

"Captain, how are we going to break it to them?" asked the astronaut.

Jacobson replied, slowly and coolly, "You and I both know that an event of this importance could *never* be withheld from the public indefinitely, nor should it be. But we have to consider how we deliver the news and, more importantly, who we tell first. Furthermore, we have a lot of 'unknowns' here; what we already have in front of us is obviously of enormous significance, but there's a great deal more that we *don't* know, so we might as well not encourage questions that we don't have answers to, yet."

He continued, "As you know, we have a transmission window coming up from Houston in about 30 minutes from now – it's public, like always, so we can't look like anything unusual is going on, for the folks back home. However, what you may *not* know is that I have a way of telling Houston that they need to set up a protected comm-link – the only people back there who will have access to it, are the mission project-managers – and that's what I plan to do. The protocol is for the link to be initiated no more than one minute after I give the keyword, so when you hear 'message received', you might want to start thinking about what you're going to say when we start talking to them."

"Almost too much excitement for one day, Martian or Earth-day, that is," joked White.

"What more do you want?" added Boyd.

"I guess we'll see," replied Jacobson. "Comm-link on."

The next thirty minutes were spent as casually as each could muster the self-control to do, secretly considering and re-considering what to say, when the time came. Eventually it did.

The overhead screen lit up, showing Hector Ramirez' roundish, poker-faced Tex-Mex peasant visage.

"Greetings, *Eagle*, this is Mission Control," he said. "We can see you've had a busy day down there today, and we should let you know, we've got a whole lot of onlookers on-line following the good news of Mars exploration as you continue your mission. Anything to report?"

As if in real-time, Jacobson replied, "Message received, Houston, but nothing really more than what you've seen on the video-cams today. We are continuing the preliminaries for our exploration of the surface, with Professor Tanaka working closely with Major Chkalov in *Infinity* to co-ordinate the best routes for us to examine local geological features. We're all looking forward to eventually heading down to the mesa-formations," – at this, Boyd and White both suppressed an urge to smirk – "To the south, as the terrain around here is pretty boring. That's about it, Houston. *Eagle* Oberg Base out."

They sat around the table, just looking at each other, waiting for the communications propagation delay to run its course. After an interminable six or so minutes, the screen crackled to life again, this time with a reddish framing around the screen's interior periphery.

White pushed the switches on the panel to "Receive".

Just like a walkie-talkie, he thought, *Except for a few million kilometers.*

Again, it was Ramirez, but this time accompanied by two others, a thin, almost gaunt, dark-brown-and-gray-haired fortyish Italian-American Cher Bono lookalike– whom Boyd recognized as Sylvia Abruzzio, Chief Mission Technical Team Leader, and an elderly man that he had never seen.

Ramirez' countenance was strange, like a man halfway between penitence and dread.

"*Eagle* Oberg, this is Ramirez at Mission Control. I recognized your message and have therefore set up this private link to discuss whatever the anomaly is. I'm joined by Sylvia Abruzzio, who you know already, and also by White House Chief Internal Technical Advisor, Mr. Fred McPherson."

The two others waved reflexively at the camera.

Ramirez continued, "I have to tell you, that is, by protocol, as you should know, these matters – you *know* what I'm talking about – are supposed to be discussed only between yourself and our team back here. Why is the rest of your team being involved, here? I request an explanation. Standing by until we hear from you."

White switched the communications-link to, "Send".

Without missing a beat, Jacobson replied, "Thanks for the reminder, Hector, but when I tell you what we have to report on here, I think you'll concur with my decision. I have not revealed the subject of our mid-course discussion, just to clear *that* up, but I'm now requesting clearance to do so. We have something very important to tell you about what's been going on down here and it seems only fair, from my point of view, that my team knows the whole picture."

He stopped, cleared his throat, stared deliberately at the camera and said,

"Houston, we have a LGM class discovery down here. I say again : *a LGM class discovery, here.* Do you copy, Houston?"

White switched to "Receive".

"Commander," asked Boyd, taking advantage of the ten-minute window, "What were you talking to them about, there?"

"Hate to be keeping secrets, Brent," Jacobson evaded, "Hopefully I won't have to keep doing so, in a few minutes from now."

His countenance took on a far-away look.

"But I want you to understand something," stated the commander. "Whatever the news... we have a *mission* to complete here, and we're going to do that, one way or another. No 'ifs', 'ands' or 'buts'. *Whatever* may come."

"Of course," replied Boyd.

The look on Jacobson's face worried him, though.

After a few minutes, the transmission indicator re-lit.

"*Eagle* Oberg Base," spoke Ramirez, "We reluctantly concur with your request. I have to tell you, Sam, that as you have no doubt concluded yourself, the irony of this discovery coming at the current time, what with how things look down here, has a lot of us shaking our heads – it's an amazing and historic event, of course, and we're all very eager to find out the details. But it's a bit late, we all think. Permission is granted to explain the current situation to your crew. Please give us a full description of your find in your next message. Over."

White, stone-faced, pushed, "Send".

"Houston," said Jacobson, "Understood and confirmed. As I speak," – he motioned to Tanaka, who hit a panel control-button – "My Science Officer is sending you all the technical data that we have available, but for the record, I can tell you the following. This morning, Mars time, according to our pre-arranged protocol, we set out for the Mesa Anomaly, expecting only to find something of geological interest. How wrong we were."

He continued, "As we neared the Anomaly, Major Devon White, to whom this discovery should be credited, noticed an unusually flat, even formation encircling the side of the mesa; to give you an Earth equivalent, it looked a bit like those special ramps we have back home for wheelchairs. So he and Major Boyd followed it up, around the mesa, and when it terminated, it did so on a platform, the mesa-side of which contained a door-like portal formation, inset into the rock, that is *unmistakably* artificial in nature. I say again, Houston, *this portal cannot be a natural formation*. It is the first indisputable proof of extra-terrestrial life, not only that, but intelligent life. We are all humbled and astonished at what we saw, here."

"We engaged in preliminary, non-destructive scanning of the object and have sent the data resulting from this back to you in Professor Tanaka's last transmission, but with the equipment we have available here, I'm afraid that there is not a lot more that we can do, without taking some small surface samples. Houston, we are all as amazed as you are on what has transpired today, but we're unsure of how this event should be portrayed to the public. As a practical matter, if you want us to do more local investigative work, in view of the distance of the Anomaly and the complexity of the work, it may be difficult to do so without making the public suspicious that something unusual is going on. Please advise as to recommended course of action. Over."

White switched to "Receive".

They all waited.

Presently, Ramirez returned, but this time, the one doing the speaking was the older fellow. "Greetings, and congratulations on your tremendous discovery, Captain Jacobson," he said.

"As Mr. Ramirez told you earlier, my name is Fred McPherson and I'm the chief technical liaison between this mission and the White House, and, I suppose, more than anyone else here, I have the job of deciding about how much of this we let out, and when. My inclination is towards full disclosure – God knows, we could *use* some good news down here – but ultimately, that decision rests with the President. I've called him and I expect he'll concur, but in the meantime I'd ask you and your crew-members to keep mum about it. We should only have to wait a few hours for his decision, anyway. Until we *do* hear back from the President, we'll put out a cover story that there has been a temporary loss of video and audio from the *Eagle*, but that other transmissions indicate that you guys and ladies are all well and proceeding normally with your business. Until further notice, those are your orders. I hope you understand."

White switched to "Send". Jacobson spoke up.

"Houston, copied and understood. Since we won't have the curious eyes of the world looking over our shoulders, we'll continue our research on the Anomaly, to the extent that we can with what scientific tools we have at our disposal here."

He paused a few long seconds, then said, "And Houston, about the other matter, I believe that information should be conveyed directly by you, to my crew. I have them standing by. Over."

White switched to "Receive". Neither he, nor Boyd, nor Tanaka – nor Sergei Chkalov, orbiting overhead – felt it useful to question Jacobson further, on this point.

Finally, six or so minutes later, the answer was theirs. This time, the person with the floor was the woman.

"Captain Jacobson, your last request copied and understood. It has fallen to me to break the following news to the crew, who I know will react to it with the professionalism and sense of duty that we all accept, when we join the space program," she said.

Abruzzio continued, "As you know, your flight to Mars has been a long one; I guess a lot can happen during that time, and this time, it sure *has*, unfortunately. About a month after the *Eagle* and *Infinity* started their escape-burn from orbit, telescopes on Earth detected a previously unknown comet – a big one, nearly the size of Shoemaker-Levy, on a peculiar trajectory. It was first seen outside the orbit of Jupiter, but we didn't pay much attention to it until it got just past the asteroid-belt; it has been accelerating ever since."

The scientist paused for a second or or two, then quietly stated, "Further trajectory-analysis determined that this object is virtually *certain* to impact with Earth, approximately one and a half months after your team is scheduled to set off on your return-trip back from Mars."

There was a stunned silence in the cabin of the *Eagle*. But the woman went on, trying to be as dispassionate as possible.

"We have named the comet TSO-2040C, although its more common name now is 'Lucifer', for obvious reasons," she noted. "The news leaked out within a few weeks of the discovery, despite our best efforts to keep it confidential, but so far we haven't seen any real signs of panic or despair over it, luckily. We still don't know exactly *where* the comet will impact the Earth, because of small perturbations in its trajectory that we're as yet unable to explain, but wherever it hits, given its mass, we are looking at an... *extinction-level* event."

Abruzzio cleared her throat and said, with welling eyes, "There is little chance that any higher level life forms, including human beings, will survive the impact and its immediate after-effects, since we expect that the initial impact will create a rupture in the Earth's crust of several hundreds to thousands of kilometers; the resulting release of magma and out-gassing would be enough to do wipe everything out by themselves, even if we were to discount the shock waves and *tsunami* that the impact will create. At first, we thought that we might be able to save a few of us by relocating to the highest mountain peaks, but then it was pointed out that the shock waves and super-hurricane force lower stratosphere winds that would be created by the impact would, literally, smash these hiding-places down to the ground, as well."

She stopped to catch her breath, then added, "Currently, NASA, the European Space Agency and the Russian Federation Space Agency are all working frantically on plans for 'life ark' type spacecraft to try to get some of us off the Earth before 'Lucifer' hits, but I have to tell you that the prospects aren't good here, either. Our best estimates are that it will take *decades*, at best, for the climate of Earth to stabilize enough after the impact, to be minimally suitable for human beings to return to the surface, but there appears to be no way to get enough air, water and food into space in sufficient quantities to give the project a fighting chance of success. As you're probably aware, the Moonbase is too small, really just a bit bigger than what you have there on Mars, and it was never intended for long-duration visits anyway. That's about it... all I can say."

Ramirez interrupted, "*Eagle*, when we first were told of this unhappy story here at Mission Control, your trip to Mars had just begun and we had to make a value judgment about what would be better: to burden you with this news, or to let you just go about your business as you have, up to now. As you know, Captain Jacobson, after I informed you about a month out, you and I jointly made the decision to withhold the news until the rest of the crew was on its way back to Earth, but, as we have seen, events have kind of made that set of assumptions invalid, now. We hope that your team will understand that we have only had what's best for everyone in mind, when we decided this. Over."

White turned the switch. Then he muttered, slowly and dejectedly, "Well, if that don't take the cake, ladies and gentlemen. We find the last dead civilization, then find out that we're one too. I – we – were gonna to be *heroes*, man! Now, we're just the Flying Dutchman of space, all dressed up in our space-suits with nowhere to go. I fuckin' *give up!*"

He turned his back to them in disgust.

Boyd quietly asked Tanaka, "Professor... did you know about this, too? For how long?"

She replied, "Not... *exactly*. The Captain told me that there was some very bad news from Earth, some time ago, but I thought it was a war or something like that. You know... the scientist in me understands it and comprehends it, but the human doesn't. It just can't be. It *can't*. Especially with what we just ran into here. It doesn't make any *sense*."

Now Jacobson spoke up. "Listen, everyone," he said. "At the outset I said that I expected everyone to carry on as usual, no matter what the message was; well, now you know why. I *know* that this is terrible news; but as professionals, whatever is or isn't happening with Earth shouldn't affect our own duties here, especially in view of what has happened here to us today. *Nothing* we do here is going to make any difference to the fate of life on Earth, but – if the worst comes to the worst – maybe the fact that we were here at all, will be testament enough to our species' accomplishments... and if Earth somehow manages to avoid this 'Lucifer' object, well then, our work will still have the importance that we knew it had this morning. So I want you to know that it's 'business as usual', until further notice. Is that *understood?*"

The other two just nodded, but Boyd offered, "Might as well, I guess. I mean, what else is there to do around here, anyway?"

He managed a grin.

The others just nodded, numbly.

White threw the "Off" switch on the view-screen. They all went to their respective duties and to, eventually, a fitful, doom-plagued sleep.

Enter If You Dare

The next day, oddly enough, most of them had more or less thrown off the shock of Abruzzio's revelation, however much it remained in the backs of their minds.

Perhaps it was the isolation and unfamiliarity of this place.

Earth, whatever its problems, it's so far away, out of the picture entirely, thought Boyd.

His mind tried to wander to thoughts of his wife and children, but he cut *that* off quickly and decisively, knowing how quickly thinking about it would depress him.

This day's expedition back to the Anomaly site – Boyd driving Jacobson and Tanaka, both of whom wanted to see the discovery for themselves, with White unenthusiastically manning the communications and mission control stations back in the *Eagle* – began much as had yesterday's, with each astronaut suiting up around noon-time, checking the others' equipment and awkwardly trundling on to the MMV. The group had traveled perhaps a third of the way to the site when the comm-link from the *Eagle* lit up.

"Transmission from Earth, Captain," announced White. "Should I pipe it through?"

"Affirmative," replied Jacobson. "Hello, Earth. What can the Mars team do for you today?"

The voice of Hector Ramirez sounded over the intercom. "Greetings, Oberg Base, this is Ramirez at Mission Control, along with Sylvia Abruzzio and Fred McPherson. I'll let Fred take it from here. Over."

Another voice said, "Hello, Captain Jacobson and Astronauts Boyd, White, Tanaka and Cosmonaut Chkalov, this is Fred McPherson of the White House Science Liaison office. I have a very important message for you from a very important person. I'm patching him in, now. Sir, go ahead."

A ghostly voice, yet familiar, now met their ears.

"Mars Team, this is the President speaking, via relay from the White House," it began.

"First, let me congratulate you all on the remarkable scientific and archaeological achievement you have just made," said the American leader. "Your team has fulfilled and at least partly answered one of mankind's most fundamental questions, that, is, 'are we alone'. Last night, in consultation with Fred McPherson and the National Security Council, I made the decision that an event of this importance should be shared with the rest of humanity. So, as we speak, our conversation is being transmitted all over the Earth, as will be subsequent events that occur on Mars regarding this "Anomaly", as it is called."

He continued, "As you are now aware, unfortunately, the news from and about Earth isn't so good; we're under threat of extinction from the 'Lucifer' object, which is due to strike our planet in a very short time. I can assure your team that our government is sparing no effort to find a way to overcome this threat and protect your families and loved ones. Currently, we have several options on the table, ranging from using nuclear missiles to deflect 'Lucifer' from its course, to a manned mission to place a high-yield nuclear device directly on the comet, to evacuation of the Earth itself, if it comes to that. You have my personal assurance that I'll keep your team appraised of the results of these projects, as each one is implemented. In the meantime, I can only ask you to continue to execute your own mission with the professionalism that you have so far showed us."

There was a short pause, then the President stated, "As a personal note... I have been thinking...

He paused again and then concluded, "Whatever happens to us down here, *you* will still have a fighting chance. Learn all you can about what's up there on Mars. When all's said and done, the only thing that got our ancestors out ahead of the saber-tooth tigers, was a little more know-how. Maybe you'll find out what happened to the Martians... so we can learn how not to have it happen to us Earthlings. That's all I have to say, Oberg Base; good luck, and god-speed."

Boyd wondered if the President had been reading from a script; the man was really just a *Fortune 500* business type and wasn't known for great oratory.

But it sounded quite natural; maybe it was the occasion.

Jacobson answered, "Mr. President, it's always an honor and a privilege to speak with you, sir, but no more so than under the present, difficult circumstances – we know that you've a lot on your mind. I'm sure that I speak on behalf not only of myself, but of all my other team-members, when I say that we will continue our mission as planned, until we're ordered to do otherwise. Right now, along with Professor Tanaka and Major Boyd, I'm in the Mars Mobility Vehicle, *en route* to the site of the Anomaly, where we plan to run more intensive tests than we were were able to do yesterday, since we now have better equipment with us. Major White is in charge of the *Eagle* and will keep the communications-link to Earth up, so you can see what we're doing, minute by minute. Please let us know if there's anything special that you want us to do; as you know, the plans are for us to be here for the four days at least, so we'll have plenty of time."

Now, Jacobson paused a bit, uncharacteristically. Then he stated,

"And please give our best wishes, love and prayers to our families and loved ones down there on Earth. We'd be there with them, if we could; but right now, we've got a job to do up here. We know they understand."

There was no reply from Earth.

Boyd hoped that the video-link couldn't see past the red dust fog on his visor.

The MMV continued on its bumpy way, with all three of its inhabitants each lost in his or her own morose thoughts.

Not even repeated jokes from White, trying to play the fool back at home base in the *Eagle,* could roust any of them until the the vehicle reached the bottom of the alien-smooth, winding ramp at the mesa site.

"Brent," requested Jacobson, "Your turn to play go-cart attendant here. The Professor and I will find our way up there. Keep the link up so you can see what we're seeing, as we go. Cherie, let's link up."

He fumbled for the climbing-rope, but was able to attach it to Tanaka's suit with little further ado. The two of them set off together, up the ramp, Jacobson leading the other one.

"Checking," said Boyd via intercom, as they disappeared around the first bend. "Radiation profile similar to what the Professor found yesterday, climbing as you get closer, but still safe, for a while, at least. How's it going, Captain? I'd advise you to move slowly up there, as Devon and I found out yesterday, it's harder going than it looks, at first."

"Affirmative," replied Jacobson. "Damn Martian dust is *everywhere*, I can see why you and Major White had such a tough slog up here the other day, I'm having to pay attention to every step to avoid slipping on the stuff. Professor, are you doing okay?"

"No problem," said Tanaka. "Just like figure-skating, minus the skates. You know, Captain... I gave it up, in order to finish my PH.D., then to write science-books. Right now, I'm questioning those choices."

They all could hear her smile.

For the next eighteen minutes, all that Boyd and the others heard was the strained breathing of the two adventurers. Then, finally, they were almost at the platform. Jacobson's helmet, with attached video-cam, cleared the plane of the platform.

"*Holy sh –*" he heard Boyd shout. "Captain! Do you *see!*"

"No, what?" answered Jacobson, until he righted himself and stood in front of the side of the mesa.

"I can't *believe...*" he stammered. "But it was shut *tight*, yesterday! Brent, Devon, Sergei, do you copy? It's *open* now. Earth, can you see this? I don't know what happened... I suppose we must have triggered it yesterday, without knowing that we did so. But we didn't *touch* anything... did we?"

Tanaka, now standing beside him, said, "That's correct – I'm *sure* that we didn't come into physical contact with it. Maybe it has a proximity-device of some kind? Well, in any event, we now don't have to worry about preservation protocol for whatever is inside – look at the dust, it has covered the open part of the entrance; *everything* in there has already been exposed to the atmosphere. We might as well see what's inside."

For a second, Jacobson just stood in front of her, staring into her view-visor. His mind spun with the facts and events that now confronted him and them all.

Too much, too fast, too momentous.

At length he decided, "Yeah, Professor, I concur. Earth, be it so noted, on my authority, I have decided that Professor Tanaka and I will enter the doorway and explore whatever is beyond it – the responsibility for whatever happens in there, is mine alone. I will provide Mission Control with a more full explanation of this decision later, but suffice it to say here, the President has instructed us to find out as much as we can about the Anomaly. We'll execute this order, as long as the risks involved are not unreasonable."

"Major Boyd," he inquired, "What's the radiation situation like?"

"It's definitely higher in the direction of the portal," Boyd noted, looking at his instruments. "But, the alpha, beta, gamma and X-ray levels are still easily in the safe-zone. Professor, I'm no expert in rad-analysis, but I've never *seen* readings like this; there are spikes of the unknown stuff which show up one second and then vanish the next, almost like a SAM radar that gets turned off when you fire an ARM at it... but the values for the known, dangerous types are still nominal or just above nominal... how's that *possible*?"

There was a pause.

Amazing, thought Boyd, *I've finally found something that can confound the dear Professor.*

But she eventually replied.

"I honestly don't know, Brent", evaded Tanaka. "Captain, the only plausible explanation that *I* can think of, is that either the instruments are malfunctioning, or we have encountered some new type of radiation that has never previously been seen. Either way, we're running a risk by getting closer to the source."

Jacobson thought for a second, then directed, "I'm willing to take that chance. But you don't have to if you don't want to, Cherie."

A voice interrupted, over the intercom. "Send me in, instead, Captain," said White. "Y'all *know* I can probably make it there in twenty minutes, if I run all the way."

They all laughed semi-hysterically at this comment, but Tanaka countered with, "No *way* are you going in there, alone, Captain. Besides, I can't let Devon get credit for *this* one, can I?"

"Very well, then," said Jacobson. "Here we go. Brent, Devon, Sergei, please sound off that you're getting the signal from our view-cams. I want Earth to see what's going on, here."

Three voices answered, sequentially.

"MMV link affirmative", voiced Boyd.

"*Eagle* link affirmative," added White.

"*Infinity* link and down-link to Houston, affirmative," chimed in Chkalov.

"Let's go," ordered Jacobson. He inched forward, into the entrance.

"Pretty dark beyond the entranceway, *Eagle*," Jacobson commented. "I'm activating my helmet-light, Professor, could you do so too, please? Visual check. I'm going forward. There are stairs going down, ten or twelve of them... wait a minute... I see a chamber of some kind, good size, maybe twenty by twenty meters... there are open portals to other chambers, at least two, off to the sides. Wait – Cherie, what's *that?* See it? The object in the middle of the main chamber?"

"Yes, I see it, Captain," replied Tanaka. "*Eagle*, are you getting this? It's *fascinating!* If I was on Earth, I'd say I was in a burial-chamber of some sort – there are inscriptions on some of the walls, but I'm not close enough to see them exactly yet, and there seem to be jars or containers arranged in various places in the chamber. That rectangular structure in the middle looks like a sarcophagus, maybe? It looks to be at least two meters or so long by a meter or so wide, it's about a meter and a half from the floor, with two ramps of the same silicate ramp-stuff that got us up here, on either side of it, almost level with the top of the structure. It's still pretty dark – our helmets are the only light in here – so I can't see into the side-chambers. Awfully dusty, too... but judging from the how much is on the inside compared to how fast the stuff gets deposited outside, I'd say that this chamber must have been sealed for many *thousands* of years, if not longer."

"Radiation check," called Jacobson. "I'm finding it warm in here. Professor, what about you?"

"Same readings as before," answered Boyd over the intercom. "Same *strange* readings. No change from previous status."

"Just checked my temperature-gage," added Tanaka. "Ambient temperature same as outside. I think what you're feeling is excitement and exertion. I'm feeling it too. I think we can be forgiven for that."

"Okay," acknowledged Jacobson. "Proceeding down. Let's be *very* careful, Professor; on Earth, we all know about how they booby-trap tombs to stop them from being pillaged. Taking the first step."

Step by step, foot by foot, they descended the stairs, until they were standing on the ground-floor of the chamber.

For a few seconds, they just stood there, immersed in the contrary emotions of wonder and amazement at the fantastic discovery that they were experiencing, along with sadness and worry about Earth, so far away.

Presently, Tanaka spoke.

"Captain," she requested, "I'd like to examine the structure in the center... its construction looks different from the rest of what's in here. I think if I clear some of the dust from it..."

"Granted," agreed Jacobson. "I'll help you. You start from that side, I'll do this one."

They both positioned on opposite sides of the structure, as far apart as the tow-rope would allow. Their suit-gloves started to brush the caked Martian dust from the top of the structure. Something translucent came into view.

"*Commander!*" shot the alarmed voice of Boyd, over the intercom. "Radiation energy-levels climbing *rapidly!* You'd better get out of there!"

"Wait," asked Tanaka. "Is the gamma and X-ray climbing, too?"

"Negative," replied the pilot. "The ones that we *know* about are just above nominal. It's the spikes of this damn *unknown* signature that are skyrocketing. Professor, every second as we speak, you're being exposed to it. I'm really worried."

"Captain," demanded the scientist, "What do you want to do? Should we abort?"

If any could have seen it, Jacobson bit his lip as he replied.

"I don't think so," he decided. "If this stuff were dangerous, we'd have felt it by now. I consider the risk of continuing to be acceptable. But keep us informed of any further changes, Major. Continuing to clear the object."

He resumed wiping off the dust.

"It's coming into view," noted Tanaka, for the audience of undoubted millions who were watching their every move.

"Boy, this is *hard* work," she complained. "I'm sweating more than I ever did in my worst workout back in my figure-skating days. But I can see it – wow, this is *incredible*, Captain! It's *indeed* some kind of burial-artifact – the top, which we have almost cleared now, is made of a crystalline substance, and I can almost see – wait..."

"*Jesus, Mary and Joseph,*" exclaimed Jacobson, "It's a *person*. I can *see* her!"

Tanaka, equally stunned, retorted, "Yes – you're right! A buried Martian, and it looks humanoid... a female ruler, maybe, it has all the human physical characteristics! *Amazingly* well-preserved, too – it has clearly been dead for a long time, judging from the dryness of that skin... but other than for that, it looks like it might have been buried yesterday. *Eagle, Infinity,* Houston, I'm going to get closer so you can get a good look, yourselves, I'll illuminate the face of the object so you can start Earth-side analysis."

"Confirmed, Professor," declared Boyd.

"And I thought I had seen *everythin',*" added White.

"Okay," announced Tanaka. "Illuminating now."

She bent over the casket, with her view-cam and helmet-light no more than a few centimeters from the top of the structure.

"Weird," she observed, "The crystalline substance on the top seems to be getting clearer, less translucent. I can... I can... see... wait a sec..."

She stammered incoherently, as if suddenly confused.

Tanaka braced herself on the structure, with both arms supporting the weight of her upper-body.

"Cherie!" interjected Jacobson. "You *okay?*"

"Fine... I think, Captain," she prevaricated. "Just felt a little *faint* there, for a second... I'm okay now. No, it's not radiation. Symptoms aren't the same, Sam. Let's have a good look at it."

Tanaka again bent over the structure, to – had she been able to hear it – the collective gasps of thousands of onlookers, back on Earth, as they beheld the face of this long-lost being, and now – there could be no doubt of it – a female humanoid.

It was remarkably similar to a young European human woman of perhaps her late teens or early twenties; except, that is, for four very prominent incisor-teeth, like those found on some human females but much sharper, displayed as the lip of the creature had withered and retracted with the ages.

Evidently its hair had been blond, or maybe white, at one time, and its pale forehead seemed perhaps slightly larger than for an average human woman, but not so much so as to look really unusual.

The being's visage was, even in its dessicated state, possessed of an unearthly beauty; its lambent eyelids were closed and its countenance was serene, as if it had just laid down one day to die.

Evidently it had once been covered in woven fabric, but only tiny fragments of this now remained; however, most of the creature's upper-body and trunk was still covered by a rusting chain-mail garment of some sort, revealing enough to clearly define it as female, obscuring enough to avoid scandalizing the prurient.

Its – *her* – arms were crossed, resting in repose on top of the chain-garment, clutching an elaborately-inscribed, intricately-crafted piece of jewelry.

Just looking at her, somehow brought a feeling of beauty and majesty, as if one were listening to a fine symphony, in a great concert-hall.

It wasn't just the setting; no, it was *more*, but none could tell how or why.

This was a find that would have the scientists working for centuries, if, that was, Earth *had* more than a couple of months in which to conduct archaeological affairs.

"Words fail me here," stuttered Tanaka. "This is an *incredible* discovery – one that I can't rationalize being here in its apparent form. Captain, what do you want to do now? Captain? I... uhh... I'm hearing *music? Nice* music... Celtic-rock-stuff? What's going *on?*"

Jacobson stepped back, as if rocked on his heels, like a boxer taking an unforeseen blow to the head.

"I... *what?* Oh, sorry, Cherie, I guess I'm feeling a bit faint, too," he replied.

"Listen," he went on, "I've been thinking about Boyd's radiation-readings... We'd better get out of here, run a med-scan on both of us so we can confirm that this unusual radiation isn't having any lasting effects, then return when we know we're safe. We've already done enough for a day, wouldn't you... think... Cherie... *Cherie?*"

He wheeled, then slid a bit as he tried to stop the weight of Tanaka's slumping body, from pulling him down.

"*Professor!*" came the voice of Boyd over the intercom. "What's going *on!* Can you hear me, Cherie?! Captain Jacobson! *Reply, please!*"

"She... appears...", Boyd heard the voice of Jacobson saying, straining as a man trying to lift a heavy weight, "... to be out... I'm feeling very light-headed, Brent... I'll try to get her out, but my legs... feel like lead... if I can't, stay out of here, you got that? Stay out of here... something's going on... can you hear that? It's *music*... a symphony? Who the *Hell* – ? I think..."

There was a "thud".

Jacobson hit the floor near the bottom stair, butt-down, legs-forward, facing the central structure.

He slumped slightly forward as the gray fog of unconsciousness enveloped him.

"*Sir! Captain!* I have to get –" shouted Boyd, now in a panic. "*Sir!* Can you hear me! *Captain!*"

There was no reply, other than for the sound of heavy, rhythmic breathing coming from both Tanaka and Jacobson.

"*Jaysus,*" interjected White, from the *Eagle*. "Brent – what do we do now? Sergei, y'all copy? We can't just leave them in there, whatever the Captain said! Radiation or not, they only got about another couple hours of oxygen in those suits. I'm gonna suit up now!"

"Negative," argued Boyd, "Wait a sec, Devon... let's *think* for a bit, first. Their vitals are still stable, but they're unconscious, that's for sure. I'm looking at the Professor's view-cam, now – it doesn't look like it would be too hard for me to get them out of there, one by one, if I can last long enough down there to untie them. I can drag them... hold on... something on the Captain's... *mother of God, what's that!*"

They regarded the view-screen display taken from Jacobson's helmet, which was pointed directly at the central structure.

Which was... *opening.*

As they watched in wary astonishment, the translucent material on top parted in the middle, half slowly sliding forward, half backward, exposing its contents to the thin Martian air for the first time in uncounted centuries.

A cloud of red dust billowed, then slowly fell to ground.

"Sergei... man... are you getting this?" stammered Boyd. "Jesus, what a time to be playing music. Devon, whatever you got there, turn it off!"

"Uh... Brent... I hear it, man, but it's not comin' from *this* end," replied White. "Damn nice, whatever it is. Maybe a malfunction in the comm-link? No time to troubleshoot it now. We gotta have a plan, Brent. Y'all got one? *Fast,* man, *fast.*"

"I'm... uhh... checking the radiation. *Migod...* weird stuff's off the scale, but the others are still okay. I think I can chance it... I'll set out now, the vitals from the Captain and the Professor are still good, but who knows for how long... *now* what... *you gotta be kidding me!*"

Boyd's jaw dropped, as he shot another glance at the Jacobson camera.

At first, it was just the tip of a thin, dessicated finger that uncertainly ran back and forth for a second or two, along the edge of demarcation between the former top of the structure and its sides.

Eventually, two or three more fingers appeared. Then there was a hand, which grasped the side of the structure.

They heard a soft moan, the sounds of pained, forced breathing, then a "thud".

Again, they saw and heard the same.

A third time. A fourth.

The hand grasped the side of the structure, firmly, semi-confidently. Another hand grasped the opposite side.

"Uhh... what do we do *now?*" unhelpfully demanded White. "This ain't in the briefing books, man. I'm out of my comfort-zone, man. *Seriously* out of it –"

"I don't know," answered Boyd. "But I'd bet you that's what knocked out the Professor and the Captain," he added. "If it can do *that –*"

The creature now came slowly into view, as it used its arms to raise its fore-body over the plane of the structure's sides. It faced the far end of the chamber, evidently unaware of humanity's first representatives on Mars just beside it.

Strange, exciting music, reverberated dimly in the recesses of the local humans' minds, as it took deep breaths of Martian air, coughing and wheezing.

The Mars-thing raised its body again, this time evidently kneeling. Then it turned to its right, and beheld the two strange-looking beings, looking like oddly stuffed children's toys with glassy, shining head-coverings, slumped over in front of it.

Boyd, White and Chkalov looked on in stunned amazement, holding their breath.

A select few on Earth (the public video-feeds had, of course, been switched off at Mission Control, early in the incident), along with the Mars contingent, now had their first look at the face of a living, extra-terrestrial creature, though – if the truth be known – the experience was anticlimactic.

The creature looked much more like a young, disarmingly pretty human female, than one of the bug-eyed monsters that science-fiction had traditionally expected. Her eyes, though of an alien, yellowish-orange color, were kind and gentle, and her countenance, upon seeing the humans, was more of surprise and concern, than of threat or hostility.

There was a glow about her, alien but inspiring, invisible yet somehow still perceptible.

She tried to get her legs over the side of the structure in which she had slept, and succeeded in doing so after about a minute or two of evidently painful effort.

Slowly, stiffly, as if each muscle was stabbing her with pain as it was called into service, the creature attempted to move down the ramp on the side of the structure.

Halfway down, the alien-girl lost her balance, careening into the cold Martian sand, head-first. She slowly braced herself on all fours, push-up wise, shaking off the sand, gasping and wheezing.

The cameras caught a glimpse of a face twisted in pain, which would no doubt have been accompanied by tears, had not the centuries denuded the poor being of most of her body fluids.

Semi-kneeling, she now was in front of the slumping, unconscious Jacobson.

She looked closely at the transparent face-visor.

Her hand swept forward, touching it to clear the residue of dust that had partly obscured it.

A smile came over her face – now much fuller and less dry-looking, than it had been inside the casket, even a few minutes earlier – as she saw Jacobson's slumbering face inside the suit.

"Unbelievable," whispered Boyd. "I think it understands that there's a man in there."

"And it's gettin' s*tronger*," added White. "I bet it's some kind of *vampire*. It's *feedin'* off the Professor and the Captain! We *gotta* get 'em out of there!"

But they had forgotten that the link to Jacobson was still active.

At hearing this unknown, language through the space-suit, the creature gave a sudden look of amazement. She then looked straight at Jacobson and said something in her own, chirping, burbling tongue.

"It's trying to *communicate* with us," commented White. *"Say* somethin' to it."

"This... uhh... is Major Brent Boyd, of the United Nations Earth expedition to Mars," clumsily started Boyd. "We come in peace."

It was a cliché, no doubt; but it was all he could think of.

The Mars-creature seemed to notice the message, but just gave another toothy smile and cocked her head oddly to the side, in what was evidently some kind of body gesture.

She now started to look over Jacobson's suit carefully, observing every item, looking for the source of Boyd's message.

After finding none, she cocked back her head with her hand in front of her mouth, first moving her jaw as if metaphorically drinking, then as if eating. She then knelt in front of the astronaut and clasped her hands in front of it, as if pleading.

"Man, for a Martian, does she ever look *cute,*" observed Boyd. "What a puppy-dog face."

"It is hungry and thirsty," noted Sergei Chkalov, from his vantage-point in the *Infinity.* "Major Boyd, perhaps we can turn that to our advantage."

Boyd switched off the forward comm-link to Jacobson and Tanaka's suits, then said, "You *bet,* Sergei – Devon, I think I know how we can get her – it – distracted long enough for me to get the Captain and the Professor out of there. I got my lunch-rations and my water-bottle here in the MMV. Maybe I can use it as a peace offering. And," – he checked the instrumentation – "It looks like the radiation-levels are dropping a bit. I think I can chance it. I'm heading up the pathway now. When I get to the platform I'm going to leave a rope going from the top as I go down the stairs, so that if I go under, Devon, you can at least pull me out. Anybody got a better idea?"

Sure that he could hear both other men shaking their heads, Boyd gathered what he needed, left the MMV and headed up the sloping entrance-ramp, huffing and puffing as he pushed his movement speed as high as he dared. About halfway up the ramp, another voice manifested itself over the intercom.

"Oberg Base, Major Boyd, Major White, Cosmonaut Chkalov, this is Science Officer McPherson at Mission Control in Houston, with an emergency message. We have just become aware of the events in the burial-chamber and of the status of Captain Jacobson and of Professor Tanaka. We're grieving the loss of these two fine pioneers of space-exploration, as no doubt you're doing yourself; but in view of their sudden incapacitation, we cannot allow any more of the expedition to enter the chamber and thereby expose themselves to whatever has affected the Captain and the Professor."

"I am, therefore ordering you, on the authority of the President," he continued, "To return to the *Eagle* immediately and await further orders from Mission Control as we decide them. I say again, return to the *Eagle* – do *not* attempt to rescue Jacobson and Tanaka. We know that this will be difficult, but we don't want to lose any more of you. Waiting for your acknowledgment. Over."

Saying it for all the world to hear, and not caring in the least, White shot back, "What the *fuck* he talkin' 'bout? Brent my man... y'all hear that? He probably hasn't seen what just happened, yet."

Boyd just replied, matter-of-factually, "No."

He thought for a second, and added, "Must be a communications-failure. Major White – did you hear anything from Houston lately? Tell them that I'm not leaving *anybody* in there... *period*."

He continued grimly on, up the pathway.

White replied, "Yeah, but it was garbled. Couldn't fully understand it. Good luck in there."

After a few long minutes more, Boyd was almost at the outside platform.

"Devon, what can you see on the view-screens?" he asked. "Where is she?"

"Dunno," White replied. "She – it – whatever – moved out of the Captain's field of view, when she didn't get whatever she wanted from him. Haven't seen anything for a couple of minutes."

Taking the last step, Boyd now advanced on to the platform and righted himself fully.

He stopped, instantly.

"Major White," he stuttered, "I have located the... *creature*. She is just past the portal, directly in front of me."

Despite having seen the being through the view-screen, Boyd was still paralyzed, for a moment, upon the inner realization that it was *real*, in the flesh, right here, right now, in front of him, an intelligent *something* from another world, another time, another everything.

For a second, he just studied it visually, wondering how it could *possibly* sustain itself on the negligible Martian atmosphere or survive the brutal cold of the outside environment, especially with bare feet.

Then he felt a sensation of awe – a feeling like he should fall to his knees and just beg this alien being for, well, at least the lives of his fellow crew-members – even though it outwardly looked like nothing more than a dirt-smeared, impoverished, starving human female in tattered, rusted chain-link garments.

It must have been the occasion...

No... it was *more*. Something *more*.

Boyd caught a glimpse of her now obviously, seductively female figure, slender and boyish but with too much of it for complete modesty – revealing at least as much as a risqué Earth bikini – showing through the link-mail of her garment.

He suppressed the unnaturally wild rush of lecherous urges that suddenly beset his mind. He was a married man, after all; but he tried all the while not to think of his family, or of their likely fate.

She had beaten him to the gesture.

The Mars-creature advanced a couple of paces, fell to her knees, head bowed down towards the ground, hands clasped in front. She stayed like this for about four seconds, then slowly lifted her head. She was now looking directly at the visor of his space-suit.

Boyd thought he noticed something changing subtly in the appearance of her eyes – their color, maybe – ? as the space-girl brought a hand over her eyebrows, shielding her eyes from the Martian sun.

She smiled at him, then, with pleading eyes, made the same eating- and drinking-gestures that she had made earlier, inside the chamber, saying something completely unintelligible in her chirping, whistling language.

It sounded like nothing he had ever heard on Earth – *that* was for sure.

This was his chance. "Give her the damn food!" he heard White demand, over the intercom.

Boyd fumbled for the ration-pack, found that, then took his water-bottle, complete with stop-valve sealing tube, from his side-pack. He slowly bent over and placed these two items in the thin layer of soft sand on the platform, about a meter in front of him, equidistant with the position of the creature. He backed off a bit.

She shuffled forward, still on her knees, head slightly bowed down.

"She's *afraid* of you, Major," he heard Chkalov claim, over the intercom.

"Good," replied Boyd, "Because that makes *two* of us."

The alien-girl now started examining the gifts that Boyd had left for her. She shook the water-bottle, quickly understanding that it contained liquids.

Glancing nervously at Boyd every couple of seconds, she tried to suck from the drinking-tube, but the valve had been designed for connection with a corresponding opening on the astronauts' space-suits, so this effort came to naught. Boyd saw her frustration.

"Devon," he said, "I'm going to take a chance, now."

He advanced to a spot beside the Mars-girl, then cautiously got down on his knees, kneeling beside her. He extended his hand outward.

She gave him back the bottle. He activated the retaining catch on the side of the bottle, loosening its top, giving it a slight twist. He handed the bottle back to the creature.

She looked at him with a knowingly friendly, almost desperate smile. Then she took the bottle and in one swift motion, removed the cap and partook of a quick swig of the water, sloshing it around in her mouth for a few seconds, concentrating on determining its taste and composition.

"She is taking a *big* chance," commented Chkalov. "Our germs could kill her."

"Maybe," whispered Boyd, "But there's an equal chance that Earth germs won't find her body compatible – and if her basic physiology is like ours, being without water will kill her much more quickly. Besides... it's *her* choice, not mine."

The Mars-girl had evidently made her decision, because she now quaffed the bottle in its entirety, drinking it greedily down to the last drop, making sucking-sounds as she tried to lick out the final remnants of any moisture the bottle had in it.

With each draught, her breathing became deeper, her complexion became softer and fuller and she seemed stronger. Out of the corner of his eye, Boyd could have sworn he saw something – what the *hell?* – lighting her trunk up from inside – but whatever this was, it lasted for only a fraction of a second.

The repast, however, was still not enough, because she again gave the pleading, hands-clasped gesture, asking for more.

All Boyd could do was hold out his hands, fingers outstretched, palms towards her. He hoped that she would understand what he meant.

She looked puzzled for a second or two, then slumped forward with a sad frown. Then she grabbed the ration-package.

Boyd remembered that it was vacuum-sealed and that it ordinarily required a utility-knife to open, but he had forgotten about this being's formidable teeth, which cleft through the package's alumiwrap sealing with little apparent effort.

She sniffed at the food-rations within.

Her face puckered up in disgust.

"She doesn't like our cooking," joked White. "What kind of rations did y'all bring with you out there, Brent?"

"Beef Stroganoff," Boyd replied. "Maybe she's a vegetarian."

The Mars-girl, whatever her eating-preferences, was, however, not in a position to be picky, today.

Clearly forcing herself to ignore the taste, she downed the entire ration-package as fast as Boyd had ever seen even a hungry Air Force recruit back from a ten-mile training run, do.

She bowed her head to him and clasped her hands in front. Then, with a very serious, almost wistful countenance on her face, the Mars-girl took something from a hidden side-pocket in her chain-garment – it was a jewel or personal ornament, of some kind – whispered some incomprehensible phrase in the direction of this bauble, kissed and hugged it as a mother kisses a newborn babe, and held it out in the palm of her hand, in front of Boyd.

He noticed that the fangs had somehow retracted, with her teeth looking now more or less like those of any superficially attractive human female.

"She wants to pay you back, Major Boyd," observed Chkalov. "I suggest that you take her gift."

Boyd reached out his hand to take the jewel and put it in a side-compartment of his suit.

Did I hear her voice, just now? absentmindedly reflected the astronaut.

Can't *be, she didn't move her lips... and it was more like a memory from times long past...*

Then, reflexively without even realizing what he was doing, Boyd offered his hand to the creature, as one would on Earth.

She inched forward, then grasped it, staring at him with doe-like, wondering, orange-yellow eyes.

He was caught by that alien glance and suddenly felt as if in a dream, as if he *knew* this creature on a deep and personal level. Again, he perceived, not heard, strange, beautiful music, like a few bars of a piece by a Martian Debussy, haunting, yet subtle and very far away.

I can't believe that this is really happening, thought Boyd,
I'm holding hands with a being from another world.
The first human to ever do.

For too brief a moment, they just stayed there, kneeling before each other in the soft Martian sand, man from Earth, female from somewhere else, joined by the common bonds of intelligence and mutual need. Then Boyd heard McPherson, again, over the intercom.

"Major Boyd and Oberg Base, this is McPherson again, at Mission Control. We have just seen the events in the chamber. Team, we're at a loss for words down here, but especially in view of this new and obviously unknown factor, we have to insist that you comply with our original orders. Major, it is the opinion of both myself and Ms. Abruzzio that the extraterrestrial being that the Professor and the Captain encountered down there, is the factor responsible for their incapacitation. In that light, we feel it all the more imperative that you avoid any contact with this creature until we can come up with a credible plan to fight it safely, before it becomes any stronger. I'm sure I don't have to remind you that I speak with the authority of your Commander-In-Chief. Please confirm. Over."

The voice of Sergei Chkalov now sounded.

"Perhaps, but not *my* Commander-In-Chief, Major Boyd," he reminded. "I suggest that you continue your current plan of action. I have also been remotely monitoring the radiation-levels and they have subsided substantially. I believe that you should be able to enter the chamber, now."

"Amen to *that*," agreed White.

"Yeah," confirmed Boyd, slowly releasing the creature's hand and returning to his feet. "I had better get going on this before the air runs out."

He began releasing the guide-rope, as he inched forward into the chamber-portal, turning on his helmet-light. Then he felt a tug on the end.

He wheeled and saw the Mars-girl, holding the end of the rope at midriff-height.

"She's tryin' to help," observed White. "Friendliest little green man, okay – little green *woman* – I ever met."

Boyd slowly went back to her.

He gently grabbed the rope from her grasp – she gave no struggle – and let it fall to the ground, waggling his index finger at her in an Earth gesture which she evidently understood, since she just cocked her head to the side in the same odd manner she had used earlier, leaving the end of the rope undisturbed on the ground.

Boyd turned his back to her and started rapidly down the stairs into the chamber.

In a few quick seconds he was on the chamber-floor, beside the bodies of Tanaka and Jacobson.

"Devon," he asked, "How are their vitals? Is one doing better than the other? I don't want to triage here, but I have to know the facts."

"Checking," replied White. "Vitals are okay, but their breathing is arrhythmic and most of their biometrics are depressed... pulses are slow, for example. The Professor's signs are a bit lower than the Captain's but neither one is really much better than the other."

"Understood," acknowledged Boyd. "Okay, then... I'm going to try to get the Professor, first."

He moved to Tanaka's suit and unattached it from Jacobson's, then put his gloved hands under her forearms and started to drag her towards the stairs.

Although Tanaka was a fairly petite woman and despite the lower Martian gravity, the effort was extremely difficult. Her space-suit added many kilograms to her weight, and soon Boyd found himself sweating profusely as he called upon every ounce of his military physical-training at each step.

After more than a few long minutes, he finally was able to deposit Tanaka's body at the entrance in front of the Mars-girl, who had seemingly been warming herself in an odd manner, palms outward, face directly pointed at the sun, evidently trying to catch the feeble rays of the Martian sun.

With a look of concern, she promptly knelt in front of the slumping female astronaut.

"Major Boyd," intoned the voice of McPherson, again, "Down here on Earth, we have just seen the events before and since my last message. We're astonished at what we are watching; this is the biggest scientific discovery in all of human history – we all feel incredibly privileged to be living through it. While we cannot endorse your insubordination – we'll have more to say about that, at a more appropriate time – we're prepared to let you manage the situation as you best see fit. All we can ask, which you should know already from common sense, is not to let this creature have any direct personal contact with any member of the team. You'll have to exercise decontamination protocol on any implement that it has touched; just because it may be able to withstand our collection of Earth bugs and germs, doesn't necessarily mean that *we* can survive whatever *it* carries along, itself. And –"

He paused for a few seconds, then requested,

"Major Boyd, tell it that the people of Earth want to be friends."

I've already got that covered, mused Boyd.

Now all you have to do is make sure that there still is *an Earth, for it to make friends*, with.

"Understood, affirmative, Mission Control," spoke the astronaut. "So far, the creature has not displayed any threatening behavior, so I'm reasonably sure that we are safe for the moment."

"And, for the record, Houston," apologized Boyd, "Please excuse any previous excesses in our language, today. We're all under a *lot* of stress. I'm now going back to get Captain Jacobson. After that, I'll try to get Professor Tanaka and the Captain to the MMV, then back to the *Eagle*. Time's of the essence, as we have to factor travel-time back to Oberg Base, in calculating the amount of air left to all of the Anomaly party, including myself. Over."

With every step feeling heavy now, he edged his way down to the chamber floor.

He tugged on Jacobson's shoulders, once, twice, thrice – to no avail. The Captain was just too *heavy.*

He tried again, sweating and cursing, hoping that he had remembered to mute the intercom.

No matter *what,* he could not allow things to end this way. He was *not* going to leave his commanding officer to suffocate in the cold Martian sand.

Boyd kept trying and Jacobson's body moved, but infinitesimally.

The astronaut began to realize that at *this* pace, he would likely exhaust his own air-supply before he even got Jacobson to the top of the stairs.

Despondent, he was about to sit down, take a breather, think of something, *anything.* But all of a sudden, he saw a dirty, bare hand on the Captain's other arm, followed by a mighty yank.

Boyd turned suddenly to see the Mars-girl, with a firm grip on Jacobson.

She was *helping* him!

He stared at her for a second and was met by a stare in return, but a knowing one, with those amber-hued (or were they blue? he could have *sworn* that, a few minutes ago) eyes looking at him with a look of saturnine, steely determination.

Looking into those eyes was like looking into the depths of the ocean, or maybe into the highest reaches of a clear, blue sky; Boyd felt lost, in over his head, as if dealing with something beyond his comprehension, and it was more than just a passing idea, he felt sure of that, somehow.

But the feeling lasted only a second. He had *work* to do, and his mind snapped back to reality.

He started to pull on Jacobson's other arm himself and was only partly surprised to feel the big man's body feel much easier to move.

They cleared the first step. White's voice came in over the intercom.

"Brent? Y'all there, man? Your head-cam cut out there for a second, but it's back now. How's it goin' with the Captain? His vitals are still good, so are the Professor's, but we're getting pretty close to the safety margin, air-supply wise, I mean. Hey – I see your camera display now, but how are y'all draggin' the man just with one arm? What's happenin' there?"

Hardly believing it himself, Boyd replied, "I'm *not,* Devon. I have a new friend helping me, with the other arm."

He momentarily turned his head to the left, giving White, Chkalov and, ten minutes later, Earth itself, a clear look at the Mars-girl, hands clamped on Jacobson's other arm.

She gave an obliging half-smile, in between strained breaths – evidently, this work was straining even her native ability to extract oxygen from the thin Martian atmosphere.

"And, for something so petite-looking, she's sure not lacking for upper-body strength," explained Boyd. "I could barely *budge* the Commander, but with her helping, he's easy to move. Hate to think what she could bench-press. Almost at the top, now... going through the door... here, I'll step back and give you a shot."

His helmet-camera revealed the slumped bodies of Tanaka and Jacobson, propping each other up just to one side of the chamber-portal, with the Mars-girl kneeling beside them, studying them carefully, then rapping lightly on each astronaut's helmet with one knuckle, then saying something directly at Boyd, in her inscrutable language.

She gestured in an outward-pointing motion, with a quizzical look on her face, eyebrows upwards. Then she held her hands out in front of her, palms open, fingers pointed downwards.

"Major," he heard Chkalov mentioning, "This is *fascinating*. Notice how she sees the difference between our space-suits and the human astronauts inside them – not only is she obviously intelligent, but she seems to understand technology. She is attempting to communicate with them, and with us. This creature may have been found in a cave... but she is no cave-girl, as you Americans call them."

"Sergei," Boyd muttered, "I knew *that*, within about five minutes of meeting her. Well, I've caught my breath now. Proceeding to take them down to the MMV, starting with Tanaka."

He went over to the Professor's suit and began turning it around to face the ramp.

Immediately, the Mars-girl sprang to his assistance. She grabbed the other arm as she had with Jacobson.

Slowly, they proceeded down the ramp, with the Mars-girl looking repeatedly to and fro, as if trying to recognize familiar landmarks.

Boyd noticed a look of sadness clouding her face, but when he did, the alien-girl looked away quickly. He also noted – or thought he noted – slight changes in the color of her eyes, or maybe something else about them, especially when she seemed to be looking at far-off objects. She returned the glance, but guardedly, with the same bland, half-smile he had seen earlier down in the chamber.

"Major Boyd," intoned the voice of McPherson over the intercom, "Down here, we have just seen the most recent events in the chamber, regarding the rescue of Professor Tanaka and Captain Jacobson. If this is of any interest, you might want to know that you're now the most famous person on Earth, or, should I say, your new *friend* is. There aren't many down here are watching anything on the news anymore, except for what's going on up *there*, which is a good thing, I suppose, considering what else has been on our mind these days. I'm now going to turn the floor over to Sylvia Abruzzio - she has some instructions for you. Sylvia, go ahead."

A familiar female voice said, "Major, first let me say that you are the envy of every scientist on Earth these days – along with the rest of them, I'd give anything and everything to be where you are right now. Along with you, we are all living through one of the greatest events in human scientific history."

Drawing pained breath after breath, Boyd suppressed an urge to ask her just to get to the point.

Abruzzio said, "As someone trained in science yourself, I'm sure you're aware that we have to exploit every opportunity we have to learn from this creature, to find out as much as we can about its history, its physiology, its language, and so on. I know that none of us wants to think about this, but the creature has now been exposed to contaminants from Earth, so we have no way of knowing how much longer it will stay alive. In this context, it's *vital* that we make the best use of the available time, however long that turns out to be."

Boyd reflected,

Funny that you'd be worried about how long this being, which has lasted thousands of years in an airless tomb, would stay alive... considering Earth and the human species' current survival prospects.

She continued, "I have devised a few simple tests for you to use on the creature, so, here goes..."

Boyd felt irrationally annoyed at this term – the Mars-girl *wasn't* an "it", she was a "she"; this was an intelligent fellow-being, helping to save his crew-mates, *not* an animal.

"First," instructed Abruzzio, "I want you to try to identify the various parts of your body – that is, the arms, legs, head, *et cetera* – one by one, drawing as good a picture as you can of each one in the sand, then next to each of these, write the English spelling for it also in the sand – lower-case only, please – and as you do this, turn on your suit's outside speaker and say the English word for the body part out loud."

Do you have any idea of what I'm coping with up here? thought an annoyed Boyd.

The Earth-bound scientist droned on, "See if you can get the creature to write and say the equivalent word for each body part in the sand, next to the English version; that will help us start to decipher its script and language, and perhaps the inscriptions in and around the chamber. Next, see if you can do the same thing for the number system, up to ten. Finally, draw a diagram of the solar-system and indicate to the creature that you came from the third planet. See how the creature responds to all of these stimuli and help it to communicate as much as possible. Do you understand these instructions? Please reply."

Officiously as possible, Boyd replied, "Affirmative, Houston... will do as soon as I have returned the Jacobson and Tanaka to safety. Priority task is rescue of my team-mates. And if this makes any difference, I believe that the Mars-girl understands this as well."

He hoped he was right.

He heard the voice of White say, "Second to that, man. We can play school with her, when we get the Professor and the Captain back here."

Boyd cracked a stupid grin, which the alien-girl evidently saw through his visor, and though obviously puzzled at its cause, she shot back another one of her incisor-laden smiles.

They had now turned the last corner, dragging Tanaka's body all the while. The MMV came into sight.

The Mars-girl stopped and a look of intense interest came over her face, but then she again took hold of the Professor's arm and helped Boyd hoist the unconscious woman into the back of the vehicle.

She then paced around the MMV, studying every part of it carefully.

A moment of panic overtook Boyd as he saw the Mars-girl about to throw one of the switches on the front instrument-panel; but he relented when he realized that she was pointing at the switches, one by one, each time saying something in her sometimes high-pitched, sometimes guttural language.

"Major," noted Chkalov, "I think she is asking you what each of the activating switches, does. This is proof beyond all doubt that this being is from a technological society. *Incredible!*"

Boyd just nodded.

He now noticed the alien-girl rummaging inside the storage area in the back of the MMV and quickly went over to her, grabbing her arm away from the hatch, gesturing "no" by wagging his finger back and forth. She immediately fell to her knees, head down, hands clasped in front, in the submissive gesture he had seen before. Then she gave the "thirsty" gesture.

"She's still dehydrated," Boyd commented to the other two. "And she may have used up some of the water I gave her earlier while helping me with Tanaka... maybe she sweats like we do? I have only one water bottle left in the vehicle, but she clearly needs it more than I do."

He reached inside the storage-hatch and pulled out the last water-container, handing it to the Mars-girl, who took and opened it with a look of utterly pathetic gratitude.

She gulped the liquid down in a trice, then kneed through the sand to Boyd's place, grasping his leg and rubbing her head on it, puppy-style. He felt like a rock-star, with a Martian groupie on his leg.

Her grip felt strong, almost painfully so.

Boyd absent-mindedly thought of all the science-fiction movies that he had seen as a kid, the ones in which man's first encounter with extra-terrestrial creatures resulted in astronauts being torn limb from limb by bug-eyed monsters of various sorts.

Somehow, this one wasn't going according to the familiar script.

He crouched and did the only thing he could think of – patting her on the head, then gently prying her arms from his leg. She did not seem to object to this, fortunately.

Boyd then pointed up the ramp and started off in that direction.

The Mars-girl followed behind him. She looked much stronger than she had been in the chamber; her complexion was now visibly ruddier and it seemed that her hair color was getting darker – now a light blond – by the minute, and, though it couldn't possibly have been, now he could have *sworn* that he saw little flashes of illumination upon her body, underneath the whatever-it-was chain-mail that she wore.

Boyd hoped that she didn't mind his frequent stares. The Mars-girl had a hypnotic beauty to her. He couldn't help wanting to see more, all the time.

He thought of Abruzzio's demands halfway up and realized that he would have to do something to stall Houston, so he switched on the outside speaker of his suit, paused momentarily, pointed to himself and said, "Boyd".

The Mars-girl paused too, pointed to herself and said something a bit like, "OOwaiOOah". She smiled.

They continued up the ramp and after another couple of minutes arrived at Jacobson's body. She pointed to it and proudly said, "Boi-oid", then pointed in the direction of the MMV, down the ramp and added "OOwaiOOah".

He heard a guffaw from White coming over the intercom.

"Hey Brent," he quipped, "Now *all* men, are a 'Boyd', to her. Congrats!"

"Yeah," Boyd replied, "I'd better set her straight."

He turned on his outside speaker and pointed to himself, then to Jacobson, saying "man". Hoping that this wasn't showing up too clearly to the watching Earth, he drew a crude picture of an anatomically correct male figure in the sand, with a female one beside it. He pointed to the male figure and said "man", again. He said "woman", pointing first to the female figure, then in the direction of Tanaka in the MMV.

Her face looked puzzled for a second, then lit up. She said something very fast and quite unintelligible, but quickly pointed to the male figure and said, "mhannnn". She pointed to herself and said, "woo-mhannn".

The Mars-girl then drew a few symbols in the sand, three underneath the male figure and four underneath the female. She pointed to the symbols underneath the male figure, saying first a guttural sound quite unlike anything in English, followed by "wai-YAH", then to the symbols underneath the female figure, saying, "OOwaiOOah".

The voice of Sylvia Abruzzio came in over the intercom. "Major, we have seen that the creature is helping you, but we must insist that you start the learning exercises that I explained earlier. Please copy. Over."

"Houston," Boyd stated, understanding that they would not have seen what just went on yet, "We have commenced trying to communicate with the girl, but I am doing this on the way, as we try to return Tanaka and Jacobson to the *Eagle*. So far, we seem to have taught her how to distinguish male from female humans... but I'm afraid her own language is harder for us to understand than ours is to her. If it's of any interest, she seems to be getting stronger and more healthy, not weaker. Proceeding to return Jacobson to the MMV. Will inform you of progress as it happens. Over."

He then pointed to himself again and said, "Boyd is man", hoping upon hope that she could understand the concept of personal names. He pointed to the slumbering figure and said, "Jacobson is man", followed by "Tanaka is woman". Then he pointed to himself again and said, "Boyd".

The Mars-girl put her hand over the back of her ear, so Boyd repeated what he had just said. She looked at him in an odd, guarded way, not with discomprehension, but as if she was thinking to herself, measuring what to say.

She paused for a noticeable few seconds, then stepped forward and said in a loud, clear, even voice,

"Kharr-ein iss woo-mannn." She pointed to herself. "Kharr-ein," she declared. She followed this word with something that sounded a bit like, "makay-lah", then a fast and unintelligible combination of whistling, gurgling syllables.

Boyd noted that she had a determined, confident look on her face, her feet planted firmly together, her hands on her hips, while saying this.

Her face looked like it was illuminated from below – was there some kind of ethereal light coming from her eyes, too? – for an instant, but that must have been his imagination, he thought. The weird music again sounded in his head and adrenalin flowed inexplicably, excitedly in his veins, for a brief second; then it was gone.

Boyd pointed to himself, to confirm the point. "Boyd," he said.

He then pointed to the Mars-girl. "Kharayn," he added.

She pointed to him with a broad grin and replied, "Boi-oid", then used both hands to point to her torso and said, "Kharr-ein".

She then looked at the body and spoke, "Jayy-kobb-sayn iss mannn", then, pointing again said, "Jayy-kobb-sayn".

"So *that's* her name," he heard White say. "Kar- what was it again? I didn't catch it here, all if it, that girl speaks awfully fast. Boyd, what did you hear?"

"'Karayn', or something very close to that," Boyd replied. "Nice to be on a first name basis with an extraterrestrial, but how does that saying go – 'I can believe six impossible things before breakfast'. I think this is about the fourth or fifth, I've lost count today, Devon. I'm going to try to move Jacobson now."

Motioning for her to join him in the task, he used the outside suit speaker to say, "Karéin, help me with Jacobson."

The Mars-girl nodded and said something like, "OOwoo". Then she took Jacobson's left arm to Boyd taking the right.

They proceeded down the ramp, somewhat more slowly than with Tanaka, given Jacobson's greater weight and the factor of accumulating fatigue. At a couple intervals along the way, she seemed to be asking questions of Boyd in her strange, whistling tongue, to which he could only smile and say "Yes," in return.

Huffing and puffing, they reached the MMV and, with what seemed to Boyd his last ounce of energy, managed to man-handle Jacobson's body into the back of the vehicle. With his exhausted back slouching against the side of the MMV, Boyd called White.

"I need a biovitals reading, Devon," he requested. "How are they doing?"

"Basic readings same as before, Brent," replied White. "But the air reading for the Captain's tank is below what it should be, I'm guessin' no more than fifty minutes left – maybe it sprung a small leak out there when you and Miss Mars-Girl there were carryin' him, or maybe a leak in the air line, can't tell from here. Oh, and here's one other thing – remember that weird radiation reading? It's gone now... all I see are the normal background ambients. Y'all better get those two back, I'll suit up and be ready to help you get 'em back into the *Eagle*. Copy?"

"Understood," Boyd confirmed. "I'll just drive a little faster on the way back, we should have plenty of margin for error, unless I break down completely halfway... let's not think about that. Starting out now... uh-oh, Devon, I got a *problem*."

His view-cam revealed the Mars-girl, "Karéin", sitting happily in the seat next to him, all ready to go. She seemed weirdly at ease in the vehicle, for someone who had just awoken from who-knows-how-many centuries in a stone tomb. She saw the tracks that had taken the MMV to this place and pointed confidently in the same direction, then pointed at the driving-controls and said something, maybe a question.

"Major," Chkalov said unnecessarily from space, "You *cannot* allow the creature to go along with you; as it is, the fact that she has come into contact with the MMV probably means that you will have to decontaminate it, and also the space-suits she has touched, when you get back to the *Eagle*. There is also the gift she gave you. That will have to be decontaminated, too."

"I know," said Boyd back.

But the truth of the matter was, he somehow *wanted* to bring the alien-girl along with him, even though all of his professional and scientific training reminded him of the obvious risks of doing so. He simply *trusted* her, completely and irrationally, not knowing why.

Boyd got out of the MMV, went around to the passenger side door, opened it and pointed first at the girl, then pointed in an outside direction, moving his hand back and forth repeatedly.

A palpable look of sadness instantly appeared on her face and she quickly debarked from the vehicle, kneeling before him, hands clutched in front.

He felt like a man about to take a beloved dog to that dreaded last trip to the veterinarian's office; it was actually harder telling this being that she could not go with him, than it was carrying the Captain.

But he was an astronaut with a professional duty to fulfill; so he said, as kindly as he could, hoping she would understand some fraction of it,

"Karéin, I can't take you back with me. Dangerous. You stay here."

He pointed down at the ground. "*Please* don't be sad, Karéin. Boyd will return. Boyd promises this."

The Mars-girl did not reply, only looked up at him with those big, amber eyes as if about to cry, but remained on her knees as he returned to the MMV, tested the engine, then slowly started to move off.

She watched intently as the vehicle receded into the distance, protecting her eyes from the sun with the palm of her hand.

Their new friend looked like one of those young French actresses from a 60's movie – the ones set in the Riviera or maybe in Spain or Italy – with the same distant, reserved, elegant glance, squinting enigmatically as she viewed the horizon.

Wake Up, Captain

Boyd had kept an eye on the Mars-girl intermittently through the rear-view mirror, in between navigating between Martian boulders, all the while half-hating himself for having left her behind.

He went over a low sand-dune and she was gone. He half-wondered if if it had all been a hallucination; he should have marveled again at the mesas, but he was lost in thought. Then the voice of Sylvia Abruzzio snapped him back to reality.

"Excellent work, Major Boyd," she said. "I think we can now be confident that we know the creature's words for 'man' and 'woman' – this is a big step forward from many perspectives, not the least of which is that we know that it is a sexual mammal. We've got our linguists and cryptographers going over the being's written language, now that we can relate some of its sounds to the written symbols we have seen previously. We're watching everything that it does to see if we can find any other clues regarding how it communicates and if we are able to decipher any of the inscriptions that you and we have so far seen, we'll let you know what they are. Keep it up, Major! Over."

Boyd wondered what Abruzzio would say when she found out that he had left the Mars-girl to face the Martian night alone, back at the base of the mesa.

White's voice sounded again. "Brent, I need an ETA, I'm figuring, twenty minutes or so? I'm suiting up now, I'll meet you outside the ship. Please confirm. White over."

"Affirmative," Boyd said, coping with the bumps of a definitely non-shock-absorbed ride. "I just did an air check for Jacobson and Tanaka and the Commander is getting dangerously close to the red zone on the gage, the Professor's okay, though. We'll need to hustle when I get there, and yes, your estimate is about right – I'm pushing this crate as fast as it will go. Over."

"Got that," White replied. "Any sign of life from either of them?"

Boyd shot a quick glance at the two figures, trying to see their faces through the thin layer of reddish dust that was already covering their visors.

"Seem to be sleeping like babies," he noted. "Breathing is rhythmic, like deep-REM sleep, at least that's my guess."

Listening all the way for more irrelevant instructions from Houston, but fortunately receiving none, Boyd drove on. Finally, he saw the *Eagle's* dirty-white, cylindrical shape peeking above a sand dune, rounded a boulder or two and roared into the clearing in front of the spacecraft.

White was there, suited up and waiting. Without a word, he came swiftly over to the MMV and grabbed one of Jacobson's arms, while Boyd took the other.

"Man," White exclaimed, "We gotta tell the Captain to lose some weight, this guy is *heavy.*"

"Yeah," said Boyd, huffing and puffing as the two of them manhandled the sleeping astronaut towards the airlock, "And you noticed that the girl – 'Karéin' whats-her-face – seemed to drag him around like a kid drags its back-sack. One of these days, I'll see if I can arm-wrestle her..."

With some difficulty, they managed to get Jacobson, then Tanaka, into the airlock. All four of them were now inside the relatively small space of this device, which was necessary considering that even White's suit had now possibly come into contact with the girl's fingerprints.

Boyd activated the computer's decontamination protocol and they were all bathed first with strong ultraviolet light, then by cleansing spray, then by another dose of UV. He hoped that the rescued astronauts wouldn't wake up while this dangerous light was shining in their eyes, but as far as he could tell, neither of them did.

Whoosh.

The inside airlock hatch opened up and they were all, finally, back in the *Eagle*. The two astronauts removed the helmets from Tanaka and Jacobson. They tried to revive the two.

"Commander! Professor! Can you hear us? Can you hear us?" implored Boyd.

There was no response, so White tried the old first aid trick of pressure just beneath the person's front shoulder-blades. "Hey! Hey! Y'all okay? Captain! Professor! *Say* somethin'!"

Tanaka did not respond, but they heard an incoherent grunt from Jacobson, followed by,

"Cherie... Brent... Devon... respond, please... emergency situation... not sure I can..."

"Captain, it's alright," Boyd said, visibly relieved. "You and Professor Tanaka are back with us in the *Eagle* and you're both safe and healthy, as far as we can tell. You both passed out in there, so we had to get you back. The Professor's still sleeping, but I think she's okay. Don't try to get up yet, you should take a few minutes to get your strength back."

Now semi-conscious, Jacobson mumbled, "Whaa... wait a minute, you mean we're back in the *Eagle*? That's good, that's good... wow, *bad* headache here, I feel just totally drained, like as if I'd been working for three or four days without sleep. Listen... Devon... thanks for going out there and getting me, but you shouldn't have left the ship, you know what the rules are..."

He managed a grin. "But I won't report you this time," he added.

White and Boyd exchanged glances, both unsure of what to say. Presently, the African-American astronaut said,

"Well, Captain... I really only got y'all out of the MMV when Brent brought you back. Y'all gotta thank him for getting you and the Professor back from that chamber there, I didn't have a part in that, I was back here at the *Eagle*."

Jacobson replied, "Amazing work there, then, Brent. I really owe you one. That must have been *exhausting*, getting two fully suited astronauts all the way back down the side of the mesa. What's the status of the chamber? Any new instructions from Houston?"

Boyd thought for a second and then commented, "Well, Commander, you see... I sort of had some *help* in getting you back, so I'm afraid I can't take all the credit for that, either. As far as the chamber is concerned, there have been some rather interesting developments down there, and Houston has issued us with quite a bit to do concerning that, also – "

Jacobson interrupted in an alarmed voice, "*What? Surely* you didn't have Sergei use the emergency landing module? Who's going to run *Infinity*, when we do our egress docking? I need to talk to Houston, pronto, Major!"

Tanaka moaned and rolled halfway over. White went to her, putting her right side up and trying to bring her back to full consciousness.

"Relax, Captain," Boyd stated, as reassuringly as he could. "Nothing like *that* has happened, Sergei's still up in *Infinity*. But you're right, I think we really should get you in touch with Houston, so they can fill you in from their perspective. If you want, Devon can open a channel."

"Brent," replied a confused Jacobson, "That's of course good news, but... if *you* didn't get us back by yourself, and neither Devon nor Sergei were out there with you... then... let's not play games with each other, here... *who* – "

By now Tanaka had apparently woken up too, albeit, groggy-headedly. She spoke up. "Indeed, Major. Who? Ughh. Ughh... I feel like death warmed over... I need something to eat, I feel so *weak*..."

White interjected, shaking his head as he peered out one of the view-ports,

"Why don't y'all see for yourselves, Captain, Professor? Your savior seems to have followed Major Boyd when he brought y'all back here. She's right outside, right now."

"What the –" Boyd shot back. "I was driving at thirty kilometers per hour, or more! How the *hell* could she have covered that amount of distance – "

Jacobson and Tanaka looked at each other in puzzlement. The Mars mission commander said, "*Who?*"

White just pointed at the view-port.

Painfully forcing themselves, aided by the other two, Jacobson and Tanaka struggled to their feet, shedding their space-suits and shuffling over to the view-port., crowding behind it.

A look of utter astonishment came to both their faces, simultaneously. They looked out on the Mars-girl, sitting cross-legged on a nearby rock, studying every detail of the *Eagle* and its surroundings. She had a pleasant, distant smile on her face.

"*My God,*" Tanaka exclaimed, "That's the creature from the chamber... isn't it? But she – it – was *dead*, entombed, I saw it with my own eyes! How in the *world* – "

Jacobson said, quietly, "Now I really *have* seen everything, folks."

He slumped, back to the wall, shaking his head. "I suppose this – alien – is the one who helped you get me out of there... isn't she, Major?"

He sighed wearily. "What next. *What* next."

"Captain, ah," explained Boyd, "Let me introduce, 'Karéin' of Mars, sir. As near as we can tell her name, at least, that's what it is, more or less. I think she knows my name, too, by the way. She seems to be friendly, which is lucky for us because she has already demonstrated that she's physically quite strong and also *extremely* intelligent. She figured out pretty quickly that I needed help in getting you and the Professor out of the chamber, so she helped me drag you two to the MMV. Houston has been sent us some instructions for how to communicate with her and we have already had some success in doing so."

Tanaka took another look at the Mars-girl, then commented, "She seems to be doing just fine out there, but that thin air and cold would kill any of us in a few minutes – I suppose she must be native to this planet? But it doesn't make any *sense*, look at her – this 'Karéin' is almost the picture of health, and when I saw her in the tomb, she looked like a well-preserved cadaver. Living creatures can't *survive* without food and water, let alone for however long she would have been in there, and now she seems very much alive. How is this possible?"

"Well, Professor," Boyd mentioned, "I kind of gave her some of my food and water-rations, as a confidence-building measure – "

"You shouldn't have done that," Tanaka complained, still wincing from exhaustion, "She could die from germ exposure, or just from eating something that's safe for us but poisonous to her."

"Yeah," White said with a smirk, "Houston said that, too, but so far, she seems in better shape than either y'all or the Captain."

"Professor," continued Boyd, "What happened out there, in a nutshell, is that you and the Captain both basically passed out, I guess you fainted or something like that. Very shortly thereafter, this 'Karéin' lifted herself out of the sarcophagus; she was pretty weak at first, but she gained strength and color very quickly – I'm not sure how, since that was before I gave her anything to eat or drink. From almost the first second that she saw the two of you, passed out on the chamber floor, she started trying to communicate with you, with us. I decided that we couldn't just *leave* you down there, so I went up to the chamber entrance, met her and the two of us got you out. I tried to make her wait back at the base of the Anomaly mesa, but I guess she's lonely, or something like that, because she seems to have followed me back here. As fast as a gazelle, I might add."

Slowly recovering her wits, Tanaka observed, "*Fascinating.* Captain, the fact that you and I were overcome by that sudden fatigue that hit us down there, seems to be related in some way to this creature's resurrection, wouldn't you say? A vampiric effect of some kind, like she was somehow drawing energy from us? That's the only thing that I can think of, which would explain what took place in the chamber. Has she used it on any of you, after that first incident?"

"Negative," replied Boyd. "Assuming that your theory is correct, for the moment, she hasn't affected *me* like that. But then again," – he thought for a second, then said with a wry smile – "Maybe she just likes me more than she likes either of you. I don't know. She didn't seem dangerous, at least when I was with her."

Taking another glance out the view-port., Jacobson cautioned, "Perhaps, Major, but at the very least, we are dealing with a totally *unknown* factor here, one which, if the Professor is right, may be capable of incapacitating any or all of us at will. This is obviously something that we have to talk to Houston about, to figure out our next steps. I think you can easily imagine what might happen if she decides to use that ability, if it really exists, when we're trying to get space-borne, or just when we're driving the MMV."

He looked again. "Wow. Tanaka, have a look at this. She's drawing something."

White, sitting at a control-panel, swiveled one of the outside cameras in the Mars-girl's direction. They all looked at the video-display. It revealed the girl drawing a series of concentric circles, a total of twelve in all, in the sand, with a large circle in the middle. Each of the second and successive circles had smaller circles placed on it, with the seventh one's smaller circle itself encircled by an elliptical design. The first five circles were closely packed together, nearest the innermost, while the remaining ones were at increasingly large distances from each other.

The creature then drew a big "X" symbol through the fifth circle's smaller circle, then a line towards the fourth smaller circle, then pointed to herself. Finally, she pointed towards the *Eagle*, finishing the exercise by holding her hands, palms outwards, in front of her, with a quizzical look on her face. She said something, unintelligible as usual.

"Captain," Tanaka replied, "She's drawing the solar-system... but this doesn't completely make sense. Assuming the design with the oval ring around it is Saturn, she has *three* planets between Earth and Saturn... but we know there are only two."

Jacobson inquired, "Isn't that where the asteroid-belt is? Maybe she's referring to one of the larger planetoids, Ceres, or Vesta, perhaps. The X symbol could represent where she's from. Except that none of the planetoids is even *remotely* inhabitable, by beings such as us or her. So perhaps she's depicting a solar-system that just *looks* like our own?"

"Any of these explanations is theoretically possible, I suppose," said Tanaka. "Oh, what wouldn't I *give* to be able to speak her language and ask her a few questions," she added. "This is obviously a *highly* intelligent, sophisticated being that understands the true nature of solar-systems – I bet she also has figured out that we aren't native to Mars, as well. That's probably why she is asking us where we're from. Captain, we should try to tell her."

"Not just yet," ordered Jacobson. "I want to see what Houston has to say, before we reveal too much about ourselves to this creature."

His remark was timely, because at that exact moment, the Earth video-link screen became active again, revealing the faces of McPherson, Abruzzio, Ramirez and a new, unfamiliar male figure in military dress.

"*Eagle*, this is Houston," said Ramirez. "Hector Ramirez here. We have seen the events since our last transmission, but we didn't want to interrupt you while you were on the important task of returning Captain Jacobson and Professor Tanaka to safety, which is why we haven't called until now. We are hoping that by now you have been able to get them back to the *Eagle*, and may I say, your fellow astronauts, as well as all of the rest of us, owe you one here, Major. Please let us know of their status the minute that you're able to examine them. I'm now going to turn the mike over to Air Force General Jack Symington, who's working with Fred McPherson on this project. General, you're on."

A no-nonsense, unfamiliar voice sounded, accompanied by the sight of a clean-shaved military man in his late forties, bedecked with military campaign ribbons and four stars on his shoulder-boards.

"Major Boyd," the man said, "My name is Jack Symington and I have been appointed by the President to provide a military perspective to Mr. McPherson, in view of the recent developments; I report directly to General Anderson of the Air Force and Joint Chiefs. I'm also going to bring you up to date on some things that have been going on down here."

The General continued, "First of all, Major, let me say how proud not only I, but all of your compatriots in the Air Force, are, of your historic accomplishments up there on Mars. You are following in the path of many of our previous astronauts, from Alan Shepherd and Neil Armstrong to the brave crews of the *Challenger, Columbia* and *Ares Voyager* – he nodded to someone off-screen – and of course Yuri Gagarin, Leonov, Komarov and the Soyuz 3 crew – but you have surpassed all of them."

I just wish they'd start lettin' black folk back into *the Air Force*, mused White, to himself.

Boyd looked out the view-port., again. The Mars-girl was still there, sitting on a rock, still studying the *Eagle* with the same, intense, yet pleasantly controlled, look on her face. She caught his glance, or he caught hers. He wondered for a second if she could see past the mirror glazing on the outside of the view-port.

The remote voice explained, "Now, as you – and Captain Jacobson, when, we pray, he recovers – are no doubt aware, the current situation up there is both a great opportunity and, potentially, a significant danger. From what we have seen from the latest scenes you sent us, that is, the situation at the MMV, the Mars-creature has demonstrated that she, it, has at least some understanding of technology. Therefore, and you should know that I have consulted with both Mr. McPherson and Ms. Abruzzio on this point, I'm ordering you to keep this creature away from exposure to any of our equipment, in particular the *Eagle*, until we have had more of a chance to assess its capabilities and intentions. Right now, Ms. Abruzzio and Mr. McPherson are attempting to draft a series of tests for you to use on it, to see if it has any real ability to operate our equipment in a way which might be hazardous. Longer-term, we need to get as much information out of it as possible as regards its background and own scientific knowledge, that might prove advantageous for NASA's or the Air Force's own uses."

Boyd heard White whisper, "As usual, Houston's a day late and a dollar short. Y'all think we should pipe this outside, so she knows what her orders are?"

They all smirked at this.

Symington continued, "As I mentioned, I also have some news about what we intend to do with the 'Lucifer' object. Here at the Air Force, we have been working very closely with the defense establishments of the other major nuclear powers, with a view to an anti-Lucifer strategy. After much deliberation, we have decided on a three-pronged approach."

"First, in a week or so from now, in conjunction with similar missions being launched by the European Space Agency and by the Russian Federation, NASA will be launching a manned mission to fly at high speed towards and land on, or get as close as possible to, the Lucifer object. Our objective will be to embed a group of powerful nuclear charges, each at least 100 megatons explosive yield, on the Earth-facing side of the object; as a precaution against single-point failure, we are using three separate spacecraft for this mission. When we detonate the charges, we hope to slow the object measurably, but also, if the scientists' calculations are correct, we should be able to deflect 'Lucifer' so that it misses the Earth entirely."

"Unfortunately –" he paused and mentioned, "We've been informed that given the object's present trajectory, even if this approach works, there's a chance that it will instead strike the Moon... which, as you can imagine, will present its own set of severe risks to the Earth."

Symington went on, "To attempt to mitigate this outcome, and also as a backup in case the tripartite mission fails completely, the United States, the European Union, the Russian Federation and the People's Republic of China have begun crash programs to manufacture as many heavy, high-payload ballistic missiles as each country is able to. For example, we have devoted over 30 per cent of our entire military industrial capacity to the restarting of the Titan 2 assembly line and the Russians and Chinese have done the same for their RS-20 and DF-52 production lines, respectively. The Europeans are trying to modify their civilian satellite launch-vehicles, too, but we are, ahem, running into a few political issues concerning the transfer of nuclear warheads to them, partly because they do not have fissile materials production infrastructure..."

Tanaka whispered to Jacobson, "*Plus ça change...*". He nodded, ruefully.

"If all goes according to plan, by the time that the Lucifer object is within range, Earth's nations should be able to fire more than three hundred ICBMs, each with warheads in the ten to fifty megaton range, at it," said the General. "Should we need to engage this option, by our best calculations it will occur when your own spacecraft is still quite far away from Earth orbit, so if we are not successful, you will have time to consider your options as regards actually returning and landing here."

Boyd leaned over and whispered to White, *sotto voce,* "And just *where* does he expect us to land? Venus, maybe?"

White laughed out loud, getting a quick elbow from Boyd – this *was* a *General* speaking, after all.

"Furthermore, should even the preceding plan fail, we have been working with the other nuclear powers to co-ordinate a last-ditch defense involving the endo-atmospheric interception of remaining Lucifer fragments with shorter-range, submarine-launched ballistic missiles," said Symington. "We are not sure what effect this will have, but again, in view of the urgency of the situation, we have to use all the tools within our disposal. So the bottom line, Major, is that Earth is doing all it can, to defend itself and ensure that you have a safe place to which to return. That's all I have to tell you, right now... I'm now going to turn the floor over to Ms. Abruzzio. Go ahead, Ma'am."

Sylvia Abruzzio now spoke up.

"Major Boyd," she stated, "Let me say here that you've done a great job with the Mars-creature out there, considering the other problems that you have had to contend with. We've already learned a tremendous amount from your interactions with this being so far, and in view of this, and in consultation with the White House, that is, Fred's people, as well as the scientific authorities at the United Nations, we can now inform you that the focus of the *Eagle and Infinity* mission on Mars has now been changed to deal exclusively with this creature. I say again, your existing mission schedule has now been canceled in favor of a new set of activities, which we will shortly be sending you, that will concentrate on trying to communicate and learn from this extraterrestrial."

White was heard to whisper, "No shit."

Abruzzio continued, "Although you can read the details when the tele-transmission arrives, briefly, we will be expecting you to travel to the Anomaly area each morning with a different set of learning exercises for you to try to have the Mars-creature, complete. We will monitor the process remotely here in Houston, so we can glean as much information as we can from how it reacts. Additionally, you will take the opportunity, whenever possible, to collect specimen data, for example blood, urine and stool samples, skin scrapings, *et cetera*, so we can get some objective information about the creature's basic physiology and biology. I should tell you that so far we are at a complete loss down here to figure out how it is even *alive*, given its original state and the environment in which it seems to be surviving right now, so the collection of samples is of vital importance. Please give us an update on what your current status is. Over."

Motioning to White to enable the up-link, Jacobson positioned himself in front of the view-screen and replied.

"Houston, this is Captain Jacobson, reporting back to you," he offered. "No doubt, you will be pleasantly surprised to see that Professor Tanaka and myself are now back in the *Eagle*, safe and sound, thanks mainly to actions above and beyond the call of duty, by Major Boyd, and," – he paused momentarily, not quite believing what he was saying – "And by the creature we now know of as 'Karéin' of Mars, that seems to be the name that she goes by, as near as we can tell. The bottom line, Houston, is that along with Boyd, this being saved our lives, by helping him get us out of the chamber at the Anomaly site and back into the MMV."

Tanaka interjected, "After almost taking our lives, remember."

Nodding, Jacobson continued, "Professor Tanaka is quite right about that, if you heard her there, Houston. She and I are still feeling mighty fatigued, and our best theory as to the cause of this, as well as the cause of our indisposition in the chamber, is that this 'Karéin' must have somehow fed off of our life-force – don't ask me what that *is*, it's the only theory that seems to make sense right now – when we were in the chamber, but I think she did not mean us any harm in so doing, that's fairly clear by the fact that she tried to help us later on. In any event, we're here now, so that's good, but I have to tell you, Houston, that so is the alien, that is, she seems to have followed Major Boyd back to the *Eagle's* site. She is currently loitering outside the ship, but aside from passively observing us, she does not appear to be interfering with our operations or attempting to damage any of our equipment. I have decided to try to limit our interactions with her temporarily, so we don't encourage her to get any closer until we have a better understanding of her intentions and capabilities."

Tanaka spoke up again. "Houston, we will be sending you video records of drawings that this 'Karéin' was making in the sand outside. The consensus of opinion is that she was trying to depict a solar-system, possibly our own, although some aspects of it are problematic. Which means that we are clearly dealing with a *very* advanced intelligence that understands celestial mechanics. I have my own ideas as to how to try to communicate with her on this topic but I'd be happy to see any suggestions that you have, down there. As soon as I get a more complete rundown on what happened out here while Captain Jacobson and I were unconscious, I'll send you a full report."

Jacobson asked, "Major Boyd, Major White, do you have anything to add here?"

Boyd replied. "Yeah," he said. "This is something that I – uhh – felt that it would have been out of place to mention before, but now that we're all discussing what happened today, I think that I had better let you know. It's about my relationship with the creature."

All eyes upon him, he continued, "Well, it's sort of like this... and it's hard to put into words. It's like I kind of feel that I have a *rapport* with this 'Karéin', basically. When she looks into my eyes, or I look into hers, I feel like I trust her on a very deep, personal level... you know the feeling you get when your first child asks you for a piece of candy that you know he or she really shouldn't have, but you just can't *bring* yourself to say 'no'? Sort of like that, and I can't figure out why I can't bring myself to be more objective with her, more detached, more scientific. I mean, she's an *alien* who I just met... but I get the feeling that I've known her, maybe loved her, all my life. I know it doesn't make sense, but it's how I feel."

"Brent," asked Tanaka with an obvious note of concern in her voice, "Do you think you might have been hypnotized or subjected to some kind of mind control, by this being?"

"No," he countered, "Nothing like *that*. At least, not that I'm *aware* of. I can assure you, Professor, that I'm in complete control of myself. I *can* say 'no' to her and have already done so, at least once. It's just that it somehow hurts to do so. That's about all I can really tell you."

"Interesting," commented Tanaka. "Perhaps this is some kind of low-level mental control, or telepathic, or empathetic, ability. Well, Major, all I can think of asking you to do, is just to keep track of it and let us know if it becomes stronger or less easy to resist. Captain, do you concur?"

"Yes," confirmed Jacobson. "Brent, of course we trust you, but we also trust you to report any changes. Agreed?"

"Agreed," replied Boyd.

"Very well," stated Jacobson. "Major White, any comments?"

White thought for a second and said, "Not a lot I can add to what's just been said, sir, except that I think y'all gonna see from the video recordings of what happened around the mesa, that this Mars-chick is on *our* side, anyway that's what I think, since if she wasn't, y'all probably wouldn't *be* here asking us questions right now, sir. Oh, and one other thing... remember that strange radiation signature that kind of started the whole ball rollin', yesterday?"

"Absolutely," confirmed Tanaka. "What about it?"

"Well, in between hauling y'all out of the MMV and such, I've been checking it periodically, trying to get a fix on it – now I *have*. Wasn't easy, because it's much weaker than it had been before, but surprise, surprise, guess where it is."

"I bet I know," offered Boyd. "*Her*. Right?"

"Y'all got it," replied White. "It's centered on her and it moves where she goes. Essentially, folks, this Mars-girl is like a little mobile nuclear reactor, that's the best way that I can explain it – she's radiatin' this unknown type of energy from inside, I guess, unless it's that chain-mail shirt she's got on, that's doin' it. Levels are very low, maybe at most like the amount of energy that would be in an incandescent light bulb... but it's definitely there."

He continued, "There's one other weird thing, too. There are definite bursts of higher output, again, not nearly enough, as far as I can tell, to hurt anyone, but they show up clearly on the instruments, at irregular intervals. I checked when, exactly, these occurred, and they seem to match, pretty much dead-on, events when we expended energy of our own, for example when you turned on the MMV, when y'all were draggin' the Captain and the Professor up from the chamber, and also when you gave 'Karéin' there somethin' to eat. But on three other occasions, her output just, uhh, *vanished*... like, I *knew* she was there, but there was nothin' at all on the scope."

"Curiouser and curiouser," said Tanaka. "When you add this to what happened to the two of us in the chamber, I'd say that we've got a Martian energy vampire here, for lack of a better term. I can't *imagine* what kind of physiology could support that kind of ability."

"Yeah," agreed White, "I guess she sort of *does* look like Count Dracula, Professor, with those teeth of hers, and she's already mesmerized Brent," – he noticed a dirty glance from Boyd – "But she's a *lot* nicer, from what I saw today."

"*Possibly*," replied Jacobson. "But we can't be unmindful of the fact, assuming that your hypothesis is true, that the creature may be radiating a type of energy that could eventually prove harmful to us, even in low amounts. In addition to being able to drain us, whenever she feels hungry. We should communicate this theory to Houston and see what they think of it."

Tanaka nodded. "I'll do that," she committed, hunched over the keyboard, entering data.

Taking another look out the view-port., Boyd mentioned, "She's gone."

He swiveled the outside cameras in a 360 degree swath, throwing a switch to enable the *Eagle's* outside lights.

"Confirmed," said Boyd. "I can see what appear to be her foot-tracks, leading back in the direction to the mesa. It's getting dark, maybe she wants to be inside for the night. Devon, what do the energy scopes say?"

"Almost flat now," said White, "Whereas a minute or two ago, they were clearly showing that signature. Pretty much confirms my idea, I'd say."

"It certainly *sounds* plausible," agreed Tanaka. "I'll include it in our report, but right now I'm trying to figure out how we would comply with Houston's instructions about getting physical samples from this 'Karéin' – as you can no doubt imagine, if you or I woke up in the presence of Martians and then they tried to slice off parts of *our* bodies without being able to communicate with us, we might interpret that as a threat. Considering this being's natural defenses, we will have to be very careful about how we do this. And I don't blame her for wanting to find some shelter; as we all know it can hit minus 60 Celsius out there, and even for *her*, that's probably mighty uncomfortable. Hopefully she has some better garments back in the chamber, or some other way to avoid the cold."

"True," replied Jacobson. "That's just one of the twenty or so things that I'll have to try to work out with Houston when I submit my report."

He exhaled wearily. "Boy, I still feel *mighty* washed-out – it's like I haven't eaten in a *week*. Professor, if you're feeling the same way, it may be appropriate for the two of us to get some nourishment and to have a rest, before we resume our duties. We aren't really sure to what extent the Mars-girl's energy-draining ability has affected us... let's check for any permanent damage before we get up to full speed duties. Can you do a physio on both of us?"

"Yes," she answered, "But I'll have to get Brent or Devon to help when it's time for mine. And if this is of any help, Captain, I've got a ravenous appetite myself, but imagine how *she* feels – I'd bet you good money that it's been quite a bit longer that she hasn't had anything to eat. I just hope that she survives those Earth-rations that our good Major here gave her."

"Well, *I* survived them," White interjected, "But only barely. And I'm *used* to this freeze-dried stuff."

They all laughed.

"Very well then," concluded Jacobson, "Let's get the physios done, then we'll resume our reporting duties. This has been an *amazing* day, the kind that only the luckiest of us ever gets to live through. I'm still wondering if it really happened, frankly, but I guess it has. Good work, everyone. Dismissed."

They all got up and began their various tasks, with Boyd and White assisting, somewhat lecherously but always professionally, with Tanaka's physical examination; despite marginally depressed biorhythms, neither Jacobson nor the Professor showed any signs of permanent harm from their experiences in the mesa-chamber. They made their reports to Houston and went to their sleeping-cots with a mixture of thrill, dread and wonder.

All, that is, except Boyd, for a while.

He stayed awake past when the others were first sleeping, thinking about *her*, all alone in the brutally cold Martian night, alone on a frigid, dead world, awakened without friends or family, sleeping in a stone chamber instead of the warm confines of his spaceship.

He felt guilty – not just for leaving her that way, but for thinking of her instead of his own wife, back on Earth – sorrowful, apprehensive.

Eventually he slept, but the dreams were much the same.

All he saw was *her* face, beckoning, entreating, while shivering alone in the night.

Not Our Problem

The next day, Boyd woke up, did his normal morning routine and showed up to the main area of the *Eagle*, to find Tanaka and the rest of them all huddled around the central table, studying something intently.

"Wow," he said, "I thought you guys were more tired than I was, but I must have slept in, I guess. Sorry."

"No harm done, Brent," replied Jacobson. "Actually Devon and I just got up ourselves, only to find the Professor working on *this*."

He pointed towards a small isolation chamber, in which was located the locket-encased jewel that the Mars-girl had given him the day before. Tanaka was hunched over a control-panel next to it, remotely manipulating two robotic arms that were examining the object.

"Just to bring you up to date, Major," Tanaka said, "I've been running some tests on this item for about an hour now, after decontaminating it as best we could. The results have been *very* interesting. The crafted part of your present from the Mars-girl is made up of a variety of metals – including some elements that I haven't yet been able to identify – but it's about half nickel-titanium alloy. And it's slightly radioactive. No, let me take that back... it's 'radioactive' only in the sense of giving off the same energy-signature that Devon noticed from the alien herself."

"Wow," was all Boyd could think of, to say.

"Indeed," she replied. "This combination of metals involves some *very* advanced metallurgical techniques, and when I run the microscope over the item at highest magnification, I'm seeing intricate design... it *might* be micro-circuitry... it's hard to say, the whorls and squiggles don't look exactly like what we'd produce, but they're close. So there's pretty definitive proof that this creature comes from a technological society."

"Also," continued Tanaka, "The jewel that's held in place by the metal part has some unusual resonant qualities; when I subject it to light waves and radio-waves; basically it's like a roach trap, they check in but they don't check out, as it were. I believe that it must have been *intentionally* crafted to have this capability, there's no non-synthetic gem element that I'm aware of that can do this. And finally, though it's probably my imagination getting the better of me here, a couple of times, I could have sworn that I saw some of the circuitry actually *re-arranging* itself, right in front of my eyes... forget that I said that, okay? All in all, it's much more than a simple piece of costume jewelry, Major Boyd; this 'Karéin' gave you something that must be quite valuable to her."

Thought I heard a little voice, incomprehensible words, in the back of my mind, when I turned on the microscope, mused Tanaka.

Well, so I'm hearing *things as well as* seeing *things... what else is new?*

"Well, I *did* give her something to eat and drink," noted the pilot. "Probably a fair trade, from her point of view."

"*Maybe*," cautiously stated Jacobson. "Cherie, is there any chance that it's dangerous? Like a bomb, something that might interfere with our electronic systems, or a tracking-device, perhaps?"

"I can't say for sure," she said, "Though I don't believe so. The thing is electronically inert and so far I haven't been able to find any integrated circuits or other microchips that might allow it to be remotely activated, although as I said, under the microscope you see some fantastically intricate engraving that I suppose *could* be that kind of thing. But I think it's highly unlikely that it could pose a threat to us, other than if we end up fighting over who gets to keep it."

She smiled.

"You keep it, then," directed Jacobson, "But if it shows any signs at all of electric activity, or if its radiation output rises, you are to eject it *immediately* from the *Eagle*... understood?"

"Understood, Captain," she replied. "Meanwhile, I'll keep studying it here in the vac-chamber. I'm still trying to get a micro-piece off it to put in the spectral analysis chamber, so I can isolate the unknown elements I mentioned earlier, but as you can imagine, something that's made of hardened titanium is very difficult to break apart. I'll let you know when I have some more results."

"Okay," he replied, "Keep us all up to date."

He activated the up-link to the *Infinity*.

"Sergei and *Infinity*, this is Jacobson calling from *Eagle*. Please acknowledge. Over."

A ghostly voice responded, "*Infinity* here. Nice to hear from you again, Captain. As Major White and Major Boyd have explained, we were concerned for your safety down there yesterday, and that of Professor Tanaka. I am awaiting your orders. Over."

"Indeed," said Jacobson, "That was a day for the history-books, Sergei. I'm not sure what we can do for an encore, but I wanted to co-ordinate our plans for today with you, anyway."

He motioned with his arm to the other inhabitants of the *Eagle*.

"The rest of you should also listen up, too," requested the commander. "Last night I exchanged a number of messages with Houston regarding our course of action from this point forward, and here is the upshot of our orders. Each day, we'll travel via the MMV to the Anomaly site and attempt, in a structured way, to learn more about the extraterrestrial, as well as to try to communicate with her. I have been given a set of more specific instructions for each remaining day, considering that we have only four days' more air-supply here before we start to get close to safety-limits; for example, today's job is to, hopefully with the assistance of this 'Karéin', identify any artifacts within the chamber that might be low enough in weight for us to load aboard *Eagle* and transport back to Earth."

"Captain, I have a question," said White.

"Yes?" replied Jacobson. "What?"

"Well, sir," White said, unsteadily, "It's just that... uhh... when the rest of our time here is up, what do we do, just... leave?"

"Of course," confirmed Jacobson. "Just like we always were going to."

"But what do we do with *her*?" asked White.

"We leave her," said Jacobson, to muffled gasps from both Boyd and Tanaka.

"Captain," protested Tanaka, "Are you *sure* that's what Houston means for us to do? I mean, leaving aside the humanitarian considerations – let me say for the record, I strongly disagree with this course of action, just on those grounds – it would be a *huge* mistake not to take the Mars-girl back with us. We can't *possibly* learn all there is to know from her, in four short days... but if we got her back on Earth we could almost certainly learn enough of her language, or maybe teach her enough of ours, to find out her history and other information that we would *never* find out in any other way. It would be a crime against science of unimaginable proportions to throw such an opportunity away. We'll probably never have another chance. Can't we ask Houston to reconsider?"

"Captain," added Boyd, "We would be leaving her here to *die*. You can't possibly be in favor of that."

His head hanging for a second, Jacobson muttered, "Well... that's what I *expected* to hear, I guess. I can't say I blame you for feeling that way. First of all, Cherie, I said more or less the same thing you said to me, to Houston, but they wouldn't budge. They feel that the risk of contaminating first us, then maybe the whole Earth, with some kind of virus or other bug she has immunity to, is just too great. Try to see it from their perspective; what with the 'Lucifer' thing going on, that's *all* they need, that is, a killer plague on top of a killer comet."

He looked at each of them for approval, but finding none, he went on, "Furthermore, we have no practical way of quarantining the Mars-girl for the entire trip back – *Infinity* was never built with such a purpose in mind – so she and the rest of us would have to be breathing the same air, drinking the same recycled water, and so on. And even if we *could* figure out some safe way around this issue, Earth has a lot on its mind these days and neither NASA nor the other space agencies can devote the kind of effort that would be needed to safely accommodate the alien, down there. I argued and argued with them, but their heels are dug in on this issue, I'm afraid."

He continued, "As for the ultimate fate of our friend 'Karéin', well, if you're asking if I'm concerned for her, of *course* I am, but as far as we can tell, she's native to this planet and she has existed here for thousands of years – apparently, without any external help. Houston's opinion is that if we leave her here, the most likely outcome is that she'll crawl back in that coffin of hers and just go back to sleep, until we next show up to wake her. I'm not sure how much credence I place in that theory, but you have to admit that there's a *chance* that Houston is right –"

Tanaka interrupted with a plaintive look.

"Sam, that's *wildly* speculative," she argued. "What happens if the 'coffin' was only meant to be used one time, like our emergency survival-suits? What if its power-source, whatever that may be, has been exhausted? What if she has just forgotten how to use it? We can't *possibly* risk the survival of a being with potentially irreplaceable knowledge on the unsubstantiated assumption that she'll be able to place herself back in suspended animation – especially when it was *us* who woke her up in the first place. *We* set the train of events leading up to her revival, in motion, and we therefore have both a scientific and moral responsibility to look after her. It would be a tragic mistake to do anything less. We *can't* leave her here, on this dead world."

"Amen to *that*," echoed Boyd. "I just *know* it would be wrong."

Motioning for silence, Jacobson sighed, "I know... I *know*. I said as much to Houston, but they refused to reconsider. If it helps any, they've instructed us to leave our remaining food and water for her when we go, along with two-way video up-link gear so that we can try to communicate with her remotely, for as long as she's alive, and cooperative. At the very least, that should buy her a little more time."

"Captain," pressed Tanaka, "Houston has to know that at most, our food would last a normal human for a few weeks – a month or two at the outside – leaving aside the fact that the water would run out before then. There's no *way* that another Earth expedition could get here in five *times* that amount of time, even if Houston weren't preoccupied with the 'Lucifer' problem. We've all seen from her previous behavior that the Mars-girl has the same basic needs that we do for food and water... and even if she is somehow able to live longer than we would on a small amount of these substances it's stupidly optimistic to think that she could do so for a year or more. I think what Houston is *really* attempting to do is to keep her alive just long enough to get a little more information out of her. The eventual outcome will be the same, regardless. It's *inhuman!*"

They all looked at each other in long silence.

Eventually Jacobson replied, "I think we all have the same feelings here, Professor... but we're all professionals and we have a job to do, whether or not we agree with everything we have been asked to do."

Besides," he thought a second and observed, "You know, and it's just a feeling I have – I can't really put my finger on it – something tells me that this 'Karéin' *will* find a way to survive... *somehow*. Maybe longer than the rest of us here or on Earth, will. Just a feeling."

"Yeah... I guess," half-heartedly agreed Boyd. "Well... I suppose we had better get going. That old clock is ticking."

"Agreed. Dismissed," ordered Jacobson.

They all suited up.

Getting To Know You

Their trips to the Anomaly Mesa on that day, and the next, and on the days after that, were all variations on a common theme: a bumpy, dusty ride in the MMV to the site, where they were greeted by a Mars-girl; she was visibly enthusiastic at the advent of their return, disheartened almost to the point of tears, when they departed with the late afternoon shadows.

The astronauts were relieved to confirm that the girl evidently *did* have some way of surviving the freezing Martian night-time temperatures, although clearly not comfortably; when, on the second day, they gave her Tanaka's third uniform set (which more or less fit her) as well as some thermal blankets, the creature had knelt in front of them and hugged their legs, one by one, with a pathetic look of gratitude on her face.

On the first day, after wolfing down their gifts of S-rations and water, 'Karéin' led them into the chamber and presented them with some jewelry-like artifacts from a storage-box in a side-chamber, along with – of much more real interest – a number of book-sized, marble-like stone tableaux, each inscribed with writings in the same, box-like script that had adorned the chamber-door. The team displayed these, one by one, to a two-way video-display that White set up at the bottom of the ramp to the Anomaly chamber, so that Earth-borne scientists could start work on the task of deciphering the inscriptions on them.

When this was done, the display suddenly lit up with the faces of lucky Earth children, who had evidently won some kind of competition to "ask the girl from Mars one question".

She understood nothing that was asked of her, of course; but Tanaka noted that while the pictures from Earth were coming in, the Mars-girl was transfixed with interest in what was going on, studying every element of every scene with the utmost concentration, pointing to things in the Earth-scenes from time to time and babbling questions excitedly.

She seemed especially fascinated by the faces of the children.

On the second day, she led them to a side-chamber which had, apparently, been the storage-space of, judging from their appearance, a number of technological devices, but unfortunately the internal mechanisms of these had long been rusted and disintegrated by the ages; none of these machines worked, and they were all too large and cumbersome to be seriously considered for transport back to Earth.

Tanaka tried to inquire what the original purpose of these items was, but all she received in return was incomprehensible discourse in the girl's whistling, cooing native language.

Later on the same day, the team discovered that 'Karéin' liked to play games, when Jacobson and Boyd caught her tossing a seat-cushion from the MMV back and forth over, by Earth standards, impossibly long distances with White. The instant when the former two showed up, she cartwheeled and caught the projectile effortlessly with her feet, delivering it to them with a girlish smile and a curtsy. She also developed a special relationship with Tanaka, spending long hours with the scientist.

Despite the setback about the origin of the devices in the chamber, the team did, slowly, learn to communicate with the alien-girl, after a fashion. They were able to teach her their individual names and the English words for all the parts of the human body, and Jacobson had to order a quick disconnection of the real-time video up-link to Earth, when the lesson had forced the girl, much to White's delight, to reveal that she was anatomically identical to human females, in every apparent way.

The also managed to cross-communicate about a hundred other English words describing simple items and concepts like "food", "water", "sky", "ground" and so on.

The Mars-girl had learned a few English phrases such as "thank you" and had even been able to say a couple of short sentences, but none of these shed much insight into her history or background. She came to comprehend the symbols for Earth's decimal number system as well as the phonetic sounds of each of the letters of the English alphabet, with remarkable rapidity, however.

'Karéin's' own language had proved considerably more difficult for the Oberg Base team to master; Tanaka's opinion was that its structure was somehow mixed up with its vocabulary, in a way corresponding to no known Earth tongue. It apparently used a number of very high- and low-pitched sounds that they could only roughly approximate with a human larynx – both Tanaka and the linguists back on Earth were of the opinion that these changed the meanings of the words, something like Chinese does on Earth – so they were only able to learn the names for the body parts and of certain other very basic nouns.

Furthermore, this alien language either did not have verbs at all, or action concepts were somehow communicated in some other way.

The alien-girl had tried to illustrate its principles writing down her equivalents to common English words, but even with constant consultations with the best of Earth's archaeo-linguists and cryptographers, the team made only very limited progress.

As near as Tanaka and the other experts could tell, the script was partly phonetic but also partly ideographic in nature, with the same symbol sometimes standing for different sounds or ideas, depending on its context, and certain blocks of inscriptions could be read phonetically or ideographically as a whole, but the astronauts were not able to tell by which rule you would do one or the other.

There were also a *lot* of written symbols, at least two hundred identified by the end of the second day, and they were by no means sure that there weren't in fact more; whereas most Earth languages constructed words with different meanings from different combinations of letters, this language seemed to just add more symbols when it needed to describe more complex concepts.

By the end of the third day, they had been able to identify the pictographic symbols that stood for 'Karéin''s name, as well as a few more after her name that seemed to be a title of some sort, and another series of symbols, transcribed from the coffin from which the girl had awoken, that referred to a calendar date. Tanaka had communicated the latter finding, along with the alien-girl's responses to gestures asking "how many sunrises", to Houston, in the hopes of determining her age.

What came back from Earth was, by now, only mildly surprising: if they were interpreting both the calendar-symbols and the girl's verbal responses correctly, she was more than *three hundred thousand years old.*

"Doesn't look a day over three thousand," was White's comment, on hearing this, and that was the occasion on which they first heard her gentle, girlish, giggling laugh, imitating the rest of them, though she could not have known the joke.

Each time, when they left, she had tried to clamber into the MMV with them, and each time when they ordered her hence, her pleadings had become more and more desperate.

Boyd felt certain that she knew they were soon to leave, although there was no obvious way that she could have come to that conclusion from the evidence she had at her disposal.

Finally, they had arrived on the fourth and final day. As always, the girl was there to greet them, saying first something in her inscrutable language, then saying "Hell-low, frenn-dss" with a comical solemnity, shaking their hands, one by one, as she always did.

Boyd noted with interest that she had been doing physical exercises of some sort, reminiscent of *Tai Chi* in a way, when they had interrupted her morning regime. Despite the severe environment and minimal nourishment, she looked the picture of health; indeed, she fairly *exuded* strength and self-confidence.

Immediately, they set about their work-schedule of trying to expand their ability to communicate with the Mars-girl. As always, she co-operated, enthusiastically, if perhaps to limited effect. The exercises took an hour or two, interspersed with liberal disbursements of food and water, all of which were eagerly consumed.

Tanaka now started the last of their tasks.

"Hello, Karéin," she said, motioning for the girl to sit down on a flat-topped rock near the bottom of the ramp up to the Anomaly chamber. This she did promptly, joined thereafter by Tanaka on one side and Boyd on the other. They had deliberately left this task to the last.

"Hooboy," said White, "*This* is going to be fun. Man, if I was the last Earthling and the Martians tried to stick anything into *me*, I'd stick 'em right back. Hope she's more laid-back than I would be."

"Now, Karéin," said Tanaka, addressing the girl in as friendly a manner as possible, "We have to take a blood sample," – she showed the girl the needle and syringe, using it in mock fashion on the arm of her space-suit – "And this may hurt a bit, but we don't want to hurt you, Karéin, please believe us. Do you understand?"

The Mars-girl motioned for the items, which she examined carefully, instantly becoming aware of the point of the needle. She seemed to panic, for she shook her head violently, babbling something excitedly.

She put the needle up to her arm, but a centimeter or two away, then pulled the syringe-plunger back as if drawing blood; but then, she made a "whooshing" sound, with both hands making a shaking movement from bottom to top, rapidly repeated several times.

"*Told* y'all," taunted White, "She's afraid of sharp objects. Can't say I blame her."

"That will be *enough*," retorted Jacobson. "Cherie, let *me* talk to her. I'll try to get her trust."

He sat down on a rock opposite the three, with White leaning behind on the fender of the MMV.

"Karéin, this is your friend Jacobson," he said, looking the girl straight in the face. "We don't want to hurt you. Here, let me show you that it's not dangerous. Okay?"

The girl pursed her lips for a second as if attempting to remember what to say, then replied, "Oh-kay".

"What are you *doing*, sir?" asked Boyd with alarm, as he saw Jacobson, his other hand clamped on the fabric of his suit's sleeve a bit above his left wrist, suddenly un-engage the clamp connecting his left suit gauntlet to the rest of the suit. His bare skin was now exposed to the Martian environment.

"Relax, team," reassured Jacobson, "I don't want to breathe the stuff out there, obviously – but as long as I keep my other hand on my cuff and keep it taut, only a bit of the air in the suit will leak out. Funny, you know, feels chilly but not as bad as I had expected, kind of like Mount Rainier at 8,000 feet or something like that. Cherie, take a blood sample. I want her to understand *exactly* what's going to happen."

"Uhh... yes, sure, Captain, I get it. Good idea. Here, keep your arm level," replied Tanaka.

She sterilized the needle, then stuck it a short distance into his arm, drawing a small amount of blood.

Stoic as ever, Jacobson did not wince a bit, instead continuing to look at the Mars-girl, smiling all the while as if nothing were happening.

Tanaka showed the syringe to the alien-girl, who observed it carefully, obviously interested. The Professor then got out another syringe and pointed at Karéin, while Jacobson reattached his glove to the rest of his space-suit.

"Your turn, Karéin," she requested.

The Mars-girl got up quickly from the rock with a pained – or perhaps apprehensive – look on her face.

Again, she babbled something quickly, with words that sounded similar to those she had used a few seconds ago, but with a louder, more insistent tone to them.

She grabbed the syringe from Tanaka and again attempted to simulate the act of drawing blood, making the same motions but even more forcefully. She held out one of her arms and made a strange motion up and down it with her other hand, whose fingers flickered quickly back and forth like a spider climbing a wall, as the hand itself went back and forth over the opposite arm. She then pointed at the syringe and made a motion underneath it, as one would do to depict water or a liquid dripping out of a container.

Her eyes were wide open with concern.

"I don't *understand* this, Captain," pondered Tanaka. "Judging from her reaction, she doesn't seem to be so much afraid of the needle, as from something *inside* the syringe. Maybe she doesn't understand that we're just taking a small amount of blood?"

"Or maybe she's afraid of being poisoned," suggested Boyd.

He crouched in front of the Mars-girl, taking her hand.

"Karéin," he spoke, "This is your friend, Boyd. You know I would *never* hurt you, Karéin... don't you?"

She nodded.

"Would it help if I do it, Karéin? Would that make you feel better?" he asked.

Tanaka gave him another syringe.

Fear again appeared on her face, but the alien-girl now seemed to be resigned to going through the ordeal, for she made no more motions of protest, rolling up her borrowed clothes' sleeve and extending her left arm out in front of her, feet braced firmly on the ground.

But when Boyd moved the syringe directly over her arm, she suddenly grabbed it, not to snatch it away, but to hold it up, in strange fashion, from underneath.

"Karéin," Boyd remarked, "You don't have to do that."

The alien-girl gave him a steely glare, leaving her other hand in exactly the same position.

"Okay," he said, "It's okay if you want to do it that way. Let's do it."

"Oh-kay," replied the Mars-girl.

She did not sound enthusiastic.

Her stare was now directly at the likely point of incision. She seemed to be concentrating on the spot.

As carefully as he could, Boyd moved the point of the needle closer, closer still, right up to the skin. He hurt, psychically, every step of the way, thinking about it, about how he could cause pain to this amazing, vulnerable creature. He must have winced momentarily, because he did not see the needle enter her body, but when he felt the resistance of her flesh, instinctively he pulled back on the syringe-plunger.

Dark red blood, like venous blood from a human being but darker still, oozed quickly into the tube.

He had his prize. He pulled out the needle.

That is, he *tried* to pull out the needle. It was gone, somehow, as if it had vanished into thin air.

Then, in the next instant, his glance caught the body of the syringe – which was *melting*, liquidizing, collapsing into nothingness, with that ichorous blood pouring from its disintegrated bottom half, accompanied with a pungent, metallic odor.

"Drop it, Brent!" he heard White shout, the second that he looked up from his instruments. "The damn stuff's *acid!*"

His hand reflexively dropped the syringe, or what little was left of it, right into the girl's waiting hand, itself already stained by rivulets of her own, lethal life-blood, below. It mixed with the plastic of the syringe into a kind of lumpy, dirty-white goo, which she looked at curiously for a second.

Then she dropped the entire mixture down in front of them, where it hissed malevolently, reacting with the red Martian sand and making an indentation at least two to three centimeters deep, before the blood's acidic elements had been fully exhausted.

"Goddamn," Jacobson shot back. "No *wonder* she didn't want us taking samples. She wasn't afraid for *herself*, she was afraid for *us*. With good reason, it turns out."

"Yeah," echoed White, "We got us a Martian chick who's a mobile nuclear reactor, with blood like concentrated battery acid. Wonder what *other* little tricks she's got up her sleeve. By the way, I was monitoring the radiation-levels while you were doing that. The unknown signature went *way* up just before you stuck her with your needle, then it dropped to almost nothing just as you put it in, then it skyrocketed again, centered on her hand, when she caught the syringe."

"It's like she's controlling it, somehow," noted Tanaka. "But for *what?* There certainly wasn't any visible effect to it."

The alien-girl wiped the remaining blood from her hand in the sand, then sat back on the rock, listening with apparent bemusement, to the humans talking with each other.

Boyd noted with relief that she did not look either angry or frightened, but rather seemed to be studying their reactions to the recent event carefully, her gaze shifting quickly from person to person as each spoke. He wondered for an instant if she had some way of understanding what they were saying, even if she didn't know English.

"Well, gentlemen," added Tanaka, "We already *knew* that this being, while she may *look* like us, has a significantly different physiology; after all, if she didn't, she couldn't have survived out here in the first place. I suppose this kind of thing is to be expected, if that makes it any easier, but as Major White has put it, we shouldn't be surprised if we find out that she is a lot different from us in other ways, too."

She turned to the Mars-girl, crouching in front of her.

"Karéin," Tanaka said, "Now we *know* why you tried to warn us. Thank you for warning us of the danger. Okay?"

"Oh-kay," replied the Mars-girl, evenly.

She winced a bit and pulled a tiny part of the scab that had formed over the wound, off her arm, holding it between her fingertips, showing it to Tanaka and saying something like "eey-OO-wai" in her language, with a rising tone at the end of the sentence.

Now Jacobson spoke up, again.

"Cherie, get a containment-box," he demanded. "She's offering it to us – hopefully it's not as dangerous when it's congealed."

He turned to the girl.

"Thank you very much, Karéin," he said.

"Oh-kay," she replied with a smile.

Tanaka approached, opening a plastic bio-isolation box in front of the girl, who, understanding immediately, dropped the dried blood-fragment into it, pointing to it and saying something at the same time.

She held up first three fingers, then gave a quizzical look, then a shoulder-shrug, then four fingers.

"Is that how long it will take to eat through the plastic, I wonder?" inquired Boyd.

He put his hand under the box and made the same gesture as the girl had, just before they tried to take the sample.

She nodded, held up three fingers, then four, then said, "Oh-kay".

"I think she's trying to tell us that it still has some acidic qualities, even in its dry state," opined Tanaka. "We'll have to put it into something chemically neutral when we get back to the *Eagle*."

She turned to the Mars-girl. "Thank you for warning us, Karéin."

The Mars-girl said, "Oh-kay".

White followed this with, "One of these days, y'all, we gotta teach her how to say something other than 'okay'."

The alien-girl looked at him, smiled as if she got the joke and said, "Oh-kay."

They all laughed out loud.

After a few seconds, Jacobson spoke up. "Well, team, I guess that's as good a way as we're likely to find, to say 'goodbye' – we all knew that the time would come when we had to leave, and that's time's now, I'm afraid. Let's get the stuff for her, out of the MMV."

Instantly, the mood of enjoyment changed to one of profound sadness amongst all the humans – a change not just driven by the situation, but far more, perhaps unnaturally intense it was, as if these human astronauts were being asked to say a final 'goodbye' to their own children, or someone equally dear to them.

Their emotions were instantly perceived by the Mars-girl, whose own expression changed to one of intense concern.

She shot her "deer-in-the-headlights" look at Boyd, who was, by now, sure that she didn't need to comprehend the exactitudes of everything that was being said, to understand what was going on.

Her eyes seemed to plead with him. His feet felt like lead, as he joined White and Jacobson in unloading the spare food and water from the vehicle.

"I can't *believe* we're really going to *do* this," protested Tanaka. "Captain, there *has* to be another way!"

"We've already been *over* that, Professor," answered Jacobson, huffing and puffing as he removed the last of the boxes from the MMV. "I wish there *were...* but there isn't."

He stood, rigid and silent, for a second, then said, "We should all say our 'good-byes', now. I'll start. Brent, you go last, since you were the first to meet her."

The Mars mission commander turned to face the girl.

"Karéin," he spoke, "I have to go now, back to where we came from, along with all my friends. I wish we could take you with us, but there isn't room."

He hoped that she wasn't good at detecting lies.

"Here," – he motioned first to the food-box, then to the water-container, opening the top clasps on each in turn so she could survey the contents – "We have left you things to eat and drink, until we get back. We have also left you something," – he walked over to the portable video unit, flipping a switch to turn it on – "That you can use to keep in touch with us. See, you can see people in the screen, so you won't be lonely. And I also brought you a present, because you gave us one."

He gave her a shiny, steel-and-plastic bracelet, which she obligingly held out her left arm for.

She gave an appreciative, forced smile as he put it on her.

Jacobson hung his head and tried to walk away, but she momentarily grasped his hand, then let it fall, after a second.

He addressed her one last time. "And thank you for saving my life. I owe you one, Karéin."

He overheard Tanaka swearing in frustration as she tried, to no avail, to wipe tears from her face with her space-suit gloves, which made it only as far as her visor.

A voice came in over the intercom, emanating from the speaker on the MMV.

"Captain," mentioned Chkalov, "I want to say, for the record, that I agree with Professor Tanaka. If the matter were up to me, I would *gladly* take a chance with my own life in the hope of preserving the life of this unique being."

Upon hearing her name, the alien-girl approached the speaker and put her ear to it.

Chkalov continued, "Karéin... I will always regret that I did not get to meet you, in person. I wish you well – *do sviedannya*, as we say, where I come from. I hope that we will meet again."

Now White approached the Mars-girl.

"Hey there Karéin," said the African-American astronaut, trying to be as chipper as possible, "Y'all have made this trip way more than this dude could ever hope for."

More softly, he added, "I hope – I *really* hope, lady, that y'all are still here when we get back. I'm telling you now that I plan to come back, Karéin. With all that's goin' on with Earth these days, don't ask me how, but I *will*. And if not me, my son, or my daughter, or one of *their* kids; one way or another, my folks won't leave y'all up here forever... that's a *promise*. Be well and take care of yourself – that's an *order*, y'all *hear?*"

She extended her hand to him and he took it, for a moment, as had Jacobson.

Tanaka stood in front of the alien-girl.

"Karéin," she whimpered, breathing heavily, "First of all, you know, Captain Jacobson and I owe you our lives."

She hugged the Mars-girl.

"And for that *alone*, we will never forget you. I wish," – bawled Tanaka, now crying openly – "I wish that we could take you back. I don't know *why* we can't, Karéin. Please, *please* stay alive, because you're so important to me, to us, to everybody back on Earth, where we come from. I don't want to go, Karéin, but I *have* to. Please try to understand."

The alien-girl nuzzled her and said something, softly. After a time, they let go.

Finally, it was Boyd's turn.

He embraced her, gently brushing her hair, "Karéin, there's a movie where they say, 'now I *know* I have a heart, because it's breaking'; well, that's about how I feel now."

He looked deeply into those lambent eyes and was lost for a few long seconds; it was a feeling first of emotional oneness, then of sudden panic, as he was aware of alien, unfamiliar thoughts and that strange, pseudo-music, impressed upon his own mind – or was it of his own thoughts, somehow being drawn out, examined, *accessed* – then of calm, relaxation and acceptance.

"You *know* by now that I love you," – the others suppressed gasps at hearing this, although it was by no means a surprise – "And that I have right from the first time we met. Karéin, you and I have something special, something that I will treasure for the rest of my days, whatever may become of me, my wife and family – " he paused for a second – "Or of Earth."

She gave him another long glance, then buried her head in his arm.

They stood together in silent embrace, except for the lonely sound of the Martian winds, for many seconds.

Eventually, it fell to Jacobson to perform the final activities.

"Well, everyone, I guess we're ready to go, then," he muttered. "We'd better saddle up. Everyone into the MMV."

It took all of Boyd's self-control to let go of her.

One by one, they morosely got into the vehicle. Boyd was followed by the moist-eyed Mars-girl, who this time did not try to get in herself, being content just to hold hands with Boyd and Tanaka until the MMV slowly started to move off.

As they reached the crest of the nearest sand-dune, Jacobson stopped the vehicle for a second and looked back at the slim, enigmatic figure in the distance, an unknown intelligence that they had known only for a short while, and who – in all likelihood – human beings would never see again.

"Do you want to have a last look, anyone?" he asked.

"Couldn't *bear* to," replied Boyd. "I'd have to go back to her."

White just shook his head.

But Tanaka sat upright, staring absentmindedly into the Martian sky.

"What's that *music*?" she asked.

The MMV crested the hill and drove on towards Oberg Base, with all aboard silent, lost in their thoughts.

Too Short A Time

Their last night on Mars was uneventful, even if none of them got any real sleep, each being lost in thoughts and dreams which differed only in sad detail.

Jacobson and Tanaka gave up trying altogether in the wee hours, contenting themselves instead in communicating the last bits of information to Houston and in performing a last few experiments.

Eventually, White and Boyd awoke from their repose, such as it had been. As dictated by protocol, both men suited up and went outside to perform the final, pre-liftoff check of the *Eagle*, ensuring that it was intact and fully functional.

"*Eagle*, this is Omega Egress team, White and Boyd reporting," Boyd called over the intercom. "Captain, Professor, is the video-link working? You see and hear okay?"

"Affirmative, Brent," came the voice of Jacobson. "As you know, I think we stowed the last of the stuff when we packed away the MMV yesterday, but let's go over the protocol list, anyway. Make sure you get as much of this damn red dust off of her as you can, probably won't make any difference to liftoff, but I just want to, regardless. Oh – and, any sign of our friend, out there?"

A quick three-sixty of the surroundings revealed no signs of anything except themselves, even though Boyd secretly wished for otherwise.

"Negative, Captain," he indicated, "No 'Kareins', little green men or anything else except us two."

Chkalov's voice interrupted.

"Actually," explained the orbiting cosmonaut, "She appears to be back at the mesa, *Eagle*," he said. "Your tracking-bracelet is working nominally. I have been following her movements for about an hour, they are indicative of her regular patterns. She seems to be stopping here and there for a few minutes at a time... but there is nothing out of the ordinary."

"Good," replied Jacobson, hollowly. "Let's get the check over with, Omega team."

Boyd and White now began to examine every attachment on the exterior of the spacecraft, looking for the slightest evidence of anything out of order, sealing up and locking all access fixtures, cleaning things as best they could, all the while.

This was a largely futile endeavor, considering that the Martian wind, which had picked up recently, causing a few minor dust-devils here and there, had an annoying habit of just covering any clean spots with a fresh, dull-red patina.

There turned out to be a few minor cracks on one of the landing-gear actuating struts as well as a dust buildup in one of the main rocket nozzles, but there was nothing likely to seriously jeopardize the *Eagle's* safe lift-off from Mars.

This fact was duly communicated to Jacobson, thence in turn to Houston.

"Well, Devon," Boyd found himself saying, "I guess it's time for us to get outta here."

"Yeah, I guess it is," softly agreed White. "Any last words? I mean, I was the first human to say something on Mars, man. Seems only fair that y'all get to be the last one."

They looked at each other directly, through the silvered glare of their view-visors, neither wanting to think through the implications of White's comment.

"All I'll say for now, and I hope that Earth is listening," offered Boyd, "Is that we – I – *will* be back here, somehow, some way, some day. I was trained to be a scientis;, but sometimes, the facts alone aren't enough... you have to *believe* in things that you can't see, or explain. I don't know why, but I believe in Earth being able to pull through."

He paused a second – imagining, absentmindedly, that he saw her again, out of the corner of his eye – then, as if in a trance, repeated,

"And I believe in... *Karéin*."

There was no need to say anything more.

They climbed the access-ladder, White first, each taking a second or two per step to survey the windswept, alien landscape, which would soon again be left in desolate solitude, except for the cairn and flag that would be the only evidence that humankind had ever visited this place.

That, and the memories – whatever they might have been, in an alien, inscrutable mind – of humans, for the being they were leaving behind.

Back To The Red Sky

They were now all reclining in their G-chairs, as they had been upon first touching down.

"Houston and *Infinity*, this is *Eagle*, Jacobson speaking," he stated. "We have completed pre-liftoff equipment and communications checks. All values are nominal; we're two minutes from start of optimal egress window. *Infinity*, please report."

The voice of Chkalov sounded, "*Infinity* here, *Eagle*. We have your beacon, tracking you perfectly. All systems are 'go' from here. May I say, Captain... I am looking forward to shaking your hand, as you return from the planet. Your expedition has far surpassed any of our expectations."

A wry smile came to Jacobson's face.

"And may *I* say, Sergei," replied the commander, "That I'm looking forward to that shot of vodka that you managed to stash away up there. It will be good to get back. Major White, telemetry test please."

"Aye-aye, sir," responded White. "Activating primary and secondary links now. I have handshake and telemetry lock with *Infinity* – backup autopilot enabled and functioning one hundred per cent. Hmm... what's *that*... thought I had an outer lower hull-integrity lock status-light there, but it's gone... must have been my imagination. Brent, can y'all verify that?"

Boyd hit some switches and studied a flat-screen display intently for a few seconds, then said, "Confirmed... seals are all good... looks like a temporary glitch with one of the sensors – there's nothing unusual in the log-file. As you'll recall, the damn things have been acting up ever since we got down here, due to that fine-grained dust. It's back on-line now, though. Captain, I'll still authorize lift-off, unless you wish to abort."

"Negative," demurred Jacobson. "As long as we're still safe to fly."

"We are, sir," confirmed Boyd. "Ready to engage on your mark."

"Check," said Jacobson. "One last thing... *Infinity*, please cross-check location of the extra-terrestrial with Major White. Last position, map co-ordinates please. We don't want her camping out under the rockets and getting hurt."

"I think that's *highly* unlikely, Captain," commented Tanaka. "She's much too intelligent."

After a short time of computer-beeps and keyboard-commands, White spoke up.

"Same as before, Captain," he stated. "Minus about 0.3 north, about 172.1 east, right by the Anomaly Mesa. Seems to have been wanderin' around there in an irregular pattern, for about the last hour or so, from what I can see, but now she's sort of stopped – Sergei, y'all confirm that? I don't see her on the video-link anymore, but that's probably because she has just wandered out of its field of view. What're you seeing up there?"

"Confirmed," answered Chkalov, over the intercom. "The tracking-gear is working normally. Last video image was about twelve minutes ago... she seems to have been speaking into that bracelet that you gave her. Perhaps she is still trying to communicate with us."

"Captain," interjected Tanaka, with an stony look on her face, "Let me again state, for the record, my *profound* disagreement with this course of action. If I could volunteer to stay behind so she could come back with us, I would."

Jacobson was about to reply, when the Earth video-link became active.

"*Eagle* Oberg Base, this is Ramirez here, with Abruzzio, McPherson and General Symington also here at Mission Control," came the voice of the Latino scientist.

"By now," said Ramirez, "You'll be almost ready for your final departure from Mars. We'd like to congratulate you for your amazing and unprecedented accomplishments on this mission – and I'm pleased to say that based on what has transpired so far, the President of the United States has now given us a tentative go-ahead to start the planning for a return-trip to Mars... assuming, of course, that we find a way to deal with the 'Lucifer' object. If any member of your team wants to volunteer to be on the second mission, you have the President's assurance that you'll have the inside track for inclusion in it. General?"

Symington's ribbon-bedecked image appeared on the screen.

"On that front, gentlemen and ladies," intoned the general, "The mission to embed nuclear detonation charges in the object, which we have now named *Salvador*, is now almost ready to go, with liftoff of the first team, from the European Union, expected from Kourou in French Guiana, tomorrow. We will of course keep your team up to date on the *Salvador* mission as it goes forward. Ms. Abruzzio, I believe you have something, too?"

Sylvia Abruzzio appeared and said, "Meanwhile, we've also been monitoring the extra-terrestrial being, 'Karéin', via your video-link equipment at the Anomaly Mesa site and have been continuing our efforts to learn her language. I have to say that progress has been slow, Oberg Base, even though she is trying to co-operate with us. One thing that I *can* tell you is that she seems to have a very advanced grasp of mathematics, especially calculus, trigonometry and geometry – she is solving every puzzle we throw at her with *amazing* speed."

"You might also be interested to know," continued Abruzzio, "That she has already had over two hundred offers of marriage from various people on Earth, some motivated no doubt from a desire to be anywhere but here these days, others by the fact that she's a kind of Martian rock-star – people are watching the lessons as a way to avoid thinking about the 'Lucifer' situation. So in that respect, she's already helping us cope with 'Lucifer'. I hope she'll eventually come to know that we appreciate this."

Boyd thought, *If I could have stayed behind and married her... I would have, and would have enjoyed however long I would have lasted.*

I hope Laura will understand this feeling, some day.

And that she'll forgive me, for having felt it.

The final person to appear was Fred McPherson.

"*Eagle*," he stated, "I don't think there's a lot I can add to what has already been said, other than to say, 'job well done'. Godspeed back home to us."

"Video up-link on", ordered Jacobson, now looking at the camera.

"Thanks for the kind send-off, Houston," he commented. "I think I speak for the rest of the *Eagle and Infinity* crew when I say that we have mixed feelings ourselves, as we prepare to leave this planet and the unique being that we have had all too short a time to come to know. We came to Mars on a mission of exploration; we have fulfilled that objective, but we leave with much yet to do. I know that if and when another spacecraft from Planet Earth comes to Mars, I'd like to be on it. Who, among us, knows what's yet to come, Houston."

He paused and added, "Who knows... what's yet to come."

They all sat in silence for a second or two, then Boyd called out, "Optimal egress window now here, Captain."

"Very well. Departure protocol, team. Major Boyd, propulsive system check," replied Jacobson.

Boyd checked the panel, the sidearm controller and the read-outs.

He used a key to uncover the engine-engagement switch.

"All nominal, one hundred, sir," he declared. "Ready on your mark."

"Goodbye, Karéin," breathed Tanaka, her lips pursed tight, her eyes watering. "I'm *so* sorry."

Boyd's arms felt like lead, again.

"Mark," ordered Jacobson.

Boyd pushed a button and pulled back on the controller.

The *Eagle* shook, gently at first, then with more force, then more, then more, then they all felt the push of gravity, compressing them into their seats.

Despite the physical discomfort and the undeniable risks of this phase of the mission – if anything went wrong here, as White said several times on the way up, much to Jacobson's displeasure, "There won't be anybody to gather the pieces, at least a bit of them guys that flamed out on Earth got picked up afterwards" – the lift-off was as anti-climatic as their original touchdown had been.

The others variously had their eyes closed, or were focused on their instruments, but Boyd's job was to get them safely off the planet, so he concentrated exclusively on maintaining the trajectory – although, if the truth be known, this job, too, was the responsibility of the computers; he was just there as a final human fail-safe, really.

"Altitude 1,000... 2,000... 5,000... climbing a bit slower than nominal, Captain," he announced. "Must be dirty thrusters – thought I cleaned 'em all off, but there's that dust again... 10,000... 20... 30... 40..."

"*Eagle*, I see you now," pronounced Chkalov over the intercom. "Velocity minus 1,000 kph negative delta, trajectory good. You're easily within the pipe, Captain Jacobson... how do the Americans say it, ah yes, 'five by five'? ETA to docking *rendez-vous* seven minutes, thirty-three seconds. Changing relative orientation of *Infinity*, now. Engaging maneuver... complete. You should be able to dock without any change in your own orientation. A trick that I have been practicing up here, Captain, while you have all been busy down there on Mars."

Smiling, Jacobson replied, "I see you have been keeping busy up there, Sergei. Can't say I blame you. Major White, docking protocol test, please."

"Checking, Captain," said White. "Comm-link engaged. Locked. *Infinity*, sending you a pulse. Please confirm."

"Confirmed," replied Chkalov. "Auto-dock enabled. Ready at any time."

"Very well then," said Jacobson. "I guess we're all just passengers, from now on, in the capable hands of Major Boyd and the computers."

He looked at a dial, and added,

"Zero-G in one minute."

"I can already feel it," remarked White.

"Hey, Captain," said the African-American astronaut, "Y'all know... wasn't much, but I'm going to miss what passed for gravity down there. Won't miss the dust, though. Or cleaning it off my face every minute just to see out my visor."

Jacobson laughed.

"Me neither," admitted Tanaka with a wry smile, "Considering that it gets *everywhere* – we'll need a month in quarantine to make sure it doesn't get to Earth, either. I'm still brushing the stuff out of my socks."

She reflected for a few seconds, then remarked, "You know, now that I'm a bit... more *removed* from the situation, although I haven't changed my opinion, Captain, I have to admit that I *could* be wrong about the extraterrestrial."

She looked out the side-portal, which revealed a magnificent view of Mars, resplendent in its ruddy glory, shimmering below them.

"She *belongs* there, in a way, with the dust, the cold and Mars," softly opined Tanaka. "As a scientist, I have to acknowledge that it's her native environment, the one that we have to assume she grew up in... what she's used to. We have no idea about how it might have affected her, were we to have taken her back to Earth."

"Yeah," Boyd replied, "Might have been like taking a polar bear down to a zoo in Florida, I guess, but she *did* seem to appreciate the extra clothes we gave her. Hope she's warm..."

Tanaka nodded.

For the next few minutes, they busied themselves with their instruments and their duties.

"Final docking approach," announced Boyd. "*Infinity*, I see you. Right on my mark."

"Confirmed," replied Chkalov. "Starting the count. 1,000 meters.. 900... 800... 700... 600... reduce velocity now, *Eagle*."

Boyd throttled back. "Velocity now 50 kph... 30... 10... residual only... stand by, folks, five seconds..."

Thud.

Click.

"Congratulations, Major," said Jacobson. "As smooth as the set-down and take-off. You can fly my rig anytime, Brent."

He turned to the video-screen.

"Houston, this is Captain Jacobson," he stated, "Reporting successful docking with *Infinity*. We're now in stable orbit over Mars and will be making de-orbit preparations over the next hour."

He spoke into a microphone.

"Sergei, confirm lock seal-integrity," said Jacobson.

"Confirmed," echoed the voice. "Seal at one-hundred, no leakage, primary and redundant locks all engaged. Captain, request permission to open the hatch."

"Permission granted," agreed Jacobson. "And... may I wish you, 'welcome aboard'."

"No, Captain," came the voice, at first mechanical, distant, then immediate and next-door, as the hatch between the two spacecraft slowly opened with a slight "whoosh", revealing the wiry, bearded face of the Russian cosmonaut, "I should welcome *you* aboard *Infinity*. After all, *my* ship is ten times the size of yours," he said with a broad grin.

"Sergei!" exclaimed White, darting effortlessly through the zero gravity, giving the Chkalov a robust handshake. "We all missed y'all down there, man. Thanks for holding the fort. Feels great to be back home... or what passes for a home these days."

"Sure *does*," confirmed Tanaka.

"Good to see ya," was all Boyd could come up with, on the spot.

White stopped for a second, and sniffed.

"Man, Sergei, is it *that* cabbage soup of yours, again?" he whined. "Tell me we don't have to smell that, all the way back."

They all laughed.

"*Our* ship, Sergei," said Jacobson, himself giving the cosmonaut a handshake. "Major White speaks the truth, at least about the mission, not the soup. It must have been lonely up here, especially with all the excitement going on down there. We all owe you. I want you to know that we're all aware of how hard it must have been to have come this close, but not actually get down there. Next time, I promise you, I'm not going if you aren't on the away-team."

Chkalov just nodded, modestly.

"Well, Captain, I suppose we should get back to business," offered Boyd. "We need to get the loose stuff secured – I'll start the pre-fire propulsive systems check."

"Agreed," said Jacobson. "We all know the drill. Stow your personal possessions and anything you find lying around loose. Major White, comm-link and astrogation checks, supplementary cross-check with Houston, please. Professor, final science activities and spacecraft life-support inventory verification. Chkalov and I will do the general systems check for *Eagle* and *Infinity* respectively. Everybody report back to me 45 minutes from now, in *Infinity's* control-center."

They all got up and went forth, with Chkalov looking over *Eagle* while the others went into the *Infinity*, enabling and checking the systems for which each was respectively responsible.

Boyd, for his part, entered the cavernous hold of the mother ship, with its rotating central hub, providing the illusion of gravity, wondering how he had put up with the confinement of the *Eagle*.

He realized that while down on Mars, he could have – at least in theory – suited up and wandered endlessly outside, while up here, he was trapped with the others, for better or worse, for the next four months.

No spaceship, however lavishly outfitted, could substitute for a planet, however desolate.

Each crew-member, Boyd certainly not least among them, attended to his or her duties with the utmost diligence, since this was not a matter of following orders, but a matter of ensuring one's own survival; on a vessel such as the *Eagle and Infinity* combination, there was no such thing as a "non-critical system". Anything that failed would have to be done without for at least four months.

All assuming, of course that there would *be* somewhere to land, at journey's end. None of them tried to spend much time considering such matters. There was too much to do, right now.

After about forty minutes, they started to congregate in the control room of the mother ship. White and Tanaka showed up first, floating in as if swimming at ten meters deep, followed shortly thereafter by Boyd, Chkalov and Jacobson.

"Status report, ladies and gentlemen," requested Jacobson. "I'll go first. I did an external via the cameras and *Infinity's* in near-perfect shape; if Sergei ran into any meteoroids above dust size while we were capering around down on Mars, I can't find any evidence of it, except that the solar panels are at about 98 per cent, so maybe we had some minor erosion there. Center hub rotation-assembly, check. Batteries, electrical, check – one minor circuit in the food prep area is marginal but still functioning. Shielding, instrumentation, auxiliaries, all check. Emergency egress module passes self-tests. Nothing else to report... so I don't believe we need an inspection EVA prior to departure. If anyone disagrees with this assessment, now's the time to voice your opinions. Professor?"

"Life-support and environmental systems fully operational, Captain," replied Tanaka. "We're of course a bit short on supplementary food and water reserves because of what we left down on the planet; but we have more than enough to last us all the way back to Earth, regardless. Sick-bay equipment is all working properly – don't forget that I owe all of you a physical, once we leave orbit and get settled down on our new trajectory. That's all, Captain."

"My turn, I guess," interjected White. "I'll keep it short and sweet. A bit of local interference here and there, 'specially on *Eagle* – can't quite pinpoint where it's comin' from, maybe a loose connector or just cosmic-rays, maybe somethin' got jarred loose at the bottom of the lander when we took off – but other than that, all communications gear and sensors are working properly, on both ships. I pinged Houston a few times via the high- and low-gain up-link arrays and they're fine, too. I updated the nav systems with some star-shots and they check against long-range GPS, so we have a good fix. That's about it."

Chkalov spoke up next.

"I will make my report now, Captain," he said. "I reviewed all general-purpose systems on the *Eagle*, and everything seems to be in working condition, if one does not count the fact that there is a surprising amount of residual surface-dust in places, which will cause some interesting problems for the decontamination team when we reach Earth, I suspect; but from a personal perspective, being able to rub some of this between my finger-tips, means that in fact, I *have*, in a way, touched Mars... so it is not *so* bad... yes?"

"Y'all still get to go back down there on the return-trip," quipped White, with a broad grin. "Even if I got to skip it myself."

Chkalov smiled appreciatively and continued, "I noticed that the locking-clasps on two of the storage bay access-hatches below the main deck level, and one in the communications relay shack, had become un-engaged. I corrected this. Also, some equipment not now relevant to the mission had been left running, causing an unnecessary load on the electrical system. I shut down the systems in question. I now judge the *Eagle* to be in good shape for departure."

"How are the engines, Major?" inquired Jacobson, nodding to Chkalov, then turning to Boyd.

"Good, in general," Boyd replied. "Of course we won't know until we do a full burn... but I tested the igniters and they're all on-line. Had to play around with number three a bit, but it seems to be nominal now. Maneuvering-thrusters are all on-line too and they've got plenty of reserve gas."

"How much reserve fuel for the main engines have we got, Brent?" asked Jacobson.

"Well," Boyd explained, "Assuming that we don't run into problems and we don't have to re-light, or anything like that, we *should* – if my calculations are correct – arrive at Earth with about a ten to twelve per cent reserve, give or take a few, Captain. Not that it matters... right?"

"Not necessarily," parried Jacobson. "This is something that I wanted to bring to everyone's attention, before we get going. As matters stand now, the flight-plan is exactly as it always has been, that is, we'll set an Earth *rendez-vous* trajectory to arrive in three months, twenty-nine days and fourteen hours, dock with ISS 2 in Earth orbit and go from there, understanding that we now have a containment and quarantine issue of a magnitude that wasn't foreseen beforehand."

He motioned the "up-link off" gesture.

White instantly complied.

Jacobson looked at each of them once, briefly, in the eye, then said, quietly, "However... we have to start considering the fact that by the time we near Earth, the situation may be so grim that returning there may not *be* a viable option."

He took a deep breath, then continued, "I know that none of us want to think about it, but there is the real possibility that Earth may not be habitable at *all* if 'Lucifer' actually impacts with it, and that it could remain that way for many human lifetimes. Even if our friends back home *do* manage to stop it, the near-Earth area of interplanetary space – at the very least, the part of it between the Earth and the Moon – may be so strewn with debris that flying in there could be very risky. At least we have the luxury, if I can call it that, of being able to know what the outcome of the 'Lucifer' object will have been, before we get back to Earth."

Jacobson continued, "I've been discussing all of this with Houston and have been trying to come up with some contingency-plans in the event that we have to adjust our flight-path, or our ultimate destination, or both, but I have to tell you, that so far, the options aren't very encouraging."

"I wonder why *that* is," Tanaka mordantly observed. "I don't suppose it would have anything to do with a severe lack of inhabitable planets around here, would it?"

Trying to force a smile, Jacobson replied, "*Something* like that. The two proposals we have been talking about involve, first, docking with ISS2, but with it in a much higher orbit, well past the Moon – Houston's been planning doing that for a long time, with the station, anyway, to get it out of the 'Lucifer' danger-zone – or, secondly, trying to get the *Eagle* and *Infinity* to touch down on the Moon near Moonbase MB1, while we're still docked. The idea here would be to do it slowly enough so that *Eagle's* landing gear could handle the impact, giving MB1 a supplemental supply of living space, air, water and food."

"Commander," Boyd protested, "With all due respect – that's *crazy! Eagle* was meant to touch down *once*, on Mars, by itself – it was never designed to handle the mass of a much larger ship like *Infinity*, even on a gravity-weak place like the Moon. And we wouldn't have enough fuel left in *Eagle's* primary thrusters afterwards, to lift off again. Besides, MB1's just a few huts and it's been uninhabited since the last mission two years ago. The last reports I remember hearing before we set off, were that it had *serious* maintenance problems – microscopic pressure-leaks they could never trace down, failures in the environmental and hydroponic systems, and so on – which the last team didn't fix because they figured they'd never be back anyway. Who knows if there's even any air left *in* it, by now? We'd be even more stranded down *there* than we are up *here*."

Tanaka interjected, "And as far as ISS2's concerned... sure, they *could* probably boost its orbit – but it's already got a full crew. Even if it manages to escape the backwash from the 'Lucifer' impact, there's no *way* that Earth would be in any shape to send up a rescue-mission before ISS2's life-support reserves run out, with or without us, whether it's in a low orbit or a high one. From what I know of that station, its oxygen recycling-system could hold out for three months for sure – four or five if we were to add ours to theirs, possibly – but after that... well, I don't have to explain what would happen, *then*."

"Yeah, and Captain, sir," slowly commented White, "I... uhh... don't really know how to say this, sir, but speaking just for myself, I'm not really big on the idea of buying myself a few more days or weeks of life either in orbit, or on the Moon, when the outcome's gonna be the same in the long run. I'd much rather be with my family down on Earth, if that's all the same with y'all. Sort of like wanting to go out with a bang rather than a whimper, if y'all know what I mean."

"If it's of any interest, Devon," Jacobson replied, "That's more or less my own opinion, and I wouldn't be surprised if a few others feel the same way –"

"*Da, etot praivielna*," interjected Chkalov in a low voice.

"But apart from the fact that we still have orders to follow, as professional astronauts and cosmonauts," explained the Mars mission commander, "We don't have any easy way of getting down to Earth, in any event. As you know, we were supposed to catch a Shuttle-NG ride back from ISS2; we certainly can't use *Eagle*, it was never designed for Earth atmospheric re-entry... it'd *melt*. Until we hear differently from Houston, we've got little choice but to stick with the original plan, and if that gets changed for whatever reason, we'll *have* to dock with something that can get us back home. Don't ask me what *that* is... because at this point your guesses are as good as mine. That's all I know... if I hear anything more from Houston I'll tell everyone here, immediately. You have my word on that."

They all went silent.

Then Tanaka mentioned, "Look, everybody... they have some pretty smart people working on things down there. I know a lot of them personally. It's amazing what human beings can accomplish when they have to stop fighting with each other and concentrate on a single purpose. Maybe we'll all be okay. We'll find a way... we've *got* to."

They all nodded, avoiding each other's glances.

Eventually, Jacobson gave the "up-link on" gesture.

Reluctantly, White again enabled the equipment.

"Very well, then, team, we're good to go – time to get back home. Take your seats, ladies and gentlemen. Pre-burn protocol," Jacobson said in his most commanding tone.

He hoped that it would sound convincing.

The team got up, fumbling for hand-grips in the zero gravity, and headed off to their posts.

Boyd reminded himself not to hold his breath, this time.

Toward A Threatened Home

The ship's systems, with the exception of *Infinity*'s rotating central drum, were enabled.

The G-chairs were doing their obtuse best to obstruct the human body, as well.

"Final pre-burn check," directed Jacobson.

"Nav systems all on-line, sir," replied White. "I have a lock on the station beacon."

"Good... let's hope there *will* be an ISS2 for us to *rendez-vous* with, by the time we get there," commented Jacobson, coolly. "Major Boyd, propulsive protocol for the pulse-nuclear-ion drive. Engage on my mark."

"Aye-aye, sir," complied Boyd. "Vernier stabilizers," he stated.

"Mark," replied Jacobson.

There was a faint "whoosh".

"Igniters, one to four in sequence," called Boyd.

"Mark," replied Jacobson.

Boyd threw four switches, one after the other.

"Igniters all nominal, sir. Awaiting your command," he spoke.

"It's been said before... but may the wind, be at our backs," Jacobson commented, looking straight forward.

"*Mark.*"

They all felt a "thump" – the kind of impact made by a hearty slap on the back, or maybe from the start of a fast ride at an exhibition park, accompanied by another faint "whoosh"; there was none of the roar that you would have expected from having watched untold science-fiction movies, thanks to the airless, soundless void of space.

But the fact that they *were* moving, was well attested by the pressure they felt on every inch of their bodies, as the *Eagle and Infinity* duo kept on accelerating at a constant rate, no more, superficially, than what one would feel in a drag racer, but, in reality, they were shortly to again become the fastest human-carrying object in history, with a velocity of untold thousands of kilometers per hour.

If they were to make it back to Earth in anything like the intended amount of time, they would need this speed.

"Check velocity against baseline," requested Jacobson.

"Eighteen point three-five thousand kph, baseline acceleration curve says nineteen point five, so we're just under," calculated Boyd. "Nothing to worry about, I'll throttle up a bit... that should correct it."

He pulled on the side-stick.

"Back on the track, zero-point-three delta, Captain," announced the pilot. "Optimal velocity of twenty-seven thousand, zero-fifty kph in twenty-five minutes, fifteen seconds."

"Very well, then," replied Jacobson. "Until then, I suggest that we all just sit back and enjoy the ride, folks," he said.

"Captain, sir? I have to go to the bathroom, sir. Are we gettin' anywhere near a truck-stop?" joked White.

They all cracked up.

"Just *think*, we're stuck with *him*, for another four months," added Tanaka, making a face at White.

"I was going to say something like that... but, trying to play officer-corps, I thought the better of it," dryly remarked Jacobson.

The next twenty-five minutes passed quickly.

From time to time each one of them shot a glance at the disc of Mars, receding slowly, its events, secrets and promise, no less the large in their minds.

Space

Traveling-Routine

After the burn was over with and the necessary post de-orbit checks had been completed, the *Eagle and Infinity* crew was able to experience something that all, save Chkalov, had not been able to partake of, since arrival at Mars : free time.

Each crew-member approached the opportunity differently, with those having immediate family spending most of their time communicating awkwardly with home; not only because of the back-and-forth delay, but because none had yet figured out how to deal with the 'Lucifer' issue.

Tanaka and Chkalov, the only two unmarried ones, busied themselves with unfinished scientific experiments and chess against the computer, respectively.

Chkalov was proud of having once beaten the accursed thing, until it was revealed that White had dropped its playing level from "Master" to "Beginner", behind the former's back.

White had, sensibly, refused Chkalov's subsequent challenge to take the computer's seat, in the next game.

On the whole, they readjusted to the new routine, or lack of it, fairly well, except for Jacobson, who seemed at loose ends, now that his command role was temporarily redundant. He had not had this problem on the outbound trip, but then, there was the excitement of what was yet to be discovered, on that leg of the journey.

Now, all was said and done, all was over with; or, so it seemed.

Jacobson tried to keep busy by jogging endless loops around the *Infinity's* central core – the only part of the ship with the illusion of gravity, and in this he was joined sometimes by one or two of the others. It thus took only a day, or perhaps not a full day, for the new routine to sink in.

After the enforced first six minimum hours of "night-time bed-rest" – ignoring, for the moment, that they hurtled through the perpetual night of space – the crew awoke for the first full day on Earthbound trajectory.

Boyd drifted lazily down the axial core passageway to the center drum and practiced his most athletic jump from the Zero-G to pseudo-grav environment, landing with a resounding "clang" on the perpetually curved inner drum track-way, followed by Tanaka's more acrobatic leap.

The two walked, unsteadily as always, the short distance to the mess-hall (really, just a partitioned part of the track-way, with non-stick surfaces in the case of an unexpected artificial gravity failure).

Chkalov was already there, lovingly savoring every last morsel of the something-or-other he had been allocated as today's "daytime food ration". Jacobson and White were evidently still asleep, judging from the fact that their meal-packets had not yet been opened.

"Morning, Sergei," greeted Tanaka. "Hungry, I see?"

"*Dobrye utra*, Professor," amicably responded Chkalov. "Alas... I used up two of my three allowed personal food-rations, that is, good Russian cabbage soup-mix, while I was waiting for you all, in my lonely time on *Infinity*. So I am forced to eat whatever is put in front of me. But I am used to that. It could be worse, as anyone who has survived as a cadet in my country's air force, can attest."

He grinned.

"I'll have to remind Devon of that, when he shows up," grunted Boyd as he sat down to survey his own rations.

"Man... what *is* this stuff?" he complained, as he tasted a bit of it. "Maybe my mind's playing tricks on me, but what we had on the away-team seemed better."

"That's no accident, Brent," responded Tanaka, with a wry smile. "If you remember your mission-briefing, they specifically stated that the rations for the away-team and the outbound leg were supposed to emphasize taste over space- and weight-efficiency by volume, to keep up morale... at least that was the idea thought up by NASA's psych analysts. They had to reverse the concept, supposedly, to be able to store enough food to comfortably make it back. You should be able to get used to it, if you just have the right *attitude*."

"Sure," he muttered, "I could get used to eating seaweed, too, if that's all I had. This stuff tastes like salted cardboard."

"Good guess," she replied, "Because that's what it *is*, more or less, seaweed, with a bit of tofu and all sorts of added vitamins and proteins. The most concentrated nutrition available – you can last a week or more on just five small helpings, or so I'm told. Keeps the... uhh... *residue*, to a minimum, too."

"Mmm," was all he could think to say back to her.

The criteria by which they had been selected for this mission, in the first place, had placed heavy emphasis on one's ability to get along with others in a confined space, over a long period of time.

Boyd wondered, idly, how White had passed the test; but perhaps a sense of humor was a good thing, in moderate proportions, so it was pointless to complain about things one couldn't change.

This monumental issue having been dealt with, the three contented themselves with chit-chat for the next half hour or so, washing their repast – such as it was – down with carefully pre-measured water-rations, allocated in valve-sealed squeeze bags, so constructed lest a few drops of the precious liquid be lost through accident or pseudo-grav failure.

Eventually, Jacobson and White dropped in, making essentially the same comments about the food as each tasted it in turn.

Boyd, and no doubt the others, reflected upon the fact that this was going to be his morning routine, for the next four months, with only minor, routine tasks to perform, for the rest of each awake period.

Well, at least he *could* catch up on his reading, via the two-way link to Earth's NeoNet; even *if* half of the 'interesting' stuff, had been censored out of its public sections, several U.S. Administrations before.

Finally, the first three had finished their meals. Boyd and Tanaka lingered behind to argue with Jacobson about the meaning of some of the symbols they had discovered on Mars, with White lounging in the background, listening via headphones to some kind of raucous music.

Now, the only real 'duty', was to wait; so, that was what they all set about to doing.

More or less the same routine had persisted for three days, when Chkalov finally had an idea to help him escape the boredom of the *Infinity*'s artificial, sterile, climate-controlled and altogether too *comfortable*, environment.

"Captain," he requested, "With your permission, I would like to examine the jewel, that is, the gift that the Mars-girl gave to Major Boyd, down on the planet. I will not remove it from its containment-chamber."

"Sure, I guess," replied Jacobson. "Considering that that's as close as you'll get to our friend 'Karéin', I don't blame you for wanting to see it. Feel free to use any of the imaging or investigative tools on it – but non-destructive tests only, understood? Perhaps you'll notice something that we all didn't, while we were down there."

"Of course," agreed Chkalov. "And did you know, Captain, that I took metallurgy as my minor, back in my college days at the Tula Institute? I am looking forward to seeing the spectral results from this unique object. I will let you know if I see anything interesting."

Jacobson gave him the thumbs-up.

Chkalov bounded off, towards the axial passageway hatch, disappearing around the curve of the central hub track-way.

Surprise In The Hold

Cosmonaut First Class Sergei Chkalov, Master Instructor Pilot of the Russian Air Force, Ph.D in Exotic Gas Dynamics from Tula State University – these were but a few of the lean, almost gaunt, Russian's previous accomplishments – cleared the aft hatch of the *Infinity*'s axial passageway, leaving it open so he could practice his favorite Zero-G swan-dive through it on the way back to "Gravity-Land", as the crew had so named the rotating center drum.

Ahead of him, at the other end of the maintenance and communications demi-chamber in which he was now located, was the airlock to the *Eagle*, sealed and shut as a precaution against the one-in-a-million chance of an accidental loss of dock-lock between the two spacecraft.

Chkalov found his heart-rate increasing unexpectedly, as he entered the hatch unlock codes on the side-panel beside the hatch itself, doing this by feel.

One part of him resented the fact that examining the artifacts from Mars, would likely – despite Jacobson's promises, earnest, no doubt, but beyond the man's ability to deliver – be as close as he would ever get to touching the mysteries that he had seen, so near yet so far, from his vantage-point up in *Infinity* while in orbit around the planet.

His other side, the rigidly disciplined, professional part, was immensely proud of the not inconsiderable role he had played in the whole affair, one that would have all of his fellow Russian Air Force cadet friends – no, in fact, *all* of his fellow citizens, back home – remember him forever.

He recalled Iosef Stalin's famous saying, "The death of one man is a tragedy; but the death of a million, is a statistic."

Although those terrible days were now long past, life for the average man or woman in Mother Russia was still mundane, exhausting and, ultimately, just an existence – not much more.

But Sergei Chkalov, like his forebears Gagarin, Titov, Leonov, Kurbenko and a score of others, would not die a statistic, however things turned out.

He had been to the mountain... and, he was coming back.

He just hoped that there would *be* a Russia, to welcome him.

The hatch opened, followed quickly by the corresponding one on the *Eagle* side of the space-dock : the two were electronically synchronized.

Chkalov self-catapulted into the *Eagle's* upper chamber, grasping the central pole surrounded by its spiral staircase, then pulled himself down to the main deck, re-engaging the lights he had turned off earlier during his inspection.

Floating just in front of the metal grid-panels that had served as a floor when the spacecraft was upright on Mars, he found the access-hatch leading to the lower storage-chamber, disengaged its locking-clamp, then moved gracefully into this more confined space – with a remaining free area perhaps big enough to hold three adult humans, when cluttered, as it was, with storage-boxes of various sizes and shapes.

Chkalov looked around, trying to find the box labeled "Mars Artifacts"; despite his years of training in the West, his mind still perceived writing in Cyrillic, so it took a slight bit longer than would otherwise have been the case, to decipher each item's description.

He noticed, to his dismay, that several of the boxes had somehow been flung open – curses, it must have been the shock of the de-orbit engine firing, but he *thought* that he had locked the things, properly – and that a few of the items that had been contained therein, were now floating aimlessly, here and there.

To his immense relief, he did not see any of the Martian *bric-a-brac* among this flotsam and jetsam.

That was good, because to have had *those* damaged due to his negligence in the pre-burn check would have been a shame he could *never* have lived down.

Now, he saw the "Mars Artifacts" box.

It was, thank God, locked shut.

If he could just put things back before anyone else called him, the others would never know that anything had been amiss.

The cosmonaut set about to returning the loose items to where they belonged, allowing for the fact that he did not exactly know where each had originally been put, brushing off fine red-brown dust from some things while trying as hard as he could not to breathe in the stuff, as it wafted within the storage-chamber.

While grasping for a hand-hold on a box to his left, Chkalov's right foot collided with a flashlight, propelling it into the dark interior of an open box, where it evidently landed with a soft "thunk".

He looked at the label on the box, which was marked, "Reserve Food / Water". Clearly, a flashlight did not belong there, so reflexively, he reached in to retrieve the item, wondering idly if any would miss a few spare food-rations – after all, he had learned the fine art of pilfering supplies as a Russian Air Force cadet, long before he had even learned to parachute, much less fly a fighter-plane – but decided quickly against the idea.

Tanaka had, after all, said they had plenty, and the stuff wasn't very tasty, anyway.

The Russian rummaged around inside the box, again and again, brushing up against what appeared to be discarded food-wrappers (he remembered the rules against waste disposal on Mars) and against something solid a couple of times, but not finding the flashlight, somehow.

Chkalov swore in his native language, hoping that the microphones on the mid-deck of the *Eagle* couldn't pick up the sound, not understanding why such a large item could be so hard to get a grasp on.

Perplexed, he came closer, grasping the side of the box so as to be able to propel himself inside it.

Then he saw the flashlight being slowly presented to him, by a slim, light-skinned, female hand.

A small, friendly-sounding voice came from inside the box, timidly asking, "Oh-kay?"

Was the next set of emotions that washed instantly over the cosmonaut plain fear, or horror, or astonishment, or the ecstasy of realized hopes, or all of these, in some proportion? His mind raced, regardless, trying to think what to do next.

Should he bolt? Should he slam the box shut?

Should he... *what?*

He observed his legs kicking reflexively against the front of the box, propelling him straight backwards, coming to rest on the far side of the chamber, next to the opened hatch to the *Eagle's* middle level.

With his military training snapping him into action, Chkalov somersaulted backwards through the hatch, rocketing over to the nearest microphone, fumbling in utter panic as he tried to open a channel.

After what seemed like an eternity, a voice came over the speaker.

"Yo, Sergei," he heard White say. "What's up there? Y'all figured out how to get that thing she gave us, to sing and dance?"

"Major," shouted Chkalov, "*I have an emergency situation down here in Eagle!*"

He heard another voice, that of Boyd, respond, loud, clear and concerned.

"What *kind* of emergency, Sergei?" asked the pilot. "Systems-failure? Is the hatch secure?"

Calming himself ever so slightly, the Russian responded, "I... do not know exactly how to say this, Major Boyd, but... well... you can tell Major White that I do not have the jewel... but I *do* have its *owner*, here with me. She is in the cargo-hold."

The intercom worked well enough to transmit the universal gasp from those in the *Infinity*, as all froze upon hearing this news.

For a few seconds there was silence, then Chkalov requested, "May I speak with the Captain, please?"

"Yes, Sergei," replied Jacobson, heavily. "Go ahead."

"Sir," asked Chkalov, "Should I close the hatch? So far I am the only one who has come into close contact with the alien-girl. If the air down here is contaminated... I should quarantine myself, should I not?"

"Yes, for the time being," commanded Jacobson.

"Check that order," Chkalov heard the voice of Tanaka counter-command.

"Sam," she reflectively implored, "There's no *point*, now. Think it through – she must have been in the cargo-hold right from the time when we lifted off, and we've had the hatch open, on and off, since then. Sergei would have been the only one who could have kept from breathing the air in the *Eagle*, and then only until he opened the hatch to the *Infinity* when we docked. We could purge all the air out of lander, or we could permanently seal Sergei in there – both of which would kill him, of course – but *nothing* we can do now can stop us from having been exposed to her. We might as well go down and say, 'hello', for all the good it will do."

"For God's sake," sharply retorted Jacobson, "*You* think it through, Professor! We're not going to make a bad situation *worse*. Sergei, shut the hatch, now, that's a direct order! And disengage the cross-ship ventilating assembly."

Chkalov complied and the hatches connecting the two spacecraft swung shut, by remote control.

He was now trapped, alone in a confined spacecraft with an alien being of unknown intentions, powers and – he thought, morbidly, diseases.

He tried to think of coping-strategies, as he listened to the panicked conversation coming in across the intercom.

"Okay, everyone, let's take a deep breath," Jacobson directed; then, shaking his head as he realized the unintentional joke, "Let me rephrase that... let's consider our options. *Somehow* – don't ask me how – our friend 'Karéin' has managed to evade *all* of our security checks, and stow away in the *Eagle*."

He stopped a second, then burst out, angrily, "Dammit! It's just not *possible*! There's no *way* she could have got in there! She would have had to have walked right *by* us!"

He slumped down, as if instantly exhausted, in the nearest chair.

"If it helps, Captain," observed Boyd, "There actually *is* another way she could have got in there – through the rear resonant chamber, specifically. But I'll be damned if *that's* possible, either. I locked the outer access-panels, Devon cross-checked the mechanism before we lifted off... and even if she *had* gotten in there somehow, she *then* would have had to have entered the master access-code to unlock the interior-to-exterior rear hatch at the back of the storage-chamber. *And*, need I add, then found some way to remain completely un-noticed, as we all loaded up our cargo-containers in that area."

He paused and added, "You're right, Captain. I give up, too. There's just no *way*."

"Unless," Jacobson warned, "Someone *helped* her get on-board. If anyone listening to this wants to come forward, now's the time. I can assure you, if you don't, and I find out later, the consequences will be *far* more severe."

Chkalov did not need to be there, to feel the atmosphere in the *Infinity* become instantly a hundred times more tense.

After a few seconds, he heard White comment, "Hey, y'all... not to put too fine a point on it, but the fact is, whatever little Houdini act this Mars-chick may have played on us to get here, and just for the record it was *not* yours truly, she's *here* now, whether we like it or not. We got a few months to figure out how she got aboard –"

"Or less, if she's given us some especially nasty Martian version of the flu," Boyd reminded him.

"Uhh, point taken, Brent my man – but as the Professor says, there's nothin' we can do about that... it either happens or it don't. Thing that I'm thinkin' about is, what do we *do* with her, in whatever time we all got left? Seems to me that's the more important question."

"You're *so* right, Devon," replied Tanaka.

Turning to face the others in the *Infinity*, she explained, "We now have to face the possibility that we *may*, indeed, have been infected with Martian organisms, that our bodies can't ultimately fight off, although I think it's interesting that *she* was able to be exposed to *our* pathogens and didn't seem to be adversely affected by them – this may indicate that the cross-species barrier between 'Karéin' and us is greater than it would superficially seem to be. For *all* of our sakes, we had better *hope* that it is. But if we *do* eventually fall victim to whatever organisms she is carrying, then we have an obligation to science to learn as much as we can from her, while we still have the strength to do so."

The others said nothing.

Tanaka then ruefully added, "I guess this will teach me 'watch out what you wish for, you just might *get* it'. Sorry, team. It wasn't *me* who let her in, I *swear*... but I'm sorry, anyway."

Chkalov responded, saying into the microphone, "Professor, you have nothing to apologize for, on my account. I, too, wanted to meet with this being, at least once in my life. Now, I suppose I have my wish, though I may not live as long, as a result. I want everyone to know that I am at peace with this outcome. And Captain, it was *not* I, either, who let her on-board."

"I had sort of ruled you out, Sergei," noted a grimly-smiling Jacobson, "As it would have been a bit difficult for you to have engineered from up there on *Infinity*, I would think."

"Major," inquired Tanaka, breaking in, "Does she seem well? Any trouble breathing? What's she doing now?"

Chkalov turned more fully in the direction of the cargo-bay. "No activity, Professor," he indicated. "She may still be in the box."

"Ask her to come out," requested Tanaka. "You might as well. We've all been exposed, now, but you're no worse off with her beside you than with her eight meters away."

"Captain?" asked Chkalov.

"You may follow the Professor's instructions," replied Jacobson, "Except, for the moment at least, anything concerning opening the inter-ship access-hatch."

"Understood," confirmed Chkalov.

He turned towards the hatch and said, softly, "Karéin, come out. Karéin, we know you are there."

There was a rustling-sound; then he saw a hand clasp the deck, then another hand, then the face – alien, with strange, orange-yellow eyes and unnaturally-sharp incisor-teeth, but still very beautiful, he thought – that he had seen remotely, so many times.

Gradually, the Mars-girl pulled herself through the hatch, floating slowly towards Chkalov. He noted how graceful her movements were, as if she were completely at home in the Zero-G environment.

She seemed to move without expending the slightest effort.

The alien-girl sat in front of him, cross-legged, startling him for a second, by pointing at him and saying,

"Sayrr-gayy? Sayrr-gayy?"

"Yes," he replied, hardly believing what he was now doing, "I am Sergei. It is very nice to meet you, Karéin."

He very much wanted to greet her in his native Russian too, but refrained from doing so, fearing that it would be confusing.

He looked at her again. No *wonder* Boyd had fallen in love with this being.

She *was* pretty – although no more so than dozens of girls he had been with, back home – but there was something extra about *this* one, something hypnotic, above and beyond the plain fact of who she was and where she was from.

There was a regal quality to her.

The alien-girl pointed to herself, saying, "Khar-ayn," followed by a fast, unintelligible babble. Then she made a sweeping movement with her hand, saying, more slowly, "Eee-gull, zaoo-OO-aai-eyay, Eee-gull."

Tanaka's voice came over the intercom, "*Amazing*. She not only knows who you are, Sergei, but she also seems to understand that she's in the *Eagle*, now," she said.

Upon hearing this, the Mars-girl spoke, "Tann-akk-ah? Ee-oo-ai znchtwAH umai nakh, Tann-akk-ah?" with a broad smile on her face.

"Hell-lo," she added.

Her head bobbed up and down in a weird, bird-like motion. It looked to Chkalov as if she was scanning everything in the area, while maintaining the conversation.

"I'd say, Professor," commented Jacobson, "That your hypothesis is correct."

The girl responded, "Ee-oo-ai nakh Jay-kob-sayn, mna-EE-gshtATAY? ooMAI WhAI-t ta'th Boi-oid?"

"We're both here, Karéin," called Boyd.

"Yeah, I'm here, too, Karéin," White chimed in. "Nice to have y'all aboard... I think."

She advanced a little more, closer to Chkalov, and gave him the submissive curtsy they had seen several times back on Mars. She babbled something, then held up a total of five fingers, one by one, then held up a sixth, pointing to herself.

"Captain," noted Chkalov, "I believe that she is asking if the five of us are the entire crew of this spacecraft."

He addressed the alien-girl.

"Yes, that is correct, Karéin, five of us," – he counted the names off, one by one, finger by finger – "Jacobson, Boyd, Tanaka, White, Sergei," – he lifted up the last finger, pointing to her –"And Karéin."

She grinned, moving her head up and down as if to signal 'understanding'.

To his relief, Chkalov noticed that he did not again see those sharp teeth.

"Major," interrupted the voice of Jacobson, "I don't like to bring this up, but how are you feeling? Any nausea, dizziness, fever, anything out of the ordinary?"

"Not so far, Captain, I feel *fine*," replied Chkalov. "I must admit to a slight feeling of elation, however. You know that I always wanted to meet her."

Before he knew what was happening, she was grasping his hand. Her grip felt warm and friendly; more than that, it was invigorating and empowering while still being relaxing, somehow.

A flash of insight came to his mind, and in that brief second-or-two, he saw a bewildering array of weird, exotic and sort-of-threatening, alien shapes, sights and sounds.

The alien-girl gazed distantly into his eyes.

Chkalov realized, dimly, that he was the first human being to ever come into direct physical contact, skin-to-skin, with an intelligent being from another world.

It might be his death, but he did not care.

"That's good," came the voice of Tanaka, "But you should monitor your own vital signs carefully, at one hour intervals, anyway, Sergei," she said.

"I... uhh... will do that, Professor," he pledged, releasing her grasp and hoping all the while that the video cameras had not revealed the act, which would, no doubt, not have pleased either Tanaka or Jacobson. "Any other instructions, Captain?"

"Not at the moment... no," Jacobson replied. "Just get to know her, I suppose. Oh, and you may want to show her where the personal hygiene equipment is, if you don't want her answering the call of nature in the Zero-G down there, and if she asks for food or water, you can give her a moderate amount of it, just don't let her have a party with our reserve rations. We'll watch you two remotely with the cameras via *Infinity*'s communications shack, so we're aware of any emergencies that may develop in the *Eagle*. I'm going to cut the intercom now, because we have some things we have to discuss privately back here – anything else you want to ask, before I do that, Sergei?"

Chkalov noted that the Mars-girl had been listening intently to what Jacobson had been saying.

She couldn't *possibly* have understood... could she? But she seemed to be examining every word.

He wondered what their little space-borne world looked like, to the alien mind in front of him.

Presently he said, "Not really, Captain. Like you, I will have to improvise, from here on. I will do my best."

"I have no doubt you will, Sergei," stated Jacobson. "Intercom off."

Make It Up As You Go

The cross-ship intercom enabling light in the *Infinity*'s mess hall changed from green to a dull red.

"Well, folks," observed Jacobson, "*That* went well enough, I suppose. That is, Major Chkalov still seems to be alive. For how much longer, I wouldn't want to predict, though. If it need be said, the circumstances of this mission have just been completely turned inside-out; we're *way* beyond anything that the contingency-plans ever envisaged. Now, it falls upon us to make some decisions about where we go from here. I'm planning on letting Houston know about this, just for the record, but only after we have decided what to do. After all, it's *our* lives that are at stake."

White and Boyd just nodded.

"Captain," explained Tanaka, "As you know, it's my scientific opinion that quarantining Sergei with Karéin will, at best, buy us a small amount of extra time, assuming that she *does* carry any dangerous pathogens, and that it's probably largely a moot point anyway, because we have already been exposed to any airborne diseases that she might have. But let's just *assume*, for the sake of argument, that there might be some kind of safety value in restricting Sergei and her to the *Eagle*. Even if that were the case, although I'm not the systems expert here," – she shot a glance at Boyd, as if to ask for support – "We'd face some severe practical problems in trying to keep them in the descent-ship, until we get back home."

"Wherever *that* is," unhelpfully added White.

"Yeah," interjected Boyd, "You're right about that, Professor. The mission profile assumed we'd have the air, food and water reserves from *Eagle* to support us on the way back, and although we do have emergency protocols involving jettisoning the lander, these all assumed that we'd be able to remove all of the vital stuff from it *before* we cast it adrift. From what I remember of the "nightmare scenario" contingency-planning – that is, in which *Eagle* gets stuck down on Mars and is unable to get back into orbit – Sergei would have been able to make it back to Earth in *Infinity*... but I doubt they ever envisaged the possibility that we would have *four* astronauts, not one, doing that. I bet I could come up with a plan, but I'm anything *but* sure that it would work... and it would be pretty unpleasant for the last month or so of the mission."

"The other thing we have to consider," mentioned Tanaka, "Is that *Eagle's* self-contained air-supply was never supposed to last for much longer than an extended stay on Mars... let alone for *three months*. Karéin obviously can tolerate a much less oxygen-rich atmosphere than we can – and it's fascinating that she doesn't seem to have any trouble breathing our much more dense, nitrogen-heavy air – but Sergei could never survive the entire trip back home, locked in there with her. We'd be sentencing him to *death* – a very slow and unpleasant death – on top of that."

With an annoyed look, Jacobson shot back, "What are you suggesting we *do*, then, Professor? Just open the hatch and let her have breakfast with us in the *Infinity*, every day? Maybe a little arm-wrestle, too? *Surely*, as a scientist, you must understand the huge risks associated with doing anything like that!"

Tanaka took a deep breath, then proposed, "Yes, Sam, that's *exactly* what I'm suggesting. I've already told you why."

Jacobson got up, shaking his head, pacing around the table.

"Devon, Brent... what have you two got to say about the situation?" he irritably demanded. "You *know* I don't like even *thinking* about sacrificing one of my crew. But what we're talking about might be the end of *all* of us."

"Captain, sir," uneasily replied White, "It's a hell of a choice, but knowin' Sergei, if y'all decided to do that, I think he'd understand... but, uhh, that's not a bridge that I think we have to cross, sir. For what it's worth, I'm willin' to take the chance... I gotta admit that I'm a bit nervous about it – I guess I seen too many horror movies about space-vampires, even though our Martian friend seems cool, so far. Truth is... don't really know *how* to say it, so I'll just come right out and *say* it... I think our chances of makin' it back to an intact Earth are pretty damn poor, anyway. If I got to go before my time, I'd like the ride to be an *interestin'* one. Having *her* to keep us company, for however long, seems like it'd be *plenty* interesting... so there we are. I'll support y'all either way, but I won't blame y'all if we let her in, and I start gettin' little red spots all over me."

As always, White's speech had a way of cutting the tension.

Jacobson turned to Boyd, saying, "Brent?"

Thinking for a moment, Boyd offered, "That's an awfully hard one, sir... I have a wife and family back home, you know. You're right, we're *way* out of the mission-briefing book here, so all we have to go on, really, is intuition. What mine is telling me right now, is that it will be okay if we let her in, that her purpose here is to help us, not to harm us. I don't know *why* I feel like this, I just *do*; from the first time I looked into her eyes down on Mars, I have trusted her, don't ask me why. So, yeah, I suppose I could go along with a decision to open the hatch."

"If I may, Commander," elaborated Tanaka, "There's something *else*... locking the two of them in there, would inevitably cause Sergei's eventual death. That's reason enough to at the very least let Sergei out – an action which would, no "ifs, ands, or buts", expose us to exactly whatever he has encountered by being so close to the alien – but even if we just left him in there to die, think what might happen afterwards. Karéin would *certainly* be aware that the available oxygen in the *Eagle* would be diminishing and she'd already have seen that we had just let one of our own friends, perish that way. She can clearly live on less O2 than we do – but I doubt that she can exist without any at all. And she has no way of knowing that we will probably arrive at ISS2 in time to pump some more air in there. There's no telling what she might do *then*, because she might feel that her own survival was at stake."

"Professor," retorted Boyd, "She wouldn't hurt us. I just *know* that she wouldn't."

"Maybe that's true, maybe she wouldn't *mean* to," noted White, "But, Brent... y'all gotta admit, she's pretty strong, otherwise she couldn't have helped y'all rescue the Professor and the Captain down there on Mars, and all she'd have to do is push a bunch of control-panel buttons in the wrong sequence and she could do some really nasty things... like, say, force an emergency de-dock and hatch-rupture between *Eagle* and *Infinity*, or fire the lander's engines and throw us way off course. If she, say, wrecked the controls badly enough, she could make our whole little home away from home, completely un-flyable. We might have to EVA just to get out of here – but that assumes that there'd be somewhere for us to EVA *to*. And three of the suits are still in *Eagle*. We'd have to get past her, to even put them on."

Boyd thought for a moment, then affirmed, "Yeah... you're right about *that*. We can disable remote access to *Infinity*... but we *can't* stop someone *inside Eagle* from being able to control their own ship."

He grinned ruefully.

"I guess NASA's contingency-planners never thought to prevent a malicious, intelligent alien from running our space-ships," said Boyd. "Remind me to show them a few old *Star Trek* episodes, when and if we get back."

"I'll make a note to do that," sardonically promised Jacobson.

"So what we have, basically," Tanaka pointed out, "Is a situation where there are some undeniable risks associated with allowing the alien access to us and to *Infinity*... but in which there are also risks associated with trying to quarantine her. And one *other* thing, which I had hoped not to have to bring up."

"What's that?" asked Jacobson, furrowing his eyebrows.

"Well," she said, "As Devon just reminded us... you and I *owe* her... don't we?"

Three sets of eyes focused on Jacobson.

"Professor," he slowly and deliberately declared, "I've been very much aware of that fact, right from the start. But I cannot and *will* not jeopardize either my crew, or this mission, based on personal feelings or commitments, real or implied. Please believe me when I say that I don't want *anyone* – and yes, that includes our Martian friend, down there – currently aboard, to come to harm, if I can possibly prevent it."

He stopped a moment, then added, "The problem is... I don't know if I *can* prevent it. But I'll try my best. My decision is, we're going to leave them in there for a while, then re-visit the situation. Professor, on average, how long do the symptoms of serious, communicable Earth diseases take to manifest themselves?"

"Whew, *that's* a challenge to answer, with any certainty," Tanaka replied. "Depends on what you're talking about; AIDS and some of the parasitic-driven sicknesses can take *years*. If you're referring to things like, say, the flu, measles or the plague, typically, one to five days before you see things like skin-discolorations or pustules, varying according to the strength of the patient's immune system and the sub-strain of the microbe causing the disease. Most victims feel unwell within about a day, though. There's no way of knowing what the incubation period would be of a *Martian* organism, of course; I'm just guessing here, but it might be slightly longer, if the germ had to mutate itself in order to infect as unfamiliar an environment as a human body. If it can do that at all – my guess is that it can't. But there's no sure way of knowing."

"That sounds real... *encouragin'*," muttered White. "Is it too late to change my vote?"

"Afraid it is," answered Jacobson, with a mordant smile. "So the plan is, we'll leave them in there for a week, and if at the end of that time, we still have a healthy, living Sergei Chkalov, we'll again discuss opening the hatch and letting her in. Note I said, 'discuss'. I'm making no promises, here."

"Understood," Tanaka said. "And..."

"Yes?" asked Jacobson.

"*Thanks*, Sam," she gratefully replied.

Quarantine

Chkalov reclined – as much as anyone could do so, in the complete absence of gravity – in one of the G-chairs in *Eagle's* control-area, much relieved that he had eventually been able to teach the Mars-girl how to use the spacecraft's "low gravity personal hygiene units".

The lesson had taken an inordinately long amount of time, not so much because Karéin had trouble manipulating the contraption – she seemed very adept at dealing with technology – but because she had not understood what its purpose was, until the cosmonaut had to show her by using it himself.

Judging from the number of discarded food-wrappers in the storage-box in which the alien-girl had evidently secreted herself, she had had a fair bit to eat, already; she had gratefully consumed three helpings of water, when Chkalov offered them, but her metabolism evidently was very efficient and there was not much "residue", as it was euphemistically called in the NASA manuals.

Over the next few hours, the cosmonaut tried to explain the function of the various instruments in the *Eagle* to her, a task which proved surprisingly successful.

She quickly learned how to activate and deactivate the intercom and the food processing equipment, as well as the Zero-G personal shower canopy (Chkalov, ever the gentleman, turned his back while she disrobed, even if he *did* sneak a peek every so often; it turned out to be well worth the effort), tarrying in the latter, luxuriating in the thin mist of recycled water until he finally had to shoo her out.

Jacobson had initially objected to this training, until Tanaka and Boyd had pointed out that it was more to their benefit to have her understand which buttons were "oh-kay" and which ones were "no oh-kay" for her to hit, than it was for her to experiment with these by herself.

Throughout all these exercises, the alien-girl seemed fascinated, paying very close attention to every word that passed Chkalov's lips.

Sometimes she would stare overlong at the dials, instruments and displays. He thought, at these times, that something about her eyes, maybe their color or something he couldn't quite identify, was changing slightly, but he wrote that idea off to fatigue and excitement on his part. She also spent considerable time looking out of the lander's view-ports, pointing to various celestial objects and babbling something or other in her own language.

Just as he was about to doze off, with the alien-girl sitting cross-legged on the G-chair next to him, her eyes closed in what appeared to be a meditative state, the intercom sounded.

"Major Chkalov," he heard Jacobson request, "Status report, please."

He reached for the intercom microphone, but somehow it was already in her hand, even though she had been further away from it than he had been.

"Hell-lo, Jay-kob-sayn," she cheerfully greeted. "Khar-ayn, hE-eare. Hell-lo, oh-kay?"

Muttering something to himself about the absurdity of having an alien-girl from Mars answering the phone, Jacobson spoke slowly and clearly, "Uhh... nice to hear from you, Karéin. Can I speak with Sergei, please?"

She complied with, "Oh-kay. Sayyrr-gayy?", handing him the microphone.

"Thank you, Karéin," said Chkalov. "Sorry, Captain, I am a bit late with my latest status report... I must have fallen asleep, I will try to be more diligent next time. But I feel fine. Apparently, *she* does too. She has taken to performing – how do you say this, in English? – yoga exercises in front of me. She seems to be very well used to operating in zero gravity; indeed, she travels through the cabin like a fish swims in the Volga. Sometimes it looks like she is able to move around without gaining momentum by propelling herself from any solid object that I can see. It is most peculiar – you should mention this to Professor Tanaka."

"I'll do that," confirmed Jacobson. "Also, I have some news for you. Since we last spoke, I have been in communication with Houston. I explained our current situation and, much to my surprise, they supported my plan of action, but they do not want any real-time transmission of activities in the *Eagle* back to Earth, for the time being. They do not want a negative impact on morale at home, should something... *unfortunate* happen to either you, or the girl, or both of you."

Chkalov said nothing, but the Mars-girl instantly noted the change in his expression, moving her face closer to his, listening yet more closely to the conversation.

Jacobson continued, "As a matter of fact, Houston doesn't want the rest of Earth to even *know* that she's here with us; as far as everybody else down there is concerned, she's still down there on Mars, just temporarily away from the cameras at the Anomaly site –"

Hanging his head, Chkalov muttered, with a cynical laugh, "Ah, Captain... are you sure you are referring to your NASA, or to our bureaucrats back in Russia? It sounds very much like 'official truth' – not to be confused with *actual* truth, as we used to say back in Moscow."

"Yeah," explained Jacobson, "Sounds more or less like that to *me*, too, but frankly I have more important things to worry about, right now, and sooner or later they'll have to let everyone know – people will start asking questions when she doesn't show up at the Mars video relay, after a few days. But apparently interest in Karéin has dropped off quite a bit lately, anyway, because everyone on Earth is, understandably, concentrating on the *Salvador* mission, which is due to lift off in less than 24 hours from now. They're so preoccupied with it, that they have asked the Professor and I to handle the experimentation and training syllabus for Karéin, entirely on our own, until further notice. Suits me fine, the Professor too, need I add."

"May I – how do you say – second that opinion," agreed Chkalov.

"Duly noted," stated Jacobson. "But I think we're finished for today, we can resume the exercises with her tomorrow. So get your sleep, we don't want normal fatigue to be confused with the opening signs of an illness. Anything else to report?"

"Negative, Captain," Chkalov replied.

"Very well then," said the Mars mission commander. "I'll check back in a few hours. Over and out."

"Good-baii, Jay-kob-sayn," chirped the alien-girl.

Teach Me Chess

Chkalov, despite his former somnolent state, was now fully awake. He decided that he needed to do something to take his mind off the situation, so he floated over to one of the *Eagle's* computer-connected 3-D modeling displays and executed the computer chess program, resulting in the holographic image of a virtual chess-board being displayed right in front of him.

The Mars-girl, of course, came over with him, swimming through the sea of weightless air as if she had always lived in a zero gravity environment.

"Now, Karéin," he related, "This is a game called 'chess', which I play against the computer. But you can also play it with one person against another. I will show you how the pieces move."

With her eyes focused on him like two laser-beams, he named each of the pieces and demonstrated the allowed moves for the pawns, first, then tried to show her the move for a rook, but she made a back-and-forth motion, as if she wanted a pencil and paper.

The *Eagle* contained no such consumables, but Chkalov *was* able to find a spare recording tablet and stylus (or "million dollar Etch-A-Sketch", as White had labeled it), which he gave to her.

The alien-girl then motioned for him to continue, scribbling the vectors for each move in turn, along with inscriptions in her strange, blocky script, beside each one.

"I should now show you the object of the game," he explained. "You see, to win, you have to capture the other side's king. I will have the computer show you."

He adjusted the game so it auto-demonstrated a simple "Fool's Mate", with a brightly flashing "Congratulations! You Won!" message, when the Black side forced a checkmate, then demonstrated the concept of checkmate another couple of times, with more lengthy and complicated scenarios.

"Do you want to play, Karéin?" he inquired.

She gave him a giggle and an enthusiastic grin.

He noticed that those incisors *did* look rather sharp, after all.

Chkalov punched a key combination into the computer and restarted the game. His hand moved to the first pawn on his side, White; the computer's 3-D touchscreen systems detected the action and he moved the ghostly, virtual playing-piece two spaces forward.

He motioned to her.

"Your turn," he declared.

The Mars-girl extended her hand, trying to come into pseudo-contact with a black pawn, but as her finger intruded into the holographic display space, as his had, a strange interference-pattern appeared, silhouetting her finger in an elfin, golden-orange glow. The entire virtual playing board shimmered and became unstable.

Chkalov looked up, startled.

He had forgotten that this creature was radioactive.

"Eemah, eemah-Sayyrr-gayYAN-a, ooshNAYkh," she mumbled, wagging her fingers back and forth. She closed her eyes and seemed to concentrate for a second, then tried again to access the holographic playing-piece.

This time there was no glow and no interference.

Unsteadily, she guided her pawn forward, until it was directly across from his white one.

"Very good, Karéin," the cosmonaut congratulated, "You have made your first chess-move."

She giggled, girlishly, and looked him in the eye.

There was something strangely dissonant about her, because she sounded *serious*, somehow.

"Excellent. Here we go. I will make a move, and you make yours after mine. We alternate. Okay?"

"Oh-kay," she happily replied.

Resolving to play a competent, but uninspired, game, so as not to defeat her too quickly, Chkalov now moved another pawn – which she countered, one for one – then another.

He was surprised to see that the alien-girl moved a knight, next. A black pawn fell, then another, followed by the typical give-and-take of the opening phases of a chess-game between two players of moderate ability.

Chkalov saw that he was steadily gaining the upper hand in the match, but on the ninth move, the girl managed to fork one of the Russian's bishops against his queen; not only that, but a dim memory came in the recesses of his mind, that he had seen this pattern of play before... but *where?*

The Mars-girl had lost twice as many pawns as he had, but it did not seem accidental that this had come to pass.

She now attempted to move a rook, to a position where it could easily be taken, next turn.

"Karéin," he warned, "You should not do that. I can take the rook on my next turn, and you cannot take the piece that I will capture it with. Are you sure you want to make that move? I will let you take it back."

She simply gave him the odd, head-cocked-to-the-side look that he had seen much earlier, when she had first encountered Boyd, down on the planet.

"Very well then," he sighed, taking the exposed rook with a pawn.

Her hand extended into the board's virtual space, moving a knight.

"ChAYk-mAYyt, oh-kay?" the alien-girl spoke up, in a weird, friendly tone.

"No, no, you see, I can still move my king, here – ", he argued.

Then, the cosmonaut noticed that there was nowhere to move, except into check.

He had played stupidly – much more so than he had intended to.

How had he *possibly* failed to see this? He felt certain that he would not have made such a mistake against the computer. Perhaps he was just smitten with the creature; but if so, the feeling had disarmed him.

Taking a second to regain his composure, he stammered, "I am *amazed*, Karéin. You win! You have a natural talent for chess, I see. Congratulations."

He extended his hand, which she grasped and shook, heartily. But she refused to let go, until she had planted a kiss on the back of his hand, to Chkalov's mild embarrassment but secret delight.

A rush of animalistic thrill, like a teenager's first real kiss on a date, went up and down his spine.

He reset the virtual game board. "Another game?" he asked.

"Oh-kay," she replied.

This game started out almost exactly as had the last one – except for the fact that they had reversed sides – with the Mars-girl losing a few more pieces than the cosmonaut.

He started playing for real, as it was evident that while he had much more experience at chess than this alien, she had a keen, analytical ability to reason out moves, several in advance.

But by mid-game, Chkalov noticed that he was steadily losing the strategic advantage, with the center part of the board falling more and more under the girl's control. A sense of panic started to develop. He could see another checkmate coming, in two or three moves at the most.

He wondered about the kind of intellect that could, after a few minutes of instruction in a game she had never before seen, consistently defeat a man who had been playing it since his childhood.

"Karéin," he ruefully admitted, "I am afraid I have badly underestimated your ability to play games. Perhaps you can teach me some things about chess, instead of *me* teaching *you*. Good game. I concede."

He knocked over his king to signal that he was resigning, extending his hand to her, as he had the last time. Secretly, he hoped for another kiss.

She stared at the toppled virtual playing-piece for a second, seemingly puzzled at the gesture of resigning from the game. Then she half-whispered, with a tone of real concern, "Sayyrr-gayy eemah, eemah Sayyrr-gaYA-nakh."

The Mars-girl then toppled her own king, swam through the air to be next to him and grasped his hand to her boyish breasts. She nuzzled his cheek with hers.

Her touch was more than friendly, as was the lambent look in those big, orange-yellow eyes. For a second, the urge to respond, to take her, to dive into her, was almost too much to withstand, but at the last moment, Chkalov's professionalism, scientific and military training kicked in and he regained his composure.

The alien-girl's pouting lip telegraphed disappointment, but she did not press the issue.

By now, Chkalov felt sure that she must have some way, outside of spoken language, to understand another intelligent being's thoughts and intentions. He felt worried that she might be able to read his mind, but took some solace in the fact that she probably would have more trouble with thoughts in Russian, than she would with those in English.

"Major Chkalov," sounded a voice from the intercom, "This is Tanaka here. I know you spoke recently with the Captain, but I wanted just to check up myself, if you don't mind."

"No problem," he replied. This time he had managed to snatch the microphone, first.

"Nohh prawbb-LAYmm, Tann-akk-ah, oh-kay?" he heard the girl chime in.

He laughed out loud.

"I see – hah – that your friend is there with you," Tanaka commented. "What's her status? Anything new to report? Feeling good?"

"Well, Professor," he grudgingly remarked, "I have just discovered that Karéin is a *formidable* chess player – I only introduced her to the game a short while ago, and she has beaten me in two successive matches, despite the fact that I have, ahem, been playing considerably longer than she has. She seems to have a very sophisticated, built-in ability to play strategically. I shall be interested to see how well she does against the computer, if I can convince her to do that. As far as our health is concerned, no real change in that, for either me or her. Also..."

His voice trailed off, momentarily.

"Yes, Sergei?" knowingly asked Tanaka.

"I – uhh – do not exactly know how to put this, Professor, but Karéin has also proved to be quite, how do you say, *affectionate*, at times. I am not sure what to do, in this case, because I do not want to antagonize her. Any advice you can give me, would be appreciated."

"Well, Sergei," the Professor replied, "It's quite simple, you see."

"Yes?"

"Just do what she *wants*," counseled the scientist.

"Are you sure that would be... *advisable*, Professor?" asked Chkalov, nervously. "I mean, you are no doubt aware, where that might eventually *lead*. Apart from the health risks that might be involved, I am sure that becoming too – shall we say, *familiar* – with the girl, would violate one or more of NASA's rules. And she is not even of our own *species*, however much she physically *resembles* a human woman, externally. Many would say that fact raises questions of a moral nature. And – I am sorry but there there is no other clear way in which to say this – as you know, Karéin has very corrosive blood; if the mucous membranes in her sexual organs have the same agent in them, ahem, Professor, I think you can imagine why *that* possibility would be frightening for a man. Have you cleared this with the Captain?"

The girl was listening to the conversation, closely. If Chkalov didn't know better, he would have sworn that she had understood every word.

"No, Sergei, I haven't, not that the subject has come up prior to now, anyway," Tanaka explained. "I see no reason to raise it with Captain Jacobson, if you don't. It's just a *suggestion*, you don't have to act on it if you don't want to. I'm just making the point, as someone trained in behavioral psychology, that you are stuck in there with her, for an indefinite amount of time, so it makes sense for you to be on as good terms with Karéin as possible. How you achieve that, is *your* business. It's up to you."

"Tann-akk-ah," the alien-girl interrupted, then babbled something fast and completely impossible for the other two to understand.

She was obviously making a point, or trying to, although its import was lost on them.

"Yes," Chkalov replied, "I suppose it *is* up to me. Ah, Professor, how little of this situation had I anticipated. At least Major Boyd had a space-suit to protect him from close encounters, as we say, down on Mars."

"Indeed," offered Tanaka, "But I'm sure that you'll figure something out."

What She Wants, She Gets

The next couple of days passed rather swiftly, with an equilibrium of sorts – if one could call it that – establishing itself within the spacecraft.

The Mars-girl busied herself with endless hours of study of the ship's on-line information resources, eagerly browsing from topic to topic with the computer's link to Earth's third-generation Internet, or 'NeoNet', as it had been termed.

Although she could not possibly have understood the text parts of the information she was accessing, occasionally she showed an amazing ability to infer the sense of a story or multimedia presentation just from the pictures or their context. It was as if she was comparing what was in front of her, with something else, whatever that might have been.

She also spent a great deal of time listening to music of all types and genres.

Apart from a mild case of space cabin-fever here and there, neither Chkalov nor the girl showed any symptoms of untoward health, much to the relief of all. Far from it; indeed, both of them, particularly 'Karéin', seemed to virtually radiate strength and vitality, in a way in which none of the others could quite put their fingers on.

Tanaka ran repeated bio-tests, none of which revealed anything specific, other than for the fact that the mild case of adult acne that Chkalov had had, was now nowhere to be seen.

At first, the alien-girl did not make any more overt advances towards Chkalov, although she still seemed cheerfully friendly in a platonic way, taking turns with the cosmonaut in feeding each other what passed for ice cream (she had a sweet tooth, apparently) and in trying to catch the bits that flew off the spoon in the zero gravity.

But at the end of the third day, after a friendly game of chess, in which he had, much to his satisfaction, managed to stalemate her, Chkalov had dimmed the *Eagle's* lights and had headed off to his zero-G sleeping bag. He had just dozed off, when, as if in a dream, she came to him, and was somehow inside the sleeping bag without having opened it.

He was already mostly undressed, except for his shorts, and these flew off quickly as her small, lithe body entwined his own sinuously, with chains of pleasure far stronger than any iron.

He tried to say something, only to feel her tongue enter his mouth, wrapping around it, probing hungrily. He had expected to taste acid, but her saliva was instead paralyzingly, hypnotically, unnaturally sweet and arousing, made much more so by the little feminine whimpers and moans she let out all the while.

His head was spinning; having *her*, having her completely and utterly, was all he could think of, all that mattered. To have tried to have resisted her would have been as futile as trying to fly by flapping one's arms.

The most ascetic Trappist monk would have been able to deny himself for, at best, another two or three seconds!

The first drop of her saliva made him rock-hard, and she took his manhood effortlessly into the folds of her tight but very wet vagina. It must have contained some of the same stuff as in her spit (thank God, not the acid in her blood), because the instant he entered her, it was all he could do to avoid exploding, right then and there.

She pumped up and down – by God! he thought, she's doing all the work, and a damn fine job, better than any whore! – as she pushed her female mound against his thigh, and rubbed the hard nipples of her boyish, flat breasts upon his chest.

She whimpered more and more frequently, almost desperately, as she tried to force her tongue deeper and deeper into his mouth.

He could hold back no more now, and released into her in a tidal wave of pleasure and surrender, which, Chkalov could instantly tell by the spasms in her cunt and the deep moan that came from her lips, took away the girl, as well.

The whole episode had taken perhaps two minutes.

They laid entwined, both gently gasping, both reveling at the warm, comfortable feeling of skin against skin, so long denied.

"I do not know what to *say*, Karéin," whispered the cosmonaut. "I lost control –"

But she interrupted him with an index finger across his lips and a "shh" sound, accompanied by a faint, girlish giggle.

"Khar-ayn oh-kay. Sayyrr-gayy oh-kay," she purred, as she moistened his lips with a quick flick of that evil tongue inserted into his mouth.

Again, the slightest taste of her saliva – he knew, now, but did not care, that it must have contained some kind of powerful organic aphrodisiac – made him instantly harden, again, inside her.

He climaxed immediately although he had no more seed to give, but she seemed to satisfy herself with a few more rubs, a few more whimpers and then a contented sigh.

In the dim half-light of the lander's night-time illumination, the Russian caught a glimpse of her teeth, a faint glistening of lethal sharpness in the twilight.

A moment of panic overtook him as childhood vampire stories came back, but when he reflexively checked his throat for puncture marks, he found none.

And... besides... weren't vampires supposed to kill their victims, or, at least, drain them of their life-force? But he felt *better*, stronger, more potent, more confident, than he had ever felt, at any time in his life.

In the deepest recesses of his mind, he thought he heard a faint residue of that pseudo-music; this time, it was a quiet, pulsating, peaceful melody.

If there were any way that two beings of different species – man and vampire-queen, man and Martian-goddess, man and... *whatever* – could really make love to each other, as do a human man and woman; well, then, this was it.

They both drifted off into a deep, contented, truly affectionate sleep, with him still inside her.

But when Chkalov again awoke, she was in her own sleeping-bag, as if nothing had happened; except, perhaps, for a saturnine half-smile on her face.

He hoped that the *Eagle's* video-recorders would not tell a different story.

Triggered

By now, the Mars-girl had become very familiar with most of the *Eagle* and *Infinity's* systems, at least with those that Jacobson had, grudgingly, consented to allow her access to.

"*Eagle*, come in," sounded Jacobson. "I need to speak to Major Chkalov, please."

"Hell-lo, Jay-kob-sayn," Karéin said, answering the "beep" of the intercom. "Khar-ayn, hE-eare. Youu taHK Sayyrr-gayy? hE-eare."

She passed the microphone to Chkalov.

The cosmonaut tried to ignore the smug wink she gave him while doing this and hoped that it wasn't caught by the cameras.

The insanity of being worried about having been caught in bed with a centuries-old alien, almost made him laugh.

"Thank you, Karéin," acknowledged Jacobson.

By now, he had somehow become used to communicating with, and giving orders to, the "sixth crew-member", as she had come to be called.

"Yes, Captain?" replied Chkalov.

"First, just so we've got *that* over with... may I have today's morning status-check, please, Sergei?" requested Jacobson.

"Nothing very new to report, Captain," replied the cosmonaut. "Most of last night, I spent on the language lessons that the Professor and Houston have given me for the girl. She is making steady progress, but I can see as we go along that her native tongue is *very* different from either English or Russian – I tried to explain what *spasiba* and *do sviedanya* mean, for example, and she learned well enough, but I do not think that she understands that we have more than one language, back on Earth. We have also played a few more chess-games, and I am happy to report that I actually *won* one against her and stalemated another. So she is *not*, in fact, invincible. I was tempted to say, 'she is only *human*, after all', but..."

Giving a measured laugh, Jacobson agreed, "Yeah, I see your point. Anything unusual on the personal health front?"

"No," deflected Chkalov, "Other than I feel like, how do you say in English, 'a million bucks'. I have *never* felt stronger or better. I have already mentioned to Professor Tanaka that my skin blemishes, those few that I had when I began the mission, seem to have vanished, since I was confined in the *Eagle* with Karéin. Now, when I look in the mirror, my complexion seems fuller and my face has fewer skin-wrinkles, somehow. I do not know how to explain this, Captain."

"Do you think it's *her?*" worriedly inquired Jacobson.

"I do not know," Chkalov replied, "But it is certainly not the food."

They shared a laugh. The alien-girl giggled as well.

"One other thing, sir, that may have been of benefit," Chkalov offered.

"Yes?"

"Could you please report to Professor Tanaka that, in keeping with her suggestions, I have... *ahem*... done what our guest wants of me. I am pleased to report that as of yet I have not encountered any serious side-effects. The opposite is true, in fact. The experience was... *amazing,* beyond my ability to describe. That is all I can think of to say of it."

There was a painful pause.

Evidently, Tanaka had not told Jacobson.

Eventually, he stiffly replied, "Major Chkalov, it would appear that all *sorts* of 'firsts' are being established on this ship. However, if I understand you correctly, I doubt that *this* one is likely to make the history-books... at least not those in the public sections of our libraries. I think you would be wise not to mention more of it to Houston."

Chkalov nodded but did not reply.

He noticed a mischievous, sharp-toothed look from the Mars-girl, and heard a low guffaw.

"Well, Sergei," continued Jacobson, "Now that we have all of *that* over with, I have something to inform you of. Unfortunately, it's not very good news."

The cosmonaut tried not to show any emotion, but the alien-girl flew over to his side at the first sound of the change in the tone of his voice.

"What would that be, sir?" he asked.

"There's really no good way to say this, so I'll just give you the facts," Jacobson said. "The bottom line is... the *Salvador* mission has failed."

He tried, and failed, to suppress a gasp.

"How?" quietly pressed Chkalov.

"I don't have *all* the details," replied Jacobson, "But from what we have been told so far, the NASA and EU teams have both met with disaster," – he was now breathing heavily – "And it appears that all crew-members have been lost. As you know, the 'Lucifer' object is surrounded by a dense cloud of irregularly-sized rock- and ice-fragments; Earth wasn't able to tell exactly how extensive it is, and with the short time left, they had to take the chance that they could navigate through it. The NASA ship hit one of these objects at high speed and disintegrated instantly; the EU one was able to limp away after colliding with another, but their ship was too badly damaged... it lasted only another five hours, then... God, I don't want to *talk* about it."

"What of the Russian one, Captain?" demanded a horrified Chkalov.

The alien-girl's hand was grasped on his arm.

She *radiated* concern.

The voice of Boyd now came over the intercom, accompanied by a video-screen showing him and the *Infinity* crew all together.

"Sergei," he explained, "You should be very proud of your countrymen. Their ship was also badly-hit on the way in, and they sustained severe casualties, but they pressed on and managed to land, anyway. The captain, Major Olga Grishin, she... well, she realized that the *Salvador Rossiya* was too heavily-damaged to make it back to Earth, so the crew took a vote and decided to stay behind and make sure the charges went off correctly."

With tears welling in his eyes, Chkalov moaned, "Olga Grishin... Olga... no, *please... no!* She was three seats away from me in my first year in Star City. One of the finest cosmonauts I have ever known – without her help I *never* would have passed the exams. I spent many nights studying with her in the library. It is a tragedy."

He stopped for a bit, then requested, "Did they succeed, Major Boyd?"

Tanaka's face now filled the view-screen.

She interrupted, saying, "They *did* set off the charges, Sergei; they gave their lives to fulfill their mission. But they were eight charges short – their ship's cargo-hold had taken a direct hit. They used what they had left, but it wasn't enough. The 'Lucifer' object *has* been damaged – we're not sure how extensively – but it is still on course with Earth. Its trajectory seems to have been affected, but not enough to avoid impact."

Hanging his head, Chkalov observed, "That is the way we do it in Russia, you see. We will follow our orders and complete our mission... or die trying."

"We know," Boyd quietly consoled.

The alien-girl was now hung over the cosmonaut's torso like a scarf, her eyes staring intently into his, with occasional glances to the view-screen.

She spoke something fast, in a tone of voice they had never heard before, then asked, "Sayyrr-gayy eemah? Watt?"

He looked at the Mars-girl, trying to seem as professional as possible, and said, "Karéin, I do not expect you to understand this, but," – he held out one of his hands in a flat plane and mimicked it impacting with his other hand, which he clenched into a ball – "Some of my most dear friends, have just died, while doing their duty. Sergei is very sad."

He had expected a hug, perhaps, or maybe just the embrace of her hand.

What he *got*, however, shocked and astonished all of them.

The Mars-girl fixed a laser-like stare on him – for a second or two, he would have sworn that her eyes were *glowing*, literally, not figuratively – and he felt paralyzed, as if she were using some strange sixth-sense to comprehend the meaning of what he said.

And they all "heard" that weird, ethereal music again, in their heads.

But it was far louder now and it did not sound very much like what they had encountered from her down on Mars; no, not at *all*. It had a building-up pseudo-tone to it, something grimly-determined, like the first few chords of an electric guitar version of *Ride of the Valkyries*, for example – something *exciting*, something foretelling action to come.

For five or ten seconds, he stayed there, caught in her stare, unable to think, move or react.

Then, as quickly as it came, the sensation lifted as the music receded.

Chkalov stared back at her, anxiously, not quite sure of what he had just experienced.

But the alien-girl turned away, looking down at the floor as if in deep meditation, with her arms braced on the chair-arms.

A reflection from something caught her face – mouth open in an 'O' shape, eyes staring – as if she was stunned, or overwhelmed with some thought.

And something *else* had changed, as well.

"Something has *happened* to her!" warned Tanaka, back in *Infinity*. "Something's been triggered!"

"What do you mean?" responded Jacobson. "*What* has been triggered?"

"I don't know," she deflected. "But don't you *feel* it?"

"*I* do," interjected Boyd. "A wave of excitement – like an adrenaline-rush, wash right over me. Man, I still feel like jumping up, *doing* something... I don't know what. I just have this urge to *act*. Mighty strange."

"Folks," called White, "Look at the radiation-readings – shit, man! Unknown one's *way* up."

"Then we'd better –" started Jacobson, only to be cut off by the image of the girl, standing deliberately in the middle of the view-camera's field of vision, holding Chkalov's hand, her legs planted strongly, almost defiantly, apart.

"Look at her *eyes*," mentioned Boyd, *sotto voce*. "They're *green*, now."

The others stared at the screen closely. It was true.

"Jay-kob-sayn," demanded the alien-girl, staring forcefully at the screen. "Showw meee. Youu mee showw Sayyrr-gayy sadd."

It sounded like a command, not a question.

"Karéin, I understand why you want to know," the Commander replied, "But I don't think you would really understand what's going on. We will tell you as soon as you can understand."

He cut the outbound video-link.

She stared back and, loudly and firmly demanded, "NOH oh-kay, Jay-kob-sayn. Khar-ayn WHAN-tt noh. Meee showw. *Youuu showw meee!*"

There was now a faint glow around her; from what or where, none could say.

"Captain," nervously observed Tanaka, "We need to do what she says. This situation's getting out of *control* –"

"Dangerously so, sir," interrupted White. "The radiation-levels are raisin' all over down there, especially the unknown one, but gamma, beta, alpha and X-rays are leakin' out – they go up, then they drop way back, then they start to leak again, it's like she is trying to control them... but maybe she can't. Sergei may be at risk if she keeps getting annoyed."

Jacobson exclaimed, "God *damn!* I just *knew* something like this was going to happen if we kept this being on-board. Well, she won't understand anyway. Sure, I'll tell her. Open up the channel again."

"Karéin," he related in as friendly a voice as possible, "I will try to explain the situation to you... but you must listen carefully, okay?"

"Oh-kay," she replied.

Even through the indirection of the video-link, her stare felt like a vice on Jacobson's mind.

"What has happened, Karéin," explained the Mars mission commander, "Is, our planet, Earth, is at risk from a comet called 'Lucifer', that may collide with Earth in the near future. Our fellow humans from Earth flew a rocket ship called *Salvador* up to the 'Lucifer' object to try to destroy it. But instead, *Salvador* failed and the people on it all died. We are all very sad, because they were our friends, and especially, friends of Sergei. That's why Sergei is sad, Karéin, because his friends have died. We all miss our friends, when they die."

The Mars-girl sat suddenly down in the nearest chair, staring blankly into space.

She mumbled, "Errth. Khar-ayn noh errth. Errth shGRAA oo-OO-ee-OO Mailànkh . LOO-see-ferr? KOM-met? SAL-vah-dorr? Whan-tt noh," her hands clenched in frustration at not being able to comprehend.

She leaped up, whirled effortlessly in place and again faced the screen, making a gesture as if drawing with a pen on paper.

"Jay-kob-sayn," she requested, "Showw mee pik. You mee showw pik errth, LOO-see-ferr, KOM-met, SAL-vah-dorr... oh-kay?"

"I think she wants pictures," offered Tanaka. "Is that right, Karéin? You want us to draw a picture for you?"

The alien-girl nodded.

"It will take some time, Karéin," Boyd pointed out. "Will you wait, please?"

Again, she nodded. "Khar-ayn he-ere."

"radiation-levels leveling off," whispered White in the background. "Now back to what's normal for her. But *this* is weird. There's now a faint trace of ozone in there with them. Where from, I can't say. There aren't any electrical failures that I can see."

"Do you think there was any permanent damage to Sergei?" whispered Jacobson to Tanaka.

Huddled so as not to be visible on camera, she half-whispered, "No, Captain, not for as short an exposure as we had there. But I sure wouldn't want him to be stuck down there with her in *that* state, for hours or days. There's no such *thing* as a 'safe' level of hard X-rays or gamma rays... and you notice that we have seen a definite physical change in Karéin. What it *means*... I have no idea."

"Well, where's that Etch-A-Sketch, then?" demanded Jacobson.

Fumbling in a locker, Boyd fished out one of the devices, complete with stylus, giving both to Jacobson.

"Here, Karéin," Jacobson stated. "I will show you. First, here is Earth," he said, drawing a circle with a crude representation of the Western Hemisphere.

"Errth," the alien-girl replied. "Oh-kay."

Jacobson erased the Etch-A-Sketch.

"Now, here is 'Lucifer', which is a comet," – he drew a circle with a tail on it, then a dart-like object approaching it – "And here is the *Salvador*. As you can see, it is – it *was* – a space-ship like ours. But it crashed."

He drew a big "X" through the dart-like shape. "Everyone on it died, Karéin."

"SAL-vah-dorr, zaoo-OO-aai-eyay, Eee-gull, een-FEEN-tee?"

"Yes, Karéin," confirmed Tanaka. "*Salvador*, *Eagle* and *Infinity*, they are all our space-ships. You are in *Eagle*, we are in *Infinity*. But *Salvador* died."

The Mars-girl turned to Chkalov.

"Sayrr-gayy," she quietly murmured, "SAL-vah-dorr, Sayrr-gayy peep-pool?"

He nodded, sadly.

The alien-girl grasped his arm, rubbing her head on it.

"*Noh* oh-kay," she gently whispered. "Prawb-lemm."

The cosmonaut knew she only meant kindness and affection, but her mere touch now drove him crazy.

He desperately tried to avoid thinking about the previous night.

Gently, the Mars-girl put down his arm, then sat back in her chair, with the same frustrated-looking forward stare that they had seen before. "Ahn'ah SAL-vah-dorr, Errth shGRAA oo-OO-ee-OO? Ahn'ah SAL-vah-dorr KOM-met LOO-see-ferr?"

She turned to the video-screen. "Pic on kom-POO-terr. Pleez, Jay-kob-sayn. Youu pic kom-POO-terr, poot pic. Pleez."

"I can't *read* her," Jacobson muttered side-wise to the others. "What does she mean?"

He turned to the screen and held up his index finger. "Please wait just a second, Karéin," he temporized.

"She wants to see better pictures of '*Salvador*', 'Lucifer', and so on, on the computer displays, I think," stated Boyd.

"Why would she want *that?*" replied Jacobson. "She already *knows* what they are."

"I'm just guessing," commented Tanaka, "But I think she doesn't understand what the relationship is of each object to the other."

"Or maybe she just doesn't like your artistic touch, Captain," joked White.

Jacobson sat and thought for a second, then grumbled, "Well, she has already had limited access to the computer, and indirectly to NeoNet, anyway... so I suppose getting her a video-clip of the whole story wouldn't be much different. She'll find out eventually. And whether or not Houston wants us to tell her what's really going on, I don't see what harm doing so could do, what with us all stuck up here with no way to affect the situation. Devon, in preparation for the news I had to give all of you this morning before we told Sergei just now, I got a video-feed from the Disney News Network that had the whole story. Can you fish it out of the archives and pipe it in to her view-screen? It might save us the trouble of having to get individual images and then explaining each one."

"No problem, Captain, I have it on hot-key, actually. I queued it up because after y'all gave us the... uhh... news... I wanted to see it for myself. But man, sir, that one's a 'downer', don't you know."

"Well, we *owe* it to Sergei, to let him see the details, Karéin or no Karéin," Tanaka interjected, "So we might as well let them both see."

"Yeah," Jacobson agreed. "Might as well. Devon, get it ready."

He turned again to the camera.

"Karéin," he explained, "We are going to show you some 'pics', as a matter of fact, we are going to show you a movie that will give you the explanations you need. Sergei, this is going to be a presentation about the failure of the *Salvador* mission and the 'Lucifer' object, but you may have to point out some of the items she has been asking about, as we go through it. You can pause the video by using the buttons on your local multimedia control-panel down there in *Eagle*. Are you ready?"

"Affirmative, Captain," acknowledged the cosmonaut. "Although, may I say... I do not look forward to seeing it."

"None of us up here in *Infinity* did, either," agreed Tanaka. "But we must face the truth."

"Rolling video now," said White.

The faces of the *Infinity* crew were now replaced on the *Eagle* main video-screen by a combined live video and multimedia presentation by the Disney News Network, its familiar, 'happy-news' logo seeming perversely out-of-place, here.

The production began with a 3-D computer model of the 'Lucifer' object and its trajectory towards Earth.

Chkalov started to explain something, but he noticed that the Mars-girl, upon first seeing the simulation of the comet's impact with Earth, was frozen in mid-stare, as if an a deep state of shock.

At once, she bolted up from the chair, space-pacing nervously back and forth. Muttering something fast and low in her own language, she made a "T" symbol with her hands, then rotated her index finger in a circular motion several times.

Chkalov rewound the production to its start, then replayed it. When it reached the impact-sequence frames, the alien-girl requested that he stop the show, which he did.

The Mars-girl stood there in front of the video-screen, just staring. The look on her face was not only of shock and sadness... but of something *else*, as well.

It might have been the look of fear. She gave him the look of a hunted animal. She was shaking and also seemed to be sweating.

He had never seen her like this.

Eventually, she motioned for the presentation to continue.

Now, it told the story of survival preparations on Earth and on Earth's near-space colonies, for example the ISS2 space-station, and of Earth's plans to defend itself against the 'Lucifer' object, first with the *Salvador* mission, then with the massive missile barrage that General Symington had told the others of some time ago.

There were scenes of mass panic, of crowds thronging at churches, mosques, temples and synagogues, of hourglasses with the sands of time running out, followed by an obviously recent report showing the liftoff of the three *Salvador* ships.

The sombre voice of the announcer explained the loss of the first two spacecraft, but then cut to footage taken directly from the surface of the comet, aboard the *Salvador Rossiya*, as the crew had sent their last messages to their friends and family back on Earth.

"Look, Karéin," Chkalov sighed, with welling eyes, "Those are Sergei people. My friends."

The alien-girl moved effortlessly through the zero-G to hold his hand, but did not take her eyes off the presentation.

The last images from the *Salvador Rossiya* were of the crew embracing each other one by one, toasting each other with a hidden bottle of vodka (thank God *that* had survived the debris-collisions, thought Chkalov), then proudly, defiantly and above all, *nobly*, saluting to the camera while singing the Russian national anthem, as the final seconds to detonation of the charges ticked away.

There was a brilliant flash of light; then... just static.

Chkalov was weeping, openly, as he stood up, quietly singing the last verses of his nation's anthem, saluting his fallen comrades.

"I must find my own vodka... yes, I must," he managed, between tears.

"*Do sviedanya, moih droogy,*" he sobbed.

Revelation

Her hand had fallen from his grasp.

She was just floating in the zero-G, as if a body floating on the ocean-waves, numb from over-exposure.

The alien-girl's eyes still cast a dull stare upwards, as she watched the last few minutes of the presentation, in which the Earth's last, desperate plans to deflect or destroy the comet were portrayed, accurately or not, as having little chance of success.

The time remaining on the "days to impact" calendar showed only one month and a precious few extra days and hours.

"*Now*, do you understand, Karéin?" softly commented Chkalov. "I am sorry that I am so emotional, where my countrymen are concerned. You must understand that they were all my friends, my brothers and sisters... and they are all gone, now."

But she just remained there, staring in apparent disorientation at the last image on the screen, for a minute or so, her hair floating all about, obscuring her face.

Then the Mars-girl slowly turned her head and looked Chkalov dead-on... with eyes that were now *glowing* eerily and brilliantly yellow-green, then yellow-red, then blue-orange, then silver-gold, then back again.

Elfin lights of some unknown type of energy crackled and played all over her body underneath Tanaka's spare recreational-suit, silhouetting it in a dull, whitish glow.

The music was on, again, with a powerful, expectant, foreboding beat to it.

Ooo, ooo, ooo, called its haunting, beautiful, siren-song.

The air smelled of ozone.

The Russian started back in sudden fear of this again very *definitely* alien being.

"Karéin!" he exclaimed, "Your *eyes* – they are –"

Now the alien-girl flew through the interior of the *Eagle*, with no visible means of propulsion, like a swallow glides effortlessly through the summer air on Earth, arriving immediately at one of the control-panels.

She looked – kindly and lovingly, as near as he could tell, to his immense relief – at the cosmonaut with those frightening, multi-colored eyes, her body now fairly *flashing* with latent energy.

"Sayrr-gayy," she spoke, showing those sharp incisors, with a sound of deadly seriousness in her voice, "I kom een-feen-ty. Youu kom, too. Sayrr-gayy, Khar-ayn, kom oos."

Her hands flashed over the controls.

Back on *Infinity*, White was the first to notice. "Captain, what's going *on* – sir, did y'all authorize an inter-ship hatch de-lock? Sir, the hatch to *Eagle's* open!"

"When did *that* happen?" shouted Jacobson. "*Secure that hatch!*"

"I *can't*," a frustrated White replied. "It's being held open by somethin', or some*one*. Don't make no *sense* – proximity detectors aren't seein' anyone within ten meters of it... but it's like it's jammed against something."

"Sir," interjected Boyd, "Karéin is gone from the *Eagle* view-screen. I can't see Sergei, either."

"I *knew* this was going to happen, Sam," explained Tanaka. "She's *coming*."

"Well, *stop her, then!*" angrily retorted Jacobson.

"We *can't*," phlegmatically replied the science officer. "Don't you *see*. This has all been *meant* to happen. There's a *plan* going on, here. We can affect what she does, about as much as we can affect 'Lucifer', or the weather on Earth."

"Well, Professor," nervously inquired White, "Just what are we *s'posed* to do? Bake her a damn *cake*, when she gets here?"

"Professor," added Boyd, "*I* like her too... but you're not making any *sense*. A 'plan'? By *whom*? Little Green Men from Mars? For what? So she can –"

Then, in one smooth movement, the central core to rotating hub-door opened.

Through it shot the one known as "Karéin-Mayréij", the outline of her figure silhouetted with a weird, golden-silver glow, barely but definitely perceptible to the unaided eye in the artificially bright light of the spacecraft's interior.

The alien-girl landed firmly on the walkway, steadied herself for perhaps a second against the pseudo-gravity, and regarded them all with glowing, blue-green eyes. Then she raised her right hand, palm-upwards, in what must have been a peace-gesture.

There was a perceptible aura of majesty, to her.

The others backed away, with Jacobson, Tanaka and White together in a far corner behind one of the eating-tables, and Boyd on the opposite side, in the middle of the corridor.

"Karéin," he worriedly asked, "Why have you *come* here? You should have stayed in the *Eagle*, with Sergei. It's *dangerous* for you to be here."

Out of the corner of his eye, he noticed that Chkalov was peeking out of the central core passageway hatch.

"Boi-oid," called the Mars-girl, "Hel-low."

She gave a quick, submissive curtsy, but then arose again, yet more dignified, more powerful.

Little bells and chimes of some other-worldly procession of the nobility, sounded in their heads.

She addressed the rest of them. "Youu skayre. Noh skayre, noh, oh-kay? Khar-ayn muhst kom, muhst."

The alien-girl turned to Boyd. "Boi-oid," she stated. "Boi-oid luv-er Khar-ayn? Bo-oid muhst."

She advanced toward him until she was right in front of him, then turned to the others.

"Khar-ayn NOH takk, geeve pik," requested the Mars-girl. She held her hands up to either side of his head, almost cupping his ears.

He thought of trying to escape, but decided against it.

She started to imitate shaking, wincing, moaning, with a feigned look of pain on her face and as she did this, she wagged a finger at and said to the others, "Hoort if, NOH staw-awp. Ba-ad hoort, noh oh-kay, Khar-ayn staw-awp."

She turned to Boyd, saying to him, lovingly, "Luv-er Boi-oid, oh-kay?"

He nodded.

The Mars-girl pointed at the floor and fell to her knees. Boyd followed.

She now held her hands over his ears and looked at him directly, saying, quietly and gently, "Boi-oid, noh skayre. Noh skayre, luv-er, noh skayre".

Instantly, he was enslaved; he could not move, or speak, or do *anything*, as his mind felt as if it was leaving his body *entirely*, being pulled down into the kaleidoscopic shine of her eyes.

He was terrified in a way that no human being ever had been, for this was an experience utterly unlike anything even in one's deepest nightmares; all the while, he was awake and conscious of what was transpiring, but there was no waking up from *this* dream: he was completely in the grip of an alien intelligence.

Boyd felt the swell of incipient, violent insanity welling up in his mind, an inchoate, primal terror of the unknown as his mind painfully rebelled against the unfamiliar thoughts invading it, but then he was calmed by the sudden feeling of touching minds with her gentle, awesomely powerful intelligence.

His mind embraced hers in a way than no man of Earth had ever experienced; in a way, it felt like sex with someone you loved, but it was far, far more intense, more intimate and direct.

He *was* her, and she *was*, him... all at once.

He heard her music, stronger, more exciting than it had ever been, a chorus of angels in his head. Boyd could somehow tell that while he was an open book to her, she was revealing only a part of herself...

But – oh, *what* marvels he perceived, in those few brief moments!

Centuries upon ages of accumulated knowledge of strange places and beings, of scientific truths as yet unguessed by beings of his ilk, of manipulating weirding powers of the body and mind that no human had discovered, of ancient battles lost and won and, above all, of deep, profound, wisdom, the type that only a handful of human beings could ever hope to understand a small portion of, invaded his mind.

For a split-second, the Mars-girl's controls seemed to loosen, as her thoughts were preoccupied with something else, and instantly, the terror returned, ten-fold worse.

Boyd perceived dark, half-remembered, youthful visions of fleeing in fear from terrible, monstrous beings – like a dinosaur, perhaps, but much larger, jagged-toothed and more fearsome – in the midst of a burning, charred, benighted landscape; then he beheld a similar memory of an impossibly-bright light in the sky, followed by an agonizing, searing pain, as if the alien-girl had only just survived a nearby conflagration of some kind (maybe a nuclear weapon, he thought).

Even worse nightmares followed, ones suffused with the inchoate dread of being in total, absolute, endless darkness, with mortal danger somehow lurking just past arm's-reach.

Get me out! cried his mind; but thankfully, her own realized its lapse, and replaced these sombre thoughts with more happy ones of times shared with friends and lovers, some of whom looked like her, some of whom appeared to be more or less human and some who didn't look humanoid at all.

While minutes, hours and days passed in Boyd's mind, perhaps ten seconds of clock-time, as humans measure it, had passed.

The Mars-girl and the astronaut were locked in a trance-like stare, with a dull, violet-tinged white glow, surrounding both of them.

"What y'all think'is goin' on?" uneasily asked White. "They look like they're paralyzed."

"I'm not sure," Tanaka replied, "But I think we should let it run its course. They seem to be communicating... perhaps, mentally."

"Yeah, but –" noted the worried African-American astronaut, "Check out their *faces*. That looks like *pain* to me, man."

They all carefully regarded what was going on.

Both the Mars-girl's face and Boyd's, were slowly twisting in a grimace. Their breathing was becoming faster. They were sweating profusely.

Blood started to appear inside Boyd's nose and it started to drip out. A thin residue of that hot, acidic blood also appeared in the corner of the girl's eye and in her ears.

Faint discharges of some kind of electricity arced from the alien-girl to Boyd and back again.

There was a throbbing, electric-sounding music in the others' heads.

Boyd's mind, still one step from terror and insanity but now bewitched by insatiable curiosity, danced with the Mars-girl's, as he probed deeper, further, wanting to *know* more, to *touch* more... to *feel* more.

He could feel her trying to resist him, trying to protect him from what he might discover, yet he could also feel her competing desire to be one with him, to surrender... to, *submit*.

Her defenses were slipping and they both felt the wave of panic as she tried to stop him from accessing her most private, forbidden thoughts.

She mentally repeated "no, no, no", but he would not – *could* not – stop.

He *had* to know! He had to know... *everything!*

A drop of the Mars-girl's blood fell from her ear and sizzled as it hit the floor.

"Sponge! Anything! *Now!*" barked Jacobson.

White produced an insulating blanket and threw it on the spot. A large, black welt appeared in the midst of the blanket, as the alien-girl's blood oxidized it, but fortunately, the astronaut had managed to get enough of the blood so that the floor itself was not holed.

"*I'm stopping this!*" yelled a frightened Jacobson.

He lunged towards the two and tried to grab Boyd's shoulders, but as his grasp tightened, there was a flash of electricity, a loud "bang" and the smell of ozone, as the Mars mission-commander was propelled backwards against the bulkhead.

He slumped down.

Tanaka rushed to his side.

"*Sam!*" she shrieked. "Sam – can you *hear* me?"

Boyd was about to win. He was about to know the unknowable, to understand the deepest, most hidden secrets of this strange, entrancing being.

He felt her last mental barrier fall, and *then* –

As his vision went dark, he felt something grab his shoulder, then felt his head hit the floor-tiles. Not from the impact, he now had the headache to end all migraines, as he slumped over on the floor, his head pounding with such pain that his vision was clouded. He felt drained, weakened, unable to move. Through the haze, he could barely see the girl, who had fallen over backwards. She was moving slowly, moaning in pain.

"Sam! *Sam!*" he heard Tanaka cry. "Sam – can you *hear* me!"

"I think he's okay," White remarked, taking the Captain's pulse. "Just knocked out, I'd say. Heartbeat's fine."

He slapped Jacobson lightly on the cheek. "*Always* wanted to do that, y'all know," he said to Tanaka, with a half-grin.

"That... that will be *enough*," Jacobson groggily managed. "Wow... remind me not to touch live wires, or live aliens, anymore," he complained.

Sitting up, he looked at Boyd and the alien-girl. "How are they, Cherie?"

"I don't know," she stated. "When you touched Major Boyd, it seemed to break their connection. But they're both breathing, at least..."

Boyd could barely feel his legs, but he somehow managed to crawl over to the girl.

"Karéin," he apologized, "I'm *so* sorry. I shouldn't have tried to do that... I lost control of myself. Can you ever forgive me?"

The Mars-girl slowly propped herself up on her two arms, sitting semi-upright.

She slowly opened her eyes – they were now just an intense green, not a glowing color – and spoke, "Dear Major Brent Boyd, be at peace, my love. There is no harm. But my head hurts, a *lot*. Owww."

Astonished, the others, joined by Chkalov who had jumped down from the hatch, quickly surrounded Boyd and the young-looking creature.

"You can now speak our language? *How*?" inquired Tanaka.

"There is... uhh... no word in your tongue for how I did this," explained the alien-girl. "I touched my mind with Brent's one. I, uhh, sucked his speaking-knowledge into my mind, so that I would be able to learn your language quickly."

She smiled. "And also the other way. Brent, *takk ee-mah hlannish'ama oo-EE-OO-ai?*"

Without thinking, Boyd, replied, "*EE-mah oo-MAH-anaish-makayalh*".

"Very good, but you must practice your back-tongue," she corrected, with a wan smile. "Your accent marks you as a foreigner."

"This is *unbelievable*," gasped Tanaka. "Captain, do you *realize* what has transpired here? She has instantly learned English telepathically and has simultaneously taught her own language –"

"It is called '*Makailkh*', Professor Cherie Tanaka," interrupted the Mars-girl. "The same word is used for my people, my species."

"She has simultaneously taught her own to Major Boyd," continued Tanaka. "Oh Karéin, we have *so* much to ask you... *so* much to learn. This is simply the most important point in human scientific history! Where do you come from? What is your history? How do you control and use energy? Who are your people? Why are you the only one left? What is that music we hear in our heads, when you – "

The alien-girl waved her index finger.

"Professor," she said, "Friend. I will try to tell you what I know, in the time that remains. But I am afraid that there is not much time. I risked touching minds with Brent because... because I am called here for a *purpose*, my life-mission that I cannot complete without much information from you. I was slowly learning your language – what is it you call it, 'Eng-lish', is that right? – but when you showed me the danger that approaches your home-world, I realized that I would never come to know your tongue fast enough to learn what I need to, in time. So I took a big chance by touching minds with Brent. Human and *Makailkh* minds are similar, but they are not the same. It hurt a *lot* to become one with dear Brent, it was dangerous –"

"It *still* hurts," Boyd grunted, with a wince.

"Sorry," she responded. "I have a big head-ache... that is what you say, yes? Myself too. But as you can see, I learned enough of this 'Eng-lish' to be able to talk with you. I am still missing many words... please do not be angry if I do not always understand you. You will find that I learn things quickly."

"No kidding," complained Jacobson. "Like operating our space-ship's controls and opening the airlock between *Eagle* and *Infinity*, without any training or authorization."

"Air-lock? You mean the door between *Eagle* and this ship?" asked the Mars-girl. "Sorry. I *had* to come in here. I had to touch with someone who speaks only Eng-lish. I learned how to operate the door by looking at your thinking-machine recordings."

She looked at Chkalov, and said, "Sayrr-gayy, my love. I could tell that you spoke something else. If I tried to touch with you, I would have had your other language mixed up with Eng-lish. It would be *very* confusing."

"*Da*," confirmed Chkalov. "Try learning English as I did, from a book... even harder."

"Yeah, that's the door, the airlock," mentioned White. "By the way, I'm Devon White," he added, offering to shake her hand.

The contact brought a rush of strange, exotic thoughts to the astronaut's mind – not to mention a physical reaction in his loins, which he tried desperately to suppress.

The Mars-girl took the hand and kissed it, then looked him straight in the face. She shut her eyelids briefly and when she opened them, they were again back-lit with an eerie, greenish-blue glow.

She now stood fully upright, as she cast her gaze from human to human, with hints of other-worldly energy flashing inside her body.

"And *I* am Karéin-Mayréij, The Storied Watcher, The Guardian Of Ages, Who Comes At The Deepest Hour," she announced, with a resounding, Stentorian voice of the utmost profundity and seriousness, as her music, powerful, foretelling of great things, played in their minds.

"*My God*," exclaimed Tanaka, "Sam... Brent... Devon... do you remember that I said, 'there is a plan here'?"

"What plan?" demanded Jacobson.

"*She is here to save Earth*," whispered Tanaka.

I Have A Plan

The one calling herself 'The Storied Watcher', turned a knowing gaze on the science officer. "You guess well, Professor," she offered. "I think that you have one of my people's gifts, in some measure."

She turned her eyes downward and added, "At least, I *hope* that you are right."

"About... what?" interjected White.

"About saving your planet," the Mars-girl replied. "May I sit down and make talk with you, friends? We have *much* to discuss."

The glow in the eyes had ceased.

"Uhh... of course," said Jacobson. "Right here."

He pulled out a chair. She graciously accepted.

"Would you like a coffee?" he offered, cursing himself inwardly for the mundane nature of the gesture, but she nodded politely and sipped the beverage as soon as it was produced in front of her. The others all sat at the eating-table, listening intently.

"First, you have nothing to fear from my being here," explained the alien-girl. "I can indeed be infected – temporarily – by your diseases, but I can easily destroy any organism that tries to invade my body. So I do not carry any, how do you say, 'bug', at all. I have no diseases, at all. You cannot become sick from me."

"Second, my soul says that I am here because your planet is in danger. I believe from a comet or meteor, that will collide with – 'Eart', is that not its name? But what I must know as soon as possible, is... is this object very near to your home-world? How much time do we – I – have?"

"Earth," answered Boyd. "It's called 'Earth'. The third planet from our star, which we call the 'Sun'. We found you on the planet we call 'Mars'."

"Ah," she mused. "'Earth'. 'Sun'. I see. My planet is '*Mailànkh*', in my language. Yours is '*U'shné'kh*'. The star is '*Tsé'làng'k*'. But for convenience, I will use your words, until perhaps you shall all become more familiar with how I speak."

"And yes, Karéin," explained Jacobson, "Currently, our Earth is in very serious trouble. The video that we showed you described the failure of what was Earth's best chance to stop the comet, which we call 'Lucifer'... but just to set your mind at rest, according to our most recent calculations, its path will not intersect with that of Earth, for some time, yet – more than a month, in fact. So we don't have to do anything hasty... not that any of us here, understand what that might be."

"Loo-see-fer," she interrupted. "I *know* that name. It is an evil spirit, or something like that... is it not?"

"How does she *know* that?" whispered Tanaka to White.

"Yes, in our mythology," continued Jacobson. "It's an apt name for a celestial body that might be the end of everything on Earth. But as you have seen, the last mission to destroy it, failed. We have a backup plan that involves firing our most powerful weapons against the object as it nears our planet, but frankly, these are likely to prove inadequate. I'm sorry, Karéin, that you may not have the time to get to know humankind, better. But by the time we all arrive at Earth, it may not be there anymore."

Tears welled up in her eyes upon hearing this. The alien-girl glanced down at the table, then looked up, with brightly glowing eyes.

"Not if *I* can help it, sir," she answered.

"Karéin," gently proffered Tanaka, "We very much appreciate you trying to help. And we know that you have some unique abilities. But you are *one* being, trapped along with the rest of us, in a spaceship many thousands of kilometers away from Earth. There's *nothing* you can do."

"*You do not know who I am,*" stated the one called 'Karéin-Mayréij', staring regally, with glowing eyes, at Tanaka.

The music came again, with chords of electricity, energy, the thrill of power. She stood up at the table, legs defiantly apart.

The alien-girl leaned over the table.

"*As for Lucifer... I am going to destroy it,*" she pledged, with the war-music chiming in her voice.

The effect was terrifying to the others. They realized that they were in the presence of something very, very powerful, something far beyond human ken.

She slumped back in her chair, looking, suddenly, like a frail, pale shard of what she had been, scant seconds earlier.

In a small voice, full of fear, she said, "Or... I will *die*, trying."

Boyd and Chkalov huddled closer to her, on either side.

"What do you *mean*, Karéin?" asked the cosmonaut.

"It is like this, friends," explained the Mars-girl, staring at the table, trying to avoid looking at the others. "When I wake up, my powers are at their lowest. I need *time* to bring them to their fullest level. But I fear that there is not enough of an interval in which to do that, in the present situation."

"And... when your batteries are... uhh... fully charged, just how much power have y'all got, then?" asked White.

A godly gaze came back at him, with the same, electric music echoing in their heads.

She said, quietly, but measuredly, "The power to lay *worlds* to waste."

In an instant, a look of panic showed on her face.

The self-styled 'Storied Watcher' fell to her knees, hands out in front, looking down at the floor, and chanted, "I beg you to excuse my arrogance –I pray you to forgive me. Please forgive my error."

The others looked at each other, nervously. White asked, "Uhhh... forgive you, for *what*?"

She looked up at them, slowly steadying herself on her feet. "Even though I have power *over* you, I am no better *than* you."

The Mars-girl shot a sidelong glance at Boyd. "Those who have know me, who touch my mind, know how dangerous it is for me to think of myself as divine. Ruling by power leads to madness and ruin. I am *not* a god, friends; if I ever start acting like one, please make me stop."

Uneasily, Jacobson replied, "You can be sure of *that*."

White added, "All you gotta do, is show us *how* to stop you."

Then Tanaka inquired, "Karéin, we have guessed that you have an ability to somehow ingest – for the lack of a better word – various forms of electromagnetic energy, and use it thereafter. Is this what you are referring to, by talking about your 'powers'?"

"Partly," the Mars-girl replied. "Among many other weirding abilities, I use a form of energy that we call '*Amaiish*', in my language, in your own, it would translate as 'the power' or 'the *Fire*' – from what I have seen of your literature, it is one that I think is yet unknown to you..."

"Bingo," interjected White, "*That's* the unknown signature that we have been seeing, since we first came to meet you."

"Quite likely," confirmed Karéin-Mayréij. "It is something that I access – I am not sure exactly *how* I do it, I just know that I *can* do it – from another Plane of Existence, one in which energy is foremost and matter, as we know it here, is fleeting. I can use moderate amounts of *Amaiish* without any external help, but to use large amounts of it, I must use other forms of energy – fire, electricity, sunlight, food, radiation, and so on – as an 'opener' – I do not really know how to say this in your language."

"An 'opener'?" asked Boyd. "What are you 'opening'?"

"Maybe your word 'trigger' would be a better one," explained the Storied Watcher. "I can use much smaller amounts of ordinary energy, a flame for example, to 'open' a pathway to much greater amounts of *Amaiish*. When I gain access to the *Amaiish* I can then re-convert it to ordinary energy, thousands or millions of times stronger than whatever I used in the first place. But it is hard to do, when I first wake up; when my powers fully return, I can use my native energy almost as I please. That 'music' that you hear, mentally, incidentally, is my war-song, it is called *Métschaì'l* in my language. It serves to warn evil-doers, when I so desire, also to empower and fortify those who I love or lead into battle; conversely, certain kinds of music that I hear, can make my own powers stronger."

The Mars-girl looked downward..

"Right now, I feel helpless... I am *so* weak," she sighed.

"Hopefully not as weak as the Professor and I felt, right after first meeting you," commented Jacobson, unhelpfully.

The alien-girl grasped his hand, a gesture that sent chills of excitement down his spine. "Captain – that is your title of honor, is it not – Sam Jacobson, please try to understand... you too, Professor Cherie Tanaka. I did not *intentionally* try to hurt you when you opened my tomb on *Mailànkh*, but some of my powers, especially those that keep me alive and defend me, operate automatically, even if I am unconscious."

She paused, then continued, "I had been asleep for a very long time and my body was as dry as the sand in *Mailànkh's* deserts – the corrosive agent that you found in my blood does not evaporate over time, as water does, but even so, after that long a sleep it felt like sand in my veins. It hurt *terribly* to move, even to lift a finger. In this state, my body instinctively sought the nearest source of energy, in this case your life-forces, with which to replenish my own. I felt a small measure of my strength returning but then I realized that I was draining you, then I stopped it, even though I was in much pain – I sought the sunshine outside to let me access some *Amaiish*, which I can use to stay alive even without food and water, although it is not pleasant doing so."

She stopped again, thought for a second, then said,

"And thank you *so* much for awakening me, friends. I owe you my new life, here with you. Though I am poor, I will repay you, many times over. I will give you everything that I have. This I do solemnly promise."

Jacobson nodded politely, to Tanaka's warm smile.

"Karéin," she offered, "Some things are meant to *be*. I think this was one of them. You have nothing to apologize for. Neither Sam nor I hold it against you."

"The Professor is quite right," added Jacobson. "Besides, you helped get us out of there. You don't owe us anything, Karéin."

"That is good to hear, dear friends," the Mars-girl agreed. "But now I must explain what I must do... or *try* to do. You say that this space-ship is on its way towards Earth? Will it overtake the Lucifer object?"

"Yes, and no," stated Boyd. "As matters stand now, although we are heading towards Earth, we will arrive months after the object impacts with it. We cannot *possibly* speed up enough to overtake the comet, even if we had any reason to do so. We are basically on a parallel course to 'Lucifer', one that will bring us into *rendez-vous* with a space-station orbiting Earth... that is, if the station or Earth are still there, when we arrive."

"A month is four of your weeks and a week is seven of your Earth-days... correct? Who here is the expert with the thinking-machine, then?" asked the Mars-girl.

"The... *what?* The computer, you mean?" said White. "That would be me or the Professor, I guess. How you know about weeks and months, though? Nobody here ever taught you..."

"I learned by using your com-pu-ter, the machine for running the space-ship and for accessing information. Before I joined with Major Brent Boyd I could understand only a little of your writing, but the pictures and other drawings taught me a lot about your world. And now I need to use your com-pu-ter again, it is very important," she replied.

"Why?" asked Tanaka.

"I need to plot a course to the Lucifer object," answered Karéin-Mayréij.

"Karéin," said Jacobson, "We want to help, but it's out of the *question*. The comet is surrounded by a debris-field of rocks, ice and dust, that would smash the *Eagle* and *Infinity* to bits. It already destroyed two of the three ships of the *Salvador* mission on their way in, and they were specifically designed to get close to the comet, whereas our ship isn't built anywhere *nearly* that strong. Flying us there would be *suicide*. I can't permit it."

The Storied Watcher gave him a long look with those glowing green eyes, then replied,

"Captain Sam Jacobson, I do not intend to plot a course for your space-ship. I am going to plot a course for *me*."

"Say *whaat*?!" exclaimed White. "Just what space-ship y'all intendin' to *take*, lady?"

"I do not *need* a 'space-ship'," she replied, haughtily, with a steely glance.

"Karéin, are you sure you know what you're suggesting?" asked Tanaka. "We've observed that you have a much more sophisticated ability to adapt to unfamiliar environments than do we humans, but outside our space-ship it's a total vacuum, with zero pressure and lethal amounts of cold, heat and cosmic radiation. No humanoid being could go out there without a space-suit, at least –"

"I do not need a 'space-suit'," the Mars-girl shot back. "I do not need air, or water, or, indeed, even clothes-garments, either. The *Fire* and my arts will protect me. What I need, is to be taken to exactly the right point, where I can leave this ship, to begin my trip to 'Lucifer'."

"Wow," was all White could think of to say. "And I thought *I* was first in the Ironman competition around here."

They all laughed, nervously.

"But... uhh... okay, Karéin, let's say y'all manage to button up yourself real good so you can handle things out there, I don't know how, but suppose," pressed White. "When you get to the comet, what are you gonna *do* to it? It's, like, *huge*. Sergei's friends, God rest their souls, set off some pretty big bombs on it, and it hardly got scratched. And I don't even think we brought an ice pick along with us on this crate..."

She gave him a saturnine, fang-filled half-smile. "May I show you?"

They all nodded.

"Can someone find me an enclosed object... a box, something you do not mind losing?" she asked.

"Sure... just a second," said Boyd.

He rummaged around in one of the storage bins and came up with a food-container with a removable lid, just slightly larger than the girl's hand. He handed it to her.

"This will do," she pronounced. "Now when I first arrive at the comet, I will be traveling very fast, because I will have used your Sun's pulling-forces to – how do you say – sling myself around the Sun and back towards Earth – "

"Why must you do that, Karéin? Why not fly directly to the comet?" asked Tanaka.

"Because I am so pitifully *weak* right now," explained the Storied Watcher. "Your Sun emits plentiful energy which I can use to open the way to my *Amaiish*. That is..." – she looked down and bit her lip as she elaborated – "*If* I am in fact *able* to survive the trip around the star. I must get the speed exactly right, to conserve the necessary momentum and offset your star's pulling-attraction. If I over-estimate, I will fly off into space at high speed and may not be able to return; ordinarily, I would have enough control over the pulling waves – "

"Gravity, is what we call it," interjected Tanaka.

"Thank you," politely answered the Mars-girl. "I could normally control these gravity-waves, so I could easily correct my course; but now, I can barely fly around this ship. If I under-estimate, I will fall into the star... even were my powers at their fullest, I could not survive *that*."

The others were silent.

Each began to understand the risks that this being was faced with.

She continued, "But assuming that I survive *that* part of the trip, I will impact with the comet at very high speed. I will burn a passageway and travel through it to its midpoint, like *this*."

The Storied Watcher clenched her fist and held it up to the narrow end of the food-box.

Instantly, all felt a surge of heat, as the girl's fist glowed with a dull, reddish-orange aura. It melted the box-end and her fist was now inside the box.

As they watched in a mixture of awe, amazement and, for the first time in months, guarded hope, they heard her say, "When I am at the exact center, I will release my energy. Like... *this*."

Her eyes flashed, silver-white, and there was a brilliant glow inside the box, for a split-second.

It shattered into a thousand charred pieces. Luckily, there was not enough smoke to set off the fire retarding subsystems.

She looked up at them and said, "But I will be releasing a *huge* amount of the *Fire*, such as I have never used, even when my powers were at their fullest. The risk... will be great, friends. Do not be surprised if you hear no more from me, afterwards."

With a hushed voice, Tanaka managed, "You would do all *this* for *us*, Karéin? Why?"

She stared past them, with a far-off look in her eyes and with the music, haunting and dignified, in the background, then stated, "Because, the Great Spirit of the universe, the Holy Light – maybe the one you name, 'God' 'Al-lah', the Almighty – as I have learned from Major Brent Boyd's mind, you call it – calls me to this duty, Professor Cherie Tanaka. Because there are none other who can do it. I am here, I was awakened for a *purpose*... that is what I believe. Do I know for sure? No. I am *not* a god, I have no special insight, beyond what is in my heart."

"What *are* you, then, Karéin?" asked Boyd, almost whispering.

"I am, maybe, an 'angel', if I understand what your language means by that word. Perhaps it is just a conceit on my part, to think that I am *God's* Destroying Angel. But you should never doubt that I am *a* Destroying Angel... She Who Shatters Worlds."

The young-looking being went quiet for a second, then added, "And there is *another* reason. I do not remember much – my memory is another thing that comes back only slowly, when I awake – but I carry with me the curse of guilt of having failed, the last time that I was called upon to do this, or something like this. What I *do* remember, is a beautiful, blue-green planet, colder and smaller than your Earth, but inhabited by an intelligent, inquisitive people much like yourselves. Something happened... something that I do not remember, exactly. But I could not stop it, though I *tried*. The planet, and those who lived on it, are no more... they are *gone*... all *gone!* I was left all alone, all by myself, for many of your years, to ponder my failure."

She was crying, now, and wailed, "I *tried*. I *tried so hard*... but I *failed*. At the last moment, I saved *myself*, instead of them. Try to *understand*; I was younger, much weaker, less sure of my powers, and I was so *afraid*. You cannot know what it is like, to have to do gigantic tasks and not to know if you will die the first time you try – like jumping off a high cliff, not knowing if you can fly."

The Storied Watcher took a deep breath and concluded, "But *this* time it will be different. This, your 'Earth', is my second chance, my chance for redemption. I will *not* hide from my duty and I *will not* fail you. I *swear* it. Upon all that is holy, I *swear* it!"

Each looked at the others in awed silence, trying to comprehend what she had been telling them. It was all too much for the rules, or even human common sense, to fathom.

Finally, Boyd took her hand and said, "Karéin, I – we – believe you. As I did from the first time I set eyes on you, down on Mars. We *know* you will do the right thing. We just need to know how we can help. Isn't that right, Captain? Professor?"

Jacobson looked up and grunted, "Yeah. I suppose. I mean, *obviously*. I'm sorry, Karéin, this is just all coming a bit too *fast* for some of us to take in. But... I don't know how to put this, exactly, but... well, I guess I'll just say it out loud – "

"I already know the substance of what you are thinking, sir," the girl said, pleasantly. "That power has been with me from the start. It is much easier to use when I know the language of those I am... *reading*, but even without that, I can still learn a lot just from the pictures of the mind."

"So just what *am* I thinking?" irritably demanded Jacobson.

"You are wondering, 'What does a creature capable of shattering a comet, need from a crew of five human beings'... or something like that," she responded. "Am I correct?"

"More or less," muttered Jacobson.

"Do not worry," replied the alien-girl. "I will refrain from doing it, any more. It is just a habit that I had to develop, while I could not communicate with you properly, by speaking. And, if this is of any interest, it is easy for you to train your own minds, to block my mental inquiries. All that you have to do is concentrate on something that you *do* want me to see, and I will not be able to see anything else. I will teach you how to do this, if time permits."

"*That's* reassuring," commented Tanaka. "Karéin, I don't mean this in a negative way, but your powers can be quite... *intimidating*, for those of us who aren't used to you."

"Which kinda includes all of us, here and on Earth," added White.

The girl got down on her knees, with her hands in front of her in the submissive gesture and said, "Please forgive me, friends. I do not want to frighten you. When others fear me, it is a sign that I slip into arrogance. Please excuse my lapse, I *beg* you."

"For a goddess, or an angel, she sure *is* humble," remarked White.

Her eyes still looking down at the floor, her arms still clasped in front, she replied, "Necessarily so. If only you knew, Major Devon White, if only you knew. Maybe some day you *will* know."

She glanced momentarily at Boyd.

"*He* knows," she observed.

"You can get up now," said Jacobson. "But as to what I was thinking... well, just what *can* we do for you, Karéin? Unfortunately, we don't have a lot of reserve fuel on this ship, so we can't deviate substantially from the course that we are now on, back to Earth. Do you require an energy-source of some kind? Something else? You have my assurance that if we can give it to you without endangering ourselves, you'll have it."

The Storied Watcher got up and sat down again, saying, "What I most require, and as soon as possible, is being able to use your... com-pu-ter, to calculate my best course around the star, then to intersect with the path of the comet 'Lucifer', as far away from your planet as possible."

She explained, "At full power, I would not need to do this, because I would have enough control over the waves of gravity in the void, to easily correct my course, to fly up, down, sideways, backwards if I had to, with just a thought. When I am truly myself, I can fly *much* faster than this space-ship; I can handle forces of acceleration, or impacts with the debris of the void, that would kill any of you, instantly. But I am so recently awakened that right now, I can safely speed up or slow down, or change course, only very slowly, and I cannot guarantee that my full powers will return before I reach your star. So I must plan everything, assuming that I will have no more power than what I feel in my body right now. I could try to do this, that is, design my path, just with the number-knowledge that I have in my head, but if I make a mistake... I have already told you, what might happen."

She paused a second, and said, "Not only to me, but to your world."

"Sam," said Tanaka to Jacobson, "I believe that I'd be the best person to help her... I'm the only Ph.D in physics and celestial mechanics here, I think. But I have another question, Karéin. If you're so short of energy, wouldn't it be easier just to try to *deflect* the comet, so that it misses Earth, rather than trying to blow it up?"

"I considered doing that, Professor Cherie Tanaka," responded the Mars-girl. "But – and I realize that this is hard for you to understand – my powers do not work that way, exactly. I *can* use *Amaiish* to move heavy objects, that is true, but something *that* size... I do not think it would work, unfortunately. The gravity-waves would not have anything to 'push' against, I think that is how you would say it in your language. And to move a really *heavy* object, any object, in fact, I have to – how would you say – 'grasp' it with the force of my mind, more or less the same way that you would grasp this coffee-cup, in front of us. But my mind's powers can reach only a certain distance and I doubt that at this point, they would be able to encircle this 'Lucifer' thing. Furthermore, if I mis-judge how far off-course that I have moved it, the comet might still crash into your home-world. *That* is why I need to pierce it, and shatter it from inside. A big, single burst of energy. That is what I need to do."

"Professor," commented Boyd, "Just to answer your question, I think you would be the right person, yeah. But you may need Devon or myself to jury-rig a simulator. Needless to say, this kind of trajectory isn't in the standard book of maneuvers."

"Agreed," said Jacobson. "Well, we had better get going on it. Right now, we have no idea of whether our guest's ideal departure point might be two days from now, or today, or an hour from now. Let's get working, team."

"Captain Sam Jacobson," the girl said with a tone of relief, looking at him directly with doe eyes, "Thank you. Thank you *very* much, sir. I owe you a great debt."

"Think nothing of it, Karéin," Jacobson replied. "By far the least that *I* can do, for someone who wants to do so much for my people. I only hope, and pray, that we can get you what you need, soon enough."

He turned to the others and continued, "Brent, Cherie, you two see if you can find, or input, an appropriate program – I seem to remember that NASA supplied us with an emergency manual trajectory calculator for the ship, in case the autopilot got totaled. Maybe we could adapt that one for our friend, if we tweak the variables a bit. Sergei, you know the computer pretty well, why don't you accompany them in case they need to bypass some of the normal user interface."

"What about me, Captain?" asked White.

"You stay here with me and help me figure out what the hell I'm going to say to Houston," said Jacobson. "Let's get going, team."

Pissing Off An Angel

It was only a short walk – in the alien-girl's case, a short, effortless flight – from the mess-section to the computer console room.

They arrived to the sight of dozens of thin-panel displays, now mostly dull and lifeless as an energy-saving measure, accompanied by three QWERTY computer keyboards and various types of input devices.

"We had better check your mass again," said Tanaka, "We got a reading down on Mars, but I want to make sure that there haven't been any variances since then."

She went out of the room and retrieved a foot-scale from the nearby sickbay.

The Mars-girl obligingly stepped on it.

"Interesting," Tanaka commented. "87.5 kilograms – I sure wouldn't have guessed that you weighed *that* much, looking at your build, height and figure, Karéin."

"My physiology is somewhat different from your own, Professor," stated the Storied Watcher. "My bone structure is rather dense, compared to that of many of the humanoids whom I have encountered in my travels."

"Is that related to the composition of your blood, perhaps?" inquired Tanaka.

"Partly, but more because my bones, and the marrow within them, acts as a kind of – how do you say in Eng-lish – 'batter-ee', I can store *Amaiish* in them, quite a lot of it, in fact, when my powers are full," elaborated Karéin-Mayréij. "This lets me use the *Fire* over long periods of time – for example when I am in a long sleep, such as in which you found me – or in difficult situations where I cannot otherwise tap the other dimension."

Tanaka gave the young-looking alien a wistful look.

"Karéin," commented the scientist, "There's *so* much that I – we – could learn from you... and, learn *with* you. I feel terrible that we will probably not have nearly enough time to even scratch the surface of it."

Smiling kindly, the Storied Watcher replied, "*I*, too, am one who pursues knowledge, Professor. Through all the many worlds and many ages, I have never ceased to be curious... to want to know more... to *understand*. So I know exactly how you feel. How much time we have to communicate these things – that, neither of us can control. But I promise you that I will use every moment that we *do* have, as best I can. And if ever we do meet again, I will give you all the time that you need to learn about me, if you will teach me what wisdom that you have. This do I promise."

She thought a second and inquired, "But please tell me... what does it mean to 'scratch the surface'?"

A tear glistened in Tanaka's eye as she laughed.

How alien this being was; yet how very alike, the two of them were.

"Sorry, Karéin," explained the science officer, "I should have known better than to have used an idiom like that. It means, roughly, 'to be only able to do a small bit of a much larger project'."

"Ah," acknowledged Karéin-Mayréij, "I see. Your Eng-lish is like my own language: not difficult to speak at first, but hard to speak like a native."

Meanwhile, Boyd and Chkalov had been busily fiddling with the computer controls.

Boyd spoke up. "I think I have something we can use," he said. "The Captain was right – Sergei *was* able to dig up the emergency trajectory calculator. How heavy did you say she was, again?"

"87.5 kg.," said Tanaka.

"Roger that," said Boyd, working the controls. "Hmm... Sergei, it's rejecting that value. Probably thinks it's too low and it's flagging it as an out-of-range input error. Anything you can do here?"

"Let me try, Major," replied the cosmonaut.

He tapped a few commands into the console. "I have reset the program and have disabled variable bounds-checking," he said. "Try it now."

"Good, it accepted the input, this time," announced Boyd. "Now, all we have to do is input the thrust and velocity values. Uhh... Professor, I think this one falls into *your* ball park. Just what figures would we use?"

"Indeed," added Chkalov. "I do not see our guest using a rocket booster, or an engine of any kind, yet – Karéin – you fly like a bird. We cannot calculate a trajectory without knowing how much thrust you can produce."

"Thrust? What is that?" replied the alien-girl. "Oh, wait... I know. Like, the little particle-smashing reaction that you use in the engines to propel this space-ship, is that right?"

"Sort of," stated Boyd. "It's more the amount of propulsive energy, or force, that the process that you refer to, produces, and indirectly the speed at which this force is able to propel a vehicle of a certain mass, that is, the *Eagle* and *Infinity*."

"In our science, Karéin," mentioned Tanaka, "We have a statement that says, 'Force equals Mass multiplied by Velocity'. Do you understand what I am saying?"

"Yes," the girl said, "I have known principles of motion and matter like that for untold ages, and I also taught myself some of your way of expressing them on your com-pu-ter. But it does not correspond to how I move, when I am – how would you say – 'flying'. I propel myself by bending the waves of the 'gravity'-force. I can reverse these, so that I can move *away* from a source of gravity rather than towards it; and I can amplify these waves, so that I can move *very* fast... at least, when my powers are at full strength."

"*Incredible*," commented Tanaka. "I know this is a bit off the topic, Karéin, but how much concentration do you have to exercise, to do this? Do you do it naturally, or is it a skill that you have to practice?"

"Both," replied the Mars-girl. "The ability is native to my people, at least, to the greater among us; it is like walking or telling your hand to pick up an eating-utensil... it just happens automatically. But learning how to 'fly', as you say, at high speeds or altitudes, is actually very difficult and it requires many years of practice, to do safely."

With an odd look, she added, "But maybe, some day... you *will* come to understand this, yourselves."

"Really?" asked Jacobson.

The Storied Watcher nodded and continued, "For example, when I will be on my path around your star, I must use my arts to make a 'bubble' in front of me and around me, like *this*," – her eyes for flashed a second and the humans heard a background of exciting, electric-rock style music, then they saw a barely visible, shimmering barrier of light, surrounding her – "To protect me from being hurt by things I might run into, at high speed. Even a speck of dust can be deadly, at the speeds at which I can travel. But when something like that hits my 'bubble', it gives off energy, which I can recycle into *Amaiish*, so in a sense it is self-supporting. Many of my people never advance to this level, though, because learning how to do it is... *challenging*, and you have to do it *perfectly*, all the time. There is not much room for mistakes, when practicing – if one's shield drops accidentally, while flying at high speed, you can imagine –"

Gradually, the bubble flickered and then vanished, as the alien-girl stopped powering it.

The music receded.

"This *is* amazing," said Boyd, "But it doesn't get us any further ahead with the computer program. Without a thrust or velocity estimate, we can't possibly plot a valid trajectory."

"Karéin," said Tanaka, "How fast do you think you can fly now?"

"I am not sure, Professor Cherie Tanaka," the Mars-girl replied, "Although I feel my strength returning more rapidly now, I think I could fly only as fast as... perhaps... a hundred times the speed of your vehicle, the one you used down on *Mailànkh*. But I feel certain that I will be able to fly faster, tomorrow. Do you have units of measure for speeds like this?"

"Yes," confirmed Boyd. "We quantify speeds in terms of 'kilometers per hour', that is, for example, 'one kilometer per hour' refers to the speed at which you would take one hour of Earth time to travel one kilometer, which is a measure of distance. We measured your own standing height as about one point seven-two meters; a thousand of these meters, equals one kilometer".

"If this helps," said Tanaka, "We calculated the distance from the *Eagle*, when it was down on Mars – sorry, *Mailànkh* – to the door to your burial-chamber, as a little under ten kilometers."

"May I have one of your 'Etch-A-Sketch' devices, please?" requested the Mars-girl.

Chkalov fumbled about in a storage-compartment and produced one, along with its corresponding stylus, and handed it to her.

"Thank you, Major Sergei Chkalov," said the Storied Watcher, with a perhaps-more-than-friendly smile, as she took the device. Immediately, she started to inscribe a complicated-looking set of what appeared to be mathematical equations, partly in human arithmetic notation and partly in her own script.

"Hmm..." she muttered, "If I recall correctly... but remember that I was not keeping track exactly, I flew from *there* to *there* in a little more than thirty-seven of your seconds... which means..."

Furiously, she scribbled more calculations, then looked up. "I think that means my speed was, in your way of saying, nine hundred and sixty-three kilometers per hour. It was lucky that I did not stumble, as it hurts to do so when traveling so fast."

"Wow," was all Boyd could think of to say, as several of the bemused others shook heads and chuckled. "I suppose that explains how you managed to be back at the Anomaly in one minute, and... with us, in the next. Someday, you will have to tell us how you managed to stow away, too."

"Stow away?" she asked.

"To 'stow away' is to hide oneself, in this case in our space-ship," Tanaka explained.

"Actually, I just walked right *by* you," remarked the Mars-girl. "Like... *this*."

Instantly, she all but vanished from sight; the only trace of her was the slightest trace of of shimmer in the air, where her figure had been.

"I am not only able to bend gravity waves," noted a voice from nothingness. "Light waves, sound waves, other waves, too."

Then the Storied Watcher reappeared, exactly where she had been previously.

By now, Jacobson and White had rejoined them.

White complained, "So she can become *invisible,* too. What's next?"

Boyd added, "Don't forget the 'faster than a speeding bullet' part, or the force field, either," to guffaws from several of the others.

"'Faster than...' – ah, I see, than a, uhh, weapon-projectile... is that right?" the alien-girl asked. "This is another of your, 'idioms'?"

"Yes," replied Tanaka, "But it is also a phrase associated with a character named 'Superman' from our world's fantasy literature. This character is supposed to be faster, stronger and more powerful than any human, in fact, he's indestructible. He's sort of an immortal guardian of the Earth, but, as I say, he's just a fictional character, not real."

The alien-girl thought for a second, then bemusedly offered, "Someday, I would like to find out more about this, 'Superman'. I think that he would be interesting. Maybe I could learn some tricks or ideas from him. I have learned much from other, supernatural beings."

Her eyes turned down.

"Alas... I am anything *but* indestructible – I have survived many thousands of your years, but I can still die by accident or violence, friends," she warned. "You may see the truth of this, sooner than you or I would like."

"Should we tell her to stay away from Kryptonite?" joked White.

"Krypto – *what?*" asked a confused Storied Watcher. "It sounds like an element – "

"Later," interrupted Jacobson. "Major Boyd, Major Chkalov, Professor, how have we been doing here? Have we got it worked out yet?"

"Partially," replied Tanaka. "We have the program working, but we can't figure out how to quantify her thrust or velocity. Her method of self-propulsion corresponds to nothing that we have ever experienced before. We're really at the guesswork stage, as far as this is concerned."

"Well," said Boyd, "We *do* have a rough estimate of how fast she was able to travel while back on Mars – a little less than a thousand k.p.h.. Down there, she would have had to cope with atmospheric drag, friction and gravity, so we could probably safely assume that she could, say, go ten to twenty per cent faster in interplanetary space. Does this sound right, Karéin?"

"You are correct, Major Brent Boyd," she confirmed. "I could probably have gone faster, but it would have disturbed even the thin air of *Mailànkh,* a lot. I was concerned that doing so might alert you to my plan to... join you, as I have."

She gave a wry, sharp-toothed grin.

"No doubt," Boyd replied. "But there's one other thing. Whatever speed we are talking about, was this a maximum, a top speed, or can you keep accelerating? If so, for how long? How fast can you go, if you push things right to the limit?"

The alien-girl pondered this question for a second or two, then observed, "It is like this. I am sorry if it is hard to understand – there are not many words in your language that accurately describe what I am telling you about. In the past, when my powers have been strong, I have been able to increase my speed continuously, at least when I have been in the void – if one tries to do this within the atmosphere of a planet, or even worse, in denser mediums like water, the inner regions of the gas planets and so on, the amount of the *Fire* that one has to expend to shield oneself from the elements becomes *enormous*, when one's speed starts to go over a certain point. When I am in - 'outer space', I think that is the phrase you use for the void – I can keep speeding up to the point where I can quite easily fly even to the most distant planets, in only a few hours of your time –"

"You mean, like, Mars, Venus, Jupiter, and so on? Surely you don't mean planets of other star systems?" exclaimed Tanaka.

"Mars... *Mailànkh* ... Vee-nuss?" listed Karéin-Mayréij. "Ah – you must mean *Hlà'ter'àh*, the second planet, the hot cloudy one, correct? Joo-pee-ter... *Zàd'e'fùléng*... that is the big one, next outward from *Mailànkh*?"

"Yes," said Boyd.

"I can fly to all of these, even the nethermost, far out where your star is but a speck in the dark sky, yes, and I have done so, several times, largely out of curiosity," explained the Storied Watcher. "I especially like the big planet because there is plentiful energy there, lots to take into my body. *Hlà'ter'àh* is not bad, either – lots of heat-energy – but it is dull, just burning rocks, everywhere, and I cannot fly very fast because its air is so thick. Also... I do not expect you to understand this, but I have memories of having traveled the deep void between the stars, once or twice."

"My *God*," said Tanaka, in a hushed, humbled tone. "You can fly between the *stars*? *Alone*? Karéin, by any of our measurements, you really *are* a goddess. We have no other word for a being with such powers."

"Yes," replied the Storied Watcher, "But do not worship or over-estimate me. Even when I fly as fast as I am capable, I cannot exceed or even come very close to the universal barrier of the speed of radiation, so, when I travel between the stars, it takes many long years of your time, even for stars that are relatively close to each other. And what little I remember of such trips is not pleasant."

She stopped and thought a bit, then explained, "The deep void is *terribly* lonely and silent – it nearly drove me insane with isolation and monotony, though I slept for much of these trips – and it has many hidden dangers: black places of very strong gravity-waves, occasional impacts with small objects at great speeds and, above all else, the possibility of missing one's intended destination altogether if one even slightly miscalculates the path. There is also no guarantee that where one is going, will be a better or more easily inhabitable place than where one is leaving from. I only dimly remember, but I know that I only undertook these trips as a last resort, a measure of desperation when I knew that it was too dangerous to stay where I was. I am *here*, now, and it is here that I want to make my home. *If* you will have me."

"Now *that* is interesting, and not too encouraging, either," observed White.

"What do you mean?" shot back Tanaka.

"Well, Professor," White commented, "I mean, we're all happy to have Karéin here with us, for her to call our ship and – maybe – our planet, home, that's a given. But... what I was a little disturbed in hearing, was that there are places that even *she* had to get out of, elsewhere in the galaxy. I mean, if they're *that* dangerous... well... I sure wouldn't want to be on the first Earth-ship to go poking around there."

"You're *scaring* me, Major," said Tanaka.

The Storied Watcher looked up.

Her eyes were glowing and, though she tried to suppress them, there was a hint of sharp teeth as she spoke.

"No, Professor Cherie Tanaka, Major Devon White has good reason to say that," she warned. "Most of the universe, at least that small part of it that I know of, is wonderful and very beautiful and I pray that someday, I will be able to show it to you. But there *are* dark places, too, where your people should *never* go. I tried to protect him, but I believe that Major Brent Boyd has seen some of these..."

Her glance turned to Boyd and the memories flooded back, a miasma of fear, foreboding and inchoate dread.

"Whoa, whoa... *whoa*," Boyd blurted, as he got up, trying to shake the visions from his head.

Sweating profusely, he paced nervously around the room. Eventually, he regained his composure and sat down again.

"What did you *do* to him?" demanded Jacobson, his voice rising. "*Stop* it, whatever it is."

"Commander," the Mars-girl replied, eyes and teeth back to normal, "I did nothing to him. What you see is the result of Major Brent Boyd having been too... *inquisitive*, when our minds were as one. He attempted to see *all* my memories, not just the ones that I wanted him to see. It was an easy mistake to make; I do not blame him for trying. Major Brent Boyd, are you feeling better, now, my love? I hope these bad visions will go away, naturally, over time. If not, I can touch minds with you again and try to erase them, but I cannot guarantee success. And I might erase other memories, too. It is not a precise science."

Fully himself again, Boyd responded, "No, if it's quite alright, I'll pass on that, Karéin. I'm just getting over the last headache, thank you very much. I can deal with nightmares. These ones are just a little more, well, *vivid*, that's all. I'll cope with them, don't worry."

She nodded, then extended her hand to cover his, then laid a light kiss on his hand.

"Kind of makes me glad that *you* were the 'lucky one' who she picked," commented Jacobson dryly, in Boyd's direction. "But we need to get back on track here. Karéin, do you have any idea, even a rough one, as to how fast you could go now? We can't help you plot your course, without that information."

"I honestly do not know, sir," the alien-girl replied, "Because I feel my powers returning, gradually. As they return, I will be able to go faster. But I understand your question. What I *can* say, for sure, is that I could probably go a fifth faster again – as Major Brent Boyd says – than I did down on *Mailànkh* initially, and that I could keep increasing my, how do you say, 'velocity', until it was twice that; maybe three times. Ordinarily, I would try to test my abilities, but there is not enough room in this space-ship – I would hit one of the walls almost immediately. If we say that I was going at roughly three thousand of your 'kilometers per hour', I think I could certainly do that. It is much, much less than the speeds at which I usually travel."

"Brent," requested Jacobson, "Does that give you what you need to know?"

"Affirmative," replied Boyd. "Sergei, when you input that, don't forget to add our current velocity, that is of the ship, as a baseline."

"Yes, of course," promised Chkalov, busily typing instructions into the computer. "Input is complete," he continued. "I will run the simulation, now."

They all looked at the display.

It showed two parabolic plots, the familiar one representing the ship's current route back to Earth, in blue; and a new one in red, branching off from the blue path at a point just a fraction of the way further along the blue path, relative to the yellow point which showed the *Infinity*'s current position.

The red path flew close to Venus, missed Mercury altogether, disappeared behind the Sun, thence reappearing to intersect with Earth at a time when the blue path had about a fifth of its distance yet to go.

"Interesting," said Tanaka. "But even if the course is valid, you would be on your own, flying towards the Sun for *weeks* on end. Karéin, how could you possibly survive that kind of trip, weeks in a total void, with no food, air or water?"

"As I said, Professor Cherie Tanaka," the Storied Watcher politely explained, "I can use my *Amaiish* to keep myself alive in such conditions, almost *indefinitely* if I have to. I suppose that if I tried to do it for thousands of your years, that would be risky, maybe there would be parts of my body that would deteriorate, regardless... this is one other reason why I can only travel to near-by stars. I have never attempted a longer trip like that, so I do not know, and it is hard to explain what it feels like, there are no descriptive words in your language. I am aware of the discomfort of not being able to breathe – sort of like how you would feel, when 'holding your breath', for a second or two – but the *Fire*, as well as certain other arts to which I have recourse, nourishes me, keeps me alive, even so. It is not painful... just, unpleasant. To tell you the truth, I find that being alone, not being able to touch or talk to anyone, is worse than this physical discomfort. I am not really sure how this ability works, exactly. I just know that I *can* do it safely, so please do not worry about this. I face many more severe tests, on this project."

"Well then," interrupted Jacobson, "I suppose that these are the figures and the plots that we're going to use, unless anyone can see something drastically wrong in what's before us. Sergei, Brent, do we have an exact plot to give her? An exact ETA to departure?"

"Here it is, Captain," said Chkalov, transferring the data to an Etch-A-Sketch via an interface cable.

"Karéin," the cosmonaut asked, "Do you understand the notation, how we have expressed the trajectory?"

The Mars-girl took the device and examined its display carefully. "This writing here," she asked, pointing to one inscription, "This refers to the date and time I am to leave... yes?"

"Correct," said Chkalov. "Specifically, fourteen hours and six minutes from now, counting from one minute ago."

"And *this*, here," – she inquired, while pointing at another part – "Is my relative direction, compared to the path of your space-ship, *Infinity*, is it not?"

"Also correct," the Russian answered. "We call it a 'delta', which is a mathematical concept for 'change' or 'difference'."

"Ah," she said, 'tak-OO-nai'nai-OO-yay-eh'. That is how we call it. But I understand."

She thought for a second, then looked up at Jacobson and asked, "Captain Sam Jacobson, I have another favor to request. Do you have a strong, hard piece of flat metal, or some other very durable substance around here, that is surplus to your needs? That is, that I could take with me, on my trip?"

"I don't know... pretty much everything here is here for a purpose," he replied. "Brent? Devon? Sergei? Anything we could give her?"

Boyd and White just shook their heads, but Chkalov said, "I am not sure if this is exactly what Karéin wants, Captain, but when I was in the *Eagle*'s cargo-hold, just prior to my first encounter with our guest, I noticed that one or two of the inner metal lining panels on some of the heavy-duty storage boxes, had come loose. Those boxes are not full, anyway. I think we could remove one of these panels... it would not compromise anything."

"Okay," Jacobson allowed. "Why don't you go and get one."

"At once, Captain," said Chkalov. He bounded up to the center core access-hatch and disappeared.

"I thought you said you don't need shielding?" asked Tanaka.

"That is correct," said the Storied Watcher. "I do not need it for that."

"For what, then?" said Tanaka.

"I will have to transcribe what I see on your writing-device, the 'Etch-a-Sketch', on to the metal of the object," the alien-girl replied. "I can commit the trajectory to memory, and will do that regardless, but I would feel safer if I had something to refer to, in case I forget something about the direction in which I am to travel."

"Well, that makes sense," commented Boyd. "I wouldn't want to go on a trip like that without a map, either. But... you said, 'transcribe'... I think we do have some conventional writing-markers on the ship, somewhere, but I doubt their ink would last long in a total vacuum, let alone if you got it close to the Sun..."

Chkalov re-appeared, carrying a flat, square piece of what appeared to be aluminum or an alloy of that metal, perhaps a half-meter by a half-meter in size.

"Captain," he announced, "This is the item of which I told you. I presume that we can give it to her?"

"Yeah, that will do," said Jacobson. "I suppose we need to dig out the marker-pens now. Where did we put them, anyway? I remember using one of them down on Mars, to mark some sample bags. Darn – I bet they're back in the cargo bay. Sorry to ask you to make two trips, Sergei, but – "

"There is no need for that, sir," interjected Karéin-Mayréij.

She gave a lithe hand-gesture and the metal plate shot from Chkalov's hands, directly into her grasp, as if propelled by some unseen force.

"Here," she added, "I will now transcribe the path that your com-pew-ter has calculated. I hope it is correct."

Their minds perceived the music, this time an electric, exciting beat, starting from nowhere.

Then, the nonplussed humans saw tiny wisps of lightening surround her eye-sockets, followed in a fraction of a second by two beams of dazzlingly bright light, or energy, or *something*, shooting from her eyes, impacting with the metal, melting and burning it, inscribing an exact replica of the calculations and shapes that were on the Etch-a-Sketch.

In perhaps three seconds, the surface of the metal plate was completely covered with this burned-in script.

Her eyes flashed and the light-beams disappeared, along with the music.

"*Jesus*, Karéin," gasped White, "If I wasn't scared of y'all *before*..."

The African-American astronaut could see from the expressions on the others' faces, that he spoke for all of them.

For a long second, the Storied Watcher just looked at him with her regal, far-off stare, an alien goddess surveying a human man.

Then she said, "Major Devon White, I have something I want to show you. Do you trust me?"

"Do I have a choice?" he tried to joke. "Yeah, I guess. Sure."

"Open up your garment-top, so that your chest is bare, please."

"Karéin, this is *highly* irregular," interrupted a worried Jacobson. "What are you trying to prove?"

"It is oh-kay," she counseled, smiling kindly.

She put her hand over Jacobson's, grasping it. "He will not be harmed. I promise you this."

The Mars mission commander winced, trying to control a sudden physical reaction, which was accompanied by a series of fascinating, though unsettling, mental images.

Unsteadily, White stood up and unzipped the top part of his jumpsuit.

"Here it is, in all its glory," he said.

"Nice," casually replied Karéin-Mayréij. "You are *attractive*, Major Devon White. Someday," she said with a sly grin and a wink, "I would like to find out how that chest *feels*, as well as looks."

White blushed a bit.

Then, with no warning whatsoever, her eyes flashed and two beams of brilliant light struck him in the exact middle of his chest, causing a momentary glow to spread all over the front part of his trunk.

He looked shocked, as would a man shot in the heart who was living out his last seconds. But he was very much alive.

"Whoa," he exclaimed. "What was *that*? I thought I was done for, there, for a second. But it feels *nice*. Kinda like the warm feeling y'all get from a good shot of Bourbon."

"That," explained the Storied Watcher, "Was the *Fire*. I can craft its energy in many forms, from those that give life and strength, to those that can... destroy. You got the first kind, the *good* kind. Had it been the *second* kind, you would have been cleft in two, or, with more power, reduced to ashes."

White, as well as a few of the others, shot quick and nervous glances over to the inscribed metal plate.

"And there is something else, which is the *real* reason I did this with Major Devon White, friends. If I tell you, I would prefer you not to tell others on your planet, until I say the time has come to do so. Will you all promise to keep this trust?" she asked.

There was a serious tone in her voice.

"Certainly," said Tanaka. "Captain? Can you second that?"

"I *suppose* so," said Jacobson, reluctantly. "Although I'm not supposed to keep secrets from Houston, I think in this case I can make an exception. Any objections, team?"

"No," replied White, Boyd and Chkalov, in unison.

"It is like this," the Mars-girl continued. "As you know, I have access to very large, almost limitless amounts of *Amaiish*, and I have had the equivalent of many of your human lifetimes to learn how to use it, how to mold it, how to make it do my bidding. It is very unlikely that any of your species could ever come close to my powers, in this respect, because even within my *own* race I am one of the most powerful, and my body has evolved specifically with the ability to harness this energy... but *if* you learn correctly and practice..."

Tanaka's jaw dropped.

"You mean that *we – we* can – human beings can –" stuttered an amazed, overjoyed science officer.

The Storied Watcher nodded, then caught them all in an earnest, determined, but kindly and loving, stare, while her regal music played gently in the background.

"Yes, *yes*, for *sure*, dear friend, Professor Cherie Tanaka. You, too – *all* humans, as far as I can tell, from the limited time I have had to be with you – can use the power... you can use the *Fire* that I bring to this space-ark. I had suspected this from the first time I met you, because you were exposed to large amounts of *Amaiish* down on *Mailànkh* with no apparent ill-effects, but after I became one in mind with Major Brent Boyd, I was basically sure of it. You just need someone to teach you how. Should I not return from my quest, I wanted you to know that mastery over *Amaiish* lies latent in your species; for, sometimes, knowing that doing something is possible, is all that one needs, to actually *do* it."

"Y'all mean we can, like, fly around, and stuff?" asked an unbelieving White. "Y'all *gotta* be shittin' us!" he protested.

Karéin-Mayréij gave a little laugh and responded, "I think that you meant, 'am I misleading you'? No, good friend – I speak with *utmost* honesty on this subject. But as to 'flying around' and so on... I do not think so, Major Devon White, not for many years, maybe not for many generations, as your people learn to use and control the *Fire*. *Those* abilities – the ones that involve moving heavy objects, or conversion into high-powered familiar energy – are what we call 'hard' or 'greater' *Amaiish*. It is the same type of energy, but you are channeling a lot of it and not doing so correctly can hurt you, or worse – if you lose control, the results can be like coming into physical contact with a powerful source of electricity. You will probably start by using 'soft' or 'lesser' *Amaiish* for good health and to help you live longer, maybe to sharpen your perceptive abilities, as well. But I may be wrong. Everyone does it in their own way."

Stunned, Tanaka abruptly got up, pacing and shaking her head.

Turning to Jacobson, with tears of wonder and portent in her eyes, she shouted wildly, "Sam, do you *realize* what we have just learned, in less than an *hour* of being able to communicate with this being? This is knowledge of *incredible* importance, one that will mark a completely new era in human evolutionary history! It's the most important knowledge that human beings have gained since we learned how to master normal fire, a hundred thousand *years* ago! *Nothing* compares even *remotely* to this! God – we *can't* let her go!"

Jacobson, like the others trying to absorb the implications of the revelation, said, "No kidding... *wow*. Holy Crow, Karéin, now I'm *glad* that you decided to stow away with us. We almost left Prometheus down on Mars, I guess."

The Storied Watcher just lowered her eyes, smiling modestly, but obviously moved by Tanaka's outburst.

Then she said, "Friends, I feel great joy, knowing that I have been the one honored to help you this way. See how I am your servant."

She looked up at Tanaka and added, "Also, I can see that you have understood that this is very important information, which is why I wanted to make sure I had told it to you, as soon as I could properly talk in Eng-lish. But who is Pro –"

"In the mythology of one of the ancient Earth-empires," interjected Boyd, "He was a demigod who first taught men how to use fire. But the more powerful gods weren't too happy about his having done so, thus he got rather severely punished for the offense. Apparently the power of fire was too much to be entrusted to mere mortals such as us."

"I guess that makes y'all the '*Fire*-Bringer', Karéin," commented White. "I sure hope nobody gets mad at you for doin' that."

Then Chkalov, who had been listening from some distance off while fiddling with the computer controls, interjected, "Captain. Professor. And Karéin. I have something you should *see*, on the computer."

He did not have a happy look on his face.

"What?" replied Jacobson.

"I just think... you should *see* this," quietly suggested the cosmonaut. "For those of you who cannot read the display easily, let me explain. Remember that we calculated Karéin's flight-path?"

"Yes," confirmed Tanaka. "It showed a valid trajectory that would get her to Earth... right?"

"Not exactly," said Chkalov. "The course, is, indeed valid. But we forgot to check if it would intersect with 'Lucifer', at an early enough *time*. All that we calculated, was that it would arrive at the comet's last estimated *position* on its own ballistic path. I regret that I did not notice this, at first."

A look of horror appeared on Boyd's face, followed by those of Tanaka and Jacobson, in turn.

"What *exactly* are you trying to tell us, Sergei?" demanded Jacobson, icily, striding over to the computer display. Boyd was already staring at it.

"There is no other way to put this," replied the Russian. "At the speed we have calculated her to be going, by the time that she arrives at Earth... the comet will already have impacted, almost two months before. We are just too far away now... while I have taken into account that she would start from the *Infinity* at our cruising velocity, and even if she were to, how do you say, 'lift off' in the next minute, at twice the rate that we calculated for her, she could not *possibly* reach Earth's vicinity in time. I am sorry."

Shock, accompanied by fury, clouded the Storied Watcher's face.

"You *told* me –" she spat, propelling herself over to the computer display. "Major Brent Boyd, Major Sergei Chkalov, please try again. It *must* be wrong. Can we try to recalculate?"

"Sure. I'll try," said Boyd, working the controls. He hit a command sequence. The display regenerated, with exactly the same symbols, paths and figures.

"Try it again," demanded the alien-girl. "You *must* have made a mistake. You must have entered a number incorrectly. You humans are not very good with numbers. Sorry that I had to say it, but I believe that I am right. Yes... must be it. Try the numbers again, *please!*"

"It won't help, Karéin," explained Boyd, as calmly as he could. "As you can see, even if I, say, triple the speed-factor that we input," – he adjusted one variable, then forced the computer to re-run the program – "You will still be arriving at Earth, at least two months late."

Pushing him aside, firmly but gently, she stood in front of the computer controls. "Major Sergei Chkalov, show me how to put the numbers in," she commanded.

Chkalov pointed to the variable-input dialog-boxes on the computer display. "You can enter your data here, here and here," he instructed. "But I am afraid that Major Boyd is correct. If it is of any use, I have also just re-checked the computer's memory, and the program itself, for data integrity. Everything is working as it should."

Feverishly, her hands moved in rapid-fire motion over the controls. She ran the program, once, twice, three times.

"*NO!*" shouted Karéin-Mayréij. "No... it cannot *be*! Not *this* time! Not *again!*"

Her tear-filled eyes flashed red, then yellow, then white.

She sat down with a thud, slamming a fist on the table in frustration and anger.

Instantly, a chair was propelled by some unseen force against a far wall, shattering into shards of composite plastics.

"That's *enough*, Karéin!" growled Jacobson. "We don't like this news, either, to say the least. But I will *not* have you wrecking my ship just because you're upset, especially when it comes down to things not going the way we thought, because you can't fly fast enough –"

"You do not *understand*, Captain Sam Jacobson," wailed the Storied Watcher, staring at him with eyes that alternately glowed and subsided. "I will fail – *again!* I will be cheated of my destiny... my chance to redeem myself! Then I will live through more ages, reminded of how fate thus taunted me! I will have the death-screams of your people echoing through my mind, for centuries upon *centuries!* How can you know how it *feels*, to see this and be helpless, totally *helpless*, to change it! How can you know how it –"

With a speed none of them had seen before of him, Jacobson turned and slapped her, hard, on the right cheek.

"*Shut up!*" he shouted.

For a half-second, there was an astonished look on the face of the Mars-girl.

Then her countenance darkened and her eyes glowed brilliant yellow.

"Do not *ever* do that again!" she hissed. "*No-one* strikes me! I could kill you with nothing but a *thought!*"

The music shot through their minds, suddenly. It was electric, rough, thrilling but frightening.

The air smelled of ozone, as her body pulsed with energy, flashing from inside.

A wave of fear and shock took hold of the others.

"Sam," nervously advised Tanaka, "*Cool it*. We all need to think this through."

But Jacobson was not to be moved.

"That's a chance I'm prepared to *take*," he retorted.

He grabbed the Storied Watcher by both shoulders, but, to the amazement of everyone save Boyd, she did not retaliate, as he roughly sat her down in the nearest seat.

He stooped over her and bellowed, his voice quaking with indignation, "Now, you listen to *me*, you self-pitying little Martian goddess! You're *upset* that you might not get to fulfill your 'destiny'... right? Well, why don't you stop thinking of yourself and consider what the *rest* of us just found out – namely, that our hopes of seeing our families, our wives and husbands, our children, our friends, everyone, have been shattered, after you gave us a glimmer of hope that Earth might have a chance. *We're* all going to *die*, now – along with all of our loved ones. *You'll* get to live, oh yes, somehow, somewhere, maybe back in a nice warm cave – I'm sure of *that*."

As she stared at him with big, stunned eyes, Jacobson continued, sarcastically, "You'll have unpleasant *dreams*, as you survive this episode? That's *really* too bad! All of *our* dreams, our hopes and thoughts too, are about to come to an abrupt end. So forgive us for not feeling too sorry for you. For a goddess, you're a pathetic one, Karéin... a *damn* pathetic one!"

"Man, talk about 'deer in the headlights'," whispered White to Tanaka, as they all waited for a response.

But Karéin-Mayréij did not reply, at all, other than for what may have been a deep, pained moan.

She flew up, out of the chair, almost too fast for the eye to follow, streaking up to the center core hatch and thence out of sight.

"Now *that* was fucking *great*, Sam!" angrily shot Tanaka to Jacobson. "Apart from just about getting yourself killed, you may have completely antagonized the only thing that could have saved Earth. She might have been able to have saved a few of us, even if not the whole world. After that, if I were her, I might not *bother*."

"Yeah, Captain, sir," carefully added White, "And just for the record, I *know* that she needed a talkin'-to, but now we got a cute little Mars-girl with laser beam eyeballs, floating around here, freaked out of her damn *mind*. Anyone remember where the space-suits are? Or maybe just a Bible, 'case we gotta say some quick good-byes?"

All four, excepting Jacobson, whose head was in his hands, looking down at the table, nervously glanced at each other.

After a moment, the commander quietly inquired, "Major Boyd, where is the alien, now? Can you give me her position?"

Boyd punched in the radiation trace program on the computer. "She appears to be in the cargo-hold, sir," he said.

"That figures," noted White. "As far away from us, as possible."

"Captain," proposed Chkalov, "I would like your permission to go down there and talk with her. She and I... we have a, special relationship, as I believe that you know."

"I'd like to go, too," requested Boyd.

"Yeah... very well... okay, permission granted," stated Jacobson. "But be careful. I don't know if she gives second chances."

The astronaut and cosmonaut just nodded and headed out the center core hatch.

Talk To Me

With a mixture of fear and grim determination, Boyd and Chkalov opened the hatch between the *Infinity* and the *Eagle* – noting in passing that it had been deliberately closed – and swam in the zero-G through the decks of the landing-ship until they were just above the lander's cargo bay hatch.

"Which one of us gets to be the lucky guy who tries first?" asked Boyd.

"Let us go in one immediately after the other, with me leading," replied Chkalov. "I feel certain that she will at least let me talk, before doing anything."

Boyd nodded and opened the hatch.

Chkalov flew down, followed closely by the other astronaut. The two men were relieved, but not entirely surprised, to find that they were still alive upon entering the hold.

They heard a faint sobbing sound from the 'Mars Artifacts' box. Not needing to say more, they moved over to the box and peered inside.

She was in there, curled into a fetal-position, moaning and breathing heavily. They could see that she was sweating and there was a sickly, greenish color to her skin.

In the dim light, she looked miserable, in an indescribable way that could never have been the same with a human being, whatever its travails.

Gently, Chkalov said, "Karéin, it's Sergei here. You remember, Sergei, your friend. Karéin, we would like to talk with you. We promise that nobody will try to hurt you again. The Captain says that he is very sorry."

"Go away. *Leave* me," she requested, in a trembling, whimpering voice. "I am not fit to be in your sight."

"Karéin," added Boyd, "*Nobody's* angry with you. You don't have to apologize to us. Every one of us – me and Sergei, Devon and Cherie, *all* of us – have had little disagreements with each other. But eventually we make up and go on with our lives. We *have* to, because we all depend on each other. Now, you're part of our team – our *family* – and we depend on you, even if it's not for what we first thought you could do for us. What is that, I'm trying to remember, that you say in your language? I know – *Makailkh sai'YA mnOOaiOO keeALKH no'OH awOO. That's* what I mean, Karéin."

A half-smile appeared briefly on her face, staring away from them, then vanished.

"Teaching you that," ruefully mumbled the Storied Watcher, "Will have been my only accomplishment, for however long you still live, Major Brent Boyd. But it will be futile. I will *fail*... and what is worse, I will have *disgraced* myself in so doing."

She paused for a second, then commented, "You should tell Captain Sam Jacobson that he is very perceptive... he is a good judge of character. For a 'goddess', I am *indeed* a 'pathetic' being. Unworthy, in every way."

"Karéin," argued Boyd, "Don't you think you're being a little *hard* on yourself? You didn't make the facts that we're all faced with. If there's nothing you can do, there's nothing you can *do*. You shouldn't blame yourself for that."

"You do not understand, nor do I expect you to," replied Karéin-Mayréij, in a low, labored tone. "You see, there is now *nothing* I can do to save your people – your own com-pu-ter gave out the calculations. So I will survive in the way I always have – by fleeing... by running."

She let out a pained laugh.

"How do you think I have lived so *long*, human?" she whined. "By being *brave?* Hardly. Yes, I *have* fought and defeated some terrible evils, you have seen some of them, in your mind. But whenever there has been a serious risk to my life, one that would likely have overcome me, I have... saved myself. And so, I will again. I am a fraudulent godling. It is the way that I am."

The Mars-girl resumed her soft moaning.

"Karéin," countered Chkalov, "I think that you are confusing bravery with common sense. There is no shame in refusing a task that you cannot win, especially if you risk your life in doing attempting it – "

"You should have told that to your friends on the, what ship was it, ah, the *Salvador Rossiya*, Major Sergei Chkalov," interrupted the alien-girl, in between muffled sobs.

Shaking his head, Chkalov backed away.

"I do not know what to *say*, Major Boyd," he muttered. "She is *right*."

"Why do you not leave me in *peace*," complained the Storied Watcher, from the dark confines of the box. "I will suffer here for a time – when I behave as foolishly I have, my body sometimes punishes me in ways that you cannot understand – then, when I have enough power to travel outside, I will leave your ship. I promise that I will not consume any more of your food or water, so you will have as much as possible for yourselves. You will then go to whatever fate lies in wait for you, as will I. All will be as it should be, as it *will* be, no matter what you or I want."

Almost in tears himself, Boyd replied, "Karéin, Karéin, oh, *Karéin*... it doesn't have to *be* like this. We *need* you. Our fates are the same – I'm *sure* of that. You must be aware of it too. But maybe you need some time to yourself. We'll respect that. When you're ready to talk with us, please come to the *Infinity*, we'll be waiting, and I know that everything that happened back there will be forgotten."

He looked at Chkalov.

"Anything more to say?" Boyd asked.

"No, not really," regretfully stated the cosmonaut. "Except – Karéin, you and I shared something very special. You *know* what I mean : I love you and I know that Brent does, too. Whatever happens to Earth, we will still have that love... I will carry it to my last days. I want to hold you, to be with you, again, Karéin of Mars. I will wait for you."

There was no answer.

"I guess that's *it*, then," muttered Boyd.

Chkalov nodded.

The two headed back out of the cargo bay, up to the inter-ship hatch (closing it as they left) and through the center core to *Infinity*, leaving the pouting creature to her thoughts and her suffering.

You Handle It

A haggard Jacobson looked up at Boyd and Chkalov, after the two returned to the pseudo-grav cylinder in the *Infinity*.

"Well? What's her attitude? Is she going to let us live?" he demanded, half-expecting to hear a negative reply.

"I do not think we have to worry about her retaliating against you, or us, sir," answered Chkalov. "It is more the other way around. She seems to be retaliating against *herself*. She seems very ashamed of her conduct."

"Yes," added Boyd, "And not just in the way that a human would do. She seems to be undergoing some kind of psycho-somatic feedback reaction, like she's punishing herself – we didn't get too good a look at her, but from what we could see, her body appeared quite weak and pale. She was obviously in pain. I'd also say that she's pretty depressed. Several times, she spoke of herself as being 'pathetic' and 'unworthy'. I'm afraid, Captain, that you really made an impression on her."

Frowning, Tanaka remarked, "Well, that's, of course, better than having her so angry that she's about to blow up the *ship*... but not as much better as you might think. I don't know if her psychology is anything like ours is, but severe depression... that can lead to some really *bad* consequences."

White interjected, "I'm no shrink, Professor, so... just what *kinds* of 'consequences' y'all talkin' about?"

"Like, in extreme cases, depression can lead to suicidal mania," observed Tanaka. "I'm sure you can imagine what *that* might mean, in a being with powers like *hers*."

White was about to say something smart, but Boyd cut him off.

"I don't think we have to worry about *that*, Professor," he explained. "She has no intention of ending her life. Far from that, in fact. What she's *really* ashamed of, is that she intends to go on living, by surviving the 'Lucifer' issue, while all of the rest of us... well, *you* get the idea. Apparently she has a long history of doing that, one that she isn't too proud of."

"Major Boyd, Major Chkalov," interrupted Jacobson, "This is all interesting, but what I really wanted to know is, 'is she going to forgive and forget'? Absent that, what I – *we* – are all faced with, is a neurotic alien, with enough power to wreck the ship with no warning, hiding out in our cargo bay. I can't allow *that* state of affairs to continue indefinitely, although it's probably not news to you that I have no idea whatsoever how to change it. What, *exactly*, did she say she was going to do? Anything? Or just stay in the cargo bay, avoiding us?"

"Captain," noted Chkalov, "She said that she intends to regain some of her strength, then she will leave us."

"*Leave* us? What do you mean?" retorted Jacobson.

"Just what Sergei said," replied Boyd. "She is simply going to get up and fly away. She didn't say where, but I think it's a pretty safe guess that it will be somewhere quite far away from Earth. Leaving us, and everyone on our planet, pretty much where we would have been, had we never found her, down on Mars."

"Ye *Gods*," breathed Tanaka. "Sam, we can't *possibly* let her do that! Apart from the *huge* loss to science in our not being able to learn from her in the meantime, she is very likely the only thing that can save our own lives, here on this ship. If she leaves, that may spell our doom."

"Professor's got a point," stated White. "Captain, sir, we know what y'all said about what's going to happen, when and if this ship arrives back at Earth, after our friend 'Lucifer' has paid its little house-call there. I dunno about the whole 'saving the planet' thang, but I'd bet y'all good money that she's got enough of this, *Amaii – Amaii – whatever* stuff in her, to at least give us the ability to fly wherever we want to go, eventually. Maybe even pick up a lucky few others, on the way."

He looked down, then offered, "Y'all know, sir, as I said earlier, I'm not sure I want to go on living, if my family isn't. But I don't want to make that decision for the rest of us. Nor for Earth. I say we should try to talk to her again."

Jacobson sat and thought silently for a minute, then declared, "Yeah... I guess we have to. Brent, Sergei, you monitor the *Eagle* internal view-cams. I'll go talk to her."

"*Alone?*" exclaimed Tanaka. "Sam, I don't think that's a good idea. She may still be upset with you. If you get into another fight with her, the results could be *disastrous*. At least let one of us accompany you."

"I'm aware of the risk, Professor," replied Jacobson, "But *I* was the one who set her off, and it's my responsibility to resolve the matter. Besides, I have some... *other* things to discuss with her. I'd just like to do this alone. But," – he turned to look Boyd squarely in the face – "If things *do* get out of hand there, and it appears that her actions might cause serious damage to the ship, Brent, I'm giving you a direct order to perform an immediate, emergency un-dock between *Eagle* and *Infinity*. I'll shut the hatch when I go in there, so we can maintain atmospheric integrity, in that event."

"Captain, I – I mean, I'm sure you know what that *means*, sir," warned Boyd, uncertainly. "You'd be *trapped* with her in the *Eagle* and even *one* shot from those eyes of hers could rupture the hull and leak out all the air; and even if *that* didn't happen, it might be impossible to re-dock later, if the ships' trajectories started to diverge – "

"I'm very well aware of that possibility, Major," replied Jacobson, matter-of-factly, "To say nothing of the equally likely one that she just tears me limb from limb. But far better just me and the *Eagle*, than everyone in *Infinity*, too."

Boyd nodded an uneasy affirmation. The others could think of nothing constructive to say, evidently.

Jacobson jumped up to the center core hatch and was gone.

Two Idiots Are We

Methodically, Sam Jacobson, Captain of the *Eagle and Infinity* Mars exploration mission, closed the airlock hatch and glided through the zero-G weightlessness of the lander's center ladder opening until he could see the hatch to the cargo bay.

He had practiced the maneuvers of securing the links between the two spacecraft hundreds of times, as he had every other operational technique for the many intricate sub-systems that make up a spaceship. He was totally confident of his ability to manage both the spaceship and his crew.

But, to put it mildly, the rule-books didn't have any guidance for situations like *this* – having to reason with, and manage, an immensely powerful alien being who seemed even more moody than a normal human woman.

It felt sexist to think that... but it was true.

At home, there would have been ways to handle a wife or a girlfriend who was "having a bad day".

Out *here*... well, he couldn't buy Karéin a box of chocolates or a bunch of flowers, now, *could* he?

Jacobson searched his mind for things to say, tactics to use.

His predisposition was to have paused and pondered the matter, going over each option, trying to pre-think out strategies to cope with every response, but intuitively he knew that doing so wouldn't have put him very much further ahead, given the many 'unknowns' about this being.

He opened the hatch and peered into the dimly-lit compartment.

"Karéin... Karéin? This is Commander Jacobson," he called. "I came here alone. Will you speak with me? I have a *lot* that I need to discuss with you."

There was no answer, but he thought he heard a low, moaning sound coming from one of the boxes in the cargo-hold. He moved closer to it, until he was just outside its open front lid.

She was clearly in there and the surrounding atmosphere somehow fairly *radiated* anguish, shame and sadness.

Jacobson had to concentrate, to avoid it engulfing *him*, too.

"Karéin... is that *you*?" he inquired. "Listen... I don't know exactly how to *say* this, but, well, I've come to make up with you, to apologize; at least, that's what I'm *hoping* to do. You see, the thing is, well... I guess I kind of flew off the handle there in the *Infinity*, and for that I owe you an apology."

There was still no answer, but he said anyway,

"Karéin, I'm not sure that this is going to make a lot of sense, because you have lived for so long, in so many different places, but... I guess that you've met a lot of people and seen them come and go; I know that must be hard, but try to see it from our perspective... *my* perspective."

Jacobson continued, "You've got to *understand*... I have a wife and children down on Earth, so do several of my crew-members, and they're all that I and the others live for. I, *we*, love them very much. When you came along and promised to save them for us... well, however much we tried to avoid hoping, we're *desperate*, we *believed* in you because at this point we have no other possible way to save our families. So when you said that you were just giving up, well, I hit you in a fit of frustration, more than anything else; it sounded to me like you didn't care about what was going to happen to Earth and everyone on it."

The Mars mission commander listened, but did not hear a response.

He went on, "I'm really sorry that I struck you... it was not only out of character for me, but worse, it was a serious breach of my responsibility as Captain to set an example for all the others, including for yourself. If it's of any interest to you, doing what I did, to one of my fellow officers back on Earth, could *easily* lose me my job and my career – possibly even land me in prison. What I'm trying to say, Karéin, is that I *failed* you, I failed my crew and I failed myself, as well. I'm very sorry. I can't take back what happened, though God knows I'd *like* to, if I could."

All he heard was sobbing.

"You know, I've heard from Sergei and Brent that you intend to leave us, in a short while. Is that right?" Jacobson asked.

A soft voice half-whispered, "Yes. I must go. No reason to stay. Nothing that I can do here. Nobody who I can help."

Jacobson hoped profoundly that she could not, was not reading his mind, because panic was racing through it.

What he said now might not only be the difference between life and death for himself and his crew, but potentially also for thousands or *millions* of others. He hugely resented this burden, for which he felt utterly out of his depth.

"Karéin," offered Jacobson in as friendly a voice as possible, "*Why? Nobody* here, especially not *me*, wants you to leave us – *whatever* you can or can't do for us or for Earth. We just want to be friends with you, to learn from you, to *be* with you... that's all."

He paused and thought for a second, then mentioned, "You know, I have to confess, when I first found out that you stowed away on the *Eagle*, well, I was *pissed* –"

The far-away voice interrupted him, "I take it that 'pissed' means 'angry', Captain Sam Jacobson."

This was moderately encouraging; at least he got a response.

"Yeah, pretty much like that," he explained. "You see, I was – I am – completely unprepared for dealing with someone like you. You *look* like one of us... but you aren't. I *think* I know what I should say to get you to do something, but the truth is, I don't have a *clue*. Karéin, I'm a man who has always wanted to be in *charge,* to have everything down to the last detail, to leave nothing to chance, to give orders and expect to have them followed. I can't do that with *you*, and it scares and frustrates me, it really *does*, I'm telling you that honestly. Not just the fact that you have these weird powers that could be the end of us, at any time."

"Please do not fear me, I beg you of that, Commander Sam Jacobson," she replied, sounding of panic. "Indeed I *do* have the ability to destroy this ship, but hear me now – I swear on, all that is holy, that I will *never* threaten you again. I shamed myself by threatening to use my powers on a friend, still more by threatening your life, out of unjustified, impulsive anger. Please," – she was crying again – "*Please*, if you can find it in your heart to forgive me... *please*..."

The Storied Watcher let out an utterly pitiful moan.

It sounded as if she was in real physical pain.

Jacobson wondered what the hell she was *doing* to herself, but suppressed an urge to shine a light into the box and look inside.

Thinking quickly, he replied, "Of *course* I forgive you, Karéin; so do all the rest of us. That is, if you'll forgive *me* for my own stupidity. And just so you know, Karéin, despite what you may think, I'm not really that afraid of death and I don't think that the others are, either. After all, space travel – the way we humans do it – is inherently dangerous, already. All that has to happen is for *one* critical component of our ship to fail in a way that we can't repair, and, well, we might as well start writing our obituaries. Being ready for one's last day just kind of goes with the territory, up here."

He stopped and thought for a second, then, after a heavy breath, remarked, "But what we all never counted on when we left, is that *we* might be fine and our families down on Earth, might be all wiped out. For a few minutes, I let down my guard and started hoping – dreaming – that you might be able to save them for us. I shouldn't have got my hopes up, I guess."

He heard a low moan.

Jacobson looked away from the box opening and said, "But what I really *am* scared about, Karéin, is if you just get up and leave, I'll be responsible for that. I'll go down in history – that is, assuming that the human race will *have* a history, much past the present – as having made the most stupid, disastrous mistake of all time, of having antagonized the only alien who we have ever met, pardon the pun. That's a hell of a legacy... don't you think?"

"Do not blame yourself, sir, for having... as you say... 'pissed me off'," the Mars-girl said, with a sad chuckle. "No, it is not *that*, though your actions did not make things any better, I must admit."

Karéin-Mayréij paused for a second, then explained, "You say that I do not care, about your planet and the ones you love. That is not true, Captain Sam Jacobson. I *do* care... I care far too much. My body makes me sick, not only out of the shame of having stupidly broken my most sacred vow and having threatened you, but also from the guilt of not being able to help. I was awakened with this purpose, which I cannot fulfill, so I have to watch as my new home, my friends, those who I wanted to love, serve and protect, will be destroyed. Maybe including you and the others – who I have come to think of as my new family. I will be tortured by this, for many of your lifetimes. Still the more, because I have failed in this way, in the past. The memories come back to taunt me."

She groaned as if sustaining a body-blow. "I know that through your eyes, this burden seems small, compared to the likely loss of those whom you love. All I can do is beg you to *believe* me, to accept that my pain is *real*. How can I *explain*, how can I make you *know*, how it *feels*. Your language has no words."

"Karéin," answered Jacobson, as gently as he could muster the ability to do, "I *do* believe you, now. I know I said differently back in the *Infinity*, but, well, apart from the fact that I blew it there, big-time, I reacted to you as I would have to a human who said what you did. Since you look *so* much like us – except maybe for the teeth – it's hard for us humans to keep in mind that you're *different*, that we can't judge you by human standards."

Sounding every so slightly more relaxed, she spoke, "But perhaps you *should* judge me, Captain Sam Jacobson. That would save me from having to judge, and punish, myself."

The alien-girl stopped for a second, then added, "And there is something *else* that makes me say this. Another thing you do not know about me."

"Yes?" he asked.

"It is like this," she stated. "Do you remember how, when I awoke from my long sleep, I drained you of some of your life-force?"

"How could I ever *forget*," he ruefully acknowledged.

"I told you that this was to give my body the nourishment it needed to bring me back to consciousness, and in that, I told the truth. But there is more," she admitted.

"More?" he asked.

At least I've got her talking, he thought, not caring if she could hear.

Slowly, Karéin-Mayréij explained, "In my many past awakenings – so many that I can no longer remember most of them – I have often come out of my sleep, only to confront beings that look and act much differently from those that I left behind, beforehand. So I have evolved a way of integrating me with these other species, of lessening the difference between myself and them. From the time that you first came into my presence and I felt your life-force, my body began to change, so I looked like a human; not only that, but part of my *mind* too, indeed, much of my entire being. With each passing day and hour, I become more and more like a human woman, and things like close personal contact with humans can speed up that process. So if you judge me as you would one of your own kind, I cannot contest you. It would not be honest for me to say that I should be exempt from your rules, your laws, because I am *Makailkh*."

Again, Jacobson was at a loss.

But he went on, "Karéin, like so much else about you, I'm afraid I don't follow you here. You mean you're changing, turning into... a human? What did you look like *before*?"

The Professor would kill to know, he thought to himself.

"'Following me'? But you *did* follow me in here, Captain Sam Jacobson...", she said in reply.

"No, that expression means, sort of, 'I don't understand'," he corrected.

"Ah," answered the Mars-girl. "No, not exactly, *part* of me is becoming like you, and that process cannot be changed back until I next go into my long sleep, but the other, greater part, will always remain what it was – what *I* am. As for what I was before now, I do not exactly recall, but I think that I have always been female and more or less like you, two arms, two legs, one head, two eyes and ears, one mouth, one nose. Oh, and also the sharp-teeth... whose venom would have killed you instantly, had I chosen to use them, back there. You have to understand, in lives dimly-remembered, I have sometimes awoken in very hostile settings, where I have had to defend myself almost from the very second when air would again fill my lungs. Though you may not have known the fullness of it, you were wise to fear me."

"Well, *that's* nice to know," prevaricated Jacobson. "That you chose not to bite me, I mean."

Certain basic things, I cannot change," she said with a morose chuckle, then continued, "Regardless, I am in the realm of human beings... I must obey you in command of this space-ship, sir, and I am subject to your rules. As well as my own. Which I broke, shamefully."

Again, she sounded on the verge of tears. "In my fury at my luck, I forgot that. But I am not sure that I can learn how to do what you say. Which is one reason that I want to go away."

Now was the time he had to ask. Or tell.

"Karéin, we want you to stay with us. I forgive your over-reaction. Will you *please* stay with us?" he pleaded, dreading the answer.

There was a long, long silence.

He held his breath, hoping, praying, though he was not a religious man.

Finally, she quietly responded, "What, then, will be my punishment?"

Jacobson desperately hoped that she could not see, or sense, the stupid grin and urge to hysterical laughter that suddenly overcame him, not just for apparently having achieved his goal, but more for the absurdity of him, an ordinary human being, being asked to mete out punishment to an eons-old, immensely powerful alien being that had undoubtedly seen many civilizations come and go.

"Uhh... that's a good question, Karéin," he stammered. "Well... here's what I want you to do. I think this is fair, considering that it's what the equivalent would have been on Earth. You will have to do fifty push-ups on the floor of the *Infinity*'s central living-area – "

"Please, sir, what is 'push-up'?" she interjected. She sounded a bit more composed now.

"Oh, I forgot, you might not know that," replied the mission commander. "It is a physical fitness exercise in which you lie face-down on the ground, keeping your legs straight, using your arms to raise your trunk and head as far up as you can, then relaxing them so you are on the ground again. It is quite physically exerting. And no using that special power of yours to negate our pseudo-gravity... you have to do it just with the muscles in your arms."

"Ah," she answered. "Oh-kay."

"And, you may not play chess with any crew-member, including against the computer, for one week, starting now," he added.

"You are most lenient, Captain Sam Jacobson," she quietly replied. "For threatening a superior, in other places I have been, I would have been made to suffer much physical pain, or I would have been put in tight restraints, in awkward positions, in a dark place, for long times. But I suppose such punishments are not practical here... *are* they?"

Idly, he started to wonder if this being had some kind of bizarre masochistic streak, but he quickly suppressed the thought in case she might be able to read it.

"Well Karéin," he said, making it up as he went, "We... uhh... don't *do* things that way, anymore. Although if you get the time to read our history-books, you will find that human beings haven't always been so enlightened. I think what I have suggested is reasonable, under the circumstances. Have you any objections?"

"No," answered the Storied Watcher, in a small voice. "I will stay and accept my punishment."

He saw a thin, almost delicate-looking female hand, extending unsteadily from the box. A huge weight of stress and concern lifted from him as he grasped it and helped her wobble to her feet.

He beheld the alien-girl, scarcely believing what he saw.

Only once or twice in his life, had he seen anything in such a pitiful state – maybe a dog that had been starved for a month or two, or a half-deflated balloon?

She was thin and pale, almost white, except for what appeared to be bruise-marks, on some of the unclothed parts of her body.

Her clothes and skin were streaked with sweat; her eyes, which had earlier shone like the brightest stars of the sky, looked dull and sullen.

Karéin-Mayréij was but a shadow of her former self.

"*My God*, Karéin," he exclaimed, "What on Earth have you done to yourself?"

Despite the lack of gravity, the Mars-girl contrived to sit down, half slumped-over, on a nearby box.

She weakly explained, "Nothing on Earth, Captain Sam Jacobson. I assume that is another of your expressions... *this* is what sometimes happens to me, when I abuse my powers. See me now, Karéin-Mayréij, the mighty Storied Watcher, Who Shatters Worlds, Vanquisher of Demon-Princes; weak enough for a child to defeat. I can barely stand up, even in this lack of gravity-force. Impressive, am I not?"

"Karéin, if I had ever *known*... I wouldn't... you look *terrible*, like death warmed... I mean, like you are very ill," apologized the Mars mission commander. "Surely this doesn't happen *every* time that you feel that you've done something wrong? I feel personally responsible for this. Is there anything that we can do to *help* you?"

"No... and no," she responded, taking time with every breath. "See – I am learning your slang," she said with a forced smile. "I do it to myself. But only *sometimes*. I do not know when or why. Maybe it is a curse, a punishment that I merited from something especially bad I did, long ago... that is what *I* believe, anyway. And all that you can do for me now, is to let me rest and regenerate my strength. It will come back quickly, because you have forgiven me. Had you not, I would have been like... like *this*, for much longer. One other reason, why I owe you a great debt, Captain Sam Jacobson."

The alien woman-child looked at him with wounded, vulnerable eyes.

Without a second thought, he flew over to her, sat – as much as one could – next to her, and held her trembling, sickly-looking body next to his.

Instantly, she put her head underneath his chin and closed her eyes. For a second, he worried that she might be trying to drain some of his life-force, as she had back on Mars, but the only feeling that came over him was relief, mixed with sympathy – or, was it love – for the strange, unique being that he was now holding close to his heart.

They stayed like this for a few uncounted minutes. Then the intercom sounded. It was the voice of Boyd.

"Captain," he inquired, "We haven't heard from you for ten minutes. Are you all right, down there?"

"Perfectly fine," Jacobson replied. "We're on our way back."

"We? Does that mean – " sounded Tanaka's voice.

"I'll explain when I get there," reassured Jacobson. "But everything's under control."

Re-Acquainting

Cradling Karéin-Mayréij in his arms, the mentally- and physically-exhausted Mars mission commander floated out of the cargo bay, up the central access openings in the *Eagle*, through the inter-ship airlock (taking care to shut it behind him – just in case) and through *Infinity*'s center core passageway to the center drum access-hatch.

The alien-girl seemed to be asleep throughout the entire short trip, bringing back pleasant memories of having carried his own children off to bed, many times back on Earth.

Opening the hatch, Jacobson propelled himself forward, landing on his feet in the pseudo-gravity of the place.

Suddenly, she felt *heavy*, considerably more so than her frail-looking body would otherwise have suggested.

The others looked on in a mixture of astonishment and pity.

"J.H.C.," Boyd exclaimed, "From the visit that Sergei and I had, I knew she wasn't in good shape, but *man*... I had no *idea*... She seems so *small*, somehow."

White added, "Man o man, *this* thing's a goddess that was gonna to smash a comet... right? She looks like one of my kids with a bad case of the flu. Bet she couldn't smash a paper cup."

Tanaka chimed in, "Captain, unfortunately, Major White sounds like he's right. Seeing the state that she's in, I'm concerned, now. Is she sick? This may be the first symptoms of an illness of some sort, maybe contracted from us. I can't think of a therapy that we could use on her – "

Opening her eyes weakly, the Storied Watcher interrupted, "I am not ill, Professor, but thank you for your concern. I have just had a... bad *experience*, caused by my own stupidity. Captain Sam Jacobson can tell you all about it. But I will recover. I just need some time."

She looked up at him. "You can put me down, now, sir. I think that I can stand."

Jacobson obliged, gently lowering her to the drum's curving floor.

For a second, it looked like her legs would buckle, but she regained her balance and stumbled over to a nearby chair.

The Mars-girl sat down, head slightly slumped, staring blankly into space. Some of her color had returned, but she was still very pale.

Quickly, Tanaka moved to sit next to her.

"Karéin," rapidly interrogated the scientist, "Are you *sure* you're okay? If you were a human I'd say that you were suffering for a severe case of one of our infectious diseases, the flu or cholera, for example. Is there *anything* we can do to help you?"

Slowly, Karéin-Mayréij lifted her head and said, "Yes, Professor Cherie Tanaka. You can get me something to eat and something warm to drink. If that is not too much to ask, from someone as foolish as myself."

Nonplussed, Tanaka replied, "Certainly... but... a foo–, what did you say?"

She caught a disapproving glance from Jacobson and retreated, "None of our business, anyway, I suppose."

The scientist retrieved a cup of hot *ersatz* tea and a special dessert ration package from the mess-section dispenser and presented it to the Storied Watcher, who returned a look of gratitude, wolfing down the food and sipping the beverage enthusiastically.

"Karéin," uncertainly mentioned White, "Not sure this is the right time to ask, but... well, I guess what we're all wondering is, y'all still planning on flying off to parts unknown? We heard that y'all didn't want to hang out around here, much longer."

"Come here, Major Devon White. You too, Sayr-gayy," she responded, with a weak smile.

Gingerly, both White and Chkalov stepped near to her.

The Mars-girl explained, "I *was* planning on leaving... yes, that is true. But Captain Sam Jacobson convinced me not to. I will stay... *if*..."

"Yeah?" replied the African-American astronaut.

Taking White's hand in one of hers and Chkalov's in the other, looking up plaintively, she continued, "If you will *have* me, people of space-ships *Eagle* and *Infinity*."

A collective sigh of relief sounded from several of them.

Chkalov spoke up.

"Karéin," he said, "Of *course* you are welcome here, always. Our fear was not that you would stay, but that you would leave."

He grinned. "And I will even share my last ration of fine Russian soup with you, to prove that we are serious."

"And I promise not to do what I did before," she pledged. "That is why you see me, as I am now. It is what I deserved."

The Storied Watcher hid her eyes, then, with a half-smile, asked, "Is it *good* soup?"

Chkalov nodded and grinned again.

Boyd and Tanaka would both have inquired further, but for a gesture not to do so by Jacobson, who announced, "There'll be ample time later for me to explain what our guest means by this. Let me just say for the record that both she and I had things to apologize for, and so we did, down there. For now, though, I think we had better just make her comfortable and get back to our normal routine, team. I'm going to make my report to Houston, in a minute – Karéin, is there anything else you need?"

"No, sir," replied the alien-girl. "But... may I ask you, who is this 'Hoo-ston', Captain Sam Jacobson? I have heard you use his name often. Is he your king, your emperor, or someone like that?"

With a chuckle, the Mars mission commander explained, "Hah, not exactly, Karéin. Our political system is called a 'democracy', in which we rule ourselves – we don't have a king or anything like that, and Houston isn't a person, it's a *place* – specifically, the space-port on Earth from which we launched our spacecraft on this mission. Although, Houston *does* contain people to whom I make reports on what has been going on here – "

"Including about myself, sir?" she interrupted.

"Very definitely so," he affirmed. "But lately, they haven't been giving me, or us, a lot of direction on what to do with you, because they are understandably preoccupied with 'Lucifer', even more so since the failure of the *Salvador* mission. They have kind of put you in my care, as it were. If it's of any interest, I think they are still telling the rest of the people on Earth that you're still down there on Mars, but somehow away from the cameras we left."

"But I am *here*... why would they intentionally mislead their brothers and sisters about me, sir? Are they afraid of me?" inquired Karéin-Mayréij.

Jacobson motioned with both hands to say 'enough', then said, "No, I don't think so, Karéin... but as for their motives, and all the other stuff going on down there, I'll leave it to the Professor to bring you up to speed on that, if you don't mind. Okay?"

He turned to leave.

"Oh-kay," she said, with a polite smile.

"Yes, Captain, perhaps that *would* be best," commented Tanaka. "But Karéin – be aware that as a scientist, eventually I will need to know *exactly* what happened to you, down there. It's not just curiosity, I hope you understand that."

The Storied Watcher nodded, sipping on the tea.

"I will keep no secrets from you, or your people," pledged the alien-girl. "At least, none that will not hurt you to know. But I have something else to ask of you, Professor Cherie Tanaka, or perhaps of the others."

"Certainly, Karéin, anything," she replied. "What do you need?"

"Someone to watch me do fifty 'push-ups'," she requested.

Water Under The Bridge

Nonplussed, Tanaka, Boyd, White and Chkalov watched as the alien-girl laid face-down on the endlessly upward-curving floor of *Infinity*'s central drum.

In spite of her weakness and frailty and in spite of Tanaka's warnings about her physical condition, she insisted upon starting the push-up drill. She needed some help from Boyd and White, initially, in trying to get the exercise right, but as it wore on, she appeared to be getting stronger rather than weaker.

"Forty-seven... forty-eight... forty-nine... fifty...," counted off, as Karéin-Mayréij completed the last of the push-ups.

"I have the numbers right... do I not?" she asked, sitting up. "It is interesting that this is considered to be a punishment, on your world; it is refreshing, actually. It helps with blood-circulation."

"There are worse punishments," offered Boyd. "*Much* worse ones. And remember that the gravity we have here, such that it is, is a lot less than on Earth. Down there, you'd be heavy enough to make it considerably more strenuous."

"Perhaps so, Major Brent Boyd," replied Karéin-Mayréij. "But I am *used* to that kind of thing. I have been to places with a great deal of gravity, in the past, but it is not so bad if one knows how to bend it to one's own purposes. And so that this has been noted, I did not use my powers to assist me in performing this exercise... just my muscles."

"So *that* was what the Captain made you do to make amends," observed White. "Fifty, huh? Wish my drill instructors back at the Academy were *that* nice. I sorta remember more like five hundred..."

"Captain Sam Jacobson is indeed a reasonable man; I have myself endured far, far worse reprisals from those I have wronged, in the past," said the alien-girl, with a pensive look. "But that was not his *only* punishment."

She looked at Chkalov and said, "No chess-games for one week, either."

Tanaka broke out laughing, hysterically. She was immediately joined by Chkalov and White, who shook his head and muttered something incomprehensible.

Eventually Boyd said,

"Yes, that's true, Karéin, but just as a friendly piece of advice, when – if – you ever end up on Earth, don't expect *that* kind of treatment, when you threaten someone's life. They're a bit more strict, down there."

Miserably, she looked at the floor, as if to cry.

Boyd stammered, "Oh, I didn't mean it *that* way... come *on*, let's forget it. Here," he said, as he grasped her arm and helped her to her feet.

"No offense taken," she answered. "It is just that you reminded me of how this situation started... how it was *my* fault."

"It was *nobody's* fault," interjected Tanaka. "Just a *misunderstanding*, that's all. The more time you spend with us humans, the more you'll learn that these things happen all the time, with us. What's important is to learn how to manage minor conflicts, hurt feelings and so on, to avoid them escalating into something more serious. And Brent is right – let's just forget it, shall we? Besides, you and I have much more important business to attend to. To start with..."

Karéin-Mayréij motioned with a waving finger.

"Peace, Professor Cherie Tanaka," she requested, "I would prefer just to be *alone* for a few hours, if that is acceptable to all of you. I need some time to regain my strength and vitality. And I would also like to use the com-pu-ter to learn some more about your 'Earth', while I am resting, since it is evident that there is still much about your people that I do not yet understand. I will come to you when I feel better, which should not be too long from now... oh-kay?"

"Why, of *course*," politely replied the science officer. "Now that you're staying with us... well, we should have adequate time to catch up on what we need to learn from each other. You'll call on me, then?"

"I will," answered the Mars-girl.

"It's settled, then," declared Boyd. "Here, Karéin – come with me to the computer-console, you – ahem – already know the way to get there. I'll show you some basic commands you can use to access NeoNet so that you can get the information you need."

"Thank you very much, Major Brent Boyd," pleasantly responded the Storied Watcher.

Her color had almost returned and she seemed much stronger, now.

"Sayr-gayy already showed me how to use your information-picture thing, but that was when I could neither speak your language nor read your writing," she said. "So I will go back over the information that I accessed earlier and see if I can... 'fill in the missing pieces', as you say. I will accompany you."

"I'll show you how it works," proposed Boyd, "But only for a few minutes... I'm beat. I'll be hitting the sack soon after I get you set up."

"'Hitting the'...*what*?" asked the Storied Watcher.

"It means, 'time for sleep'," explained Tanaka.

"Oh," sheepishly acknowledged the young-looking woman.

Then she and Boyd went off to the computer panel room together.

"That's already plenty 'nuff for one day, I'd say," suggested White to Tanaka, when the two had left.

"Any day in which you piss off a goddess, yet live to tell of it," replied the scientist, "I'd have to count, as a *good* day."

So How Are We Doing?

For the next four hours or so, the Storied Watcher sat by the computer display, feet up on a nearby chair, reviewing pages of information at dizzying speed. She seemed to read and comprehend the data much faster than could a normal human; all the more impressive, said Chkalov in a random visit, considering that she had just learned English – but Karéin-Mayréij corrected him, explaining that her mental joining with Boyd had given her the same innate knowledge of the language and script, that he had.

Finally, after a totally exhausted Tanaka went to bed, the alien-girl turned off the display and closed her eyes, with her arms crossed in front, sphinx-like.

After a full rest-cycle worth of time, the Storied Watcher awoke (if she *had*, indeed, been completely asleep, all the while) and made her way to the eating-area, finding Tanaka, Boyd and White clustered around the central table, discussing something or other.

"Hello, friends," she greeted. "I do not see Captain Sam Jacobson or Major Sergei Chkalov. Are they busy?"

"Sergei's checking out systems in the *Eagle* and the Captain's in his private quarters... I think he's communicatin' with someone back on Earth," replied Boyd. "Want me to call them here?"

"No, Major Brent Boyd," she demurred. "I really came here just to find Professor Cherie Tanaka, as I said that I would."

"Well, here I am," Tanaka replied. "I hear you've been working our computer overtime. Find out anything interesting?"

"Almost everything that I have been learning about your planet, has been very interesting," remarked Karéin-Mayréij. "Especially about Earth's scenery and its living things – your planet is very beautiful, Professor Cherie Tanaka – and about your art and music. Your people are very creative, and they have many wonderful melodies, some of which I have been singing along with, as I listened to them and learned about the other subjects. Singing makes me feel good and strengthens me, you see. Compared to a day ago, I think that I now have a far better understanding of your world... but there is a great deal to learn and I will have to spend much more time, doing this."

"I'm not sure I want to know the answer to this," asked Boyd, "But what do you think of our planet's current state of politics, that is, wars and so on? On the galactic scale, how are we doing, good, bad or indifferent?"

"That is a difficult question to answer, objectively, Major Brent Boyd," explained the Storied Watcher. "Not only because I do not remember a lot of the other civilizations that I would compare your world to, but also because I would have to judge the people of Earth by my own standards.. I have not come to judge, or rule, but to *serve*, as you recall. And another thing; I am reluctant to speak on this issue, because in other places I have been, those in power are not very tolerant. One can be imprisoned, or worse, for questioning the system of rulership."

"True," Boyd replied, with a knowing smile, "But you're dodging. Nobody here is going to get mad at you, for honestly telling us what you think of how we're governing ourselves. Consider it 'off the record', as we say."

The alien-girl stared at him for a second, as if assessing his honesty.

Then she commented, "I would have to state that your world is not the *worst*-ruled that I have ever seen, no, not at all... from what I have observed so far, all the kings and emperors of these 'nations' you have, *claim* to be ruling in the name of justice, fairness and good, whereas, I remember that I have, in other places, seen what happens when a king explicitly embraces *evil* – you do not want to *know* how bad *that* can get. Thus, in your histories, at least the part of these that I have so far read and understood, there seem to have been only one or two that have been this cruel. You have been lucky, so far, that no truly evil ruler has been able to win, in the end. When one does, it can be the end of a civilization."

Karéin-Mayréij had a far-away look as she continued, "But if I am to be honest with you, Major Brent Boyd... I am disturbed at how little effort that the richer of your people expend to help their brothers and sisters who have less. It is not *right* that beings live unhappily in poverty and hunger. Your species does not live for a long time, compared to mine; and in what time that you *do* have, you should be *happy*, you should be merry and enjoy life, you should be able to express yourselves, to wonder at and explore the heavens – not work all the time to 'buy' food and shelter. Your world is very productive; there should be enough for all, if it were to be allocated fairly. Those who have more, should be *ashamed* that they do not share. If a person has three loaves of bread and can only eat one... what loss is it to him or her, to give the other two to those who are hungry?"

"Amen to *that*," Tanaka quietly echoed. "The human race isn't perfect, Karéin. We'd be lying to pretend that we are. We have been struggling with the very issues that you mention, for centuries. We like to *think* that we're making progress, however painfully slowly; but sometimes, frankly, I wonder if we really are going forward at all."

Boyd nodded in the affirmative.

"Karéin," interjected White, "Mind if I ask you a question?"

"Not at all," she replied.

"Why do you always refer to us like, for example, 'Major Devon White'? It sounds kinda formal, at least to me," he said.

"Is that not the... *respectful* way to address you, Major... Major... Devon White?" uncertainly responded the Mars-girl. "I did not want to give anyone offense, and in some cultures, it is bad manners to be informal with someone who has not given you permission. In *one* such society, I dimly remember, one could be flogged or imprisoned for that – they had very long titles and thirty or so words for the pronoun that your Eng-lish calls 'you'... it was all too easy to use the wrong one..."

"Fascinating," stated Tanaka. "What else do you remember about this society? Where was it? How long ago were you there? What kind of beings – my *God*, I can hardly *believe* what I'm saying here... Devon, Brent, do you realize what she has just revealed? This is something that humans have wondered about for thousands of years, other civilizations on other planets..."

Smiling, the Storied Watcher said, "It is apparent that you and I will have much to discuss, Professor Cherie –"

"Just 'Cherie' or 'Professor' to you, Karéin," Tanaka interrupted. "Consider me to be on first-person speaking terms."

"Second that," added Boyd. "Call me Brent."

"Y'all already know *my* name, Karéin," added White. "'Hey you' will be fine."

They heard her laugh, an almost-bizarrely girlish giggle.

"That is wonderful, friends," she gushed. "I would assume that Sayrr-gayy would not mind being called by his – how you say – first name, either? But should I not still be formal with the Captain, out of respect for his rank?"

"Well, it couldn't hurt, I don't think," opined Boyd. "The Captain's actually pretty easy-going, but none of us – the Professor sometimes excepted – calls him 'Sam', so, yeah, you might want to stick to 'Captain', but you can leave out the other stuff."

"Very well," stated Karéin-Mayréij.

"By now, you must know that I have some advanced abilities concerned with being able to integrate into cultures, such as yours, that are new to me," she commented, "Including the fact that my body and mind, from the first time I encountered humans, have been slowly transforming so that I look, think and *act* like you, but learning the fine points of interacting with new societies is always tricky –"

"Say *whaat*?" exclaimed White. "You mean, like a chameleon?"

"A what... oh, wait a minute, I read about those on your com-pu-ter, it is an small animal that can change its coloration, correct?" she asked.

"Exactly," confirmed Tanaka, "But this is completely *new* to us... tell us all about it! Oh, wait – we were on the other, long-gone society... there is just *so* much to discuss, I don't know where to start..."

"I have already explained as much as I can to the Captain," replied Karéin-Mayréij, "So you can find out the details from him, later. But regarding your original question, I am afraid that there is not much to tell, not much that I remember right now, although sometimes my memories come back in more clarity, later. You must understand that I have only been awake for a relatively short time, since my last sleep, at least as I measure time."

"I gotta admit, she's got a *point* there," mentioned Boyd. "Considering how *old* you are, Karéin, everything that's happened since you woke up down on Mars, so far, must seem like the blink of an eye, to you."

"The blink of an... oh, I see, it must seem fleeting," answered the alien-girl. "The truth is, in a way, yes it *does*, but in another way, no. *One* part of me – the new, human-kind part, perceives time as you do; each second, minute and hour is as meaningful to me as it is to you. If it were otherwise, I could not interact with you at all. Although – and this is something that I have not had a reason to say to you, before now – I have a power that lets me perceive fractions of seconds as you would perceive minutes; sometimes this is useful when I must perform many actions in a very short space of time... but it is very stressful on my brain, I can do it only for short periods, no more than a few seconds at each instance, or my mind overloads, overheats, and I cannot stay conscious."

The Storied Watcher paused for a second and said, "But it is a greater power and it has not yet come back to me. Like *most* of my greater powers, unfortunately..."

She continued, "The *other*, much greater, more powerful part of me, my original, unchanging being, perceives time differently, but in a way that perhaps you can understand, anyway, on a smaller scale. For example, a year of Earth-time is the same absolute amount of time, to a grown human being, as it is to a newborn babe. The clock ticks at the same speed for both. But the adult has the perspective of remembering the many years passed by, of knowing that each hour or year is but a small part of the normal lifespan of a human being, whereas the baby is comparing each hour and second against only a few passed by before. It is like that for me, except that I perceive this aspect of time in *ages*, not in one human lifetime. I wish I could explain it better for you, friends, but that is difficult to do if you cannot experience it."

"Like trying to explain color to a blind man, I guess," offered Boyd.

"Yes, or like me trying to explain to you what the colors above violet or below red, look like," remarked the alien-girl. "All I can really say is, that they look *different*."

"Completely weird," Boyd said back. "Since I was... inside your head, I have known your language's names for them – *Um'b'as'ài* and *Um'nàhr'é* – and I somehow know what these names refer to; I can't quite picture these colors in my mind, but it feels like I *almost* can... like, if I squint my eyes..."

"What I wouldn't *give* to be able to see the world through your eyes, Karéin," sighed Tanaka. "In the short time that you have been with us, you have opened doors that would have taken us thousands of years, to even guess were there."

"Perhaps, someday, you *will* see through my eyes," the Mars-girl replied. "Brent did, for a short while – and maybe the knowledge that he obtained during that time will help him to see things, to *know* things, that he could not, before. But I am afraid that I will have to know much more about how your human minds work, before I can safely try *that* experiment again. Things went, ah... how do you say, 'out of hand'..."

"You can say *that* again," ruefully commented Boyd. "It was hours ago, but I still need painkillers to think straight."

"Sorry," she sympathetically answered. "But at least you can take your drugs, to lessen the pain. My body usually neutralizes such foreign substances, so I must put up with the after-affects... although these are not as bad as what I have recently suffered..."

Hello, Earth

Jacobson's face peered around what amounted to a corner, in the *Infinity's* curved living-spaces.

"Sorry to interrupt, folks, but we have been asked to make a joint report to Houston, and they're going to be on in a minute or two," he advised.

"A 'report', Captain Jacobson, sir?" asked Karéin-Mayréij. "That is like a story which you tell to your masters, correct? If I have to tell them all that I know, we will be talking to them for a *very* long time."

Smiling mildly, he replied, "No, Karéin, I don't think you'll have to do that, not *this* time, at least. Just introduce yourself, then try to answer any questions they ask, as honestly and completely as you can."

The Mars mission commander paused a second and then added, half-shaking his head, "Man, this is going to be *another* one for the history-books, isn't it? I mean, we left Earth with a crew of five... now we have a crew of *six*, including an alien, reporting back. Not something they counted on when we lifted off... I'll bet you good money on *that*."

"Captain Jacobson, sir, I have another question," interjected the alien-girl.

"Yes?" he said.

"Who are the people to whom I will be talking? How should I address them? Should I bow down before them? I do not want to give any offense," she asked.

"Well, Karéin," offered Jacobson, "I doubt you'll be offending anyone, at least once the initial shock of simply *seeing* you here with us, wears off on them. But since you asked, the person to whom I give my reports is named Hector Ramirez; you may also run into Fred McPherson, Sylvia Abruzzio and a military man by the name of Jack Symington. You'll find them reasonably easy to get along with. You don't have to perform any special gestures, at least not in *our* culture, and if you get into any trouble, the Professor and I will help you out. Oh, and remember, there's about a ten-minute delay in between the time that we say anything, and the time when they receive it. Ready?"

"I... uhh... how do you say in Eng-lish, 'guess so'," uncertainly replied the Storied Watcher.

The red video-link "on" indicator light appeared.

The face of Hector Ramirez showed up on a screen halfway up the inside wall of the *Infinity*.

"Greetings, *Eagle* and *Infinity*," started Ramirez, in his lightly-accented Tex-Mex version of English. "The purpose of this transmission is to bring you up to date on what has been happening down here, as well as to allow the entire crew to give us any comments or suggestions that you may be thinking about. As you know, we have been communicating on a regular basis with Captain Jacobson – hi there, Sam, I hope all is well with you – but we want to periodically talk to the rest of the crew, also."

Stopping for a second, Ramirez then said, "By now, you're undoubtedly aware of the failure of the *Salvador* mission. I'd like to note, though, that, due to the heroic efforts of the crew of the Russian spacecraft, who gave their lives in fulfillment of their objective – the entire world observed a moment of silence, last Wednesday, in honor of their sacrifice, as well as of that of the NASA and European Union spacecraft – we've noticed perturbations in the trajectory of the Lucifer object; it seems to have started slowly rotating since the *Salvador Rossiya* set off their charges. Unfortunately, that doesn't leave Earth any better off, I'm afraid."

Ramirez continued, "Given these facts, we are now left with the second stage of our defenses, but even here, we are not very optimistic – I'll let General Symington fill you in on the details, but what I wanted to say is, Earth's governments are now concentrating on a massive effort, which we have named the *Arks* project, to evacuate a contingent of the human race to space, so they can avoid the effects of Lucifer's eventual impact. Here at NASA, we believe that by scraping up each and every space-capable launch vehicle at our disposal – everything from Shuttles to single-person capsules based on low-weight satellite boosters – we should be able to get at least 1,200 individuals into space by a few days before Lucifer gets here. The Russians and Europeans have similar objectives, the Chinese and a few other nations like Japan and India somewhat less."

The Earth-borne scientist concluded, "Now, as I'm saying this, I know you're all thinking, 'where are these people planning to *go*, when they get to Earth orbit', and I hope what I'm about to say next, doesn't shock you too much, but... well, you must understand, that we're in a position of *desperation* here, which calls for desperate measures."

At this point, the lean, almost gaunt but still attractive, Italian-American face of Sylvia Abruzzio, appeared on the screen.

She stated, "I'll explain what Hector means. The bottom line, *Eagle* and *Infinity*, is that we'll be lifting these people into space with the full knowledge – and this is something that all the candidates for the *Arks* mission will be fully aware of themselves, too – that most of them will not be returning to Earth, alive. We're still working out the details, as you might expect, given the diversity of launch-vehicles, crew payloads and launch-trajectories... but the plan is for as many as possible of the 'rescue flights', as we're calling them, to dock with ISS2, as well as with another space-station, ISS3, that we're almost ready to launch and start building now –"

Tanaka whispered to Jacobson, "This is *madness*, Sam... those stations were meant to handle three to ten secondary ships, not *thousands* – where the hell do they –"

Abruzzio continued, "And according to a pre-agreed protocol, the 'best and the brightest', as it were – that is, that small fraction of the refugees who, we have judged, will give the human race the best chance to repopulate the Earth, and who actually make it to either of the two space-stations, will be taken on-board ISS2 or ISS3, which will then be boosted into higher, safer orbits, along with enough re-entry vehicles to accommodate all of the selected refugees when we judge it safe to return to the planet."

She paused and said, "The rest of the *Arks* refugee ships will remain in low Earth orbit; they will have to take their chances, first with the near-Earth after-effects of the Lucifer impact and then with manually controlled re-entry, when and if it can be attempted. Of course, the plan applies only to the rescue capsules that *have* a re-entry capability; due to various technical factors, we have not been able to equip all the ships with enough shielding to make it back to Earth in one piece."

She again stopped talking, and then, looking directly at them, said, "We're well aware that this plan will inevitably result in the loss of most of the refugees, perhaps up to ninety-six per cent of them, according to our best guesses. I'm sure you can appreciate, as Hector earlier pointed out, that this is an act of desperation. If it's of any interest, every person who has enrolled in the refugee program is a volunteer. Considering what's likely to happen to those of us who remain on Earth... it's still the best game in town, I guess."

Karéin-Mayréij looked at the first face of the crew – it might have been Boyd's, or White's, there was no difference – then the next and the next.

Her mind felt waves of horror, mixed with depression and hopelessness.

"But," Abruzzio mentioned, "We may still not have to put this plan into action. I'll hand the floor over to General Symington, who can explain this."

Bedecked in medals and ribbons, Symington stated in a gravelly voice, "Greetings, Captain Jacobson and crew. General Jack Symington here, to bring you up to date on the status of our second stage defenses. I'm afraid that the news here isn't that great, although we're still not out of the game, as they say."

He continued, "We have launched a specially modified first volley of ICBMs at the Lucifer object, as a data-gathering exercise; these missiles were adapted for very long range, which of course came at the expense of payload, so we still have some hope that our real, final barrage will do better. But based on the observed results of these first impacts – if I recall correctly, we delivered a total of about 75 megatons to the object – other than for creating a large cloud of vaporized surface particles, our attack had only a minor effect on Lucifer's trajectory, much too little to stop it from eventually colliding with Earth."

"If these results," he went on, "Are substantially the same for our final barrage, while we will indeed influence *where* the object will impact on Earth, impact it will, unfortunately. The problem is partly," – he almost shot a glance at Abruzzio, off-screen – "that due to the 'Arks' project that Ms. Abruzzio informed you of earlier, we do not have access to all the launch-vehicles that would otherwise be capable of carrying a high-yield nuclear warhead; we are basically limited to military missiles only. Some of us, as you might imagine, have advocated that the allocation of resources be otherwise than it is today."

"The long bomb versus trying for the next down at fourth and fifteen," commented Boyd, not caring who heard.

"What is the 'next down' –" whispered the alien-girl, until Jacobson made the "shh" symbol with his finger.

Symington demanded, "But in the context of the *Arks* refugee mission, *Eagle* and *Infinity*, I have an order to give you now – this is the *real* reason that we wanted your entire crew to be present, when we explained this to you. Before I tell you what it is, you should be aware that it comes directly from the President – Mr. McPherson can provide verification of that, if you need it. The intent of this mission is to boost the two space-stations – the existing one and the new one – into a very high orbit, far past the Moon, actually, so as to be out of the danger-zone when the Lucifer object gets to the Earth. When this occurs, we will need all the environmental reserves, mainly air and water of course, that we can get, for these stations."

He cleared his throat, then stated, "This being the case, it's the order of NASA and the President that the *Eagle and Infinity* spacecraft fire its engines so as to *rendez-vous* with ISS2 – I believe it's ISS2 and not the other station, but don't quote me on that, just yet – at a time and space co-ordinate that we are now sending you via computer-link. You will travel as fast as possible to that location, then decelerate and remain there until, God willing, you are joined by the space-station and its attendant vehicles; after that, you will follow the instructions of the commander of the station, regarding surrender and disposition of personnel and environmental resources. I'm aware of how this must sound, so I'll give you a minute or two, then I will resume what I have to say."

Frozen, Tanaka said out loud, staring straight ahead, "I think you all know what that *means*... don't you, everyone?"

Jacobson made a motion and White turned off the up-link feed.

"What is *that*, Cherie?" worriedly asked Karéin-Mayréij.

Quietly, Boyd explained, "They intend for us to hand over the *Eagle* and *Infinity* to the space-station and to anyone that the *Ark* project hand-picked, to be a survivor. Then... we... *leave*."

"Uhh... I do not understand, Brent," she replied. "*I* can leave, because I can use my powers to survive in space. But your species cannot... you could use your 'space-suits', as you call them, but where would you go? I think they do not have a lot of air-supply in them... is that not correct?"

"Karéin," wearily answered Jacobson, "I'm afraid you're missing the point. We, don't go *anywhere*. Not *alive*, anyway. They may not even let us use the air in the space-suits. They might need it in the station, for the ones that are going to travel back to Earth."

The alien-girl looked at him with wide, unbelieving eyes, then stared at the floor for a second or two.

"I do not know what to *say*," she muttered. "First your planet... now, *you*. Fortune does not smile on you, friends. Or on me. I cannot *believe* that your people would ask this of you. It is against all the laws of life and justice that I have ever known of."

"I wonder how they'll do it," dejectedly commented White. "A pill, maybe? Or just 'bye-bye' and out the airlock? Can't leave our *corpus delictus* to stink up the station, after all..."

"I bet Karéin could help us on that front," opined Boyd.

"I can kill painlessly, if that is what you mean," she retorted, first sending a hurt look at Boyd for revealing painful memories, then deliberately looking away from the group. "It causes a massive overload of the thinking-parts of the brain; the victim's entire nervous system shuts down, instantly. It does not hurt at all... I *believe*. It requires the target to be asleep, or to be unwilling to resist, and requires me to touch you in the back of the neck, if you want to know how I do it, exactly. But I will *not* do it – no! Not to my friends! There *must* be another way. There *must!*"

She sounded on the verge of tears.

"What if the alternative was watching us die slowly and painfully?" persisted Jacobson. "If I gave you an order under those circumstances... would you do it then?"

"Sir, I know I have promised to obey you, but I could *never* –" she was going to respond, but White cut in, "Transmission resuming."

Jacobson added immediately, "Come to order, crew. Let's hear them out."

"This is Symington again, *Eagle* and *Infinity*," resumed the General. "By now you have had a short time to absorb the impact of our latest orders. I don't think I have to spell out their implications here... I trust and expect that as professionals, you will obey both the letter and spirit of these orders and do your duty, both to NASA and to the human race."

"But I'd also like to say," he offered, "That the outlook's not *entirely* bleak. You all still have the opportunity to volunteer for the *Ark* program, and since you are all trained astronauts or, Major Chkalov, cosmonauts – which is a skill with a *very* high priority under the selection criteria for the program – you would have at least a fighting chance of being accepted, allowing for the fact that we have quite a few astronauts down on Earth also competing for the same spaces."

"However –" he cleared his throat again, then said, "There *is* the fact that, as far as I'm aware, the upper age limit for anyone in the 'Ark' project is –" he looked at Abruzzio, who muttered something in the background, then Symington turned again to the camera, "Thirty-five for men and thirty for women; this is, of course, to ensure maximum fertility in that portion of our species which is eventually able to return to Earth."

"Thirty-eight here," commented Boyd, *sotto voce.*

He looked at the others, pressingly, while Symington droned on, saying something about the need for 'healthy, young individuals'.

"Thirty-two," absentmindedly stated Tanaka.

"Thirty-fifth birthday will be two weeks from Earth... don't bake me a cake, y'all hear?" added White, with a mordant laugh.

"Captain, Sergei... what about you two?" asked Boyd.

"Forty-six," said a stone-faced Jacobson.

"Thirty-three," remarked Chkalov, saying, "But somehow... I do not feel so lucky, Brent."

"I suppose that an age of three hundred thousand or so of your Earth-years, would place me over the limit... and I did not hear him say that the program is available to non-humans, anyway," mused the Storied Watcher.

White and a couple of the others laughed heartily.

The African-American astronaut added, "Hey, y'all got a good sense of humor there, Karéin! Y'all gonna tell us some more jokes, after all this is over with?"

Jacobson again motioned them to silence and they resumed listening to Symington, who concluded with, "To sum up, team, that's about all I have to say, today, until we hear your report, down here. Obviously, this hasn't been the easiest news to break to you, but remember that we still have hope; our secondary defenses *may* still stop Lucifer, and we are thinking of several other last-ditch things to try – I'll inform you of those, if and when they become reality."

He stopped to catch his breath, then said, "Well, it looks like none of the group down here has anything to add, so we'll turn the floor over to you. Captain Jacobson, awaiting your report."

"Ready, everyone?" inquired Jacobson, to universal nods.

White threw a switch and the up-link activated.

"This is Captain Sam Jacobson and the crew of the *Eagle* and *Infinity*, reporting," he announced. "And I will get right to the most important item, one which you have no doubt become aware of, as soon as you will have seen the video-feed that accompanies my words – namely, that we have a new crew-member on-board. I'll let her introduce herself. Karéin... here's your chance."

Nervously at first but with building confidence in every word, the alien-girl looked directly at the camera and said, "I am Karéin-Mayréij, the Storied Watcher of many ages and worlds, Houston and people of Earth. I bring you greetings and my love and concern, in these times of danger to your planet and your race. My friends here on the spaceships *Eagle* and *Infinity*, woke me up from a long sleep on the planet that you call 'Mars'. The name of my species, of which – as far as I know – I am the only one in this part of the cloud of stars, is *'Makailkh'*; I am like human beings in form, but rather unlike you in many other ways; for example, I am many of your centuries old. I still have much to learn about humans and Earth, but from what I know so far, I am sure that you are my kin, my dear younger brothers and sisters – and that your planet is meant to be my new home."

They all heard low, haunting, Celtic-rock music in their heads. A few of them wondered whether Earth could hear it, too.

She paused, looked down for a second, then looked up with shining eyes and said, in a loud, strong voice, "Brothers and sisters of Earth, I *will* help you if I can. Right now... I do not know how. But I pray that *somehow*, I will find a way."

She looked at Jacobson.

"Is that sufficient, sir?" she politely asked.

"Perfectly," confirmed Jacobson. "Now, Houston... I know you'll have a very long list of questions pertaining to Karéin's sudden appearance; I have answered most of these in my written report, which will accompany this transmission. As you will no doubt be worried about health matters, though, I'm going to turn the mike over to Professor Tanaka, who will be able to explain that more fully. Cherie?"

"Thanks, Captain," replied Tanaka.

Smoothly and professionally, she explained, "Houston, this is Professor Cherie Tanaka here, with the science report from *Eagle* and *Infinity*. First off, I'd like to say that so far, neither we nor our new guest have suffered any ill-effects whatsoever from her close proximity to us, nor do we expect any later on. As Karéin mentioned, morphologically she looks very much like a young, Caucasian human woman, except for a few distinguishing characteristics," – the Mars-girl smiled and gave a fleeting glimpse of her fangs – "But physiologically, especially in terms of her internal organs and circulatory systems, she is *dramatically* different from us... so much so, in fact, that my own opinion is that there is zero chance of cross-species infection from her to us or *vice versa*."

Tanaka continued, "For example, you can see that Karéin's incisor-teeth are retractable and are considerably sharper than are our own. Also, she has some kind of bio-luminescent ability, which you have just seen in her eyes; this mostly manifests itself when she is... well, when she is using certain forms of energy. Kind of like, how the human body can act as an electrical conductor, but," Tanaka paused and cleared her throat, "A *bit* more powerful."

"Just a bit... like a firecracker is to an H-Bomb," White jokingly whispered to Boyd's rueful acknowledgment.

"But that's not the *most* important thing," remarked Tanaka. "In the very short time that Karéin has been with us, we have – well, there's just no other way to put this – we have gained an *unbelievable* amount of scientific and other knowledge from her. My written report will include a summary of this, but suffice it to say, Houston, that communicating with this being will advance the cause of human scientific knowledge more than any other single event since, perhaps, the invention of written language on Earth. I'm *serious* about this, Houston – it's no exaggeration. Karéin has a fantastically rich and sophisticated knowledge of the universe, including many things that humans have never even *dreamed* of –"

They heard a giggle, then the Mars-girl interjected, "You flatter me, Professor; to have lived as long as I have and *not* to have learned a few things... now *that* would be sad, would it not? Oh, sorry... I forgot that it was *your* turn..."

"Don't worry about it," pleasantly answered the scientist. "Anyway, Houston, as you can see, I'm *thrilled* to have Karéin along with us for the ride; every time I speak to her, I learn things that would otherwise take years, perhaps *lifetimes*, to understand. It's poignant, of course, that we have only encountered her at a time when as a species, there may not be much time left for us. But in whatever time I have left, I intend to pump her for every last ounce of knowledge I can get... and hope for the best. That's all I have to say, I guess."

Jacobson again spoke up.

"Houston," he said, "I'll leave it to you to ask our guest questions, in a minute, but first – Brent, Devon, Sergei – do any of you have anything that you'd like to say?"

Each looked at the other with a "you go first" regard, then, finally, White was the only one to speak up.

He remarked, "Hi there Houston, Hector and your team, this is Major Devon White, reporting. I... uhh... don't have a lot to add to what the Captain and the Professor had to say, but I just wanted to tell all of y'all down there that, except for one minor little incident," – he shot a quick glance at Jacobson, as the Mars-girl hid her face looking at the floor – "She has fit into our crew so well that I'd swear she's been here from the beginning. It's totally weird... I mean, when y'all consider that she's an *alien*, many thousands of years old, who we found in a coffin down on Mars. Despite this, or maybe because of it, I don't know, I – we – all feel very comfortable with her around. And one *other* thing, Houston."

The African-American astronaut paused.

"Go ahead, Major White," Jacobson evenly responded.

"I'm not sure how much sense this is going to make to you folks down on Earth," White stated, slowly and deliberately, "But I know that we, up here, we *believe* in her. If she says that she will do something... well, she *will*."

He had a far-off look in his eyes. "I guess what I'm tryin' to say is, 'we have *faith* in her', Houston. And that's all I have to tell y'all."

A little voice – perceived, not heard – sounded in his head. Somehow he knew it was from the alien-girl, speaking directly into his mind.

How can you say that, she sent to him, *When you should* know *that I am a fraud... that I run from danger?*

Startled, he would have said something back to her, but at the last moment he remembered that every word would be sent back to Houston.

"Okay, thanks for the comment, Major White," Jacobson said. "Last chance for anything else, from the other two? No? Very well then. Houston, that's the end of our first transmission. Awaiting your reply. Over."

As White turned off the "transmit" switch, he quipped, "Man, what I wouldn't *give* to see the look on their faces, right now."

"Probably more or less like what *we* looked like, when Sergei first found her in the cargo bay," Boyd observed. "But they'll get used to her, just like we did," he added.

"I hope that they *do*," commented Karéin-Mayréij. "You all here, on your spaceship, did not have a choice : I suspected that would be the case, when I decided to, how do you say, 'stow away'. Your fellow humans down on Earth, *do* have a choice. I hope that they accept me."

"I'm sure you won't have any trouble with that," agreed Tanaka. "But under the current circumstances, you may have some trouble getting their attention, for very long. Particularly since Sam and I were careful not to put too much about those special powers of yours, in the written reports we filed with them. We don't want to raise unrealistic expectations about you... do we?"

The alien-girl looked at her intently, not sure if the comment was meant to be interpreted just as a neutral statement, or as a kind of oblique insult.

The urge to mind-read to find out the truth was strong, but she overcame it.

Finally, she quietly replied, "No... we do not, Professor. I have shamed myself and terribly disappointed all of you, because I boasted, without knowing for sure if I could prove my claim. I have no intention of doing so, to your entire *planet*. Better that they should try to save themselves, however they can."

"Seems to me that y'all couldn't do much worse than them, even if y'all tried to," unhelpfully commented White. "Especially from the perspective of us 'expendable' space explorers, at least that's how *I* see it."

"I understand how you feel, Devon," offered Jacobson, "But it's not going to help the situation, to complain about it. We have our orders and I expect each and every one of us to carry them out."

"Captain, sir," White shot back, "Let's not shit each other about this, if y'all don't mind, sir? Houston is askin' us to commit *suicide*, to support this half-baked *Ark* scheme that they've got cooked up... y'all know that it's not the idea of *dyin'* that gets me, sir, especially when my folks back home are likely to get the same thing; what I can't handle is the idea of just being thrown out of the lifeboat. It just doesn't feel like the right way to *go*, man. Just not the right *way*."

"What *I* can't imagine," added Boyd, "Is who on ISS2, or maybe this new ISS3 thing, could give an order to do something like that. No responsible astronaut that I know of, would *ever* voluntarily sacrifice crew-members. It goes against every creed, every code of conduct, that we have. I know that I never would do it, not even if my own life were at stake."

"Da," interjected Chkalov. "In Russia, we know much about hard decisions. But Majors White and Boyd speak the truth here. No cosmonaut would order another to simply give up and die. We would give the affected person, a chance, maybe not a *good* one, but a chance. On the *Salvador Rossiya*, the crew – God rest their souls – all *decided* to sacrifice themselves. It was not decided *for* them, by someone down on Earth."

"Brent, Sergei," Tanaka commented in as detached a manner as she could, "That's true right now – but as they said... these are desperate times. People behave... *differently*, when their survival, not to say that of the whole species, may be at stake. And anyway... who says that it would be an *astronaut* in command of the station? Far more likely, some general or military guy, or a politician or two. I have no doubt that they'd give the order."

A palpable aura of gloom and guilt emanated from the Mars-girl, upon listening to this conversation. She tried to avoid looking them in the eyes, instead staring at the floor.

The others fell silent.

Eventually, after a few uncomfortable minutes, the "incoming transmission" light awoke.

They saw the face of McPherson, with the others clustered closely around her, obviously trying to get as close a look at the Storied Watcher, as possible.

"This is Fred McPherson, Chief Internal White House Technical Adviser, speaking on behalf of the President of the United States of America, who, just for your guest's information, is the primary political leader on our planet," he said. "I'd like to address my comments to 'Karéin', as you call her. First, Karéin, Earth and its many diverse nations and peoples welcome you. We are *amazed* and *very* excited to be able to communicate with you – as Professor Tanaka has said, your awakening and subsequent interactions with us have been some of the most important events in human scientific history. Personally – and I'm sure that I speak for everyone else here, too – I just find it *incredible* that I'm having the opportunity to speak with an intelligent alien being, in my own lifetime. I have to tell you, I never thought that I'd see this day."

He continued, "Unfortunately, as, evidently, you already know, our species is currently faced with an extinction-level crisis, specifically the imminent impact on our planet of the 'Lucifer' object. No doubt the *Eagle and Infinity* crew, in this respect, share our frustration at the possibility that now, on the cusp of one of the most important chances in human history, for us to advance our understanding of the universe – that is, our newly-found ability to converse with yourself – we face the very real prospect of not being left alive to learn anything at all. There are two reasons why I mention this fact now. One is just so you know that nearly *all* of our scientific and technical resources are being devoted to finding a solution to this crisis, so if we do not seem very responsive, it's not for lack of interest in you... it's just that we are fighting for our lives."

Looking at the camera and view-screen, the alien-girl answered, softly and compassionately, "Yes, I *do* understand, people of Earth. Many times, have I seen beings struggle against fate, to claim the most basic dignity... that is, the right to exist. I hope and pray that your own efforts will be successful."

McPherson then said, "Our second reason for bringing the Lucifer situation to your attention, is more selfish : Karéin, this may be – well, it probably *is* – unfair to ask of you right now, because you are still learning about us, but if there is *anything* you can do to help, any knowledge that you have, I'm asking you, on behalf of both the President and the Secretary-General of the United Nations, and indeed of all the people of the Earth, *please* share it with us. From what I gather from Professor Tanaka's reports, as well as from what she just said now, you have considerable insight into aspects of the universe that we haven't yet explored. Maybe some of your knowledge might come in handy, in our battle against the comet. We would be eternally grateful if you could help us, in however small a way."

As he went on talking, with glowing eyes, Karéin-Mayréij said back, "You have my word on that, sir. I *swear* it."

McPherson concluded by saying, "In the meantime, please co-operate with Professor Tanaka, as she asks you for other information related to your background, your history and so on. Should Earth make it through the present crisis, what you can tell us will be of great scientific and historical importance. You will be *well* rewarded for helping us with this. Well... that's all I have to say right now, but be of no doubt, Karéin, I'm looking forward to talking with you much more, later on. I'll turn the floor over to Sylvia, now. Sylvia, go ahead."

The Mars-girl wryly remarked, "Ah yes... a *reward*. Nice food, money, a comfortable bed to sleep on, servants to attend to my needs, perhaps? I have had to work *much* harder for such things, at other times, in other places."

"I wouldn't get your hopes up," interjected White. "The way things are going, y'all might not have a lot to spend your cash on."

She nodded, as Abruzzio spoke up.

"Karéin of Mars, this is Sylvia Abruzzio, I'm the Chief Technical Team Leader down here on Earth for the *Eagle and Infinity* mission, of which, I guess, you're now a part. All I can do here, to start, is to echo Fred's sense of wonder at just *seeing* you," she gushed. "Knowing that you're here with us, being able to *speak* with you... well, it's more than any scientist on Earth could ever hope for. I hope you understand how thrilled and amazed we are."

The alien-girl smiled modestly and reflexively gave the curtsy they had seen on Mars; and as she did, she mused,

Voices... what do ye say? This woman, Sylvia... she is destined for greatness? How it may be, is beyond my knowing... but thus shall it be... this do I pray.

Abruzzio went on, "I'll be brief, because we'll be communicating with each other extensively in the near future; but I *do* have a few questions that I just can't have wait until then, so I hope you don't mind if I ask you for answers to them, right now. First, exactly how *old* are you, as quantified in Earth years? Second, where are you from? That is, where were you born? Mars, or somewhere else? And third... what, exactly, does the term 'Storied Watcher' mean? I take it that it's some kind of title?"

She concluded, "Since we first saw you down there, I've wanted to ask you these types of questions, but as you no doubt have yourself noticed, your language and ours are significantly different, so we had to concentrate on basic communications, until you somehow – we're still not sure *how*, here on Earth – managed to learn to speak English. I'll hold the rest of our transmission, until you can respond. I can't *wait* until I hear back from you... Abruzzio out, for the moment."

The "incoming transmission" light went off.

"Might as well go ahead now, Karéin," Jacobson directed. "Your chance to get off on a good note with them."

"A 'good note', sir? That means to be friends, right?" asked the young-looking woman.

"More or less, yeah," he replied.

White enabled the up-link switch.

"You're on," he announced.

Staring with determination at the screen and the camera, the alien-girl said, "Hello, Chief Technical Team Leader Sylvia Abruzzio, this is Karéin-Mayréij. I am pleased and honored to meet you and I welcome the opportunity to teach you and to learn *from* you, as well. I hope that fate will allow us to meet in person, some day soon."

The Storied Watcher explained, "I will try to answer your questions as briefly and completely as I can, but to start, I should tell you that there is much about myself that I do not remember, although I have only been awake a relatively short time. Sometimes these memories come back to me later, sometimes they do not – I do not know how or why."

She went on, "I will answer the last question, regarding my title, first. I am called the 'Storied Watcher' because, in past lives, people have told legends about me and the things that I am alleged to have done. I suppose that many of these are true, if perhaps exaggerated... but I am proud of the title. Please try to understand – it is one of the very few things that I can call my own, wherever I go; most everything else, must be left behind, or crumbles to dust, when I sleep. The term 'Watcher', incidentally, is as close as I could come in your language for the word '*Khul-Algrenàthu'* in my own *Makailkh;* it means, roughly, 'they who watch over the Gods'."

The others looked on, startled, at this.

White whispered, "'They watch over the Gods', huh. I wonder who watches over *them*."

A little voice said soundlessly in his head, *I heard that.*

And the answer is, 'you do, Devon'.

Not straying from her gaze, Karéin-Mayréij continued, "Now... as to where I come from. Those memories are the most dim ones that I have, but I *do* remember being a young female-child on an island kingdom, I remember coming of age... and making many mistakes..."

She hung her head for a second, then elaborated, "I think that world, I can almost remember its name but not quite, was probably where I was born. This was not *your* world, nor, I believe, any planet near here, either; it had two suns, one much like your own, and also another, smaller one that lit up the night sky, once every fifty or so of their years. This world's years were longer than your planet's, incidentally, but its level of technology was greatly less than that of your own, however they had certain... *other* abilities to compensate. They were humanoids, like yourselves, but not just ones that looked like you humans, others too, different sizes and colors... I remember going back there several times, after sleeping; along with a few other of my own kind, and some friends, I fought in some very big battles against a terrible, evil foe. I almost died... but I won, *that* I remember clearly."

The alien-girl stated, "It must have been many thousands of your years ago, because in between my time there and now, I have awoken at least six or seven times after the long sleeps – the most recent of which was, of course, the one from which Captain Jacobson and Professor Tanaka freed me. Unfortunately I do not remember how long each has been, but from what I can tell from the difference between what the outside looked like when I finally willed myself to sleep and now, it must have been quite a long time. Much of *Mailànkh* – the planet you call 'Mars' – was mostly still green when I went to sleep and its air was thicker, more like yours now. It was an unpleasant surprise to find it so dry and barren, with thin air, and it took my body some time to adapt to it, but it was, how you say, 'oh-kay'."

Tanaka interrupted, "Sylvia, if this is of any interest, assuming that Karéin is at least as old as the artifacts with which we found her, we estimate her age to be over three hundred thousand Earth years."

"Yes, that is probably right," said the alien-girl, "But you must remember that when I sleep, I do not age as you do. In fact, I do not age past my current state of physical maturity while awake, either, so in that sense I think you would call me 'immortal'... but I can very *definitely* die from violence or mishap... so I am very careful, when I am alive."

Karéin-Mayréij gave a rueful laugh.

Then she mentioned, "When I sleep, the many years pass by, as would a few days of deep sleep, for yourselves. Sort of. I dream, but slowly. The experience is very hard to describe, in your language. I hope that I have provided some of the information you wanted to know, Chief Technical Team Leader Sylvia Abruzzio. Like Cherie Tanaka here on the space-ship, you and Hector Ramirez are people who have devoted their lives to the learning and knowing of things; behold, therefore, how much you and I have in common, for this is also a love that I have carried through the ages. I *so* much want to be your friend... I will send more information as my memories return. I will now wait for your next appearance on our com-pu-ter screen."

White turned the link off, saying, "It'll be a few minutes until they get back to us, given how far away they are".

"*Fascinating*," offered Tanaka. "Like everything else, this is information of *historic* importance. Karéin, I know your memory isn't what it should be right now, but do you think there's a chance that at some point, you might remember where your home-world, or any of the other places you have gone, are located in the galaxy? If we knew that, we could send them radio messages... eventually maybe even communicate with them. You could be the key that unlocks the whole thing."

"Or the key that unlocks Pandora's Box," retorted Boyd. "I've *seen* some of these places, in my head. The less they know about us, the better, in my opinion."

"Pandora's Box? That is a *bad* thing, is it not?" asked the Mars-girl.

"In one of our legends, Karéin," Jacobson explained, "It was a box containing all the bad things – evil spirits, goblins, ill feelings and so on – owned by a girl named 'Pandora'. She couldn't resist peeking inside it, and when she opened the box, all these things escaped, to plague mankind forever after. Although the spirit named 'Hope' also got out, which was the one good thing about the whole episode."

"Ah," acknowledged the Storied Watcher. "As Brent says, that legend certainly seems like an appropriate warning, for several of the places where I have been. Curiosity can be dangerous – my own has nearly been my undoing several times – but I know that I can never stop being inquisitive; I suspect that the same is true of your species, Captain. If I knew where these dark places now are, or how to get to them, I would *not* tell you... I love you too much to let you bring that kind of a risk upon yourselves."

"But apart from the fact that I might, just *might*, be able to remember one or two of my former homes, later, Professor," she explained, "Consider the complexity and difficulty of what you are asking of me. Some of these places may not even be within your planet's plane of existence – that is, its 'dimension', to use the closest word that your language has for this concept – and of those that are, they would have drifted far from where they were, when I knew them. Considering the amount of time that has passed since those times, the civilizations in those places have probably either evolved into forms that even I am not familiar with... or, perhaps, they have already fallen victim to perils such as your planet now confronts. The chances of you getting a meaningful response to your radio transmissions, are likely *very* small. But I will try to remember, none the less. And I have other ways of calling out to my fellow-*Makailkh*, across the gulfs of space and time; here again, the chances are poor, but they are at least more than zero."

"Reply coming in from Houston," White announced. "Putting them on."

The screen lit up, this time with Symington in the foreground, with the others behind and to the sides of him.

"Greetings," he barked, in a polite-but-firm voice. "I have no intent of duplicating what the others have said, but for the record, let me say to the alien named 'Karéin-Mayréij', 'welcome to Earth' – we hope that you'll feel at home here and that you'll understand, we mean you no harm. It truly is an event of great significance that we have encountered you."

He went on, "Now, since your last transmission, actually a bit before it, Fred McPherson and I immediately communicated the news of your improved linguistic skills, to the President of the United States, who I would remind you is the leader of the Earth – "

"I would like to see him say *that* in Moscow, on May Day," Chkalov muttered.

Karéin-Mayréij said nothing, but she *did* arch an eyebrow in his direction.

Symington stated, "And, in that context, as well as in view of the fact that you have, please correct me if I'm wrong here, volunteered to be a member of Captain Jacobson's crew, the President has asked me to relay an ord – a special request, to you on his behalf. I'll be brief about this."

He continued, "As you know, the spaceship that you are currently inside, will shortly be making a course correction, so as to dock with the ISS2 space-station, which we will be sending into high orbit under Earth's *Ark* program. What we'd like you to do, Karéin, is just to stay with the *Eagle* and *Infinity*, until they arrive at ISS2, then go aboard the space-station and await further... directions, from us."

Symington added, "This all presumes, of course, that Professor Tanaka's assessment regarding the non-communicability of disease, between yourself and the rest of us humans, holds up for the rest of the trip that the *Infinity* and *Eagle* will be making towards the space-station. If a disease *does* develop, we ask you to report it to Captain Jacobson and us as soon as possible, so we can make other plans. I hope that these instructions are clear; please let me know if you need clarification on any point. And, Karéin, may I say, when and if we get past the 'Lucifer' situation, madam, I would like the privilege of being able to shake your hand, to meet you in person. But that must wait for later. Symington out."

The "incoming" light went out.

Immediately the Storied Watcher asked, "I do not fully *understand* – what is a 'madam'? He wants to shake my hand? In one place I went, people would greet another by rubbing their cheeks... is it like that?"

"Here, I'll show you," demonstrated Boyd, grasping her hand and giving it a business-like shake.

"That's what he means," he said. "And 'madam' is just like 'sir', but for a woman."

"And a few other things, it means, as well," joked White, with a smirk.

"Hmm... I like the embrace, at least," she commented.

Then, with a slight frown, Karéin-Mayréij inquired, "But Captain Jacobson... sir, do I have to obey his – this 'Symington's, orders, too? Is he your lord, or your war-commander? He says that he represents the king, the emperor, of your planet... but I thought that you had many *different* kingdoms, that in turn had a supreme council of some kind... the 'United Nations', yes, *that's* what it is, am I right?"

Jacobson replied, "Yeah... yeah, I guess you *do* have to, Karéin, since General Symington is what we call my 'superior officer', in fact he's *several* levels of rank higher than where I am – that is, within the army of my 'kingdom', the United States, as you call it. In your terminology, he would be my war-commander, more of less. All assuming, of course, that you choose to obey either, or neither, of us."

"I don't remember her volunteering for the U.S. Air Force, Sam," Tanaka shot back, with a hint of sarcasm. "I'd hate to think of her as our next secret weapon."

Chkalov vigorously nodded in agreement.

"Karéin," he warned, "The United States is definitely *not* the only 'kingdom' on Earth. Many others exist. You do *not* have to take orders from any one leader."

The alien-girl appeared to be absorbed in thought for a few seconds, then spoke to Jacobson, "I think that both you and Professor Tanaka are right, Captain Jacobson. I know you and trust you, but I have no way to tell if these other people are asking me to do good or bad things. So I will obey *you*, for as long as I am on this ship. If you tell me to obey the orders of this 'General Symington', then I will do that, to the best of my ability. Is that acceptable, sir?"

"It'll have to do, I suppose," replied Jacobson. "The bloody rule-book doesn't say anything about the chain of command, for super-powerful alien beings."

"Sam," interjected Tanaka, "We're talking around the *real* issue here, anyway. It's pretty obvious what their ultimate goal is – to get us to take her to ISS2, then they get rid of us, while they keep *her* for who knows what."

"Y'all got a *problem* with that, Professor?" cynically inquired White. "Maybe they'll try to breed her so that we get a better species of human being to repopulate the planet with."

"Major White," sharply remonstrated Jacobson, "That comment is *way* out of order."

White shrugged.

Karéin-Mayréij advised, "Do not be angry with him, Captain. If you knew some of the things that have been done to, and with, this soft body of mine..."

"Devon's got a point," commented Boyd. "It's completely consistent with their previous orders to us. I wouldn't be at all surprised if they're thinking about *exactly* that kind of thing. After all, up to now, when Cherie told them the facts, they didn't know how different she really *is* from us, despite what she looks like."

Looking at the Storied Watcher, Tanaka asked, "Well, how do *you* feel about it, Karéin? You realize, don't you, that you'll have to leave us to our... fate, when we arrive at the space-station? You're *comfortable* with that, and everything else they might demand of you, of course?"

"No," the Mars-girl answered, looking down, her long, straight, blond hair hiding her face, "I am *not* comfortable with that, Professor Tanaka. And it will *not* happen."

"There may not be a lot you can do to *stop* it," mentioned Boyd. "Orders *are* orders, after all."

"This may not mean very much to you, Major Boyd," parried the alien-girl, "But many times in my former lives, I made such promises – not really knowing how I would carry them out – and all of them... except one or two... have been fulfilled."

Karéin-Mayréij looked pensive.

"Except one or two," she observed, softly and guiltily.

"And," she added, "Though I *can*, indeed, mate with your species, in the mundane physical sense... I very much doubt that I could have offspring by a human man. My blood-chemistry and internal reproductive system are *far* different from yours. For all I know, I may be too old to have children, anyway. I think that I had a daughter and a son, once; but it is another dim memory, and I do not know where they are now. It is probably a foolish dream... but I still hope to meet them, one day, some day. *If*, they are yet alive."

The others thought they saw the trace of a tear in her eye.

Silently, they shared her loneliness.

Presently, Jacobson proposed, "Well, I guess you should say something back to the General, Karéin. Ready to talk to him?"

"Yes, sir, I... 'guess', as you say," she replied.

White threw the switch and she spoke.

"General General Jack Symington," she started, "This is Karéin-Mayréij, responding to your last message, sir. I understand what you ask of me. I am the guest of Captain Sam Jacobson and he has asked me to obey this order, that is, to go to the space-station with the *Eagle* and *Infinity* and then wait for further instructions. I might point out that right now, I have little choice but to do so, anyway – since I am – how do you say, 'stuck' on this space-ship. I hope that you and the other Generals of Earth approve of this course of action. That is all I have to say, sir. Karéin-Mayréij out."

As White cut the link, Boyd whispered to Tanaka, "Our guest has learned the first lesson in dealing with humans, that is, to be selective with the truth – she's anything *but* stuck here."

Tanaka grinned and nodded, whispering back, "Unlike us."

"I think that's enough for now," directed Jacobson. "Sergei, Brent, you two come with me, we have to go over plans for the course correction towards ISS2. Dismissed."

They all got up and went about their duties, practical or recreational.

Slightly Different From You

Night-time, or what served as it in the artificially-maintained environment of the spacecraft, came and went, with the alien-girl having been assigned new sleeping-quarters in a spare space within Tanaka's private area.

When she was tired enough to finally close her own eyes, the Professor noted that 'Karéin' was still awake and was busily reviewing information about the Earth on a computer terminal, with her curious up-and-down head motion, as she scanned each page of information at rapid-fire pace.

The Storied Watcher had donned a set of headphones – evidently, she had a strong interest in music – and Tanaka was interested to hear her softly singing or chanting, from time to time.

The voice of Karéin-Mayréij, at least that part of it which could be heard above the background drone of the ship's systems, was entrancing; it was occasionally in soprano but mostly in alto, though the tones seemed to mix in a way that would undoubtedly have needed more than one human *chanteuse* to accomplish.

Secretly, Tanaka wished that she could get her new companion to sing loudly enough to be properly recorded.

Evidently Karéin-Mayréij *did* require some amount of rest, because she was soundly asleep in the early pseudo-morning, when Tanaka herself awoke. The scientist did not have to wake the alien-girl, though, because the latter's eyes opened instantly when the Tanaka approached within about a meter or so.

Another one of those built-in defenses, mused the science officer.

The group had again congregated in the eating-area, with the usual grumbling by White and Boyd about the quality of the food.

"Hmm... well, it is more pleasing than what you gave me down on *Mailànkh*," the Mars-girl commented, amicably. "Lots of protein... I can detect that in it. But not very spicy or tasty."

"You're welcome *to* it," Boyd replied. "I was meaning to ask you about that, by the way. You really turned your nose up at my little gift, down there. Not what you were expecting, or was it just that you don't like Beef Stroganoff?"

"Beef – animal-flesh – *ugh*," retorted the Storied Watcher, puckering her nostrils. "I do not like eating animals; doing so is cruel to these lesser beings... at least that is my opinion. Every living thing, especially animals who are capable of thought – even if at a lower level than yours, or mine – has the right not to have its life ended, just because someone more powerful finds it more 'tasty' than other things. Especially, when there are alternatives easily available. I have few moral taboos... but that is one of them. However, on *Mailànkh* I was very hungry, so I could not be overly selective. I have had to eat animals many other times, too, when I have woken up. Many primitive societies think that by offering one this kind of meal, it is an honor, because meat is usually expensive. So I – how do you say – 'put up with it'. I become used to the taste... but I feel guilty when I do."

"Yeah," allowed White, "If *I* had been asleep for a few hundred thousand years, I wouldn't be too picky, either. As for me, well, I guess I'm just as primitive as these other places are – were – I can't wait for my next steak, down on Earth, when we get back there..."

His voice trailed off.

She shot him a glance that was both dismissive and sympathetic, all at once, and said, showing her fangs, "Easy to say, if you are the dominant species on your planet, Devon... but what if, say, someone like *me* found *you* to be tasty?"

She sardonically licked her lips.

"To Serve Man," maliciously interjected Boyd. "Num, num."

"Yeah, no *kiddin'*," echoed White. "Sure hope she didn't watch *that* particular episode."

"Well then, what *do* you normally like to eat, Karéin?" asked Tanaka.

"Vegetables, fruits, bread, and such," answered the Storied Watcher. "My body needs the same proteins that other living creatures do. And sweets, things with lots of sugar, especially. I like the taste and the chemicals in the sugar help me generate the *Fire*, too... sometimes enough for a lot of it, in fact. If my memory does not fail, I remember having escaped from imprisonment a few times when I was otherwise weak, just by eating something sweet that a kind prison-guard offered me. My *Gaze* burned through the bars. Munch, swallow, digest... *zap!*"

She gave an impish smirk.

"Must be hard keeping those teeth nice and sharp, if that's what you spend your time eating," commented Jacobson, slurping a cup of fake coffee.

"Not really, sir," explained Karéin-Mayréij. "I eliminate bacteria and other bad things from my mouth, just by making it really hot in there... like *this*," she said, as she opened her mouth.

A dull glow, accompanied by a burst of hot air like having opened an oven, issued forth.

"But I still prefer to 'brush my teeth', as you people describe this method of personal hygiene," she added. "Burning out the food particles that are left in there, can leave a bad taste... like eating charcoal. It also can stain the teeth, an ugly brown color. Then it takes *much* cleaning to fix."

"Breathes fire, too. What's next... naw, should have 'spected something like that," observed White, no longer surprised.

"Oh no, Devon," she replied, "*That* is not flame – want to see me *really* do it? This is quite a trick... I have to ignite the oxygen in my mouth with a very intense, brief burst of *Amaiish*. But you should not be directly in front of me, because –"

Motioning 'stop', Jacobson pleaded, "No, that's okay, Karéin, we'll just take your word for it."

The others smiled, at this.

"Well, everyone," continued the Mars mission commander, "Once we're finished with this meal and our other morning routines, we will have to get to the matter at hand, that is, heading for ISS2. Sergei, you got the trajectory calculations verified, yet? Brent, how are the engines looking?"

The Storied Watcher's glance started to switch rapidly back and forth to each man, speaking in turn.

"Affirmative, Captain," noted Chkalov. "I had Major Boyd check the figures, and I ran them through the computer, twice. The results were interesting. If nothing else happens, for example if they decide to modify the final position of the space-station, between now and when we arrive, we should have about thirty per cent residual fuel left, at the *rendez-vous* point. We would still have enough to reach Earth."

"Or to provide the thrust needed to push ISS2 back down there, without us to burden the load," dryly remarked White.

Chkalov did not reply.

Boyd spoke up.

"Engines are fine, Captain," he indicated. "I can confirm Sergei's fuel estimates – as a matter of fact I think he's being a bit conservative – because we have been consuming some of our supplies since we left Mars, and we could jettison the refuse we're now carrying to lighten us up, if we don't mind littering outer space, that is."

"Let's just eliminate as much as we can in the incinerators and chuck the rest," requested Jacobson. "Very well, then... I guess we're good to go. I'll set our tentative burn-time for twelve o'clock noon local time today – everyone, get prepared, lock down everything you see lying loose around here, follow the normal procedures otherwise. Any comments, or questions, team?"

"I suppose it's not a good time for a mutiny?" half-jested Tanaka.

"Yo! I vote 'yes'," chimed in White.

"Presumably that was a rhetorical comment, Cherie," replied Jacobson, evenly. "And it will be taken as such. *Look*, everyone... as has happened repeatedly on this trip, I'm not very happy with what we're about to do, about where we've been told to go, but those are the orders, and we have to execute them as best we can –"

"'Execute', that's certainly an appropriate way of putting it," Tanaka retorted. "But I know what you're saying, Sam. I'm just frustrated by all of it. This isn't how the mission was supposed to *end*. To say the least."

"Captain," added Boyd, "I don't think you have to worry about any of us not going along with this – after all, where else would we *go*, and we're not going to do anything insubordinate... but I think what's bothering a lot of us is, we don't have a plan for what to do when we get to ISS2. I mean, separately from whatever, if anything, NASA has in mind for us. If we don't have a plan for our own survival, it just takes them off the *hook*, they don't even have to say 'no'."

"Excuse me, Brent," the Mars-girl interjected, "But what does 'take them off the hook' mean?"

"It means, 'to escape someone from a responsibility that he or she would otherwise have to carry out, presumably an unpleasant one," Boyd explained.

"Yeah, Brent," Jacobson grunted, "I get your point, and I've been thinking about it, but... well, you tell *me*, what I'm supposed to come up with, here. I'm pretty sure that they are factoring all of *Eagle* and *Infinity's* resources into this *Ark* project of theirs. Leaving us with... well, we can't just get on a life raft and row away from the damn space-station, now *can* we? I'm afraid the logic is bleak, and relentless. If you can think of a plan, one that doesn't just say 'we're taking our ship and going home', to Houston... by all means inform us."

The alien-girl's eyes started eerily glowing.

"Maybe *I* could take you to somewhere safe, sir," she offered, to her nonplussed new friends.

"With all due respect, Karéin," Jacobson answered, as inoffensively as he could, "I seem to remember some earlier promises you made for us. I don't want to revisit that issue unnecessarily; but, just as an example, you wouldn't have anywhere to *take* us, would you? And how would you keep us alive, in space? That, uhh, '*Fire*', stuff? It works for you... but for *us*?"

Hanging her head, Karéin-Mayréij quietly replied, "I do not believe that it would, sir. It only works for me because my own – I do not know how exactly to say this in your language – 'flavor' of *Amaiish* is intimately attuned to my own body. I am sure that I could keep you safe from the vacuum of space, as well as from radiation, with my little 'bubble', and I can provide enough heat to offset the cold out there; but when the air runs out..."

She paused for a second, then continued, "I could *try* to use my *Amaiish* on your bodies as I do mine, but if you turn out not to be compatible, as I suspect, you might very will die painfully. It would be like having some of the air in your lungs, some of the blood in your veins, turned at once to electricity, because my *Amaiish* would revert to ordinary Earth heat- and particle-energy – your minds and bodies could not keep it in its native state or use it for sustenance. Somehow I remember having tried this, in the past. I do not think that I killed the being to whom I did this, because I always try just a little bit, at first... but recovering from it must have been a long and painful experience."

"My, Karéin," White commented, "Y'all sure have a lot of creative ways to kill people. If we all get through this, I'm sure there'll be *lots* of jobs for y'all down on Earth. Starting with the Air Force, or maybe the CIA."

He received an accusatory, upset look from the Mars-girl, who protested, "I cannot change who I am, Devon. No more than you can. Both of us can use our powers to hurt, or to help. *You* could use your hands to kill someone, by stopping them from breathing. *I* can use mine to do the same... just more easily, more quickly. It is only a matter of will, and degree."

"And she's leaving aside the fact," Boyd philosophically mentioned, "That the only other place that I can think of to go, would be the Moonbase, assuming, of course, that they haven't claimed *that* for the *Ark* project, as well."

"I think we can pretty much take it for granted that they *have*... they'd be remiss not to," said Tanaka. "Of course, we could just show up there and try to crash the party, as it were."

"What do we do if they just don't open the door," cynically remarked White. "Get her to open it *for* us, maybe?"

"Crash the... oh, do not worry about that one," mumbled the Storied Watcher. "Surely you would not have me endanger your fellow space-travelers, to enter this 'Moon-base'? But what about *Mailànkh*, friends? I could take you back there, and I would not have to use as much *Amaiish* on you, to substitute for the missing oxygen... and I could use my bubble to keep the pressure up... you would be welcome in my home there. I know that it is dirty and plain, but..."

She looked anxiously at each of them for approval.

"An interesting idea," observed Jacobson, wagging a finger. "And thanks very much for the invite, Karéin. Someday, if I'm still alive, I intend to take you up on it... in a nice, warm, well-supplied space-suit, that is. But you forget that we're a considerable distance from Mars now; even if you took us at maximum speed, we'd be out of air *long* before we got there... am I right about that, Sergei?"

Chkalov reluctantly nodded.

"And your plan would still involve us getting – how would you say this – 'lit up' with that weird energy of yours, only in lesser amounts... right?" pressed Jacobson. "I don't think I like the sound of that... just sounds like a slower way to go, no offense."

"I will travel faster, yes, *faster*, to take you there. Not as far as Earth, yet. And I could... I could try to vaporize some rocks on that world," the Storied Watcher stammered. "There is some oxygen in some of them... and water in *Mailànkh*'s polar regions, too... it might help... I could tunnel deep into the rock... more air pressure..."

She rested her head on her palms, elbows on the table.

"I think the phrase you're looking for here is, 'I give up'," gently consoled Tanaka.

"I *never* 'give up', Professor Cherie Tanaka," the alien-girl replied in a determined-but-frustrated tone, not looking up. "Not for the sake of my friends."

White was about to say something, but Jacobson motioned him to silence, saying, "Look, everyone, this is an interesting subject; we could talk it to death – pun not intended – but if we want to do that, we can do it *en route*. Right now, we've all got jobs to do, so let's get going with them, please. Are there any more questions?"

"Yes, sir," indicated Karéin-Mayréij.

"Go ahead," replied Jacobson.

"I would like to ask your permission to go outside the ship – that is, into space, for a short time. I understand that you have a device, an 'air lock', that enables someone to do this, without the air in here escaping... is that correct?" she requested.

"Well, I can't see an obvious reason to *stop* you... other than the fact that you had better be back in here by the time that we fire the engines," Jacobson allowed. "But *why*? What are you trying to accomplish?"

"As I believe that I mentioned some time earlier, sir," the Mars-girl explained, "There is far too little room in this ship for me to practice my skills at high-speed travel. If I go outside, I can experiment, try to push my limits – it is sort of like you, when you exercise your muscles – so perhaps I can go faster than we have calculated."

"Hmm," mused Jacobson, "I *guess* that would be okay, then; the thought of something going wrong here, really worries me, but in the end it's *your* life and *your* decision. Any objections from anyone else?"

"I have to admit being nervous at seeing you step out there without a space-suit, Karéin," commented Tanaka. "You look and sound so much like one of us humans, that it's hard for me – I'm betting, for the others, too – to keep in the back of my mind, that you're really *very* different. I guess I just have nightmare visions of you suffering the same fate that *we* would, if we were to try something like that."

With a half-smile, the Storied Watcher replied, "I do not blame you, Professor. If it is of any interest, what I am about to do, is normally attempted by only the most powerful and highly skilled of the *Makailkh*, who are called the *Khùl-Algrenàthi'i-Atailh*, in my language. As you correctly point out, the void is a very unforgiving environment... I do not remember how or when I first learned how to master it, but I *do* remember having been very scared at trying. Last night I read something on your com-pu-ter about 'taking the first step in, how do you say, 'bungee jumping'. I think that this is how I must have felt."

Chkalov grinned.

"Or like *my* first time, when learning how to use a parachute," he offered, "I am afraid of heights. But I did not tell the instructors that, because I wanted to be a cosmonaut."

They all laughed, then Jacobson said, "Very well then. Brent, Cherie, would you two help our guest with her little... excursion, please, oh and – make sure you get some recordings of it, just for posterity, and so that people don't say we were making it up. Karéin, I'll give you one hour out there, but please be back *promptly* after that, as we have to lock down the exterior entrances to the ship in preparation for our course change burn. Does everyone understand these orders?"

"Perfectly, sir," acknowledged the Mars-girl. "One hour of your time should be more than enough. As I mentioned, I can use the *Fire* for my body's needs out there; but I have not done so for a long time, so perhaps I should just try it for a short while, to begin with. I will knock on your outside air-lock door, when I am ready to come back in."

"Captain," requested Tanaka, "With your permission, I'd like to give Karéin one of our mobile tracking-devices to wear, when she goes out. It will give her the ability to find the direction to the ship, just by pointing it – Karéin, is that okay by you?"

The Storied Watcher nodded in the affirmative.

"As long as you understand that I speed up very quickly, Professor," she warned. "I do not want to damage this techno-thing, but I cannot let its presence stop me from trying to use my full powers. I should be able to locate your ship by its energy-signature, anyway, but having a backup is not a bad idea."

"We'll have to take that chance," Tanaka replied. "I'd say that it's well worth the risk. Sam?"

"Fine by me," Jacobson agreed. "Let me know how it goes."

They finished the last fragments of their meal, got up and got to work.

No Gear Necessary

Tanaka, Boyd and the alien-girl navigated through the zero-G of the *Infinity*'s central core access-shaft, to the maintenance and technical area at the end of the ship opposite to the end to which the *Eagle* was now docked.

"The airlock's in there," Boyd indicated. "There are two other sets of pressure doors in between here and there, just to be on the safe side. I'll open them."

One by one, he activated each set of doors with a private numeric code, combined with his fingerprint for biometric confirmation.

"I'll tell you a funny story," related the astronaut, while performing this process. "As you can see, I have to confirm each change in door status with my finger, since, supposedly, my fingerprint is unique to me and it can't be faked."

While he worked, Boyd continued, "So the story goes, NASA thought that this was the perfect system, so they implemented it for both ingress and egress, that's to say, both on the inside and the outside, for all the doors and hatches in this area of the ship, including those for the airlock itself – "

"But," interjected Karéin-Mayréij, "Unlike me, you cannot expose your bodies to the vacuum of the void... so, once outside –"

"*Precisely*," he chuckled. "One week before liftoff, NASA realized that if they left the system as it was designed and installed, we could get out, but we couldn't get back *in* again, because we didn't dare take off our gloves to work the bloody thing. Sort of like a roach-trap in reverse, I'd say."

"A 'roach-trap'? That must be, something to catch insects... correct? I read about these 'roaches' – apparently, they are very robust," observed the Storied Watcher.

"If Devon were here, I'm sure he'd have something smart to say about *that*, too," commented Tanaka. "But you got the idea, Karéin. Another great theory ruined by an inconvenient set of facts, as it were. One more to go – right, Brent?"

"Yeah... just a sec... okay, got it now," Boyd announced, as the last hatch opened, revealing a smallish chamber, capable of comfortably holding perhaps four people. "Here's where we get off, I'm afraid."

Turning to the alien-girl, he explained, "This is how it works... you wait in here, while we pump out the air and equalize the environment in the chamber to reflect what's outside. I'll do it gradually, so you have a chance to get used to it. As you can see, there's a view-port here on the door, and we have a video-display here at the inside control-panel with which we can see everything that's going on in there. So, if something goes wrong, if you don't want to go through with it, just wave your hands above your head and we'll abort the process and re-oxygenate the chamber. If you *do* want to continue, I'll disable the outside access locking mechanism, so all you have to do is move the handle on the opposite hatch. Understood?"

"Yes, perfectly," confirmed the Storied Watcher. "And if it is of any interest, I must admit to being a *little* nervous. After all, I have not tried this for many thousands of your years, if you are correct about my age. I hope that I remember how to do it," she said, with a wry grin.

"Well, if anything looks even *slightly* wrong, we'll make sure you can get back in here *tout de suite*," reassured Tanaka. "Oh, by the way, that's French – another one of our Earth languages – it means, 'right away'. And do you have your tracking-device? Oh, wait, now I see it."

"Why would you use a phrase from another language, if you are speaking Eng-lish, Professor? It seems strange..." the Mars-girl inquired.

"Can we have the linguistics class a bit later, folks?" impatiently demanded Boyd. "Remember, we're still on a countdown to a noon-time engine-burn."

"Yes... of course," complied the young-looking woman. She entered the chamber and motioned with her hand to request that the inside hatch be closed.

"*God*, Brent," Tanaka complained to Boyd, as the latter worked the airlock controls, "I know she *said* she'd be fine, but it still gives me the creeps. For all her differences, she's still basically flesh and blood... creatures like us – or *her* – were never *meant* to survive out there in a total vacuum. I keep having this stupid idea that it's some kind of a suicide plan on her part. I know it's irrational, but I'm *scared* for her."

"Not irrational at all," Boyd professionally answered, as he disabled the last fail-safe control. "Considering that it would be nearly instant death for any of us, and that we think of her as one of us. But she *isn't*, Professor – I can *personally* attest to that. Compared to some of the places *she* has been, I'm sure that outer space seems relatively benign."

He paused for a second, then stated, "Starting decompression. Equalizing temperature, fifteen degrees per second."

Tanaka peered through the view-port and observed the Mars-girl, who was holding a microphone as close as possible to her lips, as the air slowly whooshed out of the chamber. Her eyes were closed, as if she was concentrating.

"How do you feel, Karéin?" Tanaka asked nervously, over the intercom.

"Fine, Professor," replied the Storied Watcher. "It comes back to me, ah *yes*, it comes *back*," she hummed. The soundless music, this time a haunting, lilting melody, started to reverberate in their heads.

The alien-girl's eyes slowly opened. They were shining as brightly as any star or planet. Tanaka noted a dull, yellowish glow, silhouetting the Mars-girl's figure, as if she was standing in front of a bright light directly behind.

"Brent, what's the environment like, now?" asked the scientist.

"Pressure now twenty-five per cent of normal, temperature minus ninety-seven point nine. How's she doing?" he said.

"I can't *believe* it," Tanaka stammered. "She's not affected at all. She's... uhh... *glowing*. I'm sure you know what I mean."

"Yeah," he commented. "Devon rigged the sensors up to try to track that *Amaiish*-energy of hers, I'm reading the one in the chamber right now; whoa, right off the *scale*. We got no shielding for that stuff, but it didn't seem to affect us down on Mars, so I guess it's too late to ask her to turn it off now."

Turning to the intercom, he addressed the Mars-girl.

"Karéin," Boyd asked, "How's it going? Want us to stop? We'll only be able to talk for a few more seconds, until the air runs out."

"It feels... *cold*, dear Brent," came a faint voice. "But it is something to which I am accustomed... like immersing your hand in the air at night on *Mailànkh*, but much colder. I can definitely feel the difference in temperature – think of how you would tell cool water from really cold water... but it does not hurt. Same thing for really hot environments, too, but in the opposite way. I wish *so* much that you could experience this, yourself... it will be so easy to move, to fly wherever I want to... *thrilling...*"

Her voice trailed off, as the last of the air left the chamber.

The alien-girl was now in an almost-total vacuum, with the temperature fast approaching the terrible cold of the outside environment, a frigid void that would suck the very life from any human, in a trice.

They both looked through the port-hole, beholding the Storied Watcher, whose face wore a saturnine, regal smile. Her eyes were still shining, perhaps not so brightly now, but the glow around her body was stronger and flickering outbursts of energy jumped up and down her frame, encasing her in mimicry of the common symbol for atomic energy.

She stood in front of them, a proud and defiant alien queen, absolutely sure of herself.

The weirding music shot through their heads, deafening yet soundless, playing an eerily exciting tune that had their adrenaline flowing to the point of discomfort.

"Boy, I wish I could *talk* to her," offered Boyd. "But without a space-suit..."

They both heard – or felt – a voice in their heads, simultaneously.

I cannot talk to you with sound in the air, it explained, accompanied by an indescribable feeling of companionship and sympathy, *but I can still let you know that I am, oh-kay, this way, by speaking into your minds.*

I am going now, friends; I will be back, soon.

Someday, I want to show you how wonderful it is to do this – to fly anywhere with no walls, no boundaries, at the speed of lightening.

We will fly together. I promise *you that, Brent, Cherie. Someday."*

They saw the same flickering, almost transparent 'bubble' that they had seen earlier, form around her, as the Storied Watcher's mind – not her hand – threw the lever that opened the outside access-door, exposing her and the inside of the chamber to the full effects of the total vacuum of outer space.

Karéin-Mayréij turned to look at them one more time, giving them an enigmatically serene smile, then, she posed, with her fists in the air as if about to engage another in a boxing ring.

The music now roared even louder in their heads, rising to an enervating, exciting crescendo.

Then, in half the blink of an eye, she was gone, hurtling away from the *Infinity* at unbelievable speed.

The music faded quickly to nothing.

Tanaka knew that she had been looking at someone – *something* – far different from and intimidatingly superior to every man and woman born of the planet called Earth.

Yet this creature was now a close friend, someone who she laughed with, shared conversation with; it – *she* – made mistakes, had feelings, had a personality, had to guess at things, had to learn.

Years of scientific training hadn't prepared Tanaka for anything remotely like this – she felt like a laboratory rat, being asked to run experiments on a human.

Punching way above my weight, mused the scientist, as she absent-mindedly stared into the porthole.

The intercom crackled. "She off and about, yet?" inquired Jacobson.

"Affirmative," answered Boyd. "She shot out of here 'faster than a speeding bullet', to use the cliché," he added. "Didn't look like she got so much as a mild chill, from what's outside."

"Okay," responded Jacobson. "Major White, are you tracking her? Got any data, yet?"

"Wait a sec... yeah, got it, although the signal's fadin' in and fadin' out, as if she's testing something," White noted. "She seems to be circling the ship, as far as I can tell... but she's increasing the distance, each time... *whoa* Jack, that's *some* speed she's getting up there – over ten *thousand* kph so far, and it's increasing fast... the signal's becoming kinda faint... damn... lost it now."

Tanaka came over to the terminal in the airlock bay. "Devon, can you please pipe the results in here?" she requested. "Wait... okay, I see where they are now... accessing. *Wow*. She must have been running *hundreds* of equivalent Earth G-forces as she circled out there. How the hell wasn't she *squashed?*"

"Just another one we'll have to ask her in the debrief," Boyd commented, matter-of-factly. "Well, Professor, I suppose that's all we can do down here for the time being, until she gets back," he said. "If it's alright with you, I have some tests to run before we do the burn."

"Sure," she replied, "But I think I'll wait here, anyway."

"You sound like a mother waiting for her daughter to get home after her first date, Cherie," observed Jacobson, over the intercom.

"Funny," Tanaka replied, "That's sort of how I feel, too."

Flying In The Void

The one called "Karéin-Mayréij" had left the spaceship, circling it slowly – or, what was for *her*, slowly – at first, unsure of her abilities, unused as they were, for so many thousands of years.

But the knowledge of these is burned into the very *being* of the greater of the *Makailkh*, suchlike cannot ever be lost; so, with each passing, her confidence waxed as she exulted in the thrill of speed, this increasing dramatically with each circumnavigation of the *Infinity* and *Eagle*.

A mental message was broadcast outward, but not in the direction of the Jacobson ship.

My blessed, beloved war-companions of old, she communicated,

Stay ye with me, as we soar; though formless now ye be... soon enough, again, I shall give ye life, body, and mind...

The Storied Watcher could not tell precisely how fast she was going – there are no speedometers for a godling, no signposts in space with which to easily measure distance versus time – but her mind could still tell, just as a human being's inner ear provides one's sense of balance, that she was accelerating constantly, that her power of speed was now many times what it had been when she had been on *Mailànkh*.

She used her gravity-bending powers to offset the crushing centrifugal forces that came with her circular path, and to compensate for the acceleration itself, until finally she elected to shoot off into the void at a tangent from the Earth-ship.

The young-looking woman was now by herself, navigating the cold emptiness of space with only innate powers and knowledge to protect herself – a tiny, shining spark of intellect and energy in a frigid sea of darkness. No son or daughter of Earth, on any boat on any ocean, could be so alone, so far from help.

She flew outwards for perhaps three or four minutes, as the people of Earth measure time, then used her gravity-mastery to stop still, to anchor herself motionless in this particular place.

She closed her eyes and meditated, far from the noise echoing through atmospheres and the polluting confusion of other sentient minds, as she had countless other times in the past.

The mind of Karéin-Mayréij perceived the heavens wheeling around her, the energy and gravity waves from the stars, planets, moons and, yes, the 'Lucifer' thing, arrayed all in a magnificent display, at once chaotic, yet with an unknowable, inscrutable purpose.

No human, whatever his or her pretensions or eventual powers, would ever understand the majestic beauty of the universe at *this* level; not like *her*, the greatest of the *Makailkh*. She was at one with this firmament, asking, praying to, use the words that you like – the Great Spirit of the universe for guidance, for comfort, for power, but most of all, for *wisdom*.

The Great Spirit communicated with her as It does (or does not) with the millions of humans that call upon It every day, for affairs mundane and serious. But unlike the people of Earth, the Storied Watcher knew what to ask and how to interpret what she had felt, in return.

Though no sound was to be heard, yet her mind perceived the haunting, eerie, yet beautiful, echoes of the melody that had accompanied her, throughout ages uncounted.

Ye come to comfort me yet again, old friend, she mused.

Are ye a spirit, or just a blessing?

Always have I wondered, never have I pressed to know; for just the inward sound of thy gentle chords, this should be enough for the likes of me...

She left her contemplation strengthened, but still uncertain, still consumed by worry.

She rotated in all directions, using her visual and extra-sensory powers to get a sense of the surroundings, as much as this can be done in outer space. To human beings, the stars and planets are all just a set of twinkling lights, after all; but to *her*, they showed off a glorious, much richer display in the upper and lower wavelengths.

The Storied Watcher was easily able to see *Mailànkh* behind her, the blue-green home of the Earth people ahead of her, several of the other planets and the Earth spaceship, several thousand kilometers away in one direction.

Karéin-Mayréij fixed her gaze on the Earth-home and instantly perceived the barrage of electromagnetic chatter issuing from it. Instinctively filtering this out, she stared wonderingly at it for several long minutes, trying to feel the thoughts of the whole planet at once. This effort failed, as it often had before. But she *did* sense the thoughts of *some* of the humans, and what came across was a miasma of fear, combined with hopelessness.

A surge of responsibility and guilt welled up, as she looked at that blue jewel of a planet, millions of kilometers away, knowing that it contained billions of sapient lives, each of them unique and precious. She yearned to meet them, to communicate with them, to learn about them, to *be* with them.

To not be lonely, again. To not be... *alone.*

She *had* to save the beings on that world. But she did not know how.

The one called "Karéin-Mayréij" could move fast, yes, *very* fast; she could feel that power returning, quickly.

But to channel *that* much *Amaiish*, or the same amount of star-power? Enough to shatter an entire *sub-planet*? She had never dared try something on *this* scale, before. She had lifted cities, crushed mountains... but *this* was far, far more ambitious. What fit of insanity had lead her to boast about doing it? What had put the words in her head?

The near absolute-zero of outer space did not send a chill through her, but idea of attempting such a feat, *did*.

The Storied Watcher privately despaired.

It would be *suicide*.

Her little 'bubble', all that protected her from the dreadful environments through which she ordinarily flew, would overload, it would collapse, leaving only her body's native ability to absorb energy to save her. She would burn out from within, like an overloaded electron-flow wire.

Hopefully, when – if – this should come to pass, she would not suffer long; there would certainly not be much left to bury, if the humans were to honor her with that custom.

Once before, she had had *this* kind of opportunity, *this* kind of choice to make.

The Angel Brings Fire Book 1 : Angel of Mailànkh

Yes, Storied Watcher, she thought, *you could have tried it then, too. But instead, you flew away, you saved yourself, you fled. And we all know how that turned out, do we not?*

Her heart felt like lead, as she cringed at the cruel memories, pushed to the outskirts of her consciousness.

You promised the humans that you would try, an inner voice reminded her. *But if you do not, at least you will have Brent, Captain Jacobson, Cherie Tanaka, Devon and Sergei, you will still have them to keep you company; far easier to keep a few alive, than to risk your life to save the rest,* her alter ego responded.

And you will give them the Fire, added the unrequited, ethereal counselor. *It will light their long way back... will it not? Then – after a thousand times ten generations – perhaps their nobility, their greatness, will be close to your own; then they might look to you as a brother or sister... not as a god...*

She felt ashamed at the thoughts. But they were the rational way to look at the situation.

Again, Karéin-Mayréij fixed her senses, all of them, on the feeble signals of the *Infinity* and *Eagle*, as the two-ship group continued its maddeningly-slow journey towards, well, wherever Jacobson's masters bid it go.

She felt trapped by the pledges that she had made to the man. But she was resolved not to break them. She carried naught but faint memories and her integrity, or perhaps the pretension of it, throughout the eons. All else would crumble to dust.

Just this once, said a voice, *try to act like you did, when you were noble and daring, back on the oldest world, when you kept your promises and defeated the Dark One of the Shadowed Empire. When you were not afraid of everything, when you had not seen so many make one little mistake and perish thereby.*

Making a mental note of the position of the Earth spaceship, the Storied Watcher now set off on a tangent, flying towards Earth itself, faster, faster still, pushing the boundaries of her powers to the very limit.

Tiny grains of space-stuff, and the atoms of the solar wind, flashed brilliantly – she was far out and cared not about being detected, so she did not mask their appearance – as they impacted against her *Amaiish*-shield and released bursts of high-energy ionizing radiation that would have been instantly deadly to any other humanoid.

But the Storied Watcher, the greatest of the *Khul-Algrenàthu* – the senior sub-race of the *Makailkh*, the defenders of worlds across the continuum of space and time – was no *ordinary* humanoid. Neither mortal, nor deity, but something in between, a far higher stage in sapient evolution that the Earth-tongues had no real words to describe, she absorbed the essence of these dying grains of matter into her vast, other-dimensional pool of *Amaiish*, reinforcing her powers in a kind of superhuman feedback loop.

211

She thought of the man named Sergei Chkalov, who had told her, back on the Earth spaceship, of how good it was to feel the warming rays of a wood fire, on a cold Russian night. (Sergei's own body had felt good enough, at that, she remembered, fondly.) How much *better*, then, did it feel, being warmed by these nuclear emissions, thousands of times more potent, in the frigid wastes of space.

It was very sad that the humans would, probably, never experience it, or understand it.

On she sped, mentally estimating her relative velocity by how her body mass felt as if increasing with each second, wondering if the humans were close enough to hear the song, in their minds.

Even though the planet that the humans called Earth seemed only fractionally nearer, the alien-girl could tell that the flying-power had substantially returned; she was still not as fast as she *could* be, but she knew that she was far faster than she had been down on *Mailànkh*. Fast enough to travel in only a few hours between the planets of this system, at least the inner ones, for sure.

The Storied Watcher stopped, wheeled and searched again for the Earth-ship. Momentarily, panic seized her, as a first look revealed nothing – had she gone too far? She *could*, of course, just continue to the blue planet, but so doing would be an immediate betrayal of her new human family. She could not forgive herself... but, all of a sudden, the faint heat-signature of the Earth-ship revealed itself.

Happily now, she headed back, working up to nearly her highest speed for a few seconds, then gradually slowing down – no need for gravity wave disturbances, here – until she was traveling at no more than a few thousand Earth kilometers per hour, as she approached the *Infinity* and *Eagle*.

Her protective bubble shimmering in the dim outside surroundings of the Earth-ship, the alien-girl found the airlock door from which she had exited, collapsed her bubble until it merely enveloped her fore-body, extended a hand and rapped lightly, three times, on the outside hatch, soundlessly laughing to herself as she observed the redundant fingerprint access control system that Boyd had told her of earlier.

She could not resist the urge to press it herself, but was disappointed to see the status display strip beside the fingerprint reader merely display, "UNKNOWN BIOMETRIC – ACCESS DENIED".

Karéin-Mayréij knocked again, with slightly more force, broadcasting the thought, *I am back, friends, would you be kind enough to let me in? It is good to be home. Oh, and I suppose I should say the words... 'knock, knock'*.

After a few seconds, the hatch started to slowly open. As soon as enough of a space appeared to admit her, she slipped in and stood where she had been originally.

She saw the face of Tanaka, then that of Boyd, as well, through the porthole.

The outside hatch closed, after a few seconds more, and she smelled Earth's oxygen-rich air being pumped into the chamber. After the thin atmosphere of *Mailànkh*, this had felt uncomfortably, almost oppressively, dense, but she had adapted... as she had always done, without exactly knowing how.

Her bubble faded to nothingness, just as the inside hatch opened.

"Who's there? Oh, it's *you*, I see. Welcome back, star trekker," greeted a grinning Boyd. "I guess you were right about not needing a space-suit," he said.

"I'll enthusiastically second that, Karéin," added Tanaka, as she observed the Storied Watcher, with wondering eyes. "I have to tell you, even though it's irrational, I have this tremendous urge to get down on my knees. To do what *you* just did... I just can't *imagine* it. I'm running out of adjectives, I'm afraid. For example, we tracked the G-forces that you were generating out there. They must have been *enormous* – how on Earth did you avoid being, well, 'squashed'?"

The Mars-girl advanced quickly and took hold of Tanaka's hand.

"But, sister, Cherie," explained Karéin-Mayréij, with a half-suppressed giggle, "I am not worthy of undue admiration... you know that. Besides... am I not flesh and blood, as are you? You can feel this, in my hand – I hope that it is not *too* cold, since I have just been outside. I just know some special tricks... that is all. They *can* be pretty impressive, I will admit – my one lapse into pride, that I will allow myself."

The Storied Watcher continued, "And I was not on Earth, of course. To answer your question, what I do to avoid the pulling-outwards forces is, I bend gravity waves to offset them, just like how I fly. It takes much practice to do so, but it is not as difficult to do as you might think, because if you do not use enough force, you very quickly become aware of the need to push harder. How would I explain it... oh-kay, *I* know – try to imagine running upwards on the downwards version of those moving stairs you have on your planet, you know, the ones in buildings where one can buy things. If you move exactly fast enough, you stay in one place, or you can go faster, with more effort. It is like that."

"Very interesting. And they're called 'escalators', by the way, Karéin. For what it's worth," interjected Boyd, "You might want to know that the good Professor waited up for you, all the while, like a mother hen waiting for her chicks to come home. She was apparently afraid that you wouldn't be okay out there... she was worried for your safety."

Squeezing Tanaka's hand and looking at her sincerely in the eyes, the young-looking being replied, "Thank you very much for your concern, Cherie. Though I was, of course, never in any real danger... remember that I am – how you say – a 'scientist', too, so I know that this was a completely unknown experience for you. The method of science is not to take chances, not to assume things. You acted as I would have, or as I hope I would have."

She let go.

"We have *so* much in common, and so many differences, Karéin-Mayréij," was all that an overwhelmed Tanaka could think of to say.

"Well, now that *that's* over with," Boyd announced, "It's time to get back to our posts, folks. Captain just informed me that we're a bit ahead of schedule for the burn – he's moved it up an hour. Why he'd be so anxious to get going, is beyond me, but those are the orders. I'm off, I'll see you back there."

Boyd disappeared into the central core, followed shortly thereafter by the two others.

First Of The *Fire*

As they floated forward, Karéin-Mayréij waited for Boyd to disappear and then remarked, "You know, Professor, in a way, you are now experiencing what I did, out there. If you can try to imagine this – that is, moving just through inertia, without gravity to constrain yourself – *that* is what flying in space is like. Excepting, of course, that I would be moving somewhat faster, than we are now. I tell you this, because, both as a fellow being and as a scientist, I want you to know how it *feels*, even though this is subjective and your language does not describe it very well."

Tanaka smiled knowingly and replied, "Yeah, excepting the several hundred thousand kilometers per hour difference in speed, I suppose. But I think I *sort* of know what you mean, Karéin. Sometimes I regret having to come back to a gravity environment – it feels *limiting*, in a way. But it's the environment in which we humans were meant to function... it's natural for us. Too much free motion in zero-G, and all kinds of negative things happen to us, which is why we created the pseudo-grav in the center drum, of course."

The Mars-girl stopped both of them, somehow, then counseled, in an odd, portentous tone, "What is 'natural' for beings like you and I, Cherie, is what we make *for* ourselves, *by* ourselves. And there is *another* thing. Remember how I told you, earlier, that you could use the *Fire*, too?"

"How could I ever *forget*, Karéin," Tanaka answered. "I think every little boy and girl on Earth has always imagined himself or herself as a super-hero, able to do things like... well, like *you* do. Your special power, this energy-source you use, it's what could set us on the course to doing that... correct?"

Karéin-Mayréij nodded.

"It is so," she confirmed, "Although I have many other powers that are not related to *Amaiish*. And for this reason, now I want to entrust you with something *very* special, Cherie. But first, you must make a promise to me, one that comes from the deepest part of your heart, one that you will never, *ever*, violate. Do you trust me enough to do this?"

The alien-girl sounded serious, as much so as Tanaka could ever remember.

Tanaka looked at her, searchingly.

Then she stated, "Yes, Karéin... I do. I should not say so, without knowing what you will ask. But Devon was right. I *trust* you, Karéin-Mayréij, Storied Watcher."

"Now take my hand, Professor," requested the other.

Tanaka grasped it.

"Close your eyes and clear your mind of all other thoughts," demanded Karéin-Mayréij. "Forget about where we are, about what your duties are, forget *everything* – except what we are concentrating on now. Repeat the words I will now say after me, Cherie Tanaka of Earth, first of your race to be given the gift of the *Fire*. And do so, *meaning* what you say, as if the fate of your *life*, of worlds, and of untold generations-to-come, depend upon it. And know that I can tell if your heart is in it, or is not."

Utmost care was in her voice.

Alien music sounded in Tanaka's head. It was moving, uplifting, like the *Ave Maria*.

The science officer closed her eyes and tried to meditate.

Thank God for the Yoga classes, she thought.

Now, Karéin-Mayréij softly sang, using a hauntingly melodious, prayerful cadence that must have come from time before time,

"'Upon my most sacred honor, I will use my power, save that the hour be dire to my life, to *help*, not to *harm*; to *love*, not to *hate*; to *heal*, not to *wound*; to *rescue*, not to *endanger*, but foremost, to *serve*, not to *rule*; ever to follow the Holy Light, not the Darkness of Evil, until I pass from this life. With this oath freely taken, I now bind myself, and all others who I will in turn give the *Fire*. Thus do I swear, for now unto eternity, never to revoke'. *Say it*, Cherie Tanaka. Say it, and begin the long journey into greatness, for your people."

Tanaka thought that it would be difficult to remember this long oath, but to her surprise, every word came easily.

She hoped that Karéin-Mayréij could not sense the tears of wonder and anticipation in her eyes, though they were shut tight.

She took a breath, then reverently repeated, "Upon my most sacred honor, I will use my power, save that the hour be dire to my life, to help, not to harm; to love, not to hate; to heal, not to wound; to rescue, not to endanger, but foremost, to serve, not to rule; ever to follow the Holy Light, not the Darkness of Evil, until I pass from this life. With this oath freely taken, I now bind myself, and all others who I will in turn give the *Fire*. Thus do I swear, for now unto eternity, never to revoke."

The woman did not feel any different, apart from waves of emotion engulfing her.

"Tears are oh-kay," the alien-girl warmly congratulated, "For today, you have crossed a *great* divide. It is appropriate that you be moved... as am I."

She stopped for a moment, then instructed, "Now, keeping your eyes shut, I want you to imagine that you are just floating on a cloud, free of all cares or worries. Breathe deeply, relax. There is no comet, no spaceship, nowhere that you have to go, nothing that you have to do. Take your time. Your mind must be at rest."

Tanaka tried; but she was excited, not knowing what had transpired.

"You are still too tense, Cherie," observed the Storied Watcher, moving behind her student and gently massaging her shoulders.

"In time," she explained, "You will learn how to do this, while thinking other thoughts... doing other things. But you are now exercising parts of your brain, mind, senses and soul, that you did not know you had, that have laid dormant in your species for thousands of years, awaiting this blessed day. Thus, you need to concentrate on *this*, in singular fashion. Take another breath. It will only take a second or two, once you figure out how, anyway. We have plenty of time."

"I'm trying, Karéin," Tanaka muttered, "But... time to do *what*?"

"I am – how do you say – 'getting to that'," the Mars-girl answered. "Eyes still closed? Good. Now relax and think that you are in the cloud, again. You are floating, completely still."

Tanaka tried again, relaxing slightly, trying to keep the excitement from her mind.

"Okay," she offered, "I think I'm a bit less hyper now... not hard to imagine I'm floating, because that's what we're both doing now, anyway..."

"Very good," replied the alien-girl. "I slightly violated my own promise not to mind-read – I looked in and I think that you are ready, now... but keep your mind on the cloud... oh-kay?"

"Sure," answered Tanaka.

She was anything *but* sure.

"Now, Professor, I want you to imagine that a little gust of wind has appeared behind you," requested Karéin-Mayréij. "It is moving you forward, ever *so* slowly. Just a breeze, enough to put your hair in slight disarray. It feels *good*... it feels pleasant. You feel the wind on your face, too, made by the air as you move forward. *That* feels good as well. Try it. Tell me if you are thinking of the scene."

"A breeze... okay. Yes, I'm thinking of that. Go ahead," requested Tanaka.

She heard a suppressed gasp from the Storied Watcher and tried not to think about why it had been made.

"Cherie, it is working – it is *working!*" gushed an excited, obviously-proud Karéin-Mayréij. "I always *thought* that you could do it, but there was doubt – not any more!"

Hastily, she added, "Now, I want you to imagine that you are Cherie Tanaka on-board a spaceship, in the no-gravity center place of the ship; you are moving forward, towards the access-hatch. Tell me if you can see *that* scene, as well."

"Well, that's not so hard to do," Tanaka responded, "Since it's where we are now."

"Indeed," confirmed the Storied Watcher. "Now, open your eyes."

Tanaka did so.

They were still in the center shaft, apparently where they had been before.

"I... uhh... don't *understand*," Tanaka protested. "What's this great power, anyway?"

With a knowing smile, the Mars-girl let go of Tanaka's hand and replied, "See that hatch over there, the one leading to where the others are, Cherie?"

"Yes, of *course* I do," Tanaka replied.

"Move to it," ordered Karéin-Mayréij.

"Can you give me a push?" requested the science officer. "I'm out of reach of the wall... I need something to hold on to, or something to brace myself against so I can push off it. 'Action and reaction' – you know."

"No, I will *not* assist," countered the Storied Watcher, with a beaming smile that partly showed those sharp teeth. "You do not *need* any help. Just *move* there."

"I don't *understand*," a frustrated Tanaka shot back. "How am I supposed to –"

"Remember your little gust of wind, propelling you forward, Cherie?" tutored Karéin-Mayréij. "*Think* of it now. You do not have to close your eyes, but instead, concentrate on the idea of moving forward. Just imagine it pushing you, slowly but surely."

"Well... alright," muttered Tanaka, concentrating and trying to recall the scene, "But I don't –"

Her voice froze.

She was... *moving*.

At a snail's pace, but she was moving... *forward*.

With no apparent means of propulsion.

"*Oh my God!*" she gasped, stunned and overjoyed. "How am I *doing* this? I just *think* it, and I *move!*"

Again, the tears came to her eyes, matched by those of her godly tutor.

"Welcome to the knowing of the Holy *Fire*, blessed Cherie Tanaka... first of your kind," sang Karéin-Mayréij.

Status-Check

Tanaka and the Storied Watcher caught up with the others in the eating-area, all chattering away about the technical details of the course change preparations.

The woman, still partly in shock, sat down next to the Mars-girl, and Tanaka's absent-minded stare caught Boyd's attention.

"Whoa, Cherie," he commented, "You look like you just saw a ghost. Everything okay over there? You look like you've been crying."

Tanaka hesitated for a second, wiping the traces of a tear, then replied, "Oh, no, Brent... nothing like that. I've just been chatting with Karéin, about... well, about some rather... 'moving', topics... I guess that's how you would describe it."

Karéin-Mayréij giggled a bit, then observed, "I am beginning to appreciate the finer points of your language, Professor. That was – how do you say – a 'pun', right? When one word has two meanings, one of them funny?"

"Yep," said Tanaka.

"Care to share the conversation with us, Professor?" asked Jacobson.

"Uhh... sure, but later, if you don't mind, Sam," Tanaka hastily replied. "Don't worry – it's nothing that would affect the mission. And it's a *good* thing, too. Not bad news."

Jacobson looked at her quizzically for a second, then said, "Very well, then, Professor, you and Karéin can tell us later... I'm sure that we can use something other than bad news, once we get under way... God knows, there's been precious little positive news these days."

He continued, "Okay, then, team, it's time for our pre-burn reports. As usual, I'll go first. Basically there's no negative change from our status prior to leaving Mars orbit; solar panels, still over 95, center hub, check, batteries, electrical, check, and the food prep circuit is back up and running, thanks for that, Sergei. Shielding, auxiliaries, instrumentation, all good. The egress module passes self-tests and," – he allowed himself a gruff smile and gave a slight cough – "Obviously the airlock works... not that the last person to use it, really *needed* it to. On *that* score, by the way, I'd like to ask the newest crew-member if she noticed anything damaged or out of order, as she flew around outside the ship. I'm not planning an EVA anyway, but it can't hurt to get a, umm, neutral opinion, on this matter."

"Who, me?" answered the Storied Watcher. "Oh... hmm... please understand, Captain, that I was not *looking* for damage to your space-ship when I was out there – I had to pay much more attention to remembering how to protect myself in space and also how to offset the pulling forces that affect one, when one starts to fly faster and faster. To answer your question, no, I did not see anything seriously wrong with either the *Eagle* or the *Infinity*, nothing like a big hole in the ships' skin, pieces broken off, or anything like that, and I am *sure* that anything like that would have been easily visible, they show up as bright blotches of *Um'nàhr'é* –"

"Infra-red, for those of you who don't speak *Makailkh*," interjected Boyd.

"Brent speaks correctly," said the smiling Mars-girl. "That is the word that your language uses for it, but in truth, it does not really *look* like red... I wish that I could make you understand. But anyway, Captain, I *do* have one malfunction to report about your ship, which I discovered while I was outside it."

"What? A malfunction? Please tell us!" retorted a visibly concerned Jacobson.

"When I wanted to re-enter your ship, sir," explained Karéin-Mayréij, "I tried to use your – how do you say – 'finger-reader', but it did not recognize me, so I could not open the airlock hatch. I had to call upon those inside, to let me in. I think that you should fix this, because otherwise, I will have to bother Major Boyd, or someone else from your crew, every time that I want to... oh, how would you say this... 'step outside'."

With a guffaw, White quipped, "See, Captain? She's earning her pay already! I bet you none of *us* would have been able to test that thing with our bare hands!"

Laughing himself, Jacobson replied, "Karéin, for a second or two, you had me worried, there. Anyway, that one is what we refer to as a 'low-priority task'... I doubt it will get fixed anytime soon, due to some... conceptual issues with its design –"

"Major Boyd told me about those," said the alien-girl. "I have seen many such oversights, in the past. Sometimes the most obvious things, are the most difficult for us to see."

"You got *that* right," agreed the Mars mission commander, "But I guess NASA didn't quite count on *you* being up here with us, to make use of their little security-device. In any event, Karéin, thanks very much for the report and the request, it never hurts to share information or to ask. If and when you next get out there, may I ask for you to just have a quick look around?"

"Certainly, sir," she politely replied. "I suppose that is my full report, then."

The Storied Watcher paused, gave a weird-looking smile and requested, as if the idea had just come to her, "Since I have done my job, sir... as a reward, may I have one of those nice candies that you have retained for, uhh, 'special occasions'?"

"Good job, on the report," Jacobson congratulated. "And go ahead, just don't eat *all* of them, if you don't mind... they may have to last us for a while. Brent?"

What on Earth motivates this creature? thought Jacobson and Tanaka, both privately, as the Mars-girl happily munched on a lemon drop from Jacobson's personal collection.

"My report's basically same as before, Captain," stated Boyd. "I have checked Sergei's fuel estimates and he's right, we're actually a bit ahead of the game on that front, probably an extra three to five per cent reserve. Igniters and maneuvering-thrusters all nominal. Propulsion systems are all fully functional, that's my opinion. Just give the word and we'll be off like a flash."

"It would be fun to race your ship," the alien-girl mischievously mentioned. "I am faster now. I think that I would win."

"I doubt that anyone would want to bet against you on *that*, Karéin," Jacobson philosophically noted, "But the protocol that *we* use around here is, all crew-members have to actually *be* on the ship, when we take off; it's just a little formality we use to ensure that nobody gets stranded, somewhere like, say, on the surface of Mars, you see. And if you *lost* the race... well, it would be rather difficult for us to go back and pick you up. I'm afraid, therefore, that we'll have to take a rain-check on your offer."

Leaning over to a confused-looking Karéin-Mayréij while the rest of them chuckled, Tanaka whispered, "A 'rain-check' is used in stores on Earth where you buy food, when they can't provide an item that they advertised to sell you – it's a promise to do something, later."

The alien-girl nodded in acknowledgment.

"I guess I'll go next," said White. "Nothing out of the ordinary with the communications subsystems, except that I can't raise the space-station or get a fix on it – probably they haven't got it on its way, yet. I'll keep trying every so often, though... who knows, Captain, maybe we'll get lucky and find out that it's not going to make it there, after all. Up-links and down-links all check out, one hundred per cent. Oh, and one other thing, I discovered that some of the systems can hiccup a bit, when our guest turns on that power of hers... must be interference of some sort, but I was able to compensate for it."

He turned to the Storied Watcher and added, "Thinking about that, Karéin, I thought y'all would like to know, I was trackin' y'all out to about twenty meters or so, by filterin' out everything except the background trace of that *Amaiish*-stuff. After that, the signal became unstable, couldn't lock on to it, disappeared a second or two later... don't know why. That's about it for me."

"That *is* interesting, Devon," replied Karéin-Mayréij. "I thought that the *Fire* was not detectable, because it is – how do you say this in your language – partly 'outside this dimension'; it is not like ordinary energy, like heat, electricity, the little particle-shine, magnetism and so on. What you say worries me, because sometimes, I want to travel without being seen. If the little instruments on your ship here can track me this far, I suppose that those on your planet might be able to see me at greater distances. I must find a way to hide, to mask my presence..."

"Ah yes, stealth, deception, the first rules of warfare," interrupted Jacobson. "You know, ordinarily, as a military commander, I'd box Devon's ears for revealing what he just did... but you're on *our* side now, right?"

He laughed cynically.

"I am on the side of all who follow justice, truth, mercy and the Holy Light," she demurely answered, while her music played hauntingly in their subconscious.

Her eyes were dimly glowing.

"That's good enough for *me*," Jacobson said, with a nervous half-wince. "Anyway, I think we should discuss it later, if you don't mind, Karéin. Professor?"

"Nothing important to report," mentioned Tanaka, "I haven't had a lot of time to check, since I have been preoccupied with Karéin's little excursion earlier, but while I was waiting for her I ran some numbers on the computers, and it turns out that there's lots of food left... considering that we might not be eating very much more of it, after we get to ISS. Air reserves are slightly lower than what had been anticipated, reflecting the fact that we have one more person here, but they're down less than I would have expected. Same situation for water. Environmental systems are running perfectly."

"Should make for a nice new home for those guys from Earth," White opined.

Nobody responded.

"Sergei, I suppose that makes you the wrap-up report," indicated Jacobson.

"All general-purpose systems are fine, Captain," Chkalov responded. "The *Eagle* is in the same condition as in which we last left it – I started all its systems, one by one, to verify their functionality, then shut them down in reverse sequence. The interlink between the two ships is stable and all cargo has been securely stowed. I reviewed the course change co-ordinates that Major Boyd entered into the computer, based on instructions from Houston, and I can verify that they are correct. I therefore judge the *Eagle* and *Infinity* to be fully ready for the course correction, sir. That is all."

"Very well, then, team," Jacobson declared, "It looks like we're ready to do our second burn, although I suppose it's not news to any of you that I'm not terribly enthusiastic about where we're heading. You're dismissed – I'll expect you at your stations, in your anti-G chairs, fifteen minutes from now. That's when we'll start the final countdown. Any questions?"

"Yes, sir," the alien-girl replied.

"Go ahead, Karéin," he said.

"I do not think that your ship has one of these 'anti-G' chairs for me to sit in, sir, because my presence here was not anticipated." she explained, "But I believe that I will be alright without one – I did not encounter any problems when I was in the box where I hid, at first. Where would you like me to stay, when you fire your engines?"

"Captain," interjected White, "I can second that opinion... from what I saw when she was flying around out there, she was pulling *thousands* of G's. If she had been in one of our chairs while doin' it, I'd be afraid for the chair... not for her."

"Heh," Jacobson chuckled, "Point well taken, from both of you. But just for the sake of obeying the rules, Karéin, could you please at least sit in *a* chair, somewhere? Right here would be fine, unless you want to bring a seat up to the control-area so you can see the procedure, first-hand. Understood?"

"Perfectly, sir," answered the Storied Watcher. "I would like that. I have always found techno-devices, and the functions that they provide, to be fascinating."

"You're very welcome to be with us... just don't press any buttons or pull any switches," Jacobson requested.

With a toothy grin, Karéin-Mayréij pledged, "I promise not to, sir. Though I *do* know how some of them work. Fifteen minutes, then?"

"Fourteen and a half," he replied.

Ghosts And Goblins

They were now all – including the Mars-girl, who sat upright in a chair borrowed from the food-area, fastened to the floor between Boyd and White – in the control-room, awaiting the course change that many of them feared would be their last.

"Well, we'd better get this over with, team," started Jacobson. "Final check, beginning now. Oh, and, Karéin, I'd appreciate it if we could just do this ourselves, since the book says we have to follow the sequence... so no questions for the time being, please. Major White, communications status."

The Storied Watcher nodded and lowered her eyes submissively, for a second, then returned to a rapid-fire visual and mental assessment of each and every movement and command.

"Navigation and comm systems all up and on-line, sir," mentioned White. "Still no fix on the station, but equivalent spatial co-ordinates are keyed in. I got us locked on it. Ready, whenever you want."

"Okay," said Jacobson. "Major Boyd, propulsive protocol. Engage on my mark."

"Yes, sir," replied Boyd. "Vernier stabilizers, now engaging," he said.

"Mark," replied Jacobson.

A faint "whoosh" sounded.

"Igniters, one to four in sequence," said Boyd.

"Mark," replied Jacobson.

Boyd threw the same four switches that he had earlier, one after the other.

The alien-girl felt the energy systems coming alive, and this excited her, as her body absorbed the stray energy associated with the event; but, remembering Jacobson's command, she kept silent.

"Igniters all on-line, one hundred per cent, Captain. Awaiting your command," he said.

"You all know I'm not given for speeches," Jacobson reflectively commented, "But I *will* say this: who knows, what awaits us. We *think* we do, but we've been wrong before, folks... *very* wrong. I have faith that we'll be wrong now, that fate will not let us down. Let's bravely go towards that fate, whatever it may be."

He paused for a second, then said, "Mark."

They all felt a bump, an only moderately uncomfortable jolt, as if on a car coming quickly to stop at a red light.

The Mars-girl noticed the humans carefully reviewing the numbers and symbols of a half-dozen computer status displays.

"Nineteen thousand kph – a good start, better than before," Boyd announced, addressing Jacobson. "Ramping up to twenty-seven oh-fifty in ten seconds, then I'll cut them... nine... eight... seven... six... five... four... three... two... one... burn complete, sir," he said, as he threw a switch, covered it with a locking mechanism and reclined back in his chair.

"It's always anti-climactic for me, after lifting off from Earth... now *that* was a ride," remarked Tanaka. "I guess I was raised to believe that you could *hear* the warp-engines going off, when a space-ship starts its journey into the Final Frontier," she said.

"Captain... may I speak now, sir?" asked Karéin-Mayréij.

Jacobson nodded in the affirmative.

"Cherie, what is a 'warp-engine'?" the alien-girl inquired of Tanaka.

"She ain't seen *Star Trek*, I guess, Professor," White joked. "Funny, I thought that was, like, English 101 for outer space people..."

"It's an imaginary form of interstellar propulsion, first made popular in an old television science-fiction show, Karéin," amicably explained Tanaka. "Supposedly it worked by warping the fabric of space itself, so you could travel directly between two places in the universe, each very distant from each other – like bending a piece of paper and poking a hole through the part that's folded upwards. It's purely *theoretical*, of course – I find it pretty far-fetched... but then, it's nice to imagine that someone could find a way around the limitation of the speed of light."

"Ah, I see," replied the Storied Watcher. "'Bending' space-time so that one can exceed the speed of light – I must admit that I have never thought of doing something like *that*, although I *have* encountered some nexus-points... anyway. It certainly *is* a fascinating idea... maybe I should try it some time!"

A nonplussed Jacobson quickly interrupted, "You're not going to attempt anything like *that*, around here... *are* you?"

He got only a wink and mischievous giggle in return, although White mentioned, "I think y'all just had your leg pulled there, Captain."

"If it is of any interest," noted Karéin-Mayréij, "I have spent – probably – several-score human lifetimes, in search of the same thing... that is, a way to fly faster than light; but the more rapidly that one goes, the more and more energy that one must expend... it quickly becomes overwhelming. The first time that I experienced the hundred years or so needed to travel between even two moderately close stars, I quickly became aware of the need for such a trick. I hope that I will find one, or build one, someday."

She stopped for a second, then added, "And 'television' – yes, I know *that*, too. Motion pictures, broadcast with electromagnetic waves. I watched some old episodes of – how do they call it, wait, I remember now – a tee-vee show called 'I Dream of a Genie', or something like that, on your com-pu-ter, last night. I selected it because it was about astronauts, like all of you... but one of them had a magical girl living with him. It was funny, but worrisome at first. I hope that I did not keep the Professor awake, because it made me laugh."

"Well," offered Boyd, "You're right, that show *was* about astronauts, but just for your information, it's many years out of date, by now. I wouldn't want you to think that Earth is exactly like how it's portrayed, there. Our societies are a bit more... *progressive*, these days. And none of us have magical housemaids, though God knows most of us could use one every so often. But why would you be *worried* about it? It's just a comedy show."

"Ah," the Mars-girl replied, "I had suspected that. But I found the show interesting not only because of the astronauts, but because the girl had magical powers. At first this concerned me, in that it might be a humorous depiction of reality – that is, there might be people who use magic on Earth. So I did some more research on your com-pu-ter and discovered that although you *do* have those who falsely claim the ability, your world is completely free of supernatural powers. That sure was a relief! But it only made sense, I suppose. If it had been otherwise, *surely* your greatest wizards and sorceresses would have banded together, to stop this 'Lucifer' thing, with their most powerful incantations. And you would not have had to use a space-ship to fly to *Mailànkh*, you would just have been sent there with the same, magical spells..."

All eyes, even those of Jacobson, who was supposed to be preoccupied with the flight details, focused on the Storied Watcher.

Tanaka spoke up.

"Karéin," she asked, "What, exactly, do you *mean*? About magic, I mean, 'wizards' and so on. You're talking as if it was *real*."

"I do not know why I confused you," replied Karéin-Mayréij. "I only said that I was relieved that Earth is free of that power. I hope that it does not offend you to hear this... but I *hate* magic. It has been the bane of my existence, since before I can remember. It is the one thing that I *really* have trouble fighting and defending myself against. On some worlds, I can have all my own powers at their greatest strength... and yet, fall victim to an otherwise very weak enchantment. I can use *Amaiish* to negate the Weirding Arts or to protect myself against their effects, but doing so is very difficult and can require huge amounts of energy. So... magic is very annoying and a few times, it has almost killed me. That is why I do not like it, friends."

"Karéin," White asked, "Y'all trying to tell us that there are places where there really *are* magicians, the Wizard of Oz, turn you into a frog, that kind of thing? I know you've been some pretty funky places, lady, but even for yours truly, *that* sounds a bit hard to swallow."

"You mean that Earth people do not know of this power?" incredulously replied the Storied Watcher. "If so, they should consider themselves lucky."

"Karéin," pressed Tanaka, "You *can't* be serious – I want to be sure that we're using the same terminology, here. We certainly *do* know of something called 'magic', that is, an imaginary ability to produce an effect without a scientifically describable cause, for example to 'conjure' an animal out of thin air, to 'teleport' oneself between two places without moving between them, to instantly cure an otherwise fatal disease, even to bring people back to life after they have died. It's something that violates all the known laws of the universe and something that you find in fiction only – it's not real, it *can't* be. You can't have an effect without a logical cause, nor can you create something from 'nothing'. Only children and people with overly vivid imaginations, believe in 'magic', at least on Earth, that's how it is."

"As I said, Cherie," the alien-girl explained, "If this is how things are on Earth, then your planet is fortunate. However, please be assured that there *are*, indeed, other places, where *exactly* the types of events that you just described, can and do occur, all the time. Why some places have magic and others – such as your own – do not, I do not know. I only know that where this power exists, it usually causes many negative consequences, such as retarding or completely ending the natural evolution of society, or by giving those who believe in darkness, chaos and unreason, the same abilities as those who support knowledge and justice. When and if the former prevail, it can mean the end of an entire civilization... or worse. Fortunately, not many planets are 'magic-rich', as you would call it. When I arrive one, usually my first objective is to find a way to leave. I am very glad that I do not have to worry about that, here."

"*Wow*," mused Tanaka. "Sam, Devon, Sergei, Brent, I hope you all are aware of what our guest has just explained... another *unbelievably* important revelation about the universe, *our* universe. That there are places where our familiar rules of physics, of cause and effect, don't apply. Where, yes, Devon, you might very well run into a 'Wizard of Oz', or – "

"Or the Wicked Witch of the West?" commented Jacobson.

"Or," said Karéin-Mayréij, staring off into space with a darkening, warning countenance, "A *Vaeran Roahon*."

She paused for a moment, then, with a shudder, quietly elaborated, "Yes, I see that my memory is coming back, friends. That was his – *its* – name. He was one of the greatest of my own kind, less powerful than me in some ways but more potent in others... he was *Makailkh*, a necromancer and a High Priest of the Forbidden Gods, all three at once – a *very* dangerous combination..."

The sudden hush that came over the others was broken by Boyd.

"One of those dark things that you hid from me," he quietly observed. "I suppose I shouldn't ask... but I can't resist... so what happened with this, uhh. 'Roahon' guy?"

"He was a traitor who became drunk on a quest for power," explained the alien-girl. "He turned from his most solemn pledges of morality, seeking instead the sinister forces of darkness... and in turn, he was possessed by these hateful entities. Disaster ensued on the world where he and I found ourselves. Many thousands died cruel, senseless deaths."

Her gaze turned to directly stare at the pilot.

"Think on it, sometime, if you dare, my brother Brent Boyd," warned Karéin-Mayréij. "But if you do... be prepared to give up peaceful sleep, for a good long while."

"Thanks for the tip," Boyd replied, "But I think I'll pass, for the time being. I've seen enough of your memories – especially the bad ones – to last a *lifetime*, thank you."

"boost-phase now off," interjected Jacobson.

"You know, Cherie," he added, "I'm no physicist but I seem to remember that what Karéin has just informed us of, isn't as completely far-fetched as it seems – didn't Einstein, or someone, have a theory that there might be alternate universes, where our laws of physics don't apply? Maybe *that's* where you have been, in earlier lives, Karéin. Must have been quite an experience. You might even have met a hobbit, I suppose."

"A... what?" inquired the Mars-girl.

"A 'hobbit' is a demi-human being in one of our world's most popular works of fantasy fiction," explained Tanaka. "They were depicted as small, about the size of a child, with hairy feet, and one of them defeats the most evil demon of all, in the final book of the series," she said.

"Hmm..." observed the Storied Watcher, "I have never met anyone who looks like *that*, but if these little people are good at fighting demons, I certainly could have used their help, in my past... I *have* encountered all sorts of other beings... green ones similar to you humans, except for their skin color, and tall, purple ones; there were also reddish-skinned creatures with four legs that did not look at *all* like humans, and furry beings with cloven hooves. That is how I remember it, more or less."

"Karéin," interrupted Tanaka, "Were these creatures all intelligent, like us?"

"Very definitely so, Professor," stated Karéin-Mayréij, "Though there were others that were not – for example, the walking dead, who yet could fight in an army, as a man does. I *hate* the memory, frankly. The world that I am thinking of, though, was riddled with accursed magic, and its civilization was much less advanced than your own – from reading your history on the com-pu-ter, I would say that it would have been like the Empire of the Romans... that was the big one that existed about two thousand of your years ago, correct?"

"Yes," confirmed Tanaka. "Do you remember anything else about this world? What its name was? Where we could look for it, in the universe?"

She turned to Jacobson and excitedly exclaimed, "My *God*, Sam, this is even *more* astounding information than she's given us before – we're hearing the details about our first extraterrestrial civilization... and it's wildly different from anything we had ever imagined."

Before the Storied Watcher could reply, Jacobson observed, "Yeah, no doubt, Cherie. I just wonder how – if – we're going to tell Houston about it. They're going to think we're *crazy*... I mean, the 'ghosts and goblins' stuff. If I were in their position, I'd probably think that the stress of being up here is getting to us."

"To be honest with you, Captain, sir," admitted the Storied Watcher, "Sometimes I, too, wonder if these memories are real – it has been a *long* time, such a long time. Many thousands of your years, in fact, because I was there – I think – several long sleeps before the one from which you awakened me. And, since Cherie asked me, its name was Te – Teh – ahh, I am sorry, I do not remember the whole word. I am not even sure that this world is within your own universe; maybe it is in another one, where, as you say, the laws of physics-science are different. No, on second thought, I believe that it *is* here, in this galaxy. I have this thought in my head that it lies towards the central core, where the stars fill the night sky, much brighter than would be the case here. Maybe I am wrong. I am not sure of *any* of this, though. Sorry."

She stopped for a second, then surveyed all of them, especially Boyd, with a look of steely defiance in her eyes, now dimly-glowing, again.

"But there is *one* thing that I *am* certain of, friends," she added, slowly and firmly, while her eyes began to shine.

Her war-music sounded in the dim recesses of their minds.

"When all was done and the field of battle lay silent," recounted the Storied Watcher, "The Evil One was defeated, cast out forever, by the might of mine own hand. I suffered grievously in the doing of this... but I *won*. The long night was ended and the people there, again live free of fear. This do I *swear*."

"Y'all sure sound *seriou*s about that, Karéin," offered White. "I think we all believe you. *I* sure do."

The others just nodded.

Regaining her composure and hiding her godly demeanor, the Mars-girl apologized, "I am sorry if I disturbed or scared you, in saying that. It is just that it is very important to me, to remember it. Especially as I have also failed, at other times."

"No harm done," joked Boyd. "I guess even a *goddess* has her good days and bad days."

"I am not such – that is, a deity... you know that," countered Karéin-Mayréij, with a wan smile, "But I will not contradict you... maybe there *is* some of the divine in this soul... it is not for me to judge. You know me all too well, Brent."

Jacobson spoke up.

"Well, that's it for the burn, folks," he announced. "We can all unstrap and get up – as always, keep in mind that we have some slight G-forces to deal with, as we're still speeding up, but you've all been through this before. And," he said with a slight grin, "I doubt that our guest will have too much of a problem with the forces of acceleration that she's now encountering, either."

"None at all," the Mars-girl politely responded. "I am, how do you say, 'used to a lot more'."

"Captain," inquired Boyd, "Do we have an updated ETA to the station, or at least to the *rendez-vous* point?"

"Sergei?" said Jacobson.

"About three weeks from now, Captain," replied Chkalov, "Assuming that we reach cruising speed according to present plans, and that we can start our deceleration burn at the right time. Also, I have been monitoring the progress of the project to boost the orbit of ISS2, and it seems to be behind schedule, so when we arrive at the place that Houston wants us to, we will be waiting for the station to get there."

"Tell them not to hurry," commented White.

"Amen to that," added Tanaka.

Time For Practice

The next week passed quickly, with most of the crew – excepting Tanaka, who pressed Karéin-Mayréij for every last tidbit of knowledge that the latter would reveal about her origins, history and physiology – finding something, *anything*, to do, to avoid dealing with the reality that was fast approaching at the *rendez-vous* point. (The science officer, however, made a point of encrypting much of the information that she was able to glean from the alien-girl, using an extremely long key that was shared only between the two of them. This subterfuge was, of course, not divulged to the other crew-members.)

They joked, they indulged in rather more than their proper share of the remaining food-rations (neither Jacobson nor Tanaka voiced any objection to this) and they amused themselves however they could.

Boyd bested Chkalov, three out of five, in a chess tournament, much to the chagrin of the Mars-girl, who, remembering her 'punishment' from Jacobson, had decided to merely observe from the sidelines.

But one night, midway through the week, the girl found *another* way to console the Russian for his loss, and it was not by counseling him on gaming strategy. This session was every bit as good as its predecessor had been; both the cosmonaut and alien-girl had to take care not to show its after-effects at breakfast-time, the next day.

As they also had to, on two other occasions.

For her part, Karéin-Mayréij managed to give as good as she got in dealing with the Professor; the alien-girl was as insistent in learning about Earth, especially its social customs, languages and military technology, as Tanaka was in learning about the Storied Watcher. And the two of them spent many secret minutes away from the others, practicing the new power that the science officer had been taught. White almost caught them doing this, once; he said nothing, though he no doubt suspected that something unusual was going on.

By the end of the week, Tanaka had discovered, to her delight, that she could not only move relatively easily in zero-G by using *Amaiish* to master gravity waves, but could also cause a pencil to roll slowly across the table in the same way, even in the spaceship's pseudo-gravity environment.

This latter feat resulted in serious headaches, however, and the scientist might have given up, had it not been for constant encouragement by the Storied Watcher.

"Exercising your mind to use *Amaiish*", the alien-girl had remarked, after one especially painful session, "Is like exercising your muscles by building a great castle : it hurts while you do it; but when you see what you have done, you know you are a noble, and the pain goes away."

None the less, the ship's supply of analgesic tablets steadily dwindled.

Tanaka hoped that nobody would notice.

Too Hot... We Believe

More time had passed. Jacobson summoned them all into the eating-area at mid-day (if such a concept made sense at all, in the artificial environment of the ship).

"Official message just received from Earth," he stated. "Probably something more important than the regular bulletins, so I thought we should all see it together. Devon, can you pipe it through?"

"Got it, Cap'n," White cheerfully replied.

"Up now. Here we are," he said.

The visage of General Symington appeared.

"Greetings, *Eagle* and *Infinity*, Captain Jacobson and crew, including our new guest, of course," came his gruff, no-nonsense voice. "This is Jack Symington here, speaking on behalf of the President. I have a status and orders report for you, so listen up; we have some major developments. Oh, and incidentally, I'm here by myself today; Ramirez, Abruzzio and McPherson are all tied up with preparations for the *Arks* project. They tell me to inform you that they'll try to be back for our next communications session."

He continued, "First, although we are about to announce this to the rest of the world, since you're part of the family, as it were, we thought you should have advance notice that at GMT plus five hours today, we – along with the world's other nuclear powers – will be launching our final barrage of thermonuclear missiles at the 'Lucifer' object. Compared to our earlier plans, we will be firing at much longer range than we had first expected to; this is for a variety of reasons, principally that many of the heavier launch-vehicles that would not have been available until later, are now earmarked for the *Arks* project, so we might as well fire what we have, as soon as we have all the missiles that we're ultimately going to get."

He cleared his throat and elaborated, "On the positive side, the scientists have figured out an improved trajectory for the missiles – we'll be using the Moon's gravity to dramatically increase their velocity, hence the greater range – and also, some of the scientists down here believe that the comet will be easier to deflect, if we hit it while it's still far out, even though we could have used more firepower if it was closer. While our attack will be less powerful than the Air Force and I had originally hoped to have, I can tell you that we're still going to make a mighty *big* 'bang', *Infinity*, so make sure you don't look directly at 'Lucifer' at the exact moment of impact. This one will be Earth's biggest swing at bat, team, so wish us all the luck you can."

Boyd noticed that Karéin-Mayréij, her eyes closed, was saying something to herself, but it was not audible.

Symington added, "Secondly, regarding your own mission; ISS2 has now been boosted from its current near-Earth orbit and is on its way to the point at which we had asked you to meet it. As you're probably already aware, we're a bit late on this front, *Infinity*, but that shouldn't concern you – just wait at the *rendez-vous* point, and we'll be back on schedule."

"Wonderful," commented White, louder than would have been politic.

"Can't *wait*," added Tanaka.

Symington observed, "Now, regarding the alien – sorry, Karéin, but that's the only way we can really describe you, scientifically – we have been receiving your reports, Professor Tanaka and Captain Jacobson, but if it's okay with you, there's no need to file them with us, until further notice. Some of the data has been very interesting, but the bottom line here is, everyone is now in emergency mode... nothing 'long-term' is being down on Earth, anymore."

He concluded, "If this helps you to understand, the 'Lucifer' thing is now clearly visible to the naked eye on a Moonless night, from Earth's surface... that has sort of focused our attention. And from what we have seen so far, it's obvious that your new friend won't be able to help us, much more than she already has... so, Karéin, all you have to do now is transfer to the space-station when it arrives and docks with the space-ship that you're now traveling on. Well, team, that's about it. We trust that the rest of your flight will be uneventful. Let us know if you need further direction. Symington out."

"Captain, I –" started the Mars-girl; but she was motioned quiet by Jacobson, as the screen went dim.

"That was to the point," he grunted. "I guess the next thing we do, is wait for the 'Big Bang'. Sergei – Cherie – since we're on GMT plus zero here, I suppose that we'd be waiting exactly on the General's schedule? No time adjustment, I mean?"

Chkalov spoke up.

"That is correct, Captain," he confirmed. "We can expect to observe the impact twenty-six hours, forty-seven minutes and twelve seconds from plus five GMT today."

"Karéin," asked Tanaka, "Were you going to say something?"

The Storied Watcher got up and started pacing around, apparently nervously. She avoided eye contact with all the rest of them.

"It is just," she mentioned, "Just... that I had an idea. Probably not worth talking about. Do not worry about it. I think you people say, 'forget it'... is that not the expression?"

"Yo Karéin," offered White, "Y'all need to understand that to get one of us humans curious about something, there's no better way than to tell us *not* to think about it."

"Devon's right about that," Jacobson added. "Now that you've got our attention, you might as well tell us."

"Very well, then," replied Karéin-Mayréij. "I hope that you will not laugh when you hear this."

"Of *course* not," said Tanaka, sympathetically.

"I must first ask a question," requested the alien-girl. "And I address it to not only you, Captain Jacobson, but also Majors Boyd and White – you are all military men, warriors, is that right? So, you would know about weapons of war?"

"Yes, that's true," interjected Boyd, "So is Sergei. He just comes from, well, a slightly different army than we do."

At this, Chkalov, smiling enigmatically, gave a slight bow.

"Oh-kay," acknowledged the Mars-girl. "Now, if I understand your General Symington correctly... he plans to fire some war-rocket ships at the 'Lucifer' thing, trying to destroy it?"

"Or," explained Tanaka, "To deflect it from its current course towards Earth. From what I understand, that's really the only hope – it's much too big to blow up, even with all the nukes on Earth. Ironic, when you think about it, because we could very easily destroy our own civilization with these weapons... and, if you read our history-books, we very nearly *did* that, two or three times, since the first atom bomb was invented."

"'Atom' bomb, 'nuke', that is what you call it, correct?" inquired the Storied Watcher. "Using the energy released, by breaking apart the smallest components of matter, fusing them back together, that sort of thing? It is a power with which I am familiar – one which I have unfortunately run across, from time to time. Not the greatest power in the universe... but a very potent one, none the less."

Boyd winced as one of the alien's suppressed memories of heat and pain suddenly came to his mind.

"Indeed," elaborated Jacobson. "These are the most powerful weapons that human beings have ever created. Depending on how much 'fissile material' – uranium, plutonium, that sort of thing – that's used to build one of these warheads, a nuclear weapon can be powerful enough to destroy an entire city in one shot. We measure their explosive power in 'megatons', that is, equivalent to *millions* of tons of our most powerful chemical explosives."

"As the good Professor points out," he added, "Inventing them in the first place is thought by many of us as having been a terrible mistake; but, like so many other aspects of science, the knowledge of how to do this has always been out there... it was just a matter of time, before someone came along and actually *did* it. After that, we had one, so – forgive me, Sergei – the Russians had to have one, too. I suppose they didn't quite trust us not to wave a nuke or two at them. Pretty soon, the whole *planet* was armed to the teeth with the damn things, but, after all, if it hadn't been, we couldn't even have *tried* the General's gambit of firing them all at 'Lucifer'."

"I can also say," commented Chkalov, "That although what Captain Jacobson says regarding the history of these weapons is true, I, for one, detest them. I have always been willing to give my life for Mother Russia; this is a solemn vow that I took, when I first put on my country's uniform. But *these* weapons are the tools of mass slaughter of civilians, not of honorable combat between two or more soldiers. I know of many other military men, both in Russia and elsewhere, who feel the same way."

"Amen to that, bro'," agreed White. "When I joined the Air Force, I told those guys *specifically* that I couldn't push that button. But they let me in, anyway. I hear they've smartened up on that kinda thing, since."

Tanaka giggled at this.

Jacobson merely smiled, and said, "Well, now that you've had the nuclear age history lesson, Karéin... so, what was this great idea of yours?"

The Storied Watcher studied him and them, for a second. They heard the faint, far-away sound of her war-music, its tones telling of might and nobility.

"What if, Captain Jacobson," suggested the alien-girl, carefully and deliberately, "I flew at 'Lucifer', when your 'nukes' explode at it? Maybe if I added my attack to your planet's..."

"Say *whaat*?" exclaimed White.

"Uhh, Karéin," hesitantly protested Tanaka, "You'd be blown to *bits*. It would be like being on the surface of the Sun, if only for a few brief seconds, but that would be more than enough time to reduce you to atoms."

"Are you quite *sure* of that?" asked Karéin-Mayréij, in a measured but defiant tone.

"Karéin," Boyd noted, "I would assume that you are planning to – what was it you said about how you do this, I don't completely remember, but I think – yeah, use the energy released by our bombs to somehow reinforce your own power? Something like that?"

"*Exactly* like that," the Mars-girl replied, looking away from all of them.

"Man, she sounds *serious*," commented White. "Karéin – don't want to burst your special bubble here, lady, but, hey, that's more or less what's gonna happen, if y'all try doin' that. These things are *powerful*... as the Captain said, they can flatten a city in a half-second. Million-degree heat, radiation that could leave you looking like an overexposed X-Ray – the works. All that's left afterwards is a big, ugly hole in the ground. A bit much to bite on even with *your* teeth, if you don't mind the expression."

"And there would be *hundreds* of these nuclear bombs going off on, or very near to, the surface of 'Lucifer', all at more or less the same time," added Boyd. "Karéin, I know your powers better than any of the others do, but Devon's right, I think. I sure wouldn't try it, if I were you. That memory, we now both share –"

"Yes. I know the one to which you refer," she replied.

"I'm saying this only because it came back to me a few minutes ago," Boyd continued, "But it looked like – *felt* like – you had experienced, and survived, *one* such explosion. From a *single* bomb. Am I right?"

"Maybe. I do not know, exactly. It was a *long* time ago, in another place. It might not even have been one of your 'nukes'... it could have been something else. I was much weaker, then," she countered, avoiding Boyd's eyes.

The Storied Watcher fixed her glance on Jacobson, staring silently as the man while he mimicked the gesture.

Finally, he said, "Karéin, God knows, no-one *wants* you to stop this comet, more than we do. The survival of our *planet* hangs in the balance, everyone here knows that. But the others know what they're talking about – remember, we all have had years of experience learning and understanding the characteristics of these weapons. We *know* what they can do, how terribly destructive they are. We know that you have innate powers far greater than our own, but asking you to do what you have suggested, would be the same as asking you to commit *suicide*. I can't authorize it. The answer is 'no', I'm afraid."

Karéin-Mayréij did not answer, at least not immediately. Instead, in silence, she slumped down in her chair, looking away from the others.

Finally, in a small voice, she retreated, saying, "Yes, sir. I understand."

Jacobson hesitated for a second, then mentioned, "But, if it's any consolation, thank you for explaining your idea to us, anyway. Mind if I share an observation with you, Karéin?"

"Not at all, Captain Jacobson," she replied.

"Your idea sounded... well, it sounded a bit desperate, frankly," Jacobson offered. "Even for someone like you. But I consider that a *good* thing, not a bad thing. It proves that you're thinking about us, that you're trying as hard as we are to find some way to save Earth. At this point I'm not sure if either you or we will succeed, but give yourself some credit for trying, anyway. We need all the ideas that we can get, that's for sure. So keep them coming."

Her countenance brightened, slightly.

"Of course, sir," she answered.

"Man," whispered White to Boyd, "The old man's got her sounding like a first-year cadet."

Boyd nodded in the affirmative.

"Well, I guess that's it for now," Jacobson announced. "I'll be keeping the countdown to Big Bang Hour – I'll give everyone a few minutes of advance warning, before it happens. Let's cross our fingers, folks."

The Mars-girl whispered to Tanaka, "That is a gesture... correct? But what does it mean, Cherie?"

Tanaka thought for a second, then explained, "It means to hope that something turns out the way you want it to, Karéin. In *this* case, though, it means more that if it doesn't, we won't need just hope; we'll need a *miracle*."

The Storied Watcher looked at her, silently, then turned away. She headed to the computer, to learn more about the world that was, as far as any of them knew, soon to play its final card.

And, to learn about its weapons of war.

Too Small A Bang

The next day, and the necessary few extra hours, seemed to take longer than the whole previous week had, at least for the human members of the crew. They were all out of sorts, anxious, caught in anticipation.

The Mars-girl, conversely, seemed unaffected, burying herself in the computer terminal, studying assiduously.

"The fact that y'all spending so much time learnin' up about Earth," White joked to her, one time, "Gives me the warm and fuzzies, that there's still going to *be an* Earth."

But the Storied Watcher replied, "Or, perhaps I am just finding out what I am about to lose... so my conscience can punish me all the more."

Upon hearing this, a chastened White crept away.

Finally, it was almost the expected impact time of the Earth missiles. They had gathered in the communications area.

"T minus one minute fifteen," Jacobson announced. "Now, I hope you're all aware that we won't see the results immediately, but we'll get them before Earth, at least, since we're closer."

"I'm not sure I want to *know*," quietly commented Tanaka.

"Aye," added Boyd. "This really *is* the old 'last kick at the can', as it were."

"I assume," interjected Karéin-Mayréij, "That expression means, 'a last chance'. But it is untrue. As long as there is life, the will to fight... there is *always* hope, Major Brent Boyd. Many times, in my former lives, matters have seemed desperate. But I *never* gave up."

She fell silent, then half-whispered, "Except for once."

"Forty seconds," counted Chkalov.

"Any wishes? Prayers?" asked Jacobson.

"Just 'give it your best shot', Earth," replied Tanaka.

"Avenge the *Rossiya*," savagely muttered Chkalov. "Avenge my dear friends, Earth. Hit the monster, with the force of a million Siberian gales."

They noticed the Mars-girl, now down on her knees, eyes closed, hands folded in front, as if praying for a miracle.

"Yo, Karéin –" started White; but, thinking the better of it, he did not finish the comment.

"I invoke the Holy Light," explained Karéin-Mayréij. "I pray for good fortune. For the deliverance of your people. I send my power, what little I have, to your weapons."

Her voice sounded, singing, melodious and dignified, as a quiet, inspiring tune registered in the minds of the humans. She repeated an invocation in her weird, burbling, trilling tongue.

As the Storied Watcher sang and breathed rhythmically, the same energy-discharges that they saw earlier, danced and played all over her body. They became much brighter, then gradually faded to nothing.

Boyd could not help noticing that Tanaka almost fainted, when the alien-girl's chant was in full tilt.

"Ten... nine... eight... seven... six... five..." counted Chkalov.

"Please, God," pleaded Tanaka, wiping a trace of perspiration from her forehead.

"Four... three... two... one...", the Russian intoned.

"Happening now," Jacobson stated. "Should be about thirty-three seconds, and we see."

They all remained silent, not moving, scarcely breathing, eyes glued to the telescopic video-displays.

There was a brilliant flash. Then another, even brighter, the kind of painful, dazzling light that leaves a greenish after-image, when one closes one's eyes.

A second. A third.

Static, all over the screen. It cleared, slowly.

Revealing the comet, looking – somehow – different, as a predator, wounded by its victim's last tooth, horn or claw, would appear.

But it was very much still there.

"Let's do a long-range scan," said Jacobson's voice. "Examine it for damage. Houston will need all the information we can give them."

"Well, that's *it*, then," commented Boyd, in his best, professional, detached tone.

"Sure is," dejectedly confirmed White. "For *all* of us, I'd say."

They heard someone sobbing and all eyes turned to Tanaka.

But, though hers were wet, it was not coming from the Professor. It was coming from Karéin-Mayréij, who had half-slumped forward, crouching over her folded legs with her upper-body.

"Not *enough*, friends," she wailed, "Never enough, *never* enough. I *tried* to help, I really *tried*... you have to *believe* me. But I am useless – I *failed, again*! Failed your whole planet, all your *people*..."

Her voice trailed off into a whimper.

Boyd and Tanaka rushed over to her and knelt down.

"Karéin," Tanaka consoled, "Don't blame yourself for this. There was nothing you could have done. But thank you so much, ever so much, for trying. We all appreciate it."

She hugged the Mars-girl.

Boyd added, "The Professor's right about that, Karéin. What's meant to be, is meant to be. I guess this one's just bigger than we, including you, were ever meant to handle. It's okay, Karéin. It's okay. Come on, get up."

They helped the young-looking woman to her feet.

The Storied Watcher stared at the floor, tears rolling down her cheeks. She cried, "Now it really *is* going to happen. Just like before. *Just like before!*"

Faster than the quickest falcon, she turned and flew away from the group.

"Let her go," counseled Jacobson. "She's just upset."

"Would you not say that she has the right to be?" commented Chkalov.

"Indeed, as do we all," replied Jacobson. "But we *knew* that this outcome might – was *likely to* – occur," he continued, "And it's up to *us* to pick up the pieces and move on, to start thinking about next steps. I expect everyone to do that, starting now... okay, maybe not *right* now. Maybe we all need some time to do some thinking, each one by him or herself."

"For what it's worth, guys," White interjected, "When she was... prayin', well, that's how it looked like to yours truly, I had a look at the radiation-counters; just to take my mind off the main subject, y'all know. She wasn't *kiddin'*, Captain; she *was* tryin' to help us, the indicators were through the roof again. How she thought she'd get that energy of hers, all the way over there to the comet, I don't know. But she was *tryin'*, man... that's no lie."

He hung his head.

"Just about as effectively as we – that is, the whole human race – has been able to help itself," Tanaka mused.

"Sam," she said, "I appreciate the offer, but I think I'd rather stay here with you, right now. If you don't mind."

"Me too," mentioned Boyd. "I'll have enough time to myself, later."

"No problem, Cherie," allowed Jacobson. "I'm not going anywhere. Sergei? Devon?"

"I'm gonna go start writin' a letter to my folks back home, if y'all don't mind, Captain, sir," replied White. "I'll need some time to figure out what exactly to say. I had the other letter all ready... guess I'll have to start from scratch."

"Of course," replied Jacobson. "And Devon, I'm in the same boat, by the way. I have to write one, too. I was hoping on it being a bit more cheerful... more positive."

For a moment, the man's voice faltered, and the others remembered that despite his stiff upper lip, Jacobson had a wife, a family, too.

"Captain," requested Chkalov, "By now all the attack, and its after-effects, will all have been recorded. I think that I will spend some time in the lab and on the computer. I would like to examine the results in more detail. I do not expect to find anything encouraging, but I would like to stay busy, for the next little while. It is how I – how do you say in English – how I 'cope', I think that is the word."

Jacobson nodded. "Good idea. Let me know ASAP if you find anything interesting, Sergei."

Chkalov stood up, walking away slowly and deliberately.

"So how do you mourn for an entire *species?*" offered Tanaka, to no-one in particular.

"Especially when it's our own," mused Boyd.

Eternal Questions

As he had before, White encountered the Storied Watcher at a computer screen, enmeshed in reading and reviewing pages of information from Earth's NeoNet computer network, as these were presented to her with super-human rapidity.

The astronaut had to suppress a chuckle, upon hearing the alien-girl fret at the "slowness of the moving picture-shows"; for, these were the only things that she could not absorb at multiples of human speed-reading abilities.

She seemed to have regained her composure, as near as he could tell; which was good, considering what had happened the last time.

Not knowing why, White accosted her.

"Hey, Karéin," he asked, trying to sound cheerful, "What y'all doin' there? If you were one of us, I'd bet you'd be calling home right about now... that's what we're all doin'... but I guess y'all don't have anyone *to* call. Sorry. Didn't mean it to come out that way."

"Do not worry about offending me, Devon," her friendly voice replied. "I understand how you and your crew-mates feel, so I will not hold it against you. As you saw, I was... *upset*, at the bad news, too."

"Yeah, y'all kinda flew off the handle there, I guess, but nobody's gonna get mad at you over it," he offered. "Our own problems up here seem pretty small, considerin'... right?"

"'Flew off the handle'... I will have to remember that one, Devon," stated Karéin-Mayréij. "I *did* fly away, upon hearing of the ineffective attack. Please understand – I am *so* frustrated at how weak I still am, about being so totally *helpless* to assist your people; at other times, in other places, I have had powers rivaling those of the Gods Themselves... I could overturn mountains, change the course of seas... but here, I am but a pale echo of my former self. None the less, I should not have become angry. At least *this* time, I did not threaten your Captain's life... so I *am* making progress, you see."

She smiled ruefully, then added, "But yes... you are right. We should not be angry or impatient with each other, not *now*. Not when the hour is this late."

He nodded, then asked, "So whatcha studying there? Earth's funeral customs, maybe?"

"Hmm... I believe that I understand your joke, and perhaps I should spend some time learning about that," said the Storied Watcher. "For the most part, I have been investigating how your planet is reacting to the failure of the attack against the comet, and what plans it is making now. The *Arks* project, in particular."

She hung her head, then looked up, then continued, "Since I have been such an utter failure so far, I thought I might be able to help some of your people to... *escape*. Maybe I could, I do not know – I am, how would you say, 'thinking out loud' – lift some of them to the relative safety of space, away from the surface of your planet. It is not much, I know... but I must do *something*."

"Y'all *know* what the Professor said," White gently replied. "It's not your *fault*. Much more *ours*, for being stupid enough not to prepare for somethin' like this comet. If y'all read our science history, you'll see that we were warned that it was gonna happen sooner or later. Don't go kickin' yourself over it."

She smiled at him.

"Thanks," she half-whispered.

White then asked, "Karéin, now that we're here, y'all mind if I ask a personal question? It's kinda been on my mind, since we got the bad news."

"A question about my person? Certainly," answered Karéin-Mayréij.

"*Sorta* about your person, yeah," he confirmed. "I don't exactly know how to say this elegantly... so I'll just throw it at ya, okay?"

"Sure," she replied.

"The thing is, Karéin," explained White, "I mean, as y'all gotta be aware right now, ninety-nine point nine per cent of the human species – includin', probably, yours truly and the rest of the crew of this little rust bucket, are about to meet their Makers, that is... we're fixin' to die, as the song goes."

She stared at the floor, avoiding his glance.

"Yes, I know," she observed.

"What I wanted to ask you," continued the astronaut, "Is... well... y'all must have seen this kind of thing happen, on and off, through all those former lives of yours, lady. I mean, mass destruction, end-of-the-world stuff, that kind of thing. Didn't y'all ever get curious, as to what happens to the unlucky ones?"

"I am sorry, Devon. I do not understand what you are trying to say," she evaded.

White, pressing, said, "What I'm tryin' to say, Karéin, is... haven't y'all ever wanted to die? Wondered where y'all go, afterwards?"

The Storied Watcher looked away, thought for a second or two, then answered, "Yes. Have you?"

"From time to time, yeah," he offered, "But it's *inevitable* for us miserable little human beings. Not like for yourself, if I understand what y'all been telling us about your past history. Hasn't it ever made y'all, even the *least* bit curious?"

"Do you want an *honest* answer to that, Devon?" she parried. "You may not like what you hear."

"Go ahead," allowed White. "I'm not sure I won't regret sayin' this... but how could it be *worse* than what we've already heard today?"

"Oh-kay," answered Karéin-Mayréij. "If you *must* know, here is what I believe – not what I *know*... because, you are correct, I have never passed over that most final of boundaries, for a sapient being. Although I have come frighteningly close, many times."

He waited and listened.

The Storied Watcher explained, slowly and deliberately, "First, you have to understand that because most of the intelligent races with which I have had contact are, or were, mortal, almost every one of them had after-death beliefs, theories, religions, whatever you want to call it. This is not at all surprising and I do not blame those who hold these views, one bit. If my *own* life was this finite, no doubt I would have them too."

"But, and second," she paused and elaborated, "My own, honest guess, is that when we die, we *are* no more – that is all. It is the end of consciousness, thought and understanding; a dark, blank nothingness, akin to the many ages that passed before we first have life. Let me ask you, Major Devon White... how did *you* feel before your mother first bore you into your world? *That* is what I think death feels like. It *terrifies* me, because I savor every waking moment, and every sleeping one, as well. Which is why I am so careful to avoid being killed."

White cleared his throat hastily and admitted, "Point taken, Karéin... point *really* taken. But you know, speakin' just for myself, well... I was raised a Baptist – if y'all haven't gotten to the religion section of NeoNet yet, that's one branch of the 'Christian' religion – and we believe that after we die, we go to our 'just rewards' in heaven, where we get to sit on clouds all day with God and play a harp. Sounds like *real* fun, man, but better than the other place, where the bad folk go... supposed to be *wicked* hot, down there. At least, that's what the preachers tell us."

She looked at him with lambent eyes and remarked, "If that is what you *truly* believe, Devon White, man of Earth, then I envy you for it. Your faith must give you great comfort, especially in times such as these. I wish that *I* had something alike. If it means anything, I have sought out such insight throughout the many years, worlds and dimensions... but I have yet to find it. I *have* run into hundreds of would-be guardians of the afterlife, who *claimed* to know what happens after one dies; but of all of these, I have met perhaps one or two whom I half-believed, although on some worlds, there were *indeed* necromancers – that is, creatures who seemed to be able to re-animate dead things and make the latter do their bidding... though I would not call such frightful creatures truly 'alive'. Maybe *that* is evidence of an afterlife; but, if so, it is not the type that I would want."

Inwardly, she mused, *But what about that greatest of powers that you have yourself used, once or twice, Storied Watcher? You have brought others back, you think, but there is no-one to do it for you, irony of ironies...*

White replied with a half-chuckle, "Well for us Christians, the head honcho of our religion, a guy named Jesus Christ, he was supposed to have come back from the dead, himself, wounds and all, so maybe y'all wouldn't like *him*, either, after all –"

"Yes, I have read *much* about him, on your com-pu-ter network," she interrupted. "This 'Jesus' seems to have had a very important impact on your history. He must have been an enlightened man, as were his brother-priests – I believe that their names were 'Mohmaed', 'Budda', 'Confusus', 'Kersna', and there was an ancestor of this 'Jesus' called 'Mozez', correct? It was interesting reading about them, not only because their teachings have much wisdom, but also because their accomplishments seemed to suggest that your world might, at one time, not have been as magic-poor as it is today."

Karéin-Mayréij continued, "Incidentally, I found it strange that they were all men; on *most* magic-rich worlds, women are found as religious leaders, too. It is unfortunate that these spiritual leaders died so long ago, or rather that I only woke up now. I am sure that I would have had much to discuss with them. Like, how those who followed them, violated all their rules about love, tolerance and sharing, turning instead to war and persecution. Sadly, I am not at all surprised at this outcome... I have seen it before..."

Shaking his head slightly, White replied, "Y'all always have a way of looking at things that I'd never have expected, lady, that's for sure... for a while there I was tempted to invite you to one of our Sunday church services, back on Earth, so y'all could find out for yourself... but I guess that won't work *now*, will it? Just for the record, I don't know if I really believe it myself, but man, you gotta believe in *somethin'*... don't you? Maybe that's why us humans invented the idea of God, so we'd have hope. So death wouldn't be the end. I mean, do you think it makes sense, for us to die and, well, for *nothin'* to remain, afterwards? I just can't *deal* with that, Karéin. Very few of us humans can."

"No," agreed Karéin-Mayréij, "I do not think that it makes sense, either, Devon. I wish that I could say this in a way that you would fully *understand*... but there *is* an elegant, serene, ineffable purpose to the universe, a grand, beautiful rhythm, like the rising and setting of your Sun, but on a vastly greater scale. It is far above and beyond you and me, both – way past the comprehension of creatures such as you or I. The universe creates amazing bounty and destroys without pity, both at the same time, motivated by forces that we cannot even guess at... and perhaps *that* is your 'God'. And so that you know... you may *think* of me as being much greater than you, and I suppose that in some ways I am... but in the grand scheme of the universe, I am as humble and insignificant as any human. On the cosmic scale, you and I are *infinitely* less important than is a single grain of sand on any beach, or a single drop of water in an ocean. But we are, none the less, more than nothing."

The Storied Watcher stopped and thought for a second, then, in a reflective voice, added, "You know, sometimes I catch myself believing that after a mortal being dies – remember, I am *not* immortal, I can easily die from mishap – it *must* somehow become part of that purpose; that one's energy, one's consciousness, one's intellect, and especially one's love and goodness of heart, must return to the larger whole. You and I are both *something*, Devon; it violates the laws of nature, as well as offends our common sense and intuition, to believe that 'something' can become *nothing,* with no purpose to show for one's life, other than in the transitory memories of a departed person's kin and friends.

"If our minds, our self-awareness, our *souls*, were created out of disordered atoms, whether by some deity or just by one's father and mother, and in so doing became much more than just a collection of chemically-attached molecules," she went on, "It just does not seem *right* to believe that the special supernatural property which makes us thinking, self-aware beings, can just vanish into complete nothingness. Elements and substances of the universe can change into a different state, they can lose heat and energy, but they cannot – as far as I have been able to tell, in all my years – just vanish altogether; so, if this be the case, how can one's soul, behave differently? It *may* be – how do you say – just 'wishful thinking' on my part, to suppose that the mighty cosmos has reserved a place for us after the life that we know has left our bodies... but I *believe* this without being sure how I would prove it. Yet, as far as anyone can attest, you and I *were* both nothing, before we were born, which leads us back to where we started. Do you see why I have only a little hope... yet more than none?"

"Yeah," he replied. "This whole thing's a deep subject, that's for sure. Y'all sure seem to have thought it out. And I guess you've had a *lot* of time to do that. More than I'll ever have."

The alien-girl noted, "You are assuming that pondering the imponderable, over many years, will necessarily lead to more understanding, than thinking about it just for a while, when faced with having shortly to deal with it. I am not at *all* sure that is a safe assumption."

Considering this point, after a second or two, White commented, "But honestly, lady, even though things are the way they are these days, I'm not sure I'd trade places with you. Us humans are used to livin' for a while, then... well, you know. It's the way things are *supposed* to be with us. Most of us don't mind it – I can say, for truth, that *I* don't. What makes things hard, is the idea that there won't *be* a 'next generation', to take over where we left off. *That's* definitely not according to plan, no way."

There was the trace of a tear in one of her eyes.

"You are *so* right about both those things, Devon," kindly stated Karéin-Mayréij. "To see successive generations of one's friends, one's family, fall victim to old age and death, as I do each time when I awake, is lonely, *terribly* lonely, in a way which I cannot explain to you... and I hope that you never *do* experience it. There was a time when it hurt *so* much that I refused to ever befriend or love a mortal; but, over time, I came to understand that it is, still, better to love and hurt, than never to love at all."

The alien-girl coughed, awkwardly, as if to avoid being overcome by emotion, then continued, "There *are* times, please believe me, when I wish my own destiny was as yours... but to then have to confront the present possibility that your children will not survive, as you have to now – it would break my heart. I think our ideas of the afterlife are different, but I hope and pray – yes, Devon, I *do* know how to pray, too, not exactly as you humans do, but I know what it means to ask the higher Planes and the Holy Light for guidance, for solace – that *your* belief is right and mine is wrong. I really *do*."

She took his hand and looked affectionately into his eyes. Somehow, the rush of super-normal thoughts and images was under control.

Even the glib Devon White could not think of anything smart to say, now. All he felt was a kind of awed friendship, as if he had known this woman from the time he was a child, as if she was his dearest, platonic companion. She shared his apprehension, while he shared hers.

He felt at peace, if only for a blessed moment.

Eventually, White came out of his trance and announced, "Right. Well, thanks – I *mean* it, no shit, Karéin, I really *needed* to talk to somebody about what was on my mind there girl, and y'all were there for me. Man, it's *weird*, you know, I mean here I am talking as if y'all were my minister back in the Compton Baptist, and here you just woke up on Mars. Strange days, lady... strange days."

"And," concluded the Storied Watcher, "I am learning deep insight into the most important issue that any thinking being can ponder, from a human man, untold *thousands* of years my junior. I wish that you could understand how humbling an experience *that* is, Devon. 'Strange days', you say? I think that the expression you humans use is, 'you got *that* right'. So... you got *that* right, Devon."

She grinned, showing those teeth just a bit.

White just feigned a smile and waved to her, as he forced himself to get up and go off to his quarters. He looked back just before he rounded a corner.

She was still sitting there, looking at him, peacefully.

Sliver Of Hope

Apart from White and the Mars-girl, everyone avoided each other's company after Tanaka and Boyd left Jacobson's presence, shortly after they had learned of the outcome of the attack. But on the pseudo-morning of the next day, they gathered in the eating-area on the Captain's orders.

"Hi, team," Jacobson offered, trying to look cheerful. "Did everybody get their affairs tended to, last night?"

A few of them mumbled affirmatively.

White spoke up. "So why the get-together, Captain, sir?" he asked, indifferently.

"Some interesting news, regarding our old friend 'Lucifer'," replied the Mars mission commander.

Instantly, four pairs of eyes, one of these glowing slightly, focused on Jacobson. Chkalov just nodded, knowingly.

Hands in the air, he motioned down their expectations. "Not *great* news," Jacobson cautioned, "But certainly not *bad* news, either."

"Sam, please explain," anxiously inquired Tanaka.

"Thought you'd never ask," he said, with the hint of a smile. "To get right to the point, it's like this: remember how we saw the missile attack hit, and, or so it seemed, not even *scratch* the damn thing?"

"Aye," confirmed the science officer.

"Well, it looks like we might have done *some* damage, after all," Jacobson stated. "Sergei? Want to explain?"

"Certainly, Captain," Chkalov replied.

Addressing the others, the Russian explained, "After yesterday's attack, I went off to examine the comet more closely. It was really just a way of having something to do, as I do not have the same family issues that many of you have... except for my mother... Anyway, I used the *Infinity's* terrain-mapping imaging radar and our other sensors to scan the object's surface from our perspective, which, as you should know, is opposite from that of Earth – they see the side of the comet that is approaching them, while we see the side that is steadily receding from us. Initially, the results were inconclusive, because the attack had sublimated much of the comet's surface into a dense particle cloud surrounding it, and this prevented a really good look at the surface. But eventually, I was able to acquire accurate readings and sent them in to Earth for processing."

"And...?" pressed Boyd.

"What Earth was able to detect, by digital enhancement of our radar surface readings, was that the missile attack was *not* completely ineffective, even though, apparently, a high percentage of the weapons detonated prematurely, possibly because of impact with the surrounding debris-field prior to actually encountering the main target," continued Chkalov.

"They are not sure exactly how this happened," he said, "But it appears that some of the shock waves of the nuclear detonations somehow were transmitted through the center of the comet, exiting out the other side. This has opened at least three deep fissures in the side of the object that is nearest to us. It is still intact, of course, but what neither Earth nor I can estimate, with any accuracy, is how internally stable the object is, whether it could withstand another attack similar to the one we have just subjected it to."

"May I add," interjected the Mars mission commander, "That this is in some ways good news... because, according to Sylvia Abruzzio, with whom I spoke late last night, if – when – 'Lucifer' impacts with Earth's atmosphere, it has a good chance of breaking up into four or more smaller pieces, maybe more, before any part of it hits our planet's surface. Unfortunately, the cumulative effect of the impact of all of these is, or so the scientists say, likely to be nearly as destructive as would be that of the whole object, possibly worse, if they're spread out enough. Remember, it's a *huge* comet; each of the secondary pieces would still be nearly an extinction-level event, on its own."

"Wait a minute," interjected Boyd. "Didn't Symington say that Earth had a last-ditch attack planned, using short-range nukes, submarine-launched missiles... that sort of thing? If the damn comet is already breaking up, isn't there a chance that our SLBMs might be able to shatter it entirely?"

But the look on the Mars mission commander's face was weary; Jacobson wanted to nip rising expectations in the bud.

He cautioned, "Look, team – it's not *bad* news, and what we need nowadays is a lot more non-bad news; but, neither NASA nor I think that we can count on the SLBMs, unfortunately. We need *ideas*... and, if any of the rest of you can think of something creative to do to get us out of the path we're on, by all means let me know. I'll call everybody together a few hours from now, when I've had a chance to consider our options. Agreed?"

"Agreed," simultaneously answered three of them.

Hot Air From Earth

White was the first one to see the "incoming" light come alive, on the heads-up status panel.

"Yo, Captain," he said, "Message from Houston. Want to screen it first?"

"No, Major White," replied Jacobson, "I don't think that's necessary. You may as well put them through."

White complied with a couple quick keystrokes and the view-screen lit up, revealing Symington, Ramirez and McPherson; Abruzzio did not appear to be there.

Ramirez spoke first.

"Hello, *Eagle* and *Infinity*," he greeted, "This is Hector Ramirez down here at Houston. I have General Symington and Fred McPherson here with me – Sylvia is busy with the *Arks* project which, as you can no doubt imagine, is now going into its 'full speed ahead' phase, so she's not with us today, she sends her regrets. I'm going to turn the floor over to Fred and then to the General, so they can bring you up to date on what our current status and plans are."

The camera moved slightly to the left from Ramirez, centering on McPherson. The man looked tired and he had a touch of five o'clock shadow.

"Thanks, Hector," McPherson said. "First of all, I don't think I need to inform you of the results of the missile attack on the 'Lucifer' object... it's no secret that we're, to put it mildly, disappointed in what has occurred, or rather, in what didn't happen. But," he sighed, "There's no point in dwelling on the past; we have to look to the future, and to next steps, now. Before I move to that, though, I'd like to commend Cosmonaut Sergei Chkalov for his fine work in assisting our long-range damage assessment scans on the comet. The data that he has revealed has been of tremendous importance in helping us understand the facts and to make plans. So, Sergei, thanks again... and if you find out anything else, please don't hesitate to send it our way."

Chkalov modestly nodded in acknowledgement.

After a short pause, McPherson continued, "As I said before, you're probably aware of the situation, but just so that we're sure that everyone is on the same knowledge base, I'll recap it briefly here. Bottom line is, we threw *everything* that we could scrape up against the damn comet, but, unfortunately, it appears not to have been enough – 'Lucifer' has been damaged, but not destroyed, and it is *still* on a collision course with Earth."

"Now," stated the general, "As you're aware, the story isn't *all* bad, because – thanks largely to the efforts of your cosmonaut friend up there – we have discovered that the comet's internal structure has been weakened by the attack. By how *much*, we're not sure... but we are continuing our assessment, and I should tell you that associated with this we have also initiated another manned mission – in effect, *'Salvador Two'* – against the comet to see if we can succeed in blowing it apart, by placing nuclear explosives so as to leverage the instability caused by the missile attack..."

Tanaka exclaimed, *sotto voce*, "Surely they *know* that would be a *suicide* mission – the comet's lethally radioactive and its local debris-field is even more intense as the thing has gotten closer to the sun... they'd be lucky if they make it down to the surface for an hour, before..."

McPherson, still in mid-sentence, explained, "We've got no problems getting volunteers for the crews; but launch-vehicles are going to be a challenge, because right now every last ship has been claimed by the *Arks* initiative. Frankly, in view of the outcome of the first *Salvador* mission, I'm not happy about pulling resources out of *Arks* – to get so many as one or two ships capable of even theoretically making it up to 'Lucifer', even for a one-way mission, we're sacrificing the ability to lift fifty, possibly a hundred, people off Earth to temporary safety... that's a *big* sacrifice to accept, in the current circumstances."

He paused a second to take a breath, then said, "Also, compared to the first *Salvador* mission, this one will take place under severely constrained circumstances, because we had months in which to prepare for the first mission but only a few weeks, at most, for this one. For example, we'll have to do it much closer to Earth – we simply don't have a ship that can get out as far as *Salvador I,* and on top of that, we can't manufacture bombs the size of the ones that we used on the first mission, there just isn't that amount of fissile material available – especially considering that the remaining missiles are to be used for a different mission. We'll keep you advised of progress, of course; but for now, all we can ask you do is to continue observing the comet and to send us data on any changes you see in it, ASAP."

The Mars-girl whispered, "What is an 'asap'?"

"'As Soon As Possible'", replied Boyd.

"Ha... I *see,*" said Karéin-Mayréij, smiling sheepishly.

"Captain, I have to talk to you," she requested; but Jacobson gestured her to silence.

McPherson concluded by saying, "Well, that's it from me, *Eagle* and *Infinity,* as I said, keep up the good work, we sure can use the extra pair of eyes that you've given us. I'm now going to turn the floor over to General Symington. General?"

Symington's face appeared, even more ridged with fatigue than had been McPherson's; however, the General seemed more in control, less willing to show his disposition.

"Greetings, crew," he said, "And let me start by echoing Mr. McPherson's congratulations to Cosmonaut Chkalov. Sir, I have the honor to inform you that, based on your activities so far in determining the weaknesses in the comet, your Air Force has decided to award you a medal – they haven't told me exactly which one, but as soon as that information is forthcoming, I'll send it your way."

He saluted, while saying this.

"Now, as Fred McPherson has explained, team, unfortunately, our main missile attack did not... achieve its full goals," Symington commented. "But as you know, we have been drafting a series of fail-safe measures to deal with this eventuality."

Tanaka suppressed an urge to laugh at the man's pomposity.

Symington continued, "And I won't bore you with the details, since you can easily access these on NeoNet... but here's a summary. Assuming that the second *Salvador* mission – which may or may not make it off the ground – is *not* successful, as the comet enters Earth's atmosphere, we're going to hit it with all our remaining nuclear weapons, down to sub kiloton-range tactical, in a last-ditch, co-ordinated strike."

"Yo... finally somethin' good out of all them nukes," grunted White.

"What's different is," elaborated the general, "We're going to target these so as to exactly hit the pressure-points associated with the newly-discovered fissures; we're hoping that this will induce the object to fracture and then shatter.

Inevitably, the remaining chunks of it will strike the Earth, causing catastrophic results, but this outcome can't, we hope, be worse than if the whole thing impacted. Planning this attack has been *extremely* complicated, not just because of the number of national commands and different types of weapons involved, but also because we have to be careful not to destroy too many of the *Arks* ships that may be in low Earth orbit at the time. It appears that some collateral damage on this front, may be inevitable."

"'Collateral damage'... where have we heard *that* before, I wonder?" idly asked Tanaka.

"Other than for that," Symington concluded, "Our plans, and your orders, remain unchanged; we're tracking you on course for *rendez-vous* with ISS2 in its boosted orbit, so that's good. The only variable that we can see right now is the outcome of the second *Salvador* mission, but we're not counting on that, so proceed as you would have. That's all I have to say... Mr. Ramirez?"

Ramirez took the microphone and stated, "Well... that's the update, *Eagle* and *Infinity*. Obviously, we had hoped to have had better news, or alternate plans... but life goes on, at least for the time remaining... right?"

He forced a grin and finished off with, "Awaiting your response, if any – especially if your alien-friend has some wise advise for us. Ramirez and Houston, over and out."

The light and screen both dimmed.

Now Jacobson turned to counsel the Storied Watcher.

"To make it easier, Karéin," he proposed, "I'll let *you* decide how to address this... it's up to you to set expectations; and as a bit of friendly advice, I'd suggest that you tell them only what you think you can *definitely* commit to. Devon, can you get us ready to record a message to them? Let us know when Karéin can start speaking."

"Way to put her on the spot, there Cap'n," interjected White. "But Karéin, just for the record, we all *believe* in you. Speak from the heart and y'all be fine."

"Thanks, my brother," was all she said.

I Am More Than You Thought

"Okay," White replied, "I got us rigged up. Tell me when, Captain."

"Now," directed Jacobson, looking into the camera.

He announced, "Hello, Houston, this is Sam Jacobson and the crew of the *Infinity* and *Eagle*, with our response to your latest transmission. First of all, thanks for the update – our hopes and prayers go with the *Salvador Two* and the brave men and women of its crew. On that subject, Houston, for reasons that we'll explain later, we have a pressing need to know every last detail about the *Salvador Two* mission – from its liftoff time, to its exact trajectory and ETA to 'Lucifer', as well as to the exact physical characteristics of the *Salvador Two* ship itself. Please *trust* us on this one, Houston, and get the information to us absolutely as soon as possible, within the next few hours if at all possible. Of course, we won't undertake any actions related to this mission, without your advance knowledge and approval. But we need that data, pronto."

He took a breath, then continued, "And as to the *second* issue that we want to discuss with you today, well... that has to do with our guest. I've asked her to... *clarify* some details about herself, to you. I'm going to hand the floor over to her, now, so she can do this. Karéin?"

"We are sending the transmission, now?" asked the Storied Watcher. White nodded affirmatively.

Karéin-Mayréij stood up and faced the camera, firmly, defiantly, with her legs slightly spread, hands semi-clenched at her sides.

She closed her eyes and her body began to pulse with the strange energy-discharges that they had seen before, accompanied by exciting, fast music, pounding suddenly in their heads.

Her entire body was glowing, shimmering with an aura of elfin light.

The alien-girl suddenly opened her eyes, which were now also glowing brightly. They had never heard the voice she used now. It was her same, soprano-alto pitch; but it had a musical, symphonic back-tone of grandeur to it.

Staring at the screen, she proclaimed, "Houston and people of Earth, I am Karéin-Mayréij, The Storied Watcher, The Guardian Of Ages, Who Comes At The Deepest Hour. These titles are not by accident, because I only awaken when someone needs my help... as your people do, now. You have seen me before, but I stand before you now to confess that, though I fear that I am still far below the height of my powers... neither am I like to mortal men and women.

"Sisters and brothers of Earth," she related, "I have weirding abilities that, until now, have not been fully revealed to anyone, except to my friends here on the *Eagle* and *Infinity*. For example, I can fly unaided in outer space, by controlling the force of gravity and by using a form of energy that I call "the *Fire*". I have other powers as well, which have been increasing day by day, since Captain Jacobson's crew and I left the planet that you call Mars. I believe that I can fly from where I am now, to the comet that currently imperils your planet – but, alas, I am *not* yet strong enough to destroy 'Lucifer', nor can I deflect it from its course... so do not think of me as your savior."

She paused for a second, then added, "I want everyone on Earth to know that there is *nothing* for which I pray for more earnestly, than to stop the comet. *That* power eludes me; but perhaps, working together, you and and I can try to achieve the same goal. For example, perhaps I could clear a path for your *Salvador* ship, to protect its crew from the hazards around the comet. Doing this may or may not be possible, depending on many details that Commander Jacobson and I do not yet have adequate information on. This is why the Commander asked for the new Earth-ship's information, 'ASAP'."

Finally, Karéin-Mayréij requested, "I ask for only one thing in return : that no harm comes to Captain Jacobson and his crew, who awoke me and cared for me, when I most needed someone to help. I owe these men and Professor Cherie Tanaka my new life... they are my new family. I place my trust in you, people of Earth, to see to this; and in turn, I place myself and whatever powers I have, at your disposal. I will *not* fail you, brothers and sisters of Earth... may peace, love and safety be with you, all your days."

She closed her eyes again and concluded, "That is all I have to say."

Gradually, the flashes of energy and the music subsided. Her voice returned to normal.

Jacobson motioned to White, who disengaged the video up-link.

"Nicely put," offered Tanaka.

"Well, if *that* doesn't get their attention," commented Boyd, "I think I'll try my own hand at jumping out there without a space-suit. You sure *sounded* godly there, Karéin."

"You know, Brent," quietly responded the Storied Watcher, "For a second or two... I *felt* 'godly', as you say. I thought that I felt the presence of my greater powers – I could almost tap them, use them. They are just out of reach... it is very frustrating. Maybe it was my imagination."

"You shouldn't have bargained with them, Karéin," mused Jacobson. "We're just not that important."

"Not to speak outta turn, Captain, sir, but about a little thing like us livin' or dyin' not bein' *important* –" shot back White.

Karéin-Mayréij sat down and turned to face Jacobson.

With determination, she said, "I love you and respect you, sir... but no, you *are* that important. Many of your lifetimes and many different worlds have taught me not to accept the idle sacrifice of lives, least of all those of my most dear friends. I am not – as you say – 'about to start now'."

"I wouldn't worry about it, Sam," suggested Tanaka. "From their perspective, granting her request would seem like quite a minor issue, in the grand scheme of things, don't you think? Yeah, they want the air we have on-board here, but letting us keep breathing it would just reduce the amount of stay time that all the rest of them have on ISS2 – nothing catastrophic would happen immediately. Or, they could just grant us all a free pass on that *Arks* program."

"Besides," added White, "We *know* that she'll help Earth, regardless of what happens to us. Right?"

He shot a grin at the Mars-girl.

"You may be right about that, Devon," she amicably replied, "But please do not ask them to test me. Some paths are best left unexplored."

"Damn straight," answered the astronaut. "Y'all can be *sure* of that."

Chkalov interrupted, "I am now receiving some data from Earth, Captain. It is – wait – I think it is the details of the *Salvador Two* mission. Obviously they had this information ready already, because there is quite a bit of it... interesting..."

"Let me have a look," requested Boyd, sauntering over to the display.

"Yeah, I see what Sergei means," he grunted, while looking into the computer-images. "What a bucket of bolts – excuse the simile, Captain, but it's more or less the truth – Houston's *really* scraping the bottom of the barrel, just to get this *Salvador Two* thing space-borne – old Shuttle One solid boosters, absolute minimum environmental allowances, no redundant systems and a test-ship that was never supposed to leave the ground; it sure wouldn't survive re-entry, *that's* for sure... but I guess that's not an issue with *their* mission profile, is it... *if* they make it off the ground, in the first place – I sure wouldn't want to put good money on that. They got it pretty well-shielded, though."

"No doubt they have learned from the fate of the first mission," stated Chkalov, "And the ship would have to keep the crew relatively safe from radiation, at least until they landed on the comet. Of course, neither American nor Russian space-suits would provide much protection once they disembarked... but as you said, Major Boyd, that is not a problem, for a, how you say in English, 'one-way' trip..."

"I wonder if they've given them something to take, when the radiation starts to affect them," Tanaka quietly surmised. "You know... a pill, something like that."

Chkalov mutely nodded.

Boyd said, "I don't see anything like that on the manifest, Professor... but I'd have to assume that it'll be there somewhere."

Karéin-Mayréij had now joined the cosmonaut and Boyd at the computer display.

"Sergei," she asked, "What is the new ship's mass? Can you compare it to this one, that is, the *Eagle* and *Infinity*, together?"

Chkalov mumbled something back to the alien-girl as Jacobson looked silently on. The Mars mission commander felt strangely at peace with himself as he watched his crew, and an other-worldly being, co-operating as friends to save his planet, huddled together in common cause.

No matter how things turn out, he thought, *I have done everything they could ask of a mission commander.*

I have done my duty.

Her music came briefly back to his mind. He didn't know if it meant that his thoughts were known to her, but neither did he care.

"Yes, *this* is interesting," Jacobson heard the Mars-girl say. "If you are right, Sergei... the new ship would not have even two-thirds the mass of this one. I could easily, how you say, 'drag it around' in space, although how well it would handle the stress of acceleration and deceleration, I am not sure –"

"Probably pretty well," commented Boyd. "Remember, it has to survive the boost-phase, off Earth. That's a *lot* more kinetic and equivalent-G stress than either *Eagle* or *Infinity* have to contend with. Even *Eagle*, which is as close as we come to the *Salvador* ship, only had to lift off Mars... much less atmosphere, much less gravity."

"What about the liftoff time and mission parameters?" asked Jacobson.

"I am still re-doing the simulation, using the new information," replied Chkalov, "But so far, Captain, it looks promising – there should be plenty of time for Karéin to get there, to the comet, I mean. They are planning to launch in a little less than three weeks, if all goes according to plan, with an estimated time to arrival at the comet being about three days after that, because the available Earth escape booster-rockets are relatively low in thrust. Even so, it is an impressive technical and organizational achievement, to build a viable space mission, in that little time."

"Don't I remember a saying like, 'The possibility of being hanged in the morning, concentrates the mind wonderfully'?" offered Boyd.

"Shit," exclaimed White. "We're less than two weeks out from ISS2 now, right? So we'd get our walking orders before the damn *Salvador Two* thing even takes *off.*"

"Not if Houston takes our esteemed guest up on her bargain," Tanaka reminded him.

"What if they do not, Professor?" asked Chkalov.

"Then," Tanaka phlegmatically replied, "We'll be no worse off, than we would have been, anyway."

"You have my word, Cherie," interjected Karéin-Mayréij, "That I will not leave the space-station, until I am certain that you will not be harmed."

"You know my feelings about following orders, Karéin," demanded Jacobson, "But I won't belabor the subject right now, because at the very least, when we get to ISS2, I can't imagine them... *executing*, what we believe their plans to be regarding the *Arks* mission, without going over these new options with both you and us. Doing that will probably buy us some time; how much, I'm not sure. All we can do, at this point, is try to come up with some valid plans of our own and then present them to Houston as soon as possible, before they get the chance to cook up anything else."

White looked at the control-panel, which now had a few more lights activated.

"Whoa, *that's* a fast one," he mentioned. "Looks like they're replying to Karéin's last message. But then I guess we're closer to Earth now, so the turn-around time isn't so bad. I'll pipe it through, okay, Captain?"

Jacobson nodded.

They saw a large group of people, among them McPherson, Abruzzio, Ramirez and, in the background, Symington, but there were also many with whom they were not familiar.

"Wow," commented Tanaka, "Sure looks like we *did* get their attention."

McPherson stepped up, in front of the crowd, and spoke.

"Greetings, *Infinity* and *Eagle*, to Captain Jacobson, his crew, and... especially, Karéin-Mayréij of Mars," he began. "We have just received your latest transmission and have been studying what you said, Karéin, with *great* interest. I have to say, Madam – if that's the right title, if not, please forgive us – that you've got a *lot* of people down here seeing you in a whole new light, although we're having a hard time believing what you said, a few minutes ago; it violates everything we have come to know about beings such as ourselves, what we're capable of... what we can survive. We *thought* that you were more or less like us. However, given the current situation, we're not inclined to subject your claims to the skepticism that we otherwise would."

He went on, "Which leaves us sort of at a loss as to what to ask you to do, because we don't have any experience in dealing with someone like you. So we're asking you just to continue with the instructions that I believe you were given, some time ago; that is, to get on-board the ISS2 space-station, when you, the *Eagle* and the *Infinity* arrive there. We have appointed Sylvia Abruzzio, along with Cherie Tanaka, to run some assessments of your abilities, so we can better make use of your help, once we know more."

"Well, I like this 'Sylvia' – she has the look of nobility," murmured Karéin-Mayréij, "But as to my only request, in return –"

"Oh, and one other thing," appended McPherson. "You have our solemn guarantee that the safety of Captain Jacobson and his crew, will not be compromised. We're not sure why you were afraid for them, but don't worry about that... we'll take care of them. That's a *promise*."

The others aboard the Mars mission ship took a deep breath.

Boyd commented, "*Suure*, he didn't understand why we were a little antsy about meeting our friends on ISS2. Has he bothered to talk to Symington, at all?"

"Thank you," breathed Tanaka, with tears in her eyes. "Thank you *so* much, Karéin."

"I'll second, third and fourth that," added White. "We *owe* y'all, Karéin. We *seriously* owe y'all."

"As I owe you, my brothers... my sister," the Storied Watcher replied, looking straight ahead.

McPherson continued, "I know you asked us not to see you as Earth's savior, but although we've done our best to be selective about what kind of information that we release to the news media... that's *exactly* what some of us are thinking, right about now. As you're likely aware, the people of this planet are almost out of tricks about how to deal with the comet, so we're grasping at any slim shard of hope... and I guess one of those, is you. If it's of any interest, some of our religious leaders are already calling you an 'angel' – that's a supernatural, divine being, in case you didn't already know – sent by one or more of our deities, to save Earth. Sorry to raise expectations like that, but it's human nature. I'll now turn the floor over to Sylvia Abruzzio, who has some more questions. Sylvia?"

Glumly, the Storied-Watcher muttered, "Yes... an, 'angel'. That, I *am* – a failed one."

"You haven't failed *us*, yet," Boyd reminded her.

Abruzzio took the microphone.

"Karéin," she asked, "I've been going over what you last said to us, again and again, as have been some of Earth's most senior scientists; but we're not sure of what you meant, because some of your claims seem... well, a bit far-fetched. For example, did we understand correctly, that you claim to be able to fly around in *outer space*, without a ship or a space-suit? Is there any proof of this? And what did you mean by, 'other powers'? Would these include anything that could affect the comet? We *want* to believe you, Karéin – but without some scientifically valid evidence that you can do what you claim to be capable of doing, we can't make any of our plans for self-defense depend on you – surely, as a rational being, you can understand why we have to proceed in this manner."

"What do they *want* her to do?" complained White, "Drop in on them and deliver a hand-written note, saying, 'Godly Greetin's From Mars'?"

A wry grin passed her face, as Karéin-Mayréij remarked, *sotto voce*, "Not a bad idea there, Devon... I think that I *could* fly to Earth and back here in plenty of time... but they would probably not be happy about me showing up there, as I believe that they are still afraid of me contaminating them. And they just ordered me to the space-station."

Abruzzio concluded, "So, basically, what we're looking for, here, is evidence, proof, anything concrete that you can show us. Once we have that, please believe me when I say, you'll have more to do than you could ever have *hoped* for. Let us know soon, Karéin, because events are moving forward... there isn't a lot of time. Awaiting your reply, *Eagle*, *Infinity*, and... 'Storied Watcher'."

As the transmission light went dim, the Mars-girl inquired, "Devon, you have a radio tracking signal, between this ship and the space-station... do you not?"

"Yep," White replied, "Been up and locked-in, since we first got our orders to divert there. Three point seven-two gigahertz, not a lot of Joules of energy in it, of course, but you don't need much, just to see the beacon, at least with the computer's noise suppression. Whoa, *I* get it – there's your tow-line... right?"

She nodded.

"Can you play the signal for me, please?" requested the Storied Watcher. White obliged, saying, "But it's just on a sub-carrier... there's nothin' to hear." The alien-girl closed her eyes and looked as if she was concentrating on something.

Then she said, "I hear it, in my mind. You are right... it *is* faint, but it is a back-and-forth tone, yes, that must be it. If this is of any interest, it is certainly easier detecting *this* kind of thing, compared to those accursed magic auras. Captain, I need to leave your ship, for a short time. But I will be back."

"What, exactly, do you have in mind?" asked Jacobson, already knowing the answer.

"Sylvia Abruzzio of Earth said that she needed some proof of my powers," replied the Storied Watcher. "Now, as Professor Tanaka has pointed out, anything that you all say on my behalf, might be interpreted by them as some sort of mental-problem. But if were to I travel to the ISS2 space-station and, how do you say, 'knock on their door'... they could not deny *that*, could they? If they do not let me in to that place, I will just come back here, immediately. If *do* they let me in, I will explain in person, then return. Either way, your people on Earth will know that I am not deceiving them. May I, sir?"

"Karéin," uneasily answered Jacobson, "Have you stopped to consider the possibility that, if they let you on to the ISS2 station – which, recall, they are planning to do when we eventually get there, anyway – they won't let you get *off*? That you won't be able to get back here, to us?"

"Seems to me," interjected Boyd, "That they'd have a hard time stopping her, if she really *wanted* to get off ISS2. One or two well-placed shots by that 'Gaze' of hers..."

"You know that I would never do something like that," disputed Karéin-Mayréij. "But I have *other* ways of making my preferences known – remember, I can put thoughts in your minds; I can be, how you say, 'very persuasive', when I want to be, but I do not like doing that unless I have to... it is a violation of another being's mental integrity. In any event, Captain Jacobson sir, I am willing to take the chance. It is not much of a sacrifice, anyway, since I will shortly be re-united with you and the rest, when the *Eagle* and *Infinity* arrive at the space-station."

"Very well, then," grumbled Jacobson.

Despite his stiff upper lip, the man looked unhappy. Like all the rest, he had grown fond of her, despite all the misadventures.

"Karéin," cautioned Tanaka, "ISS2 is still quite far away from us. Even at the highest speed we observed for you, it would take... just a second, let me figure it out... a *week* or more to get there. Not to say, to get back here, even accounting for our closing relative motion."

"I am faster now, Professor, *much* faster. I have checked the distance. A few hours, at most," confidently argued the alien-girl.

She had a steely, regal look, in her eyes.

Chkalov suppressed a gasp. He started saying, "But *that* would mean...", but as he did, the Storied Watcher got up, gave a brief curtsy and headed towards the center core and the maintenance area.

"Brent," she requested, looking at Boyd, "Would you come and help me, please? I do not want to make any mistakes, while operating your equipment."

After a wave from Jacobson, Boyd followed the alien-girl out through the hatch, with Tanaka tagging along behind. He noticed that Karéin had already made it to the outer pressure door of the airlock room.

"I could probably open it," she noted, "But I will respect your authority, my brother."

Tanaka, several body-lengths behind Boyd, cruised through the middle of the center core, positioning herself so that he could not see her, unless he looked behind, which he did not.

She did not push off from any surface, nor did she pull herself along the wall. She reached the two of them just as Boyd half-turned, so as to operate the door's unlocking mechanism.

I stopped myself... I stopped my forward motion, she thought, *just by thinking I wanted to.*

There is nothing *finer than this – I feel a thrill, a rush of adrenaline, a chill down my spine, each time when I use the power, I'm somehow more aware of my surroundings, like being on some weird, perception-enhancing drug – no* wonder *Karéin has to remind herself, that she's not a god.*

Boyd either didn't notice her abrupt stop, or didn't say anything about it, if he *had* noticed. Nor did he notice a very faint glow, that, unknown to her, had briefly come from the back of Tanaka's eyes.

But the Mars-girl gave the Professor a knowing smile, as the two of them met up.

"After you, ladies," Boyd directed, and first the two of them, then him, went through the double set of pressure doors, to the airlock ante-chamber.

"Well, we've been over this before, Karéin – we all know the drill. You got anything to say, before we shove you out into the cold and the dark?", he said.

"Yes, Brent – two things," answered the Storied Watcher. "First... you can let the air out and you can equalize the temperature in the chamber, faster, if you want – now that I remember what the deep void environment is like, I am pretty sure that I could just jump out there, with no preparation at all; my bubble would appear automatically, although it might feel a bit cold, at first..."

Tanaka said, "Heh. Sort of like jumping right into a swimming-pool in May, without taking a shower first, I guess?"

"You are correct, Cherie," confirmed Karéin-Mayréij, "Give or take a few hundred of your, how you say, Celsius degrees."

"I'm tempted to say, 'How cold *was* it, Johnnie, but that would date me'," interjected Boyd. "I'll tell you what that means, when you get back, Karéin... which means that you *do* have to return here, back to us... *promise*?"

"Oh-kay, Brent, my love," she responded. "I promise that I *will* be back, knocking at your door, sooner than you can guess."

The alien-girl regarded both of them with big, friendly eyes.

"Oh, I am *so* excited, I should tell you," she gushed. "Nobody will ever replace Captain Sam Jacobson and his crew – including you two – in my eyes; but now I will get to meet some more humans. It will be most interesting, to interact with more of your people. Maybe to help them deal with the comet."

The Storied Watcher paused for a second, then said, "I should go, now."

Mutely, Boyd opened the airlock access-door and the Mars-girl stepped into the chamber.

The door closed.

"Starting decompression and temperature-equalization," Boyd announced, professionally. "I'll run us at double the rate we tried last time, per Karéin's suggestion. Cherie, can you monitor things visually, please? Sergei and I input the values from her energy output from her last trip as a baseline, so the computer can tell if anything's going wrong."

"Yeah, I've got my eyes on her," added Tanaka. "Same glow, same aura, we saw last time, and wow, that *music*... you hear it, too? Just electrifying – I tell you, Brent, if we could just transcribe these tunes that she plays in our heads, we'd be rock-stars... makes me want to dance..."

I honestly do not know what sounds it plays, or why it plays, they heard a mental voice say.

Many years ago, I was told that it serves to warn our enemies, that the Makailkh *are coming, that evildoers should flee... you see, friends, there are many things that I still strive to understand, 'Storied Watcher' though I am...*

Then Tanaka perceived an inscrutable thought, which she somehow knew, had been meant for someone... else.

Blessed Venerable One, it respectfully implored,

Guide thy daughter, back to this ark, if ever her aim should fail... and keep my new brothers and sisters, safe.

The science officer pondered the meaning, while she and Boyd heard a faint "whoosh" as the air left the chamber containing the Mars-girl. They saw the same, martial arts-style pose that they had seen the first time, felt the surge of *Amaiish*-energy, heard the crescendo of psycho-music.

Then, she was gone, in half the blink of an eye.

"I sure hope she knows what she's doing," remarked Tanaka.

"I have little doubt of that, Professor," replied Boyd, "What *I'm* worried about, is the people on ISS2... I'm not nearly as confident, that *they'll* know what to do."

Toward The Station

Shooting effortlessly through the void of space, the Storied Watcher first flew up to the *Infinity*'s dish-shaped high-gain antenna, closed her eyes and concentrated until she had filtered the bedlam of thousands of wavelengths of random space noise, from the thin, almost imperceptible thread of the carrier signal that linked the ship she had just come from, to her new destination.

She flew directly between the antenna and its remote target – momentarily interrupting the signal, but in so doing, touching, experiencing it, as a mortal human might do, in touching a fine piece of cloth, to understand its texture, its feel – then flew to the opposite side of the antenna.

The signal, and its corresponding computer-link to the ISS2 space-station, automatically re-established itself.

Now the Storied Watcher was ready, and she cast her gaze – not just in visual light, but using powers of perception far unknown to human beings – toward the destination of the tracking beam. She saw nothing, but could just sense the energy-source at the beam's far end.

At first slowly, a few tens of thousands of kilometers per hour, the alien-girl started the journey towards the space-station. As she steadily accelerated, she discovered that she had to use all her powers of concentration to keep the tracking beam within her perception, since, as the velocity of the trip started to reach the hundreds of thousands of kilometers per hour, the radiation-bursts given off by small space-dust particles against her protective force bubble interfered with the signal's weak energy.

At just under six and a half-million kilometers per hour, she found she had reached her fastest practical speed. She could go faster, she knew; but doing so would so degrade the signal that she could no longer track it.

The young-looking woman settled in for a flight of many hours, meditating on the events of her life since she had awoken on *Mailànkh*, wondering about the new humans that she might meet, about how she could convince them of the need to approve her friends' plans for the comet.

But not only can the *Khul-Algrenàthu* make seconds seem like minutes, for their own purposes; also can they make hours, days, weeks, months, even *years*, seem like minutes. Such are the necessities of flying between the planets, even the stars.

After a few minutes of this relative time, the Storied Watcher's senses saw the energy-signature of the space-station, increasing rapidly. Instinctively, she started to apply her powers to slow down. She did so gradually and carefully, so as not to inadvertently affect this newfound, fragile, space-borne home of the humans, although, even at this, the forces of deceleration that she experienced, would have crushed any lesser being in a trice.

After synchronizing her relative motion to that of the space-station, she circled it several times, examining its outside details with intense interest and not a little admiration.

These humans are certainly an advanced race, she thought, *to have built something like this, and to have sent it out here; without the* Fire, *they have learned to use their skills of artifice to fly in space – very impressive... they are past the swords and shields stage, but why do they fight among themselves, so?*

Why do they not feed their brothers and sisters, who I saw starving, on the com-pu-ter screen?

The white-and-silver space-station was huge – twenty to fifty times the size of the *Infinity* and *Eagle* together – although she could tell that it was not meant for space travel, so much as space accommodation : it looked like a bunch of interconnected tubes and girders, except for two rotating center sections, much like *Infinity's* central core drum, no doubt for the illusion of gravity. Floating at various distances in all directions, or (in a few cases) docked with the main structure, were dozens of smaller space-vessels, all of them seemingly-abandoned or otherwise powered-down.

Unlike Jacobson's ship, the station had no obvious means of propulsion, other than a cylindrical object, now cold and dead, which seemed to have been attached to it as an afterthought, and, using the special sight, she could see stress-marks in some of the station's metal structures, as if these had been subjected to pressures that they had not been built to withstand.

There were access-doors all over the station, at least twenty of them in total... but which one to use?

Karéin-Mayréij flew up to the door nearest her and extended her hand, rapping on it three times, as the humans back on the other ship had recommended.

She waited four or five minutes, knocking on the door intermittently all the while, but nothing happened. There was no response.

Feeling a slight sense of frustration, the Storied Watcher now flew low over the space-station's structure, looking for clues as to how to gain ingress, preferably without releasing too much air into the void. But all the doors, and the levers and buttons surrounding them, looked the same.

She searched in vain for one of the finger-panels that she had seen on the *Infinity*, but found none.

Maybe the humans fixed that one, when they built this thing, she thought ruefully. *I like them for that,* she reflected, *...They learn quickly. Considering the circumstances, they will need to.*

Maybe if they see me, they will let me in, mused the young-looking being. *Ah yes – that transparent section, at the one end – it looks like the shiny, glass-stuff that Brent Boyd's space-hat had at the front, when I first saw him on* Mailànkh.

I will go in front of that and wave to them. The gold-metal film they have on it makes it hard to see through it in ordinary light, but I can still see them with the other sight...

She flew to what amounted to the front end of the station, stopped dead-center in front of a large, concave, glassed section, and waved her arms as she had seen the humans do, when they wanted to get each other's attention. Looking through the glass structure with the heat-seeing vision, she noticed three or more figures, obviously human, judging from how they compared exactly with the signatures of the humans back on the *Infinity*.

Oh yes, I forgot, she thought, *I forgot to smile.*

First rule of interacting with unfamiliar, intelligent beings.

The Storied Watcher gave her best Earth-girl's grin, taking care to retract the sharp teeth, and waited to see if they would notice her.

Knock, Knock

"Transmission coming in from ISS2, sir," announced White to Jacobson. "We're close enough now so it's only delayed a few seconds."

"Put 'em on, Devon," ordered Jacobson.

"Three guesses as to what *this* is all about," commented Boyd, who had returned to the *Infinity*'s control-center to join the other two, leaving Tanaka back in the airlock room.

Strange, he had thought, *Cherie told me she wanted to "practice some exercises", whatever* that *means...*

"Yeah," retorted White, "'See, we got this cute-lookin' chick floating around out here, *Infinity*... what the fu–'"

A previously unfamiliar face appeared on the view-screen, that of a youngish, handsome, olive-skinned man with wiry, dark hair, intense, brown eyes, a thin mustache and the stubble of a half-finished shaving job.

"*Infinity*," the man said, "This is Commander Ariel Cohen of Earth International space-station Two, calling for Commander Sam Jacobson. I have a... well, I guess you would call it, 'emergency' situation here. At least, a situation that we had not anticipated having to deal with. We need some guidance from you. Are you there, Commander? Over."

Jacobson, now wearing a knowing smile, spoke into the microphone.

"This is Sam Jacobson, ready to assist you, Commander," he said. "Don't tell me, let me guess – your question wouldn't have something to do with a pretty girl with nice, pointy-sharp teeth, showing up in your neighborhood... would it?"

Boyd and White both cracked up.

It took a few seconds for them to calm down, and just as they did, the screen lit up again. Cohen's face appeared.

"I see that you had anticipated this," the commander of the space-station said. "Just so you're aware, about two minutes ago, three of my crew came to me with a very *strange* story – namely, that something resembling a human female surrounded by a glowing aura, but completely *without* a space-suit or any other protective gear of any kind, had suddenly appeared in front of ISS2's forward observation bay. I went to see for myself and, may I say frankly, at first I thought that someone had drugged the air-supply here – but there she was... and is, floating outside, as I say this."

Cohen continued, "I'd assume that this is your 'Karéin-Mayréij', that is, the alien from Mars, Commander;, but I'm unsure as to how to proceed. Did she come here on your orders? She, or it, seems to be gesturing to us, I think to be let in; per instructions from the Multi-National Space Committee, we *had* been planning on eventually accommodating the alien on-board ISS2... but this was to happen with suitable isolation and decontamination measures, not all of which are yet in place. Awaiting your response."

"How hard is it to just open the door?" rhetorically asked Boyd.

"Yeah, certainly didn't hurt *us* any," added White.

"Well, Commander Cohen," explained Jacobson, speaking into the microphone, "I will have to leave *that* decision to yourself, but just to fill you in on the facts as I know them, first, yes, your assumption *is* correct, the person who you see outside ISS2 *is* definitely Karéin-Mayréij, the 'Storied Watcher', as she calls herself."

"We have known for some time," he went on, "That she is capable of unassisted travel in outer space at very high speeds, via a heretofore unknown form of energy that she calls the '*Fire*', alternatively, '*Amaiish*', in her own language. She is able to use and manipulate this energy in large amounts, but, frankly, we had no idea that she could travel from here to there as fast as she evidently has... I'll have to rap her knuckles about that, when she gets back here, it looks like our guest may have been less than completely forthcoming with us, about *that* aspect of her powers –"

Sotto voce, White muttered to Boyd, "Yo, I sure wouldn't want to be the one who raps *her* knuckles... if y'all draw blood, it'll melt your ruler, and if she gives you a dirty look..."

Jacobson continued, "As for why she's now with you... well, yes, I *did* authorize the trip. The purpose was to give NASA – specifically, Sylvia Abruzzio, who's got the usual scientific skepticism about what Karéin can and can't do – some hard evidence that she *can* fly in space, and, possibly, assist the *Salvador Two* mission to attack the comet. If you'd be good enough to transmit some pictures of what you're now seeing to Houston, Commander, I'd say that even Ms. Abruzzio will have the proof she needs to let Karéin try to help us with the 'Lucifer' thing."

"In the meantime," he advised, "I'd suggest that you *do* let her in to ISS2 – we've been living in close proximity to her for weeks now, with not the slightest ill-effects; Cherie Tanaka, my science officer, believes that whatever bugs that

Karéin might be carrying with her, are so alien to us humans, as not to pose a meaningful threat."

Jacobson concluded by saying, "Another consideration is, or so Major Brent Boyd, my flight officer, tells me, that Karéin is... how do I say this, exactly... 'excited' about meeting all of you, down there on the space-station. I can't claim to really *understand* how she thinks – I don't think any human being could do *that* – but she definitely has emotions, as we do... and sometimes she has trouble controlling them. Please don't misunderstand me when I say this, Commander, because she would never *intentionally* harm you; but I don't think it's in our mutual best interest to disappoint her. Besides, she's a fascinating being, once you get to know her. It's *your* ship, not mine, Commander, but I'd open the door. Jacobson out, over."

"Now we get to see," offered Boyd, "If he runs his ship with the rule-book, or with common sense."

Let Me In

The Storied Watcher had waited ten or more of the Earth-minutes, now, drifting in front of the glass-thing, watching a large number of the humans – there were clearly many more than were on the *Eagle* and *Infinity*, she had counted at least fifteen distinct heat-signatures – show up in the part of the ship behind the glass-wall, stare at her in amazement for a minute or two, then retreat to other places within the station.

She wanted to read their thoughts, to know what they intended to do; but the alien-girl refrained, remembering the discipline of her vows.

Never invade another's mind out of curiosity, never save for the need be real; you would wish no less for yourself, she remembered.

But she was growing impatient.

Why did these humans not want to meet her, to talk with her, to welcome her, as had her friends back on the *Infinity* and *Eagle*?

Were they of a different tribe, a different kingdom? Perhaps they worshiped a different deity, one less friendly than those of Jacobson and his crew?

She had *so* much to discuss with them; not least, what to do with the comet. Only a few minutes, a few minutes more; but these could be minutes she would need later.

I can shatter mountains and streak through the void, fast as lightening, reflected Karéin-Mayréij, *but I cannot make these beings come to a decision.*

Annoyed, but not knowing a better course of action, nor wanting to fly back to her home-ship in defeat, the Storied Watcher continued to wait, silently meditating as she idly counted the stars of the void.

Meet Me And Be Blessed

"Should we request a senior command-decision, first, sir?" inquired Senior First Lieutenant Li-Ho Chen of the Chinese People's Liberation Army Space Force.

"I have been thinking of that, Li," replied Commander Ariel Cohen, acting captain of Earth's ISS2 space-station. "Especially as we are effectively one half of Earth's only reliable resources, for the *Arks* program. If anything goes *wrong*... I don't know. Seems risky, to me. But I can't make every major decision that I take up here, contingent on hearing back from them. Especially as we may not have them to issue orders, sooner or later..."

His words trailed off.

A third voice, that of a short, stocky, black woman, spoke up.

"Commander," she remarked, pointing at the creature directly ahead of and above them, as she – it – *whatever* – floated in front of the space-station, apparently studying them as carefully as they were her, "You *heard* Commander Jacobson. I've also been going over his science officer's logs, at least, the few of them that I've been able to access – there are some gaps that I can't explain, but that's something we can ask her about later. There's nothing remotely indicative of a cross-contamination risk, here. I'm just a botanist, of course... but I've read two of Cherie Tanaka's books; she's not the type to overlook that kind of thing. This may be the only chance we ever get to interact with an alien. We simply *can't* pass it up."

Cohen looked lost in thought for a second or two.

Finally, he replied, "Point taken, Benetha. After all, according to the plan, we're supposed to get her – I *assume* it's a 'her' – on-board, eventually. But there's no point in taking undue chances. I'll tell you what – Li, do you think that you could isolate the air-supply in one section of the station, say, Red Three? I think there's just some spare gear in there, if I remember correctly. We could keep her there for a short while, until we've had a chance to find out what she's got on her mind. If whomever of us goes in there, drops dead, we'll know that letting her in the rest of the station is a bad idea."

"Certainly, sir," answered the taikonaut. "I will do it here, from the environment console... it is just a matter of closing a few intake and output valves. But note, Commander, that we only have one primary and one backup oxygen reconditioning systems, and neither of these can operate just in one subsection. Unless we want to *permanently* isolate the air in Red Three, we will have to mix it in with the station's general supply, at *some* point. Or, pump it out into space..."

Cohen nodded. "Let's hope that we don't have to do that," he said. "There's far too little of it, as matters stand now, especially after that damn post-boost breach in Green Seven. And can you please try to get the isolation area as small as possible, so we're not contaminating any more air than is absolutely necessary."

"Commander," interrupted the woman, "I'd like to be among the welcoming party."

"You're aware of the risks?" shot back Cohen. "If you become ill... I presume you know the *Arks* program protocol?"

"I certainly do," she replied. "I helped *define* it – as a matter of fact, I was on the team that wrote the final draft. I'll even help to mix and administer the injection, if necessary."

"I won't stand in your way," said the base-commander, "But we'll try to communicate with her remotely, at first. If, after that, you still feel it necessary to be in her physical company, well, Ms. Davidson, that's *your* call, not mine. It's your life. Oh, and you're lucky that you volunteered now... there are already two others who want the same thing, and I'm not going to risk more than three of the crew, anyway."

"Understood," said the black woman. "Who are the others?"

"Abu Bashir Samukhan – the Muslim cleric from Jakarta – and Cathrine Daladier, the French novelist... you know, the one from Tahiti," explained Cohen. "Quite a few have already asked for the privilege, but I picked only the ones with... 'non-essential' skills. You are an exception to that, so stay alive – that's an *order*, Madam," he said, smiling.

"Commander Cohen," interrupted the Chinese man, "I have created something to help us direct her. See – here it is – a sign."

He held an 'Etch-A-Sketch' in front of Cohen. It read "Door with a Red '3'" and had an arrow pointing left, underneath.

"Do you think that she will understand?" Chen asked.

"There's only one way to find out," said Cohen. "I think she has some way of seeing us, I have noticed that she seems to be following our movements. Hold it up."

Chen held the computer writing tablet up, as close to the outside-facing window as possible.

The space-girl noticed immediately and flew downwards, until she was directly in front of him.

Even through the barrier of the station's triple-layer, reinforced, anti-radiation transparent Kevlar window, Chen, along with the others, instantly felt a surge of awe, as he found himself transfixed, staring at the alien-girl's weirdly-growing eyes.

Strange music – a Tibetan *mantra*, perhaps, but set to electric guitar, a better tune than he had ever heard in the best Shanghai clubs – what the hell? sounded in his head, and although his gaze was locked on the Storied Watcher, he barely noticed her lips soundlessly making the movements that would have pronounced the English words 'Red Three Door'.

Then, she was gone.

She had disappeared from their sight faster than their eyes could track, or even blink.

"Commander," came a voice over the intercom, "Theodikas in Communications, here. I have been monitoring the outside cameras, per your request, when the... anomaly, appeared. I have her outside Red Three section – she seems to be circling the outside of the Red Three cylinder, repeatedly. I am also picking up a number of strange radiation signatures, but nothing so strong as to be worrisome. Over."

"Copy," answered Cohen. "I'm on my way to the Red Three ante-chamber. Keep me posted, if her relative position or actions change."

He turned and floated through the zero-G of the forward observation-deck, rapidly towards the main structural cylinder that formed ISS2's central axis, followed in quick succession by Chen and the black woman.

Using the omnipresent handrails and hand-holds, they propelled themselves through the station's labyrinthine collection of connecting-cylinders, interrupting their actions only to plant their feet firmly down as they passed through one of the station's two pseudo-gravity areas.

Finally, after several twists and turns, the three arrived at a small room, big enough to hold five or so adult humans, with a smaller room, separated by a double set of pressure doors, beyond, towards the exterior of the station.

"Michael," spoke Cohen, to the intercom, "Where is she now?"

"Still circling the cylinder that you're in," replied Theodikas' ghostly voice. "The alien has been flying closer for some time; she seems to be investigating every outside component. But she has not stopped in one place."

"Can you try to flash the emergency docking lights around the primary Red Three egress airlock, please?" asked the station-commander.

"Understood – activating now," said Theodikas' voice. "We seem to have her attention – yes, she has slowed. Stopped now, she is hovering just above the door."

"Thanks, Michael," said Cohen. "I'll take it from here."

Carefully, he manipulated the controls, forcing as much of ISS2's precious air-supply as possible, from the outside room.

"De-pressurized," he announced. "Outside door opening."

He cringed as he heard a slight "whoosh" – damn the engineers, anyway, why hadn't they fixed *that*, before Earth had boosted his station way up here – and waited.

It took the Mars-girl less than a full second to travel the distance from being outside, in the frigid void of space, to the relative safety and comfort of the space-station's airlock.

Through the chamber's double-paned view-port, they beheld the alien incarnation of a blond-haired, apparently Caucasian woman of perhaps eighteen to twenty years of age standing in front of them, eyes glowing alternately blue and green, a golden aura outlining her slim, boyish figure, with a translucent, shimmering 'bubble' of some sort, about a fifth of a meter from her in all directions.

She was *beautiful*, amazingly so in a disarming, 'at-first-I-didn't-notice' kind of way, much more so than the remote pictures from Jacobson's ship could ever have portrayed, despite a hint of sharp incisor-teeth behind her serenely-smiling lips.

All three of them felt a sudden urge to kneel, as the outside airlock door slammed shut.

Then, in the first of what each knew was likely to be a long series of amazements, all three of them heard a dignified, friendly 'voice' – soundless, but somehow none the less with all the attributes of spoken language – say to their minds,

Hello, brothers and sisters of Earth-ship ISS2.

I am Karéin-Mayréij, the Storied Watcher. I come with greetings from Captain Sam Jacobson and all my other friends from space-ships Infinity *and* Eagle, *who rescued me from my long sleep on Mailànkh – the planet that your people call 'Mars'. I would like to meet you, be friends with you, as well. We have much to discuss.*

May I come aboard, please?

They saw her perform a strange, submissive curtsy, or something like that, despite the fact that there was no gravity surrounding.

Israel is a place with many ghosts and goblins, Cohen thought, *but* nothing *in the IDF's training manual prepared me for meeting* this – *an alien princess from Mars.*

For a few seconds, he could do naught but stand and stare. But, coming to his senses, he fumbled for the controls, saying, "Re-pressurizing... she obviously *can* communicate with us, but we can't talk to her, without sound waves... so I have to use at least *some* air. I'll put it at fifty per cent of Earth sea level, yes, that should be enough..."

It only took a few seconds for the gas to re-enter the chamber and it appeared that the alien-girl instantly noticed its presence.

"Hello, Karéin," stammered the base commander, speaking into the outside speaker microphone. "I am Ariel Cohen, I am in charge of ISS2. We... uhh... welcome you to our station. It's a great honor to have you here with us," he added. "I mean, we're so pleased that you have come here. And there's nothing that we would like more than to meet you, but... well, we have a few *procedures* that we have to follow, first. Did Commander Jacobson explain these to you?"

Now speaking out loud, the Storied Watcher replied, "No, he did not. But I can guess. Are you afraid that I will make you sick, infect you with a contagious disease... something like that? I cannot *completely* guarantee that you will not suffer such a fate, but so far none of my friends on the *Infinity* have been adversely affected by my presence. I have turned off most of my energy-powers, too. You do not have to worry about radiation."

Looking over his shoulder, Cohen noticed that two more crew-members – a short, bald, bearded South Asian man, notable only in being apparently well past the maximum age of admission for the *Arks* program, and a shapely, dark-haired, well-tanned French woman, white but with perhaps a hint of North African influence in her, carrying an 'Etch-A-Sketch' tablet – had drifted in to join them.

The new two could not see the alien-girl, however, because the view-port was already blocked by Cohen, Benetha Davidson and Chen.

"Uhh... understood, Karéin," explained Cohen, "But we just need a little time, to look you over, sorry, maybe that did not come out right, English is not my mother tongue.".

"That is oh-kay," replied Karéin-Mayréij, with a friendly smile. "It is not *my* native language, either."

Davidson, suppressing a chuckle, said, "Well then, Commander, it looks like you and our guest have something in common, don't you? But you'd better tell her how long she'll be waiting."

"Yes, thank you for asking that, Madam – I am sorry, I do not know your name," apologized the space-girl. "That question was what I was going to ask, next. I do not have an unlimited amount of time here... at some point I will have to return to the *Infinity*."

"Benetha Davidson, Chief Botany Subject Matter Expert for the *Arks* project, at your service," the short woman replied. "Karéin, like Commander Cohen here, I'm very excited at having met you... I just wish it was in better circumstances," she said. "I don't want to take up too much time here because the Commander undoubtedly has much to discuss with you, but there's one thing that I just can't pass up, as a scientist. Is it true that you flew here, *unaided*? That is, without a space-ship, without a space-suit, without *anything*? It's awfully hard for me to imagine, that's for sure. All the way from the *Infinity*? How long did it take you?"

"Yes, that is completely true," answered the Storied Watcher. "I see that you are a colleague of Professor Cherie Tanaka; that is good, as she and I share an appreciation for science. To answer your question, Ms. Benetha Davidson, I have abilities that allow me to travel safely in the deep void of space, although – and here I find myself repeating what I explained to the crew of the *Infinity* – doing so takes a *lot* of practice; it is certainly not something that one would do without being very sure of oneself... sort of like para-choot-jumping, as you call that sport, on your planet."

"As far as the time the trip took," she said, "It was about eleven hours – I am not sure of the exact duration. I could perhaps have gone faster, but then it would have been difficult to perceive the tracking-signal that connects this ship to the *Infinity*; going too far off course in outer space, is *not* a wise thing to do."

She gave a toothy grin.

The Mars-girl continued, "I have already become acquainted with Commander Ariel Cohen, but I think I should also know the name of the third man who is up by the view-port with you, and those of the two others, the man and woman, who have just joined you, so we can be friends. For those who have just arrived, my name is 'Karéin-Mayréij'; I am called the 'Storied Watcher' by my friends on the *Infinity* and *Eagle*... and also by others, in earlier lives..."

Davidson whispered to Cohen, "How the *H* did she know that they're here – she couldn't *possibly* have seen them – "

Smiling, the alien-girl unexpectedly revealed, "I have certain powers of perception that exceed those of humans, Ms. Davidson. For example, like most intelligent beings, you radiate energy, although at a low level, and men and women look a little different in this respect, after becoming familiar with the crew of the *Eagle*, I found that I could easily tell Cherie Tanaka from, say, Brent Boyd. At ranges as close as this, I can detect your energy-signatures, even through the barriers that are now between us. But I could not do it when I was outside your space-station, except when you were in front of me, in the glass-walled front section – that part is easier to see through, in both the visual and extra-visual wavelengths."

Breaking in, Cohen commented, "Very interesting – as, no doubt, Commander Jacobson and his crew, found it. But just to answer Benetha's question, Karéin, what we had intended to do was to keep you in there for one Earth-day, along with three volunteers from my crew, one of which is Ms. Davidson herself, incidentally. The other two – the ones who, as you evidently noticed, have just arrived – are Imam Abu Bashir Samukhan, a cleric of the Islamic Republic of Indonesia, and Madame Cathrine Daladier from France. Oh, and I don't think I introduced Li-Ho Chen of the Chinese People's Liberation Army Air Force, my second-in-command here aboard ISS2. If none of the volunteers develop any symptoms of infection, then we'll take the chance and allow you to enter the rest of the station."

"'Imam', that means a religious leader... does it not?" asked the Storied Watcher. "Is Mr. Imam Abu Bashir Samukhan from your own Temple, Commander Cohen? I have noticed that on these space-ships, everyone has a particular job to do. For example, botany has to do with plants, farming, growing things to eat... correct? May I ask what Madame Daladier's responsibility is? And, Mr. Li-Ho Chen, thank you for coming here to welcome me with your sign. Your directions were easy to follow."

The Chinese man said, "You are most welcome, Storied Watcher."

"You're right about our duties, Karéin," answered Cohen. "Imam? Madame Daladier? Do you have anything to add to that?"

"Only that I am a follower of the Prophet Mohammed, peace be upon him, which is a different 'Temple' from that of the Commander – you are Jewish, I'd assume, Commander? Hello, Karéin. My name is Abu Bashir Samukhan and I am really looking forward to meeting you to discuss spiritual matters. I am sure that we will have a great deal to talk about," said the older man, in a fatherly, even-toned voice.

"You know, the faiths of Earth, never counted on encountering someone like *you*," he offered.

With a wry smile, the Storied Watcher replied, "The universe is *full* of unexpected things, sir. But I *am* very interested in religion, about how your Temples work, what they teach – as long as you are not a magician. I respect religious faith... but if you practice the weirding arts, sir, I am afraid that we will not have a lot to talk about. It is, yes, this is how you say it, 'nothing personal'. I just do *not* like wizards, that is all."

Samukhan, Cohen and Davidson exchanged puzzled looks. But then Daladier spoke up.

"*Bonjour*, Karéin," said the second woman, in heavily accented English. "I am – how do you say, in English – 'pleased to meet you'. I, Cathrine Daladier, am a writer, I write books, novels, *les romans*... that kind of thing. They give me a place on the *Arks projet* because they need someone to keep the Earth tradition of fiction, of writing, *vivant*. I would love to know about your culture, how your people experience the life. Also how your language expresses things, it is, *probablement*, different from ours, yes? Oh, *so* much to say!"

Karéin-Mayréij looked as if she was pondering something for a second, then replied, "You use some words with which I am not familiar, not from the English language, is that right, Madame Cathrine Daladier? At least, I do not *think* that they are from English, not as I learned it from Brent Boyd... I can see that your world has quite a few different tongues, for example, Sergei Chkalov on the *Eagle* taught me a few words from his Russian language. But I am pleased to meet you, too, Madame Cathrine Daladier, although I am afraid that I will not have much time, on this trip, anyway, to discuss culture, writing, the arts and so on. Maybe when I come back – right now, I have a problem with a comet, unfortunately. I hope that this does not disappoint you."

She gave a submissive bow, upon saying this.

"*Oui, je comprends*," answered Daladier, "But we will be in there with you, for a while. You may become tired of the science-talk. We chat a little, then."

The Mars-girl smiled, obligingly, then said, "Madame Cathrine Daladier, you may be right about being in here, longer than is comfortable. Commander Ariel Cohen, is a full *day* in this confined space, really necessary? Doing so may seriously impede my ability to make plans with you, to help your brothers and sisters on Earth to stop the comet. If no exception to this rule can be made, may I use your com-pu-ter to communicate with Commander Jacobson on the *Infinity*, to ask for his permission to stay here longer than we had planned, when he let me leave that ship? He gave me an order to return as soon as I could."

"Uhh... certainly," agreed Cohen, uncertainly, "There is a computer terminal and view-screen in the airlock chamber, and my Communications Officer, Michael Theodikas, can easily patch you in to the *Infinity* – I assume you're aware that there will be a short delay in between when you say something, and when they receive it, right?"

A disembodied voice from a ceiling speaker said, "All ready to go, Commander. Just have her hit the 'Send' button on the touch-screen in the chamber, she'll get a link with the *Infinity*."

"Thanks, Michael," acknowledged Cohen.

"Commander Jacobson seems to have enlisted the Storied Watcher into the American Air Force – she is taking *orders* from him, yes?" observed Chen, *sotto voce* to Cohen. "That certainly *is* an impressive accomplishment, considering that the United States could not have done the Mars project at all, without extensive support from both your Europeans and my own country. There should have been two taikonauts on that lander –"

"Sergei Chkalov, who is from a different Earth empire's army – the Russian one, I believe – said much the same thing to me, one time," interjected Karéin-Mayréij. "He told me that he wished *Russia* had been in charge of the *Mailànkh* mission, so *they* would be able to give me orders... not that he does not trust or obey Commander Sam Jacobson, of course. I seem to be very popular with you humans, at least the ones that I have so far met; but since I am here to *serve*, not to *rule*, it seems logical, does it not, that I should have to take orders from *someone*. That person happens to be Commander Jacobson because he is in charge of the ship that rescued me and because he helped me... remember, that I am here to serve *you*, not the other way around."

She looked down, for a second, then said, "My loyalty is to no particular king, queen or emperor of Earth, no one Temple or army, friends. I am here to help *all* of you... if I can."

"That's good, Karéin," offered Cohen. "And if it's of any interest, the crews on-board most of our space-ships – including *this* one – are multi-national; that's to say that we're selected on the basis of merit and ability, not necessarily national affiliation. Our American and Russian friends naturally have most of the positions, since their two nations have the most highly developed space programs, with the European Union and the Chinese People's Republic – as represented by Li-Ho here – running a close second and third, respectively."

"Frankly," he said, "With the 'Lucifer' issue hanging over all of us, national distinctions, which formerly were quite important on Earth, seem rather trivial, to many of us, these days. But I have become long-winded, here – I should let you speak with Commander Jacobson. You heard what my communications officer said, regarding the procedure to contact him?"

"Yes, sir," replied the alien-girl. "Ah yes – I see the 'virtual' button, as you say, the green one. I will touch it now... wow, you humans have very advanced communications equipment, I see... ah, yes, I am looking at the interior of the *Infinity*. There is Devon White. Hello, Devon! This is Karéin, here. I am oh-kay... how are you?"

After a flicker and a few-score seconds, they all saw White's face, with the ISS2 staff looking at a duplicate screen in the ante-room.

"Yo, Karéin!" he exclaimed. "Y'all made it down there in record time, I see. Man, that's *good* news, lady – y'all think you can speed up enough to get us, say, to Alpha Centauri, in a few weeks from now?"

She saw him turn around momentarily and shout, "Captain! We got a Storied Watcher on the screen, sir... looks like she made it to ISS2."

Smiling, Karéin-Mayréij explained, knowing that the words would not register for some time, "It is good to hear from you, Devon. But as to Al-fa Sentarri... that is the nearest star to your solar-system... correct? If I recall the relative distance from here to that star, and I only spent a short time studying the local stellar neighborhood, you would need to find something to do for more than a few weeks... more like a thousand of your Earth-years. A good chance to catch up on your reading, as you humans say."

The Storied Watcher's visage showed a wry grin.

Cohen just nodded as Chen whispered to him, "No *wonder* the Americans wanted to control this being... think of the *power* involved in doing something like that..."

The faces of Jacobson, Boyd and Tanaka were now visible.

The Mars mission commander came to the front and remarked, "Nice to see you made it down there, Karéin... but then again, I never really doubted that you would. I had a brief chat with Commander Cohen, when you first showed up there – I take it you're now aboard ISS2?"

"Yes, sir," answered Karéin-Mayréij, "And I have so far met Commander Ariel Cohen, as well as Ms. Benetha Davidson, Mr. Li-Ho Chen, the Imam Abu Bashir Samukhan and Madame Cathrine Daladier, of this ship; but I have so far not done so directly, because Commander Cohen has ordered me to stay in this little air-lock room for an Earth-day – twenty-four of your hours – with Mr. Samukhan, Ms. Davidson and Madame Daladier. This is to make sure that I do not infect the ISS2 ship's other people with the huge collection of terrible *Mailànkh* germs that I carry with me."

"She certainly has a sense of humor," observed Samukhan, under his voice, to Davidson and Daladier.

"Excuse me," whispered the French woman back, "But what is the... '*Mailànkh*'?"

"Well," answered Jacobson, "I can certainly understand that; you may remember that it's how I first reacted, when we found you were – ahem – 'along with us', Karéin. But you're right, that *would*, certainly, amount to a long stay there, for you. My understanding of the reason for your trip is so we could convince Houston that you're capable of such things, in the first place – by any reasonable criteria, I think you've accomplished that already. So why would you need to stay for a full day, anyway?"

"To meet with the people of ISS2, to get to know them better, sir," the Storied Watcher replied, earnestly. "And also to discuss plans for dealing with the comet. You know, what we were talking about on the *Infinity*, after your Earth missile attack failed."

"Commander Jacobson," commented Cohen, breaking in to the conversation from the ante-chamber terminal, "If allowing your... 'Storied Watcher' to come here to prove her abilities to Houston was your goal, well, I think you can consider *that* objective to have been accomplished; by now they will have seen images of your Karéin outside ISS2's forward observation-deck, as my comm officer, Michael Theodikas, has relayed the event down to them."

"But what," he demanded, "Are these plans she speaks of? Could we discuss them right now, over the link? I don't want to expose my crew to the alien – sorry, Karéin, it the only word that I could think of – unnecessarily, at least, before we have made the preparations that Houston has requested. If you have a plan for dealing with the comet, Commander, all of us here on ISS2 would be most interested in hearing about it."

His eyebrows furrowed, Jacobson responded with a half-sigh, "It seems that keeping things in confidence, is not my guest's strong suit. But yes, Commander, we *did* have some plans of that nature in the works."

"Since the cat's out of the bag – oh, yeah, Karéin, that means, 'since they already know the secret'," he explained, "I *can* tell you is that we were evaluating the possibility of having Karéin accompany the *Salvador Two* and protect it from local hazards around the comet. We could possibly ask her to do some other things, as well. Nothing's been decided, yet, but hopefully, that will be changing soon. Anyway, I'd like her just to come home to the *Infinity*, if it's alright with you – as I said in our first conversation, she's no threat, infection-wise... but if you'd prefer to err on the safe side, that's fine by me."

The Mars-girl looked unhappy, crestfallen even, while Chen whispered to Cohen, "How would she protect the *Salvador Two* ship from the debris-field? We saw what happened to the first *Salvador* mission... those are *large* meteoroids, sir..."

In much the same voice as that of a daughter asking a father to be allowed a Saturday night date, the Storied Watcher pleaded, "I wanted to make some new *friends*, Commander Jacobson sir – could I not stay for just a *short* while?"

"I don't have a problem with two or three hours, Karéin," replied Jacobson, "But in view of the fact that you won't be allowed to tour the ship during that time, I think you should get back after that... okay?"

"Commander Jacobson," interrupted the African-American woman, "Are you *sure* that you can't part with her just for one or two days? Oh, sorry, you don't know me, I'm Benetha Davidson, I'm the botany expert here on ISS2. In any event, Commander, surely what you have for her to do back there can wait a bit, can't it?"

"I'm afraid not," answered Jacobson, "She and I have a few things to discuss, just between us. But relax, Ms. Davidson... Karéin, myself and my whole crew, are only a few days away from docking with ISS2, anyway. When we get there you'll see more of us than you ever wanted to. Karéin, do you understand what I'd like you to do?"

"Yes, sir," the Storied Watcher quietly responded.

She looked more than a little disappointed, as did the three erstwhile members of the airlock welcoming committee.

"I will not object to that course of action," mentioned Cohen. "Karéin, we will prepare better quarters for you, when you return."

To himself, he thought, *Jacobson seems very possessive of this being. Considering her powers, I don't blame him...*

"Very well, then," stated Jacobson.

Turning to the others in the *Infinity*, he said, "Anybody here got anything to add?"

"Only, 'come home soon, girl'," joked White.

"Yeah, we all miss you already," added Tanaka. "And you owe me a lesson."

"What –" started Boyd, looking at the scientist, but Jacobson motioned him silent.

"Okay, ISS2," the Mars mission commander said, "I think we all understand each other. We'll be going along now, unless you have anything else to ask."

"Negative, Commander Jacobson," inquired Cohen, "Except that your guest will no doubt have some catching-up to do, when she gets back here... when *is* that, incidentally? I mean, when *Infinity* will meet up with ISS2?"

Jacobson again turned his back to the camera, for a moment, as he asked, "Where's Sergei? Oh, okay, Brent, you got it?"

Boyd's face showed on the screen, now.

"Major Brent Boyd, USAF, here, Commander Cohen," he stated. "We should be at the *rendez-vous* co-ordinates shortly, Commander, and we'll hold at that point when we get there, but from what we see about your velocity and relative motion, it'll be another ten or so days, approximately, until ISS2 itself arrives. By the way – I didn't want to prolong this conversation unnecessarily, but, well, Commander, how are you going to *stop*? ISS2 doesn't have any engines, other than for local power and life-support, does it?"

"No, it does not, Major Boyd," answered Cohen. "The plan was to have braking-thrust applied by using what's left of the fuel in the strap-on booster that sent us on our way here. Unfortunately, we have run into a few little mechanical problems with that, in that we have so far been unable to re-light it. But we have a few days left in which to overcome these issues... and I have my best engineering staff working on it. So I'm reasonably confident that we'll be able to reach the specified point, decelerate and then dock with you."

"I don't mean to pry, Commander... but what's the backup plan, if you can't get the booster to retro-brake you at the agreed place?" asked Boyd.

"There... *is* none, Major," guardedly admitted Cohen. "Earth is *critically* short of advanced chemical-nuclear rocket boosters and components, given the situation. It was decided only to allocate a single one, to the task of sending the station into its planned, higher orbit... and, later, for returning us back down. I really can't complain too much, since our booster has exceeded our expectations; ISS2 isn't matching *your* speed, of course, but we're already traveling much faster than the designers of this ship had ever anticipated. We just have to hope that our luck in this department continues to hold up."

"Whoa," some of them heard White exclaim, from the *Infinity*. "She'd go whizzin' right *past* us... and where she stops, nobody knows..."

"Let's hope we don't have to deal with *that* situation, folks," interrupted Jacobson. "I'm sure that Commander Cohen has the matter well under control, or at least *will* have it under control, by the necessary time. In any event, it's nothing that we can do anything about, except, Commander, if it looks like this issue might interfere with our docking maneuvers, please inform either myself, or Major Boyd here, ASAP. Agreed?"

"Agreed," replied Cohen.

Turning to the others in the ante-chamber, he directed, "You are all free to stay here for the next three hours, until, per Commander Jacobson's orders, our 'guest' will have to go back to her home ship. I would suggest that you all make the best use of the time to ask her what you want. I have some other duties to attend to, but I will be monitoring the conversation remotely – Karéin, if I think of something that I need to ask you, I assume you will not mind if I interrupt?"

"Not at all, sir," the Storied Watcher politely confirmed, "As long as your sister and brother humans here, do not object, themselves."

"My goodness," interjected Daladier, "Madame Storied Watcher Karéin, you have better manners than most people that I *conference* with, back here on Earth."

All of them tittered, at this.

"Only what I know, from observing my friends on the *Eagle* and *Infinity*, Madame Cathrine Daladier," replied the Storied Watcher. "But yours seems to be lenient culture, compared to some others that I have encountered... in one such, one had to bow and curtsy between two and sixteen times, before addressing someone, depending on who they were."

And my memory returns to me, she mused, with inner satisfaction.

I do not think that the gift of the Fire can be given through a sealed door like this... perhaps that is for the best... yet...

How can it be a good thing not to give a blessing, on a moment fleeting... then forever gone?

"Let's talk about societies, cultures, and... *beliefs*, if you please, Miss Karéin," requested Samukhan.

With an oddly saturnine look in her dimly-glowing eyes, the Storied Watcher replied, "Indeed. I have *much* to share with those who would call me a friend, who would discuss the great questions of life with me."

"No doubt, she'll have plenty to keep you occupied with," noted Jacobson. "*Infinity* out."

The view-screen went dead.

Cohen and Chen turned and floated off to their respective duties, while the three members of the welcoming committee settled in for what was for them, the most unexpected conversation they ever had, or were likely to have.

Just A Quick Little Test

It was time for her to go.

Karéin-Mayréij said her 'good-byes' to the three in the ante-chamber, promising to visit each of them in turn when she returned to ISS2.

She motioned for the remaining air to be pumped out of the airlock and then, to the amazement of both the three and of the many others who were watching attentively on the station's computer network, her eyes shone incandescent blue and green, her figure was silhouetted in a golden glow and, surrounded by a shimmering, translucent, faintly blue bubble of energy, she flew effortlessly out into space.

The alien-girl circled the structure several more times, eventually flying down to where she had earlier detected the add-on booster.

Compared to this huge, blunt-ended, cylindrical object – itself at least the size of a Prairie grain silo – the Storied Watcher was tiny, a small figure almost lost in the complex array of struts, beams and cylinders that together made up the space-station.

But she had faced tasks as large as this, or larger, many times in the past.

They said they may not be able to stop, mused the young-looking being.

But maybe I can *stop, them. Or teach someone else, how to...*

Floating in the airless, soundless void of space, she closed her eyes and concentrated, sensing, perceiving the ripple in the patterns of interplanetary gravity waves, caused by the space-station's mass.

She tried to lock her powers of force-control onto it, but her grip slipped, once, twice, thrice; this object was *big*, both its dimensions and its mass were much bigger than Jacobson's little two-ship convoy. It was difficult to fit it all in her mind, to visualize where she had to apply her force-powers.

On the fourth attempt, however, she felt her grasp fix securely on the station. Her mind felt a small flinch, like one's arm-muscles feel, when they first turn a wrench.

The one known as 'Karéin-Mayréij' concentrated again; and, to her delight, found that, yes! she *could* affect the space-station's velocity, its direction, by focusing all of her gravity-bending powers.

Satisfied with this accomplishment, after returning the station to its original position and speed, she released her grasp.

Alarm

All aboard ISS2 felt it – the shudder that suddenly ricocheted through the station's structure, followed by a feeling of faint G-force, as if in a car on a leisurely Sunday cruise.

"What's *that*?" exclaimed Cohen, who had been taking his daily work-out on the treadmill in ISS2's secondary pseudo-gravity drum, into the computer view-screen next to him. "Li? Shivani? Did we *hit* something? Michael, outside scan please – any signs of damage?"

"Working on it," he heard the voice of Theodikas say.

"No, Commander... I don't see anything on the wide-angle," remarked the communications manager. "I have checked all six, now. I *do* see the alien, though... she seems to be floating by the booster, but she does not seem to be doing anything, in fact it appears that she is having a nap. I'll run a narrow-scan over the exterior to check for micro-damage, but that will take a few minutes. I will let you know if I find anything significant. Theodikas out."

"Chen here, Commander," announced a second voice, followed shortly by the taikonaut's face on the view-screen. "Everyone here felt it, too... like when we boosted out of Earth orbit, but not as powerful. I will check for interior damage, but so far, other than for a few access-doors that have self-opened... all seems normal."

"Shivani Parmar here, Commander Cohen," sounded a third voice.

Cohen saw the dark-haired, chocolate-colored visage of his environmental systems officer.

"I'm at the other end of the station, compared to Senior Lieutenant Chen," she said, "But we too felt the impact, or whatever it was. Per protocol, I have run life-support integrity tests, but everything seems to be nominal, sir. I do not think that we have lost any air, water or other consumables. There are no hull breaches, at least none that I can detect. Should I order a manual external check, via EVA, sir?"

"No, not for the moment," replied Cohen, instantly relieved. "Li, go ahead and do a visual for the interior, but I don't think that we need an EVA, unless you later see some marginal losses, Shivani. Does anybody know what that *was*, anyway? Any guesses?"

"The best I can come up with would be a structural stress-release, sir," commented Chen. "Any impact with a meteoroid or piece of space debris big enough to have been felt throughout the ship, would *certainly* have left a notable mark on our exterior... so it cannot be that."

"Hmm... yes, I suppose you *could* be right," reflected Cohen. "But should that not have occurred earlier – say, after we had reached full egress velocity? Why *now*?"

"I do not know, sir," replied the Chinese airman. "I agree... it *is* strange."

"Very well, then," stated Cohen. "Let's all be vigilant and look for anything – however small – that seems out of place. Need I remind you all that especially considering recent events and even more, what's to come... we do *not* get second chances."

"Understood, Commander," replied both Chen and Parmar.

Cohen, temporarily satisfied but still apprehensive, went back to his exercise routine.

Welcome Back, Storied Watcher

After bidding a silent, fond farewell to the inhabitants of the space-station – with whom she had come tantalizingly, maddeningly close to meeting, only to have the damn humans' fear of non-existent diseases, to frustrate her – the Storied Watcher turned to face the tracking beam back to Jacobson's ships.

Yet I did send them my love, she mused.

There was a metal-and-plastic-stuff barrier between them all and myself – which probably would stop it...

I believe.

If not those ones... then maybe the blessing will come to their children, in the fullness of time, though only in generations to come... I will know of it.

The background electro-magnetic interference in this part of space was considerably worse than where she had originally come from, but after some difficulty, Karéin-Mayréij was able to isolate the tracking signal. She started the journey home as she had its out-bound leg, slowly, surely, then with rapid acceleration, up to the maximum speed that she could maintain and still know where she was going.

The Storied Watcher spent the trip thinking, pondering, not yet daring to imagine. She knew that her powers were returning, she could tell by having had the station in her grasp, knowing – but not ever telling, no, she would not, not even to *Jacobson*, that she could have crushed his little ship as easily as a human can crumple a sheet of paper.

Instinctively, she willed these thoughts of raw power, the might to destroy, to the back of her mind. But the luxurious call of the Fire – both her saving grace and her personal devil – resonated even *there*, begging her to release it, to show the humans what she was *really* capable of.

To show a comet, who was the more powerful.

The alien-girl wondered how Tanaka, and the humans who would come after her, would measure up to the responsibility of this new power, as useful and as destructive as mundane combustion had been, eons ago.

But the humans *had* to be told, they *had* to be enlightened – they *had* to be shown the way. It was the natural progression of the universe, the intended path of their species. It would be up to *them*, to choose how to use it, for ill or for good.

"She's here," announced White, having seen the proximity alert indicator light up on the computer display. "Came back as fast as she got there... maybe a little more."

"On my way," quickly responded Boyd, as he disappeared through the central core access-hatch.

He floated down the axial passageway and arrived at the airlock ante-chamber, finding, when he entered that room, that Chkalov and Tanaka had beaten him to the task.

"Hi, Brent," came Tanaka's greeting. "Sergei calculated her ETA back here from the length of her trip to ISS2 and he has been trying to track her via gravimetric distortions," she explained. "Seems that she's putting out a *lot* more energy now, than she had been, before."

"Y'all know, it's funny," mentioned White. "At first it wasn't too hard to get a lock on that *Amaii*-whatever shit, when she's out *there*; but just as an experiment, I tried to track her movements while she's in here with us, and the damn stuff barely *registers*... gives out after only a few meters. Maybe it gets obscured by a gas atmosphere, and the thicker *that* gets, the less our range... it was easier down on Mars, which kinda supports the theory."

"Or," offered Boyd, "She could be deliberately trying to cloak herself... right?"

"Yeah," acknowledged the black astronaut. "She's been learnin' all *about* us humans and our history, I reckon."

Suddenly, Tanaka's face wore a far-off look, as if an unexpected thought had overtaken her psyche.

"Professor...?" bemusedly asked Boyd.

"Oh, I – I was just *thinking*," Tanaka explained, "What must it *feel* like, I mean, having enough of her power, you know, *Amaiish*, as she calls it, enough to fly like *that*, across space. Enough to melt metal, just by staring at it. Just a *little* of it feels like –"

Inquisitively, Boyd asked, "And just how would you know *that*?"

Flustered, the woman stammered, "I – uhh – well, she *told* me."

She looked at the pilot for a second, checking for signs of disbelief, then continued, "Besides... if anyone should know that... *you* should, Brent. You experienced her thoughts, didn't you?"

"I suppose I *did*," he replied, "And you know, just from that fleeting experience – as much as I remember it – man, she felt *good* using it, as if she could never get enough. Like good Jack Daniels, I suppose."

He allowed himself a smile.

"I am opening the outside door," interrupted Chkalov. "Activating now."

Through the porthole, the three saw the shining, glowing-eyed alien-girl float regally into the airlock, then heard her mental projection, to the accompaniment of her psycho-music.

It is good to be home, friends, she broadcasted.

Did I miss any great events, while I was away? Like, Devon winning a chess-game against Sergei?

"Major White said that our guest has a good sense of humor," Chkalov stiffly commented, "But I do not think I will use this statement as further evidence."

To no-one in particular, he said, *"Zdravtvoitsye,* Karéin."

The airlock soon became filled and Karéin-Mayréij floated into the *Infinity,* as Chkalov opened the pressure-doors between the airlock and the ante-chamber.

"Good to have you back," greeted Boyd. "This place is rather boring without you around, frankly."

"Welcome home, Karéin," added Tanaka. "A few of us here, not least the Captain, were a bit afraid that you'd be so taken by ISS2 that you'd choose just to stay there."

"Hmm, well," peevishly replied the Storied Watcher, "As you are no doubt aware, Cherie, they would not let me loose, amongst their crew. I guess that I am too, ahh, 'dangerous', for that. Besides, you all are my family and this is my home. But you are right... in my short time there, I *did* meet some people with whom I would like to continue conversing. I learned a great deal about Earth, especially about its belief systems and its culture. These are things that would not matter much, to an exploration mission to *Mailànkh,* I suppose."

As the four of them moved through the center core of the ship towards the pseudo-gravity drum, Tanaka asked the alien-girl, "You know, Karéin, you made that trip in record time, and Sergei noticed that your energy-signature is now significantly bigger than it had been, before. Is there anything you'd care to tell us, about that?"

"I will tell Captain Jacobson," the Storied Watcher, evenly, "And you can listen to my explanation of it, then."

She paused for a second, then said, with a slight smile,

"Or, you can feel it for yourself."

Sharing The *Fire*

They reached the access-door and, one by one, practiced the zero-to-pseudo-gravity transition-jumps needed to avoid pratfalls on the curving floor of the central drum.

All, that is, except for the Storied Watcher, who simply floated down, feather-like.

They walked briskly towards the eating-area.

Jacobson and White were waiting for them.

"Coffee?" asked the Captain.

"Certainly, thank you," answered Karéin-Mayréij. "Oh, Captain Jacobson sir... did you mean *me*?"

"*All* of you, in fact," replied the commander.

"Four drinks poured – that must mean a homecoming party," joked White.

"Good to see y'all, Storied Watcher lady," he said, in a friendly voice, as he embraced her hand and gave it a good shake, followed by a kiss on his cheek from the alien-girl.

"Wish they had let us bring some booze, though," complained Boyd, "Other than for that stuff that Sergei smuggled aboard, we're dry up here."

As they sipped the *ersatz* coffee through the precautionary anti-spill spouts of NASA's zero-G cups, Jacobson commented, "Well, first of all, Karéin, I should say, 'good work' and 'welcome home', not necessarily in that order. I know it must have been difficult to have pulled yourself away from the sights and sounds of ISS2 and come back here to us. Thanks for having done so; and don't worry, you'll get another chance, soon."

"What does one say – oh, *I* know, 'no problem'," responded Karéin-Mayréij. "As I mentioned to Cherie, they thought I was a bringer of dread diseases, sort of like your 'Pandora' that you told me about, some time ago. Evidently the fact that you are all still alive was not enough for them, so I did not really get a chance to explore. Ah, well – I have waited several hundred thousand of your years for this type of thing. I suppose that I can wait a little longer."

"Can't argue with you on *that* point," amicably noted Jacobson, "But about return-trips... I think you may be a bit busy for that, in the next little while."

"Why, sir?" anxiously asked the Storied Watcher.

"Well," Jacobson explained, "Shortly after you set out on the return-leg of your trip, I received a message from Fred McPherson and Sylvia Abruzzio at Houston – I've saved it on the computer, in case you want to see it for yourself, but the gist of it is that they mostly *believe* you now. That is, that you can do a few things that us mere mortals can't. So," – Jacobson took a second to clear his throat – "They've informed me that they have *plans* for you. More specifically, plans that involve you, ahem, 'postponing' your stay on ISS2."

To a palpable sense of gloom, Tanaka mumbled, "Congratulations, Karéin – on to bigger and better things, it is, I guess."

"Yeah," added White, "Lucky you... lucky *us*."

"What, exactly, do they want me to do, sir?" guardedly inquired the alien-girl.

"I'm not sure of that, yet, Karéin," Jacobson answered. "But if it's of any interest, when I responded to Sylvia's message, Sergei and I sat down together and did a formal draft of our proposal for you to help *Salvador Two*, after that, we sent it in to Houston. They received it politely, but the impression I got when they had had a look at it was that they were stand-offish : that is, they seem to have other plans in mind for you – also, they don't seem to be very confident about the chances for success of *Salvador Two*, so they don't want to risk you with that mission. What their *real* plans are, I'm not sure. I suppose we'll just have to wait and see."

"Sir," asked Karéin-Mayréij, "If we do not return the *Salvador Two* spaceship to the vicinity of the ISS2 station and the *Eagle* and *Infinity*... what becomes of all of you?"

"*You* heard them," Jacobson said. "They promised to look after us."

"Yeah," muttered Tanaka, "After all, they wouldn't *lie* to us, *would* they?"

"No point in worrying about things that we can't change," suggested Jacobson. "But in the meantime, Karéin, I have a few other things that I'd like to ask you about. If you don't mind, that is."

"By all means, sir," the Mars-girl politely replied.

"Well," observed the Mars mission commander, "Looking only at the facts we know for sure, it appears that you *were* able to go back and forth between the *Infinity* and ISS2, at quite a good clip – much faster, in fact, than *any* Earth-ship, even unmanned probes that don't have to deal with human frailties, has ever been able to travel. Plus, Sergei informs me that your energy-signature out there was quite a bit more 'shiny' than it had been, before. And there's one *other* thing that I'm curious about, too..."

"Yes, sir?" she replied.

"Shortly after you left ISS2, I got a bulletin from Ariel Cohen, whom I believe you met while you were there, saying that the station had encountered what he termed a 'transitory emergency' – that is, there was some kind of reverberation in ISS2's structure, as if it had suffered a mid-space impact from a meteoroid; however, there was no external damage, and, luckily, other than for a few popped storage panels, no internal damage, either. Apparently this event happened while you were still in the vicinity. Care to comment about it?"

"Are you asking me if *I* caused the disturbance, sir?" she asked. "If so, the answer is, 'yes'. Please understand... I meant them no harm. I am glad that none has resulted. It was a calculated risk."

"What exactly did you *do*, Karéin?" inquired Boyd.

The Storied Watcher looked down at the floor, then quickly looked up, with brilliantly shining eyes and the hint of her psycho-music, playing in the background.

"I took *hold* of them," she stated, matter-of-factually.

Karéin-Mayréij nodded, looking serenely at Tanaka, mutely sharing a secret knowledge.

Then she closed her eyes and said, "Like *this*."

Instantly, a shudder raced through the *Infinity*'s walls, as the Storied Watcher opened her eyes again. They were still eerily shining, as the psycho-music, playing a tune of potency and majesty, raced through their minds.

She explained, "I now hold this ship, in my grasp, sir. Like you would hold something in your hand... except that I grasp with my mind. I can move it around, speed it up, slow it down, as I would do to myself, when I fly in space. I wanted to try it on the space-station, to test if I could manage something that big. And I was successful."

"Oh *God*," whispered Tanaka, suddenly gasping for air. "Oh God... I *feel* it... I feel it in you – the *power* – I *feel* it coming *from* you..."

The scientist bent over, a pale sheen of sweat on her face, stopping from slumping on the floor only by supporting her weight with an arm on the table.

"Okay," Jacobson replied, uneasily. "Point taken! You can let us go now... *please.*"

The alien-girl nodded and closed her eyes, resulting in the cessation of the music and a smaller, fainter reverberation.

Turning to Tanaka, she held the woman's hand and sent to the latter's mind,

It flowers within you, Cherie – that is good.

Think of these as 'growing pains'.

You become strong, *woman of Earth; in time, mighty* indeed, *shall you be.*

I rejoice for you... be proud of who you are become... but, remember your vows.

"I'll get back to my original line of questioning, in a minute, but I think I need to know something else, first," requested Jacobson. "Cherie, you seemed ill there, for a second. Anything you care to tell us about?"

"No... never better," Tanaka evaded. "Just felt a little *faint* there, Sam, that's all."

"*Really?*" retorted the Mars mission commander. "You know, we're not supposed to be keeping *secrets* from each other, here, Professor."

"*Definitely* not," added an obviously-suspicious Boyd.

Tanaka shot an inquisitive glance to Karéin-Mayréij, who nodded and said,

"*Tell* them, Cherie. It is time that they know."

Glancing from person to person, Tanaka explained, "It's... uhh... like *this*. She, well... she taught me how to *do* some things. With her *power*, that is, that thing she calls 'Amaiish'. So when *she* uses it, it's like I can feel it... hooboy, can I *ever* feel it. Especially when she uses as much as she just did. How can I explain it... it, uhh, felt like I was holding a flashlight... and she turns on a fifty thousand Watt searchlight, right next to me. Quite an overwhelming feeling, I can assure you."

"Man o man – that's *wicked* cool, Professor," whistled White. "Like... what kinds of things can y'all *do* with this power? Maybe fly out into space, while we're not watching?"

"Crudely put," added Jacobson, "But that's more or less what *I* was going to ask."

"Don't I *wish*," sheepishly answered the scientist. "No... nothing like *that*. Just a small 'push', here and there. Nothing you couldn't do with your little finger. It requires concentration, and if I try to use too much of it – wow, you've *never* had a headache like *that*, I can assure you, Sam. Don't take my word for it... check the supply locker for aspirin – I think you'll find that we're running a bit low."

"Can you show us?" requested a fascinated Boyd.

"Cherie, my sister," proposed the Storied Watcher, in a sympathetic, encouraging voice, "Send your coffee-cup to Captain Sam Jacobson, without moving your body. I think that he needs a, how do you say, 'sip'."

Startled, Tanaka answered back, "Karéin, I love you, but you're *nuts* – I can barely move a *pencil* –"

"Just *do* it, noble sister of Earth, blessed pioneer of the *Fire*," sang Karéin-Mayréij, serene majesty rising in her voice. "*Believe* in yourself – for were you not worthy, neither could you do it... nor would I so ask. It will be lighter than it appears to be – the gravity here is weak. You are *ready*."

Reluctantly, Tanaka announced, "Okay... no laughs at spilled beverages or frustrated science officers, please, folks. Imagine me trying to bench-press say, two hundred kilos, that's what we're about to try. Here *goes*..."

She closed her eyes; for her mentor had instructed, "Feel your mind encircle it; imagine it moving, like we did before, Cherie. Think of nothing else, other than your concentration on the cup. Then open your eyes and guide it."

Initially, the cup stayed seemingly rooted on the table.

But after a second, it started to move, infinitesimally slowly at first; it rose off the table, with Tanaka's gaze locked on it.

"Ooh, Karéin," gasped the scientist, breathing heavily, "God, it feels *good*, it hurts my head like hell but it feels so *good*, I feel powerful, like an effing *goddess*... how do you *cope* with it, how do you avoid *wallowing* in it... Sam, grab the damn thing, before I pass out with a smile on my face."

A shocked Chkalov whispered to Boyd, "Look at the Professor's *eyes*, Major – the *light* in them –"

Jacobson obliged, snatching the cup that was hovering in front of his face, as Tanaka slumped back in her chair, wiping the sweat from her brow, massaging her forehead.

"If it's okay with you, Sam," she pleaded, "No more demonstrations today, please. I feel like I just ran a mental marathon in seven seconds."

"Holy *shit*," gasped a half-stunned White, staring in awe. "*Gotta* get me some of that, man. *Seriously* gotta get me some of that."

"Wow," added an amazed Boyd. "Karéin, you sure weren't kidding when you said that *we* could do it, to. Us humans, I mean. I got to tell you... I didn't know whether to believe you or not, but, well, I guess that question has been settled."

Smiling, the Storied Watcher got up and gave the submissive bow and curtsy that they had seen before.

Standing upright in front of all of them, she explained, "This is my blessing to Cherie Tanaka, and, I hope, eventually, for all humanity. But you must understand that I am merely hastening a gift that your brothers and sisters were always meant to possess. It starts with Cherie... but it will not *end* with her. My brothers – my sister – your future, lit by the immortal, holy *Fire*, now burns bright."

Jacobson, staring absentmindedly at the cup that he now held in his hand, slowly stated, "Here's your coffee back, Professor – looks like you can *use* some, after that ordeal. But... 'bravo', to the both of you. It's an amazing accomplishment, of *that* there can be no doubt. I *do* have a question, though, Karéin. Without trying to sound jealous... why just Cherie? Why not the rest of us?"

He passed the cup back to a grateful Tanaka.

Sitting down again, Karéin-Mayréij explained, "No single reason for that, Captain Sam Jacobson, sir. First of all, I was not one hundred per cent sure that you humans could, in fact, use *Amaiish*, which is why I wanted to start with a single person, so I would not disappoint more than one person if I failed."

"Second," she went on, "And this factor may be more difficult for you to appreciate...Cherie is, among you, the most 'sensitive' to my *Fire*; all of you should be able to use it, to one extent or another, but I wanted to start with the person whom I sensed would be most easily able to unlock her mind's innate access to the power. Third, Cherie is, how you say, a 'professor'; that is, one who teaches others, a scientist who helps people learn. I felt that such a person would be well suited to pass on the knowledge of *Amaiish*, should I not be able to do so myself, later. Do you agree with my reasoning, sir?"

"As always," Jacobson replied, "Your logic is impeccable, Karéin."

"Yo, Karéin," interjected White, "Y'all know I hate to be *pushy*, but, well... like, when can I sign up for lessons? I may not have the Professor's talent, but my teachers back on Earth all said that I'm a fast learner, that's no lie."

The Storied Watcher arose and walked over to a vacant chair, next to where White was sitting.

With her beautiful, yet regally serious, visage seemingly illuminated from below, she looked deeply into his eyes and the man looked transfixed, lost, mesmerized.

After a second or two she counseled, "Devon... you *know* that I love you, trust you, respect you and honor you. But this is *not* a joke. The knowledge of *Amaiish* is a gift neither to be given, nor used, lightly. Like the gift of ordinary fire that your people first experienced many years ago, it can burn you – and much worse – if you misuse it. In time, humans will come to understand how important it is to know this."

She held his hand, again caught him in a godly stare, and demanded, "Devon White, do you accept the truth of what I say to you, now? Do you promise to follow, as I lead?"

"Yes, Storied Watcher... I *do*," White softly and seriously answered, most unlike himself. "As the Lord my God Almighty is my witness – I *swear* it."

The air shimmered with power, with the anticipation of mighty things.

Karéin-Mayréij looked up at the others and asked, "And do all of you? Think *very* carefully, brothers and sister, before you answer."

Each one, except Jacobson at first, nodded approval, not saying a word.

They all looked at the Captain, who looked totally unmanned, as if realizing that he was overtaken by events far outside his control.

Helplessly, he, too, consented.

"Then," instructed the Storied Watcher, her voice almost god-like, "Go to your knees, humans of the spaceship *Infinity*. Make a circle around me, holding each others' hands, and clear your minds of all impure thoughts, all ideas of power, all wishes of riches, of rulership... of *anything*, except the service of others."

She found an open part of the floor and knelt in the middle of it, motioning the others to come hither.

One by one, they came, kneeling as instructed, hands intertwined, Tanaka between Jacobson and Boyd, White and Chkalov next.

The alien-girl, still kneeling, placed one hand over those of Boyd and Tanaka and the other over those of White and the cosmonaut.

"Now," she explained, speaking as if recounting a story told many times, "You all begin the long, ever-winding journey upon which your sister Cherie, has already embarked. Know that you are about to receive a weirding power that will radically change your lives; and before I give you this gift, you must swear an oath to use it wisely – but the task will be *yours*, to do so, and to impart the same wisdom, to those to whom you may later pass on this same spark, this same *Fire*. I may not always be here to teach you her arts; you must learn to use her, mastering her but never letting her master *you*, each one by himself or herself. Her gifts will come to you in different ways, at different times; but come... they *will*."

"And when the unenlightened come to know that you have this power," she warned, "Beware that they may fear you, resent you... *despise* you. It will be *your* quest to lead them, to make the truth clear to them, without using the *Fire* to hurt or rule them. If you do not think that you can abide by anything that I have said, now is the time to break from our circle. I will in no way hold it against you, if you do; for knowing one's limits, is one of the first steps towards a noble spirit... and you can always take the *Fire*, later."

None moved.

All – except Tanaka – doubted.

The Storied Watcher paused for a second, then said, "Close your eyes, beloved friends; take this, the oath of the *Makailkh*, fully and honestly, forever into your hearts, with no evasions and no exceptions, saying the words yourselves, after your sister has given them to you. Cherie – lead your brothers... help them take the first step. You know what to say."

The music, akin to the most stirring choral within or beyond human understanding, reverberated noiselessly in their minds.

They all closed their eyes, and a couple of them also, remembering many days at church, also bowed their heads.

Breathlessly, Tanaka repeated, "Upon my most sacred honor, I will use my power, save that the hour be dire to my life, to *help*, not to *harm*; to *love*, not to *hate*; to *heal*, not to *wound*; to *rescue*, not to *endanger*, but foremost, to *serve*, not to *rule*; ever to follow the Holy Light, not the Darkness of Evil, until I pass from this life. With this oath freely taken, I now bind myself, and all others who I will in turn give the *Fire*. Thus do I swear, for now unto eternity, never to revoke *Say it*, all of you, Sam, Brent, Devon, Sergei, say it *now*, for the love of God!"

In unison, the others slowly began to chant the oath perfectly to the last word, even though several of them – Chkalov, in particular – worried that they would forget some part of it, or that Karéin-Mayréij would somehow take note of the fact.

A feeling of warmth, of peace, of serenity, washed over them, for the briefest of moments. Then the music slowly faded to nothingness.

"Congratulations, brothers of the *Infinity* and *Eagle*," called out the Storied Watcher, her face showing a joyful, relieved expression. "You have just taken a giant step; a great light has this day come to your people. I will sing of your bravery... your willingness to take on the task that you have just accepted. You will not regret what you have done – I *swear* it."

She paused a second, wiped the trace of a tear from her eye, then added, "If I accomplish *nothing* else while I am here, I will be content, that I have passed this on to you. You can all open your eyes now, and go back to the table, if you wish."

As their arms fell to their sides, Boyd asked, "That's... uhh... *it*?"

"Yeah... I felt good for a second or two," offered White, "I'm back to normal... that's what it looks like from here."

"Ah, *yes*," replied Tanaka, with a knowing smile, "But it's the *new* normal, Devon. Believe me, you'll find out, soon enough."

The scientist extended a hand to Jacobson, who was still semi-reclining on the floor.

"Welcome to the *alien* side, Sam," she said, emulating the Storied Watcher in drying her eyes, as she helped the man to his feet.

Regaining his composure, Jacobson offered, "Well, that was an – *interesting* experience, that's for sure. But Devon's right... I don't feel any more powerful than I was, five minutes ago. In fact, I feel exactly *like* I did, five minutes ago. If I was a scientist, Professor, I'd say that the experiment showed a null result... wouldn't you?"

"Captain," interjected the Storied Watcher, "Come here. I have something that I want to show you."

"I have a feeling I'll regret this," observed the Mars mission commander, "But, okay."

He walked over to the alien-girl.

She ripped a small piece of fabric from one of the pocket-enclosures on the jumpsuit that she had borrowed from Cherie Tanaka.

I assume that this item is not essential," she stated. "Take it and hold it in your hand, concentrating on it, sir."

"How do I... uhh... *do* that, Karéin?" he asked, uneasily.

"All you have to do, sir," explained Karéin-Mayréij, "Is to fix your gaze on it – just do not look at anything else. Oh... and by the way, this demonstration may hurt, for a second, but it will be nothing serious. Oh-kay?"

"Now I *really* regret having said 'yes', but, I suppose I'm in too deep to back out... so, fine, let's get it over with," grunted Jacobson.

"If anything starts to hurt," the Mars-girl said, grasping the man's other hand, "Just drop it, oh-kay?"

"You can *bet* on that," he replied.

The alien-girl's eyes glowed, dimly, but what caught the attention of the others was not that – rather, it was an arc of other-worldly energy, like a discharge of electrical current, complete with the smell of ozone but somehow different from electricity, that instantly shot from her, through Jacobson's trunk and down his other arm.

The energy hit the fabric, which started smoking, followed, a second later, by it bursting into bright flames.

With a quickly suppressed yelp, the wounded man dropped the fabric and stamped it out with his foot.

"Oww!" he complained. "What was the point of *that* little magic-trick?"

He began to suck on the tips of his fingers, which had been reddened by contact with the flare-up.

"First of all," dispassionately noted the Storied Watcher, "Would it help to know that, had I sent that much *Amaiish* through you, ten minutes ago, this would have killed you instantly, sir?"

"You don't... *say*," anxiously replied Jacobson, suddenly pale. "Just for the record... what would have happened to me? I mean, if we *hadn't* had our little ceremony?"

"Hmm... it has been a very long time since I actually *saw* something like that happen, sir, thankfully," the Mars-girl answered, "But if I remember correctly, you would have been – how do you say – 'cooked from the inside out'... like what happens when living tissue is subjected to much more heat than its molecules can safely absorb. But your nervous system would have shut down, first, if that would be any comfort."

"*Wonderful*," was the only thing that Jacobson could think of to say.

"Y'all got a great future as a electric-company lineman, Captain, sir," joked White, "Y'all won't even have to avoid groundin' yourself."

"And think of the *advantages*, the next time your battery dies and you don't have booster-cables," added Boyd, to guffaws from the other men, even the normally reserved Chkalov.

"I'll get some salve for your fingers," proposed Tanaka. "Looks like you touched a hot-pot, there, Sam."

"There is no need to do that, Cherie," countered Karéin-Mayréij. "For our demonstration is not yet over. Captain, come over here and put your hands in mine. Sit next to me, please."

"Is *this* one going to hurt, too?" nervously asked the Mars mission commander. "If it's alright with you, let's not have any more tests that involve the risk of any of us dying painfully. Oh, and by the way – that's an *order*."

"Yes, *sir*, and, it will not hurt, in fact the opposite of that," pleasantly promised the alien-girl. "Captain Sam Jacobson, sir, hold up your wounded fingers, look at them, concentrate on them, as you did the fabric, if you please."

"Alright," Jacobson said. "Oww... the more that I look at them, the more I *feel* them. Cherie, did you say you ate *all* the aspirin?"

"Now," serenely directed the Mars-girl, "Blow over them. With your mouth, I mean."

Jacobson, complying with this instruction, said, "Yeah, okay, they *do* feel a bit better. Cools them down. So?"

"Close your eyes, Captain," she requested. "And imagine the feeling of coolness – of relief – that you just experienced. Envision it enveloping the tips of your fingers. When you have done that, open your eyes again."

He opened his eyes and saw two reddened, painful, finger-tips.

"Can she get the salve now, please?" pleaded the man.

"No," instructed the Storied Watcher. "Instead – I want you to form that mental picture of coolness and relief, while staring at your fingertips, thinking of nothing else. Make your eyes strain to focus on the hurt spot, so that you cannot see *anything* but that. Block the pain from your mind and repeat, in your mind – you do not have to say it out loud – the words, 'they are healing, they are healing, look at them healing'. Do it now, Captain, sir."

"What have I got to *lose*," muttered Jacobson, with a tone of resignation. "Okay – I'm trying to do that now – you know, I was always known of as a stubborn S.O.B., I could accomplish *anything* just with willpower, so – what the *hell* –"

Jacobson, and the others, all save Karéin-Mayréij, watched in amazement, as the red, inflamed color gradually left his fingers, as if washed away by some ethereal spring rain.

After two or three seconds, they looked as good as new.

Stunned, the man slumped back in his chair, staring at his repaired digits.

"They're *fine*... they don't hurt at all," he gasped.

"This is *too* much," commented an amazed Boyd. "You mean we can *all* heal ourselves like that?"

"I would not go around deliberately injuring yourselves, just to find out, dear Brent," answered the Storied Watcher. "The, uhh, short answer is, yes, you *can*, but I could tell that Captain Sam Jacobson's innate ability to use *Amaiish* for this purpose was – how would I say this, in your language – fairly 'close to the surface'... so I knew that he would be easily able to fix himself. Much greater, more noble and potent powers await you; but here in the strange, unnatural circumstances of a little ark against the void of space, my intuition fails me, in trying to foretell what *exact* manner of arts, shall come to each of you individually... alas, were we down on your planet, perhaps then could I so counsel you. But as to the healing-skill, it may prove more difficult for the rest of you, and there *are* definite limits to this ability; for example, do not let someone cut off your head and expect to grow it back..."

"Damn... and here I thought I might get a better one, second time around," interjected White.

Even Karéin-Mayréij laughed at this.

"Leaving Devon's plans for self-made plastic surgery aside," dryly remarked Jacobson, "He's asked a valid question – that is, it appears that Cherie's 'talent', if you want to call it that, is telekinesis; mine seems to be healing... but what about Majors White, Boyd and Chkalov? I'd assume that *they* can use this power of yours too... right?"

"Yes," replied the alien-girl, "But your question is based on a partly false premise, sir. You *all* should, eventually, be able to move objects around – as Cherie does – and also heal yourself, as you did. From what I can tell just by touching them, Brent, Devon and Sergei do not have the same amount of easily accessible *Amaiish*-based powers as you and Cherie do; but with a little practice and patience, they will catch up to where you and she are now, Captain. It takes willpower and the wisdom to know when one is at the limits of one's power... that is all."

"Yeah, but Karéin," inquired White, "How are we gonna practice that healin'-trick? I don't feel like burnin' my fingers, six times every day..."

"You do not have to do anything so dramatic, Devon," she counseled. "Where I come from, this skill is first taught by the student spending ten minutes every morning, silently meditating on a thought such as, 'I feel wonderful today, my body is getting stronger, each minute'. Another good way to practice is to find a skin blemish – say, a pimple, or a discolored skin-mark – and concentrate on it, telling yourself, while shutting out all other thoughts, that it is being healed, that it is being made well. If you do this, you will find that the wish will slowly become reality."

"You know, Karéin," observed Boyd, "From the first time I saw you back on Mars, something instinctively told me that someone as old as you – forgive me, but there's no other way to say this, descriptively – could look as *good* as you do, I mean, no imperfections, no lines, no wrinkles. Now I know why, I guess."

Karéin-Mayréij smiled coquettishly and said, "I am flattered, Brent – that is nice to hear. And you are partly right... I use the skill myself continuously not only because it helps my physical appearance, but also my overall health, as it will yours, if you practice it and become proficient. Actually, though, what most restored my complexion down on *Mailànkh*, was simply you giving me some water. It is hard avoiding the wrinkles, even with *Amaiish*, when one has slept for several hundred thousand years."

She whispered into his mind, hoping that none of the others had yet started to evolve the thought-hearing ability, *And I think that you look pretty good too, Brent.*

"I don't know if any of you have stopped to think about stuff like this," commented Tanaka, "But she's going to put the whole cosmetics industry on Earth, out of business."

"Yeah," added White, "Along with a lot of the doctors and nurses."

"Your assumptions are reasonable, Cherie and Devon," countered the Storied Watcher, "But they are incorrect. *Amaiish*, and most of the powers that flow from her, are a *supplement* to a being's ordinary measures – for example cleanliness, physical exercise, eating the right foods, and so on – taken to maintain health and good appearance, not a *substitute* for them."

"For example," she explained, "When I awoke on *Mailànkh*, yes, my powers kept me alive, that is true; but I was *terribly* hungry and thirsty, in a way that I hope that you will never experience. It is an easy conceit to suppose that one can just use this power and abandon the more simple, basic disciplines of life – all the more so because, as I believe Cherie has already discovered, the *Fire* feels good – comforting – to use. If you try, you will find out soon enough that doing so is *not* a good idea. How do you say, in English – 'trust me on this one', friends."

"You're sure not kidding about how it feels," ruefully admitted Tanaka. "The only thing I can compare it to is a chemical stimulant, an 'upper', basically... after a while, I was almost *welcoming* the headaches, as they made me stop using this power of yours..."

"Well, team," said Jacobson, "I know you're all excited at the change that we've just been through – I have to confess that *I* am, too... as a kid, I always wanted to be a super-hero... and somehow, I guess I *am* one, now. We *all* are. Karéin, I know I'm speaking for everyone here when I say 'thank you, from the bottom of our hearts, for entrusting us with your power', even the small portion of it that we have so far experienced. It's an amazing and humbling experience, to think that we're the first."

He turned to the others and elaborated, in his most commanding voice, "Just from what we have already seen, I can tell that you weren't exaggerating when you warned us about the responsibility we now carry in learning how to use this power safely."

"So," directed Jacobson, "I'm asking the human members of my crew – Devon, Brent, Sergei and Cherie – not to try anything 'adventuresome' with this

Amaiish-stuff, particularly while we're on-board this ship, or on-board ISS2. Team, I'm trusting you to exercise good judgment here, we have already seen this power burning holes in metal; I don't think I have to elaborate on what might happen if, for example, one of you started experimenting with that kind of thing and then found out that you *can* do it... by firing at the hull of the ship –"

"That sort of thing is *very* unlikely, sir," interrupted the Storied Watcher, "Since, my *Gaze*, and other similar offensive abilities, are 'higher' powers, sometimes requiring many years of careful, intentional training – or my intentional gifting – to employ or master. Still, I think that your words are wise ones."

"Why's that?" simultaneously inquired several of them.

"Rarely – but, I *have*, indeed, seen this, a few times," she noted, "A being will suddenly develop a prodigious talent at one or more *Amaiish*-fueled powers, for no apparent reason and with no prior warning. If such an ability is exercised inappropriately, something like the consequences you have just described, might well occur. For example, if, say, Devon were somehow to unlock the *Gaze* without fully understanding it or being prepared, by myself... yes, he might be able to fire it, once – but he would burn out his optic-nerves and possibly his retinas, in so doing; that is, he would blind himself. That would be a very high price to pay, for burning a hole."

"Indeed," confirmed Chkalov.

"We *Makailkh* have a saying," commented Karéin-Mayréij. "It is, 'the *Fire* is a raging animal inside you, making you strong... but she tests always to see if you are strong *enough*, not to let her escape'. Your crew would do well to remember that."

"Whoa," exclaimed White, "Maybe I'll just stick to gettin' rid of zits, then."

Suppressing a chuckle, Jacobson continued, "The other thing I wanted to say here, team – and this is something that I'm not going to *order* you on, but I'd like everyone's opinion – is that I don't think it's a good idea, at least not for the time being, for us to inform Houston, Earth or ISS2 on our new... *attributes*. How does everyone feel about this?"

"Agreed, Sam," quickly agreed Tanaka. "For a whole bunch of reasons. We're just at the start of this experiment, after all, and I can tell you, from what I have so far experienced, that it's likely to be some time before any of these powers develop to the point where they'll let us accomplish anything more than we could do anyway – isn't that right, Karéin?"

"Maybe," guardedly responded the Storied Watcher. "If I were you, the scientist in me would assume *exactly* that. But..."

"But...?" pressed Boyd.

"However," replied the alien-girl, deliberately staring past them, "The hero in me, would wish for more – *far* more – than that. The first step to becoming greater than you are, is in so dreaming. You should dream of being the greatest among your race. Perhaps the Gods will grant your wish..."

"Interesting..." offered Tanaka. "But, Sam, another reason why I think we should not spill the beans to Houston is simply that they might not *believe* us; we had a hard enough time convincing them of our guest's abilities, and *that* took an unassisted flight on her part, across millions of kilometers of space. *Now*, here we come along and claim to be sharing in this power, except that we can't do more than a few parlor-tricks to prove it. I think it would just distract them and waste a lot of time... at least, until we have something substantial to demonstrate."

"I'm not sure I completely agree with that. Let me play Devil's Advocate here, for a minute, Professor," argued Boyd.

"What is –" interrupted the Mars-girl.

"It means, 'someone who takes a contrary position, just for the purposes of argument', Karéin," explained Jacobson. "Major... you were saying?"

"What I mean, Captain," Boyd replied, "Is that what happened here a few minutes ago, has just made us substantially more valuable to Earth in general, and to the 'Arks' program, in particular – stop to think about it, sir... if *you* were a mission planner for that program, and you had the choice of saving a survival berth on, say, ISS2, for either a normal human or one of *us*, with our amazing new powers –"

"Yeah, man! The next step up the evolutionary ladder – indispensable – I *like* the sound of that..." added White, to the obviously growing discomfort of the alien-girl.

"Well, as I was saying," continued Boyd, "The fact is that from a scientific, strictly rational perspective... I don't think there would be much of a choice at all, do you? I mean, what if one or more of these powers might be the difference between being able to survive, or not to, when we get back to Earth... whenever that is, in whatever shape in which we find it? Wouldn't *that* kind of factor be relevant to Houston? If so, what right do we have to hide it from them?"

"Point well taken," commented Jacobson. "But just running with your argument for a second, Brent... exactly what would we tell them? That we've found an exciting new way to remove pimples? I'd prefer to wait until we have something worthwhile to report, especially since – *if* our friend Mr. McPherson is to be believed – we'll have a berth on ISS2 anyway. Cherie, you got anything to say here?"

"Yes, Sam," answered Tanaka. "There's something else that worries me... if, as Brent says, Karéin's 'gift' to us is that valuable – something which, I'd remind you, the jury is still out on – then it follows logically that the minute that NASA found out about it, they'd have to order her to also start giving it, for lack of a better term, to everyone else... starting with, at the very least, everyone on the *Arks* program. Karéin, how do you feel about that?"

"How do I feel about that?" shot back the Storied Watcher, with a tone of disgust. "I will tell you. *I will not do it, that is what, whether or not I am ordered to.* Does that answer your question, Professor Cherie Tanaka?"

"If you don't mind my asking, Karéin," Jacobson carefully inquired, "Why not?"

"Because," explained Karéin-Mayréij, again deliberately avoiding their eyes, "I know you and your crew, Captain Sam Jacobson – I love and trust you because all of you have *earned* that trust, not only when you freed me from my sleep, but how you taught me and kept me safe, when I was weak. And you have taken the Oath of the *Makailkh* – to which I will hold you; let there be no doubt of that."

She went on, "*None* of what I just said, is – as far as I know – applicable to just any rough and unenlightened human from Earth; though as for my friends – my family – *they*, I will trust with the holy *Fire*. To indiscriminately give the gift of *Amaiish* to beings who do not understand its power, its capability to beguile and destroy –"

A voice called from the back of her mind.

Liar.

But I cannot *forebear,* answered the other half of her conscience.

And what if all those now here, should perish... as may well come to pass?

Would that not be worse, that the Fire *be snuffed out in my own ending... and theirs?*

"– Would be an act of folly," continued the Storied Watcher, trying to suppress an unwelcome cough. "Please believe me when I say : if I did this, and if the comet did not destroy your race... the unchecked use of my power might very well finish the rest of them, all by itself. I will not be a party to that."

She stopped for a second and lowered her eyes, then quietly resolved, "I have been a party to the destruction of too many, as it is. I wish for no more."

"Yeah," offered White, "I mean, Brent my man, try to imagine if she started handin' this thing out like candy and a few of the kids who got it, started firing that *Gaze* thing of hers – it'd be like the old days back in Compton, only this time with death rays, not AK's 'n Saturday Night Specials. Y'all know the saying, 'an armed society is a polite society' – well, I can tell y'all from personal experience... it's a *lie,* man. I don't blame her for only givin' it to folks she knows."

"Well," said Jacobson, philosophically, "I think that's your answer, Brent."

The others, including a reluctant Boyd, nodded silent approval.

"Orders Are Orders"

"Now that *that's* settled, for the moment, and as it's going to take us some time to sort out our new abilities, I'd suggest we get back to the business of ensuring that there will *be* an Earth," proposed Jacobson. "Karéin, when you were down on ISS2, did you get a chance to discuss our plans for the *Salvador Two* with them, at all?"

The Angel Brings Fire Book 1 : Angel of Mailànkh

"Unfortunately, not in depth, sir," replied the Storied Watcher. "I *did* mention to Commander Cohen that you were working on something like this; but as I did not have the exact details, he suggested that I wait until you could send the plan to himself and Houston in its entirety. I also was... how do you say... a little 'side-tracked', speaking to Madame Daladier and the Imam Abu Bashir Samukhan, regarding other subjects about Earth. Sorry."

"Don't worry about it," reassured Jacobson, "I doubt that Ariel could have authorized anything on his own authority, anyway. I guess we'll just all have to sit tight, while –"

"Message from Earth, sir," interrupted White. "Putting it through."

The visage of Sylvia Abruzzio appeared on the view-screen.

"Hello, *Infinity* and crew – Sylvia here, again," began the scientist. "We've just received an extensive report on the recent events on, in and around ISS2 and, well, all I can say is, we're *stunned* at what we saw. We are at a loss to explain how a flesh-and-blood being like Karéin can do this type of thing... and it's now evident that she possesses greater powers than we had *ever* imagined – if she's watching, please give her my sincere apologies for ever having doubted her."

"No offense taken," mused the Storied Watcher, "For doubting my powers is something I do, myself, all the time – for good reason..."

"Now," continued Abruzzio, "We are currently doing a serious re-think of our plans for dealing with the 'Lucifer' crisis, including consideration of the plan for the Storied Watcher to assist the *Salvador Two* mission. However, while we very much *do* appreciate the ideas that you two came up with, NASA will probably have different priorities for how we use this new asset – we don't have an easy way of quantifying what your guest is capable of, although, we've been doing some calculations based on what we believe her energy-output must have been, to have traveled the distance between your ships and ISS2, in the time that she did. If our assumptions are anywhere near correct, Captain... you have an *amazingly* powerful being on-board *Infinity*, with you. Karéin, we're glad that you're on *our* side, that's for sure."

"No shit," commented Devon. "That's Houston, right on top of things."

An odd, far-away, loving look came over the face of Karéin-Mayréij, for a second or two.

Perhaps, she mused, *one day, my sister Sylvia... men and women shall see a rainbow, and shall sing also of your own, new-found might...*

But all that the Storied Watcher said, out loud, was, "'Dispose of'... I am not certain that I like the sound of that."

Abruzzio concluded, "To explain what options are now on the table, I'm going to turn the floor over to Fred McPherson... Fred?"

McPherson's wizened, gray-haired face appeared on the screen.

He said, "Hello, *Infinity* and Karéin. As Sylvia just explained, while we are, for the time being, continuing with our existing plans – those are, *Salvador Two*, *Arks* and a few other ones – for dealing with the comet, in view of Karéin's newly-discovered abilities, we're also thinking of how we can deploy her most effectively. I should point out, not only to your guest but to everyone else on the *Infinity* and *Eagle*, that I've discussed this matter extensively with the President, and that I have his full authority in negotiating with the Storied Watcher."

Chkalov muttered, mostly to the alien-girl but loudly enough for the others to hear as well, "He speaks for the American President – well, how do you say in English, 'bully for *him*'."

The Mars-girl sent the Russian a knowing glance and nodded in his direction.

McPherson went on, "The most important new consideration is simply that we now obviously have a mechanism for very high-speed, interplanetary travel, without the need for rocket boosters, deep-space spacecraft, or even a space-suit... as Sylvia said, don't ask me, how *that* happens... we're just glad that it does."

Karéin-Mayréij arose and, her eyes glowing dimly, gave an insouciant little curtsy, accompanied with a mischievous smirk, showing two wicked-looking incisors.

White was only just able to restrain himself from laughing out loud.

The American Presidential Science Advisor continued, "Now, judging from how fast she was able to get from *Infinity* to ISS2, and back again, we figure that she could easily travel from where she is now, to Earth, *dozens* of times, before the comet gets too close. For that matter, she could travel between Earth and the Moon many times more than that. Maybe even to Mars... the possibilities are almost *endless*, but the problem is, we have to isolate the one or two options that would allow her to save the most people, or, alternatively, that would give us the best chance of stopping or deflecting the comet. We don't have all the answers, but here are the two plans that we're evaluating, currently, in this context."

They all held their breath.

"The first option, which is being advocated by those in charge of the *Arks* project, is for Karéin to fly to Earth and, in effect, act as a 'taxi' service, lifting people, if necessary, one by one, off the planet, into orbital habitation modules that we would custom-build for this purpose, then boost out of harm's way, as 'Lucifer' approaches," he said.

"As you are no doubt aware," continued McPherson, "The most problematic issue with the *Arks* program is simply that we have a very limited ability to supply chemical rockets capable of lifting a human in a space-capsule, into orbit. If we could get Karéin to help offload this part of the *Arks* program, we estimate that we could at least double, maybe triple or quadruple, the number of people that we would save."

"He is assuming, without appropriate evidence," whispered the Storied Watcher, "That I even *can* escape the gravity of your planet and travel through its atmosphere, while carrying one or more human beings. Fortunately, his assumption is correct. It is conservative, in fact."

McPherson stopped for a second, then mentioned, "Of course, if we pursue *this* route, at the end of it... even if we're successful, we still don't have an Earth to come back to... do we?"

"They got *geniuses* working down there," acidly commented Tanaka.

"So," explained the adviser, "The other option that we're considering asking Karéin to help us with is, destroying 'Lucifer', or, at least, deflecting it so that it doesn't hit Earth. Various ideas are being kicked around – for example, having her deposit nuclear demolition charges in the comet's fissures to shatter it, or having her place them on one side of the object to try to divert its course – but their relative chances of success are more difficult for us to assess because we don't have a clear idea of how much weight that your guest can lift. This is an important factor, when we may be asking her to carry nuclear weapons... which, as you're aware, can be a bit on the heavy side."

"So," requested McPherson, "Any additional information that you or she could give us on this subject, would be most appreciated. Another issue is that if we use Karéin for a project like this, we're kind of putting all of our eggs in one basket. In view of what happened to the first *Salvador* project, *Salvador Two* will not be lifting off with a lot of confidence in its chances of success... I guess I should update you on that project, it's already seriously behind schedule due to shortages of parts and qualified ground technicians to put the ship together – and anyway, we're not at all sure that a few more H-bombs will make much difference, either. It comes down to whether we want to try for a field goal, or throw the long bomb... pun intended."

"What is a 'field goal', sir?" asked the Mars-girl, *sotto voce*. "But I understand what he means by 'bomb'..."

McPherson stated, "We'll give you more information when we've made a decision. In the meantime, however, I have something *very* important to communicate to you here, and before I say this, I'd like to remind you that this request comes directly from the President of the United States. Karéin, we would like you to travel – as fast as you are safely able – to an orbit one hundred kilometers above the Earth, where we'll arrange for you to *rendez-vous* with one of our New Generation Shuttle spacecraft. This will, after suitable isolation and decontamination measures have been performed, take you back to Earth so we can more fully assess your capabilities and powers. We'll give you until the end of the day today, based on GMT... what's that, Sylvia... about another seven hours, right? to finish up whatever affairs you have on *Infinity;* then, we'd like you to set forth, immediately."

"We have," he concluded, "Already sent the exact spatial co-ordinates to the *Infinity*'s computer – but so you don't have any trouble finding the Shuttle, it will be equipped with a powerful light-emitting device that should be easily visible from at least two thousand kilometers away, in space. We trust and expect that you'll acknowledge receipt of this request... please understand, the future of our *planet* may very well depend on you. We're *counting* on you, Karéin... we know that you won't let us down. That's about it for me. Awaiting your reply – McPherson out."

While the funereal atmosphere induced by McPherson's words descended on the group, White commented, "Damn lucky we got your little knowledge transfer when we did, Karéin, girl. But now we got nobody to continue the lessons... do we?"

"That is oh-kay, Devon, my brother" softly replied Karéin-Mayréij, "You will find your own ways to the knowledge that you need, teaching and learning from each other. Thus it has always been, in the ways of my people."

"This *stinks*," protested Tanaka. "We can provide them with all the information that they need about Karéin, from out here. They have no legitimate need – their equipment is no better than ours –"

"You're *rationalizing*, Professor," countered Jacobson. "Nobody wants her to stay here with us, more than I do. But we have to face facts, to say nothing of the chain of command. If we were to keep Karéin here, in addition to it being a direct act of insubordination –"

"To *your* President, Captain Jacobson sir, not mine," interrupted Chkalov, through clenched teeth. "Sir, I have always followed you loyally, but I must remind you that Karéin's loyalty is to *all* of humankind – not to one nation of Earth. She has *said* so, in that many words."

"That I have, Sergei," quietly, confirmed the Storied Watcher, still looking at the floor, her long, golden hair hiding her face from the others. "And I *meant* it."

"I'm *aware* of that, Major," retorted Jacobson, "But this mission is under *NASA* control, something that you were aware of, and that you and your government agreed to, when you joined it. NASA reports to the U.S. Air Force and President, in that order – so unless and until I receive information to the contrary, it's *their* commands that we have to follow. Is that clear?"

"Yes, Captain, *sir*," icily shot back the Russian. "But in these special circumstances, I believe it appropriate for me to contact the Russian Federation Space Agency and inform them of what has transpired. And, for the record, to say that I strongly disagree with the idea that the Storied Watcher must obey, directly or indirectly, the orders of the American President."

Chkalov leaned forward a bit, and with an intense stare, added, "Need I *remind* you, sir, that this mission's original plans, which were agreed to by the Multi-National Steering Committee only after extensive discussions between the various space-faring nations, *never* – to put the matter mildly – anticipated encountering a being such as *her*. Therefore, it is *not* reasonable to assume that control over someone like Karéin should automatically fall to one nation of Earth – the U.S.A., Russia or any other – as opposed to, say, the United Nations, or a neutral, scientific body of some sort. I believe that I am entitled to send a message to this effect... am I not, Captain?"

Jacobson sat and thought for a long, pregnant moment, then offered, "You know, Major, I think that in theory I *do* have the authority to prevent you from doing that... but I won't. Whether or not you believe this, I'm not in the 'dictator' business up here; I'm just a good soldier, trying to follow orders, while being very aware of my own limitations and prejudices. All that I *can* ask, Sergei, is that you keep those same factors in mind, when you talk to your own people. Does that sound fair?"

"Yes, sir, it does," politely answered Chkalov. "There are obviously real differences between us; but conversely, we still must come to a mutually acceptable arrangement."

"It appears that the two empires to which you and Sergei respectively belong," commented Karéin-Mayréij, "Do not always see – how do you say – 'eye to eye', Captain. Or so I have read, on your com-pu-ter."

"We like to think," mentioned Boyd, "That these little differences are behind us, now."

"Or... we like to *pretend* so," sighed Tanaka.

"I would suggest, for the sake of all the people on your Earth," observed the Mars-girl, "That you all try to continue doing a good job of this 'pretending'. I have *enough* problems to deal with, already – I have no desire to mediate disagreements between two or more Earth empires... nor to have to choose between them."

Jacobson and Chkalov looked each other over, but neither said anything.

"But," asked Boyd, "We haven't really addressed the main question, yet. Have we?"

"Which is – ?" replied Jacobson.

"Which is," explained Boyd, colorlessly, "Is she going... or is she staying?"

"You *heard* McPherson's request, Karéin... did you not?" stated Jacobson, looking away from the Mars-girl.

"Yes... of course I did, sir," she replied.

"Well, then?" asked Tanaka.

"If Captain Sam Jacobson tells me to go, then I will leave," unenthusiastically pledged the Storied Watcher. "So far, I have not heard him say that."

All eyes were trained on Jacobson.

But his own were shut, as he stated, painfully forcing out every word as if pulling slivers from his flesh, "Karéin, you should go."

Tanaka got up, her demeanor reeking of anger and frustration.

"Well, that's *that*, isn't it?" exclaimed the scientist. "Orders *are* orders, after all, *aren't* they, Sam... even *goddesses* have to follow them, these days! Funny, I don't remember reading *that* kind of thing in *The Iliad*... I guess that the Greek goddesses had a bit more independence. Oh well. Don't forget to *write!*"

Fuming, she headed for the exit.

"Cherie, you know that I am not –", Karéin-Mayréij started to say, but Tanaka had gone before the alien-girl could finish the sentence.

Morosely, she slumped back in the chair, blackness clouding her face.

"Let her go and calm down a bit," suggested Jacobson. "We've been through this thing before... and I seem to remember that some of the *rest* of us, don't handle bad news particularly well..."

"Look," commented Boyd, "I think everyone here is over-reacting, anyway. I mean, there's every possibility that we'll all get together again, when this little – ahem – problem of the comet, is dealt with. Or maybe even sooner than that; for example, what if NASA wants Karéin to help ISS2 get back down to its regular orbit? Remember, its braking-rocket is shot. They may want to hire us on as 'experts' in dealing with her strange, alien psychology – sorry, Karéin, but from their point of view it would be a valid concern... we're really jumping to conclusions, here. This mission has been *full* of surprises. There'll probably be many more."

"That I will be back to meet you someday, if only to monitor the progress you have been making with the gift I have given," carefully offered the Storied Watcher, carefully, "Of *that*, there should be no doubt."

"Assumin'," unhelpfully added White, "That y'all and we are still *alive*, whenever you get your first break from your new job... whatever NASA says that is."

"Captain," interrupted Chkalov, "I believe that I will go and file my report, now. May I be excused, please? Do you want to see what I will be saying to Moscow, before I send my message?"

"Certainly," replied the Mars mission commander. "And, no, I don't... that is, I don't need to see it."

"With all due respect, sir," added Chkalov, staring his erstwhile commander straight in the eye, "I would strongly suggest that these actions should not be undertaken, until *all* the stakeholder parties in this affair – including but not limited to my own government – have had a chance to make their wishes known. To do otherwise would, in my opinion, be... *provocative.*"

"Your comments have been noted," evenly replied Jacobson.

The Russian got up, stiffly, nodded to the other man and walked off toward his quarters.

"I think I'll head off, too," stated Jacobson. "I owe Houston a reply. No need to keep you all here for that."

With that, the Captain went in the other direction, leaving Karéin-Mayréij sitting sullenly, her eyes staring in private contemplation.

Playing With The *Fire*

"So, here we are, the three of us, with seven hours, give or take a few, to kill. Read any good books lately?" half-joked White.

"I had started reading some works of the stage-craft-writer called – what was his name, yes, 'Shak-spear'," answered the Mars-girl, "Because the com-pu-ter said that he was the greatest of all human writers. But it was difficult; he uses many words that are unfamiliar to me. I have only read halfway through the play called 'Mac-beth', so far."

"Not surprising," explained Boyd, "Because William Shakespeare wrote in 'Old English', an obsolete dialect of the language that we're all speaking now – it hasn't been spoken in everyday use for hundreds of years. But I'm curious, Karéin... what did you think of 'Macbeth', so far?"

"It is very violent; several characters have died already, due to the lust for power, for wealth," offered Karéin-Mayréij.

"Sadly, this is a theme with which I am *very* familiar – mortal societies are frequently preoccupied with such things. But at least it makes an interesting story," she added, with a wan smile.

"Heh," commented White, "Did y'all ever think you'd be chattin' about English Lit with someone like *her*, when you started this trip, Brent?"

"Can't say that I did," replied Boyd, "But there've been a *lot* of things about this trip that I didn't anticipate. Like, for example, having access to that weird power that you use, Karéin. Though, I still can't seem to get it to work for *me*. Disappointing... but I guess we've had *worse* disappointments, today."

"Want to try an experiment, Devon, Brent?" requested the Storied Watcher. "I have something to teach you."

She tore another pocket-flap from her jumpsuit, then tore the resulting piece of fabric, again in two.

"Y'all tear too much more of that off your clothes, things could become *interestin'*," smirked White.

The alien-girl arched an eyebrow and sent him a wicked look, accompanied by a suitably off-color, verbally indescribable thought.

"You know, Devon," she invitingly observed, "Your society seems to have a lot of implied sexual taboos... that is, there seems to be a prejudice against people giving each other pleasure by the touch of skin to skin, without all sorts of long-term commitments or mating-ceremonies. I do not want to say that I do not respect your peoples' customs, but these ways... are not *my* ways, if you know what I mean."

"Ah, Karéin," ruefully mused Boyd, "It is *such* a pity that we only have you with us for another few hours. On second thought, don't tell my wife I said that... okay?"

"Agreed, Brent," primly replied Karéin-Mayréij, "If I ever am fortunate enough to meet her, that is. Now – how do you humans say – 'down to business'."

She produced the torn slips of fabric, giving one to each man.

"Uhh, I don't feel like burnin' my fingers today..." wavered White.

"Do not worry, Devon – you will not," answered the alien-girl. "At least, not if you pass the test."

"I never *was* very good at tests," muttered the African-American astronaut. "But I'll try *anything* once, I s'pose."

"Now," said the Storied Watcher, "What I will do, is to set these two pieces of fabric, on fire. The exercise, and the test, is for the two of you – I will let Brent go first – to extinguish the flame."

"Don't tell me... let me guess," interjected Boyd. "Without using a fire extinguisher, or a cup of water."

"You learn *quickly*, Major Brent Boyd, do you not?" answered the Storied Watcher, with a wry smile. "Indeed, yes, that is what I want you to do."

"But," she explained, "I should explain the principle here, more fully. Recall that some time ago, I mentioned that I can use mundane sources of energy – fire, electricity, radioactivity and so on – as an 'opener', to tap into much larger supplies of *Amaiish*. Basically, you will try a slight variation of the same procedure – you will absorb the flame's energy into your bodies, in so doing converting it into the *Fire*. It should be easy – this is a more or less instinctive process – except for *one* thing that you should beware of."

"And what would *that* be?" uneasily asked Boyd.

"As Cherie Tanaka noted," the alien-girl instructed, "You will find the experience of doing this, to be quite seductive. You will feel powerful, noble, capable of 'leaping over tall buildings', as your 'Super-Man' character is supposedly able to do. A *little* of this feeling is good to have; too much, and you may lose your focus on the real world. Just the small amount of energy contained in the flame that I will shortly light in this fabric should not be a problem, but later, you will be doing the same thing with larger sources, so be vigilant... do not let it overpower you."

"That's *dread*, man," commented White, "It used to take lightin' a joint or usin' an needle, to get high – now we can get a buzz just by lightin' a *match*. No *wonder* she don't want this thing shared too widely."

"I see you are learning to appreciate this power, Devon... and to respect it," professionally counseled the Storied Watcher. "That is good. Oh-kay – we will start, now. Brent, hold the fabric in your hand, just hang on to as little as you can, to ensure it does not fall."

The Mars mission pilot complied, though inwardly, he hadn't the foggiest idea of what he was really expected to do.

"Now," directed Karéin-Mayréij , "When I set the flame, I want you to concentrate on it, stare at it, in the same manner as in which I instructed Captain Sam Jacobson, with his fingers. What will be different, are the thoughts that you should have in your minds. There are two such that I know of, and you may use one or the other. One thought is to remember the warmth of a wood-fire, on a cold night – how good it felt, how much you appreciated the rays of heat, how you wanted more of them and got closer to the fire – until the heat became painful. Another is the more basic idea of 'I am hungry, I am weak, I need food'. Use either of these, as you concentrate on the fire, and you should feel the pleasant glow of *Amaiish* entering your mind and body. Are you ready?"

"As I'll ever be," replied Boyd. "Go ahead."

The Mars-girl lightly touched the far tip of the fabric (the analytical part of Boyd's mind noted that she did not use her laser-gaze to do this, so evidently the girl could emit this type of energy from even a finger), which immediately began to smoke, then, a half-second later, to burn.

"Stare at it, think on it," she instructed. "Put your other hand close enough to feel the heat, and keep what I told you, in your mind. Think of *nothing* else."

I feel warm, I feel nice, I'm at the lodge in Vail, knocking back a hot rum... I'm soaking it in..., he forced himself to think.

Whoa, realized Boyd, *This feels* nice. Damn *nice. I want more – like the rays of that bomb, from the dream –*

The fire sputtered and went out.

All of a sudden, he felt a chill in his fingers. The fabric felt cold, as if he had just pulled it from the freezer.

Boyd felt frustrated, irrationally so, as he came out of his near-trance.

He heard White clapping.

"Quite a performance, Brent my man," he said. "There's *another* Earth industry about to go the way of the dodo – them guys on the fire truck."

"May I have the fabric, please, Brent?" requested Karéin-Mayréij.

Boyd handed it to her.

"Nicely done, Major Brent Boyd," she congratulated. "You not only drained the heat-energy from the fire, but you also sucked some of it from the remaining fabric. An excellent first try, as you would say."

"Yeah... thank you," was all Boyd could think of to reply, at first. "And... I got a bit of advice for you, Devon – she sure wasn't *kidding* about how addictive that stuff is. But it packs quite a punch, too – now I *know* all about Cherie's headaches... oww."

"Your turn, Devon," announced the Storied Watcher. "Same instructions as for Brent."

She touched the edge of the fabric that White was holding and it burst into a bright flame.

Eyes bulging, White stared at the fire. "Wood fire... campfire... barbecue..." he muttered.

The fire, not affected at all, raced down the fabric, approaching his fingertips.

"What do I do now?" he demanded, sweating, gaze locked on the flame, as a moth drawn to a fire.

"You are hungry, Devon," calmly cooed the Storied Watcher. "Feed on it, eat it, *consume* it," she intoned.

"Okay," White nervously answered. "Cheeseburger... T-bone steak... Fettucine Alfredo..."

The fire was now a few millimeters from his fingers.

"*Karein*," he exclaimed, "It's not *workinnggg*..."

"Let it almost reach your fingers, Devon, trust me," she counseled, seemingly not in the least concerned. "It will *hurt* when it touches you. Pain, pain... *pain*. Think of that. Think of how much you do not want it to hurt you."

"How does thinking *that* help, girl..." gasped the man, now sweating profusely.

The fire was a hair's-breadth from his fingers. He started to feel a sharp pain.

"Now, Devon," she shouted, "Order it away – stop it from hurting you! Suck it dry! *Destroy* it!"

"*Shiiittt!!!!*", screamed White, as a sharp stinging sensation, electrified his senses.

A thought of pure, violent self-preservation – familiar enough, to be sure, but somehow calling upon a part of his psyche as yet unknown – shot through his mind. He felt a rush of near-orgasmic pleasure, far offsetting the pain, brief as the first thought but no less intense.

As if watching a movie, or something else equally unreal, he watched the flame vanish in a cloud of freezing, condensing vapors. Remembering the pain, he let go, but a second or two thereafter, the fabric, freeze-frozen into a delicate resemblance of its former self, hit the floor and shattered into a thousand icy fragments.

"My fingers – my damn *fingers!*" cursed White. "Y'all *promised* y'all wouldn't –"

"Rub them together, Devon," suggested the Storied Watcher, in the tones of a schoolmarm. "Do they hurt?"

White complied, anticipating a burning ache, only to find... nothing at all.

His finger-tips felt fine.

"No... no, they don't," he admitted. "But I could swear that *did*, a second ago... but now I got Brent's headache, that's for sure," he stammered.

"Looks like you passed the test with flying colors, Devon," commented Boyd. "Congratulations. But, Karéin... mind telling us what *that* was all about?"

"Yeah, do tell," complained White, slowly regaining his composure.

"Like, it seemed *easy* for Brent. But I couldn't get it to work, and I tried to do exactly what *he* did. Guess I ain't much of a superman," he glumly offered.

"Quite the opposite, Devon," countered Karéin-Mayréij. "This may be difficult for you to understand, but although I can guess at your native abilities with the *Fire* beforehand, when you first start to call upon it, that is when I can see how much of it is 'at the surface'. In *your* case, Devon, I sensed that you had trouble at first, but then your powers came rapidly. So I made the test a little... *harder,* to see how far you could progress."

"Thanks... I think," grunted the African-American astronaut.

"You did very well – not only did you draw even more heat-energy from the fabric – enough to cause the results that are now on the floor – but you healed your fingers with the same burst of *Amaiish* that you 'opened' by draining the flame. You have excellent potential, Major Devon White. And if it is of any interest... I believe that you have an affinity with the cold *Fire* of the Frozen

Desert. In time, your arts may surpass even those of the fell-demons of the Icy Hells."

"Remind me not to challenge 'em to a duel, though, Karéin," he said. "Y'all mind explainin' how I *did* that, though? I wasn't *tryin'* to freeze it, or to heal my fingers... not specifically, anyways."

"Some of your powers work automatically, as do mine," explained the alien-girl. "Some work automatically for one person and require thought or concentration, for others to invoke the same effect. Some can even work while you are asleep, unconscious or otherwise constrained. The use of the *Fire* is a subject in itself, as complex and multi-faceted as, say, playing one of your musical instruments... all can do a simple tune, but it takes both talent and years of practice, to become a great musician."

"Well, I always was pretty good with a harmonica," White joked. "But seriously, Karéin... thank you. Thank you very much, lady. Y'all can be *sure* I'll study up on this, every day. That's a *promise*."

She smiled warmly.

"The only thing I regret," mentioned Boyd, "Is that Sergei wasn't here. He's the only one, so far, that hasn't had a chance to do something interesting with this 'Fire' stuff."

"Do not worry about Major Sergei Chkalov," answered Karéin-Mayréij. "Be assured that I will see to his... *needs*, before I go."

Boyd and White exchanged glances.

"Damn," said White, "Now I'm *really* upset that you're leavin' us."

"Yes," she answered, "You are entitled to be, Devon. And it is time that I go see Sergei, anyway."

The Storied Watcher arose, gave a perfunctory curtsy and headed off in the direction of Chkalov's quarters, followed by the envious glances of the two men who stayed behind.

Russian Point Of View

Chkalov had just finished making his report to Moscow – none too complementary to NASA, it was, although the cosmonaut did not mention Jacobson by name – when the Storied Watcher showed up unexpectedly in the entranceway to his private quarters.

"Sergei," she requested, "I have a couple of things that I need to discuss and do with you, before I leave. May I come in?"

"Of course," answered the Russian.

"You know, Karéin," he wistfully offered, "Over the last few minutes, as I have been writing and then sending my report to my country's Space Agency, I have been thinking about the time when we first met. About you and me... and how this may be the last time that we share each other's company. Sad, is it not?"

"Parting with friends is always sad, Sergei," she replied, "Especially when that parting is to an uncertain future. But you have my word that if I am able, I will again find my way to you. I *promise*."

Karéin-Mayréij regarded him compassionately.

"It makes me feel very good to hear that," Chkalov commented. "But there is not much time left, now. So what did you want to discuss?"

"First," the Mars-girl inquired, "I want to ask you a question about your world – please answer as honestly as you can."

"Certainly," he agreed.

"It is like this," started the Storied Watcher. "It has become evident that Earth is not ruled by one empire, or even one or two in alliance, but rather, it has many smaller kingdoms – two of the largest of which, are your 'Russia' and Captain Jacobson's 'America'... is that right?"

"Yes, definitely," he explained. "And may I just say one thing about the terms you are using... you call these states 'empires', 'kingdoms', when, in fact, they suppose themselves to be 'democracies' – that is a form of government in which the people are allowed to collectively choose, or replace, their leaders, by means of voting for or against the former. Monarchies and empires are an obsolete form of government that officially were replaced years ago. Although, one could make a case that nothing much has really changed... both Russia and its main rivals, America and China, I think, are democracies in name, only. The rich and powerful have many ways of ensuring that their views, and none other, are adopted, in all three of these nations. Other countries are perhaps more democratic, but they do not have as much power."

"Ah," knowingly replied the alien-girl. "But reading from the history-files on the com-pu-ter, these three countries – America, Russia and China – looked, to me, much more like kingdoms, with hereditary rulers, than they did this 'democracy' thing you speak of. There is another one – 'You-Rope', I think is what it is called – that seems more like a democracy... but it is an alliance of several nations, not one state. In any case, that was not my main question. What I *really* wanted to know, Sergei, is, do you think that your Russia and Captain Jacobson's America, will be able to come to an agreement as to how to employ my humble powers, when your Space Agency finds out exactly what has just transpired up here?"

"Forgive me for saying this," Chkalov cautiously replied, "But why do you want to know? Of what importance is it to you? I believe that you said that you would follow the Captain's orders... and he is an American – he will have to do whatever his nation commands him, in turn. As would I, if I received an order from Russia. It is the way of things. Captain Jacobson is not a *bad* man, Karéin; he just answers to a different master... that is all."

"I have many reasons for being concerned," mentioned Karéin-Mayréij. "First, I want to help your people avoid the comet, and any dispute between Earth's rulers would delay both their, and my own, abilities to work against 'Lucifer'. More fundamentally, I do not want my presence here to become a cause for tension – or even armed conflict – between America, Russia or anyone else. Your history-books are *filled* with examples of wars having started over much less important issues – there was one, I recall, over someone's ear having been cut off – and all that the people of Earth need now, is a war in a burning house between two great nations, as the comet approaches to destroy everyone."

"And... most importantly," she hesitatingly continued, "I do not know what to *do*, Sergei. I have *thousands* of years of experience in dealing with kings, emperors and other rulers... but this provides no insight into what to do now. And I cannot talk to the others about this problem."

"What do you mean?" he asked, sympathetically. "I am sure that they all would listen."

"I cannot talk to them because they are all from this 'America' – that is, the place that launched the space-ship – and because they report to Captain Jacobson," observed the alien-girl. "They would have to tell him that I am having... *doubts*. To do otherwise would be to betray their oaths of loyalty to their commander. I would not have them do that, on my account. They are still my friends and my family."

Chkalov nodded in agreement.

"It is true that I promised to obey Captain Jacobson," the Storied Watcher went on, "And until I leave this ship, I will be under his command, it would be shameful not to at least *try* to follow his orders. But my intuition, and my conscience, tells me that to *blindly* obey the instructions of only one of your Earth emp – sorry, nations – when those issuing these demands, have no understanding of who I am, of why I have come here, of what is important to me... of the burden for which I am trying to make amends, *that*, Cosmonaut Sergei Chkalov, would be a grave mistake. At least, so it seems to me, here and now. Does any of this make sense to you?"

"It makes very *good* sense," quickly confirmed Chkalov. "And although neither I, nor any other human, can truly claim to understand you, I think that in some ways I can appreciate what you say, more than the others can. You and I are both strangers here, Karéin; I, because of the nation I represent, and you, because of who you are and where you come from."

"Aye," she solemnly agreed.

"We are both outsiders – how do the Americans say this, 'along for the ride' – but we will *never* be the same as the others, however much we try to be their friends, to cöoperate with them," noted the Russian. "It does not mean that you or I are the Americans' *enemies*... only that we are different; we do not want all of the same things that they do, we do not see the world in the same way. There is nothing wrong in acknowledging that, from my point of view."

Karéin-Mayréij smiled gratefully.

"You are very right about that, Sergei; differences are to be celebrated, not avoided," she said. "If this is of any interest, from almost the first moment that you and I encountered each other on the *Eagle*, I could tell – just from the way in which your mind formed its thoughts, although at that point I could understand neither your Russian language, nor Eng-lish – that you were different from the others... that you came from a place foreign to the Americans. That made me feel a certain kinship with you... yes, we *were*, and are, both strangers on another person's ship, I suppose."

"You and I have much more in common," she added, "Than just the need to feel the warmth and joy of each other's bodies."

He looked at her, anxiously.

Sensing his disquiet, the Storied Watcher offered, "No, do not worry – I have not come here looking for *that*, anyway, and I would not use my arts to make you give me pleasure, if you are not – how do the Earth people say, 'in the mood' – however much you would then give in to your own urges, and thus enjoy yourself. You *have* enjoyed it, Sergei... have you not?"

The Russian mutely nodded confirmation.

She cast a knowing glance and counseled, "I say that as a female who has felt ecstasy at having your manhood inside her, as a friend who you can talk to and share your troubles with, and as an intelligent fellow being, equal to you. I cannot see why I cannot be *all* of these, at once."

"You know, Karéin," he commented, "Even if you were a *human* woman, I would find that question difficult to answer, with complete honesty; sex, and the relationship between the human genders, has always been a mystery, both to men and to women, since the dawn of our civilization. When you first came to me – that is, back in the *Eagle* – I, I... went along at first, because I did not want to upset you... but, yes, I cannot deny it."

He paused for a second and then said, "Karéin, you are every man's – or at least, *this* man's – ideal lover. You gave me pleasure such as I had never experienced, and I am very grateful for that. It is just – I am sorry but I do not know a good way to say this in English, you are an *alien*... of a different *species*. Something in my moral upbringing, says that it was wrong to have, as you say, 'pleasured myself' with you. It is irrational, I know. But then sex itself is irrational."

He let forth a low chuckle and added, "It is one of the few basic human needs that we have not yet had a computer take care of, for us. But not for lack of trying."

The Mars-girl reclined back in a chair and mused, "Ah, yes... we *are* of different species; that, I cannot deny. But we are far more alike, than not – there are many intelligent creatures in this universe, Sergei, that resemble you or I, as much as would a fish or insect. And since I first met humans, my emotions, my motivations – my most basic needs and instincts – have become more and more like those of a human woman... it is one way by which I adapt to each new setting, when I re-awake in it. So it seems silly to worry about the few features that divide us."

She continued, thoughtfully, "I only wish, Sergei Chkalov, that you could see life as I do: joyfully, mortal beings like yourself are born into this world; they live a very short life, then, sadly, they die. You should be *happy*, you should experience the richness of life – including, the pleasures of sex – while you can. All too soon, your time in this life will be over. Yes, it is sad to die; but how much sadder, to die, knowing that you have never really *lived*."

"I cannot argue with wisdom like that," quietly agreed Chkalov. "I only hope that I will live to see the day, when you are again beside me, as both my lover and my friend, Karéin."

She held his hand and nodded.

After a few seconds, she asked, "But you did not answer my original question, Sergei. What do you think will happen when you tell your 'Russia' about the orders?"

"I cannot predict that for certain," the cosmonaut replied, "But if past history is any guide, my guess would be that they will not be very happy about you taking orders directly from the American Air Force – because that is how they *will* perceive the situation, even if your loyalty is personally to Captain Jacobson, Karéin. Then, they will protest to NASA and ask for both an explanation and the right to speak to you directly. And Russia will probably not be the only Earth nation that will take such a position. Many others would also want you to be under the control of no single country, particularly, of its military organization."

He paused for a second, then gravely elaborated, "If one thinks in the long run, this only makes sense, Karéin – assuming that Earth *does*, somehow, avoid the comet, you would be a very important... *weapon*, in the arsenal of whomever controls you, thereafter. I could easily see a dispute over this fact developing, possibly to the point of a war, between the nations of Earth."

Staring off into space, the Storied Watcher replied, "I do not suppose that I need to point out, that I am a servant – a tool – in the service of *all* humanity, not a weapon to be used for one Earth nation to win dominance over the others. Nor need I remind you, that I will *not* accept anything like the latter role."

"An ax can be used to cut down trees for firewood, or to cut down enemies, for one's king," countered Chkalov. "A tool with powers such as yours could easily be misused as a weapon. And regarding how you view your place with us humans, *you* may know that, Karéin, and *I* may know that; but I doubt that NASA, or my nation's space agency, know it. It may be to your advantage to make the point clear to them."

The alien-girl got up and paced around, as if deep in thought.

Finally, she requested, "Sergei... can you send them a private message on my behalf? One that will not be revealed, until later?"

"I suppose that I could," he answered, "But is it your intention to hide it from me, too? If so, the process will be more involved."

"Can I trust you to keep a secret, Sergei Chkalov, my dear friend and first lover of Earth, to whom I have entrusted my most sacred power?" demanded Karéin-Mayréij.

"When you put it *that* way, Karéin," he grinned, "How could I say 'no'?"

"It is good to have friends upon whom one can rely," she warmly replied.

"Go ahead when you are ready," he stated, "I will type it into my secured connection to Moscow, as you speak the words. But try not to go too fast... I would be able to do this much faster in Cyrillic... I have never gotten completely used to this Roman alphabet they use in English."

"Very well then – here it is," she stated.

Staring intensely at him, the alien-girl dictated, "Tell them that the Storied Watcher will shortly leave this ship on the orders of her commander, Captain Sam Jacobson; but that when she leaves her brothers and sisters here for the last time, she will decide for *herself*, how to help Earth against the threat that it now faces. It will be up to the nations of Earth to ask her to work in their service, speaking with one voice. And that Karéin-Mayréij brings her power and gifts not to any one nation of Earth – America, Russia or any else – but to all the people of Earth."

She fell silent, for a second.

"Is there anything else, Karéin?" he inquired.

"Yes," she indicated.

"Please tell me, then," asked the Russian.

"No," she countered, "Close your eyes and find it for yourself."

"What do you *mean*, Karéin?" he uncertainly asked. "If you do not tell me, then I cannot –"

"Yes you *can*," she promised, looking at him with big, affectionate eyes. "Take my hand now, brother Sergei Chkalov. Clear your mind of all thoughts, ideas, or anything else; try to forget that you are even in this room with me. Then, close your eyes and concentrate on the mental image of my face, how you last remembered me. Say the *first* thing that enters your mind, out loud, no matter how strange that it may sound."

"I – uhh – okay," he mumbled. "But I do not understand how..."

He tried to blank out his mind and succeeded in doing so only with considerable difficulty, since the touch of her flesh immediately reminded him of other things.

Then he pictured her face, as if seen receding in the rear-view mirror of a departing car, as Boyd had told him of, when the other man was down on Mars.

"*Tye goveryesh shto...*" stammered the Russian, not knowing where the words came from. Then, correcting himself, he managed, "You say that you will return, when it is time."

Bewildered, Chkalov looked at her and mumbled, "I still do not understand, Karéin... I do not *know* how I got that idea. I must have made it up... yes?"

"No," she replied, smiling warmly, "It was *exactly* what I was thinking. How does it *feel*, Sergei, to be a – how do the Americans say – 'mind-reader'?"

Overwhelmed, he stared at her for a long second, then inquired, "Is this one of the powers that you gave us earlier, Storied Watcher?"

"Indeed," explained Karéin-Mayréij, "I made it easier by being in physical contact with you, but as you practice with the others, eventually you will be able to guess their thoughts without touching them. Later, you will discern more complex thoughts and at greater distances. But remember, Sergei, it is very rude to do this, to someone who does not know or agree. It is kind of like using some kind of *Amaiish*-power to see through their clothes, if they do not want you to see their whole bodies. You would not want others to read *your* private thoughts, without permission; so treat them with respect, in turn."

"I swear I will do so," he pledged.

Reclining back in his chair, half in delight, half in shock, he offered, "You know, Karéin, I had doubted that I, or the others, *had*, in fact received this power of yours: where *I* come from, we are used to many false promises. I see that now, I indeed *am* changed, from who I was before. You kept your word... thank you, thank you again. I owe you a debt that I can never repay."

"I *always* keep my promises, Sergei... that is why it hurts so much to know that I did not do so, once, and the consequences were... *terrible*," confessed the alien-girl, moving beside him and again taking hold of his hand, grasping it firmly to her heart. "But you owe me nothing... other than, to remember the vow you took, when you received my gift."

"Well, perhaps *one* thing, my love," added the Storied Watcher, mischievously, with a wicked grin on her face. "When all of this is over, and when we do not have to worry about being interrupted."

Catching her meaning and acting on impulse, the Russian kissed her hand and said, "And I will hold you to *that* promise, Storied Watcher. Both *that* one, and the one that you will return."

She kissed his hand in turn and answered, "Then it is – how do you say in English – a 'contract'. An incentive for me to return, yes, of the best sort, would you not say? Ah, but that means my work here is done, for the moment. Not forever."

He nodded, unhappily, and watched as Karéin-Mayréij arose.

The Mars-girl tarried by the door with a long, doe-eyed glance.

She demanded, "And tell me, Sergei... what am I thinking, *now*?"

Chkalov shut his eyes and concentrated.

When he opened them, he was blushing with both surprise and arousal at what his mind had perceived in hers; but the Storied Watcher had vanished, as insubstantially as does a daydream broken by a sudden summer rain.

Sing For Your Angel

The alien-girl was passing by White's quarters – apparently coming from the direction of Chkalov's quarters, and the computer-room – but the African-American astronaut had left the hatchway door open.

Out of the corner of his eye, he saw her.

Inwardly, he wondered if he would have noticed her before the 'event' of earlier that day; his senses felt sharper, more active; or so he imagined.

"Yo, Karéin," White called, in a loud voice. "Y'all got a moment? I got something I wanted to show you."

The Storied Watcher had already gone past the door on her way, but a second or so after he called out, she had re-appeared in the doorway.

"I was heading back to the eating-area – you know, the one where we have breakfast, since the Captain wanted to have a final meeting... it is nearly time for me to go," mentioned Karéin-Mayréij, "But... oh-kay, Devon. What is it?"

"Well," he explained, "I sent one of my messages – 'telegrams', is what we call 'em, even though they're in video – back home to my wife and kids back on Earth, like I do every couple of days or so. This time, I mentioned that y'all would be leaving us shortly... don't worry, I didn't give away any secrets or anything like that. Anyway, when I got the reply, my son Martin, he said that he told his school-class that they'd be able to talk to you sometime... sorry, Karéin, but I kinda *promised* them that, way back when y'all were back on Mars. So I said that I'd try to get y'all on the video-link to them ASAP – they're at school right now, they're hooked up to a NeoNet video-feed. Would y'all mind talking to them, just for few minutes? It'd mean a *lot* to my son."

"Your *son*, Devon," she softly remarked. "Your *child*, back on Earth."

The Storied Watcher appeared as if she had been strongly affected by this revelation.

After a second, she asked, "'school-class'? What is that?"

"Oh, right... guess y'all don't know all the details of our educational systems," White hastily replied. "Sorry. It's what we call 'elementary school' – the kids there are about nine years old – oops, there they are now..."

The view-screen lit up, revealing a brightly-lit, indifferently-decorated American elementary school-classroom, populated by one somewhat bedraggled-looking, middle-aged black female teacher and twenty to thirty enthusiastic, mostly black and Hispanic children of various shapes and sizes.

The teacher stepped forward and reached past the camera's field of view, reaching and fumbling for something to one side.

"Is it on?" she asked. "Yes? It is?"

"*Children,*" the Mars-girl joyfully gasped. "*Little* ones. Oh, there are *children*, there, Devon! When I first saw them down on *Mailànkh*, I could not believe it..."

The teacher continued, "Okay, then. Hello, Major Devon White, this is East Compton Primary School #23 calling, Mrs. Atasha Jones here. We hope that you can see us – I'm not so good with these computers. I should mention that you, and your special guest up there, have a whole school worth of pint-sized astronaut and alien fans... oh, *look*, kids, there they *are!*"

White and the Storied Watcher saw a dozen or more small, fascinated-looking faces crowd around the camera at the other end, followed shortly by a voice in the background saying, "Now, children, please back up a little – we want *everyone* to get a look... here, Charles, you're bigger, get up on the stool and stand behind the others... Juanita, just kneel down in front, you'll still be able to see..."

"Hi there, all you kids down there!" exclaimed White, in a friendly, paternal kind of voice. "This is Major Devon White of the U.S. Air Force aboard the spaceship *Infinity*, heading back to Earth... the long way. And I have beside me our number one alien crew-member, Karéin-Mayréij, the 'Storied Watcher' of Mars. I'm sure y'all have already heard of her, but you'll have to be patient... it's been awhile since she's seen kids, or so she tells me."

Sotto voce, he requested, "Now's the time for you to say something."

"I... umm... ah... hello, children," stammered the alien-girl, uncharacteristically off guard. "I am Karéin-Mayréij, like my friend Devon here says. But you may all just call me 'Karéin', like he does, along with the rest of my family here on the *Infinity*. I would *so* like to come down to Earth and meet all of you, as well as the nice woman who leads you in learning things. I hope that some time soon, I will be able to do that."

She looked at White and whispered, "Is that oh-kay?"

"Sure," he confirmed. "Let's see what they say back. One thousand, two thousand, three thousand... should be comin' in any second..."

The view-screen's display now showed two rows of children, neatly seated one row slightly higher than the next, as if in a classroom portrait picture.

The teacher said, "I should say that the children are just *thrilled* to be able to speak to an astronaut – I don't think I have to tell you how proud Martin is of his Daddy – and to the first alien that we have ever encountered. Ms. Karéin-Mayréij, you can be sure that they will want you to show up here, as soon as you can."

"Karéin," White whispered to the Mars-girl, "See that one on the top row, three from the left? That's my son."

Karéin-Mayréij nodded numbly in acknowledgment.

"A fine-looking young man..." she forced out.

"Now," the teacher continued, "We know you don't have a great deal of time, as a matter of fact we're not sure how long we can keep this computer and network link up and running, so, we have two things to do for and with you today. First, the children have chosen three from amongst themselves to ask one question each, to either of you – I'm informed that it has come down to one for Major White and two for Ms. Karéin-Mayréij. I hope that won't be too much. Then, we have a little surprise for the two of you. Are you ready, *Infinity*?"

"Yes, go ahead, kids!" said White, into a nearby microphone.

"Questions?" worriedly asked the Storied Watcher. "What might they ask about? I do not want to disappoint them."

"Almost anythin'," White replied. "Just try to act natural and be as honest as y'all can afford to be. After all, they're not going to call y'all back... they're just kids."

"'Call me back'? Does that mean – " she inquired, but at that moment, the screen became active again.

The rotund, chocolate-brown face of a girl appeared.

She looked quickly behind her, soliciting the teacher for encouragement, then said, "Hello, Major White and Ms. Mayréij, I'm Serena Alvarez and I have a question."

The youngster hesitated for a second, then asked, "A question for Ms. Mayréij. I would like to know, do you have any children of your own? Kids like us, I mean. Are they back on Mars, waiting for you?"

Karéin-Mayréij took a few long seconds to compose herself, then she replied, "It is nice to meet you, Serena Alvarez... thank you for your... interesting question. I do not know if anyone has yet told you this, but, I was asleep for many, many of your years, and my memory is not as good as it should be, so there is only a little I can tell you about this. But I will try."

Looking as if she was on the verge of tears, the Storied Watcher continued, "Yes, little Serena Alvarez, I *do* – or *did* – have children, whom I loved very dearly. One girl, named 'Divi-Nialla', and a boy, named 'Mokh'... 'Mokha'... curse it anyway, I forget! I am very sorry, children – please forgive my bad temper, it is just that I became separated from my young ones a *very* long time ago, long before your parents were themselves little children, or even before your parents' parents."

Flustered but trying not to show it, she added, "My daughter and son had different fathers, and they were born many of your years apart – the girl is the elder of the two – but they were on the same world... until I fell from that place, to another, and I could not return... I miss my children *very* much. All this is hard to explain in words that you would understand, here. Maybe when we meet down there on Earth, I will be able to remember more. Is that oh-kay?"

The Mars-girl looked at her feet, miserably.

"Listen, Karéin," whispered White, quickly muting the audio signal, "If this is too *stressful* for you, lady..."

"It *is* very, how you say, 'stressful', Devon White," she replied, breathing heavily. "Remembering my children is painful for me, second only to my shame about the last... *failed*, duty. But do not stop it, not now... put them back on."

The teacher's face appeared on the view-screen. "Next question is for Major White. Jamal?"

The handsome face of a young, ebon-black African-American boy, tall for his age, now filled the screen.

"Hello, Major White, this is Jamal Kingsley," he said. "First, sir, I'd like to say that I want to be an astronaut like y'all some day. I think it's so neat that y'all was the first man on Mars, and the first to find the first signs of Ms. Mayréij's presence – y'all *awesome*, man!"

Grinning, White elbowed the alien-girl, as he quipped, "Sign that kid up!"

She managed a slight smile, in return.

"Anyway, sir, what I'd like to know," the boy asked, "Is, when this 'Lucifer' thing is over with, where y'all want to explore next? That is, in the solar-system? Y'all gonna to fly to Jupiter, or back to Mars, or to Venus, maybe? How about Saturn and that neat moon it has... you know, the one with the atmosphere? Have y'all talked it over with Captain Jacobson and NASA? I mean, with your credentials, sir, they *can't* turn you down."

Now White looked like *he* had a question for which he wasn't prepared, but he took it in stride, waited the obligatory five seconds and replied, "Yo, Jamal, good to hear from y'all, and as a word of advice, y'all keep your goals locked on in sight – I think you'll make a *fantastic* astronaut. When I started out, I was just a kid from Compton with some big dreams, ambition, and no money, but y'all know *what*? You need the first two, plus talent... not the last part. Don't ever forget that... promise?"

White bit his lip for a second, then continued, "Now as to your question. Y'all might be interested to know that in spite of the comet problem, I *have* been thinking, from time to time, about exactly what y'all asked me. Right now, the way I feel is, once the 'comet' thing is sorted out, I'd kinda like to go back to Mars, to finish explorin' where we started – only this time, I'm planning to bring one of the natives with me, to give me a tour of her quarters, so to speak."

"And I can show you the underground passageways and rooms, the ones that you, Brent, Cherie and Captain Jacobson missed, incidentally," interjected Karéin-Mayréij. "You and your people – including all the children that are hearing this, now – will *always* be welcome in my home, Devon; though you might find it not as comfortable as, say, that nice classroom down on Earth. Jamal, you may find it interesting to know that Earth-air felt very thick and heavy to me, when I first... came aboard the *Eagle*. I was used to breathing the atmosphere on *Mailànkh* – that is my name for the planet that you call 'Mars'. I became accustomed to all the extra oxygen and so on, pretty quickly... but you might find it a little harder, doing it the other way around."

She smiled warmly.

"Wow, well, there y'all go, Jamal – there's my next assignment! After that, I think I'd like to see Saturn and Titan, yeah, that would be a good one, too. As for Captain Jacobson and NASA, well, they're kinda preoccupied with *other* things right now – but I promise, the minute their minds are off that, I'll start pesterin' them. As my friend here knows, I can be *very* persistent. Can't I?"

"Oh yes," mimicked the Storied Watcher, "You certainly *can*, Devon. But being several hundred thousand of your years old, has taught me patience."

She giggled, but then added, seriously, "May I echo what Major Devon White has said here, earlier. There is *great* power in you, Jamal Kingsley, and in everyone; and it can only be released, by believing in yourself... by dreaming that you can do things that seem impossible. You should never forget that."

White whispered, hoping that it would not be picked up by the microphone, "I can personally attest to the fact, y'all sure ain't kiddin' about all that."

That half-familiar, far-away visage reappeared for a second or two.

As if in a trance, Karéin-Mayréij returned the whisper.

"And... Jamal," she voiced, "Who *knows*, how noble and mighty, you may yet be. Perhaps that day... is nearer than you think."

After a few seconds delay, they saw the teacher motion to the young man, who reluctantly gave up the microphone to a petite black girl, who, after fumbling with it, introduced herself.

"Hi, Mr. White and Ms. Mayréij, this is Latisha Johnson, with a question for Ms. Mayréij," said the child. "Although I didn't make it up myself – I got picked to be one of the people who could ask you, but then I didn't know what to say, so I went to Martin – you know, he's Mr. White's boy – and the two of us came up with my question..."

The teacher interrupted, "Okay, Latisha, that's great, but I think they should hear your question now."

"Okay," complied the little girl. "Well, here it is. Ms. Mayréij, a lot of the ministers, like the one in my mommy and daddy's church, are saying that you were sent by God to save us from the comet, and that as long as you are up there, we still have hope. The guy at Jamal's mosque is saying the same thing."

Karéin-Mayréij froze at the instant of hearing this.

The child on Earth hesitated for a second and then said, simply and innocently, "Are you an angel who is going to *save* us, Ms. Karéin-Mayréij?"

"Turn it off – put them on hold!" gasped the Storied Watcher.

White instantly complied.

"Listen, Karéin, I understand if that's a bit hard for y'all to handle right now... y'all can say we'll get back to them... they're just *kids*, after all..." he counseled.

"*Shut up* and take hold of my hand, Devon," she demanded, pale with desperation, eyes welling up with tears. "*Now*, I cannot evade, cheat... make excuses. Close your eyes, man, and ask your God for wisdom... for guidance! I do not know what to *say* to that dear little girl. I need *help* – Devon, help me, *please!*"

"Hey, no problem," he answered, gently taking hold of her hand.

Eyes closed, concentrating desperately, he quietly intoned, "Look, there, Big Guy... y'all and I usually don't see eye to eye, y'all know I'm not good at askin' for things or takin' orders, but, *this* time, well, we need to know the truth. Not for *me*, but for *her*. I don't say this often, but, *please*, Big Guy, please help us know what to do. I have *faith* that y'all won't let us down. Somehow I know that, Big Guy."

God of Earth, his mind heard the Storied Watcher plead, *show me the way. Give me the power.* Help *me!*

For a few interminable seconds, they just sat there, hands clasped in mutual need, the improbable, yet inevitable, companionship of man and *Makailkh*. But a feeling of peace, serenity and, above all, finality, enveloped them.

White opened his eyes and, just before he flicked the "on" switch, he ordered, "Trust yourself, Karéin. Say the first thing that enters your mind."

The video up-link light again engaged, and the Storied Watcher's voice sounded clear and true, her psycho-music rising rapidly in the background, her eyes shining brilliantly as any star in the firmament,

"Yes, Latisha," she sang, "*I am the angel who will save you, and all the people of Earth.*"

Looking straight at her, White remarked, firmly but reverently, "Karéin, I *believe* you, and so do they."

He turned the up-link off.

She avoided his glance, and his question, saying simply, "I have two more things to tell them, both quite important. We can wait until they hear what we just said, though."

After a few more seconds delay, they again saw the images from Earth, showing a non-plussed teacher who was still trying to regain her composure, accompanied by a classroom of children who seemed to be taking the Mars-girl's latest promise completely in stride.

"Well, uh..." announced Jones, "That's *great* news, for sure, children... isn't it? I think it's time for our little surprise, now, anyway. Are we all ready? Bobby, have you got the karaoke player ready?"

"Yes, Mrs. Jones," they heard a young voice say from off-screen.

The teacher explained, "Now, the song that our class is going to sing for you, is meant for all the brave astronauts who are trying to help us out there in space, but we'd like to especially dedicate it to Ms. Mayréij... all the more so, in view of what you've just said, I guess. Are we ready, class?"

A dozen or so small heads nodded.

"Okay," Jones went on, "The song is one of them 'oldies but goodies' – it's called, *Believe In You*. We've shortened it and changed a few words, but hopefully at least Major White will remember the tune... sing along if you want to, Major."

White commented, with a quiet chuckle, "Yes I *do* remember it... couldn't have picked better myself."

"Holy Spirit, please – not *this* –" pleaded Karéin-Mayréij; but the karaoke background music – a catchy, but dignified, collection of finely-crafted electric guitar chords from Earth's 1990's hit parade – started to play, followed a split-second later by the sound of thirty or so cherubic young voices, singing these words:

"Somewhere there's a river
Lookin' for a stream
Somewhere there's a dreamer
Lookin' for a dream
Somewhere there's a drifter
Trying to find her way
Somewhere someone's waitin'
To hear somebody say,
Weeee, believe in you
We can't even count the ways
That weeee believe in you
And all we want to do
Is help you to believe in you..."

"*Ohhhhhh,*" moaned the alien-girl, sweating profusely with flashes of light and energy shooting throughout her body, now bracing her hands against White's writing-table, as the psycho-music – somehow now in perfect harmony with the tune coming from Earth – cascaded, roared through the man's mind and – had he known it – those of all the others on-board the *Infinity*, as well.

The Storied Watcher looked like she was being slowly electrocuted, with shimmering waves of heat emanating from her, a smell of ozone and the sweat vaporizing from her flesh almost as fast as it arrived there.

White's first instinct was to turn it off, to help he; but some inner voice told him not to intervene.

Instead, he began to softly sing along, as the class continued with the next verse.

"Somewhere someone's reachin'
Trying to grab that ring
Somewhere there's a silent voice
Learnin' how to sing
Now some of us can't *move ahead*
We're paralyzed with fear
And everybody's *listening*
'Cause we all need to hear..."

"Sing, children, *sing* for me!" cried Karéin-Mayréij, her voice burning with passion, as the music reverberated throughout their minds and the spaceship, sending a perceptible shudder through the ship's structure.

"*Sing for your angel!*"

She gasped for air and moaned as the transformation enveloped her.

White, though less attuned to the power than Tanaka, nevertheless felt the presence of endless amounts of her special energy. It was all he could do to keep singing.

The children continued,

"Weeee, believe in you
We can't even count the ways
That weeee believe in you
And what else can we do
But help you to believe, to believe in *you*!"

As the Earth-music subsided, so did the Mars-girl's psycho-music.

Moaning, she slumped back in her chair, at once both newly empowered and totally exhausted, the glow in her eyes slowly waning before she closed them, obviously trying to recover from the ordeal.

The Storied Watcher forced herself to say, "Thank you, *thank you*, children. You do not know how much you have helped me, and, in turn, yourselves. Someday, I will explain this to you."

"Karéin," White sympathetically observed, "Y'all seem... *changed* by that, girl, and ordinarily I'd just say 'goodbye' to all our little friends down there, but y'all said that you had a couple more messages to pass on to them? Y'all probably won't get another chance any time soon, so if you're still up to it, tell them now. Then we'll let them go."

Slowly, Karéin-Mayréij, a demeanor of majesty all about her, opened her eyes, sat more or less straight up and replied, "Yes, honored Major Devon White, I *do* have two more things to say to the children of Mrs. Jones' class, and I lay upon them the solemn duty of informing everyone on Earth, of what I am about to say."

"I have no doubt that they'll be paying attention," White offered, with a chuckle.

"First," instructed the Storied Watcher, with a deadly-serious tone of dignity, "Tell them to cancel the *Salvador Two* mission – henceforth, no living humans should approach the comet. Attack it with your weapons, if you must; but do not send people there. Lest I hurt them, without meaning to."

"Wow. Alright, I guess," he replied. "What else?"

"Second – and this is by far the most important thing – people of Earth, when you hear my music, shield your eyes, lest you be blinded by the light. When they hear my music, the men, women and children of Earth will know that I have come to fulfill my oath."

"I trust you," mentioned White, "But they may want a bit more, uhh, *detail* to those instructions, Karéin. Y'all got anything more to add to that?"

From the corner of his eye, he noticed several faces – he could see Tanaka, Boyd and Jacobson, for sure – that had suddenly appeared in his doorway, evidently brought hither by the commotion.

Or, he thought, *by the Fire.*

Looking straight at him with the eyes of a goddess, she answered, "No. That is all they need to know. By my music, and my light, will they know that I have returned."

"Okay, then," White uneasily concluded. "There you have it, Earth. Mrs. Jones and class of East Compton Primary School #23, y'all got your orders, straight from NASA and the Storied Watcher, our newly-revealed... *angel*. We'd like to thank y'all down there so much for your questions and especially your song – it's a cliché, but y'all have really lifted our spirits here... that's no lie. Be well, everybody."

He paused and quietly added, "Y'all in *good* hands, Earth."

He flicked the link switch to "off".

Immediately, Jacobson demanded, "What was *that* all about? We all heard the music, so we came here. Oh, and it's almost time to say our good-byes. Hate to be the one to bring the bad news, but you two seemed kind of tied up doing something..."

"Yeah," interjected Tanaka, "I felt a *huge* surge of your energy, Karéin – like when you took hold of the ship – only stronger, *way* stronger, if that's possible. Who were you talking to?"

"Just some kids from my son's fourth grade class, down on Earth," evenly answered White. "I promised my son that I'd let them contact us... they asked us a few questions about ourselves, our mission, you know, the usual kind of stuff... then they sang us a song. That must have been what got y'all over here, I guess."

Boyd came through the doorway and crouched down beside the Mars-girl.

Looking at her condition, he remarked, "Holy cow, Karéin, you look a bit... *exhausted*, there. Not as bad as the other time, but *still* – are you okay?"

"Never better, Brent," the Storied Watcher replied, with a smile.

She slowly arose, and in so doing, they saw her strength and composure return, almost instantaneously.

More than that, she had a special, new glow; the others could *feel* the energy radiating from it.

"Listen, Karéin," started Tanaka, again, "About what happened a few hours ago... I should apologize for storming off like that. I didn't *mean* to insult you, but please forgive me if I did. It's just that it seems *crazy* to me that you're being ordered around by a bunch of bureaucrats on Earth, no doubt for the crassest of reasons. And, I can't *bear* the thought of you leaving... we still have *so* much to discuss, to learn about... you know how it is..."

Her voice, small and defeated, trailed off.

"No offense taken," amicably replied Karéin-Mayréij. "As the Commander has correctly pointed out, I have my... *moods*, too. But remember that as your powers grow, it will become all the more important to try to keep control. It is a lesson that I seem to keep forgetting, to my own repeated misfortune."

She stopped for a second and then said, "And I will regret leaving here, too. Cherie, you and the others are my family... but you must trust that there *is* a purpose to things. There is a reason, why I must obey, and go."

"Major White's explanation of recent events certainly sounds reasonable," commented Jacobson. "Except for what we heard from you, Karéin, just before the conversation ended. Care to explain what *that* meant? I mean, the part about the light and the music."

"No," parried the alien-girl, avoiding his stare. "No, with respect, Captain Sam Jacobson, sir."

"Karéin," Jacobson complained, his voice rising slightly, "We aren't supposed to be keeping *secrets* from each other here... are we?"

"I know, sir," she countered. "It is just that... well, that I do not exactly know what it *means*, myself – it came from deep within me, sir : a call from the heart. Although I suspect that I know what it means... more or less."

"Such as...?" he pressed.

"Such as," she calmly stated, "What the people of Earth should look for, when I destroy the comet."

Taking a seat and reclining back in it, Jacobson muttered, "Oh my, we're back to *that*, are we? I thought we had... 'dealt' with that set of issues earlier... had we not?"

"No... *this* time, I mean what I say, Captain Jacobson sir," declared Karéin-Mayréij. "You are one of us – a man becoming *Makailkh*, akin to me, now, Sam Jacobson, and you *know* that what I say is true. Use your power and you can *feel* it. *Think*, sir – ponder, meditate. *Read* me, sir... what does your mind say? Do I tell you truly, or do I lie?"

For a few seconds, Jacobson just stood there, studying her, trying to call upon some unnamed ability, without any instruction as to how to do so.

Then he slowly offered, "I suppose you *do* mean it... don't you, Karéin? I don't know *how* I know, but something tells me... like intuition on steroids. These... these powers of yours... *whew!* They take a little getting used to, that's for sure."

The Mars mission commander looked humbled, if more than pleased with himself. "But what about the *Salvador Two* project, and our plans for that?"

"I will try to save *them* as well, sir," she uneasily promised. "If I can."

The alien-girl's tone seemed suddenly weaker, less confident, somehow.

"Well," Jacobson grumbled, "What will be... will be, I guess. Anyway, as long as you're here, you're still answering to me... right?"

"Definitely, sir," politely agreed the Storied Watcher. "So what would you have me do?"

"We all know what the orders are," Jacobson replied, "That is, about you shoving off from here and flying to Earth orbit, the better to please our friends at NASA. It's almost time to get going on that."

Looking at the others, he said, "You all want to accompany us down to the airlock, I assume?"

Glumly, they all nodded.

Looking at a display, Boyd noted, "Sergei's already there, according to the computer."

"Hmm," commented Jacobson, "That's funny; he must have heard that weird music, and felt the energy-surge, too – I have a rather thicker skin for these things than, say, the Professor, here... but even *I* felt it wash over me. Why wouldn't he have come here? Isn't he interested?"

"Sir," the Storied Watcher evenly offered, "He did not *have* to. He knows what has gone on here."

"Oh, so he engaged the remote video... wait a minute, didn't we disable that for the private quarters?" asked the Mars mission commander.

"Sure did," answered White. "Resultin' in what passes for privacy up here."

"Well then, how *did* he..." wondered Jacobson. "Oh... *I* get it."

Shaking his head, he quietly remarked, "You know, Karéin... you've really set us on an uncharted course here. I don't know *how* we are going to cope, without you to teach us how to handle our new abilities. I really don't."

"You will do as my ancestors did, sir," sympathetically counseled Karéin-Mayréij. "And as have others, in the past. You will make mistakes and learn from them, and you will learn from each other, day by day, little by little. Thus has *always* been the way. I have brought you the *Fire*; now, it is up to *you*, to use it wisely, remembering the oath you took. You do not need me, any more, Captain Sam Jacobson: but others *do*. *That*, is the real reason why I must go, not some order from some Earth-nation."

"Yeah," he said, trying to mask the fact that his voice was shaking. "Yeah. That's right. Okay, well... I guess it's time to go, now. Ugh. Just for the record, folks, I mightily resent having had to be the one to say that. Wouldn't have been *my* choice, you understand."

He motioned to the others and led the way to the access-tunnel hatch.

We Believe In You

One by one, the four humans, and their alien guest, disappeared from the *Infinity*'s pseudo-gravity drum, into the weightless environment of the central tunnel. Once there, three of them propelled themselves in the familiar ways, hand-holds and pushes; two of them simply flew, by power of will.

"You have become better, *much* better, Cherie," said the Storied Watcher to Tanaka. "Try it with gravity, sometime. But do not go higher than you can afford to fall," she added with a slight grin.

"Yeah," Tanaka replied, "Like learning to skate... the hardest thing – the ice."

After a few short moments the group arrived in the maintenance area and noticed that Chkalov had already opened the access-hatches. One by one, they crowded into the ante-chamber, which was barely large enough to hold all of them, even with White halfway out the center core access-hatch.

They formed a rough circle around the Mars-girl.

"Well, this is it, I guess," morosely announced Jacobson. "Time to say our last 'good-byes'."

He looked from person to person, but none said anything, at first, so Jacobson did.

"Karéin," he offered, "I'm not a man for long speeches, and it's hard saying this... so I'll try to keep it short and sweet. Despite the fact that it has only been a little while, we've all been through a *lot*, together; God knows, when I set out on this mission, I never anticipated having to deal with someone like yourself. All I can say is that you've given me the experience of twenty lifetimes. Out of stupidity I very nearly lost you, both for this crew and for all mankind. Thank you for being bigger than I was... and, most of all, for entrusting me with your power – you have my word that I will *never* abuse your *Fire*. Take care of yourself. Oh... and one other thing."

"Yes, sir?" quietly inquired the Storied Watcher.

"I'm ordering you to leave this ship, per the instructions from NASA," he stated, *"But*... the instant when you go out that outside door, I release you from my service, Karéin-Mayréij of *Mailànkh*. You must go, and do, as your conscience tells you. If that means coming right back here, so be it. If it means going to meet the boys down at NASA or if it means going elsewhere... then, promise me that *someday*, we'll see you again. Promise?"

He gave her a fatherly smile, hugging her much smaller frame to his barrel-like chest.

"On all my honor and by the Thousand Suns, I do so promise, sir," she replied, closing her eyes, then releasing her grasp.

Then, as if recalling a duty carelessly overlooked, Karéin-Mayréij hastily spoke up.

"Brent," she asked, "Do you remember the little pendant that I gave you, when first we met, back on *Mailànkh*?"

"Certainly do," answered Boyd. "It was very touching... I could tell that it meant a lot to you."

"I took a look at it under our microscope," added Tanaka. "It's *amazingly* intricate. Is it a device of some kind?"

"Fully explaining the answers to those questions would take many days, but in time, you will come to know how greatly you have under-stated the value of this other gift," explained the alien-girl. "Her name is '*Vìrya Quü'j*', and she is *most* noble, ancient and powerful... but where *I* am about to go, I cannot take her. Promise me that you will guard her with your *life*. Promise it now, Brent Boyd, this I *implore*."

"I promise, Storied Watcher," he responded, with genuine sincerity. "I will make sure that this amulet of yours isn't subjected to any kind of testing that might be destructive... would that be okay?"

"Yes," gladly replied the Storied Watcher. "Although she is anything *but*, an 'amulet'. And do not fail in protecting her; for if venerable *Vìrya Quü'j* feels that her safety may be in doubt... if would just be better, if you do not find out how she would try to defend herself. Oh-kay?"

"Oh-kay," gently mimicked Boyd.

"Karéin," spoke up Tanaka, her voice quivering, "I don't have much to add to that. Except... except..."

Tears started to flow.

"*You* say something, Brent," sobbed the scientist, "I *can't*. I'm the Tin Man."

"Yeah, okay, Cherie... no problem," compassionately responded Boyd. "Ours are all breaking, too."

Turning to the Storied Watcher, he confessed, "Karéin... first of all, you know that I have loved you – yes, that's the right word – from the first moment when I set eyes on you, down on, *Mailànkh*... don't you?"

"Yes, I do, dear Brent, my love," confirmed Karéin-Mayréij. "You and I have been one in mind. You could hardly hide it... nor should you. Nor do I. You should not think of this as a betrayal of anyone, especially not of your beloved, down on Earth. There is no such thing as 'too much love', after all."

"Then you know that this is as hard for me, as it is for any here," he stammered. "But I, too, release you."

He looked at his feet, then added, "You have bigger things, *far* bigger ones, to deal with, than the feelings of any one man. But, Karéin..."

"Hold me, Brent," she interrupted, embracing him. "Hold me and *dream* with me. I trust you to go, only where it is wise."

The two stayed locked in each others' arms for as much as a minute, eyes closed, silently exchanging thoughts, dreams, memories.

Eventually Boyd and the girl dis-embraced, with the man looking utterly exhausted, emotionally drained.

"Sergei," he mumbled, "Would you mind running the airlock controls? I'm kind of... *out* of it, right now."

"Keep these dreams close to your heart, remembering them often, Brent Boyd," she counseled. "I will be back to share more with you."

"Please," Boyd gasped, "Please, Karéin, *do* come back. Soon. Please."

He stumbled backwards, supporting himself on the bulkhead.

Chkalov stepped forward and embraced the alien-girl.

He said, "Remember your promise to me, Storied Watcher, we have, how they say in English, a 'date', yes? And – Karéin – do not judge the people on Earth too harshly, when you meet them. You do not *want* to, I know this, but you must lead them... by example, by showing them that things do not have to be the way they always have been, down there."

He kissed the top of her head and softly and expressively breathed, "*Do sviedanya*, Karéin-Mayréij."

They heard a low "whoosh" as the Russian opened the airlock pressure-hatch.

The Storied Watcher started towards it, but then froze.

She turned around and said, with panic developing in her voice, "Listen, humans... I... I have reconsidered... I cannot *do* this..."

"What do you *mean*, Karéin?" asked Jacobson. "You're not going? But I thought you said –"

Her voice trembling with an icy fear, the alien-girl quailed, "Sir... if I go out that door – into the Void, I mean – I am *not* coming back – I fear it – not up to the task that I must complete – I am *so* afraid – so *afraid*."

Instantly, she looked small and terrified, like they had seen, shortly after she had first started to speak their language.

"Please do not make me go. *Please*, sir. I *beg* you!" she cried.

A tear ran down her cheek.

"What's the risk in going to see NASA, Karéin? All they're going to do is subject you to a bunch of tests... demeaning, maybe, but *certainly* not fatal...?" Jacobson asked.

"You do not *understand*, sir," wailed Karéin-Mayréij, in a voice full of dread. "But you should. I am *not* going to the NASA ship, or *any* space-ship. I am going to do something that the com-pu-ter says I cannot possibly do, and live. *Save me, sir!* Let me carry the people from Earth to their *Ark*-things! Let me protect the *Salvador* ship! Let me do *anything* but this!"

Her lip trembled. She started to cry.

"Then *stay* with us, Karéin," implored Tanaka, her own voice still breaking. "We don't *want* you to go!"

"Or just fly out aways – then come straight back," added Boyd, still almost out of breath. "I'm as loyal an Air Force man as the Captain... but when you go, well, you'll have done what he ordered. All bets are off, when you return."

Jacobson knew what the alien-girl meant, now.

He countered, "You don't *understand*, Brent... do you? She's got to make a *decision*. Crossing the Rubicon. One that only *she* can make."

"Indeed," agreed Chkalov. "If she goes to NASA, she is entrapped in an entire, new set of orders, procedures and distractions. My superiors back in Star City in Russia demanded that I try to stop her from doing this, forcibly if necessary, on the grounds that the American President might try to make her into a weapon... but I refused that request. Mortal men are not in a position to decide such things."

"Why does she have to decide, *now?*" complained Tanaka. "There's still plenty of time. And she has to save the new *Salvador* ship, too."

"No... there is not enough time, Professor," warned Chkalov. "For anything but her essential task, that is. Her inner thoughts have told me this. She says that the hour is late. And it is a decision she must face at some time, anyway."

Jacobson would have said something about orders, plans and suchlike things, the better to take the mind of Karéin-Mayréij off her *real* task; but he was interrupted by White, who suddenly forced his way through the throng, grabbing the alien-girl and holding her as one would a frightened child.

Trembling in his arms, she let out a pained breath, but did not say anything.

"Folks," requested White, quietly to the others, "I need your help. Come closer."

"Let's all hold hands again," he suggested, "Like how we did when she gave us her gift."

They all complied, huddled together much closer than any found comfortable.

"Let's all just close our eyes, and try to send her some good karma," White explained. "I know she can tell what we're thinking. Can't y'all as well?"

The alien-girl just whimpered.

"I got no clue how to do this," White reflected. "So think with your *hearts*, not your *heads*."

For a second, a minute, an hour – how long it was, none could measure – while haunting, powerful music reverberated in the distance, five humans, or more-than-humans, as they were now, held hands and meditated, sensitive to each other's thoughts and emotions as no-one of their race ever had done, before.

Not knowing how, they tried to support her, to send her their own small fragments of power, using instincts long latent in the human psyche. None had the slightest idea of whether the effort was working or useless, but all hoped and prayed that it would help her.

Finally, White woke up from the trance, still embracing the Storied Watcher.

He heard her say, "Friends, your power glows in me... thank you. But you *know* I that am a fraud. I told the children that I would save them – the *children*, Devon – because for a moment I felt like I could – I really *did*. I tell people that I can do impossible things, because I cannot *bear* to tell them the truth. I was a knave... an impostor... before; and I am still one, now. *No-one* should believe me. Least of all, you."

"But, Karéin, *I* believe in you," he came back, with a dignity and confidence that he had never possessed, any time before. "With all my heart, as the Lord God Almighty is my witness."

"And so do I," said Boyd.

"So do I," said Jacobson.

"So do I," said Tanaka.

"I do, too," added Chkalov.

Karéin-Mayréij looked torn, between intellect, instinct and fear; and so she was, in a way that no human could ever comprehend.

But a look of peace, of resignation to the inevitable, slowly came over her.

"Do you all *understand*," she quietly observed, "That if I now fly on the wings of your faith... I will not return? That I will *sacrifice* myself."

None answered, although Tanaka nodded affirmatively.

A few seconds passed.

Then the alien-girl said, sadly but with resolve,

"If that is what must pass, for my redemption... then, so be it."

"Storied Watcher," White softly counseled, "Don't be scared. Y'all don't have to be afraid, sister, because I – we – everyone down on Earth, too – we all have the real kind of *faith*. Remember that song... the one them kids picked? That was for a *reason*, Karéin – same as why y'all were woke up in the first place, same as why y'all stowed away with us... same, *everything*. This was *meant* to be, right from the start; I know that now, I know it as surely as I'm holding y'all right now. Karéin, y'all don't have to be brave; what y'all gotta do – *all* y'all gotta do, nothin' more – is *believe* in yourself. Like *I* do... like *we* do."

The Mars-girl silently looked up at White – the man was much taller than her, by at least a head – with the eyes of a child looking for encouragement, on her first school-day.

She broke from his embrace and stepped slowly toward the airlock, turning to face them when she was in the hatchway.

The Storied Watcher looked down at her feet, as one from whom all the fight had been beaten, then, they saw one arm extend, and instantly, the metal plate upon which she had inscribed her original flight-path, shot from where it had been hidden, to her hand.

A surge of infernal heat – surely powerful enough to have flash-burned the flesh of ordinary human beings, but strangely pleasant to *these* five – washed over them. The plate softened, then enveloped her torso in a kind of other-worldly cuirass.

Now her war-music began to echo, as the eyes and body of Karéin-Mayréij started to glow. Her power radiated out, bathing them in a frightening, intimidating refulgence of demi-godly potency.

To the relief of Jacobson and his crew – now to be less by one, enigmatic, member – they saw the same, saturnine half-smile that they had, on several occasions before.

"Humans are a strange lot, with many faults," she reflected, "But they *are* my dear kin... and the Storied Watcher will give all, even unto her *life*... for them."

The alien-girl slowly waved her hand, as the hatchway began to close.

"De-pressurizing," whispered Chkalov, glancing back and forth, between the being in the chamber and his instrument display. "Outside hatch open, now."

I go willingly to my fate, dear sister and brothers, she sent to their minds.

Remember your vows and keep me in your hearts; thus I pass from this life... yet, will I live forever.

Then – in the flash of a god's eye – she was gone.

The Station

Time For Explaining

Captain Sam Jacobson – ex-commander of the NASA space-ships *Infinity* and *Eagle* – sat uncomfortably in the main boardroom of Earth's ISS2 pseudo-gravity module; although, the latter craft could now hardly be called an "Earth" station, given the fact that it was further out from the planet than almost all previous manned space-missions, notably excepting the one over which he had previously had command, had ever gone.

Jacobson fidgeted with small objects in his vicinity, as, along with the others in the room, he waited for today's scheduled transmission from Houston's Mission Control.

Nervousness, not to say irritability, like this, was not his nature; but since he had had to sequester control over his ship to his counterpart, Ariel Cohen of ISS2, Jacobson felt like the proverbial 'third wheel'.

Yes, Cohen *had* awarded him the title of 'Station Second-In-Command', but both of them knew that the *real* chain of command went from Cohen to the latter's Chinese understudy.

A ship, whether it traveled over the waves or through the void of space, could have only *one* captain and only *one* first mate. Jacobson knew that this was the way things had to be, but that knowledge did not make his situation any more palatable.

As he tried to kill time while waiting for today's 'Earthlight Follies', as the crew of ISS2 had sarcastically termed their daily briefings, Jacobson recalled the events of the past few days, after the Mars-girl had flown from the *Infinity*.

They had reached the *rendez-vous* point in good time, but Cohen's ship, or station, or call it what you want, had been late, and indeed almost missed the maneuver altogether, as its braking rocket had repeatedly malfunctioned right up to the most critical point. Luckily, Herculean efforts on the part of ISS2's technical team had finally managed to get the accursed thing working; albeit, at the cost of using almost all of the booster's remaining fuel.

There would now be no way to get the station back to Earth, but, considering the circumstances, that issue seemed to be of very minor importance.

In any event, *Infinity*, along with its attached daughter-ship, *Eagle*, now sitting silent and forlorn, its one intended purpose now over and done with, had docked successfully with ISS2. The former Mars mission commander's own crew – minus the most interesting and unique one of them, of course – had all transferred over to the station, with little ado.

To his relief, they had mostly been given productive jobs to do; White, with ISS2's communications officer (some Greek guy, as Jacobson recalled); Chkalov and Boyd, both assigned to engineering and repair duties, and, finally, Tanaka, who had volunteered to help the space-station's environmental officer.

Jacobson himself was the only one with too much spare time on his hands, he noted, ruefully; but he was glad for the others being busy. Doing so helped keep their minds off experimentation with the weird new abilities that they all possessed.

He had reminded them that displaying these to ISS2's crew might cause, well, *problems*. Boyd had protested, but in the end, he, too, realized that anything that might jeopardize their welcome on-board the station – and humans mutating into something like a 'more-than-human', would certainly fit *that* bill – was not a good risk to take, when the alternative might be the airlock. When the 'Lucifer' thing was dealt with... then, yes, they would tell the full story of what had transpired, with the one called 'Karéin-Mayréij'.

But *that* was, in fact, the subject of today's transmission, as Jacobson was acutely aware.

The static on the cinema-sized view-screen suddenly shimmered, crackled and eventually gave way to an image of five people – Ramirez, Abruzzio and McPherson, with whom Jacobson had long been familiar, plus two new ones that he had only lately come to know, as they had been assigned specifically to liaison with the space-station.

"Hello, Commander Cohen and ISS2," he heard Ramirez' Tex-Mex voice announce. "This is Hector Ramirez here at Houston, along with Sylvia Abruzzio, Fred McPherson, Sanjay Chopra and Irina Kulakovsy, you guys all know each other. Oh, and, may I also say 'hi' to Captain Sam Jacobson and the crew of *Infinity* and *Eagle*... I know I welcomed you aboard last week, but good to see you there, anyway."

Everyone nodded politely as Ramirez went on, "A bit of housekeeping, first... Commander, I received your environmental and life-support inventories as of yesterday, more or less a good story, we're aware that you're down a bit compared to plan, but it's nothing too serious as far as we can tell. I do have to say, however, that we're concerned about the propulsion issue. If the booster is really gone for good, it'd require a re-supply mission to send you up another... and I don't think I got to tell you, the chances of *that* in the immediate future, are next to non-existent. So all we can do is ask you to pull a rabbit out of your hat and get that rocket working again, *somehow*. I guess that's all I have to say. I'll turn it over to Sylvia, now."

Abruzzio now appeared in the center of the camera's field of vision.

"Hi, everyone up there on ISS2... my turn for an update," she said. "We're nearing completion of the first phase of the *Arks* project, in that we have begun final assembly of all the boosters that we're officially going to launch – we *might* be able to scrape up a few more before L-Hour, but if that doesn't happen, that's okay."

Cherie Tanaka, who was the only one of Jacobson's former crew invited to the briefing, whispered in her ex-commander's ear, "If I were one of the ones that were supposed to go, but *didn't*... I might not think that it's okay."

Realizing that he did not have to play the senior-officer part any more, Jacobson laughed, under his breath.

Abruzzio continued, "...So, *Arks* is actually a bit ahead of schedule. However, I'm afraid the news isn't so good with *Salvador Two*. As you know, that mission was due to have taken off some time ago, and several of you have asked NASA why it is that it's still sitting on the launch-pad. We'd appreciate it if you would keep this to yourselves, when you communicate with loved ones back on Earth, given the sensitivity of the situation – but, well, at the last moment we discovered serious problems with the hull and structural integrity of the *Salvador* ship itself."

"Surprise... *surprise*," muttered Tanaka.

The Houston space scientist admitted, "The boosters and other subsystems seem good to go, but the ship has turned out to be in *such* bad shape that in our opinion it won't even survive the lift-off phase... it would probably disintegrate before it even leaves the atmosphere. Fred's been working tirelessly to resolve these problems and I'm about to move from the *Arks* program to help him get *Salvador Two* caught up... but there's a very real possibility that we may not be able to get that ship off the ground, in enough time to safely intercept 'Lucifer'."

A muffled groan erupted from the twelve people in the boardroom, as Abruzzio's words registered upon them.

She concluded, "But don't lose hope completely, team. If it turns out that the *Salvador Two* ship is only marginally boost-worthy, we've got a backup plan to fly her solely by computer; the idea would be to crash her into the comet and detonate the charges remotely. Of course, the risk to this, apart from non-optimal placement of the nukes, is that the ship might fall apart in the upper atmosphere, possibly detonating the bombs at that point... not something we would ordinarily want to happen, but it's a chance we may have to take, considering the current situation. Okay, well, that's all from me... Fred?"

McPherson's face, even more fatigued than normal, appeared on the view-screen.

"Thanks, Sylvia, this is Fred McPherson here," he started. "My main reason for being here today, that is, for taking time off the *Salvador* project, is just to let you know that we still do not have any sign of the alien... that is, former Commander Jacobson's 'Karéin-Mayréij'.

"No shit," whispered Tanaka to Jacobson.

"As you know," mentioned McPherson, "She was due to *rendez-vous* with one of our Shuttles in Earth orbit a bit more than a week ago, but, basically, she's gone AWOL – we tracked her trajectory, based on information supplied by Major Chkalov of the *Infinity*'s former crew, shortly after she left that ship, and everything seemed okay... then, she just *vanished*. Unfortunately, the Shuttle is now nearing the limit of its on-board environmental supplies and it will soon have to abort the mission and return to Earth. We obviously couldn't leave it up there indefinitely, anyway – it's one of the most important components of the *Arks* mission."

McPherson cleared his throat and commented, "The bottom line, ladies and gentlemen, is that we are back to where we were, prior to the alien's little trip from *Infinity* to ISS2 and back again. That is... we're on our own."

"No we aren't –"started Tanaka; but she was "shusshed" by Jacobson, as McPherson went on, "Personally, I view this as a *good* thing... not a bad one. Along with rumors that this 'Karéin-Mayréij' was herself responsible for sending the comet our way – 'she's the devil', that kind of nonsense – there has been *wild* speculation going on down here, mostly fueled by the less scrupulous of our religious leaders – sorry if I offended anyone in saying that, but it's the *truth* – that the 'Storied Watcher' was some kind of a savior... it was starting to induce a kind of stupid fatalism amongst some people on Earth – you know, 'the angel will save us', et cetera. It's a nice *idea*, of course... but not the kind of thing that you'd want to stake the future of your whole *planet* on... right?"

"*I* would," said Tanaka, *sotto voce.*

Jacobson did not respond.

The Presidential Science Advisor explained, "Now, although the alien is obviously no longer a factor, and although we *have* gone over this, just to tidy matters up, I have a few questions about her actions just before her departure, that I'd like to ask Captain Jacobson – ah yes, *there* he is, I see him... hello, Captain. First of all... did she say anything about where she was going, what she was planning to do? Any insight you can give us on this might help us locate her... not that doing so would really help the matter any, since we have no way to then bring her back."

"Second," he inquired, "Did something happen on the *Infinity* that might have upset her or cause her to disobey our directives? Third, assuming – and we know this isn't likely – but just in case we *are* able to locate her... do you know of any way that we could reliably communicate with the alien? Did she perhaps have a long-range radio or laser tracking-device... something like that?"

Tanaka rolled her eyes and shook her head.

"Please try to answer these questions honestly and to the best of your ability," instructed McPherson, "And please accept my word that nothing you say will be held against either yourself or your crew. We're aware that in dealing with this being you were called upon to handle a situation that none of us could have foreseen. I'll await your response... McPherson over."

Cohen, from across the table, looked at Jacobson and asked, "Need some time to think about your answers, first, Sam?"

"No," replied Jacobson, "But thanks for offering me the opportunity, Commander. I don't have much to add... and, anyway, they asked me this all before, just after we docked. I don't know *why* he's belaboring the subject. You can put me on, if you like."

Theodikas threw a switch and Jacobson, facing the screen, spoke up.

"Hello Fred, this is Captain Sam Jacobson, ex-of the *Infinity* and *Eagle* Mars mission," he stated, calmly and impassively. "I'll try to answer your questions in sequence, but before I get going – it's something that I've discussed previously with yourself, I'm really just saying it for the benefit of those in the room who are not as well... *acquainted* with 'Karéin' as I am, or was – I think we all have to understand that we are dealing with a largely unknown quantity, here."

"What I mean is," said the former Mars mission commander, "I *think* I know Karéin as well as any human being can; but what's very easy to lose sight of, particularly because she *looks* so much like us, is... well, she's *not* like us, in a number of very important ways. Some aspects of her personality are exactly like those of a normal human woman; many other things about her are, to say the least... 'alien'. So please keep that in mind, as I try to answer your questions."

Jacobson went on, "Now, as to your first question... at various times, Karéin said that she was going to just leave us, go away somewhere – fortunately, I believe that I dissuaded her from *that* course of action – then, she said that she would follow NASA's instructions and fly to the Shuttle in Earth orbit, or that she was going to help the *Salvador Two* mission avoid the 'Lucifer''s local debris-field, and –", he took a deep breath and stated, "– Twice, she said that she was going to destroy the comet."

A gasp issued from several of the people in the room.

"Excuse me," interrupted Chen, "But why did you not inform NASA – or us – of this comment? It would seem to be very relevant to the situation that now confronts us... would it not, Captain?"

Suppressing a momentary flash of irritation, Jacobson replied, "Because, First Lieutenant – I hope I have your title right, please excuse me if I got it wrong – she *also* repeatedly told us that she was in no way capable of actually *accomplishing* that task. Karéin obviously *does* have some pretty amazing abilities... as you people on ISS2 yourself found out, when she paid you her last little visit. But the point is, as ordinary humans –"

He noticed Tanaka wincing at this, but continued talking, in stride.

"We have no way at all of knowing when she's telling us the truth about this kind of thing," noted Jacobson. "For example, if a normal human being tells me that he can jump over a tall building, I know that's not likely; if he says that he can't jump over a crack in the pavement, I know *that's* not likely, either. If he says that he can't do the high jump over a five-foot bar, maybe yes, maybe no, depending on how athletic the person is."

"Now," he elaborated, "Imagine you have an alien being who first tells you that she *can* do something, then that she *can't*... and all of this depends on her use of a power – *Amaiish*, or the *Fire,* as she calls it – that we've never previously encountered and know next to nothing about. I chose not to report her boasts, First Lieutenant, so as not to raise false hopes amongst the peoples of Earth; although it appears, from what Fred has been saying, that this may have happened anyway... I'm comfortable with that decision. If I had the same set of facts in front of me, I'd make the same decision, again."

Chen did not look at all convinced.

Cohen said, "Interesting. But go ahead, Sam."

"Okay," acknowledged the former Mars mission commander. "Thanks. As to your second question, Fred, no... I don't believe that her leaving us, if that's what she really has *done*, is attributable to anything that happened on the *Infinity*, or to anything that she heard from Earth."

"Well, that's a good thing, I suppose," politely offered Cohen.

"Look," disclosed Jacobson, "I can't deny that we had – *ahem* – our 'ups and downs' with Karéin; for God's sake, the rest of us on the ship had our fights with each other, every so often... now try to imagine how much more difficult it must have been for *her*, coming out of a hundred-thousand-year trance, to learn to interact with *us* – but actually Karéin is very easy to get along with. She can have her moods – don't we all – but when we had to say 'goodbye', I can *assure* you that none of us wanted to see her go."

"You can say *that* again, Sam," interjected Tanaka, out loud. "She is, or was, the most fascinating being I have ever encountered, or am likely to encounter. She taught us things that we could *never* learn on our own, not in ten thousand years. *Never*."

Jacobson was afraid that Tanaka would go on and say more, but she evidently thought better of it and quickly buttoned up.

He took over, saying, "So, just to finish off *that* issue... no, Fred, we were on good terms with Karéin when she left. As far as NASA was concerned, I'll be honest with you – there *were* some things that you asked her to do, especially concerning leaving the *Infinity* prematurely, traveling to the Shuttle and so on, that she didn't like. From her own point of view, we are, or were, her 'family' – I suppose if you wake up all alone after thousands of years of hibernation, that's a reasonable way to look at whomever woke you up – so she didn't like being ordered to leave us. But, again, keep in mind that Karéin is a rational being; she's very intelligent, sometimes *frighteningly* so. So I doubt that she would fly off somewhere just out of petulance or rebellion.."

Jacobson explained, "Now, regarding the tracking-device, no, I'm afraid we weren't able to give her anything like that. Not that we didn't want to – but Karéin-Mayréij accelerates so rapidly that anything we might try to equip her with would be pretty much instantly wrecked. There are other technical reasons, as well, why she didn't think that would work."

He concluded, "As far as communicating with her is concerned, *if* you can locate her – a tall order, considering that she's a human-sized object in the vastness of space – and *if* you can shoot a modulated signal at her, yes, in theory you might be able to send her a message, or at least get her attention. But she'd have to be 'listening', for lack of a better word... like, if you're out in the forest, hearing a thousand subtle sounds from as many different sources, and all of a sudden a single cricket starts chirping, "Hey – look at *me!*" Even if you *could* understand it, you'd have to be listening for cricket-chatter, or it would just get lost in the background... she said that to us, once. Not very encouraging, I know... but it's the truth, as much as any of us can really know the truth, about her."

As Theodikas switched the system to receive mode, another of Cohen's entourage – this time, an East Indian woman – spoke up.

"Captain Jacobson," she commented, "You told us that you did not think that this 'Karéin' of yours has vanished out of spite or anger. Fair enough... but if that is the case, where has she gone? Why has she not made contact with someone, *anyone*, from Earth? I seem to remember several members of ISS2, among them, Mme. Daladier from the culture subsection of the *Arks* project, mentioning that the alien had said that she wanted to return to ISS2, to spend more time with us..."

"That's right, Shivani," interjected Cohen. "She said that to me in almost so many words. I believe that you were in on the same conversations, Sam?"

"Yeah, that's true," admitted Jacobson. "And I'll acknowledge that it doesn't seem to make much sense... at least, from where we are now. All I can tell you, ladies and gentlemen, is... 'I don't know'. Like I said – some things about Karéin, I can read easily, but there are other aspects of her motivation and behavior that, well, I know the dark side of the Moon a lot better, if you get my drift. If she ever *does* come back, I'll ask her to explain herself... I think she'd listen to me..."

The view-screen again came into motion, showing McPherson.

"Message received and understood, Captain Jacobson," he said. "What you say is disappointing, but, as I stated earlier, it was highly irrational for us to have placed any hope or trust in this being, in the first place. Now, at least, we have her off our minds, so we can concentrate on the tasks at hand. All we can reasonably ask you to do, in view of your special relationship with 'Karéin', is to report any contact with her ASAP, and to ask her to stay put in one place where we can communicate with her, should she again grace us with her presence."

He let out a sigh.

"You know," philosophically offered McPherson, "I'll say for the record that what's actually *more* disappointing for me, is simply that I'll now never have a chance to meet 'Karéin-Mayréij' in person. I *so* much envy you, Commander, that you've had that opportunity. Just to become *friends* with a living, breathing, intelligent, alien, I mean... to have her in your presence... to shake hands with her. Ah, well."

Softly, with a far-off look in her eyes, Tanaka whispered, "Don't lose hope, Fred. Where did I hear it being said, 'with faith, all things are possible'..."

"I don't begrudge you feeling that way," gently responded Jacobson. "Living with the Storied Watcher, you get used to things like sitting down for a coffee with a goddess who's also your best friend... it's an *amazing* experience. I wish you'd been there with us, Fred."

McPherson nodded.

"We'll be keeping you all informed on progress on the *Arks* and *Salvador* missions, as developments warrant," he concluded. "In the meantime, our thoughts and wishes are all with you; it's no secret that much of the future of mankind, or what's left of it, may rest with your ability to survive the 'Lucifer' object. Good luck, ISS2... McPherson out."

Theodikas threw a switch and the screen went blank.

"Well... that's *that*," observed Cohen. "Nothing new in that one... other than for the news about *Salvador*, I suppose. Not that it really concerns *us*, of course, since there's nothing we can do to affect that mission, either for good or bad. Captain Jacobson and Professor Tanaka – you're excused if you want to leave, since we will be dealing only with housekeeping issues from here on, but you're welcome to stay, if you want to."

"I'll stay, if you don't mind," answered Jacobson.

"So will I," added Tanaka, "But don't worry, Commander... I'll only speak if spoken to," she said, with a grin.

"Okay," amicably replied Cohen.

Steering A Space Supertanker

At least he's trying to accommodate me, and us, silently thought Jacobson.

More than a lot of commanders, with what he's got on his mind these days, would do.

"Well, let's get down to business," Cohen stated. "Li, how are the propulsion system repairs going?"

"Better than expected," Chen answered, "But not so good, even at that. I believe that we can fire the booster once or twice, for five-second bursts, each time; after that, we will be completely out of propellant. Furthermore, I doubt that we will be able to achieve anything close to the unit's nominally-rated thrust... we are probably looking at about sixty per cent of the propulsive energy to which we had access, on the out-bound leg of this trip."

"I... see," evenly replied the station-commander.

"Second Officer Muller and I have been working with the other teams to identify locally-available substances – chemicals from the food-recycling systems, for example – that we might be able to reprocess, to create a substitute propellant," elaborated Chen, "But I am not optimistic about the outcome. As you are no doubt aware, for reasons of safety, chemicals with high volatility are scarce up here... and if we try to commandeer other substances in their place, we will be causing shortages in other vital areas. But I will keep on trying."

"Good. Do so. At least we have some time on this front," ordered Cohen. "Shivani? Environmental report, please."

Parmar spoke up, saying, in a petite, only slightly-accented voice, "The news is not all good... but neither is it hopeless. We were falling seriously behind in our reserve supplies of breathable air; but, fortunately, last week we completed full decontamination of the contents of the airlock that earlier contained the alien – so we were able to return that to our available stock – and at the same time, we had the reserves from Captain Jacobson's two ships added, as well."

"How much does that count for?" asked the station-commander.

"Since those craft had not yet completed the outbound leg of what had earlier been expected as their trajectory to Earth," stated Parmar, "The addition of the *Infinity* and *Eagle* reserves have, I am happy to say, now given us an extra margin for error... perhaps as much as three to five days' worth for the station as a whole."

"I haven't heard any of them say 'thank you', yet, Sam," muttered Tanaka, privately to Jacobson.

He nodded, subliminally.

The East Indian woman continued, "food-reserves are still holding up well, better than plan, actually. water-consumption is more or less where we had anticipated. However, sir, all of these calculations were based on certain assumptions that may no longer be valid – in particular, that we would be away from Earth resupply for no longer than about seventy days, give or take three to six days' worth of error-margin..."

"I know I promised not to speak out of turn, Shivani," interrupted Tanaka, "But this is something that you and I had been discussing a day or so ago... I hope you remember me saying that I was going to ask it, at this meeting. What I'm getting at, Commander, is... 'resupply'? What did NASA have in *mind*, when they said this? Even assuming that you can get this station safely back down to a low orbit – what's going to 'resupply' you? By that time, there might not *be* a NASA, a Houston, or even a living thing above the level of a small mammal, left on Earth. In that eventuality... what's the plan?"

"The plan is, Professor," noted Cohen, matter-of-factually, "That we work out the plan, ourselves, using whatever resources that have survived the first two phases of the *Arks* project."

"I don't follow you," Tanaka retorted. "Under the *best* of circumstances, they'll be a bunch of semi-space-worthy rescue capsules, floating around in Earth orbit, waiting for *you* to rescue *them*. Not the other way around."

"That may well prove to be the case," remarked Chen, "But under the parameters of that project, Commander Cohen will be empowered to make any necessary decisions as to the apportionment of available resources, when we are able to locate surviving *Arks* ships. His word will be *final*, in this respect."

"I... see," answered Tanaka, knowing what was meant, but not wanting to make them say it out loud.

"Nothing that we weren't told earlier by Sylvia Abruzzio," Jacobson reminded her.

"If I may?" requested Parmar.

Tanaka nodded.

The East Indian woman concluded, "As I was saying, Commander, should our original assumptions about the length of our stay in this higher orbit, or about how long it takes for us to return to low Earth orbit, prove inaccurate on the low side, as we go on our return-trip, we may be forced to make some *very* difficult decisions."

"Such as?" rhetorically asked Jacobson.

"What I am trying to say, Captain Jacobson – and this is certainly not something with which you are not familiar, given your own training in space navigation – is that should we *not* start our trip back to Earth at the pre-arranged time, or should anything else unexpected happen to our propulsion systems and therefore our trajectory... we will likely run low on breathable air, before we even get back to low orbit," said Parmar.

There was a grim silence, as she continued, "I have been consulting with Mr. Chen regarding our new maximum velocity. Based on those calculations, if we are, for example, a week late on the burn-schedule, we very well might run out completely, anywhere from about two days to a few hours before reaching that orbit... although of course this is subject to a number of variables that I do not yet have the final data for. If our return speed is greater, then we would have correspondingly more margin for error."

She paused a moment, then added, "To answer your question... we would then have to engage in triage measures. This would mean sacrificing some members of the crew, so that the rest could survive."

"Well, let's hope that we do not have to deal with *that* possibility," offered Cohen.

He looked at a short, bald-headed, clean-shaven Caucasian European man with a small gold ring in one ear, two seats down from him.

"Alan? You got the engineering-stuff?" inquired the station-commander. "Then we're done – Michael, I know that the communications systems are all okay... we talked about that before, no need to keep everyone here to go over it. Oh, by the way, Professor Tanaka and Captain Jacobson, I don't think I introduced Alan Humber, my chief mechanical systems officer."

In a cheery Midlands English accent, the man with the earring said, "Hello... good to meet the two of you blokes, Captain, Professor, Alan Humber, European Space Agency, here."

He went on, "My report's basically a short one – electrical and hydraulic systems are all one hundred per cent, Commander, *although*," – he shot a semi-sarcastic glance at Chen – "Me mates and I have had to defend some of hydraulics from cannibalization by roaming propulsion-technicians. What he got away with, I think we can spare, though... no harm done there. Other than that, I've been spending my time checking for structural integrity, after that mysterious incident we had just after the alien left ISS2. So far, everything checks out... this tub's built as strong as a battleship and she's still holding together fine. That's it."

Theodikas put his hand up.

"One short comment. I have been running local and long-range scans, using the radiation signatures that we established for the alien, when she was in our vicinity," he explained. "Nothing, yet."

"Well, don't waste too much time, or power, on it, Michael," Cohen ordered, "As Fred McPherson mentioned earlier, this 'Karéin'... she certainly *was* interesting – that I'll admit – but she was, as it turned out, just a distraction. Personally I regret not having gotten to know her better, but at least *someone* did – Sam, Cherie, I sort of envy you for the experience... but it's history, now. Or so it appears."

"Yes," replied Jacobson, looking off into space, lost in contemplation, "Or so it appears."

Karéin, Tanaka thought, silently, *Where* are *you?*

As the group packed up their belongings and left the meeting-room, Jacobson's mind wandered to the chamber on Mars, to life on the *Infinity*, to where he was now, and back again.

Then, for a fleeting second, he thought he saw *her*, somewhere.

It was just an illusion... a dream, he thought.

Angel's Duty

The Storied Watcher had left Jacobson's little space-ship – and, in so doing, her home and her family – with a thousand contradictory feelings and emotions wracking her consciousness, as she hurtled through the void, her protective bubble crackling with impact-energy.

After only a few hours, the alien-girl flashed past the space-station, correctly suspecting that she had done so much faster than the humans' equipment could detect or track.

The one called 'Karéin-Mayréij' approached the Earth's moon, and, knowing that she was in a part of the void that might contain the humans' space-ships and other such objects, she gradually slowed, taking care not to do so in a way that might draw attention. She cruised above the Moon's surface, circumnavigating the body several times, observing the its unusual size, relative to its parent planet – *Mailànkh* had two such, but each was considerably smaller.

As the Storied Watcher flew over the demi-planet, her mind perceived the life-forces of several score humans, already ensconced in what must have been the "Moonbase" that Jacobson and his people had discussed, some time ago.

They have started their evacuation, she thought.

As they would have done, as their fate commands... whether or not I had awoken.

Moving at a small fraction of her maximum speed, Karéin-Mayréij quickly flew the short distance between the Moon and the Earth. She identified the NASA space-ship – what did the humans call it, yes, a 'Shuttle' – that they had prepared to accommodate her; the signals that the thing was broadcasting were useful in positively identifying it, but the ship proved easy enough to spot, with or without them.

Invisible to all but the very narrow band of radiation that she allowed to traverse her bubble – else, she would have no way to navigate, at all – the Storied Watcher floated outside the Shuttle, for a few minutes, silently contemplating her options.

All the instincts that had kept her safe, across ten times a thousand human lifetimes, told that there would be friends, safety, comfort, new experiences, inside the ship. It would keep her, feed her, entertain her.

But it would also *capture* her, *possess* her. And it would prevent her from fulfilling her vow.

You fool, her intellect, as well as her self-instinct said.

Knock on their door and all will be well.

Jacobson, Devon, Cherie, Brent, Sergei – they will all understand.

No-one expects more from you.

One hand of Karéin-Mayréij extended in the direction of the hatchway on the side of the ship's cabin, even though she knew that her power would work whether she used that appendage, or not.

She ached to make the gesture, to do the safe thing, to do what the humans – or, at least, *some* of them – wanted her to.

For a few interminable seconds, thus torn between nobility and ignobility, fear and safety, duty and gratification, the alien-girl remained immobile.

She agonized.

Now another voice, from she knew not where, sounded in the psyche of the Storied Watcher.

Not this *time,* it said.

It must be different *this time.*

She recalled the voices of Devon White's school-children, singing their melody of faith.

What did you tell them, Storied Watcher? the second voice pressed, as cruelly as any torture she had ever endured.

What did you have them believe?

A river of tears froze on her cheek, then vanished into the coldness of space, even within her bubble.

Now Karéin-Mayréij flew away, slowly, until she was a thousand meters or so from the Earth-ship.

Longingly, she took a sad, frustrated look at it.

You know *that they are not up to the task... their world will* die.

All of them, with it.

Including the children, the second voice warned, imprisoning her with a dark mantle of inevitability, holding her heart in a pitiless vice-grip of duty.

Closing her eyes – not that this mattered for more than the gesture – the Storied Watcher called to the only companion who she knew would never fail.

Holy Light, fortify my will, make me strong, take away my fear... humbly, this do I pray, she meditated.

Thus shall be my last quest, resolved Karéin-Mayréij, with her song of might and valor echoing noiselessly across the heavens.

I shall welcome the fate that I have spent ages uncounted, fighting to avoid.

Summoning all her powers, she flew away from the Earth-world, rapidly accelerating towards the second planet, the hot, cloudy one.

As the beautiful, blue-and-green planet receded behind the Storied Watcher, the second voice said,

Peace be with you.

Failure, Live And In Color

A few more boring days had passed on the station, now, with Jacobson increasingly at loose ends, while his former underlings tried, with varying degrees of success, to keep themselves busy, working with the ISS2 departments to which they had been assigned.

Boyd and Chkalov had done alright, working with Cohen's officious Chinese second-in-command on the propulsion systems, and after many man-hours of painstaking effort, they had managed to procure enough propellant to, perhaps, fire the booster rocket a couple times more than they could have, before.

No-one knew if this would be enough to get ISS2 back to Earth, not that any of them had much faith in the trip ultimately being worth the effort.

Meanwhile, general standards of behavior on the station, despite admirable efforts on the part of Ariel Cohen, had become more and more undisciplined and fatalistic, over time.

Not that anyone was disobeying orders, or anything like that; no, it was the *little* things – everything from not wearing regulation uniforms at the appropriate time, to basic scientific research schedules falling further and further behind, to petty arguments between crew-members who should have known better – that concerned both Cohen and Jacobson, on those few occasions when the station's actual commander had asked the latter his opinion.

Both men knew the warning signs of a breakdown in authority, but both had only limited tools at their disposal to prevent it, or, at least, delay it. Like so many other things, this one was out of their hands, especially, as the comet was now almost as close to the Earth as was the Moon.

Time was not long for the Earth, now.

Jacobson himself had lately taken to hanging around increasingly with Tanaka – who, despite her theoretical assignment as an understudy to Shivani Parmar, Cohen's life sciences officer, had been complaining about the lack of anything productive to do.

He had also spent one or two nights in her private quarters, cursing himself, with a sinking feeling in his stomach, for his unfaithfulness, each time thereafter.

"Don't worry about it, Sam," Tanaka had reassured him, "No woman worthy of the name, would blame you, considering the circumstances."

Jacobson had tried to take her words to heart, but still found thoughts of stepping out of the airlock drifting into his mind.

One time, he told Tanaka about these, about his guilt about his wife and family down on Earth, but she had replied, with a cynical laugh, "I wouldn't, if I were you; after all, you may get to do it anyway, when we run out of air."

God bless Cherie, he mused.

If I didn't already have *one, I'd ask you to be my wife.*

Today, though, there was an event set to take place, one which had captured the attention of most of the space-station's inhabitants, all, that is, save Jacobson and – strangely, White, who had seemed, over the last few days, unusually withdrawn, lacking his usual, irritatingly juvenile, yet refreshing, sense of humor.

"Captain Jacobson," he heard the loudspeaker in his quarters say, "This is Theodikas, in Communications. Commander Cohen has asked me to inform you that the *Salvador Two* liftoff will be happening in fifteen minutes. We have set up a large view-screen in the forward observation bay, where the proceedings will be televised up to us."

"Thanks," answered Jacobson, "I suppose I'll float on down there. But tell them not to hold it up just on my account."

"No problem, Captain," said Theodikas. "From what I hear, they have quite a few more serious issues to deal with. Such as it being weeks late, already."

Trying unsuccessfully to think of excuses not to watch the proceedings, but coming up with none, Jacobson eventually gave in and exited the pseudo-gravity area of the station, floating through its many twists and turns until he reached the bow observation-deck, the same one from which, Cohen had told him, they had first seen the Mars-girl appear.

The observation-deck was crammed with crew-members – *so* many, in fact, that for a few seconds Jacobson's commanding instincts worried about it somehow collapsing, or unbalancing the station's center of gravity – but, no doubt, Cohen and his people had already considered those hazards.

None of my business, anyway, the mind of the former Mars mission commander told him.

The view-screen became illuminated with a scene that must have been shot from the Cape Canaveral visitors' area, several miles from the launch-pad itself, looking directly at the latter across a tidal inlet.

A sad smile came to Jacobson's face as he realized that this might very well be the last time that he would ever see those familiar sand dunes, palm trees and shorebirds.

What I wouldn't give to walk barefoot in that sand, just one more time, he thought. *Or to race one of my kids through it –*

Never a very expressive man, he none the less had to fight back a tear.

The voice-over for the Disney News network started up, saying, "...And, ladies and gentlemen, we're approximately thirty seconds away from the launch of *Salvador Two*, Earth's last and best shot against the terrible menace of 'Lucifer', as the comet draws ever nearer... if you look up there in the sky – can I get a camera shot, please, Emilio – yeah, there it *is* – you can see 'Lucifer', even in daylight, now..."

As he caught a glimpse of the sinister point of light within the TV camera's field of vision, Jacobson's heart was heavy with dread.

He imagined what it must look like, *feel* like, to everyone down on Earth, as they helplessly watched their nemesis inexorably bear down on them.

He thought of what it must look like to his wife and children, without a father to be there with them.

Luckily for his sanity, the former Mars mission commander's mind was snapped back to the present by the announcer. "Okay, Cassie, we're almost ready, now... here's the countdown... ten... nine... eight... seven... six..."

A cloud of smoke billowed, as the *Salvador Two*'s main engines ignited.

To no-one in particular, Jacobson found himself saying, "You know, when I entered the program, it used to take *years* to put together a space mission; these guys have done it in *weeks*. Damn impressive, I'd say."

"That is true, sir," a black man with an East African accent, next to him said. "Where I come from they could not even agree on the plans for such a mission, in that time."

"Five... four... three..."

Fire, brilliant orange-red, erupted from the ship's engines.

"Two... one... liftoff!", the TV man exclaimed. "Liftoff of *Salvador Two*, and its heroic crew of astronauts and cosmonauts, pledged to sacrifice their own lives, to save ours!"

I'd trade that walk in the sand for one chance to shake each of their hands, Jacobson thought.

Or, to offer to take the place of one or two of them.

Slowly, the ship – an ungainly-looking parody of one of the late Twentieth Century first generation Space Shuttles, to which a collection of mismatched solid booster-rockets had been uneasily attached, cleared the launch-pad and roared upwards.

"Telemetry from Mission Control," said the TV announcer, as the view-screen changed to a scene within NASA's control-center, with a large computer trajectory display showing the path of the spacecraft so far. "All systems nominal... *Salvador* now at fifty thousand feet... seventy-five... one-hundred... Emilio, can we still see them from the ground?"

The scene again shifted to the ground. By now, the spacecraft was a tiny point of light on top of a pillar of smoke.

All of a sudden, a few, irregular puffs of smoke appeared at the top of the pillar, which, itself, stopped issuing forth.

"Houston, we have a problem," the announcer's voice sounded, apprehensively. "Emilio, can we get an idea of what's going on... okay, switching to Mission Control, again... what's that? An *explosion*? That's what it looked like from down here..."

The crowd on Earth gasped and held their breath, as did the crowd on-board the space-station.

"You know," observed the African man, "If that ship is lost... so are we."

"Yes," responded Jacobson, as if describing a failed high school science experiment, "So... are we."

"Hello, viewers," the announcer interrupted. "We have some breaking information from Mission Control. From what they're telling us, they are still in contact with *Salvador Two* – thank God, it's still intact – what's *that*? It appears that two of the spacecraft's boosters began to burn asymmetrically... Commander Nguyen had to jettison them prematurely, they were on the brink of exploding... she's fighting to get into a stable orbit..."

"*Bollocks*," he heard someone – it sounded like Humber – shout out. "God *damn* it, anyway! She's probably using the main engines to compensate. But even if she gets it into orbit, the damn thing won't be able to fly off to the comet – no fuel. We're *fucked*, my friends, we're *fucked* now, that's about the lot of it!"

"...Okay, Cassie, yes, I got that," the Disney News announcer said. "People, we now have a good idea of what has just transpired – it appears that the *Salvador Two* mission has suffered a serious setback, due to a booster engine malfunction in the upper atmosphere."

"From what I'm being told," ominously noted the newscast, "The ship has now been able to park itself in a stable orbit around the Earth, but its available fuel for what was to have been the escape-burn part of its trajectory has been almost all used up. I repeat, *Salvador Two* will *not* be able to leave Earth or intercept the comet, not unless a miracle occurs. Commander Annie Nguyen and her crew are all okay and they are in contact with Mission Control regarding what to do with the nuclear devices they carry on-board. We'll keep you informed as we hear things... this is Frank Dayton, reporting, live."

Jacobson looked from face to miserable face for some sign of optimism, of hope.

He found none, as the crowd slowly started to melt away to other places.

Feeling a tap on his shoulder, Jacobson wheeled in place and beheld Tanaka's pleasing visage. Considering her reaction to certain other events, the woman seemed very well-composed, after this one.

She commented, "Well, Sam... so much for *that* idea, eh? Think they've got something for an encore?"

"I'm glad you're not as disappointed as some of us are, Cherie," he quietly replied. "My guess is that someone down there is trying to scrounge up some more boosters, right now. If there *are* any... which I doubt."

"Which I doubt, too," interjected Cohen, joining the conversation after having pushed through the crowd. "Captain, I'd appreciate it if you and the Professor would join me for a quick meeting that I've called for my senior advisors. Without getting into the details, I think we have to consider our options from here on in, in view of what we've just seen. Same place as before, the boardroom."

"Delighted to," Jacobson said.

He lied, of course.

"Let's go, then," added Tanaka.

All of them floated out of the observation bay, disappointed to the very depths of their bones, but not surprised.

Not Enough *Fire*

As Karéin-Mayréij began the latest of her seemingly-endless training flights over the hot, gray-clouded planet that she knew as *Hlà'ter'àh* – so similar in mass, the gravity-sense told her, to the humans' own, yet so forbiddingly different... evidence, yes, of how fate and the universe punish those who take the wrong path, the wrong turn – she was building up speed such as started to even worry one of the greatest of the *Khul-Algrenàthu*.

At velocities like *this*, there were no second chances.

She hurtled past the first planet, paying that tiny ball of rock scarcely a second glance, praying that her speed, plus the trajectory that she had memorized from Jacobson's computer and his metal plate, would be enough to keep her from falling into the fatal well of the star's immense gravity-forces.

Nearer and nearer she flew, the chords of the psycho-music sounding in her mind, until the Sun – *that* was what the humans called, it, was it not – bathed the Storied Watcher with a terrible brilliance, such as would have instantly returned any Earth man or woman, or any Earth-ship, for that matter, to its constituent atoms in a millionth of a second.

But her 'bubble' – praise her ancestors, praise the Holy Light – was *holding*.

The brutal, incinerating radiation from the star infused the alien-girl's body and mind; the pain of its infernal heat lit up every nerve, but it was more than offset by the luxury of raging, insensate, scarcely intelligible *Amaiish*-power, such as none of her race had ever experienced.

All her intellect and force of will was focused to avoid giving in to this siren call, to avoid the urge to fly into the heart of the star, for one, final, orgasmic ecstasy of godly potency.

The energies that the one called 'Karéin-Mayréij' was absorbing, with each passing second, were greater than she had ever felt, or used. She tried to hold them at bay, to take only a small fraction of what she could easily have at her disposal.

A candle burns bright, she remembered,
But it does not burn long.

Her heart racing with fear and excitement, the alien-girl shot around the side of the star opposite to Earth, using all of her skills to at once resist the Sun's gigantic attraction-forces, balancing these expertly against the crushing G-forces of her trajectory.

Once or twice, her grip slipped and, frantically, she instantly compensated as she felt the trajectory changing; but, sooner than she had expected, and to her immense self-satisfaction, she began to feel and master the art of flying in this dangerous place.

The Storied Watcher rounded the far side of the star and the inner planets again came into view. As she flew low over the first, rocky planet, she released what she had just absorbed.

A brilliant flash briefly illuminated the pockmarked face of this barren, lifeless world.

The young-looking creature decelerated madly, knowing that doing so would not disturb anything in this never-traveled place, and went down to survey the results.

Her heart fell. She had burned the top from a mountain peak.

Even on this small, forgettable planet – itself no more than ten or fifteen times the size of the 'Lucifer' object – yet *again*, after countless attempts, she had failed to do much more than inflict a pin-prick.

The humans would awe and worship a being such as I, who can do this manner of thing, akin to incinerating a whole city, ruefully mused Karéin-Mayréij.

But that is because they do not know how insignificant I really am, compared to the forces of nature... compared to a comet.

As the Storied Watcher floated silently above the planet that she called *Vai'k'tai*, she pondered what had happened.

I could not hold it all, she reflected. *My spirit, my bubble, kept it out, so it would not burn me out from within.*

Yes, that *must have been why.*

I am too small... too... weak.

The alien-girl considered her options, as the *Amaiish*-power fueled her very ability to survive, despite the pleading in her lungs and heart for oxygen.

She could just give up, go back to the humans' doomed world and help them save whomever they were able to. No-one would fault her for *that*, especially if she were honest about what had just transpired – not that they would have any way of knowing if she was telling the truth, or just what was convenient.

But the voice came again, counseling,

Or, Storied Watcher... you can try again.

And thus she flew into the void, heading for the star, building up speed.

Planning For The Worst

"On the face of it," announced Cohen to the group assembled in front of him in the station's meeting-room, "Nothing's changed. That's what we're going to say to Houston. Now... the *rest* of what we're going to discuss, is off the record. Is that understood?"

All there, including Jacobson and Tanaka, nodded reluctant agreement.

"However," explained the station-commander, "Something really *has* changed, now... specifically, with the apparent failure of the *Salvador Two* project, what once was only a likely possibility – that is, the impact of the comet with Earth – we now have to consider as a near certainty. A 'done deal', as the Americans say. I know that none of us wants to think about it... but, the reality of the situation with which we are now confronted, is that *we*, plus whomever else has managed to make it into trans-lunar space, will probably represent the entire surviving membership of the human race."

Tearfully, but doing a masterful job of hiding it, Tanaka mumbled, "Yeah, that's right."

"Agreed, Commander," morosely commented Jacobson. "But how does that change *our* plans, here on ISS2?"

"In the short term, Captain," Cohen replied, "It doesn't. But in the longer term – and this is really why I've called you all here today – we have to start considering our... *options*."

"I am not sure what you mean, sir," voiced Chen. "We have received extensive contingency-plans from Houston to cover an eventuality such as this... have we not?"

Think for yourself, *for once,* thought Jacobson.

I thought NASA *was bad for beating the initiative out of people, but compared to the* Chinese...

"Yes, I'm fully aware of that, Li," Cohen answered. "What I mean is... by their own admission, NASA's plans regarding the post-impact phases of rescue and survival activities are highly speculative, if only for the obvious reason that nothing like what we may be about to witness, has ever occurred before. I think everyone in this room is aware that once the comet hits, there won't *be* a NASA, anymore."

"Won't be an *Earth*," Tanaka interjected.

"Probably not," Cohen confirmed, not losing control. "The point is that for all intents and purposes, we'll be on our own. We'll have to survive, by ourselves. We can use NASA's existing orders and plans as guidelines, there's nothing wrong with *that*, but..."

"Excuse me, sir," inquired Parmar, with a worried frown, "But was not the idea that we would be a central part of the *Arks* plan? That we would rescue all those escape ships...?"

"Yes," Cohen responded, "And until further notice, that's the way it will be. *But* – just for purposes of our own planning, within this room – and I want whatever is said, to stay in this room – we must discuss whether it would be entirely wise to implement the *Arks* plan exactly as it has been presented to us."

"Go ahead, Commander," said an interested Jacobson. "You have my word that I will not pass on anything that you say, to anyone outside this room."

"Nor will I, sir," added Chen. "I am aware that sometimes a senior-officer needs to have the confidence of his staff, for private matters."

"Very good. What I'm getting at, to put the matter bluntly, ladies and gentlemen," continued the station-commander, "Is that the *Arks* program sets a hierarchy – basically, each person within the program gets a numeric rating as to his or her 'desirability', 'viability', 'importance', call it whatever you want – and when it comes down to whether you get a berth, or don't, the higher number wins. This means, in effect, that 'survival of the fittest', under the parameters of this program, comes down to a number."

"That has *always* been known, sir," mentioned Parmar. "Why should anything be different now?"

"Because, Shivani," Cohen stated, "About two days before we had the liftoff, such as it was, of the *Salvador Two*, I finally received an answer from Sylvia Abruzzio on a question that I had submitted to her some time ago; initially, she didn't want to share the information with me – it was 'confidential', or so I was told, but I worked on her and eventually she relented. Apparently she felt that as station-commander, I had the right to know. What I asked for, was the *Arks* program rating scores of everyone on-board ISS2, myself included, as well as the equivalent scores for all of the escape ships, and of the inhabitants of them. When I ran these through the computer up here, the results... *concerned* me."

"How so?" asked Jacobson.

"The long and short of it," explained Cohen, drawing a deep breath, "Is that assuming that only, say, twenty per cent of the *Arks* rescue ships survive to *rendez-vous* with ISS2 in Earth orbit – this *itself* assumes, of course, that we have enough fuel to make it there, in the first place – on average, the *Arks* program score of those on-board the rescue ships, exceeds that of the crew of ISS2 by a rather dramatic amount, over three hundred points out of one thousand, as a matter of fact. The more *Arks* ships that survive, the worse the difference becomes."

"Oh, wow... *now* I get it," exclaimed Jacobson. "If they outrank all of us, or even *most* of us..."

"Precisely," confirmed the space-station-commander. "What we would be faced with, is having to tell at least two-thirds to three-quarters of the current crew of ISS2, to voluntarily surrender their places on this station, to incoming *Arks* program members."

"And then to go... *where*, Commander?" asked Tanaka.

"Out the door," Cohen replied, quietly. "That has always been the plan."

Parmar nodded unwillingly.

"They would still have the ships that the incoming *Arks* people used to get here, in the first place... wouldn't they?" asked Tanaka in a 'clutching-at-straws' tone.

"Theoretically, yes, Professor," interjected Humber, who had been listening to the exchange, in silence, up to this point. "Not that it would do those wankers much good, I'm afraid."

"*Do* fill us in," muttered Tanaka.

"Well, Professor," elaborated the technician, "Just out of morbid curiosity, if you want to call it that, I've been keeping track of each and every one of those ships – you know, their design, what they're made of, booster configurations, *et cetera*. From what I see, half of 'em will be very lucky just to make it out of the atmosphere – and of those that *do*, I doubt that more than one out of twenty would stand more than a snowball's chance of surviving re-entry, later on... and that's assuming that they have a competent pilot, someone trained in atmospheric braking. Basically, there'd be a better chance of me football goalie scoring on the other one, from a kick in my end."

"I don't suppose there's anywhere else for them to go, other than Earth, or what's left of it," observed Tanaka.

"Moonbase is already over capacity, and ISS1 is in the same boat that we're in," countered Humber. "Except, they're an older ship and they have even *less* capacity. Other than for those two, if you know of somewhere to go, other than Earth, I'm sure we'd all pay your bar-bill for now until forever, luv."

"You don't even know if I'm a drinking girl," deadpanned Tanaka.

"The upshot of all of this is," said Cohen, "The surviving *Arks* ships aren't a realistic option – simply delaying the inevitable – and besides, the *Arks* plan mandates that we keep the ships either docked or otherwise fastened to *us*, in case we need to cannibalize them for spare parts. So we'd be faced with telling a very large portion of the crew to simply commit *suicide*... and that's just the *start* of it. Even assuming that the crew – possibly including several of us in this room, here – would be willing just to meekly step out the airlock, whomever ended up in ISS2, would then have to run it..."

"Right you are," forcefully echoed Humber. "I'm sure this isn't news to *you*, sir... but there ain't a snowball's chance in *hell* of that working out – you'd have this station – a very *complicated* piece of technology, yours truly can attest to *that* personally – all of a sudden in the hands of a grab-bag of people from Earth, ninety-nine per cent of which would have no experience whatsoever in operating a deep space vessel, or maybe in operating anything more complex than an automobile."

"So what would happen?" inquired Parmar.

"My guess is," said Humber, "That ISS2, and them, won't last more than a *week*, under those conditions. All it would take is some wanker to throw the wrong switch and vent out the master air-circulation conduits..."

"Not to play Devil's Advocate here, Commander," asked Jacobson, "But didn't I see something in the *Arks* program notes about 'incoming selectees to be cross-trained by outgoing participants', or words to that effect?"

"Again, in *theory*, yes," replied Cohen. "But consider – what kind of training are they likely to *get*, by someone who is being told to commit suicide, in favor of the 'trainee', the minute that the instruction process is completed?"

"Yeah, if it were *me*, I'd find the venting switch, and then tell 'em it was for air-conditioning," joked Humber.

"You should meet Devon White... I'm sure you two would have a lot in common," commented a smiling Tanaka. "But Mr. Humber has a very valid point, as do you, Commander. I have some professional training in both personal and mass psychology... and I can tell you that the chances of riots, chaos, or just total disorganization, under circumstances such as this, are *very* high. I have no idea how Sylvia Abruzzio and the rest of the *Arks* planners could have failed to have foreseen it. I suppose they had a lot else on their minds."

"That is true, Cherie," mentioned Parmar, "But it works the other way, too. Imagine being one of these *Arks* program people, surviving the long odds just to get here, expecting to be let on-board and then being told that the rules have changed and you are no longer welcome. They would feel betrayed in a *most* profound way. And they would have little to lose, by acting irrationally or destructively."

"Shivani has a point, unfortunately," added Humber. "If we let 'em anywhere near ISS2, so we can get our mitts on those lovely spare parts and air reserves they have in their ships, we're also letting them get close enough to, say, ram us, when they get the bad news. An equally unpleasant outcome, or worse, mates. We have no defenses of any kind on this tub."

"Commander," inquired Chen, "With all of what we have just discussed in mind, what do you propose to *do*, sir? What is your plan?"

"I'm not sure that I *have* a complete plan, right now," answered the station-commander, "And I'm still open to ideas – as long as they preserve as many human lives as possible, not least our own, and as long as they do not involve a significant risk to the survival and viability of this station. The latter point, I think, is the most important one. Any catastrophic failure of ISS2 would probably eliminate half of the human race's chances for long-term survival, at – how do you Americans say this – 'one fell swoop'. As Commander, I *cannot* responsibly allow that to happen. Captain, do you agree?"

"One hundred per cent," affirmed Jacobson. "And if it means anything, Ariel, when I first got on-board here, I kind of envied your authority, just coming off a command myself. But you have a hell of a lot riding on the decisions that you make, now. Frankly, I wouldn't want to be in your shoes."

Cohen nodded, appreciatively. "You may yet get the chance to, Sam... if my number comes up low enough. And how about everyone else?"

"Yes," issued from all the others at the table.

"Well, that's it for now," Cohen concluded. "But start thinking fast, everyone, because, as Alan would say, 'we're down by at least a goal, and there's not much time left in the match'".

Scientist In The Void

Karéin-Mayréij hurtled past the Earth, observing its alarming proximity to the comet, resplendent with a long, shimmering tail that would have been beautiful under any other circumstances.

It could be no more than a short time, now, before this doom would arrive at the humans' home.

It was a counsel of despair; for, no matter how many times she had tried, like a feeble campfire in the depths of a frigid Arctic night, her *Amaiish* had burned brightly... but insufficiently.

No more may I obey the bounds of safety, she resolved.

Not even in the practicing of my death-quest.

Reaching the near end of her parabola about a third of the way between the Moon and *Mailànkh*, the alien-girl now accelerated yet more, ever pushing the envelope of her speed.

Avoiding G-forces such as no human – nor, she realized, none of her own, greater race, had ever contended with, she sped inwards, again towards the star.

I am in uncharted waters, she knew.

No wisdom to recall, to guide me.

Only instinct, the Holy Light, and... the faith of men like Devon.

Again approaching the Sun's infernal brilliance, she shot around it, the path now familiar, as much as can be so in the trackless wastes of space.

The Storied Watcher felt her bubble burning, roiling under the relentless bombardment of the star's radiation, testing both her bubble and herself in every frequency of what the humans called 'electromagnetism', constantly seeking an opening, even the slightest chance to leak through and thus end all her days.

But it found none, even as she dared to force herself to a closer path, with each second feeling more confident, more powerful.

More like a *goddess*.

The psycho-music roared a tune of defiance, as Karéin-Mayréij approached the 'Mercury' planet, swooping lower over it than she had on the last pass. She reached deep down, trying to pull all from the well of *Amaiish*-power that she could feel tantalizingly close, just outside her reach, and released a paroxysm of light, heat and fire.

Flying too fast to see what had transpired, she quickly circled this small ball of rock and slowed down, over where she had let loose a fraction of the Beast, within.

Now, there was a large, black, scar, on the 'Mercury'-thing, accompanied by a deep crater.

The alien-girl descended almost to the surface of this desolate world, her eyes observing the results of her attack in both visible light and in the other wavelengths, calculating what had happened with cold, analytical precision.

Even in the soundless, airless void of space, she smelled the changes in the chemical and molecular composition of the rocks that she had just shattered, incinerated and irradiated.

The humans had thought of her as an 'angel', working only from instinctive, supernatural power; a reasonable enough supposition, considering their limited understanding of her past, but, in fact, the Storied Watcher was far more of a scientist than any of them, with a greater understanding of the mechanics and physics of the universe than any of the humans could ever hope to achieve.

That one's atoms split, her mind counseled, as Karéin-Mayréij strained to remember the formulas, the rules of matter and energy that she had committed to memory, so many long lives ago.

The one over there, I burned; but there were two that just melted... that means...

There is hope, came a scarcely-dared-for revelation.

If I can just reach down deeper, get more heat...

Never before have I, but never have I done this, below me, either...

Wheeling in place, she looked upwards, towards first the hot, cloudy planet, then the humans' home-world.

She focused her view, and her mind, on the accursed 'Lucifer'-thing, as it bore down on Earth, ready to unfairly end the story of her new brothers and sisters.

Karéin-Mayréij heard the music – *her* music – again, growling a song of nobility, might and determination.

She stared at the comet, while her body roiled with the silver-white tendrils of the *Fire*, while the anger in her eyes glowed an infernal, incandescent red.

I am coming for you, she sent to it.

Sensei... Where Are You?

As they sat down for their regulation 'forty minutes of reserved time' in the food-eating-area, Jacobson requested of Tanaka, "So, any news, Cherie? I've missed the broadcasts over the last little while... been catching up on my reading..."

"First of the *Arks* ships have lifted off," Tanaka offered, matter-of-factually. "They're starting with the largest and most viable ones, first. I'm happy to report that they all appear to have made it, to orbit, that is. Whether there's an ultimate destination for them... well, you know about *that*, already."

"Hmm," grunted the former Mars mission commander.

"Oh," added the science officer, "The *Salvador Two's* still stuck in orbit, too. They're trying to boost it so that it's at least heading in the direction of the comet... but at *this* range, the chances are one in a thousand of them cracking it up and having the pieces miss Earth. Incidentally, they're starting to worry about what might happen to the *Arks* ships, if *Salvador Two* detonates too close to Earth. They're carrying a *lot* of megatons up there."

"Swell... now I *remember* why I'm not following the news," muttered Jacobson.

"Yo, well... who do I see here?" they heard White's familiar, cheerful voice say.

"Mind if I join y'all, Captain, Professor?" he requested. "I was gonna meet Brent for lunch, here – he'll probably be by, any minute now."

"By all means, Devon," invited Jacobson. "I don't know about the Professor, here, but I haven't seen much of either yourself, or of the rest of our crew, lately... funny, I *know* it's a big ship, but I thought that I'd run into one or two of you, eventually. Oh well."

"So what's up with you, Devon?" asked Tanaka. "I've been stuck with Shivani Parmar – a nice lady, and very competent, but a bit on the boring side, too much of a rule-follower for my liking. How are things at your end?"

"I've been mostly hangin' out with Mike Theodikas, y'all know, Cohen's comms officer," White replied, munching on what appeared to be *ersatz* bread of some sort, "He's a decent guy... leastaways he's let me play around with his gear, get to know its ins and outs. We've been monkeyin' with some of the long-range scanners to get a better look at the, uh, goings-on, around Earth. But y'all *know* it's just busy-work; Mike don't really *need* me around to get his job done, so to avoid botherin' him too much I spend a lot of time down in the gym, tryin' to stay fit. I run into Brent quite a bit down there – oh, *there* he is, now. Yo, Brent! Over here, man!"

Boyd shuffled over in the pseudo-gravity until he had found a seat opposite Jacobson, next to White.

"Hello, Captain," he politely greeted. "Just like old times here, I guess. Oh... except for Sergei."

"Where is he? Does anyone know?" asked Jacobson.

"Last I saw him, he was working with that Chinese guy – Chen, I believe his name is – in the propulsion engineering-bay," explained Jacobson's former pilot. "I worked with the two of them for awhile, but they had it pretty much under control, so I went off to other things. Haven't seen Sergei in a couple of days, though."

"I've hardly seen him since we got off *Infinity*," reflected Jacobson. "I hope that the little argument we had about the report – you know, the one to Russia – hasn't upset him too much. He certainly didn't show it, for the last day or so when we were approaching the station. If he *is* upset, I'd regret that... I really *would*."

"I can understand you being concerned, Sam," mentioned Tanaka, "But I *did* run into Sergei myself a few days ago, and, if it was on his mind, he didn't mention it to *me*. All he said was that he wanted a bit of time to work on his own, to get to know how the station was put together. Nothing unusual in that... it's busy-work, like Devon said."

"Yeah... I hope you're right, Professor," Jacobson opined, "Because, even though I'm now just another member of the crew of ISS2, and so are all of us ex-*Infinity* folk, we're... *different*, you know. You, me, Brent, Devon and Sergei, we'll always be our own team, regardless of where we go, or what happens to us. I'd just hate for one member of the team not to want to belong, any more."

"You know, Captain," commented White, "I agree with y'all about the teamwork thing, but you off on your count. Our team is *six* people – okay, five people and one somethin' else. Not five."

"Yeah," agreed Boyd, pensively. "Not five. We're missing the most *important* one... aren't we?"

"I *see*," quietly observed Jacobson, yet above the din of the eating-room, "That you've all been thinking about *her*, too."

"Every day, man, ev'ry *day*," replied White. "Near to every minute, 'matter of fact."

"Me too," Boyd noted. "Captain... Karéin touched us all, not just in the way that we all share; she was something *different*, for each of us. I guess Devon's not the only one who can't get her out of his mind – her dreams invade mine, from time to time, however much I try to just go back to the way it was, before. Sometimes I regret ever having *met* her, but mostly, I regret ever having let her go out that door, for the last time."

He was silent for a second or two, then added, "Well, at least I kept that locket of hers safe... sort of. Made Cohen promise to keep it under lock and key and not do any experiments on it, until we get back down to Earth –"

"Which is probably nine-tenths of the battle," cynically remarked Tanaka, "Considering that Earth won't be *there*, a short time from now."

The scientist herself paused, then continued, "I wonder where she *is*... I just can't *believe* that she has gone away and left us – left Earth – to our fate."

"She said that she was going to try to destroy the comet," reminded Boyd. "And that she would never be able to *do* it. I hate myself for even *thinking* this, but what if she has already tried... and failed... remember what she feared would happen..."

"That ain't true, Brent – it *can't* be," retorted White. "She's still out there, somewhere. With a good reason. She'll be back. I *know* she will, man."

"Well, Devon," offered Jacobson, "If that's correct – and, like everybody here, I sure *hope* it is – she had better get back here soon... *real* soon. We're almost out of time and tricks, team."

"Listen, guys, not to change the subject," Tanaka interjected, "But as long as we're all, okay, *almost* all here, I wanted to ask you, have any of you been using... *it*? Practicing? You *know* what I mean."

"I... uhh... thought the Captain asked us not to, Professor," answered White, uneasily.

"That's correct," cautioned Jacobson. "Besides, this is a public place. I don't think it's a good idea to discuss –"

"Point taken, Sam... but relax," replied Tanaka. "Nobody's paying attention to us here, anyway. Why *would* they? Everybody else has much more important things on their minds. Such as their own survival."

Jacobson straightened out his hair with his hand and looked down at the table for a second, unwillingly acknowledging that he no longer had the authority to issue orders; at least, not to do so and have them instantly obeyed.

"If you want an honest answer, Professor," admitted Boyd, "I *have* tried, once or twice, but, well... the results have been underwhelming, as they say. It was much easier when *she* was here with us, to help us 'unlock' the power, I think that's how she described it."

"Yeah, no shit, man," ruefully echoed White. "I didn't want to try the fire-extinguisher trick she taught me, 'cause I figured setting fires on this crate might attract *attention*. So I've been tryin' to bend paper-clips, make things rattle on the table, even just move a piece of paper back and forth. Nada, zippo, zilch... that's what I've been able to accomplish. Actually, that's not completely true. I *have* cooked up some mighty fine headaches. If that counts in the super-hero scheme of things, y'all know."

"For the record, my own abilities have neither improved, nor decreased, since I left *Infinity*," noted Tanaka. "I can still move things, and move myself, slowly and painfully. But nothing more."

"I think we should all keep in mind, Professor," commented Boyd, "That she specifically pointed out that fully developing these abilities might require *years* of training and practice. I don't see why that should be a surprise: after all, you can't learn karate, or expert piano-playing, or professional figure-skating, or any one of a hundred *normal* human skills, in any other way... at least, that's true for ninety-nine per cent of us. We just have to keep at it, as long as it takes."

"Need I remind you," Jacobson observed, "That 'long-term' instruction or training, may be a rather problematic idea, these days."

"Yeah, you got me *there*, Captain," allowed Boyd. "But what about *you*, sir? Any luck on your end?"

"You're asking him to admit that he's been breaking his own rules," wryly observed Tanaka. "If I know Sam Jacobson..."

"My way out of *that* one will be to say that I didn't want any of us using this ability *publicly*, Cherie," Jacobson replied, with a slightly cynical smile. "And what I'm willing to say, in that context, is, yes, I *have* been trying, but to little effect. I think I'm a bit ahead of Devon, in that I have been able to make a pen on my desk, roll over, once or twice... I gave up when it started feeling like one of my old migraines. The point is that all of these powers are really just a novelty thing, with very little practical use, that I can see. There's not much purpose in displaying them to an already tense ISS2 crew – we'd have a lot to lose and not a lot to gain."

"Unless we're able to develop them quite a bit further," pointed out Boyd. "Doesn't seem likely, does it?"

"Sam," asked Tanaka, "What if we were to practice together?"

"Yeah," agreed White. "The old mutual-encouragement thing... works for aerobics, it might work for us. Whaddya *say*, Captain?"

"I can't... I mean... I don't *know*," Jacobson hesitated. "I suppose that it *might* work. But what are you out to accomplish, Cherie? Even if we were to double, triple, quadruple, what we're capable of now, it would still be *far* less than what a normal human can do with arms, legs and hands. I just don't see the *purpose* here, Professor."

"Neither do I," argued Boyd, "But that's not necessarily a reason not to do it. We can't expect to know the outcome before we get to it... can we? And if nothing else, it'll help pass the time."

"You know, Brent," Jacobson warned, "Something like this might attract attention, suspicion. That's something we don't need, under the current circumstances. Remember, we're *guests* here."

"I don't see how they can reasonably object to the commander of the *Eagle and Infinity* Mars mission, holding a daily briefing meeting, for his crew," observed Tanaka. "Once we close the door, they have no business knowing what goes on in there. Do they?"

"In where?" inquired White. "How about the gym? It's empty a lot of the time and it's got plenty of space. I'd offer my quarters, but I'm sharin' with two other ISS2 folk, and they might wander in at any time."

Jacobson sat and thought to himself for a second, then decided, "No, Devon, we'll do it in *my* quarters, I'd suggest tomorrow morning at eight o'clock ISS2 time so we don't attract too much attention going to and fro. Lots of room, in there, more than I can use, in fact. I still outrank everybody here, you know," he said with a wry smile.

"Heh," quipped Boyd, "Still got the title and the perks, but nothing much to do, I guess, sir?"

"You got *that* right, Brent," muttered Jacobson.

"I'll try to get in touch with Sergei," proposed Tanaka. "I'll let him know, but I can't predict how he'll react, obviously. We owe it to him to offer him the chance, however."

"Yeah, that's true," agreed White. "If I see him first, I'll fill him in myself. One thing we forgot though, which I'll have to tell that Rooshian guy, is... how long are we gonna do it for? Fifteen minutes? An hour? All day? Anybody got an idea about that?"

"As long as it *takes,* I suppose," said Jacobson, with a shrug.

"Aye," added Tanaka, "But, I just wish I had *her,* to be our *Sensei.*"

Mutely, all nodded agreement, as they downed their meals, counting the bites and the days left.

Trouble Up Here, Too

Jacobson, against his better instincts, had turned on the video-feed from NeoNet, just before writing his report – going to no-one, any more, he realized, but he continued to commit the day's events to cyber-memory none the less – and before preparing to go to bed.

As the comet – now impossible to miss by the naked eye, even in daylight – had drawn ever closer, the situation on Earth, although better than Jacobson had anticipated, was getting increasingly out of control.

Apart from the emergence of the inevitable millenarian cults on every continent, nihilistic rioting had started to break out in many of the world's larger cities – including, ominously, all over Los Angeles, where White had kept his residence, against the advice of some of his well-heeled friends – as the lower strata of society, sensing that there could be no long-term retribution, began to help themselves to the finer things in life, at gunpoint.

Martial law had been declared in parts of urban America and in much of the Third World, but it was proving to be of limited effectiveness : what deterrence a soldier with a gun, compared to certain annihilation in a fortnight?

Overall, however, humanity was facing the prospect of its imminent destruction with remarkable *sang-froid*; the churches were filled to overflowing, of course, but the stock markets and the professional sports leagues were still operating and people were still, by and large, going about their daily routines.

Perhaps they just could not reconcile what was about to befall them, with the objective realities of life, work and family.

Yes, individual *people* could die; but a race, a *species*? It *couldn't* happen.

If Jacobson had been on Earth, holding down a desk-job somewhere, cheering at his son's Little League tournament, encouraging his younger daughter just before her piano-recital, it would seem completely unreal to him, too.

Only the fact of him being already in space, looking out at *it,* as *it* greedily hurtled towards Earth, allowed him to sort of understand the events that were unfolding.

"This is Commander Cohen, with a Priority Two announcement for everyone on-board," sounded the loudspeaker, shaking the former Mars mission commander out of his contemplation. "We have completed lock-down in preparation for Earth transit-burn. All essential personnel are already accounted for at their stations, but for the rest of you... please brace yourselves, as you may experience some temporary discomfort as ISS2 begins its flight back to Earth orbit. Burn will commence in fifty-seven... sorry, fifty-three, seconds from now. Cohen out."

Jacobson quickly stowed the few loose objects that he had allowed to collect in various places. He jumped back into bed with a few seconds to spare.

"Pre-burn countdown," announced the loudspeaker. "Five... four... three... two... one..."

A small shudder raced through his room, his bed and through Jacobson himself. Then, just as he began to relax, it was followed by a sharp **BANG!**, as if the bed's underside had been hit by a strong arm wielding a baseball-bat.

"Priority One emergency procedure!" exclaimed an unfamiliar voice through the overhead, as his cabin's normal florescent white lighting instantly shut off, being replaced by two or three dim, red light-emitting diodes.

"repair-crews to Blue sections Ten, Eleven and Twelve!" half-shouted the announcer. "Breach containment protocol in effect – non-essential personnel confined to quarters until further notice, please refrain from using ship systems! I repeat, *emergency* procedure – Priority One – repair-crews, please acknowledge!"

God damn, thought Jacobson, sitting helplessly in his bed.

If I was Commander again... at least I'd know *what the hell's going on.*

He waited, nervous and frustrated, in his dimly-illuminated personal quarters, for an interminable time, which he later learned amounted to about eighteen minutes.

Then the lights came back on, accompanied by another bulletin.

"This is Cohen, speaking to everyone on ISS2 with a status report," the station-commander stated in a flat, professional voice. "As you know, a few minutes, according to plan, we initiated our Earth transit-burn. Unfortunately, although the burn *itself* was successful, we had a serious malfunction in the booster immediately afterwards – we're still not completely sure what happened, but there has been an explosion in the booster's engine chamber. It seems to be damaged beyond local repair, and shrapnel from the explosion caused severe damage and a local hull breach in section Blue Eleven."

Cohen paused, then, slowly, added, "With deep regret, I have to report that we have lost three crew-members – William DeLonghi from Engineering, Alexi Romanov, also from Engineering, and Katrina Van Gelsbergen, from Environmental Services – all of whom were caught in Blue Eleven, at the time of the accident. Our thoughts and prayers go out to their friends and family. We are attempting to locate and inform next of kin on Earth as I speak."

Thank God, Jacobson thought,

I didn't hear the name, 'Sergei Chkalov', just now.

Cohen continued, "Now, I should take this opportunity to explain where this unfortunate sequence of events leaves us, to the extent that we know the facts, right now. The booster is damaged beyond our ability to repair it; we have sustained *severe* damage to Blue Eleven, *so* severe, in fact, that it has lost all atmospheric pressure – it has been isolated from surrounding sections, but it will require extensive repairs, probably including multiple EVA sessions, to make it inhabitable again. We are currently evaluating whether doing this will be cost-effective in terms of risk, materiel and work-effort."

He elaborated, "Sections Blue Ten and Twelve have sustained some damage, apparently only to the outer hull, and while they're still pressurized, travel to any of these areas is hereby prohibited until we can fully assess their status and integrity. The consequences could have been far worse, especially if the explosion had hit the main environmental plant, which is only a short distance away from the sections that were in fact affected."

The station-commander stated, "I want to reassure everyone that ISS2 is still very much intact and capable of supporting us for the immediate future. We're on a trajectory towards Earth and will arrive there after the 'Lucifer' object has either impacted, or has been destroyed. Alan Humber and Li-Ho Chen have formed a working-group to reconfigure our maneuvering-thrusters so we can use them to decelerate as we reach our intended orbit. In the meantime, I'd ask you all to go about your normal duties, when we lift quarters curfew, which will be seven o'clock tomorrow morning, local time. We are planning a memorial-service for our fallen comrades; the time and location of this will be announced shortly."

Cohen took a deep breath and concluded by saying, "You know, fellow crew-members... this was a close one, and while we mourn the tragic loss of our friends, we have to understand that these are desperate times; we all may have to learn to accept outcomes that we otherwise would not, so that *some* of us may survive. I hope and pray that such things will not come to pass – but they may. If and when they do, we should be ready. Cohen, over and out."

Well done, mused Jacobson.

I don't know where you earned your stripes, Ariel... but you're a damn good leader.

Tempted to use his rank to go out and wander despite the orders, he instead turned out the lights and went to bed, saying a silent prayer for the dead.

Four Heads Better Than One

Tanaka and Boyd were the first to arrive, within a few seconds of each other. "Where's Devon?" asked Jacobson.

"Don't know," answered Boyd. "His berth isn't too far from mine, and I went by to roust him out, but he must have already gone – he wasn't there."

"Well, I suppose we can wait a few more minutes," said the former Mars mission commander. "As long as we have to, did anyone hear any more about the problem we had with the Earth transit-burn, yesterday? I presume you all heard Cohen's broadcast?"

"Aye," confirmed Tanaka. "*Awfully* sad story, need it be said... I had trouble sleeping, but the Commander had said to stay in our quarters, so I called up Shivani on the intercom... I just got her voice-mail at first, but after about an hour and a half she had returned from the scene, or at least as close to it as they'd let her get. She said that we lost all the air in Blue Eleven, as well as a portion – she didn't know exactly how much – of what was in Ten and Twelve until they sealed the inter-section pressure-hatches. In the near term, of course, it's not the end of the world, but in the *long* term... considering that we were short already... you know, I met Katrina Van Gelsbergen a couple of times – she was Dutch, from ESA. A very nice lady..."

They all nodded, silently and sympathetically.

"Yeah, that pretty much jives with what I heard from my new acquaintances in Propulsion and Engineering," commented Boyd. "Talk has it that the explosion tore a *big* hole – large enough for a man to comfortably pass through, apparently – and it riddled the Blue Eleven main working area with dozens of smaller shrapnel holes, like a cluster-bomb going off outside... the booster itself, so they say, had most of its aft section blown off– it hardly has a combustion-chamber anymore. From what I hear, Blue Eleven, as well as the booster, are both so badly damaged that they may be *completely* beyond repair, at least with the resources that we have at our disposal up here."

"Well, *that's* just great," sighed Tanaka. "Those poor people..."

"If it's of any use to know this," mentioned Boyd, "They think that the three people we lost were killed almost instantly – that is, they didn't have time to suffer. But Alan Humber's taking it *very* hard; he was their boss, after all, and he had personally assigned the two casualties from Engineering to duty in that section, that day. Hell of a thing... there's no doubt about that."

"It's the worst thing that can happen to a commander, for sure," observed Jacobson. "Do they have any theories about what caused the explosion?"

"Well," uneasily explained Boyd, "The thing that's on everyone's minds, but nobody wants to say out loud, is whether the jury-rigged propellant mixture that Chen and his group had added to what was left of the booster's original fuel, might have been unstable, whether – to put it bluntly – if they hadn't used the stuff, the three people in Blue Eleven might still be alive. I heard a rumor that Humber had let out a curse saying *exactly* that, when he found out about the loss of his staff, and that Chen was very angry at being blamed in that way... but nobody's saying anything officially."

"I believe you worked with Chen on that project, didn't you?" asked Tanaka. "Did it look like it was properly managed?"

"If you want *my* opinion, Professor," defensively replied Boyd, "While I completely understand how Mr. Humber feels, I don't think it's fair to blame Chen for this; he was doing the best he could under very difficult circumstances... after all, for God's sake, we wouldn't have had enough propellant to properly fire the booster at *all*, without what he was able to scrounge up. Just getting the damn thing to sputter and cough isn't enough – if we didn't get a substantial percentage of its rated maximum thrust, then we'd be going back so slowly that we'd run out of air before we get anywhere *near* Earth. Chen took some chances – as would I, if the decision was mine to take."

"Yeah," mentioned Jacobson, "But I think it would be wise for all of us to stay out of this dispute, if that's what it turns out to be. We've got *enough* problems to deal with, already. The *last* thing we need is to get in the middle of – excuse my French, please – a pissing-contest between two senior-officers of this station."

"Agreed," said both the other two.

The face of White appeared at almost the same second.

"Knock, knock, sir," he greeted, in his usual, friendly manner. "Sorry I'm a bit late... I was tryin' to find Sergei, but no dice, he don't seem to be anywhere on this boat. Hope I didn't hold y'all up too much."

"No harm done," amicably answered Jacobson. "It'd have been nice to have had Major Chkalov with us for the first session, but I'm sure he'll be able to catch up later. That is, if there turns out to be anything to catch up *to*."

As Tanaka hit a door-side panel button and closed the hatch to Jacobson's quarters, the Captain announced, "Well, I guess we should get going – I don't think we should spend more than an hour at a time doing this. More and we might attract a little too much attention."

"Sounds reasonable," agreed Boyd, as they all found seats around Jacobson's uncomfortably narrow writing-table. "Okay, Professor. Let's get going. You first."

"I... *what*?" responded Tanaka.

"You start us off. With the lesson, I mean," said the former Mars expedition pilot.

"And how should I do *that*?" evaded Tanaka.

"I thought that *she* taught you... how to teach us," said Boyd, the enthusiasm in his voice waning.

"*She*, didn't teach me anything of the *sort*," complained Tanaka. "We barely had time for me to learn how to swim around in Zero-G. Now, if we hadn't sent her packing on such short order..."

"*We*, didn't," corrected Jacobson. "NASA, did."

With a knowing grin, White interjected, "The blind leadin' the blind... ain't that how it goes, Professor?"

"So what do we do *now*?" asked Boyd.

For more than a few awkward seconds, each one of the Mars expedition crew stared at the others, hoping for someone else to take the lead.

"Well," finally offered Tanaka, "Like I *said*... I don't have any special training in this field, but it occurs to me that we need to have a goal – an objective to measure progress by. Something very modest and achievable, something that we already know that at least *one* of us can do... we can build from there."

"How about moving around the fancy Zero-G pen that Commander Cohen gave me as a welcoming present, when we first docked?" suggested Jacobson. "As I said some time ago, I've been experimenting with that one and I've found that I can budge it. Just a bit, but I have to say that I *was* quite pleased with myself, when I did it. If one doesn't count the headache, afterwards."

"So be it," muttered Boyd. "I certainly can't think of anything better. Devon, is it okay with you?"

"Yeah, sure, man, I guess," White replied, uneasily. "Except... y'all *know* that I never was able to do anything like what the Captain just described. So no laughin' at me when it just *sits* there, y'all got that?"

"I'm sure you're not the *only* one who feels that way, that is, unsure of his or her abilities," observed Jacobson. "Frankly, this whole exercise seems a bit too touchy-feely for me – I'd *never* participate in it, except that, well, *she* gave us incontrovertible proof that it's not just a Ouija board session, it's real."

He seemed lost in thought for a second, then he went on, "You know, in a way, *everything* that has happened to us from the time we found out about the Anomaly on Mars, seems unreal to me... it's just so contrary to everything that I have spent a *lifetime* of military and scientific training, learning *can't* happen, like alien beings within our own solar-system, some weird, semi-magical power – sorry, Karéin, if you heard me say that, somehow – that we had absolutely no prior knowledge of, story-book civilizations... I could go on and on. I find me asking myself, 'did it really *happen*?'. But it *did*... didn't it?"

He seemed far away.

"It sure *did*, Sam," said Tanaka, sensing the man's mood. "And it's *in* us, now, it's a *part* of us. For better or worse, we *can't* go back to what we were, before. Not that I'd want to."

"I know what y'all mean, Captain, sir," added White. "I mean, here we are back with a bunch of normal people, back with science, technology and so on, back with what we grew up to know. Believin' in her bein' still out there, somewhere – that's only a bit more plausible than believin' in God, I guess; but I believe in both of 'em, y'all should know that by now. And I believe that both of 'em will do what they *have* to, to save us. I really *do*, man."

Jacobson looked up at White with big, searching eyes, as if wanting to know the truth in what his former crewmember had said.

But shortly thereafter, Boyd returned both of them to the present, saying, "Interesting ideas there guys, I'm sure we've all been thinking stuff like that, but we're eating into our time, here. Shall we get going?"

"Yes," confirmed Jacobson, pensively. "We shall."

"Okay," started Tanaka. "There it is – I've placed it in the middle of the table, so it's the same distance from each of us, more or less. Now, what I *thought* that we could do, is basically a pushing contest... the person who pushes it the furthest away from himself or himself, wins the game."

"If I win, what's the prize, Professor?" asked White.

"A whopping big headache," answered Tanaka, not missing a beat.

"Yeah, but the *good* news is, you get that even if you lose," joked Boyd. "Okay. I'm in. Let's go."

Tanaka and Boyd, seated opposite each other, propped their heads up by their hands, elbows on the table, staring at the pen with determination. Jacobson glared at it too, hands folded in his lap. White kept his hands at his sides, his glance going back and forth between the pen and the others.

After a few seconds, the pen started to move, toward Boyd. He looked up in frustration for a split-second, as Tanaka, a confident smile on her face, just continued to stare. But Boyd again rested his head on the palms of his hands and re-entered the fight.

The pen moved backwards towards the woman, more quickly now. All of a sudden, it flew off to Tanaka's left and Boyd's right, in a perpendicular direction.

Boyd and Tanaka both slumped back in their chairs, rubbing their temples.

"Whew," said the wincing former space-pilot, "I think I won – but man oh *man*, at what a cost... now I *know* what a migraine feels like."

"Welcome to the club," answered Tanaka. "But I don't understand... apart from the fact that you hadn't done that before, Brent – congratulations, by the way – did you send it off to the side?"

"No, he didn't," interrupted Jacobson, smiling in serene self-satisfaction. "*I* did. It's *my* pen, after all. I know what it takes to affect it... to 'get my grasp on it', so to speak. You know, I think I'm starting to understand what our former guest meant, when she told us that English doesn't have words for a lot of these processes. She was right about that."

"Looks like I'm kinda the odd man out," complained White. "I told y'all, this ain't my bag. Don't know why I *tried*, really," he dejectedly added.

"You weren't *concentrating*, you know," countered Boyd. "I bet you don't even have a headache. No pain, no gain..."

"I don't know what I'm supposed to be concentrating *on*, man!" retorted White. "Like tryin' to shoot an arrow at a target I can't see."

"Well, I didn't have any training in this, either," argued Boyd.

"Don't give up so easily, Devon," counseled Tanaka. "But, you know, guys," she said to Boyd and Jacobson, "He has a point – sorry I didn't think of this earlier, Devon. It's fun competing, but maybe we can help each other grow our *Amaiish*-powers more, if we all co-operate. I mean, she told me that I had the telekinetic ability inside me beforehand... all she did was show me where to think, how to visualize it, to 'turn it on'. Perhaps Devon's just having trouble doing exactly that, but if we all try to use the power *together*... maybe he'll catch on."

"Certainly seems like it's worth a try," agreed Jacobson. "But how are we supposed to *do* that?"

"Why don't we try holding hands, like we did when we first got 'initiated' by Karéin, or like we did when she finally left us?" suggested Tanaka.

"Well, that seems kind of touchy-feely, like the Captain said," objected Boyd, "But I'll put up with *anything* not to hear him complaining about it."

"Now, *now*," lectured Jacobson, looking at Boyd and White in succession. "Let's not get into one-upmanship here. This is bound to be a slow and incremental process – we've known that from the start, after all – that's what she *said* would happen. It's not surprising that some of us are better at some things and others, at other things. We all just have to do our best and hope it all works out. Ready?"

"Yeah... I guess," muttered White.

"No problem," voiced Boyd.

Half-willingly, the men extended their hands, with White linked to Tanaka and Jacobson, who was in turn linked to Boyd.

"Now," directed Tanaka, trying to summon her best schoolmarm voice, "The objective of this exercise is to visualize the pen – to imagine that it's moving. If we all think this at the same time, I'm hoping we'll multiply the cumulative effect. At least, that's what I *think* that she meant, when she was teaching me..."

"*Riight*," said Boyd, without the slightest bit of conviction. "Concentrating now."

"Me, too," grunted White. "But y'all *know* I'm just along for the ride."

"Shut up and *work* at it, Devon," ordered Jacobson, in a firm but friendly tone.

The pen started to jiggle a bit; then, without warning, it started spinning, rapidly, in place.

They all opened their eyes, suddenly.

"Man, look at it *go!*" exclaimed White. "But... uhh... Professor, we were supposed to be *movin'* it, weren't we? Like, back and forth, and all?"

"Yeah, that was the plan," replied Tanaka. "I wonder why... oh, and by the way, I opened my eyes because I *saw* it spinning, somehow... but I did that while my eyes were still closed. Totally weird feeling..."

"You know, Professor, I think I know what happened here," explained Jacobson. "We said that we were going to move it, but we didn't agree on a direction. I tried to push it away from myself, because that's the motion I know best. What about the rest of you?"

"Hah, yeah, you got us there, Captain," sheepishly admitted Boyd. "I was trying to push it away from myself, too. What about the other two of you?"

"Tried to push it away," said Tanaka. "*Now* I understand."

"So was I," added White. "For whatever *that's* worth."

Tanaka bent over to White, taking his hand and staring at the man deeply in his eyes.

"Devon," she said, "We were all trying to push it, and yet it stayed where it was. You said you can't use *Amaiish* for telekinesis, right?"

"Yeah," complained the African-American astronaut. "And I can't. Y'all *know* it."

"*Bullshit*, Devon," countered Tanaka. "Don't you remember your basic physics, 'action and reaction', *that* kind of thing? If there are three forces pushing it away from each other, and you *hadn't* been pushing back – would it have stayed there?"

"It'd be embedded in your chest right now," commented Jacobson, smiling. "Good thing you came through for yourself. On second thought..."

He chuckled, warmly.

A look of wonder and joy came over White's face.

"Y'all mean – man, oh *man*! I *was* using it, too!" he exclaimed.

The former communications officer suddenly had a far-off look.

He spoke, to no-one in particular, "Thank you. Thank y'all. Really."

"Welcome back to the team," said a smiling Jacobson. "But let's try one more thing, today – I'm just curious as to how it will work. First of all, you guys sit this one out, just for a second."

He closed his eyes and was obviously concentrating. The pen started shaking for a second, then stopped.

"Alas," he said, "I'm afraid I'm no good at levitating it."

"But what a good way to see how having the rest of us helping you, might change that," offered Tanaka, picking up the idea. "Okay, team. Hands, please."

They all closed their eyes, gingerly holding hands, concentrating on the mental prototype of a levitating gift pen. Their minds saw the object slowly flying upwards; and they heard a faint hum of strange, other-worldly music, echoing in the background of their psyches.

"I think we're pretty much there," commented Tanaka, still concentrating, "But let's try opening our eyes and trying to visualize it going upwards. Open them slowly... now."

The others complied with the request. The pen shot straight up as if launched by some ethereal rocket booster, colliding with the rather low ceiling of the room with a hollow-sounding 'thwang'.

As soon as it passed out of their field of vision, it fell quickly back to the table, making a similar noise.

"*Whoa*," exclaimed Boyd. "That's... that's really *something*," he said, nervously. "I sure felt a rush, too, like pleasure, but not the same... there isn't a *chance* that any one of us could have done that, by ourselves... am I right?"

"I'd bet so, Brent," answered Jacobson. "It seems to have a multiplier effect – 'the whole is more than the sum of its parts', I suppose. You know, I'm beginning to see what she meant when she said that to master some of the uses of this power can take years of practice, of study. Something tells me that it has many more tricks, hidden away, waiting for us to stumble on them..."

"I think we can take that for granted, Sam," earnestly confirmed Tanaka. "When you consider that it's like *nothing* we've ever been familiar with, back on Earth... a whole new ball game, I guess. A whole, *new*, ball game."

In silence, they all stared at each other for a few seconds.

"And we – not leavin' out Sergei – we're the *only* folks in the whole human race who have it. Who can pass it on. *Big* responsibility, man. The *biggest*," pronounced White.

"Yeah," agreed Boyd. "And I think we owe it to him to get him here, by hook or by crook, for next time. I don't think he realizes, or can realize, what he's missing."

"Aye," replied Tanaka. "Furthermore, based on what we saw today, having him with us, may further empower us as a group. It might unlock some doors."

"Enough super-hero lessons for today, team?" asked Jacobson, reclining with satisfaction in his chair.

They all nodded. White joked, "Tomorrow, same Bat-place, same Bat-channel, sir?"

"Don't touch that dial," replied the former Mars mission commander.

They all, including Tanaka for once, saluted, then, one by one, they left the Captain in his cabin, each lost in the realization of what they had experienced, and in what it implied for what they would become.

As Tanaka was about to round the corner out of Jacobson's room, she turned to him one last time and said,

"And, by the way, Sam... I don't have a headache, today."

Jacobson smiled guiltily at the *double-entendre*, as the woman disappeared down the corridor.

Portent Of Disaster

The comet was now the size of the Moon in the daytime sky; but it was brighter, far brighter, and it was growing hatefully more so with each passing minute.

The scientists had said that in no more than hours, now, no-one on the face of the planet, would see it, again in this way.

Or would see *anything*, at all.

The men and women of Earth gathered their children, or just themselves, to their sides, some at home, many more in houses of worship, some in other, private places, each as seemed appropriate to his or her faith and disposition.

Some despaired, some acted out in fits of insanity, but the vast majority just looked on with a mixture of disbelief and resignation.

A very few – the children of one elementary school-class in the minority ghetto of Compton, Los Angeles, for example – looked up to the skies, searching for an angel.

Meanwhile, Earth's scientists and military personnel, bloodied by repeated failure but still determined to strike back one last, defiant time, set the countdown for the final attack.

All over the world, submarines surfaced and short-range missiles, most nuclear-tipped but some not, were set up on their launch-stations; fighter jets, bred to seek out and destroy each other, instead prepared to undertake one last, suicidal zoom climb to the far reaches of their maximum altitudes, trying to impart as much momentum as they could to whatever weapons they could carry, as they shot one last volley at the onrushing target.

Tens of thousands of pencil-thin contrails began to arc up through Earth's atmosphere, towards a common enemy. The projectiles could fly but for a few minutes, before they would exhaust their fuel and fall lifelessly backwards.

But only a few minutes remained, anyway.

Angel's Last Run

Karéin-Mayréij streaked past Earth's Moon, faster than any object had ever traveled in this solar-system, while her mind frantically scanned, observed and calculated.

The comet was now very close – far *too* close – to the humans' beautiful, blue-green home. As the humans measured time, there were only hours left, before it would begin its final, fatal plunge into the blue-world's life-giving atmosphere.

One more run, she reflected.

Only one more will I have, to get it right.

To sing my death-song, so brightly that all will see.

Pushing her speed to still more desperate rates – as fast as she dared, before the inexorably waxing mass-forces would start to exceed her controlling-abilities – the alien-girl streaked past the clouded planet, past the hot, rocky one, heading on a close-following path that would have been suicidal a scant few days before.

There was just too little energy, the last time, she understood.

Too easy – too... safe.

It did not hurt enough.

Holy Light... prepare me, make me strong.

With a heart pounding in fear, rage and excitement, the mighty one named 'Karéin-Mayréij' hurtled inwards, skirting the star's corona.

She rounded its far side, exposing herself to intensities of radiation that none of her noble race – not even the greatest of the elders of the *Khul-Algrenàthu* a thousand generations past – had ever felt, or survived.

Her bubble appeared to hold, but inexplicably, she sensed some of the killing energy leaking through it, illuminating every cell in her body with cruel, burning pain – but, also, with the luxurious, exhilarating knowledge of the *Fire*, its seductive feeling of pleasure at a level that would have driven a thousand lesser beings, instantly mad.

The Storied Watcher looked downward, for a second, at the flesh in her forearm. With morbid curiosity mixed with the objective fascination of a scientist, she realized that it was *glowing*, red-hot, like a cinder in a hearth-fire.

That, and the feeling of being consumed by an inferno within, told her that she should already be... *dead*.

But somehow, she was not.

If I live but a few minutes hence, the alien-girl began to daydream,

To have experienced this... the ultimate balance of pleasure and pain, yes, my life will have been worth it...

The forbidden knowledge, the final ecstasy –

She would have given in to the urges; but her psycho-music, roaring in her mind with electric chords of energy, of duty, of *determination* – snapped her back to consciousness.

Instantly, and instinctively, Karéin-Mayréij knew what she must do, although her intellect screamed to the contrary.

She had to *trust*.

She had to *believe*.

God of Earth, let thy own Fire come to me, she prayed.

Let thy magic *come into me... I will not resist.*

She moaned soundlessly in the void of space, shrieking both in limitless pleasure and simultaneous pain, as the star's power took full hold, cascading through her bubble and body as if both were one and the same.

Her senses all but overwhelmed, not only by the sensations, but also by the fantastic outpouring of energy carried within, the Storied Watcher hurtled forward, scarcely able to tell if she was on the right path, or if she was actually flying off on some fatal tangent, away from the humans' entire system.

But presently, the hot, cloudy planet appeared up ahead, and the alien-girl was again able to think and reason. Through the haze of the surrounding, hellish radiation, she could clearly see it.

Working at lightening-speed, her mind calculated, estimated, as her hands touched the breast-plate – itself softening, almost putty-like, in the murderous heat – for the figures that had earlier been inscribed upon it.

If I can bounce off the hot-cloud world, reasoned Karéin-Mayréij, all the while fighting off the siren calls of the demons of pain and pleasure, *I can go around the Earth and hit the comet.*

No need to waste precious time by again circling their Moon.

Her bubble burning brilliantly, the Storied Watcher descended toward *Hlà'ter'àh*, hurtling toward its upper reaches. Behind, she left a mighty trail of turbulence thousands of kilometers long, a huge scar on the otherwise changeless visage that this failed planet presented to the heavens.

She absorbed the impact – a force that would have shattered a thousand Earth-ships – with the gravity-bending skills.

Onward she shot towards the humans' world, her psycho-music roaring ever louder, her bubble glowing ever brighter with *Amaiish*-energy.

Ahead loomed the 'Lucifer' thing, barely visible against the cusp of the far side of Earth, as she approached the blue-world from the other side. It was already starting to glow as it encountered the first few atoms of the Earth's upper atmosphere; and it was surrounded by a thousand twinkling lights that flashed on and off, like little fireflies over a summer lake.

Somehow, she also perceived the *Salvador* ship, careening directly at the comet. She tried to send her love to the humans in it, to make them strong, in awe of their willingness to make the ultimate sacrifice.

Great Spirit bless them, gasped Karéin-Mayréij, fighting back tears.

They are a brave race. Even now, they fight.

The hate started to build, fueling an infernal furnace within, star-like, burning, consuming.

Not this *time, not like the* last *time,* she sent to it, her eyes glowing brilliantly, with all the colors in the spectrum.

This *time – I am ready!*

The Storied Watcher, her speed ebbing slightly, started to come round the planet's dark side, away from the Sun.

A million amazed, newly hopeful eyes, stared in disbelief, into the night sky.

Guilt In A Bad Time

"I don't want to *watch* this, Sam," pleaded Tanaka, as the two of them slowly fumbled for their ISS2-regulation utility work-garments. "You can tell me what happened. *Afterwards.*"

"Cherie," the man argued, "You *know*, that *I* know how you feel. Not far from how I'm taking it myself – *that's* for sure. But we both have a duty to... *witness* it. For future generations, so we can tell them what happened, that we saw it with our own *eyes*. God knows... I don't *want* to... but I *have* to. *We* have to."

He now had his pants on.

"Intellectually, I understand what you're saying," she stammered, "But the human being in me, can't *bear* it. I have *people* down there... friends, relatives. And I have to see them... *you* have loved ones down there, too, Sam. Why put yourself through it?"

"You're damn right, Cherie, I *do*. My kids. My *wife*. Who I've not even been *faithful* to, while she..." mumbled Jacobson, breathing each word heavily, as if he was about to cry.

"Don't *torture* yourself, Sam," she implored, rushing to his side and holding him. "It's *not* your fault. *None* of this is."

"Well, I at least have to wave them goodbye," whimpered Jacobson, wiping a tear from his face. "If only to beg her to forgive me."

A defeated Tanaka merely looked up and nodded.

As he left the cabin, Jacobson said, "Join me, if you can. If you can't... I'll understand, Cherie."

He left.

Meeting-Place

Jacobson found White and Chkalov already there, in the forward observation-deck, semi-standing, as much as anyone could in the lack of gravity, along with a strangely thin crowd, in front of the large computer projection screen that had been erected in the front of ISS2's curved, glassed bow.

He moved forward, and as he did, the two men noticed him and turned in his direction.

"Sergei," Jacobson said, extending his hand, "Good to see you again."

Chkalov shook it, saying, "Please do not take this in the wrong way, Commander... but *nothing* good will happen, today."

Ruefully, Jacobson replied, "No... I guess it won't, *that's* for sure. But thanks for coming to be with us, anyway. There are fewer people here than I expected."

"I think, Captain," Chkalov commented, "That many crew-members have decided to stay in their quarters, talking to their families, right up to the final moments. I was unable to reach my mother, today, unfortunately; but I had talked with her, yesterday... so it will be alright... I think..."

He hung his head.

Jacobson paused for a second, then asked, "How long is it going to be... until..."

"Five minutes and seventeen seconds, apparently," replied White, with an uncharacteristic lack of humor in his voice.

"Hi, Devon," interjected a newly-arrived Tanaka.

Looking at Jacobson, she said, "I decided that I couldn't make you face this alone, Sam."

Not caring that the others could see him, Jacobson embraced Tanaka close to his heart, hugging her with all his might.

"Thank you, Cherie... thank you *so* much," was all that he could manage.

"Y'all know," philosophically offered White, "When we set off, I don't think any of us figured that things would end like... *this*. I mean, Karéin, by herself, would have been strange *enough*, but..."

"That is certainly true, Major White," agreed Chkalov. "You know, Captain... I was thinking about our little disagreement, the one about the report. I take back nothing that I said – nor do I expect you to – but it all seems rather... *unimportant*, now... does it not?"

Managing to tear himself away from Tanaka, Jacobson answered, "That it *does*, Sergei... that it does."

Boyd had now arrived, having evidently heard the tail-end of the conversation.

"Not much point in having disputes between nations, when there are no nations – no *nothing*, anymore," he stated, in a flat monotone.

"Good to see that you made it," said Jacobson. "Not the most pleasant of get-togethers."

"Well," Boyd replied, heavily, "I'm a bit late because I just got off the video-link with my wife... and kids. We said our good-byes. My youngest daughter Nicole... Nicky's what I call her... she's... she's almost four, you see... and she said, 'Daddy'..."

He choked up and couldn't continue.

All of them – including Chkalov – stared compassionately at Major Brent Boyd : ace Air Force pilot, accomplished astronaut, All-American boy – but a beaten man, numb with emotional pain.

Tanaka rushed to him, not needing a push, embracing and holding him, for a few seconds.

"Thanks, Professor," he gasped. "I *needed* that. I guess I won't be getting many more, from now on."

"Brent," she counseled, "There *will* be a way."

They watched the video-screen, waiting for the countdown.

Fire, Take Me

As the brilliant point of light hurtled across the night-sky of Planet Earth, for the first time, its people – at least, a goodly number of them – heard the war-music of mighty Karéin-Mayréij, the greatest of the *Makailkh*.

Their minds reverberated with its electrifying, uplifting sounds; at first, they perceived a few faint, faraway chords of a haunting, wailing, Celtic-like song, then it transitioned with rapidly-increasing volume into something like the last third of *Stairway To Heaven*, but much *more* dignified, powerful and exciting in an alien, supernatural way that the words of mortals could never describe or do justice to.

The Storied Watcher heard it, too; and as she did, her self-assurance grew a thousand-fold. She had found the key – the secret to unlock the highest of her abilities – the one that she had never *dared* use or even think of.

If any could have beheld her visage, now, they would have seen a face glowing with grim determination, combined with the thrill of having finally achieved the zenith of her great powers, exulting in these as she streaked towards Earth's nemesis.

The people of Earth looked up and beheld a shining, dazzlingly-bright *something*, rocketing directly at 'Lucifer', illuminating all the night sky, as the alien-girl shot rays of scintillating death at the clouds of debris that surrounded her, blasting each one that blocked her way into dust.

The humans fell on their knees, rubbing their eyes, as her majesty and brilliance overwhelmed them.

Her mind, empowered by the power of the star, and by something else besides, broadcast, now, to all the consciousnesses below :

By my song and my light, you shall know that the Destroying Angel has returned.

Reaching now for all her arts, Karéin-Mayréij called upon the fast-thinking one, and she perceived the few remaining seconds as others would, minutes.

She hurtled towards the comet, but even with the fast-thinking, she now perceived the comet a scant-score seconds away, with several more waves of the Earth-missiles fast approaching from underneath.

'Lucifer' was falling towards the planet, faster and faster. The Storied Watcher sensed the fissures that had been riven into its surface, wounds newly-opened and -widened by the humans' last, desperate attacks.

Into your black heart! she cursed.

My life for yours and theirs – a fair trade!

In a second for her – a *thousandth* of a second, in objective time – Karéin-Mayréij had burned her way down the largest fissure.

Her bubble and the cloud of shrieking radioactive energies that surrounded it, instantly disintegrated the many, jagged ridges and outcroppings that any lesser being, would have impacted and died upon.

I hear *you, dear ones*, she broadcasted.

Do not fear for me.

In her last second, she was almost at the comet's center, with the end of the fissure imminent.

Devon, she sent, trying to aim away from the planet,

I believe, *now.*

Tell the children... at long last... I am at peace.

While her psycho-music reached a deafening, kaleidoscopic crescendo, Karéin-Mayréij, the mighty Storied Watcher of eternal ages, God's Destroying Angel, reached down, *deep* down, further than she or any of her race ever had, releasing the Beast that she knew she could never control.

Every mote of her electrified consciousness instantly lit up with an ultimate ecstasy – one without parallel – without equal.

Take me! cried her passionate mind, across the Heavens.

Fire – **take me!**

A great light, brighter than a million stars, blew the comet to bits. And her mind faded into the whiteness of oblivion.

Witnesses To The Turn Of History

A voice from the intercom said, "Two minutes, thirty-six seconds until projected impact."

"What's with the screen?" asked Boyd.

"Split image, man," quietly explained White. "Left is the view from Earth, London, specifically, that's because they think it'll hit in the southern Pacific, somewhere. Give 'em more time, y'all know. Right is from a satellite in low orbit. Ringside *seat*, man."

"You always *did* have a way with words, Devon," offered Tanaka, forcing a laugh.

Jacobson received a tap on the shoulder and, turning, he recognized the visage of Alan Humber, fatigue and loss etched in every ridge and wrinkle.

"Hello, Commander," said the Englishman. "Rest of the ISS2 blokes are up in the meeting-room, I guess they wanted to take it sitting down, or something. I just wanted to be alone, but I changed my mind... I didn't want to go *there*, though. Mind if I join you?"

"Of *course* not," answered Jacobson.

"Alan," sympathetically inquired Tanaka, "Do you *have* anyone down on Earth? Stupid question, I know."

"No, *not* stupid, Professor," he answered, amicably. "Me... partner. Charlie, that's his name. A merchant banker, by trade... we live just outside Norwich. We've got two adopted kids – one boy, one girl. Cutest little tykes you ever *could* see... raised 'em from when they was *babies*..."

His voice broke, and he wiped a tear.

Laughing miserably, Boyd commented, "*What* an epitaph for a race, you know? The minute that we manage to build a society that includes *all* of us... there ends up being *none* of us. Well... *almost* none of us."

"That," dryly observed the Russian, "Remains to be *seen*, Major Boyd. It rests upon the slender shoulders of us, and the others up here."

Boyd nodded.

"There are still the last missiles," they heard an unknown voice from the crowd call out. "There's still one more chance."

"Yeah," echoed White, speaking in a strange, quiet, distant tone, "There *is* still one more chance... but it ain't *that*."

"Forty-two seconds," announced the intercom.

All of them somehow forced themselves to watch the images being displayed on the right side of the video-display.

Mutely, they stared, transfixed, each saying a prayer, or whatever one says, for a dying planet.

"Looks like it's in the outer atmosphere, now," Boyd pointed out. "It's starting to glow."

"Hit it, *hit* it, come *on*, Earth!" inveighed a desperate, tearful Tanaka.

They saw a thousand missiles strike 'Lucifer', blowing away first tiny bits, then small chunks, then larger pieces.

A much larger flash ripped away perhaps a sixth of it, on its sun-facing side.

"God *bless* you, *Salvador*, for doing your duty so *very* well," reverently remarked Jacobson.

"If they only had a *day* of doing that..." raged a sweating, red-faced, desperate Boyd. "*Damn it!* Damn it to *hell*! This isn't *fair!*"

"Thirty seconds," sounded the intercom.

"God bless Mike," muttered Humber. "A real *professional*, that man is."

Suddenly, a voice sounded from the left-hand side of the display, accompanied by images of a camera rapidly moving back and forth, scanning upward.

"Nigel... Nigel? You copying me? What's *that*, mate? You see it too? It's *brilliant*... heading right *at* the damn thing! What the – who's playing *music* at a time like *this..*?"

"*Oh, God!!!*" shrieked Tanaka, the tears flying from her eyes. "It's her – **it's her!!!**"

The intercom counted, "Twenty seconds," as the voice on the video-screen exclaimed, "Ladies and gentlemen, we're seeing some kind of new weapon, flying right at the comet – too *bright*, I can't *look* at it, directly – what's that *music*, goddammit – I can't *believe* this, I've just heard something saying, 'by my light, you shall know' –"

"**Jesus, Mary and Joseph!**" frantically shouted Jacobson. "*Quickly*, all of you! *Move together! Hold hands!*"

A bewildered Humber looked on as the five original members of the *Eagle and Infinity* crew effortlessly flew through the zero-G, meeting each other in a semicircle, holding hands, with White in the middle.

The African-American astronaut, his voice ringing with the sound of faith, with a song never-before heard and with something much more besides, counseled, "Send her your *power*, y'all! Tell her that you *believe!* No need to close your eyes!"

"We believe – we believe – we **believe!**" replied a more-than-human chorus, as one, as if repeating a prayer known from childhood.

"Alan," demanded Tanaka, quietly, never taking her eyes from the screen, "Do you hear music?"

"Yes," he answered. "Yes, I *do*... strange... where..."

"Take my hand, *right now*, man!" she commanded. "Take my hand and think, 'I believe'!"

Humber hastily complied, at first uneasily, but, a split-second later, a look of astonishment and wonder possessed him.

"Ten seconds," warned the intercom.

The announcement was barely comprehensible, over the enervating, powerful and ethereal song of Karéin-Mayréij, which invaded minds and sound-circuits, all over the station and the planet below.

The eyes of those in the observation-deck shot rapid-fire from the left to the right sides of the video-display, as the latter showed a brilliant speck hurtling from across the dark side of the Earth, straight at 'Lucifer'.

"Let us be thy shield and sword, mighty Destroying Angel... Fist of God!" breathed a radiant-faced White, with calm dignity.

"Two... One..."

Now they beheld a light to end all lights – terrible but beautiful all the same – as the comet disintegrated into a thousand pieces.

Its shards, some still of appreciable size but none catastrophically so, burned brightly as they slowly tumbled towards the planet that, scant seconds ago, they would have denuded of all life and hope.

The music fell silent.

Humber and the Mars mission astronauts finally released their grasp; but White's shoulders immediately slumped.

"Devon?" asked Tanaka.

His round, watering eyes stared over his shoulder, at the others.

"She's at *peace*, now," he sadly replied.

End of Book One

Epilogue

Over and over it careened – this fragile ark, this dull-glowing cocoon of strange, latterly unknown, other-worldly energy – as it hurtled toward the blue-green planet, illuminating the sky with a fire only slightly brighter than the many thousands of other fragments of a now-dead comet, as all fell into the Earth's fatal gravity well.

Now and again it flickered and briefly failed in small places, allowing demonic bursts of the raging incandescence that surrounded it to inflict hateful burns on what was inside.

But mostly – inexplicably, it held firm – as it had so many times, in eons past human understanding, when all else had seemed lost.

The numbed, shocked, unconscious, all-but-lifeless mind of the not-really-a-meteor's inhabitant saw and sensed nothing, as she and it fell ever faster Earthward.

Over Shenyang in China went the thing, lighting up the sky like some unexpected firecracker; shortly thereafter, it passed over the straits between Honshu and Hokkaido.

As the drag of this rocky, small planet's stratosphere started to brake its speed, had she been aware, the one within it would have seen the vast reaches of the Pacific opening up beneath her.

Lower and lower now the fire-bubble fell, until, just as it descended into the troposphere, it cleared the cloud layer, revealing the western coasts of North America, with the mighty north-south mountain range looming to the east.

The meteor-shower that accompanied this strange projectile was also now overcome by the gravity of the planet that, scant minutes ago, might have been denuded by 'Lucifer', as the humans called their erstwhile nemesis.

Instead, on this day, it would be the defeated shards of that almost-apocalyptic body, that would instead fall, flaming, to their demise. But as they did, the larger of them were still able to strike back, one last time.

One by one, the larger of the fragments crashed down, striking cities, roads, power plants, railways and the occasional unlucky traveler, in a last orgy of destruction.

Finally, it was time, as the blue-green planet's gravity at last overcame the momentum imparted by the greatest nearby explosion that humankind had ever witnessed.

Four brightly glowing fireballs – three natural ones, after a fashion, one something else entirely – cleared the lower reaches of the Rocky Mountains and landed, thundering for all within many miles to hear, somewhere beyond.

One fell in a lake; one hit a highway, wrecking six abandoned cars and cratering the roadway in impressive fashion; one hit the side of a mountain, promptly burying itself in the resulting avalanche; but the last one, glowing differently, in some indescribable way, crashed through the tree-tops of an evergreen mountain forest, charring all these as it roared by.

The special meteor etched a furrow of charcoal black upon the heart of the woodland, snow all around hissing and steaming at the brief touch of fire. It came to rest between two large, granite boulders, not far from a half-frozen stream that perhaps, somewhere, would feed the Snake River.

The fire upon the meteor was soon snuffed out by the wintry touch of this place, revealing only a faint, bluish-silver something-or-other – to the untutored eye, most akin to a very large soap-bubble – that, last reserves of energy spent, itself slowly faded away.

And now, there was a frail-looking young woman-like thing with, long, once-blond, now gray-and-black hair and otherwise immaculate European or maybe East Coast North American skin, filthy with congealed blood-stuff and charred wounds, garbed only in the burned, torn remnants of what might at one time have been a military uniform of some sort, lying cold, still and – most of all, *alone* – at the head of the furrow that the *faux*-meteor had created.

No breath came from her nostrils, nor her lips; nor did her pulse carry forth, nor did any of the outward signs that would have told a passing human, had there ever been any in this remote place, that she was alive.

Snow was falling; and its soft, white caress laid upon her like a delicate shroud.

Don't miss Book Two of *The Angel Brings Fire...*

Doubt Me Not